PATRICIA CO

Hornet's Nest
Southern Cross

Also by Patricia Cornwell

THE SCARPETTA NOVELS

Postmortem
Body of Evidence
All That Remains
Cruel and Unusual
The Body Farm
From Potter's Field
Cause of Death
Unnatural Exposure
Black Notice
The Last Precinct
Blow Fly
Trace
Predator

ANDY BRAZIL SERIES
Isle of Dogs

NON-FICTION
Portrait of a Killer: Jack the Ripper – Case Closed

BIOGRAPHY
Ruth, A Portrait: The Story of Ruth Bell Graham

OTHER WORKS
Food to Die For: Secrets from Scarpetta's Kitchen
Life's Little Fable
Scarpetta's Winter Table

PATRICIA CORNWELL OMNIBUS

Hornet's Nest
Southern Cross

PATRICIA CORNWELL

TIME WARNER BOOKS

This omnibus edition first published in Great Britain by
Time Warner Books in 2005

Previously published separately:
Hornet's Nest published in the United States in 1997 by G. P. Putnam's Sons
First published in Great Britain in 1997 by Little, Brown and Company
First published in paperback by Warner Books in 1997
Reprinted 1998 (four times), 1999, 2000 (four times), 2001, 2002, 2004
Reprinted by Time Warner Books in 2005

Southern Cross published in the United States in 1998 by G. P. Putnam's Sons
First published in Great Britain in 1999 by Little, Brown and Company
First published in paperback by Warner Books in 1999
Reprinted 2001, 2002
Reprinted by Time Warner Paperbacks in 2004

A CIP catalogue record for this book is available from the British Library.

Visit the author's website at www.patriciacornwell.com

ISBN-10: 0-7515-3902-3
ISBN-13: 978-0-7515-3902-8

Printed and bound in Great Britain by
Clays Ltd, St Ives plc

Time Warner Books
An imprint of
Time Warner Book Group UK
Brettenham House
Lancaster Place
London WC2E 7EN

www.twbg.co.uk

Hornet's Nest

To Cops

Chapter One

That morning, summer sulked and gathered darkly over Charlotte, and heat shimmered on pavement. Traffic teemed, people pushing forward to promise as they drove through new construction, and the past was bulldozed away. The USBank Corporate Center soared sixty stories above downtown, topped by a crown that looked like organ pipes playing a hymn to the god of money. This was a city of ambition and change. It had grown so fast, it could not always find its own streets. Like a boy in puberty, it was rapidly unfolding and clumsy at times, and a little too full of what its original settlers had called pride.

The city and its county were named for Princess Charlotte Sophia of Mecklenburg-Strelitz before she became George III's queen. The Germans, who wanted the same freedoms the Scotch-Irish did, were one thing. The English were another. When Lord Cornwallis decided to come to town in 1780 and occupied what became known as the Queen City, he was met with such hostility by these stubborn Presbyterians that he dubbed Charlotte 'the hornet's nest of America.' Two centuries later, the swarming symbol was the official seal of the city and its NBA basketball team and the police department that protected all.

It was the white whirling dervish against midnight blue that Deputy Chief Virginia West wore on the shoulders of her crisp white uniform shirt with all its brass. Most cops, frankly, had not a clue as to what the symbol meant. Some thought it was a tornado, a white owl, a beard. Others were certain it had to do with sports events in the coliseum or the new two-hundred-and-thirty-million-dollar stadium that hovered downtown like an alien spacecraft. But West had been stung more than once and knew exactly what the hornet's nest was about. It was what awaited her when she drove to work and read the *Charlotte Observer* every morning. Violence swarmed, and everybody talked at once. This Monday, she was in a dark angry mood, ready to really stir things up.

The city police department recently had relocated to the new pearly concrete complex known as the Law Enforcement Center, or LEC, in the heart of downtown on Trade Street, the very road British oppressors long ago had followed into town. Construction in the area seemed endless, as if change were a virus taking over West's life. Parking at the LEC remained a mess, and she had not completely moved into her office yet. There were plenty of mud puddles, and dust, and her unmarked car was new and a striking uniform blue that sent her to the carwash at least three times a week.

When she reached the reserved parking spaces in front of the LEC, she couldn't believe it. Occupying her spot was a drug dealer's set of chrome mags and parrot-green iridescent paint, a Suzuki, which she knew people flipped over in more ways than one.

'Goddamn it!' She looked around, as if she might recognize the person who had dared this perpetration.

Other cops were pulling in and out, and transporting prisoners in this constantly moving department of sixteen hundred police and unsworn support. For a moment, West sat and scanned, teased by the aroma of the Bojangles bacon and egg biscuit that by now was cold. Settling on a fifteen-minute slot in front of sparkling glass doors, she parked and climbed out, doing the best she could with briefcase, pocketbook, files, newspapers, breakfast, a large coffee.

She slammed her door shut with a hip as the dude she was looking for emerged from the building. He was jailing, jeans at low tide in that cool lockup look of six inches of pastel undershorts showing. The fashion statement got started in jail when inmates had their belts confiscated so they wouldn't hang themselves or someone else. The trend had crossed over every racial and socioeconomic line until half of the city's pants were falling off. West did not understand it. She left her car right where it was, fought with her armload as the dude mumbled good morning, trotting past.

'Brewster!' Her voice halted him like a pointed gun. 'What the hell you think you're doing parking in my space!'

He grinned, flashing rings and a fake Rolex as he swept arms open wide, the pistol beneath his jacket peeking out. 'Look around. Tell me what you see. Not one damn parking place in all of Charlotte.'

'That's why important people like me are assigned one,' she said to this detective she supervised as she tossed him her keys. 'Bring them back when you've moved my car,' she ordered.

West was forty-two, a woman who still turned heads

and had never been married to anything beyond what she thought she was here on earth to do. She had deep red hair, a little unattended and longer than she liked it, her eyes dark and quick, and a serious body that she did not deserve, for she did nothing to maintain curves and straightness in the right places. She wore her uniform in a way that made other women want one, but that was not why she chose police blues over plain clothes. She supervised more than three hundred wiseass investigators like Ronald Brewster who needed every reminder of law and order West could muster.

Cops greeted her on her way in. She turned right, headed to offices where Chief Judy Hammer decided everything that mattered in law enforcement in this hundred-mile area of almost six million people. West loved her boss but right now didn't like her. West knew why she had been called in early for a meeting, and it was a situation beyond reason or her control. This was insane. She walked into Hammer's outer office, where Captain Fred Horgess was talking on the phone. He held his hand over the receiver and shook his head in a *there's nothing I can do* way to West as she walked up to the dark wooden door, where Hammer's name was announced brightly in brass.

'It's not good,' he warned with a shrug.

'Why is it I didn't need you to tell me that?' West irritably said.

Balancing her burdens, she knocked with the toe of her Bates hi-gloss black shoe and nudged up the door handle with a knee, coffee almost spilling but caught in time. Inside, Hammer sat behind her overwhelmed desk, surrounded by framed photographs of children and grandbabies, her mission statement, *Prevent the Next Crime*, on the wall behind her. She was early fifties, in a smart houndstooth business suit, her telephone line buzzing relentlessly, but she had more important matters on her mind at the moment.

West dumped her load on one chair and sat in another one near the brass Winged Victory award the International Association of Chiefs of Police had presented to Hammer last year. She had never bothered to get a stand or give it an honored place. In fact, the trophy, which was three feet high, continued to occupy the same square of carpet next to her desk, as if waiting for a ride to someplace better. Judy Hammer won such things because she wasn't motivated by them. West removed the lid off her coffee, and steam wafted up.

'I already know what this is about,' she said, 'and you know what I think.'

Hammer gestured to silence her. She leaned forward, folding her hands on top of her desk. 'Virginia. At long last I have gotten the support of city council, the city manager, the mayor,' she started to say.

'And every one of them, including you, is wrong,' West said, stirring cream and sugar into her coffee. 'I can't believe you've talked them into this, and I can tell you right now, they're going to find some way to screw it up because they don't really want it to happen. You shouldn't want it to happen, either. It's a damn conflict of interests for a police reporter to become a volunteer cop and go out on the street with us.'

Paper crackled as West unwrapped a greasy Bojangles biscuit that Hammer would never raise to her lips, not even back in the old days when she was underweight and on her feet all day long, working the jail, juvenile division, crime analysis, records, inspections, auto theft, all those exciting assignments women got back in the days when they weren't allowed in patrol. She did not believe in fat.

'I mean, come on!' West said after a bite. 'The last *Observer* cop reporter screwed us so bad you sued the newspaper.'

Hammer did not like to think about Weinstein, the worthless wonder, a criminal, really, whose MO was to walk into the duty captain's office or the investigative division when no one was around. He stole reports right off desks, printers, and fax machines. This collaborative behavior culminated in his writing a front-page Sunday profile about Hammer, claiming she commandeered the police helicopter for personal use. She ordered off-duty cops to chauffeur her and do domestic jobs around her house. When her daughter was picked up for drunk driving, Hammer had the charges fixed. None of it was true. She did not even have a daughter.

Hammer got up, clearly frustrated and disturbed by the mess the world was in. She looked out a window, hands in the pockets of her skirt, her back to West.

'The *Charlotte Observer*, the city, think we don't understand them or care,' she started her evangelism again. 'And I know they don't understand us. Or care.'

West crumpled breakfast trash, and scored two points in disgust. 'All the *Observer* cares about is winning another Pulitzer Prize,' she said.

Hammer turned around, as serious as West had ever seen her. 'I had lunch with the new publisher yesterday. First time any of us have had a civilized conversation with anyone from there in a decade, at least. A miracle.' She began her habitual pacing, gesturing with passion. She loved her mission in life. 'We really want to try this. Could it blow up in our faces? Absolutely.' She paused. 'But what if it worked? Andy Brazil . . .'

'Who?' West scowled.

'Very, very determined,' Hammer went on, 'completed

our academy for volunteers, highest marks we've ever had. Impressed the hell out of the instructors. Does that mean he won't burn us, Virginia? No, no. But what I'm not going to have is this young reporter out there screwing up an investigation, getting the wrong view of what we do. He's not going to be lied to, stonewalled, hit on, hurt.'

West put her head in her hands, groaning. Hammer returned to her desk and sat.

'If this goes well,' the chief went on, 'think how good it could be for the department, for community policing here and around the world. How many times have I heard you say, "If only every citizen could ride just one night with us"?'

'I'll never say it again.' West meant it.

Hammer leaned over her desk, pointing her finger at a deputy chief she admired and sometimes wanted to shake for thinking too small. 'I want you out on the street again,' she ordered. 'With Andy Brazil. Give him a dose he won't forget.'

'Goddamn it, Judy!' West exclaimed. 'Don't do this to me. I'm up to my ears decentralizing investigations. The street crime unit's all screwed up, two of my captains out. Goode and I can't agree on anything, as usual . . .'

Hammer wasn't listening. She put on reading glasses, and began reviewing a memo. 'Set it up today,' she said.

Andy Brazil ran hard and fast. He blew out loudly, checking the time on his Casio watch as he sprinted around the Davidson College track, in the small town of the same name, north of the big city. It was here he had grown up and gone to school on tennis and academic scholarships. He had lived at the college all his life, really, in a dilapidated frame house on Main Street, across from a cemetery that, like the recently turned co-ed school, was older than the Civil War.

Until several years ago, his mother had worked in the college food service, and Brazil had grown up on the campus, watching rich kids and Rhodes scholars on their way in a hurry. Even when he was about to graduate magna cum laude, some of his classmates, usually the cheerleaders, thought he was a townie. They flirted with him as he ladled eggs and grits on their plates. They were always startled in a dense sort of way when he trotted past in a hallway, loaded with books and afraid of being late to class.

Brazil had never felt he belonged here or anywhere, really. It was as if he watched people through a pane of glass. He could not touch others no matter how hard he tried, and they could not touch him, unless they were mentors. He had been falling in love with teachers, coaches, ministers, campus security, administrators, deans, doctors, nurses since he could remember. They were accepting, even appreciative, of his unusual reflections and solitary peregrinations, and the writings he shyly shared when he visited after hours, usually bearing limeades from the M&M soda shop or cookies from his mother's kitchen. Brazil, simply put, was a writer, a scribe of life and all in it. He had accepted his calling with humility and a brave heart.

It was too early for anybody else to be out this morning except a faculty wife whose lumpy shape would never be transformed by anything but death, and two other women in baggy sweats breathlessly complaining about the husbands who made it possible for them to be walking while most of the world worked. Brazil wore a *Charlotte Observer* T-shirt and shorts, and looked younger than twenty-two. He was handsome and fierce, with cheekbones high, hair streaked blond, body firm and athletically splendid. He did not seem aware of how others reacted to the sight of him, or perhaps it didn't matter. Mostly, his attention was elsewhere.

Brazil had been writing ever since he could, and when he had looked for a job after graduating from Davidson, he had promised *Observer* publisher Richard Panesa that if Panesa would give Brazil a chance, the newspaper would not be sorry. Panesa had hired him as a *TV Week* clerk, updating TV shows and movie blurbs. Brazil hated typing in programming updates for something he did not even watch. He did not like the other clerks or his hypertensive, overweight editor. Other than a promised cover story one of these days, there was no future for Brazil, and he began going to the newsroom at four in the morning so he could have all of the updates completed by noon.

The rest of the day he would roam desk to desk, begging for garbage-picking stories the seasoned reporters wanted to duck. There were always plenty of those. The business desk tossed him the scoop on Ingersoll-Rand's newest air compressor. Brazil got to cover the *Ebony* fashion show when it came to town, and the stamp collectors, and the world championship backgammon tournament at the Radisson Hotel. He interviewed wrestler Rick Flair with his long platinum hair when he was the celebrity guest at the Boy Scout convention. Brazil covered the Coca-Cola 600, interviewing spectators drinking beer while stock cars blasted past.

He turned in a hundred hours' overtime five months in a row, writing more stories than most of Panesa's reporters. Panesa held a meeting, gathering the executive editor, managing editor, and features editor behind closed doors to discuss the idea of making Brazil a reporter when his first six months were up. Panesa couldn't wait to see Brazil's reaction, knowing he would be thrilled beyond belief when Panesa offered him general assignment. Brazil wasn't.

Brazil had already applied to the Charlotte Police Department's academy for volunteers. He had passed the background check, and was enrolled in the class that was to start the following spring. In the meantime, his plan was to carry on with his usual boring job with the TV magazine because the hours were flexible. Upon graduation, Brazil hoped the publisher would give him the police beat, and Brazil would do his job for the paper and keep up his volunteer hours at the same time. He would write the most informed and insightful police stories the city had ever seen. If the *Observer* wouldn't go along with this, Brazil would find a news organization that would, or he would become a cop. No matter how anybody looked at it, Andy Brazil would not be told no.

The morning was hot and steamy, and sweat was streaming as he began his sixth mile, looking at graceful antebellum buildings of ivy and brick, at the Chambers classroom building with its dome, and the indoor tennis center where he had battled other college students as if losing meant death. He had spent his life fighting for the right to move ahead eighteen miles, along I-77, to South Tryon Street, in the heart of the city, where he could write for a living. He remembered when he first started driving to Charlotte when he was sixteen, when the skyline was simple, downtown a place to go. Now it seemed an overachieving stone and glass empire that kept growing. He wasn't sure he liked it much anymore. He wasn't sure it liked him, either.

Mile eight, he dropped in the grass and began plunging into push-ups. Arms were strong and sculpted, with veins that gracefully fed his strength. Hair on wet skin was gold, his face red. He rolled over on his back and breathed good air, enjoying the afterglow. Slowly, he sat up, stretching, easing himself into the vertical position that meant getting on with it.

Andy Brazil trotted back to his twenty-five-year-old black BMW 2002 parked on the street. It was waxed, and shellacked with Armor All, the original blue and white emblem on the hood worn off forever ago and lovingly retouched with model paint. The car had almost a hundred and twenty thousand miles on it, and something broke about once a month, but Brazil could fix anything. Inside, the interior was saddle leather, and there was a new police scanner and a two-way radio. He wasn't due on his beat until four, but he rolled into his very own spot at noon. He was the *Observer*'s police reporter and got to park in a special spot near the door, so he could take off in a hurry when trouble blew.

The instant he entered the lobby, he smelled newsprint and ink the way a creature smells blood. The scent excited him like police lights and sirens, and he was happy because the guard in the console didn't make him sign in anymore. Brazil took the escalator, trotting up moving metal stairs, as if he was late somewhere. People were statues coming down the other side. They glanced curiously at him. Everyone in the *Observer* newsroom knew who Brazil was, and he had no friends.

The newsroom was big and drab, filled with the sounds of keys clicking, phones ringing, and printers grabbing fast-breaking stories off the wire. Reporters were intense in front of computer screens, flipping through notepads with the paper's name on cardboard covers. They walked around, and the woman who covered local politics was running out the door after a scoop. Brazil still could not believe he was a player in this important, heady world, where words could change destinies and the way people thought. He thrived on drama, perhaps because he had been fed it since birth, although not generally in a good way.

His new desk was in the metro section, just beyond the glass-enclosed office of the publisher, Panesa, who Brazil liked and was desperate to impress. Panesa was a handsome man, with silver-blond hair, and a lean look that had not become less striking as he had skated beyond forty. The publisher stood tall and straight in fine suits dark blue or black, and wore cologne. Brazil thought Panesa wise but had no reason to know it yet.

Each Sunday, Panesa had a column in the Sunday paper, and women in the greater Charlotte area wrote fan letters and secretly wondered what Richard Panesa was like in bed, or at least Brazil imagined this was so. Panesa was in a meeting when Brazil sat behind his desk and covertly glanced into the publisher's transparent kingdom as Brazil tried to look busy opening notepads, drawers, glancing at old printouts of long-published stories. It did not escape Panesa's notice that his boyish, intense police reporter had arrived four hours early his first day on his new beat. Panesa was not surprised.

The first item on Brazil's agenda was that Tommy Axel had left another 7-Eleven rose on Brazil's desk. It had the sad, unhealthy complexion of the people who shopped in establishments that sold dark red, tightly furled passion at the counter for a dollar ninety-eight. It was still wrapped in clear plastic, and Axel had stuck it inside a Snapple bottle filled with water. Axel was the music critic, and Brazil knew he was watching this very minute from not very far away, in features. Brazil slid a cardboard box out from under his desk.

He had not finished moving in, not that the task was especially formidable. But he had been assigned nothing yet and had finished the first draft of a self-assigned piece on what it had been like to go through the volunteer police academy. He could add and cut and polish only so many times, and was terrified by the thought of sitting in the newsroom with nothing to do. He had made it a habit to scan all six editions of the newspaper from wooden spools near the city directories. He often read the bulletin board, checked his empty mailbox, and had been meticulous and deliberately slow in moving his professional possessions the very short distance of forty-five feet.

This included a Rolodex with few meaningful phone numbers, for how to reach television networks and various shows, and stamp collectors or Rick Flair, was of little importance now. Brazil had plenty of notepads, pens, pencils, copies of his stories, city maps, and almost all of it could fit in the briefcase he had found on sale at Belk department store when he had been hired. It was glossy burgundy leather with brass clasps, and he felt very proud when he gripped it.

He had no photographs to arrange on his desk, for he was an only child and had no pets. It entered his mind that he might call his house to check on things. When Brazil had returned from the track to shower and change, his mother had been doing the usual, sleeping on the couch in the living room, TV loudly tuned in to a soap opera she would not remember later. Mrs Brazil watched life every day on Channel 7, and could not describe a single plot. Television was her only connection to humans, unless she counted the relationship with her son.

Half an hour after Brazil appeared in the newsroom, the telephone rang on his desk, startling him. He snatched it up, pulse trotting ahead as he glanced around, wondering who knew he worked here.

'Andy Brazil,' he said very professionally.

The heavy breathing was recognizable, the voice of the same pervert who had been calling for months. Brazil could hear her lying on her bed, sofa, fainting couch, wherever she got the job done.

'In my hand,' the pervert said in her low, creepy tone. 'Got it. Sliding in, out like a trombone . . .'

Brazil dropped the receiver into its cradle and shot Axel an accusing glance, but Axel was talking to the food critic. This was the first time in Brazil's life that he had ever gotten obscene phone calls. The only other situation to come even close was when he was blasting his BMW at the Wash & Shine in nearby Cornelius one day and a pasty-faced creep in a yellow VW bug pulled up and asked him if he wanted to earn twenty dollars.

Brazil's first thought was he was being offered a job washing the guy's car since Brazil was doing such a fine job on his own. This had been wrong. Brazil had turned the high pressure wand on the guy for free. He had memorized the creep's plate number and still had it in his wallet, waiting for the day when he could get him locked up. What the man in the VW bug had proposed was a crime against nature, an ancient North Carolina law no one could interpret. But what he had wanted in exchange for his cash had been clear. Brazil could not fathom why anyone would want to do such a thing to a stranger. He wouldn't even drink out of the same bottle with most people he knew.

Brazil was not naive, but his sexual experiences at Davidson had been more incomplete than those of his roommate, this he knew. The last semester of his senior year, Brazil had spent most nights in the men's room inside

Chambers. There was a perfectly comfortable couch in there, and while his roommate slept with a girlfriend, Brazil slept with books. No one was the wiser, except the custodians, who routinely saw Brazil coming out of, not going into, the building around six o'clock every morning as he headed back to the second floor of the condemned building he and his roommate shared on Main Street. Certainly, Brazil had his own small private space in this dump, but walls were very thin and it was difficult to concentrate when Jennifer and Todd were active. Brazil could hear every word, everything they did.

Brazil dated Sophie, from San Diego, on and off during college. He did not fall in love with her, and this made her desire uncontrollable. It more or less ruined her Davidson career. First she lost weight. When that didn't work, she gained it. She took up smoking, and quit, got mononucleosis and got better, went to a therapist and told him all about it. None of this turned out to be the aphrodisiac Sophie had hoped, and their sophomore year, she stabilized and slept with her piano teacher during Christmas break. She confessed her sin to Brazil. She and Brazil started making out in her Saab and her dorm room. Sophie was experienced, rich, and pre-med. She was more than willing to patiently explain anatomical realities, and he was open to research he really did not need.

At one P.M., Brazil had just logged onto his computer and gone into his basket to retrieve his police academy story, when his editor sat next to him. Ed Packer was at least sixty, with fly-away white hair and distant gray eyes. He wore bad ties haphazardly knotted, sleeves shoved up. At one point he must have been fat. His pants were huge, and he was always jamming a hand inside his waistband, tucking in his shirttail all around, as he was doing right now. Brazil gave him his attention.

'Looks like tonight's the night,' Packer said as he tucked.

Brazil knew exactly what his editor meant and punched the air in triumph, as if he'd just won the US Open.

'Yes!' he exclaimed.

Packer couldn't help but look at what was on the computer screen. It grabbed his interest, and he slipped glasses out of his shirt pocket.

'Sort of a first-person account of my going through the academy,' Brazil said, new and nervous about pleasing. 'I know it wasn't assigned, but . . .'

Packer really liked what he was reading and tapped the screen with a knuckle. 'This graph's your lead. I'd move it up.'

'Right. Right.' Brazil was excited as he cut the paragraph and pasted it higher.

Packer rolled his chair closer, nudging him out of the way to read more. He started scrolling through what was a very long story. It would have to be a Sunday feature, and he wondered when the hell Brazil wrote it. For the past two months, Brazil had worked days and gone to the police academy at night. Did the kid ever sleep? Packer had never seen anything like it. In a way, Brazil unnerved him, made him feel inadequate and old. Packer remembered how exciting journalism was when he was Brazil's age and the world filled him with wonder.

'I just got off the phone with Deputy Chief Virginia West,' he said to his protégé as he read. 'Head of investigations . . .'

'So who am I riding with?' Brazil interrupted, so eager to ride with the police, he couldn't contain himself.

'You're to meet West at four this afternoon, in her office, will ride with her until midnight.'

Brazil had just been screwed and couldn't believe it. He

stared at his editor, who had just failed the only thing Brazil had ever expected of him.

'No way I'm being babysat, censored by the brass!' Brazil exclaimed and didn't care who heard. 'I didn't go to their damn academy to . . .'

Packer didn't care who heard for a different reason. He had been a complaint department for the past thirty years, here and at home, and his attention span tended to flicker in and out as he mentally drove through different cells, picking up garbled snippets of different conversations. He suddenly recalled what his wife had said at breakfast about stopping for dog food on the way home. He remembered he had to take his wife's puppy to the veterinarian at three for some sort of shot, then Packer had a doctor's appointment after that.

'Don't you understand?' Brazil went on. 'They're just handling me. They're just trying to use me for PR!'

Packer got up. He towered wearily over Brazil like a weathered tree gathering more shadow the older it grows.

'What can I say?' Packer said, and his shirt was untucked again. 'We've never done this before. It's what the cops, the city, are offering. You'll have to sign a waiver. Take notes. No pictures. No videotapes. Do what you're told. I don't want you getting shot out there.'

'Well, I've got to go back home to change into my uniform,' Brazil decided.

Packer walked off, hitching up his pants, heading to the men's room. Brazil slumped back in his chair and looked up at the ceiling as if the only stock he owned had just crashed. Panesa watched him through glass, interested in how he was going to turn this around, and convinced he would. Systems analyst Brenda Bond blatantly glared at him from a nearby computer she was fixing. Brazil never paid her any mind. She was repulsive to him, thin and pale, with coarse black hair. She was hateful and jealous, and certain she was smarter than Brazil and all because computer experts and scientists were like that. He imagined Brenda Bond spending her life on the Internet inside chat rooms, because who would have her?

Sighing, Brazil got up from his chair. Panesa watched Brazil pick up an ugly red rose in a Snapple bottle, and the publisher smiled. Panesa and his wife had desperately wanted a son, and after five daughters it was either move to a larger home, become Catholic or Mormon, or practice safe sex. Instead, they had gotten divorced. He could not imagine what it must be like to have a son like Andy Brazil. Brazil was striking to look at, and sensitive, and, though all the results weren't in, the biggest talent ever to walk through Panesa's door.

Tommy Axel was typing a big review of a new k.d. lang album that he was listening to on earphones. He was a goofball, sort of a Matt Dillon who wasn't famous and never would be, Brazil thought. He walked up to Axel's desk and clunked the rose next to the keyboard as Axel boogied in his Star Trek T-shirt. Surprised, Axel pushed the earphones down around his neck, faint, thin music leaking out. Axel's face was smitten. This was the One for him. He had known it since he was six, somehow had a premonition that a divine creature like this would overlap orbits with his when the planets were aligned.

'Axel,' Brazil's heavenly voice sounded like a thunder-clap, 'no more flowers.'

Axel stared at his lovely rose as Brazil stalked off. Brazil didn't mean it, Axel was certain, as he watched Brazil. Axel was grateful for his desk. He scooted his chair in closer and crossed his legs, aching for the blond god walking with purpose out of the newsroom. Axel wondered where he was going. Brazil carried his briefcase as if he wasn't coming back. Axel had Brazil's home phone number because he had looked it up in the book. Brazil didn't live in the city, sort of out in the sticks, and Axel didn't quite understand it.

Of course, Brazil probably didn't make twenty thousand dollars a year, but he had a *bad* car. Axel drove a Ford Escort that wasn't new. The paint job was beginning to remind him of Keith Richards's face. There was no CD player and the *Observer* wouldn't buy him one, and he planned to remind everyone there of that someday when he landed a job with *Rolling Stone*. Axel was thirty-two. He had been married once, for exactly a year, when he and his wife looked at each other during a candlelight dinner, their relationship the mystery of all time, she from one planet, he from another.

They, the aliens, agreeably left for new frontiers where no person had gone before. It had nothing to do with his habit of picking up groupies at concerts after Meatloaf, Gloria Estefan, Michael Bolton, had worked them into a lather. Axel would get a few quotes. He'd put the boys and their winking lighted shoes, shaved heads, dreadlocks, and body piercing, in the newspaper. They called Axel excited, wanting extra copies, eight-by-ten photographs, followup interviews, concert tickets, backstage passes. One thing usually led to another.

While Axel was thinking about Brazil, Brazil was not thinking about him. Brazil was in his BMW and trying to calculate when he might need gas next since neither that gauge nor the speedometer had worked in more than forty thousand miles. BMW parts on a scale this grand were, in his mind, aviation instrumentation and simply beyond his means. This was not good for one who drove too fast and did not enjoy being stranded on a roadside waiting for the next non-serial killer to offer a ride to the nearest gas station.

His mother was still snoring in front of the TV. Brazil had learned to walk through his decaying home and the family life it represented without seeing any of it. He headed straight to his small bedroom, unlocked the door and shut it behind him. He turned on a boom box, but not too loud, and let Joan Osborne envelop him as he went into his closet. Putting on his uniform was a ritual, and he did not see how he could ever get tired of it.

First, he always laid it out on the bed and indulged himself, just looking for a moment, not quite believing someone had given him permission to wear such a glorious thing. His Charlotte uniform was midnight blue, creased and new with a bright white hornet's nest that seemed in motion, like a white twister, on each shoulder patch. He always put socks on first, black cotton, and these had not come from the city. Next he carefully pulled on summer trousers that were hot no matter how light the material, a subtle stripe down each leg.

The shirt was his favourite because of the patches and everything else that he would pin on. He worked his arms through thc short sleeves, began buttoning in the mirror, all the way up to his chin, and clipped on the tie. Next was his name plate and whistle. To the heavy black leather belt he attached the holder with its Mag-Lite, and his pager, saving room for the radio he would check out at the LEC. His soft Hi-Tec boots weren't patent leather like the military type he had seen most of his life, but more like high-top athletic shoes. He could run in these if the need ever arose, and he hoped it would. He did not wear a hat because Chief Hammer did not believe in them.

Brazil inspected himself in the mirror to make sure all was perfect. He headed back downtown with the windows and sunroof open, and propped his arm up whenever he could because he enjoyed the reaction of drivers in the next lane when they saw his patch. People suddenly slowed down. They let him pass when the light turned green. Someone asked him directions. A man spat, eyes filled with resentment Brazil did not deserve, for he had done nothing to him. Two teenaged boys in a truck began making fun of him, and he stared straight ahead and drove, as if none of this was new. He had been a cop forever.

The LEC was several blocks from the newspaper, and Brazil knew the way as if he were going home. He pulled into the parking deck for visitors, and tucked his BMW in a press slot, angling it the way he always did so people didn't hit his doors. He got out and followed polished hallways to the duty captain's office, because he had no idea where the investigative division was or if he could just stroll in without asking permission. In the academy, his time had been spent in a classroom, the radio room, or out on a street learning how to direct traffic and work nonreportable accidents. He did not know his way around this four-story complex, and stood in a doorway, suddenly shy in a uniform that did not include gun, baton, pepper spray, or anything helpful.

'Excuse me,' he announced himself.

The duty captain was big and old at his desk, and going

through pages of mug shots with a sergeant. They ignored him. For a moment Brazil watched Channel 3 television reporter Brent Webb, perched over the press baskets, going through reports, stealing whatever he wanted. It was amazing. Brazil watched the asshole tuck the reports into his zip-up briefcase, where no other journalist in the city would ever see them, as if it were perfectly acceptable for him to cheat Brazil and everyone trying to report the news. Brazil stared at Webb, then at this sergeant and captain who did not seem to care what crimes were committed in plain view.

'Excuse me,' Brazil tried again, louder.

He walked in, rudely ignored by cops who had hated the paper so long they no longer remembered why.

'I need to find Deputy Chief West's office.' Brazil would not be ignored.

The duty captain lifted another plastic-sheathed page of hard-boiled mugs up to the light. The sergeant turned his back to Brazil. Webb stopped what he was doing, his smile amused, maybe even mocking as he looked Brazil up and down, assessing this unfamiliar guy playing dress-up. Brazil had seen Webb enough on television to recognize him anywhere, and had heard a lot about him, too. Other reporters called Webb *The Scoop*, for reasons Brazil had just witnessed.

'So how do you like being a volunteer?' Webb was condescending and had no idea who Brazil was.

'Which way to investigations,' Brazil replied, as if it were an order, his eyes piercing.

Webb nodded. 'Up the stairs, can't miss it.'

Webb studied the way Brazil was dressed and started laughing, as did the sergeant and duty captain. Brazil helped himself to the TV reporter's briefcase and pulled out a handful of purloined offense reports. Brazil smoothed and shuffled them. He perused and stacked them neatly, taking his time, while everyone watched and Webb's face turned red.

'Believe Chief Hammer might like to see *The Scoop* in action.' Brazil smiled at him.

Brazil's boots were quiet as he walked off.

Chapter Two

Patrol was the largest division of the Charlotte Police Department, but investigations was the most treacherous, it was Virginia West's belief. Citizens followed burglaries, rapes, and homicides with fearful eyes. They complained when violent offenders weren't instantly snatched off the street, as if the Rapture had come. West's phone had not stopped ringing all day.

The trouble started three weeks ago when Jay Rule, a businessman from Orlando, arrived in the Queen City for a textile meeting. Hours after Rule left the airport in a rental Maxima, the car was found abandoned in a dark, overgrown vacant lot off South College Street, in the heart of downtown. The interior bell was dinging its complaint that the driver's door was open and headlights on. Λ bricfcasc and overnight bag had been gone through in the backseat. Cash, jewelry, portable phone, pager, and no one was quite sure what else, were gone.

Jay Rule, thirty-three, was shot five times in the head with a .45 caliber pistol loaded with a high-velocity, extremely destructive hollowpoint ammunition called Silvertips. His body was dragged fifteen feet into kudzu, his pants and undershorts pulled down to his knees, his genital area spray-painted bright orange in the shape of a large hourglass. No one, including the FBI, had ever seen anything like this. Then the following week, it happened again.

The second homicide was less than two blocks from the first, just off West Trade Street, behind the Cadillac Grill, which wasn't open at night, because of crime. Jeff Calley, forty-two, was a Baptist minister visiting Charlotte from Knoxville, Tennessee. His mission in the city was simple. He was moving his failing mother into a nursing home called The Pines, and staying in the Hyatt while he did so. He never checked in. Late that night, his rental Jetta was found, driver's door open, bell dinging, same modus operandi.

Week three, the nightmare repeated itself when fifty-two-year-old Cary Luby visited from Atlanta. West was discussing his case over the phone when Brazil appeared in her doorway. West did not notice him. She was too busy shuffling through large, gory scene photographs as she continued arguing with an assistant district attorney.

'That's not correct, I don't know where you got that, okay? He was shot multiple times in the head, contact. A .45 loaded with Silvertips . . . Yeah, yeah, exactly. All within several blocks of each other.' She was beginning to get annoyed. 'Jesus Christ. Of course I've got people down there undercover, hookers, pimps, trolling, hanging out, whatever it takes. What do you think?'

She switched the phone to her other hand, wondering why she ever wore earrings, and irritated that anyone might question her ability to do her job. Checking her watch, she looked through more photographs, pausing at one that clearly showed the painted hourglass, which was rather much a solid orange figure eight. The base was over the genitals, the top over the belly. It was weird. The ADA continued asking questions about the crime scene, and West's patience was deteriorating. So far, this day had been shit.

'Just like the others,' she told him emphatically. 'Everything. Wallet, watch, wedding band.' She listened. 'No. No. Not credit cards, anything with the victim's name . . . Why? Because the killer's smart, that's why.' She sighed, her head beginning to throb. 'Jesus friggin' Christ. That's my point, John. If we're talking *carjacking*, then why wasn't his rental Thunderbird taken? *Not a single car has been.*'

She swiveled around in her chair and almost dropped the phone when she saw the young male volunteer cop standing in her doorway, writing as fast as he could in a reporter's notepad. The son of a bitch was looking around West's office, taking down every confidential word being said about the most sensational, scariest murders the city had ever known. So far, sensitive details had been kept out of the press as political pressure gathered and darkened and swarmed.

'Gotta go,' West abruptly said.

She slammed down the receiver, hanging up on the ADA. She pinned Brazil with her eyes.

'Shut the door,' she said in a quiet, hard way that would have terrified anyone who worked for her or was about to get arrested.

Brazil was unflinching as he got closer to the desk. He was not about to be intimidated by this big-shot bureaucrat who had sold him down the river. He dropped Webb's stolen offense reports in front of her.

'What do you think you're doing?' West demanded.

'I'm Andy Brazil with the *Observer*,' he said with cool politeness. 'Webb's swiping reports out of the press basket. In the off chance you might care. And I'm going to need to check out a radio. I was supposed to meet you at four.'

'And what? Eavesdrop?' West shoved back her chair, got up. 'Looks to me like you already got your story.'

'I'm going to need a radio,' Brazil reminded her again, for he couldn't imagine being out on the street and not having a lifeline to the dispatchers.

'No you're not. Trust me,' West promised him.

She angrily stuffed files into her briefcase and snapped it shut. She grabbed her pocketbook and stalked out. Brazil was on her heels.

'You've got your nerve,' she went on furiously, as if she had been mad at this young man in uniform all of her life. 'Just like every other asshole out there. Give 'em a little, want more. Can't trust anybody.'

West wasn't at all what Brazil had expected. He didn't know why he'd assumed the deputy chief would be overweight and overbearing, flat-chested, with a square, masculine face, and overprocessed hair. But no. She was maybe five-six, five-seven, with dark red hair barely brushing her collar, and very good bones. She was almost handsome, and buxom, and not the least bit fat, but he didn't care and would never be interested. She was unkind and unattractive to him.

West shoved open glass doors leading into the parking lot. She dug into her pocketbook, heading to her unmarked Crown Victoria.

'I told everyone what a bad idea this was. Would they listen?' She fumbled with keys.

'Would you?' Brazil demanded.

West paused, looking at him. She yanked open the door, and Brazil blocked it.

'It might be nice if I got a fair trial.' He shoved his

notepad at her, flipping through scribbles he had made while West was on the phone. 'I was describing your office and you,' he announced much like the ADA West had just been talking to on the phone.

She didn't have to skim much to know she'd made a wrong assumption. She sighed, stepping back, looking volunteer officer Brazil up and down, wondering how it could be possible that a reporter was dressed like this. What had policing come to? Hammer had lost her mind. Brazil should be arrested for impersonating an officer, that was the reality of things.

'Where do you live?' West asked him.

'Davidson.'

This was good. At least the next hour and a half would be spent in the commute. West might even be able to stretch it out. The longer she could keep him off the street, the better. She almost smiled as she climbed into her car.

'We'll go there first so you can change clothes,' she gruffly said.

For a while, they did not speak as scanner lights blinked, and dispatchers and cops cut in and out on the radio like Rollerbladers. The Mobile Data Terminal (MDT) beeped as it logged calls and displayed addresses and messages on its computer screen. West and Brazil drove through the city as rush hour peaked. It looked like it might rain. Brazil was staring out his window. He felt stupid and mistreated as he took off his police tie and unbuttoned his collar.

'How long you been with the *Observer*?' West asked him, and she felt a tug around her chest, as if her bullet-proof vest were rubbing her wrong, except she wasn't wearing one. She felt a little sorry for this ride-along.

'A year,' Brazil answered, hateful toward Deputy Chief

West and wondering if she were going to let him ride with her again.

'How come I've never heard of you before now?' she asked.

'I didn't get the police beat until I finished the academy. That was the deal.'

'What deal?'

'My deal,' Brazil continued to stare sullenly out the window.

West tried to change lanes but the jerk next to her wasn't cooperative. She gestured angrily back at him. 'Same to you, drone!' She stopped at a red light and looked at Brazil. 'What do you mean, *deal*?'

'I wanted the cop shop, told them I'd make it worth their while.'

'What's that supposed to mean?'

'I want to know cops. So I can write about them. I want to get it straight.'

West didn't believe him. Reporters always said shit like that, lied with pretty tongues, no different than people in general, really. She drove on, got out a cigarette, and lit it.

'If you're so curious about us, how come you didn't become a cop for real?' she challenged him.

'I'm a writer,' Brazil said simply, as if this were his race, his religion, or family name.

'And we all know cops can't write.' West blew out smoke. 'Can't even read unless there's pictures.'

'*There are* pictures.'

She threw up her hands and laughed. 'See?'

Brazil was silent.

'So why do you live way the hell in Davidson?' she asked.

'I went to school there.'

'I guess you must be smart.'

'I get by,' he told her.

The gleaming Crown Victoria turned onto Main Street, which was what its name suggested in this charming college town. Homes were genteel, white frame and brick, with ivy and sprawling porches and swings. West had grown up outside of Charlotte, too, but heading a different direction, where there wasn't much but red clay and fathomless farmland. She couldn't have afforded to go to a college like Davidson, and doubted her SATs would have impressed anybody in a positive way. Brazil's college was sort of like Princeton and other places West had only read about.

'While we're on the subject,' she said, 'I don't remember any police stories by you.'

'This is my first day on the beat.'

She couldn't suppress her growing dismay over what she had been saddled with this night. A dog barked and began chasing her car. Suddenly, it was raining hard.

'So what'd you do for a year?' she investigated further.

'The TV magazine,' Brazil added to his resume. 'A lot of overtime, a lot of stories nobody wanted.' He pointed, releasing his shoulder harness. 'It's that one.'

'You don't take your seatbelt off until I've stopped the car. Rule number one.' West pulled into a rutted, unpaved driveway.

'Why are you making me change clothes? I have a right . . .' Brazil finally spoke his mind.

'People wearing what you got on get killed out here,' West cut him off. 'Rule number two. You don't have a right. Not with me. I don't want anyone thinking you're a cop. I don't want anyone thinking you're my partner. I don't want to be doing this, got it?'

Brazil's house hadn't been painted in too long to tell

the color. Maybe it had been pale yellow once, maybe eggshell or white. Mostly now it was gray and flaking and peeling, like a sad old woman with a skin condition. An ancient, rusting white Cadillac was parked in the drive, and West decided that whoever lived here didn't have taste, money, or time for repairs and yard work. Brazil angrily pushed open the car door, gathering his belongings as he got out, and halfway tempted to tell this deputy chief to get the hell out of here and not come back. But his BMW was still in Charlotte, so that might pose a problem. He bent over, peering inside at her.

'My dad was a cop.' He slammed the door shut.

West was typical brass, typical anybody who had power, Brazil fumed as he strode up the walk. She didn't give a shit about helping somebody else get started. Women could be the worst, as if they didn't want anybody else to do well because no one was nice to them when they were coming along, or maybe so they could pay everybody back, persecute innocent guys who'd never even met them, whatever. Brazil imagined West at the net, a perfect lob waiting for his lethal overhead smash. He could ace her, too.

He unlocked the front door of the house he had lived in all his life. Inside, he unbuttoned his uniform shirt and looked around, suddenly conscious of a dim, depressing living room of cheap furniture and stained wall-to-wall carpet. Dirty ashtrays and dishes were wherever somebody had forgotten them last, and gospel music swelled as George Beverly Shea scratched *How Great Thou Art* for the millionth time. Brazil went to the old hi-fi and impatiently switched it off.

'Mom?' he called out.

He began tidying up, following a mess into a slovenly old kitchen where milk, V8 juice, and cottage cheese had been left out by someone who had made no effort to clean up or hide the empty fifth of Bowman's cheap vodka on top of the trash. Brazil picked up dishes and soaked them in hot sudsy water. Frustrated, he yanked out his shirttail and unbuckled his belt. He looked down at his name tag, shiny and bright. He fingered the whistle on its chain. For an instant, his eyes were filled with a sadness he could not name.

'Mom?' he called out again. 'Where are you?'

Brazil walked into the hallway, and with a key that no one else had a copy of, he unlocked a door that opened onto the small room where he lived. It was tidy and organized, with a computer on a Formica-topped desk, and dozens of tennis trophies and plaques and other athletic awards on shelves, furniture, and walls. There were hundreds of books in this complicated person's simple, unassuming space. He carefully hung up his uniform and grabbed khakis and a denim shirt off hangers. On the back of the door was a scarred leather bomber jacket that was old and extra large, and looked like it might have come from some earlier time. He put it on even though it was warm out.

'Mom!' Brazil yelled.

The light was flashing on the answering machine by his bed, and he hit the *play* button. The first message was from the newspaper credit union, and he impatiently hit the button again, then three more times, skipping past hang-ups. The last message was from Axel. He was playing guitar, singing Hootie & the Blowfish.

'I only wanna be with you . . . Yo! Andy, it's Axel-don't-axe-me. Maybe dinner? How 'bout Jack Straw's . . . ?'

Brazil impatiently cut off the recording as the phone rang. This time the caller was live and creepy, and breathing into the phone as the pervert had sex with Brazil in mind, again without asking.

'I'm holding youuu so haarrrddd, and you're touching me with your tongue, sliiiidiiing . . .' she breathed in a low tone that reminded Brazil of psycho shows he sometimes had watched as a child.

'You're sick.' He slammed the receiver back into its cradle.

He stood in the mirror over his dresser and began brushing hair out of his eyes. It was really bugging him, getting too long, streaks from the sun catching light. He had always worn his hair one of two ways, short or not as short. He was tucking an obstinate strand behind an ear when suddenly the reflection of his mother boiled up from behind, an obese, raging drunk, attacking.

'Where have you been?' his mother screamed as she tried to backhand her son across the face.

Brazil raised an arm, warding off the blow just in time. He wheeled around, grabbing his mother by both wrists, firmly but gently. This was a tired, old drama, an endless rerun of a painful play.

'Easy, easy, easy,' he said as he led his besotted mother to the bed and sat her down.

Muriel Brazil began to cry, rocking, slurring her words. 'Don't go. Don't leave me, Andy. Please, oh pleassseee.'

Brazil glanced at his watch. He looked furtively at the window, afraid West might somehow see through shut blinds and know the wretched secret of his entire life.

'Mom, I'm going to get your medicine, okay?' he said. 'You watch TV and go to bed. I'll be home soon.'

It wasn't okay. Mrs Brazil wailed, rocking, screaming hell on earth. 'Sorry, sorry, sorry! Don't know what's wrong with me, Andyeeee!'

West did not hear all of this, but she heard enough because she had opened car windows to smoke. She was suspicious that Brazil lived with a girlfriend and they were having a fight. West shook her head, flicking a butt out onto the weed-choked, eroded drive. Why would anyone move in with another human being right after college, after all those years of roommates? For what? She asked no questions of Brazil as they drove away. Whatever this reporter might have to say to explain his life, she didn't want to hear it. They headed back to the city, the lighted skyline an ambitious monument to banking and girls not allowed. This wasn't an original thought. She heard Hammer complain about it every day.

West would drive her chief through the city, and Hammer would look out, poking her finger and talking about those businessmen behind tall walls of glass who decided what went into the paper and what crimes got solved and who became the next mayor. Hammer would rail on about Fortune 500 yahoos who didn't live anywhere near here and determined whether the police needed a bicycle squad or laptops or different pistols. Rich men had decided to change the uniforms years ago and to merge the city police with the Mecklenburg County's Sheriff's Department. Every decision was unimaginative and based on economics, according to Hammer.

West believed every bit of it as she and Brazil cruised past the huge, new stadium where David Copperfield was making magic, and parking decks were jammed with thousands of cars. Brazil was oddly subdued, and not writing down a word. West looked curiously at him as the police scanner rudely announced this modern city's primitive crimes, and the radio softly played Elton John.

'Any unit in the area,' a dispatcher said. 'B&E in progress, four hundred block East Trade Street.'

West floored it and flipped on lights. She whelped the siren, gunning past other cars. 'That's us,' she said, snapping up the mike.

Brazil got interested.

'Unit 700,' West said over the air.

The dispatcher wasn't expecting a deputy chief to respond, and sounded somewhat startled and confused.

'What unit?' the dispatcher inquired.

'700,' replied West. 'In the nine hundred block. I'll take the B&E in progress.'

'Ten-four, 700!'

The radio broadcast the call. Other cars responded as West cut in and out of traffic. Brazil was staring at her with new interest. Maybe this wasn't going to be so bad after all.

'Since when do deputy chiefs answer calls?' he said to her.

'Since I got stuck with you.'

The projects on East Trade were cement barracks subsidized by the government and exploited by criminals who did deals in the dark and got their women to lie when the cops showed up. Breaking and entering around here, it had been West's experience, usually meant someone was pissed off. Most of the time, this was a girlfriend calling in a complaint on an apartment where her man was hiding and had enough outstanding warrants to be locked up twenty times.

'You stay in the car,' West ordered her ride-along as she parked behind two cruisers.

'No way.' Brazil grabbed the door handle. 'I didn't go to all this trouble to sit in the car everywhere we go. Besides, it isn't safe to be out here alone.'

West didn't comment as she scanned buildings with windows lighted and dark. She studied parking lots filled with drug dealer cars, and didn't see a soul.

'Then stay behind me, keep your mouth shut, and do what you're told,' she told him as she got out.

The plan was pretty simple. Two officers would take the front of the apartment, on the first floor, and West and Brazil would go around back to make sure no one tried to flee through that door. Brazil's heart was pounding and he was sweating beneath his leather jacket as they walked in the thick darkness beneath sagging clotheslines in one of the city's war zones. West scanned windows and unsnapped her holster as she quietly got on the radio.

'No lights on,' she said over the air. 'Closing in.'

She drew her pistol. Brazil was inches behind her and wished he were in front, as furtive officers they could not see closed in on a unit scarred by graffiti. Trash was everywhere, caught on rusting fences and in the trees, and the cops drew their guns as they reached the door.

One of them spoke into his radio, giving West, their leader, an update, 'We got the front.'

'Police!' his partner threatened.

Brazil was concerned about the uneven terrain, and clotheslines hanging low enough to choke someone, and broken glass everywhere in the tar-black night. He was afraid West might hurt herself and turned on his Mag-Lite, illuminating her in a huge circle of light. Her sneaking silhouette with drawn pistol was bigger than God.

'*Turn that fucking thing off!*' she whipped around and hissed at him.

Charlotte police caught no one on that call. West and Brazil were in a bad mood as they rode and the radio chattered. She could have gotten shot. Thank God her officers hadn't seen what this idiot reporter had done. She couldn't wait to give Hammer a piece of her mind, and was halfway tempted to call her boss at home. West needed something to give her a boost and pulled into the Starvin Marvin on South Tryon Street. Before she had shifted the car into park, Brazil was pulling up his door handle.

'You ever heard of looking before you leap?' she asked, like a severe schoolteacher.

Brazil gave her an indignant, disgusted look as he undid his seatbelt. 'I can't wait to write about you,' he threatened.

'Look.' West nodded at the store, at the plate glass in front, at customers prowling inside and making purchases. 'Pretend you're a cop. That should be easy for you. So you get out of your cop car? Don't check? Walk in on a robbery in progress? And guess what?' She climbed out and stared inside at him. 'You're dead.' She slammed the door shut.

Brazil watched Deputy Chief West walk into the convenience store. He started to make notes, gave up, and leaned back in the seat. He did not understand what was happening. It bothered him a lot that she did not want him around, even though he was convinced he didn't give a rat's ass. No wonder she wasn't married. Who would want to live with somebody like that? Brazil already knew that if he were ever successful, he wouldn't be mean to people new at life. It was heartless and said everything about West's true character.

She made him pay for his own coffee. It cost a dollar and fifteen cents, and she hadn't bothered to ask him how he drank it, which wasn't with Irish cream and twenty packs of sugar. Brazil could barely swallow it, but did the best he could as they resumed patrolling. She was smoking again. They began to cruise a downtown street, where prostitutes clutching washcloths strolled languidly along the sidewalk, following them with luminous, empty eyes.

'What are the washcloths for?' Brazil asked.

'What do you expect? Finger bowls? It's a messy profession,' West remarked.

He shot her another look.

'No matter what kind of car I drive, they know I'm here,' she went on, flicking an ash out the window.

'Really?' he asked. 'I guess the same ones have been out here, what, fifteen years, then? And they remember you. Imagine that.'

'You know, this isn't how you make points,' West warned.

He was looking out and thoughtful when he said, 'Don't you miss it?'

West watched the ladies of the night and didn't want to answer him. 'Can you tell which are men?'

'That one, maybe.'

Brazil stared at a big, ugly hooker in a vinyl miniskirt, her tight black top stretched over opera breasts. Her come-hither walk was slow and bulging as she stared hate into the cop car.

'Nope. She's real,' West let Brazil know, and not adding that the hooker was also an undercover cop, wired, armed, and married with a kid. 'The men have good legs,' she went on. 'Anatomically correct perfect fake breasts. No hips. You get close, which I don't recommend, they shave.'

Brazil was quiet.

'Guess you didn't learn all this working for the TV magazine,' she added.

He could feel her glancing at him, as if she had something else on her mind.

'So, you drive that Cadillac with shark fins?' she finally got around to it.

He continued looking out at the trade show along the street, trying to tell women from men.

'In your driveway,' West went on. 'Doesn't look like something you'd drive.'

'It isn't,' Brazil said.

'Gotcha.' West sucked on the cigarette, and flicked another ash into the wind. 'You don't live alone.'

He continued staring out his window. 'I have an old BMW 2002. It was my dad's. He got it used and fixed it up, could fix anything.'

They passed a silver rental Lincoln. West noticed it because the man inside had the interior light on and looked lost. He was talking on his portable phone, and casting about in this bad part of town. He turned off on Mint Street. Brazil was still looking out at dangerous people looking back at them when West got interested in the Toyota directly ahead, it's side window knocked out, the license plate hanging by a coat hanger. There were two young males inside. The driver was watching her in the rearview mirror.

'What you wanna bet we got a stolen car ahead,' West announced.

She typed the plate number into the MDT. It began to beep as if she'd just won at slot machines. She read the display and flipped on flashing blue and red lights. The Toyota blasted ahead of them.

'Shit!' West exclaimed.

Now she was in a high-speed pursuit, trying to be a race driver and balance a cigarette and coffee and snatch up the mike, all at the same time. Brazil didn't know what to do to help. He was having the adventure of his life.

'700!' West's voice went up as she yelled into the mike. 'I'm in pursuit!'

'Go ahead, 700,' the radio came back. 'You have the air.'

'I'm north on Pine, turning left on Seventh, give you a description in a second.'

Brazil could scarcely contain himself. Why didn't she pass, cut the car off. The Toyota was just a V6. How fast could it go?

'Hit the siren!' West shouted at him as the engine strained.

Brazil didn't have this course in the volunteer academy. Unfastening his seatbelt, he groped around under the dash, the steering column, West's knees, and was practically in her lap when he found a button that felt promising. He pressed it as they roared down the street. The trunk loudly popped up. West's car rocked into a dip as they sped after the Toyota, and crime-scene equipment, a raincoat, a bubble light, flares spilled out, scattering over pavement. West couldn't believe it as she stared into the rearview mirror at her career bouncing away in the afterburn. Brazil was very quiet as police lights were turned off. They slowed, crawled off the road, and stopped. West looked at her ride-along.

'Sorry,' Brazil said.

Chapter Three

West answered nothing more for an hour and twenty-five minutes, as she and Brazil inched their way along the street, collecting police gear that had jumped out of the trunk. The bubble light was shattered blue plastic. Flares were crushed paper cases leaking a dangerous composition. A Polaroid crime-scene camera would capture nothing any more. The raincoat was miles away, snagged on the undercarriage of a station wagon, touching the exhaust pipe and soon to catch on fire.

West and Brazil drove and stopped, picked up, and drove again. This went on without conversation. West was so angry she did not dare speak. So far, two patrol units had cruised past. There was no doubt in the deputy chief's mind that the entire four-to-midnight shift knew exactly what had happened and probably thought it was West who had hit the switch because she hadn't been in a pursuit in this life. Before tonight she had been respected. She had been admired by the troops. She stole a hateful glance at Brazil, who had recovered a jumper cable and was neatly coiling and tucking it beside the spare tire, which was the only thing that hadn't flown out, because it was bolted down.

'Look,' Brazil suddenly spoke, staring at her beneath a street light. 'I didn't do it on purpose. What more do you want me to say?'

West got back in the car. Brazil halfway wondered if she might drive off without him, and just leave him out here to be murdered by drug dealers or hookers who were really men. Maybe the consequences were occurring to West, too. She waited for him to climb in. He shut the door and pulled the seatbelt across his chest. The scanner hadn't stopped, and he was hoping they'd go on something else quick so he could redeem himself.

'I have no reason to have a detailed knowledge of your car,' Brazil said in a quiet, reasonable tone. 'The Crown Vic I got to drive during the academy was older than this. The trunk opened from the outside. And we don't get to use sirens . . .'

She shoved the car in gear and drove. 'I know all that. I'm not blaming you. You didn't do it on purpose. Enough already,' she said.

She decided to try another part of town, off Remus Road near the Dog Pound. Nothing would be going on there. Her assumption would have been accurate, were it not for an old drunk woman who decided to start screaming on the lawn of the Mount Moriah Primitive Baptist Church, near the Greyhound bus station and the Presto Grill. West heard the call over the scanner and had no choice but to back up the responding unit. She and Brazil were maybe four blocks away.

'This shouldn't be anything and we're going to make sure we keep it that way,' West pointedly told Brazil as she sped up and took a right on Lancaster.

The one-story church was yellow brick with gaudy

colored glass windows all lit up and nobody home, the patchy lawn littered with beer bottles near the JESUS CALLS sign in front. An old woman was screaming and crying hysterically, and trying to pull away from two uniformed cops. Brazil and West got out of their car, heading to the problem. When the patrolmen saw the deputy chief in all her brass, they didn't know what to make of it and got exceedingly nervous.

'What we got?' West asked when she got to them.

The woman screamed and had no teeth. Brazil could not understand a note she was wailing.

'Drunk and disorderly,' said a cop whose nameplate read *Smith*. 'We've picked her up before.'

The woman was in her sixties, at least, and Brazil could not take his eyes off her. She was drunk and writhing in the harsh glare of a street light near the sign of a church she probably did not attend. She was dressed in a faded green Hornets sweatshirt and dirty jeans, her belly swollen, her breasts wind socks on a flat day, arms and legs sticks with spider webs of long dark hair.

Brazil's mother used to make scenes outside the house, but not any more. He remembered a night long ago when he drove home from the Harris-Teeter grocery to find his mother out in front of the house. She was yelling and chopping down the picket fence as a patrol car pulled up. Brazil tried to stop her and stay out of the way of the axe. The Davidson policeman knew everyone in town, and didn't lock up Brazil's mother for disturbing the peace or being drunk in public, even though he had justification.

West was checking the old woman's cuffed wrists in back as blue and red lights strobed and her wailing went on, pierced by pain. West shot the officers a hot, angry look.

'Where's the key?' she demanded. 'These are way too tight.'

Smith had been around since primitive times and reminded West of jaded, unhappy old cops who ended up working private security for corporations. West held out her hand, and he gave her the tiny metal key. West worked it into the cuffs, springing them open. The woman instantly calmed down as cruel steel disappeared. She tenderly rubbed deep angry red impressions on her wrists, and West admonished the troops.

'You can't do that,' she continued to shame them. 'You're hurting her.'

West asked the woman to hold up drooping arms so West could pat her down, and it entered West's mind that she ought to grab a pair of gloves. But she didn't have a box in her car because she wasn't suppose to need things like that anymore, and, in truth, the woman had been put through enough indignity. West did not like searching people, never had, and she remembered in the old days finding unfortunate surprises like bird claw fetishes, feces, used condoms, and erections. She thought of rookie days, of fishing cold slimy Spam out of Chicken Wing's pocket right before he socked her with his one arm. This old lady had nothing but a black comb, and a key on a shoelace around her neck.

Her name was Ella Joneston, and she was very quiet as the police lady cuffed her again. The steel was cold but didn't have the teeth it did a minute ago when the sons-a-bitches *snaked* her. She knew exactly what it was they wrapped around her wrists in back where she couldn't see, and it bit and bit without relief, venom spreading through her, making her shake as she screamed.

Her heart swelled up big, beating against her ribs, and would have broke had that blue car with the nice lady not pulled up.

Ella Joneston had always known that death was when your heart broke. Hers had come close many times, going back to when she was twelve and boys in the projects knocked her down right after she'd washed her hair. They did things she never would speak of, and she'd gone home and picked dirt and bits of leaves out of braids and washed off while nobody asked. The police lady was sweet, and there was someone in plain clothes there to help her, a clean-looking boy with a kind face. A detective, Ella reckoned. They took each of her arms, like she was going to Easter Sunday and dressed in something fine.

'Why you out here drinking like this?' The lady in uniform meant business but she wasn't harmful.

Ella wasn't sure where *out here* was. She didn't have a way to get places. So she couldn't be far from her apartment in Earle Village, where she had been sitting in front of the TV when the phone had rung earlier this evening. It was her daughter with the awful news about Efrim, Ella's fourteen-year-old grandson, who was in the hospital. Efrim had been shot several times this morning. Everyone supposed the white doctors tried all they could, but Efrim had always been stubborn. The memory brought fresh hot tears to Ella's eyes.

Ella told the lady cop and the detective all about it as they situated her into the back of a police car with a partition to make sure Ella couldn't hurt anyone. Ella mapped out Efrim's entire short life, going back to when Ella held him in her arms right after Lorna birthed him. He was always trouble, like his father. Efrim started dancing when he was two. He used to act big beneath the streetlight out front, with those other boys and all their money.

'I'm going to get your seatbelt on,' the blond detective said, snapping her in and smelling like apples and spices.

The old woman reeked of stale bad hygiene and booze, triggering more images for Brazil. His hands were shaking slightly and not as facile as usual. He didn't understand what the woman was muttering and gumming and crying about, and every breath smelled like the inside of a Dumpster in the heat. West wasn't helping a bit now, standing back and watching, making Brazil do the dirty work. His fingers brushed the old woman's neck and he was startled by how smooth and warm it was.

'You're going to be all right.' Brazil kept saying what couldn't possibly be true.

West was not naive. She knew patrol was a problem. How could it not be with Deputy Chief Goode heading it? That beat cops might be a little too rough or simply unprofessional in general wasn't a shock, but West couldn't stomach it. She approached the two patrolmen, both older and miserable in their jobs. She got in Smith's face and remembered being a sergeant and putting up with dead wood like him. As far as she was concerned, he was so low on the food chain, she wouldn't slop hogs with him.

'Don't let me *ever* see or hear of anything like this again,' West said in that low tone that Brazil found scary.

West was close enough to see stubble that looked like sand, and a firestorm of broken blood vessels caused by what Smith did when he wasn't in a patrol car. His eyes were lifeless on hers, for his building had been vacant for years.

'We're out here to help, not hurt,' West whispered. 'Remember? That goes for you, too,' she added to his partner.

Neither cop had any idea about the boy riding with the deputy chief this night, and they sat inside the cruiser with its hornet's nests on the doors, watching the midnight-blue Crown Victoria leave. Their prisoner in back was quietly snoring.

'Maybe Deputy Chief Virgin finally found a boyfriend,' said Smith as he peeled open two sticks of Big Red gum.

'Yeah,' said the other cop, 'when she gets tired of Romper Room, I'll show her what she's missing with the big dogs.'

They laughed, pulling out. Moments later, the scanner announced more bad news.

'Thirteen-hundred block Beatties Ford Road,' it said. 'Report of an ambulance held hostage by a subject with a knife.'

'Glad we're tied up on a call,' Smith said, smacking a mouthful of cinnamon.

It was West's bad luck that Jerome Swan had not experienced a pleasant evening. It had begun at a fuzzy hour before the sun had gone down in this rundown part of the city. West had no reason to be aware of the nip joint in the area known as the Basin, off Tryon Street, very close to the Dog Pound, where she had been heading for quite some time now. So when the call went out, she was trapped, really. Two marked units got there first, and then Captain Jennings arrived with his ride-along, City Councilman Hugh Bledsoe.

'Shit,' West said when they rolled up on the scene. 'Fuck.'

She parked on the side of the narrow, dark street.

'You see that tall man right there getting out of the car, the one in the suit? You know who that is?'

Brazil reached for the door handle, then thought better of it.

'I know exactly who it is,' he said. 'Huge Bedsore.'

West shot him a surprised look. It was true the cops had a pet name for their city councilman, but she wasn't clear on how Brazil knew about it.

'Not one peep out of you,' West warned as she opened her door. 'Stay out of the way.' She got out. 'And don't touch anything.'

The ambulance was rumbling, and parked in the middle of the street with the tailgate open wide, light spilling out as red and blue flashed and strobed from cop cars. The men had convened near a rear tire to come up with a plan. West followed around to the back to assess the problem for herself, Brazil right behind her and dying to get in front. Swan was inside, as far back as he could get, wielding a pair of surgical scissors, his eyes bloody egg yolks filled with fury when the woman cop in the white shirt filled his vision.

He had knots on his head and was bleeding from the fight he had gotten into at the nip joint where he had been gambling and drinking Night Train Express fortified wine. When he was put in the ambulance, it was one of those times when he decided he really didn't feel like going anywhere just that second. Whenever this happened, Swan seized the environment. In this case, he grabbed the closest dangerous object he could, and yelled to the paramedics that he had AIDS and was going to cut every one of them. They jumped out and got the cops, all of them men, except for that one with the big tits peering in at him like she might do something.

West saw the problem plainly. The subject was holding down the lock to a side door that led out to the street, and the only way to get to him was for someone to climb inside the ambulance. This didn't require much of a plan. West went around to confer with the committee of officers still gathered by the same tire.

'I'm going to divert him,' she said as Bledsoe stared at her as if he'd never seen a woman in uniform. 'The minute he takes his hand off the door, you guys grab him,' she made sure they understood.

She got closer to the open back of the ambulance and made a face, waving a hand before her eyes.

'Who used pepper spray?' she called out.

'Even that didn't stop him,' one of the cops let her know.

Next thing Brazil knew, West had climbed inside the ambulance and picked up an aluminum stretcher to use as a shield. She did this easily, and her lips moved. Swan didn't like whatever it was she was communicating to him. His eyes were on hers, arteries bulging in his neck as he twitched and challenged her with looks and utterances. She was halfway inside when he lunged. Swan was sucked out as if he opened the door of an airplane. Brazil went around to check and found him facedown on the street being cuffed by all those men with a plan. City Councilman Bledsoe watched, hands in his pockets. His eyes followed West as she walked back to her car. Then he stared at Brazil.

'Come here,' Bledsoe said to him.

Brazil cast a furtive glance in West's direction, certain he might get left alone out on this dark, unfriendly road.

He was mindful that West had ordered him not to talk to anyone.

'You're the ride-along,' Bledsoe stated as he got closer.

'I don't know if I'm *the* ride-along,' Brazil answered.

He was just trying to be modest, but the councilman took it the wrong way. He thought the kid was being a smartass.

'Guess Superwoman there just gave you a good story, huh?' The councilman nodded his head toward West, who was getting back into her car.

Brazil was beginning to panic. 'I've got to go,' he said.

Bledsoe had a goatee and liked gloss gel. He was the minister of the Baptist church on Jeremiah Avenue. Strobing police lights flashed in his glasses as he stared at Brazil and mopped his neck with a handkerchief.

'Let me just tell you one thing,' he went on, getting unctuous. 'The city of Charlotte doesn't need people coming out here and being insensitive to humanity and poverty and crime. Even this man here is not to be ridiculed or laughed at.'

Swan was being led away, dazed. He had been minding his own business in the nip joint one minute and was sucked up by aliens the next. Bledsoe swept a hand over the lighted skyline in the distance, rising and sparkling like a kingdom.

'Why don't you write about that?' the councilman said it as if he wanted Brazil to start taking notes, so he did. 'Look at all the good, the accomplishments. Look at how we've grown. Voted the most attractive city to live in nationwide, third largest banking center in the country, with an appreciation of the arts. People are in line to move here. But no. Oh no.' He tapped Brazil's shoulder. 'I'll wake up in the morning to another depressing story. An ambulance hijacked by a man with a knife. News intended to strike fear in the hearts of citizens.'

West started pulling out and Brazil broke into a run, as if he were about to miss the school bus. Bledsoe looked surprised and annoyed for he hadn't finished talking, and West knew it was no accident that the councilman just happened to be out tonight while Andy Brazil, the experiment in community policing, was riding. Bledsoe would find his way into a story and impress his constituents this reelection year with how diligent and caring he was. CITY COUNCILMAN TAKES TIME TO RIDE WITH POLICE. She could see the headline now. Opening the glove box, she rummaged for a roll of Tums.

She stopped the car so Brazil could climb in. He wasn't even breathing hard and had just sprinted a good fifty yards. Reminders like that made West want to smoke.

'I told you not to talk to anyone,' she said, lighting up.

'What was I supposed to do?' He was indignant. 'You walked off without me and he got in my face.'

They passed more impoverished houses, most of them boarded up and not lived in anymore. Brazil was staring at West, thinking about Bledsoe calling her *Superwoman*.

'They made a mistake promoting you,' Brazil said. 'That was really something, what you did back there.'

West had been good at this once. Taking the sergeant's exam had been the first step toward paperwork and political correctness. If Hammer hadn't come to town, West was fairly certain she would have looked for something else.

'So tell me,' Brazil was saying.

'Tell you what?' West asked, blowing out a stream of smoke.

'What did you say to him?' Brazil wanted to know.

'Say to who?'

'You know, the guy in the ambulance.'

'Can't tell you.'

'Come on. You said something that really pissed him off,' Brazil insisted.

'Nope.' West flicked an ash out the window.

'Oh, come on. What?'

'I didn't say anything.'

'Yes you did.'

'I called him a pussy,' she finally confessed. 'And you can't print that.'

'You're right,' Brazil told her.

Chapter Four

The downtown skyline was huge around a terrible crime scene, minutes past ten P.M. Police were tense and sweating, their flashlights probing a parking lot behind an abandoned building, and an area overgrown with weeds where the black rental Lincoln had been abandoned. The driver's door was open, headlights burning, interior bell dinging a feeble warning that was too late. Detective Brewster had been called in from home and was standing near the Lincoln, talking on his portable phone. He was dressed in jeans and an old Izod shirt, his badge and a Smith & Wesson .40 caliber pistol and extra magazines clipped to his belt.

'Looks like we got another one,' he said to his in-transit boss.

'Can you give me a ten-thirteen?' West's voice sounded over the phone.

'Ten-thirteen's still clear.' Brewster looked around. 'But not for long. What's your ten-twenty?'

'Dilworth. Heading your way on forty-nine. EOT ten-fifteen.'

* * *

Brazil had learned how to talk on the radio in the academy and understood codes and why Brewster and West were talking in them. Something very bad had gone down, and they didn't want anyone else, a reporter for example, monitoring what they were saying. Basically, Brewster had let West know that the scene was still clear of people who shouldn't be there, but not for long. West was en route and would arrive in less than fifteen minutes.

West reached for the portable phone she had plugged into the cigarette lighter. She was on red alert, driving fast as she dialed a number. Her conversation with Chief Hammer was brief.

West shot Brazil a severe look. 'Do everything you're told,' she said. 'This is serious.'

By the time they reached the crime scene, reporters had gathered in the night, all poised as Brazil's peers tried to get close to a terrible tragedy. Webb held a microphone, talking into a camera, his pretty face sincere and full of sorrow.

'No identification of the victim, who like the first three shot to death very close to here was driving a rental car,' Webb taped for the eleven o'clock news.

West and Brazil were quiet and determined as they made their way through. They avoided microphones jabbed their way, cameras rolling in their faces as they ducked and dodged and hurried. Questions flew all around them as if some fast-breaking news bomb had gone off, and Brazil was terrified. He was acutely self-conscious and embarrassed in a way he did not understand.

'Now you know what it's like,' West said to him under her breath.

Bright yellow crime-scene tape stretched from woods to a streetlight. Big black block letters flowed across it, repeating the warning CAUTION CRIME SCENE DO

NOT ENTER. It barred reporters and the curious from the Lincoln and the senseless death beyond it. Just inside it was an ambulance with engine rumbling, cops and detectives everywhere with flashlights. Video tape was running, flashguns going off, and crime-scene technicians were preparing the car to be hauled into headquarters for processing.

Brazil was so busy taking everything in and worrying about how close he was going to be allowed to get that he did not notice Chief Hammer until he walked into her.

'Sorry,' Brazil muttered to the older woman in a suit.

Hammer was distressed and immediately began conferring with West. Brazil took in the short graying hair softly framing the pretty, sharp face, and the short stature and trim figure. He had never met the chief, but he suddenly recognized her from television and photographs he had seen. Brazil was awed, openly staring. He could get a terrible crush on this woman. West turned and pointed at him as if he were a dog.

'Stay,' she commanded.

Brazil had expected as much but wasn't happy about it. He started to protest, but no one was interested. Hammer and West ducked under the tape, and a cop gave Brazil a warning look should he think about following. Brazil watched West and Hammer stop to investigate something on the old, cracked pavement. Bloody drag marks glistened in the beam of West's flashlight, and based on the small, smeared puddle just inches from the open car door, she thought she knew what had happened.

'He was shot right here,' she told Hammer. 'And he fell.' She pointed to the puddle. 'That's where his head hit. He was dragged by his feet.'

Blood was beginning to coagulate, and Hammer could

feel the heat of the throbbing lights and the night and the horror. She could smell death. Her nose had learned to pick it up the first year she was a cop. Blood broke down fast, got runny around the edges and thick inside, and the odor was weirdly sweet and putrid at the same time. The trail led to a Gothic tangle of overgrown vines and pines, with a lot of weeds.

The victim looked middle-aged and had been dressed in a khaki suit wrinkled from travel when someone had ruined his head with gunshots. Pants and Jockey shorts were down around fleshy knees, the familiar hourglass painted bright orange, leaves and other plant debris clinging to blood.

Dr Wayne Odom had been the medical examiner in the greater Charlotte-Mecklenburg area for more than twenty years. He could tell that the spray-painting had occurred right where the body had been found, because a breeze had carried a faint orange mist up to the underside of nearby poplar leaves. Dr Odom was reloading a camera with bloody gloved hands, and was fairly certain he was dealing with homosexual serial murders. He was a deacon at Northside Baptist Church and believed that an angry God was punishing America for its perversions.

'Damn it!' Hammer muttered as crime-scene technicians scoured the area for evidence.

West was frustrated to the point of fear. 'This is what? A hundred yards from the last one? I got people all over the place out here. Nobody saw anything. How can this happen?'

'We can't watch the street every second of the day,' Hammer angrily said.

From a distance, Brazil watched a detective going through the victim's wallet. Brazil could only imagine what West and Hammer were seeing as he impatiently waited by West's car, taking notes. One thing he had learned while writing term papers was that even if he didn't have all the information, he could create a mood. He studied the back of the abandoned brick building, and decided it had been some sort of warehouse once. Every window was shattered, and an eerie dark emptiness stared out. The fire escape was solid rust and broken off halfway down.

Emergency lights were diluted and weird by the time they got to the thicket where everyone was gathered. Fireflies flickered around the dinging rental car, and Brazil could hear the sounds of far-off traffic. Paramedics were coming through, sweating in jumpsuits, and carrying a stretcher and a folded black body bag. Brazil craned his neck, writing furiously, as the paramedics reached the scene. They unfolded the stretcher's legs, and Hammer turned around when metal clacked. West and Brewster were studying the victim's driver's license. No one was interested in giving Brazil a quote.

'Carl Parsons,' Brewster read from a driver's license. 'Spartanburg, South Carolina. Forty-one years old. Cash gone, no jewelry if he had any.'

'Where was he staying?' Hammer asked him.

'Looks like we got a confirmation number for the Hyatt near Southpark.'

West crouched to see the world from a different angle. Parsons was half on his back and half on his side in a nest of bloody leaves, his eyes sleepy slits and dull. Dr Odom inflicted yet one more indignity by inserting a long chemical thermometer up the rectum to get a core temperature. Whenever the medical examiner touched the body, more blood spilled from holes in the head. West knew that whoever was doing this had no plan to stop.

Brazil wasn't going to stop, no matter how much West got in his way. He had done all he could to capture visual details and mood, and now he was on the prowl. He happened to notice a new bright blue Mustang parked near an unmarked car, where a teenaged boy sat in the front seat with a detective Brazil had seen before, running around, impersonating a drug dealer. Brazil took more notes as the teenager talked and paramedics zipped the body inside a pouch. Reporters, especially Webb, were obsessed with getting footage and photographs of the murdered man being carried away like a big black cocoon. No one but Brazil focused on the teenager climbing out of the detective's car and returning to his Mustang, in no hurry.

The top was down, and when Brazil headed toward the flashy car, the teenager's blood began to pound with excitement again. The nice-looking blond guy had a reporter's notepad in hand. Jeff Deedrick got out his Chapstick and cranked the engine, trying to look cool as his hands shook.

'I'm with the *Charlotte Observer*,' Brazil said, standing close to the driver's door. 'I'd like to ask you a few questions.'

Deedrick was going to be famous. He was seventeen but could pass for twenty-one unless he got carded. He would get all those girls who, before this night, had never paid him any mind.

'I guess it's all right,' Deedrick reluctantly said, as if weary of all the attention.

Brazil climbed inside the Mustang, which was new and did not belong to Deedrick. Brazil could tell by the dainty blue lanyard keychain that matched the color of the car. Most guys too young to drink didn't have cellular phones, either, Brazil noted, unless they were drug dealers. He was willing to bet that the Mustang belonged to Deedrick's mother.

First Brazil got name, address, phone number, and repeated every syllable back to Deedrick to make certain all was correct. This he had learned the hard way. His first month on the job, he had gotten three *We Were Wrongs* in a row for insignificant, picayune errors relating to insignificant details, such as somebody *junior* versus somebody *the third*. This had resulted in an obituary about the son, versus the father. The son was having tax problems, and didn't mind the mistake. He had called Brazil, personally, to request that the paper leave well enough alone. But Packer wouldn't.

Perhaps Brazil's most embarrassing mistake, and one he preferred not to think about, was when he covered a loud, volatile community meeting about a controversial pet ordinance. He confused a place with a person, and persisted in referring to *Latta Park* this and *Miss Park* that. Jeff Deedrick, however, he had right, of this Brazil made sure. There would be no problems here. Brazil eyed the crime scene in the distance, as paramedics loaded the body into the ambulance.

'I admit I had a few, am driving along and know I'm not going to make it home,' Deedrick kept talking, nervous and excited.

'Then you pulled back here to use the bathroom?' Brazil flipped a page, writing fast.

'Pulled in, and see this car with lights on, the door open and think someone else is taking a leak.' Deedrick hesitated. He took off his baseball cap and put it on backward. 'I wait, don't see no one. Now I'm getting curious, so I go on over and see him! Thank God I got a phone.'

Deedrick's wide stare was fixed on nothing, and sweat was beading on his forehead and rolling from his armpits. At first he thought the guy was drunk, had dropped his pants to take a piss, and had passed out. Then Deedrick saw orange paint, and blood. He had never been so frightened in his life. He galloped back to his car, peeled out, and floored it the hell out of there. He pulled off under an overpass and peed. He called 911.

'My first thought?' Deedrick went on, a little more relaxed now. 'It's not really happening. I mean, the little bell is ringing and ringing, all this blood, pants down around his knees. And I . . . Well, you know. His parts.'

Brazil looked up at him. Deedrick was stuttering.

'What about them?' Brazil wanted to know.

'It's like they were spray-painted traffic cone orange. With this shape.'

Deedrick was blushing as he outlined a figure-eight in the air.

Brazil handed him the notepad. 'Can you draw it?' he asked.

Deedrick shakily drew an hourglass, to Brazil's amazement.

'Like a black widow spider,' Brazil muttered as he watched West and Hammer duck under crime-scene tape, ready to leave.

Brazil ended the interview, in one big hurry, conditioned by now to fear being left. He also had a question that Hammer and West needed to hear. He addressed the chief first, out of respect.

'Has the killer spray-painted all his victims with an hourglass?' Brazil said earnestly and with excitement.

West went still, which was rare for her. She did not move. Brazil thought Hammer was the most overpowering person he had ever met. She waved him off with a *no comment* sort of gesture.

'I'll let you handle this,' she said to West.

Hammer headed to shadows where her car was parked. West strode to her Ford without a word, and when Brazil got in and fastened up, they had nothing to say to each other. The scanner was active and it was getting very late. It was time to return Brazil to the parking deck so he could get in his own car and get the hell out of her hair. That was the way West felt about it. What a night.

They were riding back to the LEC at almost midnight, both of them keyed up and tense. West couldn't believe she had hand-delivered a reporter to that scene. She absolutely could not take it in. This had to be somebody else's life that was happening to West on a dimension where she had no control, and she was reminded of a time she would never admit to anyone, when she was a sophomore at a very small, religious school, in Bristol, Tennessee. The trouble began with Mildred.

Mildred was very big and all the other girls on her floor were afraid of her. But not West. She saw Mildred as an opportunity because Mildred was from Miami. Mildred's parents had sent her to King College to get saved, and to straighten out. Mildred found someone in Kingsport who knew someone in Johnson City who had dealings with a guy at Eastman Kodak who sold pot. West and Mildred lit up one night on the tennis courts where no one could see anything except tiny orange coals glowing and fading by a net post on court two.

It was awful. West had never done anything this wicked, and now she knew why. She lost control, belly laughing and telling outlandish stories while Mildred confessed she had been fat all her life and knew precisely what it felt like to be black and discriminated against. Mildred was something. The two of them sat out on red and green Laykold for hours, finally lying on their backs and staring up at stars and a moon that looked like a bright yellow swing swelling with the round shadow of promise. They talked about having babies. They drank Cokes, and ate whatever Mildred had in her pocketbook.

Mostly this was Nabs, Reese's Cups, Kit Kats, and things like that. God, how West hated to think about that wretched time. It was her luck that, in the end, marijuana made her paranoid. A couple tokes into the third joint, she wanted to run as fast as she could, dive into her dorm room, punch in the lock, hide under the bed, and come back out in camouflage, a Tec-9 ready to go. When Mildred decided that West was physically attractive, the timing wasn't good.

West believed women were great. She'd loved every woman teacher and coach she'd ever known, as long as they were nice. But there were a couple of problems here. She had never really contemplated the possibility of what Mildred's interest might mean about West, or West's family, or of West's possibilities in the after-life. Plus, Mildred grabbed West no differently than a guy would. Mildred didn't even ask, and this was unfortunate, since West was in camouflage, at least in her mind. West turned into the LEC parking deck for visitors.

'You can't do anything with that,' West said to Brazil in an accusing tone.

'With what?' Brazil asked in a measured voice.

'You know *what*. In the first place, you had no business talking to a witness,' West said.

'That's what reporters do,' he replied.

'In the second place, the hourglass is something only the killer knows. Got it? So you don't put that in the paper. Period.'

'How can you say for a fact the killer's the only one who knows about it?' Brazil was about to lose his temper. 'How do you know it won't trigger information from somebody out there?'

West raised her voice and wished she had never met Andy Brazil. 'You do it, and the next homicide in this city's going to be you.'

'*Yours*,' he helped her out.

'That's it.' West turned into the police deck. She was not going to have this squirt correct her grammar one more time. 'You're dead.'

'I believe you just threatened me.' Brazil drew attention to it.

'Oh no. Not a threat,' West said. 'A promise.' She jammed the car into park. 'Find someone else to ride with.' She was the maddest she'd ever been. 'Where are you parked?'

Brazil yanked up the door handle in a murderous reply. 'Well, guess what?' he said. 'Fuck you.'

He got out and slammed the door. He stalked off into the dark, early morning. He managed to write his stories in time for the city edition, and he pulled off I-77 on his way home and bought two tallboy Miller Lites. He managed to drink both as he drove very fast. Brazil had a frightening habit of pushing his car as far it would go. Since his speedometer didn't work, he could only guess how fast he was going by the RPMs. He knew he was flying, going close to a hundred miles an hour, and it wasn't the first time he'd done this. Sometimes he wondered if he were trying to die.

At home, he checked on his mother. She was unconscious in bed, and snoring with her mouth open. Brazil leaned against the wall in the dark, the night-light a sad dim eye. He was depressed and frustrated. He thought about West and wondered why she was so heartless.

West walked into her own small house and tossed keys on her kitchen counter as Niles, her Abyssynian cat, appeared. Niles was on her heels, much like Brazil had been all day, and West flicked on her sound system and Elton John reminded her of the night. She hit another button, changing to Roy Orbison. She walked into the kitchen, popped open a beer, and felt maudlin and didn't know why. She went back into the living room and turned on the late-night news. It was all about the killing. She plopped on the couch at the same time Niles decided she should. He loved his owner and waited for his turn as the TV played bad news about a dreadful death in the city.

'Believed to be another out-of-town businessman simply in the wrong place at the wrong time,' Webb said into the camera.

West was restless, worn out and disgusted, all at the same time. She wasn't happy with Niles, either. He had climbed up her bookcases while she was out. She could always tell. How hard was it? He leapt up three shelves, just high enough to knock down bookends and a vase. As for the framed picture of West's father on the farm, well, what did Niles care about that? That cat. West hated him. She hated everyone.

'Come here, Sweetsy,' she said.

Niles made his ribs rattle, knowing how much it pleased her. It worked every time. Niles wasn't stupid. He reached around and licked his hindquarters because he could. When he looked at the lady who kept him, he made sure his eyes were very blue and crossed. Owners fell for that, and, predictably, she snatched him up and petted him. Niles was happy enough.

West wasn't. The next day when she got to work, Hammer was waiting for her deputy chief, and everybody seemed to know it. West left her Bojangles breakfast without even opening the bag. She dropped everything and hurried down the hall. West almost ran into Hammer's outer office and felt like giving Horgess the finger. He very much enjoyed West's negative reaction to being summoned like this.

'Let me call her,' Horgess said.

'Let me let you.' West didn't disguise how surly she felt.

Horgess was young, and had shaved his head. Why? Soon he would dream of hair. He would lust after it. He would watch movies starring people with hair.

'She'll see you now,' Horgess said, hanging up the phone.

'I'm sure.' West gave him a sarcastic smile.

'For God's sake, Virginia,' Hammer said the instant West walked in.

The chief was gripping the morning paper, shaking it, and pacing. Hammer didn't wear pants often, but today she was in them. Her suit was a deep royal blue, and she wore a red and white striped shirt and soft black leather shoes. West had to admit, her boss was stunning. Hammer could cover or show her legs without gender being an issue.

'Now what?' Hammer railed on. 'Four businessmen four weeks in a row. Carjackings, in which the killer changes his mind, leaves the cars? Robberies? A weird hourglass symbol spray-painted on the victims' groins? Make and model, names, professions. Everything but the damn crime-scene photos right there for all the world to see!'

The headline was huge:

BLACK WIDOW KILLER CLAIMS FOURTH VICTIM

'What was I supposed to do?' West said.

'Keep him out of trouble.'

'I'm not a babysitter.'

'A businessman from Orlando, a salesman from Atlanta, a banker from South Carolina, a Baptist minister. From Tennessee. Welcome to our lovely city.' Hammer tossed the paper on a couch. 'What do we do?'

'Letting him ride wasn't my idea,' West reminded her.

'What's done is done.' Hammer sat behind her desk. She picked up the phone and dialed. 'We can't get rid of him. Got any idea how that would look? On top of all the rest of it?' Her eyes glazed as the mayor's secretary answered. 'Listen, Ruth, get him now. I don't care what he's doing.' Hammer started drumming polished nails on the blotter.

West was in a worse mood when she left her boss's office. It wasn't fair. Life was hard enough, and she was beginning to wonder about Hammer. What did West know about her, anyway, except that she had come to Charlotte from Chicago, a huge city where people froze their asses off half the year and the mob had its way with public officials. Next thing, Hammer sailed here, that housewife husband of hers tagging along.

Brazil wasn't pleased with his circumstances, either. He was punishing himself again this morning, pounding up bleacher steps in the stadium where the Davidson Wildcats lost every football game, even some they hadn't played, it seemed. He was going at it and didn't care if he had a heart attack or was sore tomorrow. Deputy Chief West was a lowlife cowboy, and as insensitive as shit, and Chief Hammer wasn't at all what he had fantasized. Hammer could have at least smiled or glanced at him, and made him feel welcome last night. Brazil headed back up the steps again, sweat leaving gray spots on cement.

Hammer wanted to hang up on the mayor. She had had just about enough of his unimaginative way of solving problems.

'I understand the medical examiner believes these murders have a homosexual connection,' he was saying over the phone.

'That's one opinion,' Hammer answered. 'The fact is that we don't know. All the victims were married with children.'

'Exactly,' he slyly said.

'For God's sake, Chuck, don't pile this on me so early in the morning.' Hammer looked out the window and could almost see the bastard's office from where she sat.

'Point is, the theory is helpful,' he went on in his South Carolina drawl.

Mayor Charles Search was from Charleston. He was

Hammer's age and often considered what it might be like to bed her. If nothing else, it would remind her of things she seemed to have forgotten. Her place, for starters. If she wasn't married, he would swear she was a lesbian. He sat in his leather judge's chair, headset on, and doodled on a legal pad.

'The city, out of town businesses, won't be as bothered by this . . .' he was trying to say.

'Where are you so I can break your neck,' Hammer said over the phone. 'When was your lobotomy? I would have sent flowers.'

'Judy.' This doodle was really good. He focused on it, putting his glasses on. 'Calm down. I know exactly what I'm doing.'

'Of course you don't.'

Maybe she was a lesbian, or bisexual, anyway, with a grating Midwestern accent. He reached for a red pen, getting excited over his art. It was an atom with orbits of little molecules that looked weirdly like eggs. Birth. This was seminal.

To make matters ever so much worse this morning, West had to go to the morgue. North Carolina didn't have the best system, it was West's opinion. Some cases were taken care of locally, by Dr Odom and the police forensic labs. Other bodies were sent to the Chief Medical Examiner in Chapel Hill. Go figure. It was probably all about sports again. Hornets fans stayed in town, Tarheels got their lovely Y-incision in the big university town.

The Mecklenburg County Medical Examiner's office was on North College Street, across from the award-winning new public library. West was buzzed in at the glass entrance. She had to give the place credit. The building, which was the former Sears Garden Center, was brighter and more modern than most morgues, and had added another cold room the last time USAir had crashed another plane around here. It was a shame that North Carolina didn't seem inclined to hire a few more MEs for *the great state of Mecklenburg,* as some sour senators were inclined to disparage the state's fastest-growing, most progressive region.

There were only two forensic pathologists to handle more than a hundred homicides a year, and both of them were in the necropsy room when West arrived. The dead businessman didn't look any better now that Dr Odom had started on him. Brewster was at the table, wearing a disposable plastic apron and gloves. He nodded at her as she tied a gown in back, because West didn't take chances. Dr Odom was splashed with blood, and holding the scalpel like a pencil as he reflected back tissue. His patient had a lot of fat, which always looked worse inside out.

The morgue assistant was a big man who was always sweating. He plugged an autopsy saw into the overhead cord reel, and started on the skull. This West could do without. The sound was worse than the dentist's drill, the bony smell, not to mention the idea, awful. West would not be murdered or turn up dead suspiciously in any form or fashion. She would not have this done to her naked body with people like Brewster looking on while clerks passed around her pictures and made comments.

'Contact wounds, entrances here behind the right ear.' Dr Odom pointed a bloody gloved finger, mostly for her benefit. 'Large caliber. This is execution style.'

'Exactly like the others,' Brewster remarked.

'What about cartridge cases?' Dr Odom asked.

'Forty-fives, Winchester, probably Silvertips,' West

replied, thinking about Brazil's article again and all that he had revealed. 'Five each time. Perp doesn't bother picking them up, doesn't care. We need to get the FBI on this.'

'Fucking press,' Brewster said.

West had never been to Quantico. Her dream had always been to attend the FBI's National Academy, which was rather much the Oxford University of police training. But she'd been busy. Then she kept getting promoted. Finally, the only thing she was eligible for was executive training up there, for God's sake. That meant a bunch of big-bellied chiefs, assistant chiefs, and sheriffs, out on the firing range trying to make the transition from .38 specials to semiautomatic pistols. She'd heard the stories. All these guys blasting away, dumping brass into their hands, and taking the time to stuff it neatly in their pockets. Hammer offered to send West last year. Forget it. West didn't need to learn a thing from the FBI.

'I'd like to know what their profilers would have to say,' West said.

'Forget it,' Brewster said, chewing a toothpick and swiping Vicks up his nose.

Dr Odom picked up a big sponge, and squeezed water over organs. He grabbed a tan rubber hose, and suctioned blood out of the chest cavity.

'He smells like he was drinking,' said Brewster, who could no longer smell anything except childhood memories of colds.

'Maybe on the plane,' Odom agreed. 'What about those guys at Quantico?' He eyed Brewster, as if West had never brought up the subject.

'Busy as jumping beans,' Brewster replied. 'Like I said, forget it. They got what? Ten, eleven profilers and are about a thousand cases behind? Think the government's going to fund shit? Shit no. Too damn bad, too. 'Cause those profilers are damn good.'

Brewster had applied to the FBI early on, but forget that, too. They weren't hiring, or maybe it had to do with the polygraph test he wasn't about to take. He sniffed more Vicks. God, he hated death. It was ugly and it stunk. It was a tattletale. Like this fellow's dick, for example. The guy looked like a balloon with this little knot, so all his air didn't get out.

West was angry, her face hard, as she stared at the fleshy nude body opened up from neck to navel, and blaze orange paint no amount of scrubbing would wash away. She thought of his wife and family. No human should ever have to come to such a grim place and be put through something like this, and she felt fresh anger toward Brazil.

She was waiting for him when he trotted out of the Knight-Ridder building, his notepad in hand as he headed to his car and a story. West, in uniform, climbed out of her unmarked Ford, and she strode toward Brazil like she might tackle him. She wished she could have bottled that dead smell and sprayed it in Brazil's face, and rubbed his nose in the reality West had to live with every day. Brazil was in a hurry and had a lot on his mind. A Honda was on fire in the Mental Health parking lot, according to the scanner. Possibly, it was nothing, but what if someone was in it? Brazil stopped. He was startled as West jabbed a finger into his breastbone.

'Hey!' He grabbed her wrist.

'So how's the Black Widow reporter today?' West coldly said. 'I just came from the morgue, you know, where reality's laid out and carved up? Bet you've never been there. Maybe they'll let you watch someday. What a good story that would be, right? A man not old enough to be your daddy. Red hair, hundred and ninety-seven pounds. Guess what his hobby was.'

Brazil released West's arm. He groped for words but didn't have any.

'Backgammon, photography. He wrote the newsletter for his church, wife's dying of cancer. They got two kids, one grown, other a freshman at UNC. Anything else you want to know about him? Or is Mr Parsons nothing but a story to you? Little words on paper?'

Brazil was visibly shaken. He started walking off to his old BMW as the Honda in the Mental Health parking lot burned and he no longer cared. West wasn't going to let him off so easy. She grabbed his arm.

'Get your goddamn hands off me,' Brazil said. He jerked his arm free, unlocked his car door, and got in.

'You screwed me, Andy,' West told him.

Brazil cranked the engine, and squealed out of the parking deck. West returned to the LEC and didn't go straight to investigations because she had a few of her own. She stopped off at the Records Room, where women in their own special uniforms ruled the world. West really had to court these girls, especially Wanda, who weighed somewhere between two-fifty and three hundred pounds and could type a hundred and five words a minute. If West needed a record or to send a missing-person report off to NCIC, Wanda was either a hero or hell on earth, depending on when she was fed last. West brought in a bucket of KFC once a month, and sometimes Girl Scout or Christmas cookies, depending on what was in season. West approached the counter, and whistled at Wanda, who loved West. Wanda secretly wished she was a detective and worked for the deputy chief.

'Need your help,' West said, and her police belt was making her lower back ache, as usual.

Wanda scowled at a name West had scribbled on a slip of paper. 'Lord have mercy,' she said, shaking her head. 'If I don't remember that like it was yesterday.'

West couldn't be certain, but thought Wanda had gained more weight. God help her. Wanda took up two lanes of traffic.

'You sit on down.' Wanda pointed with her chin, as if she were Chinese. 'I'll get the microfilm.'

While Wanda's minions typed, stacked, and racked, West went through microfilm. She had her glasses on and was hurt by what she saw when she got to old articles about Brazil's father. His name, too, was Andrew, but people had called him Drew. He had been a cop here when West was a rookie. She had forgotten all about him, and had never made the connection. Christ, but now that she was looking at it, the tragedy came back to her and somehow put Brazil's life in focus.

Drew Brazil was a thirty-six-year-old robbery detective when he made a traffic stop in an unmarked car. He was shot close range in the chest, and died instantly. West took a long time looking at articles, and staring at his picture. She headed upstairs to her division and pulled the case, which no one had looked at in a decade, because it had been exceptionally cleared, and the dirtbag was still on death row. Drew Brazil was handsome. In one photograph, he wore a leather bomber jacket that West had seen before.

The scene photographs clubbed her somewhere in her chest. He was dead in the street, on his back, staring up at the sun on a spring Sunday morning. The .45 caliber bullet had almost ripped his heart in half, and in autopsy photographs, Odom had two thick fingers through the hole to demonstrate. This was something young Andy Brazil need never see, and West had no intention of talking to him ever again.

Chapter Five

Brazil was looking up articles, too, in the *Observer* file room. It was amazing how little had been written about Virginia West over the years. He scrolled through small stories, and black and white photographs taken back in a day when her hair was long and pinned up under her police hat. She had been the first female selected as rookie of the year, and this impressed him quite a lot.

The librarian was impressed, too. She peeked at Andy Brazil about every other second, her heart stumbling whenever he walked into her domain, which was fairly regularly. She'd never seen anyone research stories quite the way this young man did. It didn't matter what he was writing about, Brazil had to look something up or ask questions. It was especially gratifying when he spoke to her directly as she sat primly at her neat maple desk. She had been a public-school librarian before taking this job after her husband had retired and was underfoot all the time. Her name was Mrs Booth. She was well past sixty and believed that Brazil was the most beautiful human being she had ever met. He was nice and gentle, and always thanked her.

It shocked Brazil to read that West had been shot. He could not believe it. He scrolled faster, desperate for more details, but the lamebrain who had covered the incident had completely missed an opportunity for a huge 1-A story. Damn. The most that Brazil could pin down was that eleven years ago, when West was the first female homicide detective, she had gotten a tip from a snitch.

A subject West had been looking for was at the Presto Grill. By the time West and other police arrived, the subject was gone. Apparently, West answered another call in the same neighborhood, and the same subject was involved, only now he was really fried and irritable. He started firing the minute West rolled up. She killed him, but not before he winged her. Brazil was dying to ask her about it, in detail, but forget it. All he knew was that she took a bullet in the left shoulder, a flesh wound, a graze, really. Was the bullet as hot as he had heard? Did it cook surrounding tissue? How much did it hurt? Did she fall, or bravely finish the gunfight, not even realize until she held out a hand and it had blood on it, like in the movies?

The next day Brazil drove to Shelby. Because of his tennis prowess, he had heard of this small, genteel town in Cleveland County, where Buck Archer, friend of Bobby Riggs, who had lost to Billie Jean King in the Battle of the Sexes, was from. Shelby High School was a well-kept brick complex, and home of the Lions, where students with money got ready for college in big cities like Chapel Hill and Raleigh. All around was farmland and cow towns with names like Boiling Springs and Lattimore. Brazil's BMW rumbled around to the tennis courts, where the boys' team was holding a summer camp. Kids were out with hoppers of chartreuse balls. They were whacking serves, overhead smashes, cross-court shots, in pain and sweating.

The coach was prowling the fence, clipboard in hand, dressed in long white Wimbledon pants, a white shirt, a shapeless hat, zinc oxide on his nose, and all of it out of fashion and old.

'Move your feet. Move! Move!' he called out to a boy who would never move anything fast. 'I don't want to see those feet stop!'

The boy was overweight, and wore glasses. He was squinting and hurting, and Brazil remembered the suffering inflicted by coaches and drills. But Brazil had always been good at everything he tried, and he felt pity for this kid and wished he could work with him for an hour, and maybe cheer him up a little.

'Good shot,' Brazil called out when the boy managed to scoop one up and push it over the net.

The boy, who did not play in the top six positions, missed the next shot, as he searched for his fan behind the green windscreen covering the fence. The coach stopped his tour, watching this blond, well-built young man heading toward him. He was probably looking for a job, but the coach didn't need anyone else for this camp, which was the most worthless crop in recent memory.

'Coach Wagon?' Brazil asked.

'Uh huh?' The old coach was curious, wondering how this stranger knew his name. Oh God. Maybe the kid had played on the team some years back and Wagon couldn't remember. That was happening more and more these days, and it had nothing to do with Johnnie Walker Red.

'I'm a reporter for the *Charlotte Observer*,' Brazil was quick and proud to say. 'I'm doing a story on a woman who played on your boys' team a long time ago.'

Wagon might be deleting a lot of files these days, but he'd never forget Virginia West. Shelby High School had no women's team back in those days, and she was too good to ignore. What hell that had caused. At first, the state wouldn't hear of it. That kept her off the team her freshman year while Wagon battled the system on her behalf. Her sophomore year, she played third racket, and had the hardest flat serve for a girl that Wagon had ever seen, and a slice backhand that could go through hot bread and leave it standing. All the boys had crushes on her and tried to hit her with the ball whenever they could.

She never lost a match, not singles or doubles, in the three years she played tennis for Coach Wagon. There had been several stories about her in the *Shelby Star*, and the *Observer* when she blazed through spring matches, and the regionals. She had reached the quarterfinals of the state championship before Hap Core slaughtered her, thus ending her career as a male athlete. Brazil found the articles on microfilm after he got back to the newspaper. He rolled through more stories, like someone possessed, as he made copious notes.

The pervert was also possessed, but beyond that distinction, there were no similarities between her profile and Brazil's. The pervert was writhing in her chair in her dim den in her small house where she lived alone in Dilworth, not far from where Virginia West lived. The two were not acquainted. The pervert was in a La-Z-Boy brown vinyl recliner, footrest up, pants down, as she breathed hard. Information about her was not forthcoming, but the FBI would have profiled her as a white female between the ages of forty and seventy, since the female sex drive wasn't known to develop transmission problems as early as the male's. Indeed, profilers had noted that women got into overdrive about the same time they ran out of estrogen.

This was why Special Agent Gil Bird at Quantico, busy working on the Charlotte serial murders, would have pinned the female pervert's age at a reasonable forty or fifty, her biological clock a phantom-pain of time, ticking only in her imagination. Her periods were simply that, an end of sentence, a coda. It wasn't that she really wanted Brazil. She just thought she did. Her lust was far more complicated. Bird would have offered a possible scenario that might have explained it, had he been officially invited into the case.

Special Agent Bird would have accurately hypothesized that it was payback time. All those years the pervert was dissed, and not nominated for the homecoming court, and not worshiped, and not wanted. As a young woman, the pervert had worked in the cafeteria line at Gardner Webb, where basketball players, especially Ernie Presley, always grunted and pointed, as if she were as low on the food chain as the greasy scrambled eggs and grits they desired. Andy Brazil would have treated her in precisely the same fashion. She did not have to know him to prove her case. At this stage in her frustrated life, she preferred to screw him in her own time, and in her own way.

Blinds were drawn, the television turned low and playing an old Spencer Tracy and Katharine Hepburn movie. The pervert was breathless as she whispered on the phone, drawing it out, enunciating slowly.

'Saw you driving. Shifting gears. Up and down in overdrive . . .'

Her power over him was the most exciting thing she'd ever known in her nothing life. She could not contain it as she thought of his humiliation. She controlled him as completely as a fish in a tank, or a dog, or a car. Her heart was on a drum roll as she heard his confused silence over the line, and Hepburn walked into the bedroom, dressed in a satin robe. What incredible bones. The pervert hated her, and would have switched channels, but she did not have a free hand.

'Screw yourself,' Brazil's voice rewarded her with its presence. 'You have my permission.'

The pervert didn't need permission.

Packer scrolled through Brazil's latest and most masterful article.

'This is great stuff!' Packer was ecstatic about every word. 'One hell of a job! *Wild, Wild West*. Love it!'

Packer got up from a chair pulled close. He tucked in his white shirt, his hand jumping around as if his pants were a puppet. His tie was red and black striped and not the least bit elegant.

'Ship it out. This runs one-A,' Packer said.

'When?' Brazil was thrilled, because he had never been on the front page.

'Tomorrow,' Packer let him know.

That night, Brazil worked his first traffic accident. He was in uniform, with clipboard in hand, the appropriate forms clamped in. This was a lot more complicated than the average person may have supposed, even if the damage was nonreportable, or less than five hundred dollars. It appeared that a woman in a Toyota Camry was traveling on Queens Road, while a man in a Honda Prelude was also traveling on Queens Road, in this unfortunate section of the city where two roads of the same name intersected with each other.

* * *

The pervert was nearby in her Aerovan, stalking and listening to the police scanner and Brazil's voice on it. She was working her own accident about to happen as this young police boy pointed and gestured, all in dark blue and shiny steel. She watched her prey as she rolled past flares sparking orange on pavement in the dark of night, crossing Queens as she traveled west on Queens.

Streets having the same name could be attributed to rapid hormonal growth, and was similar to naming a child after oneself no matter the gender or practicality, or whether the first three were christened the same, as in George Foreman and his own. Queens and Queens, Providence and Providence, Sardis and Sardis, the list went on, and Myra Purvis had never gotten it straight. She knew that if she turned off Queens Road West onto Queens Road East and then followed Queens Road to the Orthopedic Hospital, she could visit her brother.

She was doing this in her Camry when she got to that stretch she hated so much, somewhere near Edgehill Park, where it was dark, because the day was no longer helpful. Mrs Purvis was the manager of the La Pez Mexican restaurant on Fenton Place. She had just gotten off work this busy Saturday night and was tired. None of it was her fault when Queens ran into Queens and the gray, hard-to-see Prelude ran into her.

'Ma'am, did you see the stop sign there?' The boy cop pointed.

Myra Purvis had reached her limit. She had turned seventy last February and didn't have to take this sort of shit anymore.

'Is it in Braille?' she smartly asked this whippersnapper in blue with a white tornado on his arms, reminding her of something she once used to mop her kitchen floor. What was the name of that? Genie in a Bottle? No. Lord, this happened a lot.

'I want to go to the hospital,' that man in the Honda was complaining. 'My neck hurts.'

'Lying like a rug,' Mrs Purvis told the cop, wondering why he wasn't wearing any hardware beyond a whistle. What if he got in a shoot-out?

Deputy Chief West didn't often get out to cruise so she could check on her troops. But this night she had been in the mood. She floated along rough, dark streets in David One, listening to Brazil's voice on the scanner in her car.

'One subject requesting transport to Carolinas Medical Center,' Brazil was saying.

West saw him in the distance, from the vantage of her midnight-blue car, but he was too busy to notice as he filled out a report. She circled the intersection as he worked hard, talking to subjects in barely damaged cars. Flares languished along the roadside, his grille lights silently strobing. His face was eerie in blue and red pulses, and he was smiling, and seemed to be helping an old biddy in a Camry. Brazil lifted his radio, talking into it.

He marked EOT for End Of Tour and drove to the newspaper. Brazil had a ritual few people knew about, and he indulged himself in it after zipping through a small story on Charlotte's quirky traffic problems. He went up the escalator three moving steps at a time. The workers in the press room had gotten used to him long months before, and didn't mind when he came into their off-limits area of huge machinery and deafening noise. He liked to watch some two hundred tons of paper fly along conveyor belts, heading to folders, destined for bundles and driveways, his byline on them.

Brazil stood in uniform and watched, not talking, overwhelmed by the power of it all. He was used to laboring on a term paper that took months and was read by maybe one person. Now he wrote something in days or even minutes, and millions of people followed every word. He could not comprehend it. He walked around, avoiding moving parts, wet ink, and tracks to trip on as the roar filled his ears like a nexus on this sixth night before the seventh day of his career's creation.

It was chilly out the next morning, Sunday, and sprinkling rain. West was building a high wooden fence around her yard on Elmhurst Road, in the old neighborhood of Dilworth. Her house was brick with white trim, and she had been fixing up the place since she'd bought it. This included her latest, most ambitious project, inspired, in part, by people driving through from South Boulevard, and pitching beer bottles and other trash in her yard.

West was wet, as she hammered, with tool belt on. She held nails in her mouth, and vented her spleen, as Denny Raines, an off-duty paramedic, opened her new gate and helped himself to her property. He was whistling, had jeans on, and was a big, handsome guy and no stranger to this industrious woman. She paid him no mind as she carefully measured a space between two boards.

'Anyone ever tell you you're anal-retentive?' he said.

She hammered, which was suggestive of what he felt like doing to her the first time they met, at a crime scene, when he could only suppose she had been called from home since she was in charge of investigations, and the victim was a businessman with the weird orange paint over his parts, and bullets in his head. Raines took one look at the babe in brass and that was the end of his rainbow. She hammered, eating nails, in the rain.

'I was thinking about brunch,' he said to her. 'Maybe Chili's.'

Raines approached from the rear and wrapped his arms around her. He kissed her neck, and found it wet, and a little salty. West didn't smile or respond or take the nails out of her mouth. She hammered and didn't want to be bothered. He gave up, and leaned against what she was building. He crossed his arms, and studied her as water dripped off the bill of his Panthers baseball cap.

'I take it you've seen the paper,' he said.

He would bring that up, and she had no comment. She measured another space.

'This is an affirmative. Now I know a celebrity. Right there. This big on the front page.' He exaggerated with his hands, as if the morning paper with West in it was ten feet tall. 'Above the fold, too,' he went on. 'Good story. I'm impressed.'

She measured and hammered.

'Truth is, I learned stuff even I didn't know. Like the part about high school. Shelby High. That you played on the boys' tennis team for Coach Wagon? Never lost a match? How 'bout that?'

He was more enchanted with her than ever, roaming her with his eyes and not getting charged a dime a minute. She was aware of this and feeling ripped off as she tasted metal and hammered.

'You got any idea what it does to a guy to see a good-looking woman in a tool belt?' He finally got to his fetish. 'It's like when we roll up on a scene and you're in that goddamn uniform. And I start thinking thoughts I shouldn't, people bleeding to death. Right now I got it for you so bad I'm busting out of my jeans.'

She slipped a nail from between her lips and looked at him, at his jeans. She rammed the hammer into her belt, and it was the only tool that was going to be intimate with her this day. Every Sunday, without fail, they had brunch, drank mimosas, watched TV in her bed, and all he ever talked about was calls he had been on over the weekend, as if she didn't get enough blood and misery in her life. Raines was a doll, but boring.

'Go rescue somebody and leave me alone,' she suggested to him.

His smile and playfulness fled as rain fell in a curtain from heaven. 'What the hell did I do?' he complained.

Chapter Six

West stayed outside in the rain alone, hammering, measuring, and building her fence as if it were a symbol of what she felt about people and life. When her gate opened and shut again at three P.M., she assumed it was Raines trying again. She slammed another nail into wood and felt bad about the way she had treated him. He had meant no harm, and her mood had nothing to do with him, really.

Niles could have done with the same consideration. He was in the window over the kitchen sink, looking out at his owner in a flood. She was swinging something that looked like it might hurt Niles if he got in her way. Niles had been minding his own business earlier, walking in circles, kneading the covers, finding just the right warm spot to settle on his owner's chest. Next thing, he was an astronaut, a circus acrobat shot out of a cannon. It was just a darn good thing he could land on his feet. He stared through streaming water at someone entering the yard from the north. Niles, the watch cat, had never seen this person, not once in his ancient feline life.

Brazil was aware of a skinny cat watching him from a window as he trespassed and West hammered, calling out to someone named Raines.

'Look, I'm sorry, okay?' she was saying. 'I'm in this mood.'

Brazil carried three thick Sunday papers wrapped in a dry-cleaning bag he had found in his closet. 'Apology accepted,' he said.

West wheeled around, and fixed him in her sights, hammer mid-swing. 'What the hell are you doing here?' She was startled and taken aback, and did her best to sound hateful.

'Who's Raines?' Brazil got closer, his tennis shoes getting soaked.

'None of your damn business.' She started hammering as her heart did.

He was suddenly shy and tentative in the rain as he got closer. 'I brought you some extra papers. Thought you might . . .'

'You didn't ask me.' She hammered. 'You didn't give me a warning. Like you have some right to investigate my life.' She bent a nail and clumsily pried it out. 'Ride around all night. The whole time you're a spy.'

She stopped what she was doing to look at him. He was soaked and dejected, wanting her to be pleased. He had given her the best he knew.

'You got no fucking right!' she said.

'It's a good story.' He was getting defensive. 'You're a hero.'

She went on, enraged and not certain why, 'What hero? Who cares?'

'I told you I was going to write about you.'

'Seems to me that was a threat.' She turned back to her fence and hammered. 'And I didn't believe you meant it.'

'Why not?' He didn't understand any of this, and didn't think it was fair.

'No one has before.' She hammered again, and stopped again, trying to stay mad but not doing a good job of it. 'I wouldn't have thought I was all that interesting.'

'What I did is good, Virginia,' he said.

Brazil was vulnerable and trying not to be. He told himself that what this hammer-wielding deputy chief thought didn't matter in the least. West stood in the rain, the two of them looking at each other as Niles watched from his favorite window, tail twitching.

'I know about your father,' West went on. 'I know exactly what happened. Is that why you run around playing cop morning, noon and night?'

Brazil was struggling with emotions he didn't want anyone to know about. West couldn't tell if he was angry or close to tears as she chipped away at him with her own investigation into his past.

'He's plainclothes,' she said, 'decides to pull a stolen vehicle. Number one violation. You don't do that in an unmarked car. And the asshole turns out to be a felon on the run, who points his gun close range. Last thing your father said was, "Please God no," but the fucker does it anyway. Blows a hole in your daddy's heart, dead before he hits the pavement. Your favorite newspaper made sure Detective Drew Brazil looked bad in the end. Screwed him. And now his son's out here doing the same thing.'

Brazil sat on the swampy lawn, staring hard at her. 'No, I'm not. That's not the point. And you're cruel.'

West didn't often have such a powerful effect on guys. Raines never got this intense, not even when she broke it off with him, which she had done five times now. Usually, he got mad and stormed off, then ignored her as his phone didn't ring until he couldn't stand it anymore. Brazil she did not comprehend, but then she had never known a writer or any artist, really. She sat next to him, both of them in a grassy puddle and drenched. She tossed the hammer and it splashed when it landed, its violence spent for the day. She sighed as this young volunteer-cop-reporter stared at drops streaking past, his body rigid with rage and resentment.

'Tell me why,' she said.

He wouldn't look at her. He would never speak to her again.

'I want to know,' she persisted. 'You could be a cop. You could be a reporter. But oh no. You got to be both? Huh?' She playfully punched his shoulder, and got no response. 'You still live with your mother, I got a feeling. How come? Nice-looking guy like you? No girlfriend, you don't date, I got that feeling, too. You gay? I got no problem with that, okay?'

Brazil got up.

'Live and let live, I always say,' West went on from her puddle.

He gave her a piercing look, stalking off. 'I'm not the one they call gay,' he said in the rain.

This did not threaten West. She had heard it before. Women who went into policing, the military, professional sports, coaching, construction, or physical education were oriented toward same-sex relationships. Those who succeeded in any of these professions, or owned businesses, or became doctors, lawyers, or bankers, and did not paint their nails or play round-robin tennis in a league during office hours, were also lesbians. It did not matter if one were married with children. It mattered not if one were dating a man. These were simply facades, a means of faking out family and friends.

The only absolute proof of heterosexuality was to do nothing quite as well as a man and be proud of it. West had been a known lesbian ever since she was promoted to sergeant. Certainly, the department was not without its gay women, but they were closeted and full of lies about boyfriends no one ever met. West could understand why people might assume she was living the same myth. Similar rumors even circulated about Hammer. All of it was pathetic, and West wished people would let their rivers flow as they would and get on with life.

She had decided long ago that many moral issues were really about threats. For example, when she had been growing up on the farm, people talked about the unmarried women missionaries who kept busy at Shelby Presbyterian Church, not far from Cleveland Feeds and the regional hospital. A number of these fine ladies had served together in exotic places, including the Congo, Brazil, Korea, and Bolivia. They came home on furlough or to retire, and lived together in the same dwelling. It never occurred to anyone West knew that these faithful ladies of the church had any interest beyond prayer and saving the poor.

The threat in West's formative years was to grow up a spinster, an old maid. West heard this more than once when she was better than the boys in most things and learned how to drive a tractor. Statistically, she would prove to be an old maid. Her parents still worried, and this was compounded by the nineties fear that she might be an old maid who was also inclined elsewhere. In all fairness, it wasn't that West couldn't understand women wanting each other. What she could not imagine was fighting with a woman.

It was bad enough with men, who slammed things around and didn't communicate. Women cried and screamed and were touchy about everything, especially when their hormones were a little wide and to the right. She could not imagine two lovers having PMS at the same time. Domestic violence would be inevitable, possibly escalating to homicide, especially if both were cops with guns.

After a light, solitary dinner of leftover spicy chicken pizza, West sat in her recliner chair in front of the TV, watching the Atlanta Braves clobber the Florida Marlins. Niles was in her lap because it was his wish. His owner was at ease in police sweats, drinking a Miller Genuine Draft in the bottle, and reading Brazil's article about herself because it really wasn't right to be so hard on the guy without taking a good look at what he had done. She laughed out loud again, paper rattling as she turned a page. Where the hell did he get all this stuff?

She was so caught up, she had forgotten to pet Niles for fourteen minutes, eleven seconds, and counting. He wasn't asleep, but merely pretending, biding his time to see how long this might go on that he might add to her list of infractions. When she ran out of indulgences, there was that porcelain figurine on top of the bookcase. If she thought Niles couldn't jump up there, she had another think coming. Niles could trace his lineage back to Egypt, to pharaohs and pyramids, his skills ancient and largely untested. Someone hit a home run and West didn't notice as she laughed again and reached for the phone.

Brazil didn't hear it ring at first because he was in front of his computer, typing, possessed by whatever he was writing as Annie Lennox sang loudly from the boom box. His mother was in the kitchen, fixing herself a peanut-butter sandwich on Sunbeam white bread. She slurped another mouthful of cheap vodka from a plastic glass as the phone rang from the wall. She swayed, grabbing for the counter to steady herself, and got a drawer handle as two blue phones on the wall rang and rang. Silverware crashed to the floor, and Brazil jumped up from his chair as his mother managed to grab at her double-vision of the phone and bump it out of its cradle. It banged against the wall, dangling from a snarled cord. She lunged for it again, almost falling.

'What?' she slurred into the receiver.

'I was trying to reach Andy Brazil,' West said over the line, after an uncertain pause.

'In his room going.' Mrs Brazil made drunken typing motions. 'You know. Usual! Thinks he'll amount to Hemingway, something.'

Mrs Brazil did not notice her son in the doorway, stricken as she talked on in fractured, bleary words that could not possibly make sense to anyone. It was a house rule that she did not answer the phone. Either her son got it or the answering machine did. He watched in despair, helpless as she humiliated him yet again in life.

'Ginia West,' Mrs Brazil repeated as she finally noticed two of her sons coming toward her. He took the phone out of her hand.

West's intention had been merely to confess to Brazil that his story was rather wonderful and she appreciated it, and didn't deserve it. She had not expected this impaired woman to answer, and now West knew it all. She didn't tell Brazil a thing other than that she was on her way. This was an order. West had dealt with all types in her years of police work, and was undaunted by Mrs Brazil, no matter how vile, how hateful and hostile the woman was when her son and West put her in bed and made her drink a lot of water. Mrs Brazil passed out about five minutes after West helped her into the bathroom to pee.

West and Brazil went for a walk in darkness broken by an occasional lighted window from old southern homes along Main Street. Rain was gentle like mist. He had nothing to say as they drew closer to the Davidson campus, which was quiet this time of year, even when various camps were in session. A security guard in his Cushman watched the couple pass, pleased that Andy Brazil might finally have a girlfriend. She was a lot older than him, but still worth looking at, and if any one needed a mother figure, that boy did.

The guard's name was Clyde Briddlewood, and he had headed the modest Davidson College security force since days when the only problem in the world was pranks and drunkenness. Then the school had let women in. It was a bad idea, and he had told everyone he could. Briddlewood had done his best to warn the preoccupied professors as they were hurrying to class, and he had alerted Sam Spencer, the president back then. No one listened. Now Briddlewood had a security force of eight people and three Cushmans. They had radios, guns, and drank coffee with local cops.

Briddlewood dipped Copenhagen snuff, spitting in a Styrofoam cup as Brazil and his girlfriend followed the brick walk toward the Presbyterian church. Briddlewood had always liked that boy and was sorry as heck he had to grow up. He remembered Brazil as a kid, always in a hurry somewhere with his Western Auto tennis racket and plastic bag of bald, dead tennis balls that he'd fished out of the trash or begged off the tennis coach. Brazil used to share his chewing gum and candy with Briddlewood, and this touched the security guard right down to his boots. The boy didn't have much and lived with a bad situation. True, Muriel Brazil wasn't hitting the sauce back then as bad as she did now, but her son had a lousy deal and everyone at Davidson knew it.

What Brazil didn't know was that a number of people who lived in the college community had plotted behind the scenes for years, and had raised money from wealthy alumni, even dipping into their own wallets to make certain that when Brazil was college age, he was offered an opportunity to rise above his situation. Briddlewood, himself, had put a few bucks in the pot, when he didn't have much to spare, and lived in a small house far enough away from Lake Norman that he couldn't see the water but could at least watch the endless parade of trucks hauling boats along his dirt road. He spat again, silently rolling the Cushman closer to the church, keeping his eye on the couple, to make sure they were safe out here in the dark.

'What am I going to do with you?' West was saying to Brazil.

He had his pride and was in a humorless mood. 'For the record, I don't need you to do a thing for me.'

'Yeah you do. You got serious problems.'

'And you don't,' he said. 'All you got in your life is an eccentric cat.'

This surprised West. What else had he dug up about her? 'How'd you know about Niles?' she wanted to know.

West was aware they were being stalked by some security guard in a Cushman. He was hanging back in shadows, certain West and Brazil couldn't see him creeping in the cover of boxwoods and magnolia trees. West couldn't imagine how boring that job must be.

'I have a lot in my life,' she added.

'What a fantasy,' Brazil said.

'You know what? You're a total waste of my time.' She meant it.

They walked on, moving away from the campus and cutting through narrow roads where faculty lived in restored homes with cherished lawns and old trees. Brazil used to wander these lanes as a boy, fantasizing about people inside expensive homes, imagining important professors and their nice husbands and wives. Light filled their windows and seemed so warm back then, and sometimes draperies were open and he could see people moving inside, walking across the living room with a drink, sitting in a chair reading, or at a desk working.

Brazil's loneliness was buried out of reach and unnamed. He did not know what to call the hollow hurt that started somewhere in his chest and pressed against his heart like two cold hands. He never cried when the hands pressed, but would tremble violently like a distressed flame when he thought he might lose his tennis match or when he didn't get an A. Brazil could not watch sad movies, and now and then beauty overwhelmed him, especially live music played by symphonies and string quartets.

West could feel rage building in Brazil as they walked. The mounting silence became oppressive as they passed lighted homes and dark thick trees armored in ivy and kudzu. She did not understand him and was beginning to suspect she'd made a big mistake thinking she could. So what if she'd worked hostage negotiation, homicides, and was experienced in talking people out of killing themselves or someone else? This didn't mean she was even remotely capable of helping a strange guy like Andy Brazil. In fact, she didn't have time.

'I want this killer,' Brazil started in, talking louder than was necessary or wise. 'Okay? I want him caught.'

He was obsessed, as if what this killer was doing was personal. West had no intention of getting into his space on this. They walked on. Brazil suddenly kicked a rock with a fancy black and purple Nike leather tennis shoe that looked like something Agassi would endorse.

'What he does.' Brazil kicked more rocks. 'What do you think it must be like?' His voice got louder. 'Driving somewhere in a strange city, tired, away from home, a lot on your mind. Getting lost, stopping to ask directions.' Another rock skittered across blacktop. 'Next thing, you're being led to some Godforsaken place, behind an abandoned building. A warehouse. A vacant lot.'

West stopped walking. She was staring at him as he furiously stomped ahead, wheeled around.

'Hard cold steel against your head as you beg not to die!' he yelled as if the crime had happened to him. 'As he blows your brains out anyway!'

West was frozen as she watched something she had never seen before this moment. Porch lights of nearby houses flipped on.

'He pulls your pants down and spray-paints this symbol! *How would you like to die that way?*'

More lights came on. Dogs barked. West went into her police mode without a conscious thought. She walked over to Brazil and firmly took his arm.

'Andy, you're disturbing the entire neighborhood.' She spoke with quiet calm. 'Let's go home.'

Brazil stared defiantly at her. 'I want to make a difference.'

She nervously scanned their surroundings. 'Believe me. You are.'

More lights turned on, and someone had come out on his porch to see what crazy person had wandered into his quiet neighborhood. Briddlewood had fled in his Cushman minutes earlier.

'Which is why we need to go,' West added, pulling Brazil along as they started walking back. 'You want to help. Okay. Tell me what you have to contribute besides tantrums and words.'

'Maybe we could plant something in one of my stories to trick him.' He had an idea.

'I wish it were that simple,' she said, and she meant it. 'And you're assuming he reads the paper.'

'I bet he does.' Brazil wished she would have an open mind, as he flew through possibilities of what subliminal propaganda he might plant to ensnare this monster.

'The answer's no. We don't plant stories.'

Brazil hopped ahead again, excited. 'Together we could get him! I know it.'

'What's this together stuff?' West said. 'You're just a reporter. Hate to remind you of that fact.'

'I'm a volunteer cop,' he corrected her.

'Uh huh. The gunless wonder.'

'You could give me shooting lessons,' he then said. 'My dad used to take me out to a dump in the county . . .'

'He should have left you there,' she said.

'We'd shoot cans with his .38.'

'How old were you?' West asked when they were in Brazil's driveway.

'Starting when I was seven, I think.' He had his hands in his pockets, and was looking down as he walked, a streetlight lighting up his hair. 'Seems like I was in the second grade.'

'I mean, when he died,' she gently said.

'Ten,' he said. 'I had just turned ten.'

He stopped, and did not want West to leave. He didn't want to go in and face the way he lived.

'I don't have a gun,' he told her.

'Thank you, Jesus,' she said.

Chapter Seven

Days went by. West had no intention of furthering the cause of Andy Brazil. His problems were his own, and it was time he grew up. When the following Sunday rolled around and Raines was interested in brunch, she called Brazil because she was a certified firearms instructor. If he needed help, it was only fair that she offer. He said he could be ready in ten minutes. She told him that unless she flew the Concorde to Davidson, she would not be picking him up for at least an hour.

She drove her personal car for this, a Ford Explorer with dual air bags. It was a white sports utility vehicle with four-wheel drive that ate snow for a snack. She roared into his driveway at three P.M., and he was out the door before she could open hers. The obvious range would have been the one at the police academy, but this she could not do because volunteers were not allowed, nor were guests. West chose The Firing Line on Wilkinson Boulevard, just past Bob's Pawn Shop, and a number of trailer parks, the Oakden Motel, Country City USA, and Coyote Joe's.

Had they continued another block or two, West realized, they would have ended up in the parking lot of the Paper Doll Lounge. She had been in there before on fights. It was disgusting. Topless women were on the same block as gun and pawn shops, as if breasts and g-strings somehow belonged in the same category as used merchandise and weapons. West wondered if Brazil had ever visited a topless lounge and sat stiffly in a chair, his hands in a white-knuckle grip on armrests, as a naked woman rubbed against his inner legs, and got in his face.

Probably not, West decided. She had a feeling he was a foreigner who didn't speak the language, hadn't tried the food or seen the sights. How could this have happened? He didn't have girls after him in high school, in college? Or boys? She did not understand Andy Brazil as he foraged through shelves of ammunition inside the firing range shop, picking out Winchester 95 grain full metal jacket .380, Luger 115 grain ball nine-millimeter cartridges, and contemplated .45 automatic 230 grain, Federal Hi-Power, Hydra-Shok hollowpoints, and Super X 50 Centerfire that were too expensive for practice. He was going nuts. This was a candy shop, and West was buying.

Gunshots sounded like a war going on inside this range, where NRA rednecks worshiped their pistols, and drug dealers with cash and leather hightops got better at killing. West and Brazil were loaded down with hearing protectors, safety glasses, and boxes of ammunition. She was a woman in jeans, carrying two pistol hard cases. Dangerous-looking men gave her hostile glances, not happy about girls invading their club. Brazil was picking up danger signals as he surveyed his surroundings.

The men didn't seem to like him, either. He was

suddenly conscious of being in Davidson tennis sweats and having tied a bandana around his head to keep his hair out of his eyes. These guys all had guts and big shoulders, as if they worked out with forklifts and cases of beer. He had seen their trucks in the parking lot, some of them with six wheels, as if there were mountains and streams to climb and cross along I-74 and I-40. Brazil did not understand the tribe of Male he had grown up around in North Carolina.

It was beyond biology, genitals, hormones, or testosterone. Some of these guys had naked pinups on the mudflaps of their tractor trailers, and Brazil was frankly horrified. A guy saw a foxy woman with a body, and he wanted her protecting his radials from gravel? Not Brazil. He wanted her at the movies, the drive-through, and in candlelight.

He was using the staple gun, fastening another target to cardboard and attaching it to the frame in his lane. West, the instructor, was examining her pupil's latest target. The silhouette she held up had a tight spread of bullet holes in the center of the chest. She was amazed. She watched Brazil push cartridges into the magazine of a stainless steel Sig-Sauer .380 pistol.

'You're dangerous,' she let him know.

He gripped the small gun with both hands, in the position and stance his father had taught him in a life he scarcely recalled. Brazil's form wasn't bad, but it could be improved, and he fired one round after another. He dropped out the empty magazine and smacked in a new one. He fired nonstop, as if he couldn't shoot fast enough and would kill anybody else in life who hurt him. This would not do. West knew the reality of the street.

She reached for a button in his booth and held it in. The paper target suddenly came to life and screeched along the lane toward Brazil, as if it were going to attack him. Startled, Brazil shot wildly. BAM! BAM! BAM! Bullets slammed into the target's metal frame, into the back rubber wall, and then he was out of ammo. The target screeched to a stop, rocking from its cable in his face.

'Hey! What are you doing?' He turned to West, indignant and bewildered.

She did not answer at first as she pushed cartridges into black metal magazines. She smacked one into her big bad black .40 caliber Smith & Wesson semiautomatic, then looked at her student.

'You shoot too fast.' She racked back the slide and it snapped forward. She aimed at her own target in her own lane. 'You're out of ammo.' She fired. BAM-BAM. 'And out of luck.' BAM-BAM.

She paused, and fired twice again. She set down her pistol and moved close to Brazil, taking the .380 from him, and opening the slide to make sure the gun was unloaded and safe. She pointed it down the lane, hands and arms locked, knees slightly bent, in the proper position and stance.

'Tap-tap and stop,' she told him as she demonstrated. 'Tap-tap and stop. You see what the other person's doing and adjust.' She returned the .380 to him, butt first. 'And don't slap the trigger. Take it home tonight and practice.'

That night, Brazil stayed in his room and dry-fired West's .380 until he had a significant blister on his index finger. He aimed it at himself in the mirror, that he might get used to seeing a gun pointed at him. He did this with music playing and fantasies spinning, the deadly tiny black eye staring at his head, his heart, as he thought of his father, who had not drawn his gun. His father had not had time even to key his radio. Brazil's arms were beginning to tremble, and he had not eaten supper.

It was a few minutes past nine, and his mother had refused to eat earlier when he had offered to fix her a hamburger patty and a salad of fresh tomatoes and Vidalia onions, with oil and vinegar. More alert than usual, she was watching a sitcom, and in the same faded blue flannel robe and slippers she wore most of the time. He could not grasp how she could live the way she did, and had given up thinking he could change her or the life she hated. In high school, he, her only child, had been the expert detective, rooting through the house and her Cadillac, seeking her hidden stashes of pills and liquor. Her resourcefulness was amazing. Once she had gone so far as to bury whisky in the yard beneath the rose bushes she used to prune when she still cared.

Muriel Brazil's greatest fear was to be present. She did not want to be here, and the nightmare of rehabilitation and AA meetings darkened her memory like the shadow of a monstrous bird flying over her and splaying its claws, ready to snatch her up and eat her alive. She did not want to feel. She would not sit in groups of people who had only first names and talked about the drunks they once were, and binges they used to go on, and how wonderful it was to be sober. All spoke with the sincerity of contrite sinners after a religious experience.

Their new god was sobriety, and this god allowed plenty of cigarettes and black decaffeinated coffee. Exercise, drinking copious amounts of water and talking regularly to one's sponsor was critical, and the god expected the recovering one to contact all he had ever offended and apologize. In other words, Mrs Brazil was supposed to tell her son and those she worked around at Davidson that she was an alcoholic. She had tried this once on several of the students she supervised at the ARA Slater food service that catered the cafeteria in the new Commons building.

'I've been away a month at a treatment center,' Mrs Brazil told a junior named Heather, from Connecticut. 'I'm an alcoholic.'

Mrs Brazil tried the same line on Ron, a freshman from Ashland, Virginia. The expected catharsis was not there. Students did not respond well and avoided her after that. They regarded her fearfully as rumors floated around campus. Some of what was said got back to Brazil, heightening a sense of shame that drove him deeper into his isolation. He knew he could never have friends because if anyone got close, the truth would be known. Even West had been confronted the first time she had called his house. Brazil was still perplexed, if not stunned, that this had not seemed to affect the deputy chief's opinion of him.

'Mom, how about I cook us up some eggs?' Brazil paused in the doorway. Light from the television flickered in the dark living room.

'I'm not hungry,' she said, staring at the screen.

'What have you eaten? Probably nothing, right? You know how bad that is for you, Mom.'

Pointing the remote control, she changed to another channel, where people were laughing and exchanging bad lines.

'How 'bout a grilled cheese?' her son tried again.

'Well, maybe.' She changed channels again.

It was hard for her to be still when her son was nearby. It was hard to look at his face and meet his eyes. The nicer he was to her, the more abusive she felt, and she had never figured out why. She would not make it without him. He bought food and kept the house going. Her social security checks and a small pension from the police department supplied her liquids. It didn't take as much to get drunk these days, and she knew what this said about her liver. She wished she would go on and die, and she worked at it every day. Her eyes filled with tears and her throat closed as her son rattled around in the kitchen.

Alcohol had been the enemy the first time she'd ever touched it, when she was sixteen and Micky Latham took her to Lake Norman at night and got her drunk on apricot brandy. She vaguely remembered lying in the grass, watching stars reconfigure and blur as he breathed hard and clumsily worked on her blouse as if buttons had just been invented. He was nineteen and worked in Bud's Garage, and his hands were calloused and felt like claws on breasts that had never been touched before this intoxicated moment.

That was the night sweet Muriel lost her virginity, and it had nothing to do with Micky Latham, and everything to do with the bottle in its ABC store brown paper bag. When she drank, her brain lifted as if it might sing. She was happy, brave, playful, and witty. She was driving her father's Cadillac the afternoon Officer Drew Brazil pulled her over for speeding. Muriel was seventeen and the most beautiful, worldly woman he'd ever met. If he thought he smelled alcohol on her breath that afternoon, he was too mesmerized to put it in perspective. He was rather glorious in his uniform, and the ticket never got written. Instead, they went to Big Daddy's fish camp after he got off duty. They married that Thanksgiving when she had missed her period two months in a row.

Muriel Brazil's son reappeared with grilled cheese on

wheat bread, cooked just right and cut diagonally, the way she liked it. He'd put a dollop of ketchup on the side so she could dip, and he brought her water that she had no intention of drinking. He looked so much like his father, it was more than she could bear.

'I know how much you hate water, Mom,' he said, setting the plate and napkin in her lap. 'But you got to drink it, okay? Sure you don't want salad?'

She shook her head and wished she could thank him. She was impatient because he was blocking her view of the TV.

'I'll be in my room,' he said.

He dry-fired until his finger bled. He was remarkably steady because years of tennis had strengthened the muscles of his hands and forearms. His grip was crushing. The next morning, he woke up excited. The sun was shining, and West had promised to take him to the range again late afternoon to work with him further. It was Monday, and he had the day off. He didn't know what he would do between now and then, or how he would make hours pass. Brazil could not endure free time, and usually gave it away to some project.

The grass was heavy with dew when he slipped out of the house at half past seven. Carrying tennis rackets and a hopper of balls, he walked first to the track, where he ran six miles and did push-ups, sit-ups, and crunches, to get his fix of endorphin. By now, the grass was warm and dry, and he lay in it long enough for his blood to stop pounding. He listened to the buzzing of insects in clover, and smelled bittersweet green vegetation and wild onions. His gym shorts and tank top were saturated as he trotted downhill to the outdoor tennis courts.

Ladies were playing doubles, and he politely trotted behind them on their court, going to the other end, so he could be as far away from anyone as possible. He didn't want to disturb people with the hundreds of balls he intended to kill. Brazil served in deuce court and ad court, on one side, then the other, picking up after himself with the bright yellow hopper. He was slightly annoyed. Tennis was unforgiving if he didn't practice. His usual precision wasn't there, and he knew what this boded. If he didn't start playing again, he was going to lose one of the few things he'd ever been good at. Damn. The ladies on court one noticed a marked deterioration in their own games as they continued to watch with envy the young man on court four hit balls so hard they sounded like baseballs cracking against bats.

Chief Hammer's concentration was in and out, too. She was presiding over an executive staff meeting in her private conference room, in her sizeable corner of the third floor. Windows overlooked Davidson and Trade, and she could see the mighty USBank Corporate Center topped by its silly aluminum headdress, which oddly brought to mind a wild man with a bone in his nose, perhaps from some *Little Rascals* episode from long years past. At exactly eight this morning as Hammer was carrying her first cup of coffee to her desk, the CEO of that sixty-story erection had called her.

Solomon Cahoon was Jewish, and the Old Testament factored into his mother's choice of names for her firstborn male child. Her son would be a king who would make wise decisions, such as the one this Friday, when he had informed his police chief that she would hold a press conference to let citizens know that the serial killings in Charlotte were homosexual and of no threat to normal men visiting the Queen City on business. Northside Baptist Church would be holding a prayer vigil for victims' families and the souls of those killed. Police were following very good leads.

'Just a reassurance thing,' Cahoon had relayed to the chief over the phone.

Hammer, and her six deputy chiefs, along with people from strategic planning and crime analysis, were discussing this latest commandment delivered on high. Wren Dozier, deputy chief of administration, was especially incensed. He was forty with delicate features and a soft mouth. Unmarried, he lived in a section of Fourth Ward where Tommy Axel and others had condominiums with dusky rose doors. Dozier had known he would never be promoted beyond captain. Then Hammer had come to town, a woman who rewarded people for good work. Dozier would take a bullet for her.

'What a bunch of shit,' Dozier said as he slowly and angrily twirled his coffee mug on the table. 'So what about the other side of this, huh?' He met eyes all around. 'What about the wives and kids back home? They're supposed to think the last thing Pop did was pay for a homosexual encounter out on some city street somewhere?'

'There's no evidence to support such a thing,' West said, and she was unhappy, too. 'You can't say something like this.' She stared at Hammer.

The chief and Cahoon could agree on nothing, and she knew he was going to have her fircd. It was all a matter of time, and would not be a first, either. At her level, it was all politics. The city got a new mayor, who brought along his own chief, which was what had happened to her in Atlanta, and would have in Chicago, had she not left. She really could not afford to get reshuffled again.

Each city would get only smaller, until one fine day she ended up right where she'd started, in the economically languishing one-horse town of Little Rock.

'Of course I will not get up in front of reporters and spread such crap,' the chief said. 'I won't.'

'Well, it can't hurt to remind the public that we are following leads and are on the case,' said the public information officer.

'What leads?' said West, who headed investigations, and should be privy to such things.

'If we get any, we'll follow them,' said Hammer. 'That's the point.'

'You can't say that, either,' worried the PIO. 'We have to leave out the *if we get any* part of . . .'

Hammer impatiently cut her off. 'Of course, of course. That goes without saying. I didn't mean literally. Enough of this. Let's move on. Here's what we're going to do. A press release.' She regarded the PIO over reading glasses. 'I want it on my desk by ten-thirty and out to the press by midafternoon so they can meet their deadlines. And I will see if I can get up with Cahoon, talk him down from this.'

This was very much like securing an audience with the Pope. Hammer's secretary and another assistant traded phone calls with Cahoon's people for most of the day. Finally, the meeting was barely arranged for late that afternoon, sometime between four-fifteen and five, depending when a gap appeared in the CEO's impossible schedule. Hammer had no choice but to show up at the early end of this interval and hope for the best.

At four she left her police department and walked through downtown on a lovely afternoon that, before this moment, she had not noticed. She followed Trade to Tryon to the corporate center, with its eternal torch and sculptures. Inside a huge lobby of polished stone, she walked briskly, her heels clicking over marble as she passed rich wood paneling and famous fresco paintings depicting the Shingon philosophy of chaos, creativity, making, and building. She nodded at one of the guards, who nodded back and tipped his cap. He liked that lady chief, and had always thought she walked like she knew how, and she was nice and didn't disrespect anyone, whether they were a real cop or not.

Hammer boarded a crowded elevator and was the last to get off at the top of the crown, which at this dizzying level, really was aluminum pipes. Hammer had visited Cahoon before. Rarely a month went by that he didn't summon her to his suite of mahogany and glass overlooking his city. As was true of Hampton Court Palace, visitors were required to pass through many outer layers and courts to get to the king. Should a crazed gunman decide to carry out his mission, by the time he reached the throne, many secretaries and assistants might be dead, but Cahoon, quite likely, would not have heard the noise.

Several outer offices later, Hammer entered the one occupied by the executive secretary, Mrs Mullis-Mundi, also known as M&M by those who did not like her, which was virtually all. She was candy-coated, but with nuts. She would melt in the mouth and break teeth. Hammer, frankly, had no use for this perky young thing who had gotten married and kept her name while appropriating that of her husband, Joe Mundi. Mrs Mullis-Mundi was bulimic, and had breast implants and long dyed blond hair. She wore size four Anne Klein. Her cologne was Escada. She worked out daily in Gold's Gym. She did not wear slacks, and was simply biding time before she sued for sexual harassment.

'Judy, great to see you.' The executive secretary stood and offered her hand with the same lilting style that Hammer had observed in devout bowlers. 'Let me see how he's doing.'

A half hour later, Hammer remained seated on a buttery-soft ivory leather couch. She was reviewing statistics, memos, and attending to the armies marching restlessly inside her briefcase. Mrs Mullis-Mundi never got off the phone or grew tired of it. She took one earring off, then the other, then rotated the phone again to a hand less tired, as if to emphasize the painful demands of her career. Often she looked at her large scratch-proof Rado watch, and sighed, flipping her hair. She was about to die to smoke one of her skinny menthol cigarettes that had flowers around the filter.

Cahoon was able, at last, to fit the chief in at precisely thirteen minutes past the hour. As usual, his day had been long, with far too much in it, and all insisting that they could speak to no one but him. In truth, he had never been in a hurry to let Hammer into his office, regardless of the minor fact that it was he, versus her, who had demanded a meeting. She was ornery and opinionated, and had treated him like a bad dog the first time they'd met. As a result, he was one without fail and consistently, when dealing with her. One of these days, he would send her down the road and bring in a progressive man, the sort who snapped open a briefcase with the *Wall Street Journal* and a Browning Hi-Power inside. Now, that was Cahoon's idea of a chief, someone who knew the market, would shoot to kill, and showed a little respect to leaders of the community.

Hammer's first thought whenever she was face to face with the ruler of the city was that he had made his fortune on a chicken farm and had attributed his history to someone else by another name. Frank Purdue, she almost believed, was an alias. Holly Farms was a front. Solomon Cahoon had made his millions off plump breasts and thighs. He had gotten rich off fryers and fat roasters and their little thermometers that popped up at precisely the right time when things were heating up. Clearly, Cahoon had dovetailed these experiences and resources into banking. He had been wise enough to realize that his past might pose a credibility problem for one securing a mortgage through USBank, if this person happened to see the CEO smiling on chicken parts at Harris-Teeter. Hammer couldn't blame him for coming up with an alias or two, if this was what he had in fact done.

His desk was burled maple, not old but magnificent, and much more expansive than the ninety-six inches of wood veneer, including a return, that the city furnished her. Cahoon was creaking in an apple green English leather chair with brass studs and the same burled armrests, talking on the phone, looking out spotless glass, and beyond aluminum pipes. She sat across from him, and was on hold again. It really didn't bother her all that much anymore, for Hammer could transport herself just about anywhere. She could solve problems, make decisions, come up with lists of matters to be investigated, and deliberate what would be good for dinner and who should cook it.

To her, Cahoon always looked naked from the neck up. His hair was a bristly silver fringe he wore like a crown. Cropped short, it stood up straight in different lengths, and was shaped like a crescent moon in back. He was perpetually tan and wrinkled from his passion for sailboats, and he was vital and distinguished in a black suit, crisp white shirt, and Fendi silk tie filled with gold and deep red clocks.

'Sol,' she politely greeted him, when he eventually hung up the phone.

'Judy, thanks so much for fitting me in,' he said in his soft southern voice. 'So what are we going to do about these gay bashings, these queer killin's? These fag-fisher-queens trolling in our city? You understand the false impression all of it is giving to other corporations and companies thinking of relocating here? Not to mention what it does to business in town as usual.'

'*Fag-fisher-queens*,' Hammer slowly, thoughtfully repeated. '*Trolling*.'

'Yes, ma'am.' He nodded. 'You want some Perrier or something?'

She shook her head, and measured her words. 'Gay bashings. Queer killings. This came from where?' She was not on his same planet, and that was her choice.

'Oh come on.' He leaned forward, propping elbows on his rich desk. 'We all know what this is about. Men come to our city. They cut loose, give in to their perversion, think no one will be the wiser. Well, the angel of death for these sickos is swooping in.' He nodded deeply. 'Truth, justice, and the American way. God putting his foot down.'

'Synonymous,' she said.

'Huh?' He frowned in confusion.

'All are synonymous?' she said. 'Truth. Justice. American way. God putting his foot down.'

'You bet, honey.' He smiled.

'Sol, don't call me that.' She jabbed her finger the same way she did when making points while West was driving her around the city. 'Don't. Not ever.'

He settled back in his leather chair and laughed, entertained by this lady. What a trip. Thank God she had a husband to set her straight and put her where she belonged. Cahoon was willing to bet that Hammer's man called her honey and she waited for it, apron tied in back, like Heidi, Cahoon's first and only wife. Saturday mornings, Heidi served him breakfast in bed, providing he was in town. She continued this even now, after so many faithful years, although the effect wasn't quite the same. What happened to the female body after it turned thirty? Men were ready and willing until death. They sat tall in the saddle, and were unaffected by gravity, and this was why it wasn't out of the question for the male to seek out younger females, eventually.

'You understand the definition of honey?' Hammer started in on this again. 'A food for larvae. To be flattering or obsequious. Cajolery. What you say to get your socks darned and buttons sewn on. Christ, why did I come to this city?' She shook her head, not kidding.

'Atlanta wasn't much better,' he reminded her. 'Certainly not Chicago, or it wouldn't have been for long.'

'True, true.'

'What about your press conference?' He moved on to more important matters. 'I passed along a very appropriate suggestion. And what?' He shrugged thin shoulders. 'Where's my press conference? Was it so much for me to ask? This building is a beacon bringing business to Charlotte-Mecklenburg. We need to disseminate positive information, such as our hundred and five percent clearance rate for all violent crimes last year . . .'

She interrupted him, because she couldn't let this pass. 'Sol, this is not financial smoke and mirrors. You cannot manipulate the bottom line on paper and in computers and get everyone to accept it. We're talking tangibles. Rapes, robberies, B&Es, homicides, with real flesh and blood victims. You're asking me to convince citizens that we cleared more cases than we had last year?'

'Old cases were solved, that's why the numbers . . .' he started to repeat what he had been told.

Hammer was shaking her head, and Cahoon's infamous impatience was heating up. This lady was the only one who dared talk to him in this fashion, if he didn't include his wife and children.

'What old cases?' Hammer said. 'And going back how far? You know what this is like? It's like someone asking me how much I make as chief of police and I say a million dollars because I'm going back ten years.'

'Apples and oranges.'

'No, no, Sol.' She was shaking her head more vigorously. 'No apples and oranges here. Oh no. This is fertilizer.'

'Judy.' He pointed a bent finger at her. 'What about the conventions that decide not to come here because of this . . . ?'

'Oh for God's sake.' She waved him off and stood. 'Conventions don't decide anything, people do, and I can't hear anymore of this. Just let me handle things, you mind? That's what I'm paid to do. And I'm not going to spread a lot of crap. You'll have to get someone else to do it.' She started walking out of his office with its view. 'A hundred and five percent.' She raised her hands in exasperation. 'And I'd watch out for your secretary, by the way.'

'What does she have to do with this?' Cahoon was most confused, which was fairly normal after a visit with Hammer.

'I know the type,' Hammer warned. 'How much does she want?'

'For what?' He was baffled.

'Trust me. She'll let you know,' said Hammer, shaking

her head. 'I wouldn't be alone with her or trust her. I'd get rid of her.'

Mrs Mullis-Mundi knew the meeting could not have gone well. Cahoon had not sent for water, coffee, tea, or cocktails. He had not summoned her on the intercom and asked her to show the chief out. Mrs Mullis-Mundi was conjuring up herself in her Chanel compact, checking her smile in the mirror, when Hammer suddenly was there. This was not a woman who bleached her teeth or waxed her legs. The chief tossed some sort of report in a file folder on the executive secretary's enameled Chinese desk.

'These are my stats, the real ones,' Hammer said as she left. 'See to it he gets them when he's feeling open-minded.'

School kids were getting the grand tour through the marble lobby when the chief's rapidly clicking heels carried her out. She glanced at her Breitling watch without really noting the time. Tonight was her twenty-sixth anniversary of being married to Seth. They were supposed to have a quiet evening at the Beef & Bottle, the rare steak, male hang-out that he loved and she tolerated. It was on South Boulevard, and it had been her experience whenever she had dined there that she generally represented her gender alone as she picked at her meat.

She began, as always, with baby frog legs sautéed in wine and garlic, and a Caesar salad. The din grew louder around them in this darkly paneled room, where city fathers and planners had met for decades, on their way to heart attacks. Seth, her husband, loved food better than life, and was fully engaged with shrimp cocktail, hearts of lettuce with famous blue cheese dressing, bread, butter, and a porterhouse for two that he typically did not share. Once upon a time, Seth had been an enlightened and handsome assistant to the Little Rock city manager, and he had run into Sergeant Judy Hammer, on the capitol grounds.

There had never been any question about who was the engine driving the train in this relationship, and this was part of the attraction. Seth liked her power. She liked his liking it. They were married and began a family that quickly became his responsibility as the wife soared and was called out at night, and they moved. That Hammer was her name and not his made sense for those who knew them and gave the matter a thought. He was soft, with a weak chin that called to mind the watery-eyed knights and bishops of Washington portrait galleries.

'We should pick up some of this cheese spread for the house,' Seth said, laying it on thick in candlelight.

'Seth, I worry about what you're doing to yourself,' Hammer said, reaching for her pinot noir.

'I guess it's port wine, but it doesn't look like it,' he went on. 'It might have horseradish in it. Maybe cayenne pepper.'

His hobby was studying law and the stock market. His most significant setback in life was that he had inherited money from his family, and was not obligated to work, was gentle, and tended to be mild, nonviolent, and tired much of the time. At this stage in life, he was so much like a spineless, spiteful woman that his wife wondered how it was possible she should have ended up in a lesbian relationship with a man. Lord, when Seth slipped into one of his snits, as he was in this very minute, she understood domestic violence and felt there were cases when it was justified.

'Seth, it's our anniversary,' she reminded him in a low voice. 'You haven't talked to me all evening. You've eaten everything in this goddamn restaurant, and won't look at me. You want to give me a clue as to what's wrong, for once? So I don't have to guess or read your mind or go to a psychic?'

Her stomach was balled up like a threatened opossum. Seth was the best diet she'd ever been on, and could throw her into anorexia quicker than anything. In rare, quiet moments, when Hammer walked alone on a beach or in the mountains, she knew she had not been in love with Seth for most of their marriage. But he was her weight-bearing wall. Were he knocked out, half her world would crash. That was his power over her, and he knew it like any good wife. The children, for example, might take his side. This was not possible, but Judy Hammer feared it.

'I'm not talking because I have nothing to say,' Seth reasonably replied.

'Fine.' She folded her cloth napkin, and dropped it on the table as she began searching for the waitress.

Miles away, on Wilkinson Boulevard, past Bob's Pawn Shop, trailer parks, Coyote Joe's and the topless Paper Doll Lounge, The Firing Line was conducting a war of its own. Brazil was slaughtering silhouettes screeching down the lane at him. Ejected cartridge cases sailed through the air, clinking to the floor. West's pupil was improving like nothing she'd ever seen. She was proud.

'Tap-tap, you're out!' she rudely yelled, as if he were the village idiot. 'Safety on. Dump the magazine, reload, rack it! Ready position, safety off! Tap-tap! Stop!'

This had been going on for more than an hour, and good ole boys were peering out from their booths, wondering what the hell was going on down there.

Who was that babe shouting like a drill sergeant at that faggy-looking guy? Bubba, who was begot by a Bubba and probably related to a long line of them, was leaning against a cinder-block wall, an Exxon cap low over his eyes. He was big and bad in fatigues and a camouflage vest, as he watched the target screeching closer and closer to the blond guy.

Bubba was aware of the dense, tight spread, recognizing this guy's skill at head shots. Bubba drooled snuff in a bottle, and glanced back at his own lane to make certain no one thought about touching his Glock 20 ten-millimeter combat-type handgun or his Remington XP-100 with Leupold scope and standard load of 50-grain Sierra PSP bullets and 17 grains of IMR 4198 powder. This was a handgun that rested very nicely over sandbags. His Calico model 110 auto pistol, with its 100-shot magazine and flash suppressor, wasn't half bad, either, nor was the Browning Hi-Power HP-Practical pistol, complete with Pachmayr rubber grips, round-style serrated hammer, and removable front sight.

There was little Bubba liked better than to machine-gun a couple of targets, brass flying like shrapnel, as drug dealers walked behind him, not the least bit interested in messing with the man. Bubba watched the bitch down range unfasten a target from its metal frame. She held it up and looked at her dead-eye, sweet boyfriend.

'Who pissed you off?' she asked him.

Bubba's manly stride carried him their way as more rounds exploded like strings of firecrackers.

'What is this? Some kind of school going on here?' Bubba asked, as if he owned the place.

The woman gave him her attention, and he didn't like what he saw in her eyes. This one didn't know fear. Clearly, she didn't have sense enough to appreciate what she was looking at, and Bubba went over to her lane and helped himself to her Smith & Wesson.

'Pretty big piece for a little gal like you.' Bubba grinned in his cruel way, dribbling more snuff in his jar.

'Please put it down,' West calmly told him.

Brazil was intrigued and appropriately nervous about where this was going. The big-bellied pig dressed like Ruby Ridge or Oklahoma City looked like he had hurt people in the past and was proud of it. He did not put West's gun down, but was now dropping out the magazine, checking the slide, and ejecting the cartridge from the chamber. It occurred to Brazil that West was disarmed, and he could not help her, because the .380 was out of ammunition, too.

'Put it down. Now.' West was most unfriendly. 'It's city property, and I am a city police officer.'

'How 'bout that?' Bubba was beginning to enjoy himself immensely. 'Little woman here's a cop. Well, golly gee.'

West knew better than to announce her rank, which would make matters only that much worse. She stepped so close to him, the toes of their shoes were about to touch. Her chest would have pressed against his belly had she not decided against it.

'This is the last time I ask you to put my gun right back where you found it,' she said, staring up into his homely, whisky-flushed face.

Bubba fixed his sights on Brazil, deciding this pretty boy might be in for a life lesson. Bubba strode over to West's lane, set down her gun, walked up to Brazil, tried to grab the .380 for inspection. Brazil slugged Bubba and broke his nose. Bubba bled over camouflage, and dripped on assault weaponry as he hastily packed his duffel bag.

It was Bubba's Last Stand when he cried out from the steps that the lady and her boyfriend had not heard the last from Bubba.

'Sorry,' Brazil said right off when he and West were alone again.

'Jesus Christ. You can't just hit people like that.' She was mostly embarrassed that she hadn't resolved the conflict herself.

He was loading magazines, and realizing he had never struck anybody in his life. He wasn't sure what he felt about it as he lovingly studied West's .380 pistol.

'What does one of these cost?' he asked with the reverence of the poor.

'You can't afford it,' she said.

'What if I sold your story to *Parade* magazine. My editor thinks they'd go for it. I could make some money. Maybe enough . . .'

This was just what West wanted, another story.

'How about I make a deal with you,' she said. 'No *Parade* magazine. Borrow the Sig until you can afford one of your own. I'll work with you a little more, maybe on an outdoor range. We'll set up some combat situations. The way you piss people off, it's a good idea. Rule of etiquette. Pick up your brass.'

Hundreds of shiny cartridge cases were scattered in their area. Brazil got down and began plucking them up, clinking them into a metal can while West gathered her belongings. She had an unpleasant thought, and looked at him.

'What about your mother?' she asked.

He kept working, glancing up, a shadow passing behind his eyes. 'What about her?'

'I'm just wondering about a gun being in the house.'

'I got good at hiding things a long time ago.' He loudly clanged brass into the can, making his point.

Bubba was waiting in the parking lot, inconspicuous inside his spotless chrome and black King Cab pickup truck with gun rack, Confederate flag mud flaps, roll bar, KC fog lights, Ollie North bumper sticker, PVC pipes for holding fishing poles on the front grille, and neon lights around the license plate. He held a wadded-up undershirt to his bleeding nose, watching as the lady cop and her asshole boyfriend emerged from the firing range, walking through the gathering dusk. Bubba waited long enough to see her get out keys and head for an impeccable white Ford Explorer in a corner of the unpaved lot. Her personal wheels, Bubba supposed, and this was even better. He climbed down from his cab, a tire jack in a meaty fist, ready for a little payback.

West was expecting him. She was practiced in the modus operandi of Bubbas, for whom revenge was a reflex, like getting up for a beer during commercials. She had already dipped into her totebag for what looked like a black golf club handle.

'Get in the car,' she quietly ordered Brazil.

'No way,' he said, standing his ground as Bubba strode toward them, a menacing sneer on his gory face.

Bubba didn't get within six feet of her car before West was walking to meet him. He was surprised, not expecting kick-ass aggression from this little lady cop. He tapped the tire iron against a meaty thigh as a warning, then raised it, eyeing the Ford's spotless front windshield.

'Hey!' Weasel, the manager, yelled from the range's entrance. 'Bubba, what d'ya think you're doing, man!'

The retractable steel baton snapped out like a whip,

suddenly three feet long with a hard knobby tip that West pointed at Bubba. She drew slow circles in the air, like a fencer.

'Put it down and leave,' she commanded Bubba in her police tone.

'Fuck you!' Bubba was really losing his temper now because he was losing his nerve. He had seen weapons like hers at gun shows and knew they could be mean.

'Bubba! You quit right now!' screamed Weasel, who ran a clean business.

Brazil noticed that the manager was most upset but did not get one step closer to the trouble. Brazil was casting about, wanting to help. He knew better than to get in her way. If only the .380 was loaded. He could shoot out this goon's tires or something, perhaps cause a diversion. West caused her own. Bubba raised the tire iron again, this time completely dedicated to connecting it with her car, because he had committed himself. It no longer mattered what he felt. He had to do it, especially now that Weasel and a gathering crowd were watching. If Bubba didn't carry out his threat and avenge his injured nose, everyone in the Charlotte-Mecklenburg region would know.

West smacked the bony part of Bubba's wrist with the baton, and he howled in pain as the tire iron clanked to the parking lot. That was the end of it.

'Why didn't you arrest him?' Brazil wanted to know a little later, as they drove past Latta Park in Dilworth, close to where she lived.

'Wasn't worth it,' she replied, smoking. 'He didn't damage my car or me.'

'What if he takes out warrants on us, for assault?' The thought was weirdly appealing to Brazil.

She laughed as if her ride-along hadn't lived much. 'Don't think so.' She turned into her driveway. 'Last thing he wants is the world knowing he got beat up by a woman and a kid.'

'I'm not a kid,' he said.

Her house was as he remembered it, and the fence was no further along. Brazil asked no questions, but followed her through the backyard to her small workshop, where there was a table saw and a vast collection of tools neatly organized on pegboards. West built bird houses, cabinets, even furniture, it appeared to him. He had done enough odd jobs around his house during his life to have a healthy respect for her obvious ability. He found it a strain to even assemble K-Mart bookcases.

'Wow,' he said, looking around.

'Wow what?' She shut the door behind them and turned on a radio.

'What made you decide to do all this?'

'Survival,' she said, squatting to open a small refrigerator. Bottles rattled as she brought out two long-neck Southpaw Lights.

Brazil did not like beer, in truth, even though he drank it from time to time. It tasted rotten and made him silly and sleepy. He would die before he let her find this out.

'Thanks,' he said, screwing off the cap, and tossing it in the trash.

'When I was getting started, I couldn't afford to hire people to help me out around here. So I learned on my own.' She opened hard cases and got out guns. 'Plus, as you know, I grew up on a farm. I learned whatever I could from my dad, and the hired hands.'

'What about from your mom?'

West was disassembling the pistols as if she could do

it in her sleep. 'Like what?' She glanced across the table at him.

'You know, domestic stuff. Cooking, cleaning, raising kids.'

She smiled, opening a tackle box stocked with gun-cleaning paraphernalia. 'Do I cook and clean for myself? You see a wife anywhere?' She handed him a cleaning rod and a stack of patches.

He took a big swig of beer and swallowed it as fast as he could, trying not to taste it, as usual. He was feeling braver, and trying not to notice how good she looked in her gray T-shirt and jeans.

'I've done shit like that all my life, and I'm not a wife,' he said.

'What do you know?' she asked as she dipped her rod into a small brown bottle of solvent.

'Nothing.' He said this as a sulking challenge.

'Don't give me your moods, okay?' West replied, refusing to play games, because, frankly, she was too old for them.

Brazil threaded a patch through his rod, and dipped it in Hoppes. He loved the smell, and had no intention of confessing anything else to her. But the beer had a tongue of its own.

'Let's talk about this wife-shit again,' she pushed him.

'What do you want me to say?' Brazil, the man, replied.

'You tell me what it means.' She really wanted to know.

'In theory,' – he began to clean the barrel of the .380 – 'I'm not entirely sure. Maybe something to do with roles, a caste system, a pecking order, a hierarchy, the ecosystem.'

'The ecosystem?' She frowned, blasting her barrel and other parts with Gunk Off.

'Point is,' he explained, 'that being a wife has nothing to do with what you do, but with what someone thinks you are. Just like I'm doing something you want me to do right now, but that doesn't make me a slave.'

'Don't you have the roles a little reversed here? Who was giving who firearms instruction?' She scrubbed the inside of the barrel with a toothbrush. 'You're doing what you want to do. I'm doing what you want me to do. For nothing, for the record. And who's the slave?' She sprayed again and handed him the can.

He reached for his beer. It was his limited experience that the warmer beer got, the worse it got.

'So let's say you grow up and get married someday,' she went on. 'What are you going to expect of your wife?'

'A partner.' He tossed his bottle into the trash. 'I don't want a wife. I don't need anybody to take care of me, clean for me, cook for me.' He got out two more beers, popped them open and set one within her reach. 'Saying I'm too busy to do all that shit for myself someday? I'll hire a housekeeper. But I'm not going to marry one,' he said as if this were the most ridiculous notion society had ever devised.

'Uh huh.'

She reached for the barrel of the .380, checking his work. Man talk, she thought. The difference was, this one could put words together better than most. She didn't believe a thing he said.

'It should look like a mirror inside.' She slid the barrel in front of him. 'Scrub hard. You can't hurt it.'

He picked up the barrel, then his beer. 'See, people should get married, live together, whatever, and do things just like this,' he went on as he dipped a brush in solvent and resumed scrubbing. 'There shouldn't be roles. There should be practicalities, people helping out each other like friends. One weak where the other's strong, people using their gifts, cooking together, playing tennis, fishing. Walking on the beach. Staying up late talking. Being unselfish and caring.'

'Sounds like you've thought about this a lot,' she said. 'A good script.'

He looked puzzled. 'What script?'

She drank. 'Heard it all before. Seen that rerun.'

So had Bubba's wife, Mrs Rickman, whose first name had ceased to be important when she had gotten married twenty-six years ago in the Tabernacle Baptist Church. This had been down the road in Mount Mourne where she worked every day at the B&B, known for the best breakfast in town. The B&B's hot dogs and burgers were popular, too, especially with Davidson students, and, of course, with other Bubbas on their way for a day of fishing at Lake Norman.

When gun cleaning was completed, and Brazil suggested to West that they stop for a bite to eat, neither of them had a way to know that the overweight, tired woman waiting on them was Bubba's wretched wife.

'Hi, Mrs Rickman,' Brazil said to the waitress.

He gave her his bright, irresistible smile and felt sorry for her, as he always did when he came to the B&B. Brazil knew how hard food service was, and it depressed him to think of what it had been like for his mother all those years when she could still get out and go anywhere. Mrs Rickman was happy to see him. He was always so sweet.

'How's my baby?' she chirped, setting plastic laminated

menus in front of them. She eyed West. 'Who's your pretty lady friend?'

'Deputy Chief Virginia West with the Charlotte police,' Brazil made the mistake of saying.

So it was that Bubba would learn the identities of his attackers.

'My, my.' Mrs. Rickman was mighty impressed as she got an eyeful of this important woman sitting in a B&B booth. 'A deputy chief. Didn't know they had women that high up. What'll be? The pork barbecue's extra good tonight. I'd get it minced.'

'Cheeseburger all the way, fries, Miller in the bottle,' West said. 'Extra mayonnaise and ketchup. Can you put a little butter on the bun and throw it on the grill?'

'Sure can, honey.' Mrs Rickman nodded. She didn't write down anything as she beamed at Brazil.

'The usual.' He winked at her.

She walked off, her hip killing her worse than yesterday.

'What's the usual?' West wanted to know.

'Tuna on wheat, lettuce, tomato, no mayo. Slaw, limeade. I want to ride patrol with you. In uniform,' he said.

'In the first place, I don't ride patrol. In the second place, in case you haven't noticed, I have a real job, nothing important. Just the entire investigative division. Homicide. Burglary. Rape. Arson. Fraud. Auto theft. Check theft,' she said. 'White collar, computer, organized crime, vice. Juvenile. Cold case squad. Of course, there's a serial killer on the loose, and it's my detectives on the case, getting all the heat.'

She lit a cigarette, and intercepted her beer before Mrs

Rickman could set it down. 'I would prefer not to work twenty-four hours a day, if it's all the same to you. You know how my cat gets? Won't touch me, won't sleep with me? Not to mention, I haven't gone out to a movie, to dinner, in weeks.' She drank. 'I haven't finished my fence. When was the last time I cleaned my house?'

'Is that a no?' Brazil said.

Chapter Eight

Bubba's Christian name was Joshua Rickman, and he was a forklift operator at Ingersoll-Rand in Cornelius. Perhaps the manufacturer's greatest claim to fame came and went in the early eighties when it manufactured a snow machine that was used in the winter Olympics somewhere. Bubba wasn't clear on the details, and didn't care. Air compressors were what one saw on life's highways. They were in demand all over the world. His was an international career. This early Monday morning he was deep in thought as he skillfully deposited crates on a loading dock.

His wife happened to have mentioned the Davidson kid who was dating some big-shot police woman. Yo. Bubba didn't have to strain himself to add two and two. His nose hurt like shit, but no way he was going to a doctor. For what? It was his philosophy that there was nothing to be done about a busted nose or ripped ears, knocked-out teeth and other non-life-threatening head injuries, unless one had some queerbait interest in plastic surgery, which Bubba clearly did not. His nose was a blimp and always had been, so the setback in this case was pain and pain alone. Every time he blew his nose, blood gushed and tears filled his eyes, all because of that little son of a bitch. Bubba wasn't about to forget.

He had books for life's problems, and referred to them as needed. *Make 'Em Pay* and *Get Even 1* and *2* were especially insightful. These were the ultimate revenge technique manuals penned by a master trickster and privately published out of Colorado. Bubba had discovered them at gun shows here and yon. Bombs were an idea. What about a television tube that would explode, or a Ping-Pong ball loaded with potassium chlorate and black powder? Maybe not. Bubba wanted some real damage here, but wasn't interested in the FBI Hostage Rescue Team (HRT) fast roping in or staking out his property. He didn't want prison time. Maybe what was called for was the trick where certain scents available at the hunt shop would draw every rodent, neighborhood pet, bug, reptile, and other critter into the yard, that all might ruin it during the night. Bubba slammed the forklift in reverse, thoughts buzzing.

Or he could feed beer-laced urine through a tube inserted under the police lady's front door. He could mail hair to her, anonymously. Eventually, would she move? Hell yes. She'd want to, oh yeah. Or maybe Sea Breeze in the jock strap of that blond kid she was jerking off with, unless both of them were queer, and, frankly, Bubba had his opinion. Honestly, there was no way a man could look that good or a woman could be that powerful unless they were suspect. Bubba could see it now. The pretty boy getting what he deserved, from the rear, from a manly man like Bubba, whose favorite movie was *Deliverance*. Bubba would teach the little asshole, oh yes he would. Bubba hated fags so intensely that he was on the lookout for them in every sports bar and truck stop, and in all vehicles he passed on life's highways, and in politics and the entertainment industry.

West and Brazil could not know of their personal peril. They were not thinking of themselves this Tuesday night as emergency lights flashed on broken glass and the torn, crumpled remains of a patrol car that had crashed in the affluent residential neighborhood of Myers Park. Raines and other paramedics were using hydraulic tools to get bodies out of a Mercedes 300E that was wrapped around a tree. Everyone was tense and upset as a siren screamed, and police had set up a barricade, blocking off the street. Brazil parked his BMW as close as anyone would let him. He ran towards red and blue lights and rumbling engines.

West arrived, and cops moved saw horses to let her through. She spotted Brazil taking notes. He was dazed by horror as Raines and other paramedics lifted another bloody dead body out of the Mercedes and zipped it inside a pouch. Rescuers lowered a victim next to three others on pavement stained with spilled oil and blood. West stared at the totaled Charlotte cruiser with its hornet's nest emblem on the doors. She turned her attention to another cruiser not far away, where Officer Michelle Johnson was collapsed in the back seat, holding a bloodstained handkerchief to her devastated face as she trembled and shook. West swiftly walked that way. She opened the cruiser's back door and climbed in next to the distraught officer.

'It's going to be okay,' West said, putting an arm around a young woman who could not comprehend what had just happened to her. 'We need to get you to the hospital,' West told her.

'No! No!' Johnson screamed, covering her head with her hands, as if her plane were going down. 'I didn't see him until he was through the light. Mine was green! I was responding to the ten-thirty-three, but my light was green. I swear. Oh God! No, no. Please. No. Please, please, please.'

Brazil was inching closer to the cruiser and heard what Johnson said. He stepped up to the door, and stared through the window, watching West comfort a cop who had just smashed into another car and killed all its occupants. For an instant, West looked out. Her eyes met his and held. His pen was poised and filled with quotes he now knew he would never put in any story. He lowered the pen and notepad. Slowly, he walked away, not the same reporter or person he had been.

Brazil returned to the newspaper. He walked in no hurry and not happy to be here as he headed for his desk. He took his chair, typed in his password, and went into his computer basket. Betty Cutler, the night editor, was an old crow with an underbite. She had been pacing and waiting for Brazil, and swooped in on him. She began her annoying habit of sniffing as she spoke. It had occurred to Brazil that she might have a cocaine problem.

'We got to ship this in forty-five minutes,' she said to him. 'What did the cop say?'

Brazil began typing the lead, and looking at his notes. 'What cop?' he asked, even though he knew precisely who she meant.

'The cop who just wiped out an entire family of five, for Chrissake.' Cutler sniffed, her lower teeth bared.

'I didn't interview her.'

Cutler, the night editor, didn't believe this. She refused

to believe it. Her eyes glittered as she gave him a penetrating stare. 'What the hell do you mean, you didn't interview her, Brazil!' She lifted her voice that all might hear. 'You were at the scene!'

'They had her in a patrol car,' he said, flipping pages.

'So you knock on the window,' Cutler loudly berated him. 'You open her door, do whatever you have to!'

Brazil stopped typing and looked up at a woman who truly depressed him. He didn't care if she knew it. 'Maybe that's what you would do,' he said.

When the paper thudded on his front porch at six o'clock the next morning, Brazil was already up. He had already run five miles at the track. He had showered and put on his police uniform. He opened the door, snatched the paper off the stoop, and rolled off the rubber band, eager to see his work. His angry steps carried him through the sad living room and into the cramped dingy kitchen where his mother sat at a plastic-covered table, drinking coffee held in trembling hands. She was smoking and momentarily present. Brazil tossed the paper down on the table. The front page, above the fold headline, screamed POLICE CRASH KILLS FAMILY OF FIVE. There were large color photographs of broken glass, twisted metal, and Officer Michelle Johnson weeping in the cruiser.

'I can't believe it!' Brazil exclaimed. 'Look! The damn headline makes it sound like it was the cop's fault when we don't even know who caused the wreck!'

His mother wasn't interested. She got up, moving slowly toward the screen door that led out to the side porch. Her son watched with dread as she swayed, and snatched keys from a hook on the wall.

'Where are you going?' he asked.

'The store.' She dug inside her big, old pocketbook.

'I just went yesterday,' he said.

'I need cigarettes.' She opened her billfold and scowled.

'I bought you a carton, Mom.' Brazil stared at her.

He knew where his mother was really going and felt the same old defeat. He sighed angrily as his mother clutched her pocketbook and counted dollar bills.

'You got a ten-spot?' she asked him.

'I'm not buying your booze,' he stated.

She paused at the door, regarding an only child she had never known how to love. 'Where are you going?' she said with a cruel expression that made her face ugly and unfamiliar. 'A costume party?'

'A parade,' Brazil answered. 'I'm directing traffic.'

'Parade charade.' She sneered. 'You're not police, never will be. Why do you want to be going out there to get killed?' She got sad just as quickly as she had turned mean. 'So I can end up all alone?' She yanked the door open.

The morning got no better. Brazil drove fifteen minutes through the police department deck, and finally left his BMW in a press space, even though he really wasn't on official press business. The day was lovely, but he took the tunnel from the deck to the first level of police headquarters because he was feeling especially antisocial. Whenever he had encounters with his mother, he got very quiet inside. He wanted to be alone. He did not want to talk to anyone.

At the Property Control window, he checked out a radio and was handed keys for the unmarked vehicle he would be driving in the Charlie Two response area between Tryon and Independence Boulevard for the annual Freedom Parade. It was a modest celebration sponsored by local Shriners in their tasseled hats and on their scooters, and Brazil could not have been assigned a worse car. The Ford Crown Victoria was dull, scratched black, and had been driven hard for a hundred and sixteen thousand miles. The transmission was going to drop out any moment, providing the damn thing started, which it didn't seem inclined to do.

Brazil flipped the key in the ignition again, pumping the accelerator as the old engine tried to turn over. The battery supplied enough juice to wake up the scanner and radio, but forget about going anywhere, as the car whined, and Brazil's frustration soared.

'Shit!' He pounded the steering wheel, accidentally blaring the horn. Cops in the distance turned around, staring.

Chief Hammer was causing her own commotion not too far away inside the Carpe Diem restaurant on South Tryon, across the street from the Knight-Ridder building. Two of her deputy chiefs, West and Jeannie Goode, sat at a quiet corner table, eating lunch and discussing problems. Goode was West's age and jealous of any female who did anything in life, especially if she looked good.

'This is the craziest thing I've ever heard,' Goode was saying as she poked at tarragon chicken salad. 'He shouldn't be out with us to begin with. Did you get a load of the headline this morning? Implying we caused the accident, that Johnson was pursuing the Mercedes? Unbelievable. Not to mention, skid marks indicate it wasn't us who ran the red light.'

'Andy Brazil didn't write the headline,' West said, turning to Hammer, her boss, who was working on cottage cheese and fresh fruit. 'All I'm asking is to ride routine patrol with him for maybe a week.'

'You want to respond to calls?' Hammer reached for her iced tea.

'Absolutely,' West said as Goode looked on with judgment.

Hammer put down her fork and studied West. 'Why can't he ride with regular patrol? Or for that matter, we've got fifty other volunteers. He can't ride with them?'

West hesitated, motioning to a waiter for more coffee. She asked for extra mayonnaise and ketchup for her club sandwich and fries, and returned her attention to Hammer as if Goode was not at the table.

'No one wants to ride with him,' West said. 'Because he's a reporter. You know how the cops feel about the *Observer*. That won't go away overnight. And there's a lot of jealousy.' She looked pointedly at Goode.

'Not to mention, he's an arrogant smartass with an entitlement attitude,' Goode chimed in.

'Entitlement?' West let the word linger like a vapor trail in the rarified air of Carpe Diem, where high feminine powers met regularly. 'So tell me, Jeannie, when was the last time you directed traffic?'

It was an odious job. Citizens did not take traffic cops seriously. Carbon monoxide levels got dangerously high, and the cardinal rule that one must never turn his back to traffic was irrelevant in four-way intersections. How could anyone face four directions simultaneously? Brazil had questioned this since the academy. Of course, it made no sense, and added to the mix was a basic disrespect problem. Already, he'd had half a dozen teenagers, women, and businessmen make fun or him or offer gestures that he was not allowed to reciprocate. What was it about America? Citizens were all too aware of law enforcement officers, such as himself, who wore no gun and seemed new at the job. They noticed. They commented.

'Hey Star Trek,' a middle-aged woman yelled out her window. 'Get a phaser,' she said as she gunned onto Enfield Road.

'Shooting blanks, are we, fairy queen?' screamed a dude in an Army-green Jeep with a basher bumper, sports rack, and safari doors.

Brazil directed the Jeep through with a hard stare and set jaw, halfway wishing the shithead would stop and demand a fight. Brazil was getting an itch. He wanted to deck someone, and sensed it was only a matter of time before he busted another nose.

Sometimes, Hammer got so sick of her diet. But she remembered turning thirty-nine and getting a partial hysterectomy because her uterus had pretty much quit doing anything useful. She had gained fifteen pounds in three months, moving up from a size four to an eight, and doctors told her this was because she ate too much. Well, bullshit. Hormones were always to blame, and for good reason. They were the weather of female life. Hormones moved over the face of the female planet and decided whether it was balmy or frigid or time for the storm cellar. Hormones made things wet or dried them. They made one want to walk hand-in-hand in balmy moonlight, or be alone.

'What does directing traffic have to do with anything?' Goode wanted to know.

'Point is, this guy works harder than most of your cops,' West replied to Goode. 'And he's just a volunteer. Doesn't have to. Could have a real attitude problem, but doesn't.'

Hammer wondered if salt would hurt her much. Lord, how nice it would be to taste something and not end up looking like her husband.

'I'm in charge of patrol. That's where he is right now,' Goode said, turning over lettuce leaves with her fork to see if anything good was left. Maybe a crouton or a walnut.

Brazil was sweating in his uniform and bright orange traffic vest. His feet were on fire as he blocked off a side street. He was turning cars around left and right, routing them the other way, blowing his whistle, and making crisp traffic motions. Horns were honking, and another driver began yelling rudely out the window for directions. Brazil trotted over to help, and was not appreciated or thanked. This was a terrible job, and he loved it for reasons he did not understand.

'So he relieves at least one sworn officer from traffic duty,' West was saying as Hammer chose to ignore both of her deputy chiefs.

Frankly, Hammer could take but so much of the bickering between the brass. It never ended. Hammer glanced at her watch and imagined Cahoon at the top of his crown. The fool. He would turn this city into the prick of America, peopled by yahoos with guns and USAir Gold cards and box seats for the Panthers and Hornets if someone did not stop him.

Cahoon had been stopped three times on his way to lunch on the sixtieth floor, in the corporate dining room. Awaiting him amid linen and Limoges were a president, four vice-presidents, a chairman and a vice-chairman, and a top executive with the Dominion Tobacco Company, which over the next two years would be borrowing more than four hundred million dollars from USBank for a cancer research project. Computer printouts had been stacked high by Cahoon's plate. There were fresh flowers on the table, and waiters in tuxedos hovered.

'Good afternoon.' The CEO nodded around the table, his eyes lingering on the tobacco executive.

Cahoon didn't like the woman and wasn't sure why, beyond his rabid hatred of smoking, which had begun seven years ago, after he had quit. Cahoon had serious misgivings about granting such a huge loan for a project so scientific and secretive that no one could tell him precisely what it was about, beyond the fact that USBank would be instrumental in the development of the world's first truly healthy cigarette. He had reviewed endless charts and diagrams of a long and robust cylinder with a gold crown around the filter. The amazing product was called *USChoice*. It could be smoked by all, would harm none, and contained various minerals, vitamins, and calming agents that would be inhaled and absorbed directly into the bloodstream. Cahoon was reminded of what his bank's contribution would mean to humanity, as he reached for his bubbly water, and felt happy.

The people along Eastway Drive were also happy as they waited for the Freedom Parade. It was always full of hope and bounce, Shriners zig-zagging on their scooters, waving at the crowd, reminding all of burn units and good deeds. Brazil was slightly concerned that other cops at other intersections seemed bored and restless. There were no floats. He scanned the horizon and saw nothing but a patrol car in a hurry heading his way. A horn blared and another driver yelled, this time an angry old woman in a Chevrolet. No matter how much Brazil tried to help, she was determined to be unpleasant and unreasonable.

'Ma'am,' he politely said, 'you have to turn around and take Shamrock Drive.'

She flipped him a bird and roared off, as the frantic, irritated cop in the patrol car rolled up on Brazil's intersection.

'The parade and a funeral somehow got routed through here at the same time,' the cop hastily explained.

'What?' Brazil asked, baffled. 'How . . . ?'

But the patrol car sped off.

'Doesn't matter who he relieves from traffic,' Goode was saying as she gave up on food in hopes it would give up on her. 'I don't want him. He's a spy, CIA, KGB, whatever you want to call him.'

'Now how stupid is that?' West pushed her plate away. 'For Chrissake.'

Hammer said nothing as she looked around the restaurant to see who else she recognized. The book columnist for the *Observer* and an editorial writer were eating lunch, but not together. Hammer trusted none of them. She had spent no time with Andy Brazil, but thought maybe it wouldn't be a bad idea. He sounded interesting.

When the hearses slowly appeared, they were gleaming black, with headlights burning. Brazil watched their formidable approach as he struggled to keep his side street blocked, and continued to direct cars to turn away.

The endless funeral procession crept past with precision and dignity, and hundreds of people waiting for Shriners and scooters drank sodas, and watched and waved. This wasn't exactly what they had expected when they'd headed out into the morning for a little free excitement, but they were here and would take whatever they could get.

Inside a black Lincoln Continental stretch limousine with white leather interior and a television and VCR, the bereft brother and the widow were dressed for Sunday and staring out tinted glass. They were impressed by all the spectators lining the street to pay last respects. A lot of them had brought snacks, drinks, kids, and small American flags. They were waving and cheering, which was the way it ought to be, a celebration, as one crosses over to the other side, into the loving arms of Jesus.

'I had no idea Tyvola had so many friends,' the brother marveled, waving back.

'And all these police came out.' The widow shyly waved, too.

Brazil blew his whistle and almost got run over by an old man in a Dodge Dart who didn't seem to understand that a policeman holding out both palms was a hint that the driver might want to stop. The unbroken caravan of stretch limousines, town cars, hearses, all black with lights on, didn't seem to send any direct message to Howie Song in his Dart. By now, Song was halfway out into the intersection with a line of cars bumper to bumper behind him. It was not possible he could back up unless everyone else did.

'Don't you move!' Brazil warned the impatient old man, who had his radio turned up as high as it would go, playing a country western tune.

Brazil set three traffic cones in front of the Dart. They scattered like bowling pins the instant Brazil stepped back to direct other cars to back up. Song in his Dart helped himself to the Boulevard, certain the lumbering funeral cars would let him through so he could get to the hardware store.

That's what you think, thought Chad Tilly, director of the Tilly Family Mortuary, which was famous for its air conditioned building, plush slumber parlors, and quality caskets. His big ad on page 537 of the Yellow Pages was unfortunately positioned directly next to Fungus and Mold Control. Tilly's secretary was forever telling people who called that although they had similar concerns in the funeral business, they could not help with basement moisture problems or sump pumps, for example.

Tilly had driven in more funeral processions than he could remember. He was a formidable businessman who hadn't gotten his fine suits and rings by being a pushover. He not only didn't let that little piece of law-breaking banged-up blue Dodge shit through, but Tilly got on his two-way radio. He raised his lead car on the air.

'Flip,' he said to his number-two man in the company.

'Coming at ya, boss.'

'Put the brakes on up there,' Tilly told him.

'You sure?'

'Always am,' said Tilly.

This stopped the entire line of black cars with lights burning. The Dart could not get across the Boulevard now, and Song was momentarily confused. He stopped, too, long enough for a cop to yank open his door and get the crabby old man out of the car.

'Flip,' Tilly was back on the air. 'Move along.' He chuckled.

Hammer was not amused as she applied lipstick after lunch and listened to her two female deputy chiefs bickering like rival siblings.

'I'm in charge of patrol,' Goode announced inside the Carpe Diem, as if the restaurant's name applied to her. 'And he's not riding with us. God only knows what will end up in the newspaper. You're so hot on him, let him ride with your people.'

Hammer got out her compact and glanced at her watch.

'Investigations doesn't have ride-alongs. Ever,' West replied. 'It's against department policy and always has been.'

'And what you're proposing isn't?' Goode demanded.

'Ride-alongs, volunteers, have been riding with patrol for as long as I've been here,' West reminded her in a strained voice.

Hammer got out her wallet, and studied the bill.

'I'm wondering if there's some personal agenda here,' Goode went on.

West knew exactly what the bitch was implying. It had been duly noted around the department that Andy Brazil was rather good to look at, and West had never been famous for dating. The current theory circulating was that she had found a boy toy because she couldn't get a man. Long ago, she had learned to ignore such gossip.

'The bigger issue,' Goode was saying, 'is that volunteers don't routinely ride with a deputy chief who hasn't made an arrest or written a ticket in fifty years.

He's probably not even safe out there with someone like you.'

'We've handled some situations a lot better than patrol did,' West let her know.

Hammer had heard enough. 'Here's what we're going to do,' she spoke. 'Virginia, I'm going to approve your riding patrol with him. It's an interesting idea. We might learn something new. I probably should have done the same thing a long time ago.'

She put money on the table. West and Goode did the same. Hammer nailed Goode with a look.

'You'll do everything you can to help,' Hammer said to her.

Goode was cold as she got up and turned to West for one last remark. 'Hope there's no problem. Remember, your rank is unclassified.'

'As is yours,' Hammer said to Goode. 'I can fire you without cause. Just like that.' She snapped her fingers. She wished Goode had gone into some other profession. Maybe undertaking.

Chapter Nine

Chad Tilly could have used another undertaker at exactly that moment. He had brilliantly outmaneuvered the Dodge Dart with its kamikaze old man rocking to country western. That round the funeral director had won without effort, but it had also been Tilly's experience that when he was relaxed and not looking, he usually got his butt kicked. Tilly was creeping along again when he decided to light a cigar and fiddle with the radio at the same time.

Tilly did not notice the blond kid in uniform, and no gun, suddenly halting the procession as, of all things, a Fourth of July-looking float appeared on the horizon, running the lead limo off the road. This was amazing. Sweet Jesus, this could not be so. Tilly slammed on brakes at the same moment his assistant's inability to completely shut the hearse's tailgate became known. The copper-tinted casket with deep satin lining slammed one way and ricocheted out the other like a lightweight alloy bullet. The casket and its occupant skittered over pavement and kept going, for, as luck would have it, the procession was momentarily on a slight hill.

* * *

Brazil had not been trained to handle such a situation and was on his radio in a flash as yet a second float glided into view. This was awful. It was his intersection. He would be blamed. His armpits were soaked and his heart was out of control as he tried to contain the disaster of the world. Men in dark suits with lots of rings and gold crowns on their teeth were flying out of stretch limousines, and chasing a run-away gaudy electroplated casket down the boulevard. Oh God. No. Brazil blew his whistle and stopped all traffic, including floats. He raced after the casket as it continued its lonely journey. People stared at the cop chasing it. They cheered.

'I'll get it,' Brazil called out to men in suits, as he sprinted.

The foot pursuit was brief, order restored, and a dapper man who identified himself as Mr Tilly formally thanked Brazil for all to hear.

'Is there anything else I can do to help?' replied Brazil, the community-oriented cop.

'Yeah,' the funeral home director boomed. 'Get them mother-fucking floats outa my way.'

Floats were pulled over to make room, and none moved an inch for an hour. Not one spectator went home, and others came as word traveled around. This was the best Freedom Day in the history of Charlotte.

Goode, head of patrol, did not share quite the same enthusiasm, since traffic control was her responsibility, and a runaway casket was not something she wanted to hear about on the evening news. It was a matter she intended to resolve in person, but not until it was dark out. Then she packed up her slim, soft leather satchel and headed to the parking deck, where the city paid nineteen dollars a month for her reserved parking space. She preferred driving her personal car back and forth to work, and got inside her black Miata.

Goode opened her satchel, dug for Obsession, and strategically sprayed. She dry-brushed her teeth. She worked on her hair a bit, and threw the car in reverse, loving the engine throbbing beneath her. She headed out to Myers Park, the wealthiest, oldest neighborhood, where huge mansions with slate roofs gathered their cobblestone skirts around them lest they be splashed by the dirtier elements of the city.

Myers Park Methodist Church was gray stone and rose from the horizon like a castle. Goode had never been to a service here, but the parking lot she knew very well, for she worshiped in it regularly. Brent Webb was on his break after the six o'clock news, his Porsche idling beneath a large magnolia tree in a far corner. He shut down the engine as his other one got going. He got out of his car, looking each way, as if about to cross traffic, and slid inside Goode's Miata.

Rarely did they talk, unless she had a scoop he must know. Their lips locked, sucked, bit, probed, and invaded, as did tongues and hands. They drove each other farther than either had ever been, each time more primitive and special, each frenzied by the other's power. Webb had secret fantasies of Goode in uniform, whipping out her handcuffs, and her gun. She liked to watch him on TV, when she was alone at home, savoring his every syllable as he alluded to her, and secretly quoted her to the world.

'I assume you know about the casket problem.' Goode could barely talk.

'Whose?' asked Webb, who never knew anything unless the information was stolen or leaked.

'Never mind.'

They were breathing heavily, the Pointer Sisters jumping on the radio. They made out in the front seat, maneuvering around the stick shift as best they could. Through the front windshield the lit-up city skyline was close, the USBank Corporate Center very much a symbol of Webb's good mood. He unfastened her bra, never sure why he bothered, and he imagined her tie, her police belt, and his excitement grew.

Officer Jenny Frankel was typically excited, as well, for she was young and still enthusiastic about her job. She looked for trouble, begged, and even prayed for it, so when she noticed two vehicles pulled off in a remote corner of the Myers Park Methodist Church parking lot, she had to check it out. In the first place, choir practice was yesterday, and AA didn't meet until Thursday. Plus, there were drug dealers everywhere, threatening to take over. Fuck no, was her position. She would take the city back, return it to decent, hard-working men and women if it was the last thing she did in life.

She pulled into shadows and stopped, now close enough to notice movement in the front seat of a late-model black Miata that looked vaguely familiar, for some reason. Frankel suspected the active silhouettes were two men, based on the hair. She typed plate numbers into her MDT and patiently waited as the two guys kissed, fondled, and sucked. When Deputy Chief Goode's and Brent Webb's Department of Motor Vehicle information returned to the video display, Frankel rapidly left the area. Other than her sergeant, with whom she went out drinking several times a week, Frankel told no one what she had observed this night. The sergeant also told only one person, and this discreetly went on.

* * *

Brazil's day had been long, but he did not want to go home. After working traffic, he had changed his clothes and done his eight hours for the *Observer*. Now it was almost one A.M. The late shift had been slow. For a while he had hung around the press room watching newspapers race towards their final destination of puppy crates and recycling bins. He had stood, mesmerized, unable to see his byline this time because all he had been able to bring in was a local metro story about a pedestrian run over in Mint Hill. The victim was a known drunk and night editor Cutler didn't think the story merited more than three inches.

Brazil got in his BMW and headed back toward Trade Street. This was not a safe thing to do, and no one need tell him that. He rumbled past the stadium and the Duke Power transfer station, stopping at a dead end at West Third where the old crumbling building seemed even more haunted and menacing at this hour. Brazil sat and stared, imagining murder, and believing there was a person who had heard the gunshots and spraying of paint. Somewhere, someone knew. Brazil left his engine running, the Sig Sauer between the front seats, and within reach.

He began walking around, probing with a flashlight, his eyes nervous, as if he feared he was being watched. Old blood on pavement was black, and an opossum was working on it, eyes white in the flashlight as it spied the intrusion and scuttled off. The woods teemed with restless insects, and fireflies winked. A far-off train rumbled down rusty tracks, and Brazil was chilled, his attention darting around, like static. He felt murder in this place. He sensed a sinister energy that bristled and coiled and waited to claim more. These killings were common and cold, and Brazil believed that the monster was known by the people of the night, and fear kept identity hidden.

Brazil did not believe prostitution was right. He did not think that anyone should have to pay for such a thing. He did not believe that anyone should have to sell such a thing. All of it was depressing, and he imagined being a homely middle-aged man and accepting that no woman would want him without his wallet. Brazil imagined a woman worrying about servicing the next client in order to feed her child or herself or avoid another beating from her pimp. A horrid slavery, all of it dreadful and hard to imagine. This moment, Brazil entertained little hope about the human condition when he considered that heartless behavior had evolved not one level higher since the beginning of time. It seemed that what had changed, simply, was the way people got around and communicated, and the size of the weapons they used against each another.

On Highway 277, he saw one of these very sad creations on the shoulder, walking languidly, in tight jeans and no bra, her chest thrust out. The young hooker was pointed and tattooed, in a skimpy white knit shirt. He slowed, meeting bold, mocking eyes that didn't know fear. She was about his age and missing most of her front teeth, and he tried to imagine talking to her, or picking her up. He wondered if the appeal was stolen fire, some sort of mythical thing, an ill-gotten rush that made people feel powerful, her over him, him over her, if only for a dark, degrading moment. He imagined her laughing at her johns and hating them as much as she hated herself and all. He followed the young hooker in his rearview mirror as she stared back at him, with a slight, quizzical smile, waiting for the boy to make up his mind. She could have been pretty once. Brazil sped up as a van cruised close to her and stopped.

* * *

The next night, Brazil was out on the street again, and reality seemed different and odd, and, at first, he thought it was his imagination. From the moment he left the *Observer* in his BMW, he saw cops everywhere in spotless white patrol cars. They were watching and following him, and he told himself this could not be true, that he was tired and full of fantasy. The evening was slow, with no good reports in the press basket, unless Webb had already stolen them. There were no good calls over the scanner until a fire broke out. Brazil didn't waste time. The blaze was huge and he could see it against the night sky in Adam One, close to where Nations Ford and York Roads met. Brazil's adrenaline flooded him with nervous energy. He was focused on getting to the scene and not getting lost, when suddenly a siren sounded behind him, and he checked his rearview mirror.

'Shit,' he said.

Moments later, he was in the passenger's seat of a police cruiser, getting a ticket as the distant fire burned without him.

'My speedometer is broken,' Brazil tried that shopworn line.

'Get it fixed.' The officer was unfriendly and taking her time.

'Could you please hurry with that, ma'am?' Brazil then politely said. 'I've got to get to my assignment.'

'You should have thought about that before you broke the law.' She was not nice about it.

A half hour later, Brazil was talking on the two-way radio, and leaving the fire scene, where an abandoned building was still fully involved. Flames danced from the roof, as fire fighters on cranes blasted water through broken windows. News helicopters hovered nearby. Brazil was telling a metro editor what he'd found.

'Unoccupied, an old warehouse. No injuries,' he said into the mike.

In the rearview mirror, a patrol car was following him. He couldn't believe it. Another cop was staring right at him.

'Just do a couple graphs,' the editor told him over the air.

He would get to it. Right now, Brazil had more important concerns. This was not an imagined threat, and he could afford no more tickets or points on his record. He started driving the way he played tennis, serving up this and that, slicing, sending a ball topspinning over his opponent's head. Asshole, he thought as the same car bird-dogged him. Like anybody else, Brazil could and would take but so much.

'That's it,' he snapped.

The patrol car was behind him in the right lane. Brazil continued at a steady speed, and took a left on Runnymede Lane. The cop stayed on Brazil's bumper, and they slowed to a stop at a red light. Brazil did not look over or acknowledge in any way that he was aware of the problem. He was cool in his saddle-leather seat, preoccupied with adjusting the radio, which had been silent for years. At the last second, he swerved into the left lane, and the officer pulled up beside him, with an icy smile that Brazil returned. The ruse was up. They were squared off. This was war. There was no turning back. Brazil thought fast. Officer Martin, with his .40 caliber pistol, shotgun, and 350 V8, didn't need to think.

The light turned green and Brazil threw his old car into neutral, gunning it like he was going to blast off after the space shuttle. Officer Martin gunned his car, too, only the big horsepower Ford was in drive. It was already through the intersection by the time Brazil had finished his U-turn, flying the other way on Barclay Downs. He caromed off on Morrison, and cut a tangled path that ended in a dark alleyway in the heart of Southpark Mall, next to a Dumpster.

His heart was hammering as he turned off headlights and sat, his thoughts frantic and frightened. He was trying to figure out what might happen if the cop found him again. Would the officer arrest Brazil for trying to elude, for resisting arrest? Would the cop show up with other goons and beat the shit out of Brazil in a place like this, remote and dark, with no chance of discovery by a citizen with a video camera? Brazil gasped as a burglar alarm suddenly sounded like a clanging jackhammer, shattering the absolute quiet. At first, he thought it was a siren that was somehow related to his fugitive status, then a back door swung open and slammed against brick. Two young males hurried out, loaded down with electronics they had just stolen from Radio Shack.

'911!' Brazil yelled into the mike connecting him into the newsroom. Disgusted, he yelled at himself this time, 'Oh now that was helpful.'

'What was that?' the newsroom crackled back.

Brazil squealed off in pursuit, flipping headlights on. The thieves were having a hard time moving fast and holding on to their hard-earned rewards. Smaller boxes dropped first, primarily Walkmans, portable CD players, and computer modems. Brazil could tell that these two would hang on to boom boxes and miniature televisions until the bitter end. He raised the newsroom on the radio, and this time instructed an editor to call 911 and put the phone near the base station so a dispatcher could hear what Brazil was saying.

'Burglary in progress.' He was talking like a machine

gun, weaving after his quarry. 'Southpark Mall. Two white males running east on Fairview Road. I'm in pursuit. You might want a unit at the rear of Radio Shack to collect what they've dropped before someone else does.'

The thieves cut through a parking lot, then through another alleyway. Brazil broadcast their every step, on their heels like a border collie herding sheep. Neither young man could legally buy beer, and both had been smoking dope, stealing, lying, and jailing since they were old enough for their pants to fall off. Neither was in premier shape. Shooting hoops and boogeying in front of their friends and on street corners was one thing. But running wide open for blocks was definitely another. Devon, especially, knew one lung, and possibly both, would rupture any second. Sweat was stinging his eyes. His legs might buckle, and unless he was having vision disturbances, too, the flashing red and blue lights of his childhood were closing in like UFOs from all corners of the planet.

'Man!' Devon gasped. 'Let's drop it! Run!'

'I am running, man!'

As for Ro, whose name was short for something no one could recall, he would be damned before he would relinquish what he had his arms around. The TV alone would keep him in rocks for a week, unless he traded it in on a new pistol, this time one with a holster. The Smith & Wesson stainless-steel .357 revolver with its four-inch barrel jammed in the back of his baggy jeans wasn't going to stay put much longer. Ro could feel it slipping as sweat blurred his vision and sirens screamed.

'Shit,' Ro complained.

The gun was completely submerged, now, and working its way down. Oh Lord, he hoped he didn't shoot himself in some private place. He would never live it down. The revolver slid through layers of huge boxer shorts, burrowing down his thigh, his knee, and finally peeking out at the top of a leather Fila. Ro helped it along by shaking his leg. This was no easy feat while running with half the Charlotte Police Department and some crazy-ass white boy in a BMW about to run Ro down. The gun clattered against pavement as the circle of white cars with flashing lights was complete around Devon and Ro. The two bandits simply stopped in their tracks.

'Shit,' Ro said again.

In all fairness, Brazil's reward for his valiant contribution to community policing should have been the pleasure of cuffing the suspects and tucking them into the back of a patrol car. But he had no enforcement powers. For that matter, he was on the newspaper's payroll this night, and it was no simple matter to explain why he happened to be parked in a dark alleyway behind a Radio Shack when the burglary occurred. He and Officer Weed went round and round about this as Brazil gave his statement in the front seat of Weed's cruiser.

'Let's try this again,' Weed was saying. 'You were sitting back there with your headlights off for what reason?'

'I thought I was being followed,' Brazil patiently explained again.

Weed looked at him, and had no idea what to make of

this one except that she knew the reporter was lying. All of them did. Weed was willing to bet the guy had parked back there to sleep on the job, maybe jerk off, smoke a little weed, or all of the above.

'Being followed by who?' Weed had her shiny metal clipboard in her lap, as she worked on her report.

'Some guy in a white Ford,' Brazil said. 'Wasn't anybody I knew.'

It was late by the time Brazil rolled away from the Southpark scene, without a word of thanks from any officer there, he noted. The way he calculated it, he had about an hour to kill before he needed to get back to the newsroom and write up what he'd gotten during his eight hour shift, which wasn't much, in his mind.

He wasn't far from the area of Myers Park where Michelle Johnson's horrible accident had occurred, and for some reason, Brazil was haunted by that awful night, and by her. He cruised slowly past the mansions of Eastover and fantasized about who lived inside them and what they must feel about the neighbors who were killed. The Rollins family had lived around the corner from the Mint Museum. When Brazil was in front of their stately white brick house with its copper roof, he stopped. He sat and stared. The only lights on were for the benefit of burglars, because nobody in the family was home, or ever would be. He thought of a mother, a father, and three young children, gone in one violent minute, life lines randomly intersecting in exactly the horribly wrong way, and all was lost.

Brazil had never heard much about rich people dying in car wrecks or shoot-outs. Now and then their private planes went down, and he recalled there had been a serial rapist in Myers Park back in the eighties. Brazil imagined a young male in a hood knocking on doors, his sole intention to rape a woman home alone. Was it resentment that fired such cruelty? An up yours to the rich? Brazil tried to put himself in the mindset of such a young violent man as he watched lighted windows flow past.

He realized the rapist had probably done exactly what Brazil was doing this night. He would have browsed, stalked, but most likely on foot. He would have spied and planned, the actual awful act incidental to the fantasy of it. Brazil could not think of much worse than to be sexually violated. He had been scorned by enough rednecks in his brief life to fear rape as a woman might. He would never forget what Chief Briddlewood of Davidson security told him once. *Don't ever go to jail, boy. You won't stand up straight the whole time you're there.*

The wreck was right about where Selwyn and the various Queens Roads got confused, and Brazil recognized the scene instantly as he approached. What he had not expected was the Nissan pulled off the street. As he got closer, he was shocked to realize Officer Michelle Johnson inside it, crying in the dark. Brazil parked on the shoulder. He got out and walked toward the officer's personal car, his footsteps sure and directed, as if he were in charge of whatever was going on. He stared through the driver's window, transfixed by the sight of Johnson crying, and his heart began to thud. She looked up and saw him and was startled. She grabbed her pistol, then realized it was that reporter. She relaxed but was enraged. She rolled her window down.

'Get the fuck away from me!' she said.

He stared at her and could not move. Johnson cranked the engine.

'Vultures! Fucking vultures!' she screamed.

Brazil was frozen. He was acting so oddly and atypically

for a reporter that Johnson was taken aback. She lost interest in leaving. She did not move, as they stared at each other.

'I want to help.' Brazil was impassioned.

A streetlight shone on broken glass and black stains on pavement, and illuminated the gouged tree the Mercedes had been wrapped around. Fresh tears started. Johnson wiped her face with her hands, her humiliation complete as this reporter continued to watch her. She heaved and moaned, as if overwhelmed by a seizure, and was aware of the pistol that could end all of it.

'When I was ten,' the reporter spoke, 'my dad was a cop here. About your age when he got killed on duty. Sort of like you feel you've been.'

Johnson looked up at him as she wept.

'Eight-twenty-two P.M., March twenty-ninth. A Sunday. They said it was his fault,' Brazil went on, his voice trembling. 'Was in plain clothes, followed a stolen car out of his district, wasn't supposed to make a traffic stop in Adam Two. The backup never got there. Not in time. He did the best he could, but. . .' His voice caught, and he cleared his throat. 'He never had a chance to tell his story.'

Brazil stared off into the dark, furious at a street, at a night, that had robbed him of his life, too. He pounded his fist on top of the car.

'My dad wasn't a bad cop!' he cried.

Johnson had gotten strangely quiet, and felt empty inside. 'I'd rather be him,' she said. 'I'd rather be dead.'

'No.' Brazil bent down, at her eye level. 'No.' He saw her left hand on the steering wheel, and the wedding band she wore. He reached in and gripped her arm. 'Don't leave anybody behind,' he said.

'I turned in my badge today,' Johnson told him.

'They made you do that?' he protested. 'There's no evidence you . . .'

'No one made me. I did it,' she cut him off. 'They think I'm a monster!' She broke down more.

Brazil was determined. 'We can change that,' he said. 'Let me help.'

She unlocked her car and he got in.

Chapter Ten

Chief Hammer was watering her plants when West walked in the next morning. West carried coffee and another healthy breakfast from Bojangles, this time a sausage-egg biscuit and Bo-Rounds, for a little variety. The chief's phone was going crazy, but Hammer was busy atomizing orchids. She glanced up without a greeting. Hammer was well known for one-two punch announcements in her faint Arkansas accent.

'So.' She sprayed. 'He gets in a pursuit, resulting in two arrests. Single-handedly cracking a string of Radio Shack burglaries that has plagued the city for eight months.'

She examined an exotic white blossom, and sprayed again. Hammer was striking in a black silk suit with subtle pinstripes, and a black silk blouse with a high collar, and black onyx beads. West loved the way her boss dressed. West was proud to work for a woman who looked so sharp and had good legs, and was decent to people and plants, and could still kick butt with the best of them.

'And he somehow managed to get the truth from Johnson.' Hammer nodded at the morning paper on her desk. 'Clearing up this notion that she's responsible for those poor people's deaths. Johnson's not going to quit.'

Hammer moved over to a calamondin tree near a window and plucked dead leaves from bushy branches that always bore fruit. 'I talked to her this morning,' she went on. 'All this, and Brazil wasn't even riding with us.' She stopped what she was doing, and looked up at her deputy chief. 'You're right. He can't be out by himself. God knows what he'd do if he had a uniform on. I wish I could transfer him to another city about three thousand miles from here.'

West smiled as her boss worried about spider mites and quenched a corn plant with a small plastic watering can. 'What you wish,' West said to her, 'is that he worked for you.' Paper crackled as she dug into her Bojangles bag.

'You eat too much junk,' Hammer told her. 'If I ate all the crap you do, I'd be a medicine ball.'

'Brazil called me,' West finally got around to this as she folded back a greasy wrapper. 'You know why he was behind that Radio Shack?'

'No.' Hammer started on African violets, glancing curiously at West.

Five minutes later, Hammer was walking with purpose down a long hallway on the first floor. She did not look friendly. Police she passed stared and nodded. She reached a door and opened it. Uniformed officers inside the roll call room were startled to see their well-dressed leader walk in. Deputy Chief Jeannie Goode was in the midst of briefing dozens of the troops about her latest concerns.

'All, I mean *all* inquiries get routed to the duty captain . . .' Goode was saying before the vision of Hammer walking toward her cut the meeting short. Goode knew trouble when she saw it.

'Deputy Chief Goode,' Hammer said for all to hear. 'Do you know what harassment is?'

The color drained from Goode's face. She thought she might faint, and leaned against the blackboard while cops stared, paralyzed. Goode could not believe the chief was about to dress her down in front of thirty-three lowly David One street cops, two sergeants, and one captain.

'Let's go upstairs to my office,' Goode suggested with a weak smile.

Hammer stood in front of her troops and crossed her arms. She was very calm when she replied, 'I think everyone could benefit from this. It has been reported to me that officers tailed an *Observer* reporter all over the city.'

'Says who?' Goode challenged. 'Him? And you believe him?'

'I never said it was a him,' Hammer informed her.

The chief paused for a long time and the silence in the room gave Goode chills. Goode thought about the pink Kaopectate tablets in her desk drawer. The third floor seemed very far away.

'One more time.' Hammer looked at everyone. 'It will cost you.'

High heels snapped as she walked out. When she tried to reach Andy Brazil at home, someone else answered the phone. The woman was either drunk or did not have her teeth in, perhaps both. Hammer hung up and tried Panesa.

'Judy, I will not have my reporters intimidated, bullied . . .' Panesa jumped right in.

'Richard, I know,' Hammer simply said, staring out at the skyline, and discouraged. 'Please accept my apology and my promise that something like this will not happen again. I'm also giving Brazil a special commendation for his assisting the police last night.'

'When?'

'Immediately.'

'And we can put that in the paper,' Panesa said.

Hammer had to laugh. She liked this man. 'Tell you what,' Hammer said. 'You put that in the paper, but do me a favor. Leave out the part about why Brazil was hiding in an alleyway.'

Panesa had to think about this for a moment. Generally, cops abusing their power, harassing a citizen, was a much better story than something positive, such as a citizen helping, or making a difference by doing the right thing, and demonstrating community responsibility and being appreciated for it.

'Now listen,' Hammer spoke again. 'It happens again, then run it one-A, Richard, okay? I wouldn't blame you. But don't punish the entire police department because of one asshole.'

'Which asshole?' Now Panesa was really interested, and maybe pulling Hammer's chain just a little.

'It's been taken care of.' Hammer had nothing more to say about it. 'What's Brazil's phone number? I'm going to call him.'

This impressed Panesa even more. The publisher could see Brazil beyond glass. As usual, Brazil was in early, working on something no one had asked him to do. Panesa scanned a phone sheet and gave Hammer Brazil's extension. Panesa thoroughly enjoyed watching Brazil's stunned expression when he snatched up his phone a moment later and it was the chief of police.

'Judy Hammer,' the familiar voice was strong over the line.

'Yes, ma'am.' Brazil sat up straighter, knocked over his coffee, shoved back his chair and grabbed notepads out of the way of a tepid flood.

'Look, I know all about last night,' the chief went straight to the point. 'I just want you to hear from me that this sort of behavior is absolutely not condoned by the Charlotte Police Department. It is not condoned by me and will not be repeated. Please accept my apology, Andy.'

Hearing her say his name made him warm all over. His ears turned red. 'Yes, ma'am,' was all he seemed capable of uttering, repeatedly.

He used words for a living, and were there any available when he needed them? He was devastated when she hung up. She had to think he was lobotomized, a wimp, a dolt. He could have at least thanked her, for God's sake! Brazil wiped up coffee. He stared blankly into his computer screen. She wouldn't get on the phone if he called her back, he supposed. She would be off on other important things by now. No way she'd waste any more time on him. Brazil was oblivious to the story he was writing about First Union Bank's minimal losses in a fraud case. Tommy Axel, not so far away, typically, did not exist.

Axel had been looking at Brazil all morning, and was certain Brazil's feelings were stirring. The guy was blushing even as Axel stared. That definitely was a good sign. Axel could hardly concentrate on his Wynona Judd review, which was unfortunate for her. What might have been a splashy story about her latest fabulous album was destined for mindless jargon that no doubt would cost her millions in sales. Axel had that power. He sighed, working up the courage to ask Brazil yet one more time to do dinner, a concert, or a club with male strippers. Maybe he could get Brazil drunk, get him to smoke a little dope, jazz him up and show him what life was about.

* * *

Brazil was in despair as he glanced again at the phone. Oh, what the hell. What happened to having guts? He grabbed the receiver, flipped through his Rolodex, and dialed.

'Chief Hammer's office,' a man answered.

Brazil cleared his throat. 'Andy Brazil with the *Observer*,' he said in a remarkably steady voice. 'I wonder if I might have a word with her.'

'And this is in regard to what?'

Brazil was not about to be scared off the case. It was too late. There was no place to run, really.

'I'm returning her phone call,' he bravely said, as if it were perfectly normal for the chief to call him and for him to get back to her.

Captain Horgess was thrown off. What did Hammer do? Dial this reporter's number herself? Horgess hated it when she did that instead of placing all calls through him. Damn it. He couldn't keep track of that woman. She was out of control. Horgess punched the hold button without bothering to tell Brazil. Two seconds later, Hammer's voice was on the line, shocking Brazil.

'I'm sorry to bother you,' he quickly said to her.

'That's quite all right. What can I help you with?' she replied.

'Oh, not a thing. I mean this isn't about a story. I just wanted to thank you for what you did.'

Hammer was quiet. Since when did reporters thank her for anything?

Brazil interpreted the silence wrongly. Oh God, now she really thought he was stupid. 'Well, I won't take up your time.' He was talking faster and faster, thoroughly decompensating. 'Uh, I, well. It's just that it was a big thing to do. I thought so. When you didn't have to. Someone in your position, I mean. Most wouldn't.'

Hammer smiled, drumming her nails on a stack of paperwork. She needed a manicure. 'I'll see you around the department,' she told him, and her heart was pricked as she hung up.

She had two sons and they hurt her on a regular basis. This did not prevent her from calling them every Sunday night, or setting up a college trust for the grandbabies, and offering to send plane tickets whenever a visit was possible. Hammer's sons did not have her drive, and she secretly blamed this on the bad genetic wiring of their father, who was all egg white and no yolk, in truth. No bloody wonder it had always required so many tries for Hammer to get pregnant. As it turned out, Seth's sperm count could be done on one hand. Randy and Jude were single, with families. They were still finding themselves in Venice Beach and Greenwich Village. Randy wanted to be an actor. Jude played drums in a band. Both of them were waiters. Hammer adored them. Seth did not, and this was directly related to how seldom they came to town and why their mother ached in private.

The chief was suddenly depressed. She felt as if she might be coming down with something. She buzzed Captain Horgess. 'What do I have scheduled for lunch?' she asked.

'Councilman Snider,' came the reply.

'Cancel him and get West on the phone,' she said. 'Tell her to meet me in my office at noon.'

Chapter Eleven

The Presto Grill was an acronym for Peppy Rapid Efficient Service Tops Overall, and was not in a good part of town. Every cop in the greater Charlotte-Mecklenburg area knew that Hammer and West ate breakfast at the Presto every Friday morning. This was monitored far more closely than the cops supposed either woman knew, for there wasn't an officer interested in survival who would take even the slimmest chance that something bad might happen to the chief or deputy chief on his beat.

The small grill looked as it had in the forties, when it was built. It was on West Trade Street and surrounded by eroded parking lots, just down from the Mount Moriah Primitive Baptist Church. Hammer preferred walking from headquarters when the weather was nice, as it was this day. West never walked when she could ride, but it was not her call.

'Nice suit,' Hammer said to West, who had opted to give her uniform a day off and was dressed in a red blouse, and a bright blue pants suit. 'Why do you never wear skirts?' Hammer asked her.

It was not a criticism, just curiosity. West had a very nice figure and slender legs.

'I hate skirts,' West said, breathing hard, for Hammer did not walk at a normal pace. 'I think hose and high heels are a male conspiracy. Like binding feet. To cripple us. Slow us down.' She breathed.

'Interesting,' Hammer considered.

David One Officer Troy Saunders spotted them first and was instantly palsied by indecision as he quickly turned off on Cedar Street, out of sight. Did he alert his buddies out here? He was reliving the nightmare of Hammer's surprise appearance at roll call, and her severe warning about cops following people and harassing, spying, tailing, no matter the motive. Wouldn't it be harassment, in the chief's eyes, if he, Saunders, instigated her and West being spied upon, or tailed, during lunch? Christ. Saunders came to a dead halt in an All Right parking lot, his heart out of control.

He checked his mirrors, and scanned parked cars, deliberating. It wasn't worth the risk, he decided. Especially since he had been right there, and had heard every word Hammer had said to Goode. The chief sure as hell could check roll call, and know for a fact that Saunders had been sitting three chairs away from her. She'd be all over his ass for insubordination, for disobeying a direct order. He was certain that her eyes had burned through him when she'd said, *Next time, it will cost you.* Saunders raised no one on his radio. He parked in the farthest corner of the pay lot and smoked.

By twenty minutes past noon, the regulars had found their favorite stools lining the Formica counter inside the grill. Gin Rummy was the last to sit, the usual banana in his back pocket that he planned to save for later on in the day when he got hungry again while driving his red and white Ole Dixie taxicab.

'You can fix me a hamburger?' Gin Rummy asked Spike at the grill.

'Yeah, we can fix you a hamburger,' Spike said, pushing the bacon press.

'Know it's early.'

'Man, it's not early.' Spike scraped clean an area of the grill, and slapped down a frozen hamburger patty. 'When's the last time you looked at a clock, Rummy?'

His friends called him that for short. Rummy smiled, shaking his head sheepishly. He usually came in for breakfast but was running a little late today. Seems like those two white ladies usually came in for breakfast, too. Maybe that was the problem. Everything was confusing. He shook his head again, grinned, and adjusted his banana so he didn't bruise any part of it.

'Why you carry your banana like that?' asked his neighbor, Jefferson Davis, who operated a yellow Caterpillar and still bragged that he had helped build USBank. 'Put it in your shirt pocket.' He tapped the pocket on Rummy's red-checked shirt. 'Then you don't sit on it.'

Other men at the counter, and there were eight of them, got into a deep discussion about Rummy's banana and Davis's suggestion. Some were eating beef tips and gravy, others sticking with the fried livermush, collard greens, and cheese grits.

'I put it in my shirt pocket and I see it the whole time I'm driving,' Rummy was trying to explain his philosophy. 'Then I eat it sooner. See? It never makes it till three or four o'clock.'

'Then stick it in the glove box.'

'No room in there.'

'What about the passenger's seat up front? All your fares ride in back, right?' Spike set down the burger, all the way, thousand island instead of mayo, double American cheese, and fried onions on the side.

'Won't work. Sometimes bags go up front.' Rummy neatly cut his lunch in half. 'Or I pick up four fares at the bus station, and one of 'em gotta go up there. They see a banana on the seat, think I eat on the job.'

'Well, you do, man.'

'That's so.'

'The truth.'

'Tell it, brother.'

'Not with no one in with me, I don't.' Rummy shook his head, chewing, the banana remaining in his back pocket, where it belonged.

Hammer did not recall the Presto being this loud. She eyed the men at the counter, halfway expecting them to get into a fight any minute. Seems one told another to stick something somewhere, and others were agreeing. She hadn't been in a good fight in a while, if she didn't count arguments with Seth. Of course, she was no fool. She knew there were at least twenty patrol cars cruising the area, watching every bit of Cobb salad she speared with her fork. It was annoying, but she didn't blame her troops, and in fact appreciated their attention and care. She found it touching, even though she knew the motive was their butts and not her wellbeing, really.

'I probably should have confronted her in private,' Hammer was saying.

West wished Hammer had reprimanded Goode in front of the entire police department, all sixteen hundred of them, or at a televised city council meeting.

'You're being too hard on yourself,' West diplomatically said, as she finished her Reuben and fries.

'I swear, the food here really is the best,' said Hammer. 'Look at those hash browns. Everything from scratch.'

West watched Spike cooking, flinging, slamming away, as men on their stools continued arguing about where to hide stolen goods, or maybe drugs. The glove box. Under the seat. On their persons. West couldn't believe how brazen criminals were these days. While it was true that she and her chief were both in plain clothes, everyone knew who they were, and West's portable radio was upright on the table, chattering away. Did these dudes care, were they even remotely intimidated by the law?

'Tell you what,' one of them railed on, jabbing a finger at the one with the red-checked shirt. 'You want to know what to do with it? I'm here to tell you. Eat it. Quick before anybody sees. Then what's anybody gonna say 'bout it? Huh?'

'Can't say nothing.'

'Not one thing.'

'You got that right.'

'Sitting on it ain't the answer, Rummy,' Spike spoke his mind. 'Besides, it's not like you can't get the same thing here. High quality, imported, good price. Fresh every morning.' He folded a ham and cheese omelet. 'But oh no. Every stinking day you come in with the same damn thing stuffed in your pocket. Like what? Maybe you think you're impressing the women or something? Make 'em think you're happy to see 'em?'

Everyone laughed, except West, head of investigations for the city. She was going to get some of her guys on this right away, and bust this ring wide open, trace it back to Colombia, get the DEA in on it, if need be.

'Drugs,' she mouthed to her boss.

Hammer was preoccupied, and still so angry at Goode that Hammer's blood felt hot as it raced around her body. How dare that lamebrain overpromoted bitch jeopardize the reputation of the entire police department and of women everywhere. Hammer could not remember the last time she was this furious. West was enraged, too, Hammer could tell, and found this somewhat soothing. Not many people understood what it was like to have Hammer's responsibility and stress, and West had integrity, damn it. She knew how wrong it was to abuse power.

'Can you believe it?' West asked her, angrily crumpling her napkin as she glared at the drug dealer in his red-checked shirt, with a banana in his back pocket. 'Can you believe people?'

Hammer shook her head, about to boil over. 'No,' she said. 'I never ceased to be amazed . . .'

Both of them got quiet as the call came over the radio.

'Any unit in the area, six hundred block West Trade. Robbery in progress, armed white male on a bus, robbing passengers . . .'

Hammer and West were on their feet and running out the door to the Greyhound bus terminal next door. David One units were responding, but it seemed not one car was within blocks. This baffled Hammer as she ran with some difficulty in high-heeled Ferragamos. West was slightly behind her. They ran around the station to a lane on the side where a forty-seven-passenger bus filled to capacity was idling, with doors open wide.

'We'll get on pretending to be passengers,' West whispered as they slowed their pace.

Hammer nodded, knowing exactly how this would go down. 'I'll go first,' she said.

This was not quite what West had in mind, but the last thing she intended to do now or ever was imply that

Hammer had forgotten how to be a cop. Hammer's black pumps were loud on metal steps as she smiled, climbing aboard, oblivious and on her way somewhere. People were terrorized in their seats as the sinister young white male made his way down the aisle, collecting wallets, cash, jewelry, and dropping them in a plastic trash bag.

'Excuse me,' Hammer politely said to anyone listening.

Magic the Man whipped around, and fixed on the fine lady in her fine black suit as she spotted his gun. Her smile faded and she froze, as did another lady right behind her. This was getting better. These bitches looked rich.

'Is this the bus for Kannapolis?' the older bitch in black stammered.

'This is the bus for you giving me your money.' Magic jabbed the .22 pistol her way.

'Yes sir. I don't want a problem,' the lady in black said.

Magic thought she seemed confused, as if she might pass out or pee in her pants. She shakily moved closer to him, as she rooted around in her big black leather pocketbook. Magic might just take that too, for his mama. Maybe those bad black shoes, too. Wonder what size they were? He found out as much as he would ever need to know about those shoes when the bitch suddenly kicked him so hard in the shin with a knife-pointed toe that he bit his tongue. She suddenly had a big pistol out and was poking it against his head as his gun instantly vanished from behind, and then he was face down in the aisle, and the other bitch was jerking his wrists together and wrapping them tight with a flex cuff.

'Man, oh man. That's too tight,' Magic said as his shin throbbed. 'I think my leg's broke.'

Innocent passengers on the bus stared slack-jawed, in speechless wonder as the two well-dressed ladies led that son-of-a-bitch murderer off into the bright afternoon.

Police cars were suddenly roaring up, blue and red lights whirling, and all on the bus knew the ladies somehow had made that happen, too.

'Thank you Jesus,' someone thought to say.

'Lord be praised.'

'It's a miracle.'

'Batman and Robin.'

'Hand that bag over here so I can get my gold chain back.'

'I want my ring.'

'Everybody remain where you are and don't touch anything,' said a cop as he boarded.

Officer Saunders hoped the chief wouldn't notice him as he climbed out of his cruiser.

'Where were you?' she asked him as she briskly walked past. She then commented to West, 'Don't you find that a little odd? Usually they're all over the place when we're around.'

West didn't understand it, either, but she did have more respect for the chief's skirts and pumps. Not only had they not slowed her up enough to matter, but the shoes, at least, had come in handy. She was proud of her boss as they walked back inside the Presto to pay their bill. The men at the counter were smoking now, still arguing, and oblivious to what had just gone down next door at the Greyhound station. Not that a bunch of drug dealers cared about a bunch of innocent people getting robbed, West thought. She threw them another menacing look as Hammer drank one last swallow of her unsweetened iced tea and glanced at her watch.

'Well, I guess we'd better be getting back,' Hammer suggested.

* * *

Andy Brazil had heard about the incident at the bus station when it crackled over his scanner while he was working on a substantial story about the long-term consequences of violence on victims and the relatives left behind. By the time he ran down the escalator, got into his car and raced to the six hundred block of West Trade, the drama apparently had ended in an arrest.

He was trotting past the Presto Grill when West and Hammer were walking out of it. Startled, Brazil stopped, and stared at both of them. In the first place, he didn't understand why two of the most prominent people in the city would eat in such a dive. Nor could he fathom how they could continue with lunch when lives were in danger not fifty yards away, and they had to have known. West was carrying her police radio.

'Andy.' Hammer nodded her greeting to him.

West shot him a glance that dared him to ask questions. He noted that both were in handsome business suits, and that the chief's black leather handbag included a secret compartment for her pistol. He supposed her badge was somewhere in there, too, and he liked the way her calves knotted as she briskly walked off. He wondered what West's legs looked like as he hurried on to the bus station. Cops were busy taking statements, and this was no small chore. Brazil counted forty-three passengers, not including the driver, who proved to be a pretty great interview.

Antony B. Burgess had been a professional bus driver for twenty-two years and had seen it all. He had been mugged, robbed, hijacked, and stabbed. He'd been shot at the Twilight Motel in Shreveport when he picked up a she who was a him (sh'im) by mistake. He told all this to Brazil, and more, because the blond dude was nice as hell, and discerning enough to recognize a raconteur when he met one.

'Had no idea they was cops,' Burgess said again, scratching under his cap. 'That one never would have entered my mind. They come on board all in black, and red and blue, like Batman and Robin. And next thing Batman's kicked the fool out of the little bastard and's about to blow his fucking brains all over my bus while Robin cuffs 'im. Ho-ly smoke.' He shook his head, as if he'd seen a vision. 'And that's the po-lice chief. That's what I heard. Can you believe it?'

By five P.M., the story was in the bag and destined for 1-A above the fold. Brazil had already seen the headline in the composing room:

POLICE CHIEF AND DEPUTY FOIL ABDUCTION OF BUS

BATMAN AND ROBIN IN HEELS?

West got a preview a little later when Brazil, in uniform, hopped in her car for another night out on the town. He was full of himself, and thought this story was his best yet. He was thrilled over what Hammer and West had pulled off, almost wanted their autographs, or a poster of the two of them to hang in his room.

'Jesus fucking Christ,' West exclaimed again as they sped along South Boulevard, not going anywhere in particular. 'You didn't have to put in the Batman shit.'

'Yes I did,' Brazil insisted, his mood sinking like the sun, as his world got dark and stormy. 'It was a quote. It's not like I made it up.'

'Fuck.' West would be the laughingstock of the entire department tomorrow. 'Goddam son-of-a-bitch.' She lit a cigarette, imagining Goode laughing.

'This is an ego thing.' Brazil didn't like his work criticized and could take but just so much of it. 'You're just pissed because you don't like being a sidekick, Robin instead of Batman, because it reminds you of your real situation. You aren't Batman. She is.'

West gave him a look that was heat-seeking, like a missile. He would not survive this night, and probably should have remained silent.

'I'm just being honest,' he added. 'That's all.'

'Oh yeah?' She launched another look. 'Well let me tell you *honest* for a minute. I don't give a flying fuck what someone quotes to you, okay? You know what quotes like that are called in the real world? They're called bullshit. They're called perjury, hearsay, impeaching a witness, slander, dis-fucking-respect.'

'How do you spell that last one? I guess it's hyphenated?' Brazil was trying not to laugh, and pretending to take notes as West gestured with her cigarette and got increasingly ridiculous.

'Point is, just because someone says something, Sherlock, doesn't mean it's gospel, worth repeating, worth printing. Got it?'

He nodded with mock seriousness.

'And I don't wear high heels and don't want anybody thinking I do,' she added.

'How come?' he asked.

'How come what?'

'You don't want people thinking it?' he said.

'I don't want people thinking about me, period.'

'How come you don't ever wear high heels. Or skirts?' He wasn't going to let her duck him.

'Not any of your goddamn business.' She tossed the cigarette butt out her window.

The police radio took charge, broadcasting an address on Wilkinson Boulevard that anyone who knew anything would recognize as the Paper Doll Lounge. The striptease joint had been in Charlotte longer than sex, staffed by women with nothing on but a g-string, and tormenting men with jeans full of dollar bills. This night, derelicts were swigging from quart bottles of beer brilliantly disguised by brown paper bags. Not far away, a damaged young man joyfully rooted around inside a Dumpster.

'She wasn't much older than me,' Brazil was telling West about the young hooker he'd noticed the other night. 'Most of her front teeth gone, long dirty hair, tattoos. But I bet she was pretty once. I wish I could talk to her, and find out what happened to turn her into something like that.'

'People repeat their histories, find other people to abuse them,' West said, strangely impatient with his interest in a hooker who might have been pretty once.

They got out of the car. West approached a drunk in a Chick-Fil-A cap. He was swaying, clutching his bottle of Colt .45.

'We're having a lot of fun tonight,' West said to him.

The man was staggering, but jolly. 'Cap'n,' he slurred. 'You're lookin' mighty fine. Who dat wid ya?'

'You can pour it out or go to jail,' West said.

'Yes, ma'am. That's an easy 'cision! No questi'n 'bout it!'

He emptied beer on the parking lot, almost falling headlong into it, and splashing Brazil's uniform trousers and impeccable boots. Brazil was a good sport. He jumped back a little late, wondering where the nearest men's room was and certain West would take him there straight away. She scattered the drunks, emptying their lives on pavement while they watched and counted their change in their minds, calculating how quickly they could get back to Ray's Cash & Carry, the Texaco Food Mart, or Snookies'.

Brazil followed West back to their car. They climbed in and fastened their seatbelts. Brazil was embarrassed by the sour smell seeping up from his lower legs. This part of the job he could do without. Drunks disturbed him in a deep way, and he felt anger as he watched the men through his window. They were staggering off and would be drinking something else before West and Brazil were even a mile down the road. That was the way people like that were, addicted, wasted, no good on this earth and hurting everyone.

'How can anybody sink that low?' he muttered, staring out and ready to leave.

'Any of us could,' West said. 'That's what's scary. One beer at a time. Any one of us.'

There had been times in her life when she had found herself on that same road, night after night, drinking herself to sleep, not remembering the last thing she thought or read, and sometimes waking up with lights still on. The impaired young man was joyfully ambling over to their car, and West wondered what trick in reality placed some people where she was sitting, and consigned others to parking lots and Dumpsters. It wasn't always a choice. It hadn't been for this one, who was known by the police, and was a permanent resident of the street.

'His mother tried to abort him and didn't quite pull it off,' West quietly told Brazil. 'Or that's the story.' She hummed open Brazil's window. 'He's been out here forever.' She leaned across the front seat, and called out, 'How goes it?'

He couldn't speak any language that Brazil might recognize. He was gesturing wildly, making strange sounds that shot fear through Brazil. Brazil wished West would drive off quickly and get them out of here before this creature breathed or drooled on him. God, the guy smelled like dirty beer bottles and garbage, and Brazil pulled back from the window, leaning against West's shoulder.

'You stink,' West said to him under her breath as she smiled at their visitor.

'It's not me,' Brazil said.

'Yes it is.' To their visitor, she added, 'What you doing out here?'

He gestured, getting more excited as he told the nice police lady everything he'd been up to, while she smiled and clearly enjoyed hearing about it. Her partner needed to lighten up a little.

Boy, as he had always been called, knew when cops were brand new. Boy could tell by how tense they got, by the look on their faces, and this always invited Boy to have a little fun with them. He stared at Brazil, and gave him his gummy, gaping grin, as if he were some exotic creature new to the planet. When Boy poked the rookie, the rookie flinched. This excited Boy more than ever, and he got louder, dancing around, poking the rookie again. West laughed, winking at her ride-along.

'Uh oh,' she said. 'I think he's sweet on you.'

She finally rolled up the window, and by now Brazil felt completely soiled. He had beer on his uniform and had been mauled by someone with no teeth who spent his life inside Dumpsters. Brazil thought he might throw up. He was indignant and hurt as West laughed and drove off, lighting a cigarette. Not only had she not prevented his degradation, she had made it happen and was savoring it. He fumed in silence as West headed out on West Boulevard, toward the airport.

She cut over on the Billy Graham Parkway, wondering what it would be like to have a major highway named after her. She wasn't sure she would appreciate cars and trucks rolling over her day and night, leaving ratty recaps and skid marks, while drivers made obscene comments to other drivers, and gave them the finger, and pulled out guns. There was nothing Christian about a road, the more West thought about it, unless it was used in Biblical analogies, such as the road to hell and what it was paved with. The more she contemplated all this as she drove, the sorrier she felt for the Reverend Billy Graham, who had been born in Charlotte, in a house that against his will had been appropriated by a nearby religious theme park.

Brazil had no idea where they were going, except it was not where the action was, and it was apparent West had no intention of taking him someplace where he could clean up. He was riveted to the scanner, and things were popping in Charlie Two on Central Avenue. So why were they heading in the opposite direction on this parkway? He remembered his mother watching Billy Graham on TV all the time, no matter what else was on or what Brazil might want to see. He wondered how hard it might be to get a quote from the famous evangelist, maybe inquire about the Reverend Graham's views on crime, one of these days.

'Where are we going?' Brazil asked as they turned off on Boyer toward Wilkinson Boulevard again.

This was definitely the sinful strip, but West did not stay on it long. She sped past Greenbriar Industrial Park and turned left on Alleghany Street, heading into Westerly Hills, a nothing neighborhood near Harding High School. Brazil's mood got worse. He suspected West was up to her old tricks, and it not only reminded him that she really did not want to be out here with him, but hinted rather strongly that he had no business on police calls and would not be on many, if she had her way about it.

'Any unit in the area of the twenty-five hundred block of Westerly Hills Drive,' the scanner shattered West's peace of mind. 'Suspicious subjects in the church parking lot.'

'Shit,' West said, speeding up.

What lousy luck. They were in Westerly Hills on Westerly Hills Drive, The Jesus Christ Is Lord Glorious United Church of the Living God right in front of them. The small white frame church was Pentecostal, and deserted this night, not one car in the parking lot when West turned in. But there definitely were subjects loitering, half a dozen young males with their mother, who was full of herself and feisty in a wheelchair. All stared hatefully at the cop car. Not real sure what to make of the situation, West ordered Brazil to stay put, as both their doors opened and both climbed out.

'We got a call of . . .' West started to say to Mama.

'Just passing through,' her oldest son, Rudof, volunteered.

Mama gave Rudof a killing look, holding his eyes. 'You don't got to answer to no one!' she snapped at him. 'You hear me? Not to no one!'

Rudof looked down, his pants about to fall off, and red boxer shorts showing. He was tired of being dissed by his mama and hassled by the police. What had he done? Nothing. Just walking home from the E-Z mart because she needed cigarettes, all of them going with her, taking a nice walk and cutting through the church parking lot. What was so wrong with that?

'We didn't do nothing,' Rudof folded his arms and said to the cops.

Brazil knew a fight was coming, just like he could smell a storm before the front moved in. His body tensed as he scanned the small, violent crowd standing restlessly in the dark. Mama wheeled closer to West. Mama had something on her mind she'd been wanting to deliver for a long time, and now was as good an opportunity as any. All her children would hear, and these two police didn't look like they would hurt anybody unnecessarily.

'We just got here,' Mama said to West. 'We were just coming home, walking like anybody else. I'm tired of you people prosecuting us.'

'Nobody is . . .' West tried again.

'Oh yes. Oh yes, uh huh, you are.' Mama got louder and angrier. 'This is a free country! We was white, you think anybody would've called the police?'

'You have a good point,' West reasonably replied.

Mama was amazed. Her children were baffled. For a white lady cop to admit such a thing was unheard of and miraculous.

'So you're agreeing that you were called because we're black,' Mama wanted to make sure.

'That would be my guess, and it absolutely isn't fair. But I didn't know you were black when the call came over the radio,' West went on in the same calm but sure tone. 'We didn't respond because we thought you were black, white, Asian, or anything. We responded because it's our job, and we wanted to make sure everything was all right.'

Mama tried to be hateful as she wheeled on her way, her brood in her wake. But she was wavering. She felt like she might cry and didn't know why. The police got back in their shiny new car and drove away.

'Rudof, pull up your pants, son,' Mama complained. 'You gonna trip and break your neck. Same with you, Joshua. I swear.' She wheeled ahead in the night, in the direction of their poor apartment.

Brazil and West were quiet as they got back on Wilkinson Boulevard. He was thinking about what she'd said to that family. West had said *we* several times, when most people would have said *I*, as if Brazil wasn't there. It felt really good when she included him, and he was touched by her gentleness with that wounded, hateful family. Brazil wanted to say something to West, to let her know, to somehow show his appreciation. But he was oddly tongue-tied again, just as he had been with Hammer.

West headed back into the city, thinking, and wondering why her ride-along was so quiet. Maybe he was angry with her for avoiding calls, or trying to avoid them, at any rate. She felt bad. How would she like it were the roles reversed? It wasn't very kind, and he had every right to resent her for it. West was totally ashamed of herself. She turned up the scanner, and picked up the mike.

'700,' she said.

'700,' the dispatcher came back.

'I'm ten-eight.'

Brazil couldn't believe it. West had just told the radio that she was in service, meaning she wanted to take calls like everyone else on the street. The two of them would actually be assigned situations. They were available for trouble. This wasn't long in coming. Their first call was to Our Lady of Consolation Catholic Church.

'Check for loud music coming from the club in the shopping center across the street,' came the instruction over the air.

The dispatcher's nickname was Radar, and there were reasons for this. First, Radar had started his career with the North Carolina Highway Patrol, where he was famous for clocking cars, abutments, buildings, trucks, signs, pedestrians, low-flying planes, helium balloons, and trees, and nailing all for exceeding the speed limit. He simply loved the radar gun. He deeply loved being a Smoky out on life's highways and pulling the unaware outlaws as they hurried to important places or away from them. Radar retired. He bought a RV and began a new career as a dispatcher to pay for it. It was believed by the 911 operators that Radar could sense trouble before it hit. This call at the church, for example, he had a feeling about, a real bad one.

Thus he had assigned it to Deputy Chief West, because it was Radar's personal conviction that no woman should be in a uniform unless she was naked beneath it and on the cover of those detective magazines he also loved. In addition to an intuition that bordered on the psychic, Radar knew that the respondent in this case, Fat Man's Lounge, was run by a bunch of thugs who held his same beliefs about a woman's place. Colt, the bouncer, who Radar personally knew, would not respond well when West with all her brass, ass, and big tits rolled up.

West knew none of this as she lit a cigarette and made a U-turn on Statesville Avenue. She nodded at the MDT. 'It took me forty minutes to learn how to use this thing,' she said to Brazil. 'You got ten.'

Our Lady of Consolation Catholic Church was having a special night of music, and the parking lot was packed with cars. Listings for Catholic places of worship were brief in the Charlotte Yellow Pages. Choices were far more abundant for churches that were Baptist, Advent Christian, Presbyterian, Apostolic, Assembly of God, Evangelical, Pentecostal, Non-Pentecostal, Gospel, Full Gospel, Foursquare Gospel, to name but a few. These outnumbered the Catholics about twenty-eight to one.

Indeed, Catholic places of worship were sandwiched between the one Buddhist church in the city and the charismatics who spoke in tongues. So it was, that Catholics did not take their church for granted, never knowing when it might be burned by men in disguises, or criticized in editorials. The congregation of Our Lady of Consolation was rocking the block this night, its stained glass windows glowing in the dark, Jesus bright and colorful in many poses, and sheep.

'You sure it isn't the bar complaining about the church?' Brazil wondered out loud.

West was finding the situation rather odd, too. How the hell could anyone inside that church hear a thing beyond their own choir, which was belting out some hymn, and accompanied by guitars, the organ, drums, and possibly a violin or two. She turned into the shopping center directly across the street and cut through the parking lot. Fat Man's Lounge wasn't doing nearly the business the church was. A couple of shifty-looking dudes were hanging out in front, drinking beer, smoking, and glaring.

Brazil did not hear any noise, not one sound drifting out of the Lounge. He suspected someone in the church had complained just to hassle Fat Man's, which clearly was a den of iniquity. Members of Our Lady would, without a doubt, have preferred another establishment across the street from them, something wholesome and family-oriented, like a Shoney's, a Blockbuster Video store, or maybe another sports bar. The dudes out front followed the cop car with hostile eyes as West parked. She and Brazil got out, and approached their welcoming committee.

'Where's all the noise?' West asked. 'We got a complaint.'

'Only noise is that over there,' a dude said, jutting his chin at the church. He boldly took a swig of beer, drunk and mean.

'Word's the noise is coming from here.' West held her ground.

She started walking toward the lounge, Brazil with her, the dudes moving out of their way. Fat Man's was a depressing, dark den, smoke hanging in the air, and music playing, but not too loudly. Men were drinking at wooden tables, watching a woman on stage, in g-string and tassels, as she twirled heavy, sagging breasts. Brazil didn't want to stare too hard, but he was pretty sure that the left one was tattooed with the planet Saturn, bright yellow, with rings orbiting fast. In big circles. These were, without a doubt, the biggest breasts he had ever seen in person.

The stripper, whose stage name was Minx, needed another Valium. She was thirsty, had to have a cigarette, and damn it all, the fucking cops were here. What this time? She started twirling the other way, then did two different directions at once. This usually got the men going, but tonight's stingy crowd was about as excitable as a cemetery. Minx smiled. The boy cop couldn't take his eyes off her.

'Never seen tits before?' she asked him as he went by.

Brazil was indifferent. West shot Minx a cool look, and thought the stripper's fried egg tattoo on her left breast was rather clever, not to mention apropos. Lord, this one even had stretch marks, cellulite, her clients not interested in anything that wasn't in a glass. Colt, the bouncer, was the exception. He was heading at the cops like a freight train on a mission. He was big and scary in a shiny black suit, thick gold chains, and a red leather tie. He looked like he might hurt them, starting with Brazil.

'We got a complaint of loud music,' West said to Colt.

'You hear it?' Colt lifted his heavy jaw, veins like ropes in his powerful neck.

He was full of hate toward these white cops, especially the bitch. Who did she think she was, anyway, strutting into Fat Man's, in her fancy uniform with all its shiny shit meant to hurt hardworking people like him? He glanced at Minx, making sure she wasn't letting up. It seemed not a night went by when he didn't have to smack a little more energy into her, give her pain some place where it wouldn't show, encouraging her to do her job. She was slinging away. Nobody cared. Nobody tipped. Two of the regulars were getting up and leaving, the night still young. Colt knew the cops were to blame.

Colt jerked open the side door leading out into an alleyway. He grabbed Brazil by the front of his uniform shirt with such force, it ripped.

'*Heyyyy!*' Brazil yelled.

Colt lifted the punk off his feet and threw him outside in the trash, where he belonged. Garbage cans clattered against pavement, bottles clanging. It was just a good thing Brazil was dirty, anyway. He got to his feet in time to see West whipping out her handcuffs. Colt had her by her uniform shirt, intending to pitch her, too, as the little shit yelled '*Mayday! Mayday!*' into his police radio.

Chapter Twelve

Colt gagged, and for a blinding shard of insight thought someone had shoved a pool cue into the hollow of his massive neck. It seeped into his fading consciousness that the bitch was drilling her index finger into that soft hollow over his windpipe. He couldn't breathe. His tongue protruded as she drilled and he gagged, gasping for air, his eyes bugging as he dropped to his knees, a gun barrel now staring at his nose. Colt's ears were ringing, blood roaring as the bitch screamed like she was going to eat him tartare.

'*You move I'll blow your brains out motherfucker!*'

Minx gyrated. Patrons drank. Backup cops burst through the front door, far away across the dark, smoky room. West had a knee on Colt's beefy back, and was busy snapping cuffs on his wrists, tight behind him. Brazil looked on in awe. Cops hauled Colt and the drunk dudes to jail. Minx saw her chance and walked off her runway, plucking lousy folded dollar bills out of her garter, wrapping up in a sweatshirt, and lighting a cigarette, out of here for good this time.

'Why did I let you get me into this?' West was saying

as she unlocked their car. 'I don't do this any more for a reason.' She climbed in, yanking the seatbelt across her chest, cranking the engine.

Both of them were excited and trying not to show it. Brazil held together his ruined uniform shirt, which was missing half its buttons. West noted that he had a very well-developed chest to go with those shoulders and arms and legs. She instantly stopped transmitting any and all signals, such as body language or glances or words or heat. Where was all this coming from, anyway? Outer space. Not from her. No sir. She opened the glove box, and rummaged until she found the tiny stapler she was sure was in there somewhere.

'Hold still,' she said to him, as if it were an order.

She leaned close because there was no other way to correct the situation, and gathered his shirt together, and began stapling. Brazil's heart picked up speed. He could smell her hair, his own seeming to stand on end. He did not move. He was terrified to even breathe as her fingers brushed against him. He knew she could tell what he was feeling, and if he as much as twitched and inadvertently touched her somewhere, she would never believe it was an accident. She'd think he was just one more prick out there who couldn't keep it in his pants. She'd never see him as a person, as a sensitive human being. He'd be reduced to this thing, this guy-thing. If she leaned half an inch closer to the right, he would die right there, on her front seat.

'When was the last time you had to do something like that?' he managed to ask.

West covered her repair job with his clip-on tie. The more she tried not to connect with his person, the clumsier her fingers got, fumbling, and touching. She nervously tried to put the stapler away, and dropped it.

'I use it for reports.' She groped under the seat. 'Don't

think I've ever used it on someone's shirt.' She slammed shut the glove box on the third try.

'No,' Brazil said, clearing his throat again. 'I mean, what you did in there. That guy must weigh two hundred and fifty pounds, and you decked him. All by yourself.'

West shoved the car in gear. 'You could,' she said. 'All you need is training.'

'Maybe you . . . ?'

She held up a hand as if halting traffic. 'No! I'm not a goddam one-person police academy!' She tapped the MDT. 'Clear us outa here, partner.'

Brazil was tentative as he placed his fingers on the keyboard. He started typing. The system beeped as if it liked him. 'God, this is so cool,' he said.

'Small minds,' West commented.

'Unit 700,' Radar, the dispatcher, said. 'Missing person at five-fifty-six Midland.'

'Shit. Not again.' West grabbed the mike, and tossed it to her partner. 'Let's see what they're teaching volunteers these days.'

'700,' he said on the air for all to hear. 'We're ten-eighteen five-fifty-six Midland.'

Missing person reports were so much paperwork, it was unbelievable. Such investigations were almost always fruitless, for either the person really wasn't missing, or he was and dead. Radar's preference was that West had gotten her butt kicked at Fat Man's. At least Radar could ensure that she would be filling out forms the rest of her life, and Midland was government subsidized housing, definitely not a nice place for a female or her reporter ride-along.

* * *

Luellen Wittiker lived in a one-bedroom unit. Her number, 556, like all others in Midland Court, was painted in huge numbers over the door. The city had done this free of charge so the cops could find places fast when out at night with searchlights sweeping and K-9 dogs panting. Luellen Wittiker had just moved here from Mint Hill, where she had worked as a checkout clerk in Wal-Mart until she hit her eighth month of pregnancy and got tired of Jerald coming around. How many times did she have to tell him *no*. N-O.

She paced, wringing her hands, her four-year-old daughter, Tangine, watching from the bed, which was close to the front door. Boxes were still stacked against a wall, although there were not many, since the Wittiker family traveled light. Luellen prayed every hour that Jerald would not find out where she had moved. He would show up. Oh yes. She paced some more. Where the hell were the police? They think this was the lay-away plan? Can't do it now, pick it up later?

Oh yes. He would find her. Because of that bad seed child of hers. Wheatie was out there right now, God only knew where, probably trying to find a way to get hold of Jerald, who was not Wheatie's biological father, but his mother's last boyfriend. Wheatie hero-worshiped Jerald, and that was the problem. Tangine watched her mother pacing. Tangine was eating a Popsicle. Jerald was nothing more than a lowlife drugman, who bought and sold the big stuff, and did it, too.

Cain, crack, diesel, smoke, all that shit. He walked around in his big warm-up suit and Filas like he was in the NBA, and had a diamond earring, too, and a 4×4, black with red and yellow detailing. He'd drive up, and Wheatie would start in, walking, bad-mouthing, cool-talking, just like Jerald. Next thing, Wheatie would start cussing Luellen, and even slapping her around, or smoking marijuana. Just like Jerald. She heard feet on the steps and called out to make sure.

'Police,' a woman's voice sounded.

Luellen worked a big cinderblock back from the door, and removed a concrete support steel bar that she had found on a construction site. She had the same set of improvised locks at the back door, too. Even if Jerald or his bad friends could get in, she'd at least hear things scraping and clanging, and have time to get out her matte-black nine-millimeter Baretta Model 92FS pistol with its Tritium night sights, wood grips, and fifteen-shot magazine. The gun had come from Jerald, as well, and it had been a big mistake giving her this hand-me-down. If he so much as knocked on her door, it would be his last gesture.

'Come on in,' Luellen said to the two police officers at the top of concrete steps.

Brazil's eyes adjusted to the glaring illumination of a naked lightbulb in a plastic Greek column lamp. A small TV was on, the Braves playing the Dodgers. There was a boom box in a corner, walls bare, the bed unmade and right there in the living room, a little girl sitting on it. She had braids and sad eyes. It was hot as hell in here, and Brazil started sweating. So did West. She had attached an endless form on top of her metal clipboard, and was prepared to do a lot of writing. Luellen began by telling the police lady all about Wheatie, including that he was adopted and jealous as hell of Tangine and the unborn baby, yet unnamed.

'He called you after he missed the bus,' West repeated as she wrote.

'Wanted me to come get him, and I told him I had no way,' Luellen said. 'Last time I was pregnant, he jumped on me and I lost the baby. He was fifteen then. Always been hateful because he's adopted, like I told you. Trouble from day one.'

'You got a recent picture of him?' West asked.

'Packed up. Don't know if I can get to it.'

Mother described Wheatie as small, bad skin, wearing Adidas, baggy jeans hanging off, tealgreen Hornets T-shirt and baseball cap, and a fade haircut. He could be anywhere, but Luellen worried that he was running with bad kids and into drugs. Brazil felt sorry for Tangine, who seemed unimportant in the grand scheme of things as she climbed down from the bed, fascinated by this blond man in his fancy uniform with all its shiny leather. He got out his Mag-Lite and started bouncing the beam around on the floor, playing with her like she was a cat. Tangine didn't know what to make of this and got scared. She was screaming and did not intend to stop by the time the police left. Mother watched Brazil and West feel their way down the steps in the complete dark.

'Way to go,' West said to her partner, as Tangine wailed and shrieked.

Brazil missed a step and landed on his ass.

'I'd put a light on if I had one,' Luellen said from the doorway.

The next two hours were spent in the records room. West continued to fill out forms, having no idea that there were so many of them these days. It was astonishing, and she was unfamiliar with anyone back here tonight, and all were rude and not inclined to respect West's rank. Were she paranoid, she might have suspected a conspiracy, as if someone had instructed the clerks to give the deputy chief a bad dose, to stick her but good. Mostly, West got their backs as they typed, and sipped their Frescas and Diet Cokes. West could have asserted herself, but didn't. She entered the missing person information in NCIC herself.

She and Brazil rode around for a while in the Midland area, hoping they might spot the small adopted son with bad skin and Hornets cap. They drove slowly past kids hanging out on corners, and beneath street lights, hateful eyes following. Wheatie remained at large, and as the evening wore on, Brazil had developed a relationship with him. Brazil imagined Wheatie's wretched life, his loneliness and anger. What chance did anyone like that have? Nothing but bad examples, and cops out there like cowboys waiting to lasso and round him up.

Brazil's early years weren't perfect, either, but there was no comparison. He had tennis courts and nice neighbors. Davidson security treated him like family, and he was always welcome to visit their small brick precinct, and listen to their stories and gossip and exaggerations. They made him feel special when he came in. The same was true at the laundry with its rooftop of tangled rusting metal, from students picking up laundry and tossing the wire hangers up there, where they stayed for years. Doris, Bette, and Sue always had time for Brazil. The same could be said in the snack bar, the M&M soda shop, the bookstore, anywhere he went, really.

Wheatie had never experienced any of this, and quite likely never would. At the very moment West was reprimanding a driver for not wearing a seatbelt, Wheatie was jailing with his heroes in the slums off Beatties Ford Road. There were four friends, all years older than Wheatie. His pals had big pants, big shoes, big guns, and big rolls of cash in their pockets. They were high-fiving, laughing, soaring on wings of smoke. Yes sir, the night had been good, and for one sweet minute, that hollow, hurtful spot in Wheatie's heart was full and feeling fine.

'Give me a gun, I'll go work for you,' he said to Slim.

'Little piece like you?' Slim laughed. 'Uh uh.' He shook his head. 'I give you a job, you get spanked and I end up with nothing.'

'Bullshit,' Wheatie said in his biggest, boasting tone. 'Nobody fuck with me.'

'Yeah, you bad,' said Tote.

'Yeah, you bad,' Fright imitated Tote, while popping Wheatie on the head.

'Man, I gotta go get me some food,' said Slim, who could eat tires after getting high. 'How 'bout we hit Hardee's.'

He meant this literally. Slim and company were under the influence and armed, and robbing Hardee's was as good an idea as any they had come up with this night. All of them piled into his red Geo Tracker. They headed out with the radio so loud the bass could be felt five cars away. Wheatie plotted as they drove, thinking about Jerald and how proud he would be of Wheatie right now. Jerald would be impressed with Wheatie's buddies. Wheatie wished Slim, Tote, and Fright could meet Jerald. Shit, wouldn't they step back and give Wheatie a little more respect? Fuck yeah, they would. He watched telephone poles and cars go by, his heart picking up speed. He knew what he had to do.

'Give me a gun, I'll do it,' he said loud enough to be heard over heavy metal.

Slim was driving, and laughed again, eyeing him in

the rearview mirror. 'You will? You ever hit anything before?'

'I hit my mother.'

They all laughed.

'He *hit* his mother! Woooo-weeee! Bad ass!'

They were choking, guffawing, weaving in and out of traffic. Fright slipped out his high-gloss stainless steel Ruger .357 Blackhawk revolver with its six-and-a-half-inch barrel and walnut grips and adjustable sights. It was loaded with six Hydra-Shoks. He handed his piece to Wheatie, who acted as if he knew all there was to know about guns, and owned plenty of them. They pulled up to Hardee's. The friends landed glazed eyes on Wheatie.

'All right motherfucker,' Slim said to him. 'You go in and get a twelve-piece dinner, all white meat.' He snapped out a twenty-dollar bill. 'You pay and wait. Don't do nothing 'til you got the food, you know? Then you tuck it under your arm, pull out the gun, clean out the registers, and run like hell.'

Wheatie nodded, heart drilling out of his chest.

'We ain't gonna be sitting right here.' Fright made that point, jerking his head at the Payless gas station next store. 'Back there by the Dumpster. You take long, motherfucker, we leave your ass.'

Wheatie understood. 'Get the fuck outa my face,' he said, tough and invincible as he tucked the revolver in the front of his pants and pulled his T-shirt over it.

What Wheatie did not understand was that this particular Hardee's had been robbed before, and Slim, Fright, and Tote were aware of it. They were laughing and lighting up another joint even as he walked in and they drove off. Wheatie's little butt was going to get locked up tonight. He'd learn about jailing honestly, his pants falling off because they took his belt, then dropping the rest of the way when some motherfucker got the urge for his sweet little ass.

'Twelve piece, white meat.' Wheatie's voice didn't sound quite so tough now that he was at the counter. He was shaking all over and terrified that the fat black lady in a hairnet knew all about his plan.

'What sides you want?' she asked.

Shit. Slim didn't tell him that part. Oh shit. He got it wrong and they'd kill him. His furtive, hard eyes cast about, not seeing the Tracker anywhere.

'Baked beans. Slaw. Biscuits,' he did the best he could.

She rang it up, and took his twenty. He left the change on the counter, fearful that tucking it in his pocket might draw attention to the gun. When the big bag of chicken and side orders were gripped under a frail arm, Wheatie drew the gun, not real smoothly, but he got it out and pointed it at the fat lady's startled face.

'Give me all your money, motherfucker!' he commanded in his cruelest voice as the gun shook in his small hands.

Wyona managed this Hardee's and was working the counter because two of her people were out sick tonight. She'd been robbed three times in her life and this little piece of motherfucking white meat wasn't going to make it four. She put her hands on her hips, glaring at him.

'What you gonna do, cockadoodledo? Shoot me?' she sang.

Wheatie had not anticipated this. He clicked back the hammer, hands shaking harder. He wet his lips, eyes jumping. It was decision time. No way he could let this fat chicken lady dis him. Shit man. He walked out of here without the money and that was the end of his career. He wasn't even sure he'd gotten the sides right. Oh shit, he was in trouble. He closed his eyes and pulled the trigger. The explosion was incredible and the revolver jumped in his hands. The bullet smashed through *large fries $1.99* on the lit-up sign over Wyona's head. She grabbed the big .357 magnum away from him, and he ran like hell.

Wyona was a firm believer in community intervention. She chased Wheatie out the door. She thundered after him through the parking lot, across the way to the Payless, and behind it where a red Tracker was parked, filled with teenagers smoking weed. They locked the doors. Wheatie tugged a handle to no avail, yelling, as the huge woman grabbed the back of his pants, yanking them down to his leather Adidas. He fell to the pavement in a tangle of red denim as she pointed the revolver through glass, at the driver's head.

Slim knew a determined look when he saw it. This bitch was going to shoot him if he so much as blinked. He slowly lifted his hands from the steering wheel, and held them up.

'Don't shoot,' he begged. 'Oh please don't shoot.'

'Get on your car phone and call 911 right now,' Wyona screamed.

He did.

'Tell them where you are and what you done and that if they don't get here in exactly two minutes, I'm blowing your motherfucking head off!' she screamed, her foot firmly planted on Wheatie, who was supine and shaking on the pavement, face down, hands covering his head.

'We just robbed Hardee's and are behind the Payless on Central Avenue!' Slim yelled into the phone. 'Please get here quick!'

Selma, the 911 operator who got the call, wasn't certain what this was about. But she gave it a priority one because her instinct prodded her in a tragedy-about-to-occur direction. Radar, meanwhile, had not finished with West this night. He passed the emergency along to her.

'Goddamit,' West said as she drove past Piedmont Open Middle School. She was trying to avoid other problems, and did not wish to hear her unit number one more time, ever.

Brazil couldn't grab the mike fast enough. '700,' he said.

'Unknown trouble, four thousand block of Central Avenue,' Radar said with a smile.

West floored it, flying down Tenth Street, cutting over to the one thousand block of Central, flying past the Veterans Park and Saigon Square. Other units backed her up, for by now it had occurred to every cop on the street that their deputy chief was handling a lot of dangerous calls unassisted by anyone. When she rolled into the Payless, six cars with lights flashing were behind her. This was uncommon, but West didn't question it and was grateful. She and Brazil got out. Wyona lowered the gun, now that help was here.

'They tried to rob me,' she said to Brazil.

'Who did?' West asked.

'The piece of white shit under my foot,' she said to Brazil.

West noted the fade haircut, the bad skin, the Hornets cap and shirt. The boy's pants were knotted around his basketball shoes, and he had on yellow boxer shorts. Next to him was a big bag of chicken and side orders.

'He come in, ordered twelve piece all white meat, then pulled out this thing.' Wyona handed the gun to Brazil because he was the man and Wyona had never dealt with woman police and wasn't about to start now. 'I chased him out here to where these sons of bitches are.' She gestured furiously at Slim, Fright, and Tote as they cowered inside the Tracker.

West took the gun from Brazil. She looked back at the six other officers standing nearby and observing.

'Let's lock 'em up,' she said to the troops. To Wyona, she added, 'Thanks.'

The boys were rounded up and cuffed. Now that they were official felons again and not about to be killed, their bravery returned. They stared hatefully at the police and spat. In the car, West gave Brazil a pointed look. He typed on the MDT, clearing them from the scene.

'Why do they hate us so much?' he said.

'People tend to treat others the way they've been treated,' she answered. 'Take cops. A lot of them are the same way.'

They rode in silence for a while, passing other poor landscapes, the aspiring sparkling city around them.

'What about you?' Brazil asked. 'How come you don't hate?'

'I had a good childhood.'

This made him angry. 'Well I didn't, and I don't hate everyone,' he said. 'So don't ask me to feel sorry for them.'

'What can I tell you?' She got out a cigarette. 'It goes back to Eden, the Civil War, the Cold War, Bosnia. The six days it took God to make all this.'

'You got to quit smoking,' he said, and he remembered her fingers touching him as she fixed his shirt.

Chapter Thirteen

Brazil had a lot to think about. He wrote his stories fast and shipped them out within seconds of various deadlines for various editions. He was strangely unsettled and not remotely tired. He did not want to go home, and had fallen into a funk the instant West had let him out at his car in the parking deck. He left the newsroom at quarter past midnight, and took the escalator down to the second floor.

The press room was going full tilt, yellow Ferag conveyors flying by seventy thousand papers per hour. Brazil opened the door, his ears overwhelmed by the roar inside. People wearing hearing protectors and ink-stained aprons nodded at him, yet to understand his odd peregrinations through their violent, dirty world. He walked in and stared at miles of speeding newsprint, at folding machines rat-a-tat-a-tatting, and belt ribbon conveyors streaking papers through the counting machines. The hard-working people in this seldom-thought-of place had never known a reporter to care a hoot about how his clever words and bigshot bylines ended up in the hands of citizens every day.

Brazil was inexplicably drawn to the power of these huge, frightening machines. He was awed to see his front page racing by in a blur, thousands and thousands of times. It was humbling and hard to believe that so many people out there were interested in how he saw the world and what he had to say. The big headline of the night was, of course, Batman and Robin saving the hijacked bus. But there was a pretty decent piece on WHY A BOY RAN AWAY, on the metro section front page, and a few paragraphs on the altercation at Fat Man's Lounge.

In truth, Brazil could have written stories forever about all he saw while riding with West. He wandered up a spiral metal staircase to the mail room, and thought of her calling him *partner*. He replayed her voice over and over. He liked the way she sounded, deep but resonate and womanly. It made him think of old wood and smoke, of fieldstone patched with moss, and of lady's slippers in old forests scattered with sun.

Brazil did not want to go home. He wandered out to his car, in a mood to roam and think. He felt blue and did not know the source of it. Life was good. His job couldn't be better. The cops didn't seem to despise him quite as intensely or as universally. He contemplated the possibility that his problem was physical, because he wasn't working out as much as usual, and wasn't producing enough endorphin, or pushing himself to the point of exhaustion. He cruised down West Trade, looking at the people of the night trolling, offering their bodies for cash. Sh'ims followed him with sick, glowing eyes, and the young hooker was out again, at the corner of Cedar.

She walked seductively along the sidewalk and stared brazenly at him as he slowly drove past. She had on tight cut-off jeans that barely covered firm buttocks, her T-shirt cut off, too, just below her chest. Typically, she wasn't wearing a bra, and her flesh moved as she walked and stared at the blond boy in his black BMW with its loud, rumbling engine. She wondered what he had beneath his hood, and smiled. All those Myers Park boys in their expensive cars, sneaking out here to taste the fruit.

Brazil roared ahead, daring a yellow light to be red. He turned off on Pine and entered Fourth Ward, the lovely restored area where important people like Chief Hammer lived, within walking distance of the heart of the city she was sworn to serve. Brazil had been here many times, mostly to look at huge Victorian homes painted fun colors like violet and robin's egg blue, and at graceful manors with elaborate dentil work trimming slate roofs. There were walls and big azaleas, and trees that could clarify history, for they had been here since horses, shading genteel streets traveled by the rich and well known.

He parked on that special corner on Pine where the white house and its gracious wraparound porch were lit up, as if expecting him. Hammer had liriope grass, periwinkles, pansies, yucca, ligustrum hedges, and pachysandra. Wind chimes stirred in the dark, sending friendly tones of truth, like a tuning fork, welcoming him, her protégé. Brazil would not trespass, would not even think of it. But there were numerous tiny public parks in Fourth Ward, sitting areas with fountains and a bench or two. One such cozy spot was tucked next door to Hammer's house, and Brazil had known about this secret garden for a while. Now and then he sat in the dark there, when he could not sleep, or did not want to go home. There was no harm done or imagined.

It wasn't as if he were on her property. He wasn't a stalker or a voyeur. All he wanted, really, was to sit where no one could see him. The most he invaded was the window of her living room, where he saw nothing, for the draperies were always drawn, unless a shadow passed by, someone who belonged in that house and could walk wherever he pleased. Brazil sat on a stone bench that was cold and hard beneath his dirty uniform trousers. He stared, and the sadness he felt was beyond any word he knew. He imagined Hammer inside her fine house, with her fine family, and her fine husband. She was in a fine suit, probably talking on a portable phone, busy and important. Brazil wondered what it would be like to be loved by a woman like that.

Seth knew exactly what it was like, and as he finished loading his ice cream bowl into the dish washer, he entertained violent thoughts. He had been lacing his late-night Chunky Monkey with butterscotch and hot fudge when Chief Wife came in with her bottle of Evian. So what did she do? Nag, nag, nag. About his weight, his coronary arteries, his propensity for diabetes, his laziness, his dental problems. He went into the living room, flipped on 'Seinfeld,' tried to block her out, and wondered what had ever attracted him to Judy Hammer.

She was a powerful woman in uniform the first time they met. He would never forget the way she stood out in dark blue. What a figure she cut. He had never told her his fantasies about being overpowered by her, cuffed, pinned, held, yoked, and hauled away in the paddy wagon of erotic captivity. After all these years, she did not know. None of it had happened. Judy Hammer had never restrained him physically.

She had never made love to him while she was in uniform, not even now, when she had enough brass and gold braid to impress the Pentagon. When she went to police memorial services, banquets, and showed up in dress blues, Seth turned fainthearted. He was overcome, helpless and frustrated. In the end, after all these years and disappointments, she was still splendid. If only she didn't make him feel so worthless and ugly. If only she hadn't driven him to this, forced him into it, caused it, and willed abject ruination upon his life. It was her fault that he was fat, and a failure.

The chief, his wife, honestly was not privy to any of her husband's ambitions or lustful imaginings or the complete set of his resentments. She would not have been flattered, amused, or held responsible, for Chief Hammer was not aroused by dominance, or prey to control, or quick to assume that others might be smitten and excited by her position in life. It would never occur to her that Seth was eating ice cream with butterscotch, hot fudge sauce, and maraschino cherries at this unhealthy hour because he really wished to be shackled to the bedposts, or to be searched inappropriately and for a long time. He wanted her to arrest him for animal desire and throw away the key. He wanted her to languish and doubt herself and all she had done. What did not interest him in the least was to be sentenced to the solitary confinement their marriage had become.

Chief Hammer was not in uniform or even on the portable phone. She was in a long, thick terry-cloth robe, and suffering from insomnia, and this was not unusual. She rarely slept much because her mind kept its own hours, the hell with her body. She was sitting in the living room, 'The Tonight Show' droning on as she read the *Wall Street Journal*, various memos, another long letter from her ancient mother, and a few salient pages from Marianne Williamson's *A Return to Love*. Hammer did her best to block out Seth making noise in the kitchen.

His failure in his passage through the world felt like hers. No matter what she told herself or the therapists she left in Atlanta and Chicago, profound personal failure was what she felt every hour of every day. She had done something very wrong, otherwise Seth would not be committing suicide with a fork, a spoon, or chocolate sauce. When she looked back, she realized that the woman who had married him was another entity. She, Chief Hammer, was a reincarnation of that earlier lost manifestation. She did not need a man. She did not need Seth. Everyone knew it, including him.

It was a simple fact that the best cops, Marines, Airmen, National Guards, firefighters, and military people in general who were women did not need men, personally. Hammer had commanded many such independents. She would pick them without question, as long as they weren't so much like the men they did not need that they had completely adopted bad male habits, such as getting into fights rather than not, or being clingy and demanding and domineering. What Hammer had concluded after all these years was that she had an overweight, neurotic, nonworking wife who did nothing but bitch. Judy Hammer was ready for change.

Thus it was that she made a tactical error this very early morning, in her long clean robe. She decided to go out on her wraparound porch, and sit on the swing, sipping chardonnay, alone with her thoughts, for a spell.

Brazil was mesmerized when she emerged, a vision, a god glowing in lamplight, all in white and shimmering. His heart rolled forward at such a pitch, he could not catch up with it. He sat very still on the cold cement bench, terrified she would see him. He watched every small thing she did, the way she pushed forward and let go, the bend of her wrist as she lifted the tapered glass, her head leaning back against the swing. He saw the slope of her neck as she rocked with eyes shut.

What did she think? Was she a person just like him, with those darker shades, those lonely, cold corners of existence that no one knew? She swung slowly, and alone. His chest ached. He was drawn to this woman and had no clear idea why. It must be hero worship. If he had a chance to touch her, he really wouldn't know what to do. But he did want to, as he stared, in the night, at her. She was pretty, even at her age. Not delicate, but fascinating, powerful, compelling, like a collector's car, an older BMW, in mint condition, with chrome instead of plastic. She had character and substance, and Brazil was certain that her husband was quite the contender, a Fortune 500 man, a lawyer, a surgeon, someone capable of holding an interesting conversation with his wife during their brief, busy interfaces together.

Chief Hammer pushed the swing again and sipped her wine. She would never be completely devoid of street sense, no matter her station in life. She goddamn knew when she was being watched. Abruptly, she stood, feet firmly planted on her porch. She searched the night, detecting the vague silhouette of someone sitting in that annoying little park right slam next to her house. How many times had she told the neighborhood association that she didn't want a public area adjacent to her domicile? Did anyone listen? To Brazil's horror, she walked down porch steps and stood amidst pachysandra, staring right at him.

'Who's there?' she demanded.

Brazil could not speak. Not a fire or a *Mayday* could have pried a word loose from his useless tongue.

'Who's sitting there?' she went on, irritable and tired. 'It's almost two o'clock in the morning. Normal people are home by now. So either you're not normal, or you're interested in my house. Police live in this house. They have guns and shoot to kill. And you still want to rob us?'

Brazil wondered what would happen if he ran as fast as he could. When he was a little boy, he believed that if he sprinted full speed, he would disappear, become invisible, or turn to butter like in 'Little Black Sambo'. It wasn't so. Brazil was a sculpture on his bench, watching Chief Judy Hammer step closer. A part of him wanted her to know he was there, so he could get it over with, confess his intensity, have her blow him off, laugh, dismiss him from her police department, and be done with him, as he deserved.

'I'm going to ask one more time,' she warned.

It occurred to him that she might have a gun on her person, perhaps in a pocket. Jesus Christ, how could any of this happen? He had meant no harm driving here after work. All he'd wanted was to sit, think, and contemplate his raison d'être and how he felt about it.

'Don't shoot,' he said, slowly bringing himself to his feet, and holding his hands up in surrender.

Hammer knew for a fact she had a wacko in her midst. *Don't shoot?* What the hell was this? Clearly, this was someone who knew who she was. Why else would the person assume she might be armed and wouldn't hesitate to shoot? Hammer had always nurtured the unspoken fear that in the end, she would be taken out by a loonytune with a mission. Assassinated. Go ahead and try, was her motto. She followed the brick walk through more pachysandra as Brazil's panic level crested. He cast his eyes toward his car on the street, realizing that by the time he raced to it, got in, and drove off, she would have his plate number. He decided to relax and feign innocence. He sat back down as she, in her white robe, floated closer.

'Why are you here?' she asked, hovering mere feet from him now.

'I didn't mean to be disturbing anyone,' he apologized.

Hammer hesitated, not getting quite what she had expected. 'It's almost two o'clock in the morning,' she repeated.

'Actually, it's a little later than that,' Brazil said, chin in hand, face in shadows. 'Love this place, don't you? So peaceful, great for thinking, meditating, getting into your spiritual space.'

Hammer was entertaining second thoughts about this one. She sat down on the bench, next to him.

'Who are you?' she asked, and the indirect light was an artist lovingly painting her face as she studied him.

'Nobody special,' Brazil said.

Oh yes he was. She thought of her own horrible life, of the husband in there, where she lived. This one on the bench next to her understood. He appreciated her for who and what she was. He respected her power and wanted her as a woman at the same time. He was deeply interested in her thoughts, her ideas, her memories of childhood. Brazil traced her neck deep down into her plush white terry-cloth robe, slowing down, taking his time. He kissed her, tentatively until he was sure she was kissing him back, then he worked on her lower lip until their tongues became acquainted and were friends.

When he woke up inside his locked bedroom, he wasn't finished yet and in agony. It was awful. Please Lord, why couldn't it be true? But it decidedly was not. It was a fact that he had sat in the tiny park staring at Hammer's house and she had come out to drift on her swing. It was not a fact that any of the rest of it had occurred, except in fractured dreams. She did not know that he was there in the dark, hearing her North Carolina flag snap in the wind, over her porch. She did not care. He had never touched his lips to hers, he had never caressed soft skin, and never would. He was terribly ashamed. He was frustrated and confused. She was probably thirty years older than Brazil. This was sick. Something must be terribly wrong with him.

Brazil played the messages on his answering machine when he came home at quarter of three in the morning. There were four, all of them hang-ups. This only worsened his mood. He could not help but think that the pervert was after him because he, too, was some sort of deviant. There had to be reason a sick person would be drawn to him. Brazil was angry as he yanked on running clothes at dawn. He grabbed a tennis racquet, the hopper of balls, and trotted out the door.

The morning was wet with dew, the sun already making its potent presence known. Magnolias were dense and heavy with waxy white blossoms that smelled like lemon as he passed beneath them. He cut through the Davidson campus, sprinting along the small road winding behind Jackson Court, heading to the track. He ran six fast miles, and furiously served tennis balls. He worked out with weights in the gym, sprinted several laps, and did push-ups and sit-ups until his body's natural opiates kicked in.

Hammer was preoccupied with her ruined morning. This was what she got for altering her routine and having lunch with West, who clearly could not keep out of trouble. Hammer had worn her uniform this day, which in itself was exceedingly unusual. She had not found it necessary to argue court dates with the district attorney in fifteen years, and wanted no problem here. She believed in the power of personal confrontations, and determined that the DA was about to have one. By nine A.M., Hammer was inside the big granite Criminal Court Building, waiting in the reception area of the city's top prosecutor.

Nancy Gorelick had been reelected so many times, she ran unopposed and most of the population would not have bothered to go to the polls were there not other officials to vote for or against. She and Hammer were not personal friends. The DA certainly knew very well who the chief was, and in fact had read about Hammer's heroics in the morning paper. Batman and Robin. Oh please. Gorelick was a ruthless Republican who believed in hanging first and sorting out later. She was tired of people who thought special excuses should be made for them, and there was no doubt in her mind about the reason for Hammer's impromptu visit.

Gorelick made Hammer wait long enough. By the time the DA buzzed her secretary to say that the chief could be shown in, Hammer was pacing the reception area, looking at her watch, and getting more irritated by the second. The secretary opened a dark wooden door and Hammer strode past her.

'Good morning, Nancy,' the chief said.

'Thank you.' The DA nodded with a smile, hands folded on top of her neat desk. 'What can I do for you, Judy?'

'You know about the incident at the Greyhound bus station yesterday.'

'The whole world knows,' said Gorelick.

Hammer pulled a chair around to the side of the desk, refusing to sit directly across from Gorelick with a big block of wood between them. There was little more valuable than office psychology, and Hammer was a master at it. Right now, the DA's setup was blatantly overpowering and unwelcoming. Gorelick was leaning forward with hands on the blotter, assuming a posture of superiority and dominance. She was visibly bothered that Hammer had rearranged the order, and was now facing the DA with nothing between them but crossed legs.

'The Johnny Martino case,' Gorelick said.

'Yes,' Hammer said. 'Also known as Magic the Man.'

'Thirty-three class D felony charges of robbery with a dangerous weapon,' Gorelick went on. 'He'll plea bargain. We'll sock him with maybe ten, get him to agree to consolidate sentencing under five counts. Since he's a prior record level two, he's going to be out of circulation for so long, he'll turn into a skeleton.'

'When do you anticipate setting the court date, Nancy?' Hammer wasn't impressed, and frankly, believed not a word. This guy would get the minimum. They all did.

'I've already set it.' The DA picked up her big black date book and flipped pages. 'Set for superior court, July twenty-second.'

Hammer wanted to kill her. 'I'm on vacation that entire week. In Paris. It's been set for a year. I'm taking my sons and their families, and I've already bought the tickets, Nancy. That's why I came by this morning. Both of us are busy professionals with crushing schedules and responsibilities. You know perfectly well, Nancy, that police chiefs normally do not make arrests and end up in court. When was the last time that you heard of such a thing? I'm asking you to work with me on this.'

Gorelick didn't care who anybody was, especially not this chief of police, with her personal wealth and fame. All in Gorelick's courtroom had jobs waiting for them, busy schedules, and demands on their time, except the defendants, of course, who generally had nothing in their Day Timers but empty spaces to fill with trouble. Gorelick had never been especially fond of Judy Hammer. The chief was arrogant, competitive, power drunk, noncollaborative, and vain. She spent considerable money on designer suits and pearls and accessories, and, in a word, did not suffer from the same problems, such as body fat, adult acne, estrogen volatilities, and rejection, as others.

'I was not elected to work with you or anyone,' Gorelick stated. 'It is my job to set trial dates that please the court, and that is what I have done. Vacation plans are not the business of the court, and you will have to make whatever adjustments are necessary. As will everyone else involved.'

Hammer noted that Gorelick was overbuffed as usual. She had a penchant for short skirts, bright colors, and open necklines that were an invitation whenever she bent over to look at documents, dockets, or cases. She wore too much makeup, especially mascara. There were rumors about her many affairs, but Hammer had chosen to view these as unfounded until this moment. This was the woman the cops called the DA *Whorelick*. She was lower than dirt, and a slut. Office psychology dictated that Hammer should get up from her chair.

She did, and leaned against the desk, helping herself to her opponent's domain, breathing all the air she wished, picking up a crystal paperweight of USBank, and fiddling with it. Hammer was very comfortable and in charge. She spoke rationally, softly, and sincerely.

'The press, of course, has been calling me about yesterday's incident,' Hammer confessed, and her fooling with the paperweight was clearly bothering Gorelick. 'National press. The *Washington Post, Time, Newsweek, CBS This Morning*, Jay Leno, *New York Times*, Don Imus, Howard

Stern.' She began to pace, tapping the USBank in her palm, as if it were a slapjack. 'They'll want to cover the trial, I'm sure. It's a big story, I guess.' She paced and tapped. 'I suppose when you stop to think about it, when has something like this ever happened? That reminds me.' She laughed. 'Some studio and a couple producers from Hollywood called, too. Can you imagine?'

Gorelick wasn't feeling well. 'It is an unusual situation,' she had to agree.

'An amazing example of community policing, Nancy. People doing the right thing.' Hammer paced and gestured with the little crystal building wearing a crown. 'Your treating a chief and deputy chief just like anyone else, making no special considerations.' She nodded. 'I think all those reporters are going to like that. Don't you?'

Gorelick would be ruined, would look like the dickhead she was. Someone would run against her next fall. She'd have to go work in a law firm as a lowly junior attorney to a bunch of overbearing partners who wouldn't want her to join their exclusive ranks.

'I'm going to tell them all about it.' Hammer smiled at her. 'Right now. I guess the best thing would be a press conference.'

The court date was moved ahead a week, and landed on a day convenient for all, except Johnny Martino, aka Magic the Man, who was sitting in his jail cell, dejected in a blaze orange jumpsuit with DEPT OF CORR stenciled in on the back. Everybody in the Corr wore one, and now and then, when he gave much thought to the matter, he wondered what the hell the *Corr* was. As in Marine Corps, Peace Corps, *C&O RailRoad* maybe? His old man worked for Amtrak, cleaning up cars after all those passengers got off.

No way young Martino was ever doing shitwork like

that. No fucking way. He couldn't believe how bad his leg hurt from where that bitch kicked him. The guns people carried these days, women especially. Both of them pointing *forty-fucking-caliber semiautomatics* at his head. Now where the hell did that come from? Fucking Mars? These ladies beam down, or something? He was still stunned, and had sat up on his narrow bunk this morning thinking yesterday on the bus didn't happen.

Then he focused on the steel toilet bowl that he had not bothered to flush last night. His shin was throbbing so bad, and had a lump on it the size of an orange, the skin broken in the middle, like a navel, where that pointy metal toe had connected. Now that he explored the situation a little further, he should have been suspicious of two rich ladies like that getting on the Greyhound. No way people like them take the bus. Some of the guys were talking and laughing up and down the cells, going on and on about him getting his ass kicked by some old woman with a big pocketbook, everybody making fun of Martino. He got out a cigarette, and thought about suing. He thought about getting another tattoo, might as well while he was here.

Brazil's day was not going especially well, either. He and Packer were editing another self-initiated, rather large piece Brazil was doing on mothers alone in a world without men. Brazil continued to come across typos, spaces, blank lines that he knew he had not caused. Someone had been breaking into his computer basket and going through his files. He was explaining this to his metro editor, Packer, as they rolled through paragraphs, inspecting the violation.

'See,' Brazil was hotly saying, and he was in uniform,

ready for yet another night on the street. 'It's weird. The last couple days I keep finding stuff like this.'

'You sure you're not doing it? You do tend to go through your stories a lot,' Packer said.

What the editor had observed about Brazil's remarkable productivity had now reached the level of *not humanly possible.* This kid dressed like a cop frightened Packer. Packer didn't even much want to sit next to Brazil anymore. Brazil wasn't normal. He was getting commendations from the police, and averaging three bylines every morning, even on days when he supposedly was off. Not to mention, his work was unbelievably good for someone so inexperienced who had never been to journalism school. Packer suspected that Brazil would win a Pulitzer by the time he was thirty, possibly sooner. For that reason, Packer intended to remain Brazil's editor, even if the job was exhausting, intense, and unnerving, and caused Packer to hate life more with each passing day.

This morning was a typical example. The alarm had buzzed at six, and Packer did not want to get up. But he did. Mildred, his wife, was her typical cheery self, cooking oatmeal in the kitchen, while Dufus, her purebred Boston Terrier puppy, skittered around sideways and wall-eyed and looking for something else to chew, or pee or poop on. Packer was tucking in his shirt all the way around as he entered this domestic scene, trying to wake up, and wondering if his wife was losing what marbles she had left.

'Mildred,' he said. 'It's summer. Oatmeal is not a good hot-weather food.'

'Of course it is.' She happily stirred. 'Good for your high blood pressure.'

Dufus jumped and fussed at Packer, dancing around his feet, trying to climb him, grabbing cuffs in snaggly teeth. Packer never touched his wife's puppy if he could help it, and had refused any input into its development beyond naming it, over objections from Mildred, who had made it a condition of their marriage that she would never be without one of these ugly little dogs from her childhood. Dufus did not see very well. From his perspective, Packer was a very big and unfriendly tree, a utility pole, some other edifice, maybe a fence. Whenever Packer came within scent, Dufus was airborne and in grass and squatting and relieving other basic functions that meant nothing to Dufus. He untied both of Packer's shoelaces.

Packer made his way across the newsroom as if he saw no color in the world, only gray. He was tucking in his shirt, heading to the men's room, feeling like he had to go and knowing nothing would happen again, and reminded that next Wednesday at two P.M., he had an appointment with his urologist.

Brazil was running down the escalator, deciding to take matters into his own hands. He pushed through several sets of doors, finally entering the rarified, air-conditioned space where Brenda Bond ruled the world from an ergonomically-correct green fabric chair with rollers. Her feet were on an adjustable footrest, her valuable hands poised over a contoured keyboard designed to prevent carpal tunnel syndrome.

Bond was surrounded by IBM and Hewlett Packard mainframes, multiplexor, modems, cabinets containing huge tape reels, decoders, and a satellite feed from the Associated Press. It was her cockpit, and he had come. She could not believe that Brazil was standing before her, had sought her out, and wanted to be with her and no one but her this very second in time and space. Her face got hot as she looked him up and down. God almighty, was he built, and he knew it, and was already showing his contempt for her.

'I think someone's getting into my basket and going through my files,' Brazil announced.

'Impossible,' Bond, the genius, arrogantly told him. 'Unless you've given out your password.'

'I want it changed,' he demanded.

She was studying his uniform trousers and the way they fit him, particularly in the area of his zipper, appropriating, and full of her superiority. Brazil made a big point of looking where she was looking, as if there must be something on his pants.

'What? I spill something?' he said, walking off.

It was not that his trousers were too tight, nor were they provocative in any way. Brazil never wore anything for the purpose of drawing attention to himself or impressing others. For one thing, shopping had never been an option. The entirety of his wardrobe could be accommodated by two dresser drawers and about twenty coat hangers. Mostly, he had uniforms, and tennis clothes supplied by the tennis team, and by Wilson, which had put him on a free list when he was in high school and consistently ranked in the top five juniors in the state. Brazil's uniform trousers were, in truth, baggy, if anything. Yet people like Brenda Bond still stared. So did Axel.

When Brazil was in midnight blue and black leather, he had no idea what effect it had on others. If he had paused to analyze the matter, he might have discovered that uniforms were about power, and power was an aphrodisiac. Axel knew this for a fact. He got up and trotted out of the newsroom, in pursuit. Brazil was notorious for his sprints down the escalator, and into the parking deck. Axel worked out in the Powerhouse Gym every early morning, and was rather spectacularly sculpted.

Axel drank Met-Rx twice a day, and was very much admired when he was gleaming with sweat, and in a tank top and a weight belt, pumping, veins standing out, in his skimpy shorts. Other fit people stopped what they were doing, just to watch. He had been stalked several times by residents of his apartment complex. In truth, Tommy Axel could have anybody, and probably had at any given time. But he was not into aerobic exercise, because it was not a spectator sport. He got winded easily.

'Shoot,' Axel said when he burst through glass doors leading into the parking deck, as Brazil was driving his old BMW out of it.

Publisher Panesa had a black-tie dinner this night and was going home unusually early. The publisher was starting his silver Volvo, with its unrivaled safety record and two airbags, and was witness to Axel's shameless behavior.

'Christ,' Panesa muttered, shaking his head as he pulled out of his reserved space in the center of the best wall, no more than twenty steps from the front glass doors. He rolled down a window, stopping Axel cold.

'Come here,' Panesa told him.

Axel gave his boss a crooked, sexy Matt Dillon smile, and strolled over. Who could resist? 'What's going on?' Axel said, moving in a way that showed muscle to its best advantage.

'Axel, leave him alone,' Panesa said.

'Excuse me?' Axel touched his chest in pure hurt innocence.

'You know exactly what I mean.' Panesa roared off, fastening his shoulder harness, locking doors, checking mirrors, and snapping up the mike of his private frequency two-way radio to let the housekeeper know he was en route.

The longer Panesa had worked in the newspaper business, the more paranoid he had become. Like Brazil, Panesa had started out as a police reporter, and by the time he was twenty-three, knew every filthy, nasty, cruel, and painful thing people did to one another. He had done stories on murdered children, on hit and runs, and husbands in black gloves and knit caps stabbing estranged wives and friends before cutting their throats and flying to Chicago. Panesa had interviewed women who lovingly seasoned home cooking with arsenic, and he had covered car wrecks, plane crashes, train derailments, skydiving gone bad, scuba diving gone worse, bungee jumping by drunks who forgot the cord, and fires, and drownings. Not to mention other horrors that did not end in death. His marriage, for example.

Panesa frantically ran through downtown traffic like a Green Bay Packer, cutting in and out, the hell with you, honk all you want, get out of my way. He was going to be late again. It never failed. His date tonight was Judy Hammer, who apparently was married to a slob. Hammer avoided taking her husband out in public when she could, and Panesa did not blame her, if the rumor was true. Tonight was NationBank's Public Service Awards banquet, and both Panesa and Hammer were being honored, as was District Attorney Gorelick, who had been in the news a lot lately, scorching the NC General Assembly for not coughing up enough money to hire seventeen more assistant DAs, when it was clear that what the Charlotte-Mecklenburg region really needed was another medical examiner or two. The banquet was held at the Carillon, with its wonderful paintings and mobiles. Panesa was driving.

Hammer's personal car was a Mercedes, but not new and with only one airbag, on the driver's side. Panesa would not ride in anything that did not have a passenger's side airbag, and this had been made clear up front. Hammer, too, was rushing home early from the office. Seth was working in the garden, weeding and fertilizing. He had made cookies, and Hammer smelled the baked butter and sugar. She noted the telltale traces of flour on the counter. Seth waved a handful of wild onions at her as she peered out the kitchen window at him. He was civil enough.

She was in a hurry as she headed to her bedroom. God, the image staring back at her in the mirror was frightening. She washed her face, squirted nonalcohol styling gel into her hands and riffled through her hair. She started all over again with makeup. Black-tie affairs were always a problem. Men owned one tux and wore it to everything, or they rented. What were women supposed to do? She hadn't given any thought to what she might put on until she was walking into a house that smelled like a bakery. She pulled out a black satin skirt, a gold and black beaded short-waisted jacket, and a black silk blouse with spaghetti straps.

The truth was, Hammer had gained four pounds since she had worn this ensemble last, at a Jaycee's fundraiser in Pineville, about a year ago, if memory served her well. She managed to button her skirt, but was not happy about it. Her bosom was more out front than usual, and she did not like drawing attention to what she normally kept to herself. She irritably yanked her beaded jacket around her, muttering, wondering if dry-cleaning might have shrunk anything and the fault, therefore, not hers. Changing earrings to simple diamond posts with screw-backs was always troublesome when she was rushed and out of sorts.

'Darn,' she said, closing the drain just in time before a gold back sailed down the sink.

Panesa did not need a personal shopper, had no weight concerns, and could wear whatever he wished whenever he wished. He was an officer in the Knight-Ridder newspaper chain, and preferred black-label Giorgio Armani that he did not get in Charlotte. Hornets fans had priorities other than draping their spouses in two-thousand-dollar foreign suits, it seemed, and shopping remained a difficulty in the Queen City. Panesa was, as it turned out, dazzling in a tuxedo with satin lapels, and trousers with stripes. His was black silk, and he wore a matte-finished gold watch, and black lizard shoes.

'So tell me,' Panesa said when Hammer climbed into the Volvo. 'What's your secret?'

'What secret?' Hammer had no idea what this was about as she fastened her shoulder harness.

'You look stunning.'

'Of course I don't,' Hammer said.

Panesa backed out of the driveway, checking his mirrors, noticing the fat man working on geraniums. The fat man was watching them leave, and Panesa pretended not to notice as he adjusted the air conditioning.

'Do you shop around here?' Panesa asked.

'Lord, I need to.' Hammer sighed, for when did she have time?

'Let me guess. Montaldo's.'

'Never,' Hammer told him. 'Have you noticed how they treat you in places like that? They want to sell me something because I can afford it, and then treat me like an inferior. If I'm so inferior, I ask myself, then why are they the ones selling hose and lingerie?'

'That is absolutely the truth,' said Panesa, who had never shopped in a store that did not have clothes for men. 'Same thing in some restaurants I won't go to anymore.'

'Morton's,' Hammer supposed, although she had never eaten there.

'Not if you're on their VIP list. They give you a little card, and you can always get a table and good service.' Panesa switched lanes.

'Police officials have to be careful of things like that,' Hammer reminded the publisher, whose paper would have been the first to print a story about Hammer's VIP status or any other special favors possibly resulting in one establishment getting more police protection than another.

'Truth is, I don't eat much red meat anymore,' Panesa added.

They were passing the Traveler's Hotel, upstairs from the Presto Grill, which Hammer and West had made rather famous of late. Panesa smiled as he drove, reminded of Brazil's Batman and Robin story. The hotel was a horrific dive, Hammer thought as she looked out her window. Appropriately, it was across Trade Street from the city's unemployment office, and next door to the Dirty Laundry Cleaner & Laundry. No eating or drinking was allowed in the lobby of the Traveler's. They'd had an axe murder there several years earlier. Or was that the Uptown Motel? Hammer couldn't remember.

'How do you stay in shape,' Panesa continued the small talk.

'I walk whenever I can. I don't eat fat,' Hammer replied, digging in her purse for lipstick.

'That's not fair. I know women who walk on the treadmill an hour every day, and their legs don't look like yours,' Panesa observed. 'I want to know precisely what the difference is.'

'Seth eats everything in my house,' Hammer was out with it. 'He eats so much, I lose my appetite on a regular basis. You know what it does to you to walk in at eight o'clock, after a hellish day, and see your husband parked in front of the TV, watching "Ellen," eating his third bowl of Hormel chili with beef and beans?'

Then the rumors were true, and Panesa suddenly felt sorry for Hammer. The publisher of the *Charlotte Observer* went home to no one but a housekeeper who prepared chicken breasts and spinach salads. How awful for Hammer. Panesa looked over at his peer in satin and beads. Panesa took the risk of reaching out and patting Hammer's hand.

'That sounds absolutely awful,' the publisher sympathized.

'I actually need to lose a few pounds,' Hammer confessed. 'But I tend to put it on around my middle, not my legs.'

Panesa searched for parking around the Carillon, where Morton's Of Chicago steak house was doing quite a business without them. 'Watch your door there. Sorry,' Panesa said. 'I'm a little close to the meter. I don't guess I need to put anything in it?'

'Not after six,' said Hammer, who knew.

She thought how nice it would be to have a friend like Panesa. Panesa thought how nice it would be to go sailing with Hammer, or jet skiing, or do lunch or Christmas shopping together, or just talk in front of the fire. Getting drunk was also a thought when, normally, it was a big problem for the publisher of a nationally acclaimed newspaper or the chief of a formidable police department. Hammer had overdone it with Seth now and then, but it was pointless. He ate. She passed out. Panesa had gotten drunk alone, which was worse, especially if he had forgotten to let the dog back in.

Being drunk was a rarified form of beaming-out-of-here, and it was all about timing. It was not something that Hammer ever discussed with anyone. Panesa did not, either. Neither of them had a therapist at this time. This was why it was rather much a miracle that the two of them, after three glasses of wine, got on the subject while someone from USBank was pontificating about economic incentives and development and company relocations and the nonexistent crime rate in Charlotte. Panesa and Hammer hardly touched the salmon with dill sauce. They switched to Wild Turkey. Neither of them fully recalled receiving their awards, but all who witnessed it thought Hammer and Panesa were animated, witty, gracious, and articulate.

On the way home, Panesa got the daring idea of tucking his car near Latta Park in Dilworth, and playing tunes, and talking, with headlights out. Hammer was not in the mood to go home. Panesa knew that going home was soon followed by getting up in the morning and going to work. His career was not as interesting as it used to be, but he had yet to admit this even to himself. His children were busy with involved lives. Panesa was dating a lawyer who liked watching tapes of Court TV and talking about what she would have done differently. Panesa wanted out.

'I guess we should go,' Hammer volunteered, about an hour into their sitting inside the dark Volvo and talking.

'You're right,' said Panesa, who had a trophy in the back seat and an emptiness in his heart. 'Judy, I have to say something.'

'Please,' said Hammer.

'Do you have a friend or two you just have fun with?'

'No.'

'I don't either,' Panesa confessed. 'Don't you think that's rather incredible?'

Hammer took a moment to analyze. 'No,' she decided. 'I never had a friend or two. Not in grammar school when I was better than everyone in kickball. Not in high school, when I was good in math and the president of the student body. Not in college. Not in the police academy, now that I think about it.'

'I was good in English,' Panesa thought back. 'And dodgeball, I guess. A president of the Bible Club one year, but don't hold that against me. Another year on the varsity basketball team, but horrible, fouled out the one game I played in when we were forty points behind.'

'What are you getting at, Richard?' asked Hammer, whose nature it was to walk fast and rush to the point.

Panesa was silent for a moment. 'I think people like us need friends,' he decided.

West needed friends, too, but she would never admit this to Brazil, who was determined to solve every crime in the city that night. West was smoking. Brazil was eating a Snickers bar when the scanner let them know that any unit in the area of Dundeen and Redbud might want to look for a dead body in a field. Flashlights cut across darkness, the sound of feet moving through weeds and grass, as Brazil and West searched the dark. He was obsessed and managed to get ahead of West, his flashlight sweeping. She grabbed him by the back of his shirt, yanking him behind her, like a bad puppy.

'You mind if I go first?' West asked him.

Panesa stopped in Fourth Ward, in front of Hammer's house, at twenty minutes past one A.M. 'Well, congratulations on your award,' Panesa said again.

'And to you,' Hammer said, gripping the door handle.

'Okay, Judy. Let's do this again one of these days.'

'Absolutely. Award or not.' Hammer could see the TV flickering through curtains. Seth was up, and probably eating a Tombstone pizza.

'I really appreciate your allowing Brazil to be out with your folks. It's been good for us,' Panesa said.

'For us, too.'

'So be it. Anything innovative, I'm all for it,' said Panesa. 'Doesn't happen often.'

'Rare as hen's teeth,' Hammer agreed.

'Isn't that the truth.'

'Absolutely.'

Panesa controlled his impulse to touch her. 'I need to go,' he said.

'It's late,' she completely agreed.

Hammer finally lifted the door handle, letting herself out. Panesa drove off in the direction of his empty house and felt blue. Hammer walked into her space, where Seth lived and ate, and was lonely.

* * *

West and Brazil were working hard and unmindful of the time. They had just pulled up to the federally subsidized housing project of Earle Village and entered apartment 121, where there were suspicious signs of money. A computer was on the coffee table, along with a lot of cash, a calculator, and a pager. An elderly woman was composed on the couch, her raging old drunk boyfriend dancing in front of her, his finger parried at her. Police were in the room, assessing the problem.

'She pulled a .22 revolver on me!' the boyfriend was saying.

'Ma'am,' West said. 'Do you have a gun?'

'He was threatening me,' the woman told Brazil.

Her name was Rosa Tinsley, and she was neither drunk nor excited. In fact, she didn't get this much attention except once a week, when the police came. She was having a fine time. Billy could just hop around, threaten away, like he always did when he went to the nip joint and lost money in poker.

'Come in here doing all his drug deals,' Rosa went on to Brazil. 'Gets drunk and says he's gonna cut my throat.'

'Are there drugs here?' West asked.

Rosa nodded at Brazil, and gestured toward the back of the house. 'The shoe box in my closet,' she announced.

Chapter Fourteen

There were many shoe boxes in Rosa's closet, and West and Brazil went through all of them. They found no drugs, the boyfriend was evicted, and Rosa was rewarded with instant gratification. West and Brazil headed back to their car. Brazil felt they had accomplished a good thing. That rotten, stinking, besotted old man was out of there. The poor woman would have some peace. She was safe.

'I guess we got rid of him,' Brazil commented with pride.

'She was just scaring him, like she does once a week,' West replied. 'They'll be back together by the time we drive off.'

She started the engine, watching the old boyfriend in her rearview mirror. He was standing on the sidewalk, carrying his things, staring at the dark blue Crown Victoria, waiting for it to disappear.

'One of these days he'll probably kill her,' West added.

She hated domestic cases. Those and dog bite reports were the most unpredictable and dangerous to the police. Citizens called the cops, and then resented the intervention. It was all very irrational. But perhaps the worst feature of people like Rosa and their boyfriends was the codependency, the inability to do without the other, no matter how many times partners brandished knives and guns, slapped, stole, and threatened. West had a difficult time dealing with people who wallowed in dysfunction, and went from one abusive relationship to the next, never gaining insight, and hurting life. It was her opinion that Brazil should not live with his mother.

'Why don't you get an apartment, and be on your own for once?' West said to him.

'Can't afford it.' Brazil typed on the MDT.

'Sure you can.'

'No, I can't.' He typed some more. 'A one-bedroom apartment in a decent neighborhood is about five hundred a month.'

'So?' West looked over at him. 'And your car is paid for, right? You owe any money to Davidson?'

It wasn't any of her business.

'You could afford it,' West preached on. 'What you got is a sick relationship. You don't get away from her, you'll grow old together.'

'Oh really?' Brazil looked up at West, not appreciating her remarks in the least. 'You know all about it, do you?'

'I'm afraid so,' West said. 'In case you haven't figured it out yet, Andy, you aren't the first person in the world to have a codependent, enabling relationship with a parent or spouse. Your mother's crippling, self-destructive disease is her choice. And it serves one important function. It controls her son. She doesn't want you to leave, and guess what? So far you haven't.'

* * *

This was also Hammer's problem, although she had yet to face it fully. Seth, too, was a cripple. When his powerful, handsome wife breezed in with her trophy in the early morning hours, he was surfing hundreds of cable channels made possible by his eighteen-inch satellite dish on the back porch. Seth liked country western music, and was looking for just the right band. It was not true that he was eating a Tombstone pizza. That had been earlier, when it had gotten to be midnight and his wife still was not home. Now he was working on popcorn drenched with real butter he had melted in the microwave.

Seth Bridges had never been much to look at. Physical beauty was not what had attracted Judy Hammer to him long ago in Little Rock. She had loved his intelligence and gentle patience. They had started out as friends, the way everyone would, were the world filled with good sense. The problem lay in Seth's capacity. He grew as his wife did for the first ten years. Then he maxed out, and simply could stretch no further as a spiritual, enlightened, big-thinking entity. There was no other way to broaden himself unless he did so in the flesh. Eating, frankly, was what he now did best.

Hammer locked the front door and reset the burglar alarm, making sure the motion sensors were on stay. The house smelled like a movie theater, and she detected a hint of pepperoni beneath a buttery layer of chilled air. Her husband was stretched out on the couch, crunching, fingers shiny with grease as he stuffed popcorn inside a mouth that never completely rested. She walked through the living room without comment as stations changed as fast as Seth could point and shoot. In her bedroom, she angrily set the trophy on the floor, in a closet, with others she never remembered.

She was overwhelmed with fury, and slammed the door,

tore her clothes off, and threw them in a chair. She put on her favorite nightshirt, and grabbed her pistol out of her pocketbook, and walked back out into the living room. She'd had it. No more. Enough. Every mortal had limits. Seth froze mid-shovel when his wife marched in, armed.

'Why drag it out?' she said, towering over him in blue and white striped cotton. 'Why not just kill yourself and get it over with? Go ahead.'

She racked the pistol and offered it to him, butt first. Seth stared at it. He had never seen her like this, and he propped himself up on his elbows.

'What happened tonight?' he asked. 'You and Panesa get into a fight or something?'

'Quite the opposite. If you want to end it, go ahead.'

'You're crazy,' he said.

'That's right, well on my way to it, thanks to you.' His wife lowered the gun and put the safety on. 'Seth, tomorrow you go for help. A psychiatrist and your primary care physician. You straighten yourself out. Starting this minute. You're a pig. A slob. A bore. You're committing slow suicide and I do not intend to watch a minute longer.' She snatched the bowl of popcorn out of his oily hands. 'You don't get it fixed, I'm out of here. Period.'

Brazil and West also were suffering aftershocks from their confrontation in her unmarked car. They had continued arguing about his living situation, by now both of them in a lather as they drove through another rough area of the city. Brazil was glaring at her, and not particularly cognizant of the area or its bad people who were thinking violent thoughts about the cop car cruising past. Brazil wondered what possessed him to want to spend so much of his valuable time with this rude, insensitive, inappropriate deputy chief who was old and backward and, in truth, a jerk.

It seemed that fighting was a cloud layer over the Queen City, and Panesa's pleasant mood had deteriorated as well when his lawyer friend called at the precise moment Hammer was locking her bedroom door and West was telling Brazil to grow up and Bubba was on the prowl in his King Cab. The lawyer had been thinking about Panesa, whom she had observed on the late news, in his stunning tuxedo, receiving a trophy. The lawyer was thinking about Panesa and his silver hair, and wanted to drop by and maybe stay over. Panesa made it clear that this was not possible, and never would be again, as Bubba parked in dark shadows near Latta Park.

Bubba was in camouflage, a black cap pulled low. When he stealthily reached West's house, he was pleased that she wasn't home. Bubba could only suppose that she was being screwed by her sissy boyfriend, and Bubba smiled as he imagined her getting screwed again by Bubba, as he sneaked closer to the front of the brick house. His intention wasn't felonious but would ruin the bitch's mood when she couldn't open her front or back doors because someone had filled the locks with Super Glue. This idea had come from yet another of his anarchist manuals, and might well have worked like a charm had circumstances not conspired against him as he unfolded his Buck knife and cut off the tip from the tube of glue.

A car was coming, and Bubba wisely supposed it might be the cop returning home. It was too late to run, and he dove into the hedge. The Cavalier wagon passed, carrying Ned Toms to The Fish Market, where he was about to start his shift, unpacking seafood from boxes of ice. He noticed a big dog moving around in bushes in front of a house where he often saw an unmarked cop car parked, then his Cavalier was gone like a breeze.

Bubba emerged from the hedge, his fingers glued together and left hand completely fastened to the right inner thigh of his fatigues. He rapidly hobbled away, looking remarkably like a hunchback. He could not unlock his truck or drive without freeing one hand, and this required his removing his pants, which he was in the process of doing when Officer Wood happened by on routine patrol, checking the park for perverts. Bubba was arrested for indecent exposure.

West and Brazil heard the call over the scanner, but were not even close, and were busy discussing Brazil's life.

'What the hell do you know about my mother or why I choose to take care of her?' Brazil was saying.

'I know a lot. Social services, juvenile court, are overwhelmed by cases just like yours,' West said.

'I've never been a social service case. Or in juvenile court.'

'Yet,' she reminded him.

'Mind your own business for once.'

'Get a life,' she said. 'Declare your independence. Go out on a date.'

'Oh, so now I don't date, either,' he snapped.

She laughed. 'When? While you're brushing your teeth? You're out every night working, and then show up in the newsroom by nine, after you've run your ass off around the track and hit a million tennis balls. You tell me when you date, Andy? Huh?'

Fortunately, Radar the dispatcher hailed them exactly at this moment. Apparently there was an assault on Monroe Road.

'Unit 700 responding,' Brazil irritably said into the mike.

'They call you Night Voice,' West told him.

'Who's they?' he wanted to know.

'Cops. They know when you get on the radio that you're not me.'

'Because my voice is deeper? Or maybe because I use proper grammar?' he said.

West was making her way through more menacing-looking government-subsidized housing. She was constantly checking her mirrors. 'Where the hell are my backups?' she said.

Brazil had his eye on something else, and excitedly pointed. 'White van, EWR-117,' he said. 'From the APB earlier.'

The van was moving slowly around a corner, and West sped up. She flipped on lights and siren, and twenty minutes later, cops hauled someone else to jail as West and Brazil drove on.

Radar wasn't finished with them yet. A call came in for a car broken into at Trade and Tryon, and he assigned this to unit 700, as well, while other cops rode around with nothing much to do.

'Subject a black male, no shirt, green shorts. May be armed,' Radar's voice came over the scanner.

At the scene, West and Brazil discovered a Chevrolet Caprice with a smashed windshield. The upset owner, Ben Martin, was a law-abiding citizen. He'd had his fill of crime and violence, and did not deserve to have his brand new Caprice mauled like this. For what? His wife's coupon book that looked like a wallet in the back seat? Some shithead hooligan destroyed Martin's hard-earned ride to get fifty cents off Starkist albacore tuna, or Uncle Ben's, or Maxwell House?

'Last night, same thing happened to my neighbor over there,' Martin was explaining to the cops. 'And the Baileys over there got hit the night before that.'

What had gone wrong in the world? Martin remembered being a boy in Rock Hill, South Carolina, where they did not lock their doors, and a burglar alarm was when you walked in on the sucker cleaning you out and he was surprised. So you beat the fool out of him, and that was the end of it. Now there was nothing but randomness, and strangers brutalizing a new Caprice for manufacturer's coupons camouflaged by a red fabric wallet fastened with Velcro.

Brazil happened to notice a black male in green shorts running a block away, headed toward the dark, ancient Settlers Cemetery. 'That's him!' Brazil shouted.

'Get on the radio!' West ordered.

She took off. It was instinct, and had nothing to do with reality, which revealed her as a middle-aged, out of shape, Bojangles-addicted smoker. She was at least a hundred feet behind the subject and already heaving. She was sweating and clumsy, her body and heavy Sam Browne belt simply not designed for this. The bastard had no shirt on, his muscles rippling beneath gleaming ebony skin. He was a damn lynx. How the hell was she supposed to catch something like this? No way. Subjects didn't used to be this fit. They didn't used to drink Met-Rx and have fitness clubs in every jail.

Even as she was thinking these thoughts, Brazil passed her, flying like an Olympic athlete. He was gaining on

Green Shorts, closing in as they entered the cemetery. Brazil zeroed in on the muscular V-shaped back. This dude had maybe five percent body fat, was shiny with sweat, running his scrawny butt off, and believing he would get away with stealing that coupon book. Brazil shoved him as hard as he could from the rear, and sent him sprawling to the grass, coupons fluttering. Brazil jumped on top of Green Shorts and dug a knee in the common thief's spine. Brazil pressed his Mag-Lite, like a gun, against Green Shorts's skull.

'*Move I'll blow your brains out motherfucker!*' Brazil screamed.

He looked up, proud of himself. West had finally gotten around to showing up, heaving and sweating. She would have a heart attack, of this she was certain.

'I stole that line from you,' Brazil told her.

She managed to detach handcuffs from the back of her belt, having no clear recollection of when she might have used them last. Was it when she was a sergeant and got in a foot pursuit with a sh'im in Fourth Ward, way back when, or in Fat Man's? She felt lightheaded, blood pounding her neck and ears. West traced her deterioration back to her thirty-fifth year, when coincidentally, Niles had deposited himself on her back stoop one Saturday night. Abyssinians were exotic and quite expensive. They were also difficult and eccentric, possibly explaining why Niles had been available for adoption. Even West had moments when she wanted to boot him out the car door on one of life's highways. Why the scrawny, cross-eyed kitten with memories of the pyramids had picked West remained unknown.

The stress brought on by Niles's addition to the family precipitated a self-destructiveness in West that had nothing to do with her growing isolation as she continued to get promoted in a man's world. Her increased smoking, consumption of fat and beer, and her refusal to exercise were completely unrelated to her breaking up with Jimmy Dinkins, who was allergic to Niles, and, frankly, hated the cat to the point of pulling his gun on Niles one night when Dinkins and West were arguing and Niles decided to insert himself by pouncing on Dinkins from the top of the refrigerator.

West was still sweating, her breathing labored, as she led their prisoner back to the car. She thought she might throw up.

'You got to quit smoking,' Brazil said to her.

West stuffed the subject into the back of the car, and Brazil climbed in the front.

'You got any idea how much fat's in Bojangles, and all that other shit you eat?' Brazil went on.

Their prisoner was silent, his eyes bright with hate in the rearview mirror. His name was Nate Laney. He was fourteen. He would kill these white cops. All he needed was a chance. Laney was bad and had been since birth, according to his biological mother, who also had always been bad, according to her own mother. This bad seed could be traced back to a prison in England, where the original bad seed had been shipped out to this country, around the same time the troops in the Queen City had been chasing Cornwallis down the road.

'I bet you never exercise.' Brazil did not know when to quit.

West gave him a look as she wiped her flushed face with a tissue. Brazil had just sprinted a hundred yards and wasn't even breathing. She felt old and crabby, and sick and tired of this kid and his naive, self-righteous opinions. Life was entirely more complicated that he thought, and he would begin to see it for himself after he'd been out here a year or two, with nothing but fried chicken places on every corner. Bojangles, Church's, Popeye's, Chic N Grill, Chick-Fil-A, Price's Chicken Coop. Plus, cops didn't make much money, certainly not in their early years, so even off-duty options for dining were limited to the pizza, burgers, and bar food that were plentiful in Charlotte, where citizens loved their Hornets and Panthers and Nascar race-car drivers.

'When was the last time you played tennis?' Brazil asked as their prisoner plotted in the backseat.

'I don't remember,' she said.

'Why don't we go out and hit some.'

'You need your head examined,' she said.

'Oh come on. You used to be good. I bet you used to be in shape, too,' he said.

The massive concrete jail was in the heart of downtown. It had been built at the same time as the big new police department, in this city that enjoyed a crime clearance rate that exceeded the actual number of cases, according to some. There were many levels of security to go through at the jail, starting with lockers where police were to deposit their guns on the way in. At a desk, deputies checked all who entered, and Brazil looked around, taking in yet another new, scary place. A Pakistani woman in dark clothing and a veil was being processed for shoplifting. Drunks, thieves, and the usual drug dealers were being herded by cops, while the sheriff's department supervised.

In the Central Warrant Repository, West searched her prisoner, emptying his pockets of Chap Stick, one dollar and thirteen cents, and a pack of Kools. She shuffled through his paperwork. He was happy now, laughing, full of himself, checking to see who was watching Nate the Man.

'You able to read?' West asked him.

'My bond on there?' Her prisoner was jailing, wearing three pairs of boxer shorts, two pairs of shorts, the outer ones green, falling off, no belt, looking around and unable to stand still.

''Fraid not,' West said.

Inside blue metal solitary holding cells, another young boy beyond redemption stared out with forlorn, killing eyes. Brazil stared back at him. Brazil looked at the Holding Area, where a cage was packed with men waiting to be transported to the jail on Spector Drive until the Department of Corrections transferred them to Camp Green or Central Prison. The men were quiet, peering out, gripping bars like animals in the zoo, nothing else to do in their jailhouse orange.

'I ain't been in here in a while,' West's prisoner let her know.

'How long's a while?' West completed an inventory of Nate the Man's belongings.

Nate Laney shrugged, moving around, looking. ''Bout two months,' he said.

Chapter Fifteen

West and Brazil ended their ride with breakfast at the Presto Grill. He was wide-eyed and ready for adventure. She was worn out, a new day just begun. She went home long enough to notice a tube of Super Glue in her shrubbery. Nearby was an open Buck knife. She barely remembered hearing something on the scanner about a subject exposing himself in Latta Park. It seemed glue was involved. West bagged possible evidence, getting an odd feeling about why it might have landed in her yard. She fed Niles. At nine A.M., West accompanied Hammer through the atrium of City Hall.

'What the hell are you doing with a summons book in your car?' Hammer was saying, walking fast.

This had gone too far. Her deputy chief had been out all night in foot pursuits. She had been locking people up.

'Just because I'm a deputy chief doesn't mean I can't enforce the law,' West said, trying to keep up, nodding at people they passed in the corridor.

'I can't believe you're writing tickets. Morning, John. Ben. Locking people up. Hi, Frank.' She greeted other city councilmen. 'You're going to end up in court again. As if

I can spare you. Your summons book gets turned in to me today.'

West laughed. This was one of the funniest things she'd heard in a while. 'I will not!' she said. 'What did you tell me to do? Huh? Whose idea was it for me to go back out on the street?' Her sleep deficit was making her giddy.

Hammer threw her hands up in despair as they walked into a room where a special city council meeting had been called by the mayor. It was packed with citizens, reporters, and television crews. People instantly were on their feet, in an uproar, when the two women police officials walked in.

'Chief!'

'Chief Hammer, what are we going to do about crime in the east end?'

'Police don't understand the black community!'

'We want our neighborhoods back!'

'We build a new jail but don't teach our children how to stay out of it!'

'Business downtown has dropped twenty percent since these serial killing–car jackings started!' another citizen shouted.

'What are we doing about them? My wife's scared to death.'

Hammer was up front now, taking the microphone. Councilmen sat around a polished horseshoe-shaped table, polished brass nameplates marking their place in the city's government. All eyes were on the first police chief in Charlotte's history to make people feel important, no matter where they lived or who they were. Judy Hammer was the only mother some folks had ever known, in a way, and her deputy was pretty cool, too, out there with the rest of them, trying to see for herself what the problems were.

'We will take our neighborhoods back by preventing the next crime,' Hammer spoke in her strong voice. 'Police can't do it without your help. No more looking the other way and walking past.' She, the evangelist, pointed at all. 'No more thinking that what happens to your neighbor is your neighbor's problem. We are one body.' She looked around. 'What happens to you, happens to me.'

No one moved. Eyes never left her as she stood before all and spoke a truth that power brokers from the past had not wanted the people to hear. The people had to take their streets, their neighborhoods, their cities, their states, their countries, their world, back. Each person had to start looking out his window, do his own bit of policing in his own part of life, and get irate when something happened to his neighbor. Yes sir. Rise up. Be a Minute Man, a Christian soldier.

'Onward,' Hammer told them. 'Police yourself and you won't need us.'

The room was frenzied. That night, West was ironically reminded of the overwhelming response as she and Brazil sped past the stadium rising eerily, hugely against the night, filled with crazed, cheering fans celebrating Randy Travis. West's Crown Victoria was directed and in a hurry as it passed the convention center, where a huge video display proclaimed WELCOME TO THE QUEEN CITY. In the distance, cop cars went fast, lights strobing blue and red, protesting another terrible violation. Brazil, too, could not help but think of the timing, after all Hammer had said this morning. He was angry as they drove.

West knew fear she would not show. How could this happen again? What about the task force she had handpicked, the Phantom Force, as it had been dubbed, out day and night to catch the Black Widow Killer? She could not help but think of the press conference, and its excerpts on radio and television. West was tempted to wonder if this might be more than coincidental, as if someone was making a mockery of Charlotte and its police and its people.

The killing had occurred off Trade Street, behind a crumbling brick building where the stadium and the Duke Power transfer station were in close view. West and Brazil approached the disorienting strobing of emergency lights, heading toward an area cordoned off by yellow crime-scene tape. Beyond were railroad tracks and a late-model white Maxima, its driver's door open, interior light on, and bell dinging. West flipped open her portable phone and tried her boss's number again. For the past ten minutes, the phone had been busy because Hammer had one son on call waiting, and the other on the line. When Hammer hung up, her phone immediately rang with more bad news.

Four minutes later, she drove out of her Fourth Ward neighborhood in a hurry as West folded the phone and handed it to Brazil. He returned it to the leather case on his belt, where there was plenty of room since volunteers packed light. Brazil was pleased to attach anything to his belt that was *road legal*, a Charlottean term, the etymology of which could be traced back to Nascar gods and the rockets they drove, not one of which, in fact, was permitted on life's highways unless it was chained to a trailer. Brazil envied what most cops complained about. Backaches, inconvenience, and being encumbered did not enter his mind.

Of course, he carried a radio with channels for all response areas, the antenna stubby and prone to probe very short officers' armpits. Brazil also wore a pager no one ever called, a Mini Mag-Lite with two-thousand-two-hundred candlepower in its black leather holster, and West's cellular phone, because he was not allowed to carry the *Observer*'s cellular phone when he was in uniform. Brazil had no gun or pepper spray. His ultra duty belt was without expandable baton, nightstick ring, double magazine holders, handcuffs, or double cuff case. Brazil lacked a long flashlight case, or Pro-3 duty holster, or clip holder, and had not a single molded belt keeper, or for that matter, a silent keyholder with Velcro wraparound flap.

West had all this and more. She was fully loaded, and Niles could hear her coming from the far reaches of the city. Minute by minute, the seven-pound Abyssinian waited for the sound, listening for the beloved clanking and creaking and heavy landings. His disappointment was becoming chronic and broaching unforgivable as he sat in his window over the sink, watching and waiting, and increasingly fixated by the USBank Corporate Center (USBCC) dominating the sky. Niles in his earlier lives had been intimate with the greatest erections in all of civilization, the pyramids, the magnificent tombs of pharaohs.

In the fantasies of Niles, USBCC was the giant King Usbeecee, with his silver crown, and it was simply a matter of time before his majesty shook loose of his moorings. He would turn right and left, looking at his feeble neighbors. Niles imagined the King stepping slowly, heavily, feeling his way, shaking earth, for the first time. He aroused Niles's fearful reverence because the King had no smile, and when his eyes caught the sun and turned gold, they were overpowering, as was the mighty monarch's sheer weight. King Usbeecee could step on the *Charlotte Observer*, the entire police department, all of the LEC and City Hall. He could crush the entire force of armed officers, and their chief and deputy chiefs, the mayor, the newspaper's publisher, reducing all to precast dust.

Hammer got out of her car and wasted no time striding through her detectives and uniformed police. She ducked under the tape with its bright yellow warning that always made her ache and fear, no matter where she saw it. Hammer was not in the form she would have liked, having even more on her mind than usual. Since her ultimatum to Seth, her quality of life had radically disintegrated. He had not gotten up this morning, and was mumbling about Dr Kevorkian, living wills, and the Hemlock Society. Seth had pontificated about the silliness of assuming that suicide was selfish, for every adult had the right to be absent.

'Oh for God's sake,' his wife had said. 'Get up and go for a walk.'

'No. You can't make me. I don't have to be in this life if I don't want to be.'

This had prompted her to remove all firearms from their usual spots. Hammer had collected many over the years and had strategically tucked them in various places around the house. Still at large when West had called was Hammer's old faithful Smith & Wesson stainless steel five-shot .38 special with Pachmeyer grips. Hammer was fairly certain it was supposed to be in the drawer of her vanity in her bathroom. She was almost positive this was where it had been last time she had rounded up weapons and locked them in the safe before the grandbabies came to town.

Hammer had many concerns. She was depressed and coping the best she could as anxieties from her press conference, which had involved national media, continued to pluck at her. Politics were what she hated most. They, honestly, were the bane of her existence. *A hundred and five percent clearance rate*. She wished Cahoon could be here in this Godawful place. This was what he needed to see. The Cahoons of the world lose it, wouldn't be able to handle it, would pale and flee. This gory dead businessman was not about appearances or economic development or the tourist industry. This overgrown, creepy thicket flickering with fireflies near railroad tracks, this Thrifty rental car, open and dinging, was about reality.

Hammer spoke to no one as she approached tragedy, and blue and red lights lit up her hard, distressed face. She joined West and Brazil near the Maxima as Dr Odom arranged another black pouch around another body. The medical examiner's gloved hands were bloody, and sweat dripped in his eyes as his heart beat slow and with force. He had dealt with the savagery of sexual homicide most of his life, but nothing like this. Dr Odom was a compassionate man, but he was tough. He had learned long ago to keep himself in check and not relate too closely. It was sad but true that it was easier for him to be clinical when the victims were women or obvious gays not getting along or, in some cases, foreigners. It had been comfortable for him to categorize.

Dr Odom was feeling increasingly shaky about his homosexual serial-killing theory. This victim happened to be fifty-four-year-old state senator Ken Butler from Raleigh. The last thing Dr Odom intended to imply, in any form or fashion, was that the much-beloved black leader was something less than mainstream. Dr Odom also knew, from his vast experience, that homosexual politicians didn't cruise downtown streets looking for boys. They went to public parks and men's rooms, where they could always swear they were neither exposing themselves nor offering an invitation. They were urinating.

Dr Odom zipped the pouch over blood and naked flesh, covering the blaze-orange hourglass. He looked up at Hammer, and shook his head as he stood. His back was killing him. Brazil was staring into the Maxima, hands in his pockets to make sure he didn't inadvertently touch anything and leave his prints. That would be the end of his career. He might even become a suspect. After all, didn't he coincidentally happen to be in the area every time one of these bodies turned up? He nervously glanced around him, wondering if this might remotely occur to anyone. Dr Odom was busy giving Hammer and West his opinions.

'This is a fucking nightmare,' the medical examiner was saying. 'Jesus Christ.'

He ripped off his gloves, and wasn't quite sure what to do with them. He cast about, looking for a receptacle for biological hazards. Catching the eye of Denny Raines, he gave the paramedic a nod, and the big, handsome guy came through with his stretcher and crew. Raines winked at West, drinking in the sexy sight of her in uniform. She was pretty unbelievable, and Hammer was hot, too. Brazil's eyes fixed on Raines. Brazil got a strange feeling as he watched the overbuilt ambulance attendant eyeing West and Hammer. Brazil wasn't sure what the problem was, but he was suddenly anxious and a little sick to his stomach. He wanted to get in Raines's face, beg him to start something so Brazil could finish it, or at least order Raines to leave the scene.

'Well, it's all yours now,' Dr Odom went on to Hammer as stretcher legs clacked. 'I'm not releasing a damn thing to the media. Never do. Any statement will have to come from you.'

'We're not releasing his identity tonight.' Hammer was adamant. 'Not until he's been positively identified.'

There was no doubt in her mind. His driver's license was on the floor of the Maxima, on the passenger's side. Hammer recognized the senator's imposing stature, the gray hair and goatee, and heavy face. He hadn't survived long enough to have tissue response to his horrendous injuries, no swelling or bruising. Butler did not look so different from when Hammer had seen him last, at a cocktail party in Myers Park. She was terribly upset and determined that it would not show. She approached Brazil. He was prowling around the car, taking notes.

'Andy,' she said, touching his arm. 'I'm sure I don't need to tell you how sensitive this is.'

He got still, looking at her as if she were the reason people went to church every Sunday. She was God. Hammer was distracted as her gaze wandered inside the car, to the black leather briefcase stamped with the gold initials K.O.B. It was in back, open, as were an overnight bag and a suit bag, everything dumped out. She made a silent inventory of keys, a calculator, USAir peanuts and tickets, a portable phone, pens, paper, address book, Tic Tacs, lubricated Trojan condoms, shoes, socks, and Jockey shorts, all scattered by hard, heartless hands.

'Are we sure it's the senator?' Brazil managed to ask.

Hammer gave him her upset eyes again. 'Not sure enough for you to release that yet.'

'Okay,' he said. 'As long as you don't give it to out to someone else first.'

'Never. You do the right thing, so will I,' she said the usual. 'Call me tomorrow at five P.M. I'll give you a statement.'

She walked off. His eyes followed her as she left the crime scene, and ducked under tape, walking briskly through the strobing blue and red night. Television crews, radio reporters, and mobs of reporters darted at her like barracuda. She waved them off and got into her chief's car. Brazil prowled some more, disturbed in a way he did not understand as he got closer to where the senator had been killed. Raines and other paramedics were carrying the body to the ambulance, and the Ace twenty-four-hour towing and recovery truck was rolling in to haul the Maxima to the police department.

The ambulance beeped as it backed up, carrying the dead senator to the morgue while cameras caught it all. Brent Webb watched Brazil with jealous eyes. It wasn't fair Brazil got such special treatment, and could wander around the crime scene with a flashlight as if he belonged there. Brazil's privileged position, his golden touch, would end soon enough, Webb knew. The television reporter smoothed his perfect hair and lubricated his lips with lip balm. He looked sincerely into the camera and told the world the latest tragic news as a Norfolk-Southern train loudly lumbered past.

Chapter Sixteen

Brazil's flashlight swept gravel and weeds at the edge of rusty railroad tracks as the last train car loudly rumbled through the dark, hot night. Coagulating blood glistened bright red in the strong beam, illuminating a dingy washcloth and bloody quarters, pennies, and dimes that must have come out of pockets when the murdered senator's pants were pulled down. Blood and gore clung to kudzu, and there were fragments of skull and brain. Brazil took a deep breath, looking down dark tracks, the skyline huge and bright.

Seth had images of his own blood and gore, and savored the imagined reaction of Chief Wife when she walked into his room and found him on top of his bed, where he sat up now drinking beer, the .38 revolver in his lap. He could not take his eyes off the gun, which was loaded with one Remington +P cartridge. Intermittently, Seth had been spinning the cylinder for hours as he watched 'Friends,' 'Mary Tyler Moore,' and other reruns, and tested his luck. It wasn't good.

So far, out of perhaps a hundred dry runs, he had committed suicide successfully but twice. How could that be possible? Didn't this go against the law of averages? He figured the cartridge should have lined up fatally at least twenty times, since it was a five-shot revolver, and five divided into one hundred was twenty.

He had never been good in math. Seth had never been good in anything, he decided. Everyone would be better off without him, including his wimpy sons and his emasculating wife. She'd benefit the most, walking in, finding him slumped over, shot in the head through a pillow, blood everywhere, finished, end of story. No longer a problem. No more taking fatso Seth places and being ashamed, while younger men still looked at her with interested eyes. Seth would show her. Take that. Let his final chapter haunt her the rest of her big-shot days.

He would never go through with it, Hammer was quite sure of this. Certainly, when she had slid open her vanity drawer and found the .38 missing, it had occurred to the top police officer in Charlotte that her depressed, self-destructive spouse might have a clue as to the gun's whereabouts. And for what? Self-protection. Hardly. Seth rarely remembered to set the burglar alarm. He did not like to shoot and had never carried a gun, not even in Little Rock, when he was a member of the NRA because most people were. Hammer deduced and worried as she drove.

The fool. Wouldn't this be his last and greatest revenge? Suicide was a mean and skulking act, unless one was dying anyway and desired an earlier flight out of pain and suffering. The vast majority of people killed themselves for payback purposes. Some of the nastiest notes Hammer had ever read were the last comments of just such people. She had not much sympathy because there wasn't a soul she knew who didn't bump over bad stretches of life's highways now and again, struggle over long, lonely miles where it entered the mind that maybe one should run off the road, be done with it. Hammer was not exempt. She was well aware of her own spells of destructive eating, drinking, not exercising, laziness. They happened, and she picked herself up and went on. She always chose a better lane, and got healthy again. She would not die, because she was responsible, and people needed her.

She walked into her house, not knowing what she would find. Locking the door, she reset the alarm. The TV was loud in Seth's bedroom across from the kitchen. For a moment, his wife hesitated, tempted to walk back and check, but she couldn't. Suddenly, she was afraid. She headed to her own part of the house, her heart filled with dread as she freshened up in the bathroom. It was late, but she didn't change into her nightshirt yet or pour herself a Dewar's. If he had done it, there would be people all over her property within minutes. There was no point in getting out of her clothes or smelling like booze. Judy Hammer began to cry.

Brazil was thinking about the deal he had made with Hammer as he flew through his story. Still in uniform, he sat before his computer, fingers dancing as he typed and flipped through his notepad. He included incredible detail about this night's Black Widow killing. With photographic total recall, he showed what was inside the car, describing bloody money, and what the police and medical examiner had done, and how violent death felt and smelled and looked. His piece was graphic and moving, but it did not include the victim's identity. Brazil kept his word.

This was very stressful for him. The journalist in him screamed that he had to print the truth, whether it was known for a fact. Brazil was honorable. He could not betray the police. He assuaged himself with the reality that Chief Hammer would never screw him, and he knew that West wouldn't. Brazil would get his quote tomorrow at 5 P.M., and no one, especially Webb, would catch on until they read it in the *Observer* the following morning.

Webb had just come on the air for the eleven o'clock news when Hammer walked into her husband's bedroom. Her heart slowed a little when she saw no blood. Nothing, in the least, stood out. Seth was on his side, head deep in the pillow. Webb's voice was unusually solemn, the killing the lead story.

'. . . the shocking revelation in this night's tragedy is that the victim is believed to be Senator Ken Burton . . .'

Hammer turned to stone, riveted to the TV. Seth sat straight up in bed, startled.

'My God,' Seth exclaimed. 'We just had drinks with him last month.'

'Shhhhhhhhh,' Hammer silenced her self-destructive husband.

'. . . once again, the peculiar symbol of an hourglass was spray-painted on the body. Burton was believed to have been shot at close range with a high-velocity hollowpoint ammunition known as Silvertips . . .'

Hammer snatched up the portable phone from the table by Seth's bed, where there were three Miller Lite cans and a glass of what looked like bourbon.

'Where's my .38?' she said to him as she dialed.

'Got no idea.' He could feel the revolver between his legs, which was not an ideal place for it. But it had rearranged itself when he had fallen asleep.

'. . . sources say his briefcase, tote bag and suit bag were rifled through inside the rental Maxima. Butler had picked up the Thrifty rental car at five-fifteen this afternoon. His money was gone, except for bloody change found under his body. Blood money, as the Black Widow claims number five . . .' Webb's voice lowered, resonating tragic irony.

Brazil was getting his fix of press room sound and fury, and therefore was not at his desk to receive Hammer's call. He watched thousands of newspapers speeding on a conveyor belt. His front page headline was an inch high and blurred, but he could still read it from where he stood.

BLOODY MONEY – BLACK WIDOW CLAIMS NUMBER FIVE

He couldn't quite make out his byline, but he knew it was there. Workers dozed in chairs, waiting for technical problems. Brazil watched one-ton newsprint reels eerily floating up from underground, carried slowly along tracks past barrels of liquid alum, and vats of yellow, red, blue and black ink. Metal clanked as dollies carried newsprint that reminded him of giant rolls of toilet paper. He wandered to the mail room, staring at palates of bundled papers, listening to the loud click-clicking of the Muller Martini machine feeding inserts into papers as a belt carried them into the counting machine. His enthusiasm had left him, for some reason. He felt listless. He was restless, nocturnal again, and still sort of off-line in a way he did not understand.

It was a sweet-sick feeling. His heart was heavy and ached, and when he thought of that beefcake paramedic winking at West and looking at Hammer with lust in his eyes, Brazil felt a tightness and a rage. He felt fright. He experienced the same weak, chilly sensation he associated with barely escaping a car accident or almost losing a tennis match. Was it possible either woman might like Raines, that meatloaf of a paramedic who had to have a meager mental bank account to spend so much time working out? Of late, Brazil recently had caught the rumors about Hammer's pitiful marriage to a fat guy who was unemployed. A dynamic woman like her would have needs and urges. How did Brazil know that she might not go for it, and decide to meet Raines somewhere?

It was important for Brazil's peace of mind and spiritual development that he know Hammer had, in fact, driven straight home. He could not trust her unless he knew, with certainty, that she would not betray him and the world by stooping so low as to sneak around with Denny Raines. Brazil drove quickly through Fourth Ward. He was stunned to see an ambulance parked in front of Hammer's house, and her dark blue police car gleaming in the driveway. Brazil's heart was boxing his ribs as he parked some distance away, staring in horror and disbelief. How in God's name could she be so blatant?

A madness invaded Brazil's otherwise sound mind. He got out of his BMW and strode toward the house of the woman he worshiped but no longer respected or would ever speak to or think of or wonder about again. He would air his righteous thoughts, but there would be no violence unless Raines started it. If so, Brazil would sock him to Oz, ace him, smash him. He tried not to think about Raines's size, or that the paramedic did not appear to be scared of much. Brazil was having second thoughts when Hammer's front door opened.

Raines and another paramedic wheeled out a stretcher bearing a fat older man. Chief Hammer followed and seemed in shock, and Brazil was stunned and baffled in the middle of Pine Street. Hammer was distraught as practiced hands loaded her husband into the ambulance.

'You sure you don't want me to ride with you?' Hammer asked the fat man.

'I'm sure.' The fat man was in pain and sluggish, perhaps from whatever was dripping into him intravenously.

'Well, have it your way,' Hammer told him.

'I don't want her coming,' the fat man instructed Raines.

'Not to worry.' Hammer sounded hurt as she walked back to the house.

She stood in the doorway, watching the ambulance drive off. Squinting, she noticed Brazil on her dark street, staring at her. She recognized him, and it all came back to her. Oh Christ. As if she didn't have problems enough.

'I tried to get you earlier. Give me a chance to explain,' she called out to him.

Now he was completely baffled. 'Excuse me?' He stepped closer.

'Come here.' Hammer wearily motioned to him.

He sat on her porch swing. She turned out the light and sat on the steps, certain this young man must think she was the biggest, most dishonest bureaucrat he had ever encountered. Hammer knew this might be the night her controversial community policing project would go to hell along with everything else.

'Andy,' she began, 'you've got to believe that I said nothing to anyone. I swear I kept my promise to you.'

'What?' He was getting a very bad feeling. 'What promise?'

She realized he did not know. 'Oh God,' she mumbled. 'You didn't hear the news tonight?'

'No, ma'am. What news?' He was getting excited, his voice rising.

Hammer told him about Channel 3 and Webb's scoop.

'That's impossible!' Brazil exclaimed. 'Those are my details! How could he know the stuff about the bloody money, the washcloth, any of it! He wasn't there!'

'Andy, please lower your voice.'

Lights were blinking on. Dogs were barking. Hammer stood.

'It's not fair. I play by the rules.' Brazil felt as if his life were over. 'I cooperate with you, help as much as I can. And get crucified for it.' He got up, too, the swing moving, slowly swaying, and empty.

'You can't stop doing what's right just because others do things that are wrong,' she spoke quietly, and from experience, as she opened the door that would lead her back inside her fine home. 'We've done some pretty wonderful things, Andy. I hope you won't let this ruin it.'

Her face was kind but sad as she looked at him. He felt the ache in his heart, and his stomach was doing something strange, too. He was sweating and chilled as he stared at her, unable to imagine what it must have been like for her children to be raised by such a person.

'Are you all right?' Hammer thought he was acting oddly.

'I don't know what my problem is.' He wiped his face with his hands. 'I think I've been trying to get sick or something. It's none of my business, but is your husband all right?'

'A flesh wound,' she replied, weary and depressed again as moths fluttered past, into her house, where soon they would die from pesticide.

Misfires rarely occurred with double-action revolvers. But when Hammer had demanded that Seth return the .38 to her, he had gotten angry and mean. He'd had enough of being bossed around by this woman, who next would begin searching him and his bedroom. There was no way out. Unfortunately, she'd walked in before he'd had a chance to stash the gun in a place she couldn't find it. Worse, Seth had been sleeping in a drunken position that had resulted in tingling and numbness in his right hand. When he had decided to send this same hand down to his crotch to fish out the revolver, it had not been a wise move. It was also Seth's bad luck that the one time he did not want the cartridge lined up with the firing pin was precisely then.

'His left buttock,' Hammer was explaining to Brazil, who was inside the house with her now, because she could not leave her front door open all night.

Brazil looked around at vibrant oriental rugs on polished hardwood floors, at fine oil paintings and handsome furniture in warm fabrics and rich leathers. He was standing in the foyer of Chief Hammer's splendid restored home, and no one else was around. It was just the two of them, and he began sweating profusely again. If she noticed, she did not let on.

'They'll X-ray, of course,' she was saying, 'to make certain the bullet isn't lodged close to anything important.'

There was a dark side of +P hollowpoints, Hammer

thought. The objective of their design was for the lead projectile to expand and rip through tissue like a Roto Rooter. Rarely did the bullets exit, and there was no telling how much lead was scattered through Seth's formidable lower region. Brazil was listening to all this, wondering if the chief would ever get around to calling the police.

'Chief Hammer,' Brazil finally felt compelled to speak. 'I don't guess you've called this in?'

'Oh dear.' It hadn't even occurred to her. 'You're absolutely right. I guess a report has to be taken.' She began pacing as the reality hit. 'Oh no, oh no. That's all I need! So now I get to hear about this on TV, the radio. In your paper. This is awful. Do you realize how many people will enjoy this?' She envisioned Cahoon sitting in his crown, laughing as he read about it.

POLICE CHIEF'S HUSBAND SHOOTS SELF
RUSSIAN ROULETTE SUSPECTED

No one would be fooled, not for a minute. A depressed, unemployed, obese husband in bed with his wife's .38 loaded with only one cartridge? Every cop who worked for Hammer would know that her husband had been flirting with suicide. All would know that there were serious problems in her house. Some would even suspect that she had shot her husband and knew exactly how to get away with it. Maybe it wasn't his left buttock she had been aiming at, either. Maybe he had turned around just in the nick of time. Hammer went into the kitchen and reached for the phone.

There was simply no way she was dialing 911 and having the call broadcast to every cop, paramedic, reporter, and person who owned a scanner in the region. She got the duty captain on the line. It happened to be Horgess. He was fiercely loyal to his boss, but not especially quick-thinking or known for shrewd judgment.

'Horgess,' she said. 'I need an officer over to my house ASAP to take a report. There's been an accident.'

'Oh no!' Horgess was upset. If anything ever happened to his chief, he'd answer directly to Goode. 'Are you all right?'

She paced. 'My husband's at Carolinas Medical. I'm afraid he had an accident with a handgun. He should be fine.'

Horgess immediately grabbed his upright portable radio. He ten-fived David-One unit 538, a rookie too scared to do anything other than what she was told. This decision would have been good had Horgess not failed to overlook the reason Hammer had called him, the duty captain, directly.

'Need you over there *now* to take an accidental shooting report,' Horgess excitedly said into his radio.

'Ten-four,' Unit 538 came back. 'Any injuries?'

'Ten-four. Subject en route to Carolinas Medical.'

Every officer on duty, and some who weren't, and anyone else with a scanner, heard every word of the broadcast. Most assumed Chief Hammer had been accidentally shot, meaning Jeannie Goode this very instant was the acting chief. Nothing could have sent the force into more of a panic. Hammer had a base radio station in her kitchen and it was on.

'Horgess, you idiot!' she exclaimed in disbelief to no one in particular, inside her kitchen.

She stopped pacing. It struck her that Andy Brazil was still standing in the doorway. She was not entirely sure why he was here and suddenly doubted the wisdom of a handsome young reporter dressed like a cop being in the house with her, in the wake of a domestic shooting. Hammer also knew that her entire evening shift was heading toward her address, flying to investigate the fate of their leader.

Goode never kept her radio on at home or in her car, but a source had tipped her off, and she was already putting on her uniform, preparing to take over the Charlotte Police Department, as Unit 538 sped through Fourth Ward. Unit 538 was terrified. She worried she might have to stop to vomit. She turned on Pine Street, and was stunned to find five other police cars already in front of Hammer's house, lights strobing. In Unit 538's rearview mirror, more cars came, miles of them, speeding through the night to help their fallen chief. Unit 538 parked, shakily gathered her metal clipboard, wondering if she could just leave, and deciding probably not.

Hammer went out on the porch to reassure her people. 'Everything is under control,' she spoke to them.

'Then you're not injured,' said a sergeant whose name she did not recall.

'My husband is injured. We don't think it's serious,' she said.

'So everything's okay.'

'Man, what a scare.'

'We're so relieved, Chief Hammer.'

'See you in the morning.' Hammer dismissed them with a wave.

That was all they needed to hear. Each officer secretly keyed his mike, broadcasting several clicks over the air, signaling comrades everywhere that all was ten-four.

Only Unit 538 had unfinished business, and she followed Hammer into the rich, old house. They sat in the living room.

'Before you even start,' Hammer said, 'I'm going to tell you how this is going to be done.'

'Yes, ma'am.'

'There will be no implication that the right thing was not done here, that exceptions were made, because the subject involved happens to be married to me.'

'Yes, ma'am.'

'This is routine and will be worked according to the book.'

'Yes, ma'am.'

'My husband should be charged with reckless endangerment and discharging a firearm in the city limits,' Hammer went on.

'Yes, ma'am.'

Unit 538's handwriting was unsteady as she began filling out the accidental shooting report. This was amazing. Hammer must not like her husband much. Hammer was nailing him with the maximum charge, locking him up and throwing away the key. It just proved Unit 538's theory that women like Hammer got where they were by being aggressive hardasses. They were men poured into the wrong form at the factory. Hammer recited all the necessary information. She answered Unit 538's banal questions, and got the cop out as fast as possible.

Brazil remained seated at the kitchen table in Chief Hammer's house, wondering if anyone might have recognized his distinctive BMW parked out front. If the cops ran his tag, what would they think? Who was he here to see? He remembered with a sinking feeling that the condominiums Axel and friends lived in were just around the corner. Cops with their suspicious minds might think Brazil had parked a street away, trying to fool everybody. If word got back to Axel, he'd believe Brazil was stalking him, had a thing for him.

'Andy, let's wind this up.' Hammer walked in. 'I suppose it's too late to get this in the paper for tomorrow.'

'Yes, chief. The city edition deadline was hours ago,' Brazil replied, glancing at his watch, and startled that she would want a word of this in the paper.

'I'm going to need you to help me, and have to trust that you will, even after what happened with Channel Three,' she said.

There was no one Brazil would rather assist.

Hammer looked at the clock on the wall, in despair. It was almost three A.M. She had to get to the hospital, whether Seth liked it or not, and she needed to be up in three hours. Hammer's body did not appreciate all-nighters anymore, but she would make it. She always did. Her plan was the best she could devise under circumstances which were truly extreme and upsetting. She knew tomorrow's news would bristle with Seth's bizarre shooting and what it might imply. She could not preempt the television and radio stations, but she could at least straighten out the facts the following day with a true, detailed account by Brazil.

Brazil was silent and stunned as he sat in the passenger's seat of Hammer's impeccable Crown Victoria. He took notes while she talked. She told him all about her early life and why she had gone into law enforcement. She talked about Seth, about what a support he had been as she was fighting her way through the ranks of what was truly a male militia. Hammer was exhausted and vulnerable, her personal life in shambles, and she had not been to a therapist in two years. Brazil had caught her at a remarkable time, and he was moved and honored by her trust. He would not let her down.

'It's a perfect example of the world not allowing powerful people to have problems,' Hammer was explaining as she drove along Queens Road West, beneath a canopy of great oak trees. 'But the fact is, all people have problems. We have tempestuous and tragic phases in relationships we don't have time enough to tend to, and we get discouraged and feel we have failed.'

Brazil thought she was the most wonderful person he had ever met. 'How long have you been married?' he asked.

'Twenty-six years.'

She had known the night before her wedding that she was making a mistake. She and Seth had united out of need, not want. She had been afraid to go it alone, and Seth had seemed so strong and capable back then.

As he lay on his stomach in the ER, after X-rays and scrubbing and being rolled all over the place, Seth wondered how this could have happened. His wife had once admired him, valued his opinion, and laughed at his witty stories. They were never much in bed. She had far more energy and staying power, and no matter how he might have wanted to please, he simply could not carry her same tune, didn't have as many pages, usually was snoring by the time she'd returned from the bathroom, ready for the next act.

'Ouch!' he yelled.

'Sir, you're going to have to hold still,' the stern nurse said for the hundredth time.

'Why can't you knock me out or something!' Tears welled in his eyes as he clenched his fists.

'Mr Hammer, you're very fortunate.' It was the triage surgeon's voice now, rattling X-rays that sounded like saw blades. She was a pretty little thing with long red hair. Seth was humiliated that her only perspective on him was his corpulent fanny that had never seen the sun.

Chapter Seventeen

The Carolinas Medical Center was famous for its triage, and patients were med-flighted in from all over the region. This early morning, helicopters were quiet silhouettes on red helipads centered by big H's on rooftops, and shuttle buses moved slowly from parking lots to different areas of the massive concrete complex. The medical center's fleet of ambulances were teal and white, the colors of the Hornets and much of what filled Charlotte with pride.

The entire hospital staff knew that a VIP had arrived. There would be no waiting, no bleeding in chairs, no threatening, no shortcuts or neglect. Seth Hammer, as he had been erroneously registered and referred to most of his marriage, had been taken straight into the ER. He had been rolled in and out of many rooms. He wasn't certain he understood the pretty surgeon's vernacular, but it seemed, according to her, that although the bullet's destruction of tissue had been significant, at least no major arteries or veins had been hit. However, because he was a VIP, no chances could be taken. It was explained that medical personnel would do arteriography, and shoot him full of dye, and see what they found. Then they would give him a barium enema.

Hammer parked in a police slot outside the emergency room at not quite four A.M. Brazil had filled twenty pages in his notepad, and knew more about her than any reporter who had ever lived. She fetched her large pocketbook with its secret compartment, and took a deep breath as she got out. Brazil was struggling with his next question, but had to ask. It was for her own good, too.

'Chief Hammer.' He hesitated. 'Do you suppose I could get a photographer here to maybe get something of you on your way out of the hospital, later?'

She waved him off as she walked. 'I don't care.'

The more she thought about it, the more she realized it didn't matter what he wrote. Her life was over. In the course of one short day, all was lost. A senator had been murdered, the fifth in a series of brutal slayings committed by someone the police were no closer to catching. USBank, which owned the city, was at odds with her. Now her husband had shot himself in the ass while playing Russian roulette. The jokes would be endless. What did this suggest about where he assumed his most vital organ was, after all? Hammer would lose her job. What the hell. She may as well offer her two cents worth on her way out the door. Brazil had just gotten off a pay phone, and was walking fast to keep up with her.

'We'll also be running the Black Widow story, if there's a positive ID,' he nervously reminded her.

She didn't care.

'I'm wondering,' Brazil pushed his luck, 'if you'd have a problem with my slipping in a few details or two that might trick the killer.'

'What?' Hammer glanced blankly at him.

'You know, if I messed with him a little. Well, Deputy

Chief West didn't think it was a good idea, either,' he conceded.

The enlightened chief caught on to what he was suggesting, and was interested. 'As long as you don't release sensitive case details.'

She fixed on the triage nurse in her console, and headed there. No introduction was necessary.

'He's on the way to the OR right now,' the nurse said to the police chief. 'Do you want to wait?'

'Yes,' Hammer decided.

'We have a private room the chaplain uses, if you'd like a little quiet,' the nurse said to this woman who was one of her heroes.

'I'll just sit where everybody else does,' Hammer said. 'Someone might need that room.'

The nurse certainly hoped not. Nobody had died in the last twenty-four hours, and this had better not change on her shift. Nurses always got the raw end of that deal. Doctors suddenly vanished. They were off to their next bit of drama, leaving the nurses to take out tubes, tie on toe tags, wheel the body to the morgue, and deal with bereft relatives who never believed it and were going to sue. Hammer found two chairs in a corner of the reception area. There were maybe twenty distressed people waiting, most accompanied by someone trying to comfort them, most arguing, others moaning and bleeding into towels, or cradling broken limbs, and holding ice on burns. Almost all were weeping, or limping to the restroom, and drinking water from paper cups, and fighting another wave of nausea.

Hammer looked around, pained by what she saw. This was why she had chosen her profession, or why it had chosen her. The world was falling apart, and she wanted to help. She focused on a young man who reminded her of Randy, her son. The young man was alone, five chairs away. He was burning up with fever, sweating and shivering, and having a difficult time breathing. Hammer looked as his earrings, his chiseled face and wasted body, and she knew what was wrong with him. His eyes were shut as he licked cracked lips. It seemed everyone was sitting as far from him as possible, especially those leaking body fluids. Hammer got up. Brazil never took his eyes off her.

The triage nurse smiled at Hammer's approach. 'What can I do for you?' the nurse said.

'Who's the young man over there?' Hammer pointed.

'He's got some sort of respiratory infection.' The nurse became clinical. 'I'm not allowed to release names.'

'I can get his name from him myself,' Hammer told her. 'I want a large glass of water with a lot of ice, and a blanket. And when might your folks get around to seeing him? He looks like he could pass out any minute, and if he does, I'm going to know about it.'

Some seconds later, Hammer was returning to the waiting area with water and a soft folded blanket. She sat next to the young man and wrapped him up. He opened his eyes as she held something to his lips. It was icy cold and wet and felt wonderful. Warmth began to spread over him, and his shivering calmed as his feverish eyes focused on an angel. Harrel Woods had died, and he was relieved as he drank the water of life.

'What's your name?' the angel's voice sounded from far away.

Woods wanted to smile, but his lips bled when he tried.

'Do you have a driver's license with you?' the angel wanted to know.

It blearily occurred to him that even Heaven required

a picture ID these days. He weakly zipped open his black leather butt pack, and handed the license to the angel. Hammer wrote down the information, in the event he might need a shelter somewhere, if he ever got out of here, which wasn't likely. Two nurses were making their way to him with purpose, and Harrel Woods was admitted to the ward for AIDS patients. Hammer returned to her chair, wondering if she might find coffee somewhere. She digressed more about helping people. She told Brazil that when she was growing up, it was all she had wanted to do in life.

'Unfortunately, policing seems to be part of the problem these days,' she said. 'How often do we really help?'

'You just did,' Brazil said.

She nodded. 'And that's not policing, Andy. That's humanity. And we've got to bring humanity back into what we do, or there's no hope. This is not about politics or power or merely rounding up offenders. Policing always has been and always must be about all of us getting along and helping each other. We're one body.'

Seth's body was in dire straits in the OR. His arteriogram was fine and he hadn't leaked any barium from his bowels, but because he was a VIP, no chance would be taken. They had draped and prepped him, and he was face down again, and nurses had pierced his tender flesh repeatedly with excruciatingly painful injections and a Foley catheter, to relieve pain and check his urine for blood, or so he thought he overheard. They had rolled in a tank of nitrogen and connected it to a tube. They began subjecting him to what they called a Simpulse irrigation, which was nothing more than a power wash with saline and antibiotics. They were blasting him with three thousand ccs, suctioning, debriding, as he complained.

'Put me under!' he begged.

There was too much risk.

'Anything!' he whined.

They compromised and gave him an amnesiac they called Midazolam, which did not relieve pain, but caused it to be forgotten, it seemed. Although the bullet was located on the X-ray, they would never locate it in so much fat, not without dicing Seth as if he were destined for a chef salad, the surgeon knew. Her name was Dr White. She was a thirty-year-old graduate of Harvard and Johns Hopkins, and had done her residency at the Cleveland Clinic. Dr White would not have been as concerned about leaving the bullet were it the typical semi-jacketed, round-nosed variety.

But hollowpoints opened like a flower on impact. The deformed missile in the chief's husband had cut a swath, exactly as planned by Remington, and might continue to do damage after the fact. Without question, it put him at considerable risk for infection. Dr White made an incision so the wound could drain, and it was packed and dressed. The sun was rising by the time Dr White met Chief Hammer in recovery, where Seth was groggy, lying on his side, tethered by IV lines, a curtain drawn to give him the privacy afforded VIPs, as set by the medical center's unwritten policy.

'He should be fine,' Dr White was saying to Hammer.

'Thank God,' Hammer said with relief.

'I want to keep him overnight in isolation, and continue the IV antibiotics. If he spikes a fever during the first twenty-four hours, we'll keep him longer.'

'And that could happen.' Hammer's fears returned.

Dr White could not believe she was standing here and

the police chief was looking to her for answers. Dr White had read every article written about this incredible woman. Hammer was what Dr White wanted to be when Dr White was older and powerful. Caring, strong, good-looking, kick-ass in pearls. Nobody pushed Hammer around. It wasn't possible that Hammer put up with the same shit Dr White did, from the old boy surgeons. Most were graduates of Duke, Davidson, Princeton, and UVA, and wore their school bow ties to the symphony and cocktail parties. They didn't think twice when one of their own took a day off to boat on Lake Norman or play golf. But should Dr White need a few hours to go to her gynecologist, to visit her sick mother, or give in to the flu, it was another example of why women didn't belong in medicine.

'Of course, we're not expecting any problem,' Dr White was reassuring Hammer. 'But there is extensive tissue damage.' She paused, searching for a diplomatic way to explain. 'Ordinarily, a bullet of that power and velocity would have exited, when fired at such close range. But in this case, there was too much mass for the bullet to pass through.'

The only image that came to Hammer's mind was tests the firearms examiners conducted by shooting into massive shimmering blocks of ballistic jelly, manufactured by Knox. Brazil was still taking notes. Nobody cared. He was such a respectful, helpful presence, he could have continued following Hammer for years and it would not have been a problem. It was entirely possible she would not have been fully cognizant of it. If her imminent termination were not an inevitability, she might have assigned him to her office as an assistant.

Hammer spent little time with her husband. He was checked out on morphine, and would have nothing to say to her were this not the case. She held his hand for a moment, spoke quiet words of encouragement, felt terrible about all of it, and was so angry with him she could have shot him herself. She and Brazil headed out of the hospital as the region headed to work. He hung back to allow the *Observer* photographer to get dramatic shots of her walking out the ER entrance, head down, grimly following the sidewalk as a Medvac helicopter landed on a nearby roof. Another ambulance roared in, and paramedics rushed to get another patient out as Hammer made her way past.

That photograph of her by the ambulance, a helicopter landing in the background, her eyes cast down and face bravely tragic, was sensational. The next morning, it was staring out from racks, boxes, and stacks of papers throughout the greater Charlotte-Mecklenburg area. Brazil's story was the most stunning profile of courage Packer had ever seen. The entire metro desk was in awe. How the hell did he get all this? Hammer wasn't known for divulging anything personal about herself or her family, and suddenly, in a time when discretion was most vital, she revealed all to this rookie reporter?

The mayor, city manager, city council, and Cahoon were not likewise impressed. They were interviewed by several television and radio reporters, and were openly critical of Hammer, who continued to draw far too much attention to the serial murders and other social problems in the Queen City. It was feared that several companies and a restaurant chain were reconsidering their choice of Charlotte as a new location. Businessmen were canceling meetings. It was rumored that sites for a computer chip manufacturing plant and a Disney theme park were being scouted in Virginia.

Charlotte's mayor, city manager, and several city councilmen promised that there would be a full police investigation into the accidental shooting. Cahoon, in a brief statement, agreed this was fair. The men smelled blood and were crazed by it. Panesa did not often get directly involved in choosing sides, but he rolled up his sleeves on this one and penned an impassioned editorial on the Opinion page that ran Sunday morning.

It was called HORNET'S NEST, and in it, Panesa went into great detail about the city's ills as seen through the eyes of an unflagging, humane woman, their beloved chief, who was embattled by her own demons and yet 'has never let us down or burdened us with her private pain,' Panesa wrote. 'Now is the time to support Chief Hammer, to show her respect and caring, and prove that we, too, can stand up and make the right choices.' Panesa went on to allude to Brazil's story of Hammer in the ER bringing a blanket and water to a young man dying of AIDS. 'That, citizens of Charlotte, is not only community policing, but Christianity,' Panesa wrote. 'Let Mayor Search, city council, or Solomon Cahoon throw the first stone.'

This went on for days, things stirred up, hostility rising from Cahoon's crown and swarming through the mayor's window. Telephone lines angrily buzzed as the city fathers plotted on secure phones, devising a way to run Hammer out of town.

'It's got to be the public that decides,' the mayor said to the city manager. 'The citizens have got to want it.'

'No other way,' Cahoon agreed in a conference call, from his mighty desk, as he viewed his kingdom between aluminum pipes. 'It's entirely up to the citizens.'

The last thing Cahoon wanted was pissed-off people changing banks. If enough of them did and went on to First

Union, CCB, BB&T, First Citizens Bank, or Wachovia, it could catch up with Cahoon and hurt him. It could become an epidemic, infecting the big, healthy investors, like a computer virus, Ebola, salmonella, hemorraghic fever.

'The problem, damn it, is Panesa,' opined the mayor.

Cahoon felt a fresh wave of outrage. He would not soon recover from the publisher's Sunday editorial with its comment about throwing stones. Panesa had to go, too. Cahoon's brain raced through his formidable network, contemplating allies in the Knight-Ridder chain. This would have to come from on high, at the level of chairman or president. Cahoon knew them all, but the media was a goddamn centipede. The minute he gave it a prod, it curled up tight and took care of its own.

'The only person who can control Panesa is you,' the mayor said to Cahoon. 'I've tried. He won't listen to me. It's like trying to talk sense to Hammer. Forget it.'

Both the publisher and the police chief were unreasonable. They had agendas, and had to be stopped. Andy Brazil was becoming a problem, as well. Cahoon had been around the block enough times to know exactly where he would attack.

'Talk to the boy,' Cahoon said to the mayor. 'He's probably been trying to get quotes from you anyway, right?'

'They all do.'

'So let him come see you, Chuck. Pull him over to our side, where he belongs,' Cahoon said with a smile as he gazed out at the hazy summer sky.

Brazil had turned his attention to the Black Widow killings, which he was certain would not stop. He had become obsessed with them, determined that somehow he would uncover that one detail, that important insight or clue that might lead police to the psychopath responsible.

He had gotten FBI profiler Bird on the phone, and had written a chillingly accurate but manipulative story. Last night, Brazil had returned to the train tracks on West Trade Street, to explore the razed brick building, his flashlight shining on crime-scene tape stirred by the wind. He had stood still, looking around that forsaken, frightening place, trying to read the emotion of it. He tried to imagine how the senator had stumbled upon the place.

It was possible the senator had plans to meet someone, back in the dark overgrowth where no one would see. Brazil wondered if the autopsy had revealed drugs. Did the senator have a secret vice that had cost him his life? Brazil had cruised South College Street, looking out at the hookers, still not sure which were men or vice cops. The young one he had seen many times before, and it was obvious that she now recognized him in his BMW as she languidly strolled and boldly stared.

Brazil was tired this morning. He could barely finish four miles at the track and didn't bother with tennis. He hadn't seen much of his mother, and she punished him by not speaking on those rare occasions when she was awake and up. She left him notes of chores she needed done, and was more slovenly than usual. She coughed and sighed, doing all she could to make him miserable and stung with guilt. Brazil continued to think of West's lecture to him about dysfunctional relationships. He heard her words constantly in his head. They pounded with each step he ran, and blinked in the night as he tried to sleep.

He had not seen or talked to West in days and wondered how she was, and why she never called to go shooting or to ride or just to say hi. He felt out of sorts, moody and introverted, and had given up trying to figure out what had gotten into him. He did not understand why Hammer hadn't contacted him to say thanks for his profile. Maybe something in it had pissed her off. Maybe he had gotten a fact wrong. He had really put his heart into that story, and had worked himself almost sick. Panesa seemed to be ignoring him, also, now that Brazil was making a list. Brazil told himself that if he were as important as any one of these powerful people, he would be more sensitive. He would try to think of the little person's feelings, and make that person's day by picking up the phone, or sending a note, or maybe even flowers.

The only flowers West had in her life this moment were the ones Niles had shredded all over the dining-room table. This was after he had scattered litter in the bathroom while his owner was in the shower, her wet bare feet about to step on grit and unpleasant things coated in it. West's mood was volatile, anyway. She was incensed over the storm of controversy surrounding her beloved boss, and fearful of where it all might end. The day Goode became acting chief was the day West moved back to the farm. West knew all about Brazil following Hammer into very private rooms that not even West had entered.

It was all so typical, she thought as she cussed Niles, rinsed her feet and cleaned up the bathroom floor. Brazil used West to gain a foothold with the chief. Brazil had acted like a friend, then the moment he got a chance to ingratiate himself with a higher power, West didn't hear a word from him ever again. Wasn't that the way things went? The son of a bitch. He hadn't called to go shooting, to ride, or even to make sure she was still alive. West discovered what was left of the blood lilies from her garden as Niles darted under the couch.

* * *

The resurrection lilies Hammer carried into Seth's hospital room at ten A.M. were magenta and appropriately named. Hammer set them on a table and pulled a chair close. The bed was raised, allowing her husband to eat, read, visit, and watch TV on his side. His eyes were dull with the strep infection that had invaded from unknown colonies. Fluids and antibiotics ready for combat marched nonstop through narrow tubes and into needles taped to each arm. Hammer was getting frightened. Seth had been in the hospital three nights now.

'How are you feeling, honey?' she asked, rubbing his shoulder.

'Shitty,' he said, eyes wandering back to Leeza on TV.

He had seen, heard, and read the news. Seth knew the terrible thing he had done to himself. Most of all, he knew what he had done to her and his family. Honestly, he had never meant any of it. When he was in his right mind, he'd rather die than hurt anyone. He loved his wife and could not live without her. If he ruined her career in this city, then what? She could go anywhere, and it would be ever so much easier for her to leave him behind, as she had already threatened, if she had to move anyway.

'How are things with you?' Seth mumbled as Leeza argued with a gender-reassigned plumber who had cleavage.

'Don't you worry about me,' Hammer firmly said, patting him again. 'All that matters right now is that you get better. Think positively, honey. The mind affects everything. No negativity.'

This was like telling the dark side of the moon to lighten up a bit. Seth stared at her. He couldn't remember the last time she'd called him *honey*. Maybe never.

'I don't know what to say,' he told her.

She knew precisely what he meant. He was poisoned by remorse and guilt and shame. He had set out to ruin her life and the lives of his children, and was getting good at it. He ought to feel like shit, if the truth was told.

'You don't have to say anything,' Hammer gently reassured him. 'What's done is done. Now we move on. When you leave here, we're going to get you some help. That's all that matters now.'

He shut his eyes and tears swam behind the lids. He saw a young man in baggy white trousers, and bow tie and snappy hat, grinning and happy on a sunny morning as he skipped down the granite steps of the Arkansas state capitol. Seth had been charming and sure of himself once. He had known how to have fun, and party with the rest of them, and tell funny tales. Psychiatrists had tried Prozac, Zoloft, Nortriptylene, and lithium. Seth had been on diets. He had stopped drinking once. He had been hypnotized and had gone to three meetings of Overeater's Anonymous. Then he had quit all of it.

'There's no hope,' he sobbed to his wife. 'Nothing left but to die.'

'Don't you dare say that,' she said, her voice wavering. 'You hear me, Seth? Don't you dare say that!'

'Why isn't my love enough for you!' he cried.

'What love?' She stood, anger peeking around her curtain of self-control. 'Your idea of love is waiting for me to make you happy while you do nothing for yourself. I am not your caretaker. I am not your zookeeper. I am not your innkeeper. I am not your keeper, period.' She was pacing furiously in his small private room. 'I am supposed to be your partner, Seth, your friend, your lover. But you know what? If this were tennis, I'd be playing goddamn singles in a goddamn doubles match on both sides of the net while you sat in the shade hogging all the balls and keeping your own private score!'

Brazil had spent the better part of the morning wondering if he should call West to see if she wanted to play some tennis. That would be innocent enough, wouldn't it? The last thing he wanted was to give her the satisfaction of thinking he cared a hoot that he hadn't heard from her in three and a half days. He parked at the All Right lot on West Trade, near Presto's, and went inside the grill for coffee, starved, but saving himself for something healthy. Later, he'd drop by the Just Fresh, the *eat well feels good* fast food restaurant in the atrium of First Union. That and Wendy's grilled chicken filet sandwiches with no cheese or mayonnaise were about all he lived on these days, and he was losing weight. He secretly wondered if he were getting anorexic.

He sat at the counter, stirring black S&D coffee, waiting for Spike to stop cracking eggs with one hand over a bowl. Brazil wanted to chat. The Michelob Dry clock on the wall over Spike's head read ten-forty-five. There was so much to do, and Brazil had to get it done by four P.M., when his beat for the newspaper formally began. As much as Packer loved Brazil's scoops, the regular news of burglaries, robberies, rapes, suicides, fistfights in sports bars, white-collar bank crimes, drug busts, domestic problems, dog bites, and other human interest stories needed to be covered. Most of those reports Webb stole long before anyone else could see them. In fact, the situation was so acute, that the rest of the media now referred to the Charlotte Police Department's press basket as *The Webb Site*.

* * *

West, having recalled Brazil's early complaint about this, had finally done her bit by calling Channel 3 and complaining to the general manager. This had solved nothing. Nor was Goode receptive when West had brought it up to her, not realizing that Goode, in fact, regularly logged into The Webb Site. These days she and Brent Webb parked all over the city in her Miata. This was not due to a problem with their going to her apartment, where she lived alone. The risk of exposure was a huge turn-on to the couple. It was not unusual for them to park within blocks of his house, where his wife waited dinner for him, and picked up his dirty clothes, and sorted his socks.

Chapter Eighteen

The task force West had assembled to investigate drug deals going down at the Presto Grill also had much dirt to find, sort through, and hopefully match with other crime trends in the city. Mungo was an undercover detective, and he was eating grilled chicken tips and gravy in the grill, while Brazil, whom Mungo did not know, sipped black coffee. Mungo had gotten his street name for obvious reasons. He was a mountain in jeans and Panthers T-shirt, his wallet chained to his belt, long bushy hair tied back, and a bandana around a sloping forehead. He wore an earring. Mungo was smoking, one eye squinting as he watched the blond guy quiz Spike at the grill.

'No, man.' Spike was flipping a burger and chopping hash browns. 'See, none's from around here, know what I mean?' He spoke with a heavy Portuguese accent.

'Where they come from doesn't matter,' Brazil said. 'It's what happens once they get here. Look, the source of the bad shit going down is right where we are.' He was talking the language, drumming his index finger on the counter. 'Local. I'm sure of it. What do you think?'

Spike wasn't going to explore this further, and Mungo's radar was locked in. That blond pretty-boy looked familiar. It seemed Mungo had seen him somewhere, and that made him only more convinced that he was going to develop Blondie as a suspect. But first things first. Mungo needed to sit here a little longer, see what else was going down, and he hadn't finished his breakfast.

'I need more toast,' he said to Spike as Blondie left. 'Who's he?' Mungo jerked his head in the direction of the shutting front door.

Spike shrugged, having learned long ago not to answer questions, and Mungo was a cop. Everybody knew it. Spike started filling a toothpick holder while Brazil made his next stop. Adjoining the Presto was the Traveler's Hotel, where one could get a room for as little as fifty dollars per week, depending on how well one negotiated with Bink Lydle at the desk. Brazil asked his questions to Lydle and got the same information he'd been handed next door.

Lydle was not especially hospitable, his arms folded across his narrow chest as he sat behind the scarred reception desk, with its bell and one-line telephone. He informed this white boy that Lydle knew nothing about these businessmen being whacked around here, and couldn't imagine that the 'source of this bad shit going down' was local. Lydle, personally, had never seen anyone who made him suspicious, certainly not in his hotel, which was a city landmark, and *the* place to go back in the days of the Old Southern Train Station.

Brazil walked several blocks to Fifth Street and found Jazzbone's Pool Hall. Brazil decided that somebody was going to talk to him, even if he had to take a risk. At this early hour, Jazzbone's wasn't doing much business, just a few guys sitting around drinking Colt 45, smoking, telling favorite stories about binges, and women, and winning at numbers. Pool tables with shabby green felt were deserted, balls in their triangles, waiting for tonight when the place would be crowded and dangerous until the boozy early morning. If anyone knew what was going on in the neighborhood, Jazzbone was the man.

'I'm looking for Jazzbone,' Brazil said to the drinking buddies.

One of them pointed to the bar, where Jazzbone, in plain view, was opening a case of Schlitz, and aware of the golden-hair dude dressed like college.

'Yeah!' Jazzbone called out. 'What you need.'

Brazil walked across cigarette-burned, whisky-smelling carpet. A cockroach scuttled across his path, and salt and cigarette ashes were scattered over every table Brazil passed. The closer he got to Jazzbone, the more he noticed details. Jazzbone wore gold rings, fashioned of diamond clusters and coins, on every finger. The gold crowns on his front teeth had heart and clover cut-outs. He wore a semiautomatic pistol on his right hip. Jazzbone was neatly replacing bottles of beer in the cooler.

'All we got cold right now is Pabst Blue Ribbon,' Jazzbone said.

Last night had been busy and had wiped Jazzbone out. He had a feeling this boy wanted something other than beer, but he wasn't undercover, like Mungo. Jazzbone could smell police and the Feds the minute they hit the block. He couldn't remember the last time he was fooled. Jazzbone only got spanked by the other dudes out there, people coming into his establishment looking just like him, guns and all.

'I'm with the *Charlotte Observer*,' said Brazil, who knew when it was better to be a volunteer cop, and when not. 'I'd like your help, sir.'

'Oh, yeah?' Jazzbone stopped putting away beer, and had always known he'd make a good story. 'What kind of help? This for the paper?'

'Yes, sir.'

Polite, too, giving the man respect. Jazzbone scrutinized him, and started chewing on a stirrer, cocking one eyebrow. 'So, what you want to know?' Jazzbone went around to the other side of the bar and pulled out a stool.

'Well, you know about these killings around here,' Brazil said.

Jazzbone was momentarily confused. 'Huh,' he said. 'You might want to specify.'

'The out-of-towners. The Black Widow.' Brazil lowered his voice, almost to a whisper.

'Oh, yeah. Them,' Jazzbone said, and didn't care who heard. 'Same person doing all of 'em.'

'It can't be helping your business worth a damn.' Brazil got tough, acting like he was wearing a gun, too. 'Some creep out there ruining it for everyone.'

'Now that's so, brother. Tell me about it. I run a clean business here. Don't want trouble or cause none either.' He lit a Salem. 'It's others who do. Why I wear this.' He patted his pistol.

Brazil stared enviously at it. 'Shit, man,' he said. 'What the hell you packing?'

One thing was true, Jazzbone was proud of his piece. He had got it off a drug dealer playing pool, some dude from New York who didn't know that Jazzbone owned a pool hall for a reason. In Jazzbone's mind, when he was good at something, whether it was a woman, a car, or playing pool, he may as well own it, and he was definitely one hell of a pool player. He slipped the pistol out of its holster so Brazil could look without getting too close.

'Colt Double Eagle .45 with a five-inch barrel,' Jazzbone let him know.

Brazil had seen it before in *Guns Illustrated*. Stainless steel matte finish, adjustable sights with high-profile three-dot system, wide steel trigger, and combat-style hammer. Jazzbone's pistol went for about seven hundred dollars, new, and he could tell the kid was impressed and dying to touch it, but Jazzbone didn't know him well enough for that.

'You think it's the same one whacking all these white men from out of town?' Brazil repeated.

'I didn't say they was white,' Jazzbone corrected him. 'The last one, the senator dude, wasn't. But yeah, same motherfucker's doing 'em.'

'Got any idea who?' Brazil did his best to keep the excitement out of his voice.

Jazzbone knew exactly who, and didn't want trouble like this in his neighborhood anymore than those rich men wanted it in their rental cars. Not to mention, Jazzbone was a big supporter of free enterprise, and collected change from more than pool sharking and beverages. He had an interest in a few girls out there. They earned a few extra dollars and kept him company. The Black Widow was hurting business bad. These days, Jazzbone had a feeling men came to town after watching CNN and reading the paper, and they rented adult movies, stayed in. Jazzbone didn't blame them.

'There's this one punkin head I seen out there running girls,' Jazzbone told Brazil, who was taking notes. 'I'd be looking at him.'

'What's a punkin head?'

Jazzbone flashed his gold grin at this naive reporter boy.

'A *do*.' Jazzbone pointed to his own head. 'Orange like

a punkin, rows of braids close to his head. One mean motherfucker.'

'You know his name?' Brazil wrote.

'Don't want to,' Jazzbone said.

West, in charge of investigations for the city, had never heard of a punkin head in connection with the Black Widow killings. When Brazil called her from a pay phone, because he did not trust a cellular phone for such sensitive information, he was manic, as if he had just been in a shoot-out. She wrote down what he said, but not a word of it sparked hope. Her Phantom Force had been undercover out on the streets for weeks. Brazil had spent fifteen minutes at Jazzbone's, and had cracked the case. She didn't think so. Nor was she feeling the least bit friendly toward Brazil's two-timing, user-friendly ass.

'How's the chief?' he asked her.

'Why don't you tell me,' she said.

'What?'

'Look, I don't have time to chit-chat,' she rudely added.

Brazil was on a sidewalk in front of the Federal Courthouse, hateful people looking at him. He didn't care.

'What did I do?' he fired back. 'Tell me when's the last time I've heard from you? I haven't noticed you picking up the phone, asking me to do anything or even to see how I am.'

This had not occurred to West. She never called Raines. For that matter, she did not call guys, and never had, and never would, with the occasional exception of Brazil. Now why the hell was that, and why had she suddenly gotten weird about dialing his number?

'I figured you'd get in touch with me when you had something on your mind,' she replied. 'It's been hectic.

Niles is driving me crazy. I may turn him over to the juvenile courts. I don't know why I haven't gotten around to calling you, okay? But a lot of good it's going to do for you to punish me for it.'

'You want to play tennis?' he quickly asked.

West still had a wooden Billie Jean King racquet, clamped tight in a press. Neither were manufactured anymore. She had an ancient box of Tretorn balls that never went dead but broke like eggs. Her last pair of tennis shoes were low-cut plain white canvas Converse, also no longer made. She had no idea where anything was, and owned no tennis clothes, and didn't especially enjoy watching the sport on TV, but preferred baseball at this stage in her personal evolution. There were many reasons she gave the answer she did.

'Forget it,' she said.

She hung up the phone and went straight to Hammer's office. Horgess was not his usual informative, friendly self. West felt sorry for him. No matter how many times Hammer had told him to let it go, he never would. He had picked up the radio instead of the phone. Horgess, the sycophantic duty captain, had made sure all the world knew about the embarrassing shooting at the chief's house. That's all anybody talked and speculated about. The expected jokes were ones West would never want her boss to hear. Horgess was pale and depressed. He barely nodded at West.

'She in?' West asked.

'I guess,' he said, dejected.

West knocked and walked in at the same time. Hammer was on the phone, tapping a pen on a stack of pink telephone messages. She looked amazingly put together and in charge in a tobacco-brown suit and yellow and white striped blouse. West was surprised and rather pleased to note that her boss was wearing slacks and flats again. West pulled up a chair, waiting for Hammer to slip off the headset.

'Don't mean to interrupt,' West said.

'Quite all right, quite all right,' Hammer told her.

She gave West her complete attention, hands quietly folded on top of the neatly organized desk of someone who had far too much to do but refused to be overwhelmed by it. Hammer had never been caught up, and never would be. She didn't even want to get to all of it. The older she got, the more she marveled over matters she once had considered important. These days, her perspective had shifted massively, like a glacier forming new continents to consider and cracking old worlds.

'We've not really had a chance to talk,' West proceeded delicately. 'How are you holding up?'

Hammer gave her a slight smile, sadness in her eyes before she could run it off. 'The best I can, Virginia. Thank you for asking.'

'The editorials, cartoons and everything in the paper have been really terrific,' West went on. 'And Brazil's story was great.' She hesitated at this point, the subject of Andy Brazil still disturbing, although she didn't understand it, entirely.

Hammer understood it perfectly. 'Listen, Virginia,' she said with another smile, this one kind and slightly amused. 'He's pretty sensational, I have to admit. But you have nothing to worry about where I'm concerned.'

'Excuse me?' West frowned.

Brazil was out in bright sunshine, walking along the sidewalk in an area of the city where he should not have been without armed guards. This was a very special juncture known as Five Points, where the major veins of State, Trade, and Fifth Streets, and Beatties Ford and Rozzelles Ferry Roads, branched out from the major artery of Interstate 77, carrying all traveling on them into the heart of the Queen City. This included the thousands of businessmen coming from Charlotte-Douglas International Airport, and those bad dudes waiting, including the serial killer, Punkin Head.

Punkin Head was believed to be a shi'm by those who had laid eyes on the pimp, which were few. It held its own council, as a rule, in an '84 Ford cargo van, dark blue, 351 V8, which it was especially fond of because the van had windows only in front. Whatever business Punkin Head chose to run out of the back remained private, as it should have, and this included sleeping. This fine morning, Punkin Head was parked in its usual spot on Fifth Street, in the Preferred Parking lot, where the attendant knew to leave well enough alone, and was now and then rewarded with services Punkin Head's business could provide.

Punkin Head was reading the paper, and eating its third take-out bacon and egg sandwich with hot sauce and butter, brought to him by the attendant. Punkin Head saw the white boy walking around, snooping, a notepad in hand. Word on the street was the dude's name was Blondie, and Punkin Head knew exactly who Blondie was trying to snitch on, and Punkin Head wasn't appreciative. It watched, thinking, as it finished its breakfast and popped open a Michelob Dry, taking another look at the front page story in this morning's *Observer*.

Some South American reporter named Brazil was getting far too personal about Punkin Head, and it was not pleased. In the first place, it was incensed that when the masses thought about Punkin Head, they envisioned a spider, and that all believed the orange symbol Punkin Head painted on each body was an hourglass. Punkin Head painted what it did because it liked orange. It also intended to whack and rob eight businessmen, and no more, before it moved on. To linger longer in the same area would be pressing its luck, and the figure eight was simply a reminder, a note to itself, that soon it would be time for Punkin Head and Poison to head out in the van, maybe up to the DC area.

In an article this morning, the reporter named Brazil had quoted an FBI profiler as saying that the Black Widow was a failure in interpersonal relationships, had never married or held a job long, was inadequate sexually and in every other way, and suffered from a sexual identity crisis, according to Special Agent Bird. Punkin Head, who of course was not referred to by name, but simply as 'the killer,' had read and viewed considerable violent pornography throughout its life, had come from a dysfunctional home, and had never finished college, if it had ever gone at all. It owned a vehicle, probably old and American, and still lived with its father, which it hated, or had for much of its adult life. Punkin Head was slovenly, possibly fat, and a substance abuser.

SA Bird, the article went on to say, predicted that Punkin Head would soon begin to decompensate. Punkin Head would make mistakes, overstep itself, become disorganized and lose control. All psychopaths eventually did. Punkin Head threw the newspaper into the back of the van in disgust. Someone was snitching, leaking personal details about Punkin Head to the press, and it glared out at Blondie pausing at the Cadillac Grill, where the sh'im's sandwiches had been carefully prepared. Blondie decided to go inside.

The clientele at the Cadillac Grill wasn't happy to see Blondie walk in. They knew he was a reporter and wanted nothing to do with him or his questions. What did he think? They were crazy? They're suppose to risk getting Punkin Head pissed off, turn it meaner than usual and end up with Silvertips in their heads? That sh'im was the nastiest, most hateful of all time, and the truth was that the business community of Five Points wanted it to move on or get whacked. But as was often true in fascist regimes, no one had the guts or the time to rise up against Punkin Head. Energy and lucid thought were low among soldiers who stayed up late drinking Night Train, smoking dope, and shooting pool.

The head cook at the Cadillac was Remus Wheelon, a heavyset Irishman with tattoos. He had heard all about Blondie and didn't want the snitch in his establishment. Remus was well aware that he had just fixed Punkin Head three deluxe Rise and Shine sandwiches, and the cold-blooded killing piece of shit was probably sitting out there in its van, watching, and waiting for Remus to so much as serve Blondie a cup of coffee. Remus waited on the counter. He took his time scraping the grill. He made more coffee, fried another batch of baloney, and read the *Observer*.

Brazil had helped himself to a booth and picked up a greasy plastic-laminated menu, handwritten, prices reasonable. He was aware of people staring at him in a manner that was about as unfriendly as he had ever seen. He smiled back, as if this were Aunt Sarah's Pancake House, giving them an *eat me* attitude that made all think twice. Brazil refused to be deterred from his mission. His pager went off for all to hear, and he grabbed it as if it had bitten him. He recognized the number, and was surprised. Brazil looked around, deciding that the venue probably wasn't the best for whipping out his reporter's portable phone and calling the mayor's office.

He was getting up to leave, and changed his mind when the door opened, the bell over it ringing. The young hooker walked in, and Brazil's pulse picked up. He wasn't sure why he was so fascinated, but he couldn't take his eyes off her, and felt compassion that was equaled by fear. She wore jeans cut off high, sandals with tire tread soles, and a Grateful Dead T-shirt with sleeves torn off. Her naked breasts moved in rhythm as she walked. She took the next booth over, facing him, eyes bold on his as she flipped dirty blond hair out of the way.

Remus brought her coffee before she could even pick up the menu. She studied plastic-covered writing with difficulty, the words tangling like fishing line on the shore of Lake Algae, as the rich folks in Davidson called the pond at Griffith and Main Streets, where her daddy had taken her fishing a few times. This was before she got older and Mom was working in housekeeping at the Best Western. Daddy was a truck driver for Southeastern, and kept erratic hours. Mom wasn't always home when her husband rolled in from a long trip.

In the mind of Cravon Jones, his three daughters belonged to him, and how he chose to express affection was his business and his right. There was no question he was partial to Addie, who was named after his wife's mother, who he hated. Addie was blond and pretty from the day she was born, a special child who loved to cuddle with her daddy, and with whom her mother did not bond or get along. Mrs Jones was tired of coming home to a drunk, disgusting, stinking man, who slapped her around, shoved, and on one occasion broke her nose and jaw. The daughters, understandably, were drawn to him out of fear.

Addie reached her eleventh year, and Daddy crawled in bed with her one night. He smelled like sour sweat and booze as he pressed his hard thing against her, and then drove it in while blood soaked sheets and her silent tears flowed. Addie's sisters were in the same room and heard all of it. No one spoke of the event or acknowledged that it was real, and Mrs Jones remained selectively ignorant. But she knew damn well, and Addie could tell by her mother's eyes, increased drinking, and growing indifference toward Addie. This went on until Addie turned fourteen and ran away one night while Mrs Jones was working and Daddy was on the road somewhere. Addie got as far as Winston-Salem, where she met the first man who ever took care of her.

There had been many since, giving her cain and crack, cigarettes, fried chicken, whatever she wanted. She was twenty-three when she stumbled off the Greyhound in Charlotte some months back. Addie didn't remember it much, seemed like last she recalled she was in Atlanta, getting high with some rich dude who drove a Lexus and paid an extra twenty dollars to urinate in her face. She could take anything as long as she wasn't present, and the only turnstile to that painless place was drugs. Sea, her last and final man, beat her with a coathanger because she had cramps and couldn't make any money one night. She ran off for the countless time in her life, headed to Charlotte because she knew where it was, and it was all she could afford after grabbing some old lady's purse.

Addie Jones, who had not been called by her Christian name in too many highs to remember, had an Atlanta

Braves duffel bag she'd stolen from one of her tricks. In it she had a few things, and both hands had been gripping hard as she had walked along West Trade, nearing the Presto Grill, across from the All Right parking lot, where Punkin Head was waiting in its van, fishing. Most of its best catches had come off buses, all those fuck-ups washing ashore like biological hazards, their stories all the same. Punkin Head knew this for a fact, having crawled off one of those buses itself some time back.

Fifteen minutes later, Addie had been inside that dark blue van, and Punkin Head knew it had a find this time. Not only did it want this girl for itself, but the johns out there were going to fall hard for her perky body and sultry eyes and swollen mouth. Punkin Head christened its new creature Poison, and the two of them began their unfriendly takeover. Other pimps were flip at first. Then the killings began, and cops were everywhere. There were stories of bad hollowpoints and something painted orange, and something else about a spider. All got scared.

'What'll be?' Remus asked Poison as she smoked a cigarette and stared out at the street.

'Some bacon,' she said in an accent that no longer sounded white or even American.

It had been Remus's observation throughout his career that hookers took on the accents and mannerisms of their owners. Black hookers sounded white and white hookers sounded black, white gigolos walked with an NBA spring, black gigolos strutted like John Wayne. By now Remus was used to it. He just did his cooking and ran his joint, live and let be. He didn't want trouble, and Poison troubled him like an ice pick too close to his eye. She had a mocking smile, as if she knew the joke was on him. Remus sensed that a cold-blooded killing, including his own, would amuse her.

* * *

Brazil sat in his booth for quite some time, watching the clientele thin. He was tapping his menu, his table bare since no one seemed inclined to wait on him. He watched the young hooker finish breakfast. She dropped money on the table and got up. Brazil's eyes followed as she left. He was dying to talk to her, but scared. The bell on the door got quiet in her mysterious wake, and he got up, too. Brazil forgot he had never ordered, and left a tip. He emerged from the grill, notepad out, looking up and down the sidewalk, walking around the block, his eyes scanning the parking lot across Fifth Street, not seeing her anywhere. Disappointed, he continued wandering.

A black van with dark tinted glass drove slowly past, but Brazil gave it not a second thought as his mind tried to unlock something he was certain he knew the combination to, but could not yet access.

Mungo stared out the van's windshield at Blondie, realizing that this case was getting only bigger. Mungo watched the slow, languid way the guy moved, stopping every now and then to search traffic and stare. Mungo's excitement mounted when Blondie approached Shena, one of the oldest sluts in the area.

She was perched on the front wooden steps of a dilapidated wooden house, sipping Coke, trying to get over the night before, and readying herself for the one coming up. Blondie walked up like they knew each other. He started talking to her. She shrugged, gestured, then got pissed and waved him off like he was a pigeon in her way. Uh huh, Mungo thought. This boy-bait was becoming a territorial problem out here, moving in on the other hookers' lemonade stands.

Blondie was probably luring men, maybe some women, selling them dope, committing crimes against nature, and getting rich from it.

Mungo was convinced that if he dug further he would find out that Blondie was way up there on the drug-dealing chain, probably directly connected to New York. There could be a connection to the Black Widow killings. Mungo got out the video camera and captured what was possibly the best-looking, most clean-cut male prostitute he'd ever seen, except in the movies. Mungo quickly drove back to headquarters.

West had been up all night. She had done her best to make Niles shut up his yowling and kneading. She had thrown him off the bed until her shoulder got tired. She had talked in an adult fashion with him, trying to make him understand her fatigue and need of sleep. She had yelled, threatened, and locked him out of her room. He had been well rested, and happily snoozing on his favorite windowsill when West hurried out the door this morning, late for work. She had no patience left. When Mungo walked into the conference room in the midst of her meeting with the Phantom Force, she was not welcoming.

'We're having a meeting,' she said to Mungo.

'And I got something you're going to want to hear about.' He proudly held up the videotape. 'Definitely a player, maybe even more, maybe even our killer or at least involved.' Mungo was breathless and looked like a biker.

Hammer had been on the phone ever since West had seen her last, and West got on the radio and told her boss to give her a call.

'I don't want you to get your hopes up,' West told her. 'But it sounds pretty promising.'

'Describe him,' Hammer said.

'White male, five-foot-seven, one-thirty pounds, blond, tight black jeans, tight polo-type shirt, Nikes. Strolling the area of Fifth and Trade, looking at cars, talking to hookers. Apparently he was in the Presto talking about the quality of drugs in the area, and local sources, words to that effect. Also,' West went on, 'and this bothers me considerably, chief, you're aware of Poison, a.k.a. Addie Jones?'

'Right.' Hammer had no idea.

'They were in the Cadillac Grill together for quite a long time. She left, and he went out right after her. At that point they split, seemingly off to do whatever they were up to.'

'Where's this videotape?' Hammer wanted to know.

'I've got it.'

'You looked at it yet?'

'We use these handheld JVC Grax 900 camcorders for covert operations. Mungo has gone to get the VHS adapter, and should have it for me in a minute.'

'Bring it by,' Hammer said to her. 'Let's take a look.'

Chapter Nineteen

In the mayor's office, Brazil was impatiently perched on a couch, making a note of his surroundings and watching the secretary, Ruth Lafone, answer another call. She felt a little sorry for Andy Brazil, well aware that he was being set up as others before him. Her phone rang again. Ruth answered and smiled. She was pleasant and respectful to the man elected by an overwhelming majority to serve the people of the city. She hung up as she rose from her chair, and looked at Brazil.

'The mayor will see you now,' she said.

Brazil was slightly bewildered. He had no idea how many times he had tried to get comments, interviews, and opinions from Mayor Search. Now the mayor was calling Brazil, finally following up on a request? Which request? Brazil wished he had dressed a little better this day, something beside black jeans that were too small. He had stopped in the men's room, at least, and had tucked in his faded red Head shirt, which also was a bit too small. Since Brazil had lost a few pounds, his normal clothes were falling off as if he were jailing, so he had dipped into another drawer of jeans and shirts he'd had since high school.

'If you don't mind my asking,' he said to the secretary as he got off the couch. 'Is there some purpose to this interview other than my requests to talk to the mayor that go back to the beginning of my career?'

'I'm afraid he can't always get to everything right away,' she apologized as she had learned to so well over the years.

Brazil looked at her for a moment, hesitating, detecting something in the way she averted her gaze from him. 'Okay,' he said. 'Thanks a lot.'

'You're so welcome.' She led him to the slaughter because she needed her job.

Mayor Search was a distinguished, neat man in a European-cut summer-weight gray suit. He wore a white shirt, his tie charcoal and blue paisley with matching suspenders. He did not get up from his huge block of walnut, the skyline of the city filling many windows. USBank Corporate Center was cut off about belt level, directly behind him, and the mayor could not see the crown unless he got on the floor and strained to look up.

'Thank you for finding the time to see me,' Brazil said as he sat in a chair across from Search.

'Understand you've got a rather interesting situation here in our city,' Search said.

'Yes, sir. And I appreciate it.'

This wasn't the typical smartass reporter Search dealt with morning, noon, and night. The kid was Billy Budd, Billy Graham, wide-eyed innocence, polite, respectful, and committed. Search knew the extreme danger of sincere people like this. They died for causes, would do anything for Jesus, served a higher calling, were no respecter of persons, believed in burning bushes, and were not led into sin by Potiphar's wife. This wasn't going to be as easy as Search had supposed.

'Now let me tell you something, son,' Search began in his earnest, overbearing way to this lad who was lucky to get the mayor's time. 'No one loves our police department more than I do. But you do realize, I hope, there are two sides to every story?'

'Usually more sides than that, sir, it's been my experience,' said Brazil.

Hammer was in her outer office, having a word with Horgess, while she waited for West and a videotape that she prayed might reveal what Mungo seemed to think it did. Maybe her luck would turn for the better for once.

'Fred, enough,' Hammer said, standing at the corner of his desk, hands in the pockets of her tobacco brown pants.

'It's just I feel so bad, Chief Hammer. Can't believe I did something like that. Here you trusted me, and I'm supposed to make your life better, be a faithful retainer. And look what I did when things got a little stressful,' Horgess said in his same sad, hate-me tone.

This was sounding all too much like Seth, and the last thing Hammer needed at present was an office husband as pitiful as the one in room 333 at Carolinas Medical Center.

'Fred, what do we say about mistakes? As part of our vision statement?' she quizzed him.

'I know.' He could not look at her.

'First, we allow a mistake if you were trying to do the right thing when you made it, and second, if you tell someone that you made the mistake. And third, if you are willing to talk about your mistake to others so they won't do the same thing.'

'I haven't done two and three,' he said.

'No, you haven't,' Hammer had to agree as West walked in. 'Two isn't necessary because in this instance, everybody already knows. No later than seventeen hundred hours, I want a commentary by you for the *Informer*, telling everyone about your mistake. On my desk.' She looked at him over the top of her glasses.

Mayor Search did not know the first thing about a community policing vision statement or any other vision statement, for that matter, that did not slaughter people for making mistakes, especially of the egregious nature that caused Hammer such embarrassment. This was not about to happen to him because the mayor knew how to handle people, including the media.

'It absolutely is untrue that the city is unsafe,' he stated to Brazil, and the office seemed to have gotten airless and hot, and maybe smaller.

'But five businessmen from out of town have been murdered in the last five weeks,' Brazil said. 'I don't know how you can . . .'

'Random. Isolated. Incidents.' Sweat rolled down his sides. Search felt his face getting red.

'Downtown hotels and restaurants claim business has dropped more than twenty percent.' Brazil wasn't trying to argue. He just wanted to get to the bottom of this.

'And people like you are only going to make that worse.' Search mopped his forehead, wishing Cahoon had never passed this goddamn assignment along to him.

'All I want is to tell the truth, Mayor Search,' Billy

Budd, Billy Graham, said. 'Hiding it won't help resolve this terrible situation.'

The mayor resorted to sarcasm, laughing at this simple boy's simple logic. He felt that bitter juice seep through his veins, the bile rising, as his face reddened dangerously, his rage a solar flare on the surface of his reason. Mayor Search lost control.

'I can't believe it,' he laughed derisively at this reporter who was nothing in life. '*You're* giving *me* a lecture. Look. I'm not going to sit here and tell you business isn't suffering. I wouldn't drive downtown at night right now.' He laughed harder, unstoppable, and drunk with his power.

By six P.M., at happy hour, West and Raines were on their way to being drunk at Jack Straw's A Tavern of Taste, next to La-dee-da's and Two Sisters, on East Seventh Street. West had changed out of her uniform, and was casual in jeans, a loose denim shirt, and sandals. She was drinking Sierra Nevada Stout, the beer of the month, and still in a state of disbelief over the videotape she had watched with Hammer.

'Do you have any idea how this makes me and my investigative division look?' she said for the fourth time. 'Christ. Please tell me this is a nightmare. Please, please. I'm going to wake up, right?'

Raines was drinking Field Stone chardonnay, the wine of the month. In gym shorts, Adidas with no socks, and a tank top, he was turning all heads except for the one across the table from him. What was it with her? All she ever talked about was work and that twit from the paper she rode around with. And Niles, oh yes, let's not forget that fucking, God-save-the-queen, cat. How many times had that cat ruined a building moment? Niles seemed to know exactly when to cause a distraction. A jump on Raines's back or head, a bite of a sock-covered toe. How about the time Niles sat on the remote control until the volume of Kenny G sounded like an air raid?

'It's not your fault,' Raines said again, working on the spinach dip.

West ate another pickle fried in beer batter as Jump Little Children began setting up all their equipment and instruments. This small place with blue plastic table cloths and funky art in screaming colors by someone named Tryke was going to rock tonight, jam, trot out primitive Ids and libidos. Raines hoped he could make West stay at least until the second set. Actually, Raines thought what had happened to her all in a day's work was hilarious. It was all he could do to look tender and concerned.

He imagined Mungo-Jumbo swinging into the Presto to chow down. He spots a dude with a banana in his pocket who's the head of the Geezer Grill Cartel. A task force is formed, ending with a videotape of Blondie, the King of Vice and top suspect in the Black Widow serial murders, as he cruises Five Points in his tight black jeans and reporter's notepad. What wouldn't Raines have paid to see a videotape of Hammer sitting in her important conference room watching this shit! Christ! He fought a smile again, and was losing. His face was aching and his stomach hurt.

'What's wrong with you?' West gave him a look. 'There's nothing fucking funny about this.'

'There certainly isn't,' he said weakly as he dissolved into laughter, doubled over in his chair, howling as tears streamed down his face.

This went on as Jump Little Children set up amplifiers, and checked Fender electric guitars, Pearl drums with

Zildjian medium crash cymbals, and Yamaha keyboards. They gave each other sly looks, flipping long hair out of the way, earrings glinting in the dim light. This guy was fried. Man, look at him go. Cool. The girlfriend wasn't digging it, either. Him taking a trip she's not on. Kind of weird he's drinking chardon-fucking-nay.

West was so angry she wanted to flip over the table, cowboy style. She wanted to jump on top of Raines, flex-cuff his ankles and feet and just leave his sorry ass in the middle of Jack Straw's on a hot Thursday night. She halfway believed the only person Mungo was undercover for was Goode. Maybe Goode had gotten to him, and promised him favors if he would set up West, and destroy her credibility, her good relationship with Hammer. Oh God. When they had been sitting at that polished table and the video had flickered on, at first West was certain some mistake had been made. Brazil, big as life, was walking along to the sound of traffic, making notes, for Chrissake! How many serial killers or drug kingpins walk around in the middle of the day making notes?

As for Brazil's physical description, Mungo-the-Woolly-Mammoth had missed that by about forty pounds and six inches, although West had to admit she'd never seen Brazil in clothes that tight. She didn't know what to make of it. Those black jeans were so tight she could see the muscles in the back of his thighs flex as he walked, the red polo shirt fitting like paint, muscles lean and well-defined, and he had veins. Maybe he was trying to blend out there. That would make sense.

'Tell me what she did,' Raines choked, wiping his eyes.

West motioned to the waitress for another round. 'I don't want to talk about it.'

'Oh come on, Virginia. Tell me, tell me. You got to.' He

straightened up a bit. 'Tell me what Hammer did when she saw the tape.'

'No,' West said.

Hammer hadn't done much, in truth. She'd sat in her usual spot at the head of the table, staring without comment at the twenty-four-inch Mitsubishi. She'd watched the entire tape, all forty-two minutes of it, every bit of Brazil's long promenade and indistinct conversations with the city's unsavory downtown folks. West and Hammer had watched Brazil point, shrug, jot, scan, and squat to tie shoelaces twice, before finally returning to the All Right to retrieve his BMW. After a pregnant silence, Chief Hammer had taken off her glasses and voiced her opinion.

'What was this?' she had said to her deputy chief in charge of investigations.

'I don't know what to tell you,' West had said, feeling dark hate for Mungo.

'And this all began the day we had lunch at the Presto and you saw a man with a banana in his pocket.' Hammer had wanted to make sure she was clear on the facts of the case.

'I really don't think it's fair to link the two.'

Hammer had gotten up, but West knew not to move.

'Of course it's fair,' Hammer had said, hands in her pockets again. 'Don't get me wrong, I'm not blaming you, Virginia.' She'd begun pacing. 'How could Mungo not recognize Andy Brazil? He's out there morning, noon and night, either for the *Observer* or us.'

'Mungo is deep cover,' West had explained. 'He generally avoids any place police or the press might be. I don't think he reads much, either.'

Hammer had nodded. She could understand this, actually, and she was raw. Hammer was not ready or willing to react violently to the embarrassments and honest mistakes of others, whether it was Horgess, Mungo, or even West, who really had made no error, except perhaps in her choice of Mungo to do anything in life.

'Do you want me to destroy it?' West had asked as Hammer popped the tape out of the VCR. 'I mean, I'd prefer not to. Some of that footage includes known prostitutes. Sugar, Double Fries, Butterfinger, Shooter, Lickety Split, Lemon Drop, Poison.'

'All of them were in there?' Hammer was perplexed as she had opened the conference room door.

'They blend in. You have to know where to look.'

'We'll hang on to it,' Hammer had decided.

Raines was laughing so hard, West was furious with herself for telling him the rest of the story. He had his head on the table, hands covering his face. She wiped her forehead with a napkin, perspiring and flushed, as if she were in the tropics. The band would be cranking up soon, and Jack Straw's was getting crowded. She noticed Tommy Axel walk in, recognizing him from his picture in the paper. He had another guy with him, both dressed a lot like Raines, showing off. Why was it most of the gay guys were so good-looking? West didn't think it was fair. Not only were they guys in a guy's world, with all the benefits, but their DNA had somehow managed to appropriate the good stuff women had, too, like gracefulness and beauty.

Of course, gay guys got some of the bad stuff, too. Sneakiness, game playing, compulsive grooming, vanity, and shopping. Maybe it had nothing to do with gender, after all, West considered. Maybe there was no such thing as gender. Maybe biologically people were just vehicles, like cars. She'd heard that overseas the steering wheels were on one side, while here they were on the other. Different genders? Maybe not. Maybe just different cars, the behavior of all determined by the spirit in the driver's seat.

'I've had enough,' West hissed at Raines.

She drained her Sierra Nevada and started on another one. She might just tie one on tonight. Raines was driving.

'I'm sorry. I'm sorry.' He took another deep breath and was spent. 'You look like you don't feel too good,' he said with one of his concerned expressions. 'It is a little hot in here.'

West mopped her face again, her clothes getting damp, but not in the way Raines might have hoped. She was feeling the heaviness in her lower nature, the goddess of fertility reminding West with more volatility every month that time was running out. West's gynecologist had warned her gravely and repeatedly that troubles would begin about her age. She, Dr Alice Bourgeois, spoke of punishment when there were no children and none on the way. *Never underestimate biology*, Dr Bourgeois always said.

West and Raines placed an order for cheeseburgers, fries, and another round of drinks. She wiped her face again and was getting cold. She wasn't sure she could eat anything else, not another fried pickle. She watched the band setting up, her attention wandering to people at other tables. She was quiet for a long time, overhearing a couple not so far away speaking a foreign language, maybe German. West was getting maudlin.

'You seem preoccupied,' said Raines the intuitive.

'Remember when those German tourists got whacked in Miami? What it did to the tourist industry?' she said.

Raines, as a man, took this personally. He had seen the bodies in the Black Widow slayings, or at least several of them. It was unthinkable to have a gun shoved against your head, your brains blown out. There was no telling what indignities those guys had been subjected to before the fact, and how did anyone really know that their pants hadn't been pulled down first, that maybe they hadn't been raped and then spray-painted? If the killer had been wearing a condom, who was going to know? West had said just the right thing to put Raines in a mood. Now he was totally pissed, too.

'So this is about the tourist industry,' he said, leaning across the table and gesturing. 'Forget guys being jerked out of their cars, brains blown all over, balls spray-painted with graffiti!'

West wiped her face again and dug Advil out of her butt pack. 'It's not graffiti. It's a symbol.'

Raines crossed his legs, feeling endangered. The waitress set down their dinner. He grabbed the ketchup bottle as he folded a french fry between his lips.

'It makes me sick,' he said.

'It should make everybody sick.' West could not look at food.

'Who do you think's doing it?' He dipped a bouquet of french fries into a red puddle.

'Maybe a sh'im.' She was soaked in cold sweat. Her hair was wet around her face and neck, as if she'd just been in a foot pursuit.

'Huh?' Raines glanced up at her, biting into his dripping burger.

'She-him. Woman one night, man the next, depending on the mood,' she said.

'Oh. Like you.' He reached for the dish of mayonnaise.

'Goddamn it.' West shoved her plate away. 'I must be about to start.'

Raines stopped chewing, rolling his eyes. He knew what that meant. The first twangs on electric guitars shattered the din, and sticks beat-beat and beat-beat-beat. Cymbals crashed and crashed as Axel snaked his foot around Jon's ankle and thought about Brazil for the millionth time this day.

Packer was thinking about Brazil, too, as the editor carried Dufus out the back door, like a small, squirming football, headed for the same Japanese maple. Dufus had to go in the same place, get used to it, and be able to find his smells. It didn't matter that the tree was in the hinterlands and that it had started to rain. Packer dropped his wife's wall-eyed dog in the same bald spot next to the same gnarled root. Packer was out of breath, watching Dufus curtsey to the Queen.

'Why don't you lift your leg like a man,' Packer muttered as bulging eyes watched him, speckled pink nose twitching. 'Sissy,' Packer said.

The worn-out editor's pager had vibrated earlier this evening while he was mowing the grass on his vacation day. It had been Panesa, calling to tell him that the mayor had admitted that even he wouldn't drive downtown at night right now! Jesus living God, this was unbelievable. Surely the paper was well on its way to winning a Pulitzer for a series that made a difference in society, one that changed history. Why the hell did this wait to happen when Packer was out of the newsroom? He'd been there thirty-two years. The moment he decided to put life in perspective, ward off that heart attack perched outside the window of his existence, Andy Brazil showed up.

Now it was run-through-the-yard time to get Dufus's

bowels wound up that they might unleash what, in Packer's mind, should have been a humiliation to any creature, except maybe a small domestic cat. Dufus would not chase Packer, or come, and this was not new. The editor sat on the back porch steps while his wife's dog chewed mulch until it was time to drop his niggling gifts. Packer sighed and got up. He walked back into the air-conditioned house, Dufus on his heels.

'There's my good little boy,' Mildred cooed as the dog hopped and licked until she picked him up and rocked him in loving arms.

'Don't mention it,' Packer said, falling into his recliner chair, flicking on television.

He was still sitting there hours later, eating chicken nuggets, and dipping them in Roger's barbecue sauce. He loudly dug into a big bag of chips, swiping them in sauce, too. After several Coronas with lime, he had forgotten about the window and the heart attack perched beyond it. Mildred was watching *Home for the Holidays*, again, because she thought it was their life. Go figure. In the first place, Packer did not play the organ and she did not wear a wig or smoke, and they did not live in a small town. Their daughter had never gotten fired, at least not from an art gallery. That was one place she had never worked, probably because she was color blind. Nor was their son gay that Packer knew of or cared to know of, and any intimations to the contrary by his wife went into the Bermuda Triangle of their marital news hole. The editor didn't listen and the story didn't run. The End.

Packer pointed the remote control with authority. The volume went up, the ubiquitous Webb staring at the camera in a way that Packer knew meant trouble.

'Shit,' Packer said, hitting a lever on his chair, cranking himself up.

'In a rare, if not shocking, moment of candor today,' Webb said with his sincere expression, 'Mayor Charles Search said that because of the Black Widow serial killings, hotel and restaurant business has dropped more than twenty percent, and he himself would not feel safe driving downtown at night. Mayor Search implored Charlotte's citizens to help police catch a killer who has ruthlessly murdered five . . .'

Packer was already dialing the phone, bag of potato chips falling out of his lap, scattering over the rug.

'. . . an individual the FBI has profiled as a sexual psychopath, a serial killer who will not stop . . .' Webb went on.

'Are you listening to this?' Packer exclaimed when Panesa picked up his phone.

'I'm taping it,' he said in a homicidal tone Packer rarely heard. 'This has got to stop.'

Chapter Twenty

Brazil never watched television because his mother monopolized the one at home, and he did not frequent Charlotte's many sports bars, where there were big screens in every corner. He knew nothing about what had been on the eleven o'clock news this Thursday night, and no one paged him or bothered to find him. All was peaceful as he ran on the Davidson track in complete darkness, close to midnight, no sound but the rhythm of his breathing and falling feet. As pleased as he was about his amazing nonstop journalistic home runs, he could not say that he was happy.

Other people were getting a lot of the same stuff he was. Webb, for example, and no matter how informative or compassionate the story, the bottom line was the scoop. Brazil, of late, was scooping no one, if the truth be told. It just seemed he was because what he wrote routinely ended up on the front page and changed public opinion and seemed to rattle a lot of cages. Brazil would have been satisfied to spend the rest of his days writing pieces that did just this and nothing else. Prizes didn't matter much, really. But he was realistic. If he didn't beat everybody to the quote, the revelation, or the crime scene, one of these days he might not get paid any more to write.

At which point, he could become a cop, he supposed, and this turned his mind to West again, sailing him off firm ground into a dark, tangled, painful thicket that hurt and frustrated him the more he tried to fight his way out of it. He ran harder, bending around goal posts, passing empty bleachers filled with the memories of games, mostly lost, during fall nights when he had usually been studying or walking the frosty campus beneath stars he tried to describe as no one ever had. He would tuck his chin into his hooded sweatshirt, heading to the library or a hidden corner of the student lounge, to work on a term paper or poetry, not wanting couples he passed to notice him.

Even if West hadn't wanted to play tennis, there was no need for her to have been rude about it unless she hated him. *Forget it.* Her voice saying those heartless words followed him as he ran harder, lungs beginning to burn, catching fire around the edges as his legs reached farther, and sweat left a trail of scattered spots. He tried to outrun the voice and the person who owned it, anger flinging him through the night, and past the fifty yard line. Legs wobbled as he slowed. Brazil fell into cool, damp grass. He lay on his back, panting, heart thundering, and he had a premonition that he was going to die.

Virginia West felt like it. She lay in bed, lights out, a hot water bottle held close as contractions prepared her for birth for no good cause. Ever since she was fourteen, she'd gone into labor once a month, some episodes worse than others. On occasion, the pain was debilitating enough to send her home from school, a date, or work, lying about what was wrong as she gulped Midol. After a sullen Raines, the paramedic, had dropped her off, she'd taken four Motrin, a little too late. Hadn't Dr Bourgeois told her to take two hundred milligrams of ibuprofen four times a day *three days before* trouble started so it could be prevented, *and don't cut yourself or get a nosebleed, Virginia?* West, as usual, had gotten too busy to bother with anything so mundane, so trivial, as her health. Niles recognized the cyclical emergency and responded, curling around his owner's neck and head, keeping her warm. He was pleased she wasn't going anywhere and he didn't have to share their bed.

Chief Judy Hammer was having morbid premonitions and was bedside, too, in the Surgical Intensive Care Unit (SICU) of Carolinas Medical Center, where Seth's condition was serious and on the wrong side of getting better. Hammer was in shock, dressed in gown, mask and gloves, sitting by his bed. High dose penicillin, clindamycin, and immunic globulin dripped into her husband's veins in an effort to counter necrotizing fasciitis (NF). It was a rare infection, and associated with systemic infection, and a fulminant course, according to Hammer's personal observations and the notes she had been taking every time Dr Cabel, the infectious disease doctor, spoke.

This was all somehow related to everyday group A beta-hemolytic streptococci and *Staphylococcus aureus*, which Hammer could not comprehend beyond figuring out that the microscopic bastards were eating her husband alive. Meanwhile, Seth's oxygen content in his bloodstream had dropped below normal, and the medical center was in a panic. Personnel had made Seth, the VIP, a top priority, and specialists were in and out. Hammer could not keep them straight. She could not think as she stared at her husband's slack, feverish face and smelled his death through the mask she wore.

During the Civil War, surgeons would have diagnosed her husband's condition as simple gangrene. No fancy Latin term changed the reality of flesh turning black and green at a wound site, with limbs, and eventually the person, rotting alive. The only treatment for NF was antibiotics, surgery, and amputation. About a third of the three to five hundred people who got the disease in the US annually died, or approximately thirty percent, according to what Hammer had found through searches on America Online.

Nothing she had discovered about the disease had consoled or given hope. The deadly bacteria burst upon the scene in recent years when it killed eleven people in Great Britain. KILLER BUG ATE MY FACE, screamed the *Daily Star*. DEADLY FLESH EATING BACTERIA, other tabloids proclaimed. It had killed Jim Henson of the Muppets, Hammer had discovered on the Internet, and was believed to be a virulent form of a strep that had caused scarlet fever in the 1800s. In some cases, NF spread too rapidly for antibiotics to work, and it was feared that Seth would be the latest statistic. His VIP status had insured aggressive treatment since admission, so the problem lay not in the hospital, but in his general condition.

Seth had poor nutrition. He was clinically depressed. He had a history of heavy drinking and arteriosclerotic vascular disease. He had received a trauma resulting in an open wound, and a foreign body that could not be removed. Seth, according to Dr Cabel, was immunosuppressed, and was losing approximately a pound of flesh per hour. This did not include layers lost by surgeons fileting to the next level of healthy, bleeding tissue, which soon after turned black and green, despite all efforts and prayers. Hammer was motionless in her chair, reliving every word she'd ever spoken to her husband, every deed that had been angry or unkind. None of his flaws would come to her now.

This was all her fault. It had been her .38 special, her Remington hollowpoint +P cartridge. It had been her order that he root under the sheets for that gun and hand it over to her *this minute*. It had been Hammer giving him the ultimatum about his weight, and she halfway believed that what he suffered from now was no coincidence, but a functional illness. Seth was melting before her eyes, an inch smaller every hour, slabs lighter after every surgery. This was not the weight-loss plan she would have wished for him. He was punishing her for all those years he had lived in her shadow, the wind beneath her wings, her inspiration and biggest fan.

'Chief Hammer?'

She realized someone was speaking, and her eyes focused on Dr Cabel, in surgical greens, cap, mask, gloves, and shoe covers. He was no older than Jude. God help me, Hammer thought with a deep, quiet breath as, once again, she got out of her chair.

'If you'll give me a minute with him,' Dr Cabel said to her.

Hammer went out into the antiseptic, bright corridor. She watched nurses, doctors, family members, and friends alight on different rooms where more suffering lay tethered to narrow hydraulic beds, and machines monitored the life force as it struggled on. She stood, in a daze, until Dr Cabel returned, slipping Seth's chart in the envelope on the back of the door.

'How is he?' Hammer asked the same question, pulling her mask down around her neck.

Dr Cabel left his mask on. He took no chances, and

didn't even shower at home anymore without lathering from head to toe with antibacterial soap. He shut Seth's door, eyes troubled. Hammer was shrewd, and not interested in further euphemisms, convolutions, and evasions. If this young infectious disease doctor thought he could hide the truth from her, she was about to add to his education.

'We're going to take him back into surgery,' Seth's doctor said. 'Which is fairly typical at this point.'

'And which point is this point, exactly?' Hammer wanted to know.

'Day two of progressive streptococcal gangrene and necrotizing fasciitis,' he replied. 'The necrosis is visibly beyond the margins of the original debridement.'

While Dr Cabel respected Chief Hammer, he did not want to deal with her. He cast about for a nurse. Shit. All were busy elsewhere.

'I need to get started,' he said.

'No so fast,' Hammer let him know. 'Exactly what are you going to do in surgery?'

'We'll know better when we go in.'

'How about hazarding a guess.' She might slap him.

'Generally, at this stage, the wound is debrided again down to bleeding, healthy tissue. We'll probably irrigate with saline and pack the wound with Nu-Gauze. We'll continue with hyperbaric oxygen therapy twice a day, and I recommend total parenteral nutrition.'

'Multivitamins then,' she said.

'Well, yes.' He was mildly surprised by her ability to connect the dots.

Hammer had been buying vitamins for years and failed to see anything special about the suggestion. Dr Cabel started to walk off. She snatched him back by his greens.

'Let's cut to the chase,' she said. 'Seth has had strep

throat a dozen times in his life. Why has it turned into this now? Aside from his lousy immune system.'

'It's not exactly the same thing as the strep that causes a sore throat.'

'Clearly.'

This lady was not going to let him go. Dr Cabel felt sorry for Seth in a different way, now. Living with this woman would wear out anybody. Imagine asking her to fetch coffee or take your word for it? When all else failed, Dr Cabel switched to the language that only his superrace understood.

'It's quite possible strep has acquired new genetic information, picked up genes. This can happen through infection by a bacteriophage,' Dr Cabel informed her.

'What's a bacteriophage?' She wouldn't give up.

'Uh, a virus that can incorporate its DNA into a bacterial host,' he said. 'The hypothesis is, that some M1 strain of group A strep, in approximately forty percent of recent invasive infections, seems to have acquired genetic material from a phage. This is according to WHO.'

'*Who*?' Hammer frowned.

'Exactly.' He looked at his watch long enough to give her a broad hint.

'Who the hell is *who*?' She would get an answer.

'World Health Organization. They have a strep reference laboratory. The long and short of it, this may all be connected to a gene that encodes a toxin called superantigen which is widely believed to be connected to toxic-shock syndrome.'

'My husband has the same thing you get from a tampon?' Hammer raised her voice.

'A distant cousin.'

'And since when do you amputate for that?' she demanded as passerbys glanced curiously at the two people in greens arguing in the spotless, well-lit corridor.

'No, no.' He had to get away from this woman, so he, the English major, threw Shakespeare at her. 'Ma'am, with what your husband's got, surgery remains the most effective treatment. "Be bloody, bold and resolute,"' he quoted. '*King Lear*.'

'*Macbeth*,' Hammer, who loved the theater, said as Dr Cabel hurried off.

She lingered long enough to see her husband wheeled back to the OR, then Hammer went home. By nine o'clock, she had collapsed in bed, too exhausted and distressed to remain in a conscious state effectively. She and her deputy chief, in their respective homes, one with a pet, one without, slept fitfully the rest of the night.

Brazil tossed and yanked sheets this way and that, over his feet, under them, back over them again, on his side, on his belly. Finally, he lay on his back, staring up into the dark, listening to the TV murmur through the wall as his mother lay passed out on the couch again.

He kept thinking about what West had said. He should move out, find an apartment. Yet whenever he followed this scary, exciting path a few steps further, he always ran slam into the same scarecrow that sent him fleeing the other way. What was he supposed to do about his mother? What would happen to her if he left her alone? He supposed he could still bring by groceries, stop in to check on her, fix things, and run errands. Brazil worried as he thrashed in bed, listening to the eerie strains of what must have been some three A.M. half-a-star horror flick. He thought about West and felt depressed again.

Brazil decided that he did not like West in the least.

She was not the kind, enlightened woman that Hammer was. One day, Brazil would find someone like Hammer. They would enjoy and respect each other, and play tennis, run, work out with weights, cook, fix the cars, go to the beach, read good fiction and poetry, and do everything together, except when they needed space. What did West know about any of this? She built fences. She cut her own grass with a rider mower because she was too lazy to use a push one, and her yard was barely half an acre. She had disgusting eating habits. She smoked. Brazil turned over again, hanging his arms off either side of the mattress, miserable.

At five, he gave up and went back to the track to run again. He clipped off eight more miles and could have gone farther, but he got bored and wanted to get downtown. It was strange. He'd gone from exhaustion to hyperactivity in a matter of days. Brazil could remember no other time in his life when his chemistry had swung him around like this. One minute he was dragging, the next he was high and excited with no explanation. He contemplated the possibility that his hormones were going through a phase, which he expected would be normal for one his age. It was true that if the male did not give in to his drives between the ages of sixteen and twenty, biology would punish him.

His primary care physician had told him exactly that. Dr Rush, whose family practice was in Cornelius, had warned Brazil about this very phenomenon when Brazil had a team check-up his freshman year at Davidson. Dr Rush, recognizing that Brazil had no father and needed guidance, said many young men made tragic mistakes because their bodies were in a procreation mode. This, said Dr Rush, was nothing more than a throwback to colonial times when sixteen was more than half of the male's life expectancy, assuming Indians or neighbors didn't get him first. When viewed in this fashion, sexual urges, albeit primitive, made perfect sense, and Brazil was to do his best not to act on them.

Brazil would be twenty-three next May, and the urges had not lessened with time. He had been faithful to Dr Rush, who, according to local gossip, was not faithful to his wife and never had been. Brazil thought about his sexuality as he ran a few sprints before trotting home. It seemed to him that love and sex were connected but maybe shouldn't be. Love made him sweet and thoughtful. Love prompted him to notice flowers and want to pick them. Love crafted his finest poetry, while sex throbbed in powerful, earthy pentameters he would never show to anyone or submit for publication.

He hurried home and took a longer than usual shower. At five past eight, he was moving through the cafeteria line in the Knight-Ridder building. He was in jeans, pager on his belt, people staring curiously at the boy wonder reporter who played police and always seemed alone. Brazil selected Raisin Bran and blueberries as the intercom piped in WBT's wildly popular and irreverent *Don't Go Into Morning* show, with Dave and Dave.

'In a fast-breaking story last night,' Dave was saying in his deep radio voice, 'it was revealed that even our city's mayor won't go downtown at night right now.'

'Question is, why would he anyway?' quipped Dave.

'Same thing Senator Butler should have asked.'

'Just checking on his constituents, Dave. Trying to be of service.'

'And the eensy weensy spider crawled up his water spout . . .'

'Whoa, Dave. This is getting out of control.'

'Hey, we're supposed to be able to say anything on this

show. That's in the contract.' Dave was his usual witty self, better than Howard Stern, really.

'Seriously. Mayor Search is asking everybody to help catch the Black Widow Killer,' Dave said. 'And next up is Madonna, Amy Grant, and Rod Stewart . . .'

Brazil had stopped in the middle of the line, frozen as the radio played on and people made their way around him. Packer was walking in, heading straight towards him. Brazil's world was Humpty Dumpty off the wall, cracks happening everywhere at once. He paid for his breakfast, and turned around to face his ruination.

'What's going on?' he said before his grim editor could tell him.

'Upstairs now,' Packer said. 'We got a problem.'

Brazil did not run up the escalator. He did not speak to Packer, who had nothing more to say. Packer wanted no part of this. He wasn't going to insert his foot in his mouth. The great Richard Panesa could fix this one. That's why Knight-Ridder paid Panesa those big bucks. Brazil had been marched to the principal's office only twice during his early school years. In neither case had he really done anything wrong. The first time he had poked his finger into the hamster cage and had gotten bitten. The second time of trouble occurred when he inserted his finger into the hole at the top of his clipboard and had gotten stuck.

Mr Kenny used wire cutters to free young Brazil, who had been humiliated and heartbroken. The blue Formica clipboard with its map of the United States was destroyed. Mr Kenny threw it into the trash while Brazil stood bravely by, refusing to cry, knowing his mother could not afford to buy him another one. Brazil had meekly asked if he could stay after school for a week, dusting erasers on back steps, to earn enough to buy something new to hold notebook paper and write on. That had been okay with all.

Brazil wondered what he could offer to Panesa to make up for whatever he had done to cause such a problem. When he walked into the publisher's intimidating glass office, Panesa was sitting behind his mahogany desk, in his fine Italian suit and leather chair. Panesa didn't get up or acknowledge Brazil directly, but continued reading a printout of the editorial for the Sunday paper, which slammed Mayor Search for his glib, albeit true, comment about his reluctance to travel downtown these nights.

'You might want to shut the door,' Panesa quietly said to his young reporter.

Brazil did and took a seat across from his boss.

'Andy,' he said, 'do you watch television?'

His confusion grew. 'I rarely have time . . .'

'Then you may not know that you are being scooped right and left.'

The dragon inside Brazil woke up. 'Meaning?'

Panesa saw fire in his eyes. Good. The only way this sensitive, brilliant young talent was going to last in this criminal world was if he were a fighter, like Panesa was. Panesa wasn't going to give him a breath of comfort. Andy Brazil, welcome to Hell School, the publisher thought as he picked up a remote control from his mighty desk.

'Meaning' – Panesa hit a button, and a screen unrolled from the ceiling – 'that the last four or five major stories you've done have been aired on television the night before they ran in the paper, usually on the eleven o'clock news.' He pressed another button, and the overhead projector turned on. 'Then the radio stations pick them up first thing in the morning. Before most people get a chance to read what we've plastered on the front page of our paper.'

Brazil shot up from his chair, horrified and homicidal.

'That can't be! No one's even around when I'm out there!' he exclaimed, fists balled by his sides.

Panesa pointed the remote control, pressed another button, and instantly Webb's face was huge in the room.

'. . . in a Channel Three exclusive interview said she returns to the scene of the crash late at night and sits in her car and weeps. Johnson, who turned in her badge this morning, said she wishes she had been killed, too . . .'

Panesa looked at Brazil. Brazil was speechless, his fury toward Webb coalescing into hatred for all. Moments passed before the young police reporter could gather his wits.

'Was this after my story?' Brazil asked, though he knew better.

'Before,' Panesa replied, watching him carefully, and assessing. 'The night before it ran. Like every other one that's followed. Then this bit with the mayor. Well, that clinched it. We know that was a slip on Search's part and not something Webb could know unless he's got the mayor's office bugged.'

'This can't be!' Brazil boiled over. 'It's not my fault!'

'This is not about fault.' Panesa was stern with him. 'Get to the bottom of it. Now. We're really being hurt.'

Panesa watched Brazil storm out. The publisher had a meeting, but sat at his desk, going through memos, dictating to his secretary while he observed Brazil through glass. Brazil was angrily opening desk drawers, digging in the box under it, throwing notepads and other personal effects into his briefcase. He ran out of the newsroom as if he did not plan on coming back. Panesa picked up the phone.

'Get Virginia West on the line,' the publisher said.

* * *

Tommy Axel was staring after Brazil's wake, wondering what the hell was going on, and at the same time suspicious. He knew about Webb, and had heard about the leaks, and didn't blame Brazil for being out of his mind. Axel couldn't imagine the same thing happening to him, someone stealing brilliant thoughts and analyses from his music columns. God. Poor guy.

Brenda Bond also was alert to the uproar as she worked on a computer that had gone down three days in a row because the idiot garden columnist had a knack for striking combinations of keys that somehow locked him out or translated his files into pi signs. Bond had a strange sensation as she went into System Manager. She found it hard to concentrate.

West was standing behind her desk, struggling to pack up her briefcase, and snap the lid back on her coffee, and wrap up the biscuit she didn't have time to eat. She looked worried and frantic as Panesa talked to her on the phone.

'You have any idea where he went?' West inquired.

'Home, maybe?' Panesa said over the line. 'He lives with his mother.'

West looked hopelessly at the clock. She was supposed to be in Hammer's office in ninety seconds, and there was no such thing as putting the chief on hold, or being late, or not showing up, or forgetting. West shut her briefcase, and slid her radio into the case on her belt. She was at a loss.

'I'll do what I can,' she promised Panesa. 'Unfortunately, I've got court this morning. My guess is he's just blowing off steam. As soon as he cools down, he'll be back. Andy's not a quitter.'

'I hope you're right.'

'If he hasn't shown up by the time I get back, I'll start looking,' West said.

'Good idea.'

West hoped that Johnny Martino would plead guilty. Hammer didn't. She was in a mood to cause trouble. Dr Cabel had done her a favor, really. He had ignited a few sparks of anger, and the brighter they got, the more the mist of depression and malaise burned off. She was walking the fastest West had ever seen her, a zip-up briefcase under an arm, sunglasses on. Hammer and West made their way through the sweltering piedmont morning to the Criminal Court Building, constructed of granite in 1987, and therefore older than most buildings in Charlotte. Hammer and West waited in line with everyone else at the X-ray machine.

'Quit worrying.' West tried to reassure her boss as they inched forward behind some of the city's finer citizens. 'He'll plead.' She glanced at her watch.

'I'm not worried,' said Hammer.

West was. There were a hundred cases on the docket today. In truth, this was a bigger problem than whether Martino pled guilty versus taking his chances before a jury of his peers. Deputy Octavius Able eyed the two women getting closer in line and was suddenly alert and interested in his job. West had not passed through his X-ray machine since it resided in the old courthouse. Never had Able so much as laid eyes on Hammer in person. He had never had complete control over her. West was in uniform, and walked around the door frame that was beeping every other second as pagers, change, keys, good luck charms, and pocket knives, went into a cup.

Hammer walked around, too, assuming the privilege of her position.

'Excuse me, ma'am!' Deputy Able said for all to hear. 'Ma'am! Please step through.'

'She's the chief of police,' West quietly told him, and she knew damn well it went without saying.

'Need some identification,' the powerful deputy said to Hammer.

A long line of restless feet stopped, all eyes on the well-dressed lady with the familiar face. Who was that? They'd seen her somewhere, Maybe she was on TV, the news, a talk show? Oh heck. Then Tinsley Owens, six deep in line, here for reckless driving, got it. This lady in pearls was the wife of someone famous, maybe Billy Graham. Hammer was nonplussed as she dug through her pocketbook, and this made Deputy Able's assertion of self not quite as rewarding. She smiled at him, holding up her badge.

'Thanks for checking.' She could have knocked him over when she said that. 'In case anybody had any doubts about the security of our courthouse.' She leaned close to read his nameplate. 'O.T. Able,' she repeated, committing it to memory.

Now the deputy was dead. She was going to complain.

'Just doing my job,' he weakly said as the line got longer, winding around the world, the entire human race witnessing his destruction.

'You most certainly were,' Hammer agreed. 'And I'm going to make sure the sheriff knows how much he should appreciate you.'

The deputy realized the chief meant every word of it, and Able was suddenly taller and slimmer. His khaki uniform fit perfectly. He was handsome and not nearly as old as he had been when he was at the BP pumping gas this morning and a carload of juveniles yelled, calling him *Deputy Dawg, Hawaii Five-O, Tuna Breath*, and other racial slurs. Deputy Octavius Able was ashamed of himself for throwing his weight around with this woman chief. He never used to be that way, and did not know what had happened to him over the years.

Chapter Twenty-one

Hammer and West signed in at the Court Liaison Office and punched time cards. On the second floor, they followed a long corridor crowded with people looking for a pay phone or the bathroom. Some were sleeping on maple benches, or reading the *Observer* to see if their cases might be mentioned. When West opened the door to 2107, her anxiety increased. The courtroom was packed with defendants waiting for punishment, and with cops whose fault it was. Hammer led the way to the very front, sitting on the side for lawyers and police. Assistant District Attorney Melvin Pond spotted the two powerful women instantly and got excited. He had been waiting for them. This was his chance.

Fourth Circuit Judge Tyler Bovine, of the Twenty-fifth Prosecutorial District, had been waiting, too, as had the media from far and near. *Batman and Robin*, she, Judge Bovine, thought with intense pleasure as she departed from her chambers. She'd see about that when she reigned on high in the long black robe that covered her massive body of law. West felt increasingly troubled for a number of reasons. She was worried about Brazil and afraid she'd never get out of here to check on him. Tyler Bovine, as was true of the rest of the judicial herd, was a traveling judge. She resided on the other side of the Catawba River, and despised Charlotte and all that was good about it, including its citizens. The judge was confident that it was only a matter of time before Charlotte annexed her home town of Gastonia, and all else Cornwallis had failed to seize.

'All rise for the judge.'

All got around to it, and Judge Bovine smiled to herself as she entered the courtroom and spotted Hammer and West. The judge knew that the press had been tipped not to waste their time hanging around here this day. Batman and Robin would be back on Monday. Oh yes they would. The judge sat and put on her glasses, looking important and godlike. ADA Pond stared at the docket as if he had never seen one before this morning. He knew he had a battle on his hands, but was determined he would prevail.

'The court calls the case of the State of North Carolina versus Johnny Martino,' he said with confidence he did not feel.

'I'm not ready to hear that now.' Judge Bovine sounded bored.

West nudged Hammer, who was thinking about Seth and not sure what she would do if he died. It did not matter how much they fought or drove each other crazy or proved irrefutably that men and women could not be soulmates or friends. Hammer had a tragic look on her face, and ADA Pond took it as a slight to his knighthood and professional future. He had failed this wonderful, heroic woman whose husband was shot and in the hospital. Chief Hammer did not need to be sitting here with all these cretins. Judge Bovine saw the look on Hammer's face, too, and also misinterpreted, and was further aroused. Hammer had not supported Bovine in the last election. Bovine would see how big and important Hammer was now.

'When I call out your name, please stand. Maury Anthony,' announced ADA Pond.

Pond scanned despondent faces. He searched people slumped back, pissed off and sleeping. Maury Anthony and his public defender rose near the rear. They came forward and stood before the ADA's table.

'Mr Anthony, how do you plead to possession with the intent to sell cocaine?' the ADA asked.

'Guilty,' Mr Anthony spoke.

Judge Bovine stared out at the defendant who was no different than all others. 'Mr Anthony. You realize that by pleading guilty you have no right to appeal,' she stated rather than asked.

Mr Anthony looked at his public defender, who nodded. Mr Anthony returned his attention to the judge. 'Yes, sir,' he said.

Laughter was scattered among those awake and alert. Mr Anthony realized his egregious error and grinned sheepishly. 'I'm sorry, ma'am. My eyes ain't what they once was.'

More laughter.

Judge Bovine's big flat face turned to concrete. 'What says the state,' she ordered as she sipped from a two-liter bottle of Evian.

ADA Pond looked over his notes. He glanced at Hammer and West, hoping they were attentive and impressed. This was his opportunity to be eloquent, no matter what a dog of a case it was.

'Your Honor,' the ADA began as he always did, 'on

the night of July twenty-second, at approximately eleven-thirty, Mr Anthony was drinking and socializing in an establishment on Fourth Street near Graham . . .'

'The court requires the exact address,' Judge Bovine interrupted.

'Well, Your Honor, the problem is, there's not one.'

'There has to be one,' said the judge.

'This is an area where a building was razed in nineteen-ninety-five, Your Honor. The defendant and his associates were back in weeds . . .'

'What was the address of the building that was razed?'

'I don't know,' said the ADA, after a pause.

Mr Anthony smiled. His public defender looked smug. West was getting a headache. Hammer had drifted farther off. The judge drank from her bottle of water.

'You will provide that for the court,' the judge said, screwing on the cap.

'Yes, Your Honor. Only, where this transaction occurred isn't precisely at the old address, but rather farther back, approximately eighty feet, and then another fifty feet, I'd say, at a sixty-degree angle, northeast, from the Independence Welfare building that was there, that was razed, in a thicket where Mr Anthony had set up a hobo camp, of sorts, for the purposes of buying and selling and smoking crack cocaine and eating crabs with associates on that night. Of July twenty-second.'

ADA Pond had the attention, however briefly, of Hammer, and West, plus Johnny Martino's mother, and the conscious courtroom, in addition to two bailiffs and a probation officer. All stared at him with a mixture of curiosity and lack of comprehension.

'The court requires an address,' the judge repeated.

She took another gulp of water and felt contempt for her psychiatrist, and for manic-depressive people everywhere.

Not only did lithium necessitate drinking a tub of water daily, but it caused frequent urination, which by Judge Bovine's definition, was double jeopardy. Her bladder and kidneys were a drip coffee maker that she could feel and measure as she drove back and forth from Gaston County, and sat on the bench, and went to the movies, and flew on crowded airplanes, or walked on the track and found the fieldhouse locked.

Because she was a superior court judge, she could adjourn every fifteen, twenty, or thirty minutes, or until after lunch, if her need was great and she so chose. She could wheel in a damn Porta-John, do whatever she liked, *ipso facto*. But what she would never do, not once during this life and on this planet, was to interrupt a case after it was started, because above all else, the judge was a well-bred lady who had grown up in an antebellum house and gone to Queens College. Judge Bovine was tough, but never rude. She did not tolerate fools or classless people, and no one could accuse her of anything less than impeccable manners. There was nothing more important than manners, really.

ADA Pond hesitated. Hammer had faded away again. West could not get comfortable. The bench seat was wood, and it pressed her police belt and the small of her back. She was perspiring and waiting for her pager to vibrate. Brazil was decompensating. It was something West sensed, yet she wasn't certain why, or what to do about it.

'Mr Pond,' the judge said, 'please continue.'

'Thank you, Your Honor. On this particular night of July twenty-second, Mr Anthony did sell crack cocaine to an undercover Charlotte police officer.'

'Is this officer in the courtroom?' The judge squinted at the sea of wretches below her.

Mungo stood. West turned around, dismayed when she saw who had caused such creaking and shuffling and whispering. *Oh God, not again.* West's sense of foreboding darkened. Hammer remembered Seth bringing her breakfast in bed and dropping keys on the tray. The new Triumph Spitfire was green with burl wood, and she had been a sergeant with free time, and he was the rich son of a rich land developer. Back then, they went on long drives and had picnics. She would come home from work, and music filled the house. When did Seth stop listening to Beethoven, Mozart, Mahler, and Bach, and start turning on the TV? When did Seth decide he wanted to die?

'The subject, Mr Anthony,' Mungo was saying, 'was sitting on a blanket in the thicket Mr Pond has just described. He was with two other subjects, drinking Magnum Forty-four and Colt Forty-five. Between them they had a dozen steamed crabs in a brown paper bag.'

'A dozen?' Judge Bovine queried. 'You counted them, Detective Mungo?'

'Most were gone, Your Honor. I was told there had been a dozen originally. When I looked there were three left, I believe.'

'Go on, go on.' What patience the judge had for this drivel from the dregs of humanity was inversely proportional to her filling bladder as she took another slug of water and thought of what she would eat for lunch.

'The subject, Mr Anthony, offered to sell me a rock of cocaine, in a vial, for fifteen dollars,' Mungo continued.

'Bullshit,' was Mr Anthony's comment. 'I offered you a fucking crab, man.'

'Mr Anthony, if you aren't quiet, I will hold you in contempt of court,' Judge Bovine warned.

'It was a crab. Only time I used the word *crack* was when I told him to *crack* it himself.'

Mungo said, 'Your Honor, I asked the subject what was in the bag, and he distinctly replied, "crack."'

'Did not.' Mr Anthony was about to approach the bench, his public defender restraining him by a sleeve that still had the label sewed on it.

'Did too,' Mungo said.

'Did not!'

'Too.'

'Uh uh.'

'Order!' the judge declared. 'Mr Anthony, one more outburst and . . .'

'Let me tell my side for once!' Mr Anthony went on.

'That is what you have a lawyer for,' the judge said severely, and was beginning to feel the pressure of water and a loss of composure.

'Oh yeah? This piece of shit?' Mr Anthony glowered at his free-lunch defense.

The courtroom was awake and interested, more so than ADA Pond had ever witnessed before this morning. Something was going to happen, and no one was about to miss it, people nudging each other and making silent bets. Jake on the third row, defendant's side, was putting his money on Mr Anthony ending up with his butt in jail. Shontay two rows over was betting on the undercover detective who reminded her of a haystack wearing a wrinkled pinstripe suit. Cops always won, no matter how wrong they might be, it was her belief, based on hearsay. Quik, way in the back, didn't give a fuck as he practiced flicking his thumb out like a switchblade. As soon as he could, the asshole responsible for Quik's *show cause warrant* was gonna pay. Ratting on him like that. Man.

'Detective Mungo.' Judge Bovine had had enough. 'What probable cause did you have to search Mr Anthony's brown paper bag?'

'Your Honor, it's like I said.' Mungo was unmoved. 'I asked him what was in the bag. He told me.'

'He told you crabs, and suggested you crack these crabs yourself,' said the judge, who really had to go now.

'Gee. I don't know. I thought he said crack.' Mungo tried to be fair.

This sort of thing happened to Mungo more times than not. He'd always found it easier to hear whatever he wanted, and when one was as big as him, one could. The case was dismissed, and before the judge could adjourn to her chambers, the agitated ADA called the next, and the next, and the next, and the judge did not interrupt, because it was one thing she would not do. Citizens arrested for burglaries, car thefts, rape, murder, and more drug dealers and those who patronized them stood with their public defenders. ADA Pond was mindful of the judge's constricted body language and miserable demeanor. Pond was accustomed to the judge's frequent visits to her chambers, and knew that capitalizing on her disability was his only hope.

Each time Her Honor started to rise from her bench, ADA Pond was off and running on the next case. As fast as he could, he announced the Johnny Martino once again, in hopes Pond would break the judge, wear her down, and subject her to the water treatment until she could take no more. Her Honor would hear the state of North Carolina versus Johnny Martino so Hammer and West could return to life's highways, and the hospital. ADA Pond prayed Hammer would think kindly of him when he ran for DA in three years.

'Johnny Martino,' ADA Pond said as fast as he could, again, moments later.

'I'm not ready to hear that case yet.' The judge could barely talk.

'Alex Brown,' the ADA blurted out.

'Yeah.' Mr Brown stood, as did his counsel.

'How do you plead to malicious wounding?'

'He started it,' Mr Brown stated for the record. 'What I'm supposed to do, huh? In Church's getting a quart of chicken livers and he decides he wants the same thing, only he's going to get mine and not pay.'

Hammer had tuned back in long enough to make an assessment of her surroundings and those in it. This was much more disheartening than she had imagined. No wonder her beat officers and investigators got so discouraged, so jaded and cynical. There had been a time when she'd had no sympathy or use for people like this. They were lazy, no-account, self-destructive, self-absorbed wastrels who added nothing to society and took from everyone around them. She thought of Seth, of his money, privilege, and opportunity. She thought of the love she and others had given him. Chief Hammer thought of many people she knew who were no better than anybody in this courtroom, really.

West wanted to kill Judge Bovine. It was outrageous making a chief and deputy chief sit through all this. West's attention wandered back to Brazil about every other minute. She wondered if he had returned to the newspaper, and her ominous foreshadowing got denser and more chilling. If she didn't get out of this courtroom soon, she might cause a scene. Her boss, oddly, had returned to the present and seemed fascinated by everything around her, as if Hammer could sit here all day and think those private thoughts that had made her who and what she was.

'Johnny Martino,' ADA Pond struck again.

'I'm not going to hear that case now,' the judge snapped as she carefully got to her feet.

That would be the end of it for at least half an hour, West thought with fury. So she and Hammer would get to sit in the hallway and wait. Oh great. This would have been exactly right had Johnny Martino's mother permitted it. Like West, Mrs Martino had been pushed too far. Mrs Martino knew exactly what was going on. She knew that those two ladies in front were Batman and Robin, and that the judge had to pee. Mrs Martino rose before the judge could climb down from her throne.

'Now hold on one minute,' Mrs Martino loudly said as she made her way over people and up to the bench, in her nice dress and loafers. 'I been sitting here this whole time seeing exactly what's going on.'

'Ma'am . . . !' Her Honor protested, by now standing and in crisis, as a reporter for New Country WTDR radio slipped into the back of the courtroom.

'Don't you ma'am me!' Mrs Martino wagged her finger. 'The boy who robbed all those innocent folks is my son. So I got a right to say whatever the hell I want. And I also know who these women are.' She gave them a deep nod. 'Risking themselves to help all those poor folk when that rotten-ass boy of mine climbed on that bus with the gun he got from some drug dealer out there. Well, I tell you what.'

West, Hammer, ADA Pond, and the courtroom, listened to Mrs Martino with keen interest. The judge deemed it best to reseat herself and hold tight. Mrs Martino had been waiting all her life for her day in court, and she began to pace like an experienced trial lawyer. Radio reporter Tim Nicks was writing down everything, his blood singing and playing drums in his ears. This was too good to be true.

'Let me tell you something, judge,' Mrs Martino went on. 'I know a game when I see one. And every time you could let those poor busy ladies out of here, you pass on it, say move on, no way, not now, ummm ummm.' She shook her head, striding, swinging arms wide. 'Now why you want to be doing that to people who help, to people trying to make a difference out there? It's a disgrace, that's *exactly* what it is.'

'Ma'am, please be seated. . .' Her Honor tried again.

Johnny Martino was in Mecklenburg orange and flip-flops when he was brought in from the jail. He raised his right hand and swore to tell the truth one more time in his life. Hammer was sitting up straight, filled with shining admiration for Mrs Martino, who had no intention of being silenced, and in fact, now that her son had appeared, was only getting started. West was fascinated by how Judge Cow was going to get herself out of an udder disaster, ha! West stifled laughter, suddenly on the verge of hysteria and another hot flash. ADA Pond smiled, and Reporter Nicks wrote furiously in his notepad.

'You want me to sit down, judge?' Mrs Martino walked up closer to the bench, and put her hands on her sturdy hips. 'Then I tell you what. You do the right thing. You hear Johnny's case this minute, listen to his guilty, lying, stealing ass. Then let these fine crusading ladies be on their way, out there saving more lives, helping more folks who can't help themselves, delivering us from evil.'

'Ma'am, I am hearing the case,' Judge Bovine tried to explain. 'That's what we're doing . . .'

But Mrs Martino had her mind made up about the way things were. She turned around and gave Johnny the eye.

'Tell me now.' She swept her arms over the courtroom, touching all. 'Anybody here who insists on stepping ahead of these Christian ladies?' She looked around, taking in the silence, not finding a raised hand to count. 'Speak now,' she called out. 'All right then! Do we want to set these ladies free?'

The courtroom cheered and roared, people doing high-fives for Batman and Robin, who could do nothing but watch, enchanted.

'Johnny Martino, how do you plead to ten counts of robbery with a dangerous weapon?' the ADA called out.

Judge Bovine's teeth were clamped, and a sleeve of her robe flapped empty and useless as she held in her objections, her legs crossed.

'Guilty,' Johnny Martino mumbled.

'What says the state,' the judge whispered, in pain.

'Mr Martino boarded a Greyhound bus on July eleventh at one-eleven P.M.,' ADA Pond summarized. 'He robbed ten passengers at gunpoint before being apprehended and restrained by Chief Judy Hammer and Deputy Chief Virginia West . . .'

'Yo Batman,' someone yelled.

'Robin!'

The cheering began again. Judge Bovine could endure no more. She might have called the sheriff for intervention, but she had more pressing concerns. She had been polite, well mannered, well bred, and had lost control of her courtroom. This was a first. Someone had to pay. It might as well be the son of a bitch who caused all this when he climbed on that damn bus.

'The state agrees to consolidate sentencing under ten counts,' the judge announced rapidly and with no attempt at drama. 'Defendant is a prior record level two and will receive in each of the ten counts a sentence of seventy months minimum or ninety-three months maximum, for a total of seven hundred months minimum and nine hundred and thirty months maximum. The court is recessed until one.' She gathered her robe in one hand and fled as Mr Martino checked the judge's math.

Reporter Nicks fled back to South McDowell Street, where *Today's Hot New Country and Your All Time Favorites* could be heard on 96.9. It was rare his station got breaking news, scoops, tips, or leaks, as if to imply that a country music audience didn't vote or care about crime or want crack dealers in jail. The point was, no city official or Deep Throat had ever bothered to think of Nicks when something went down. This was his day, and he was out of his '67 Chevelle with such urgency that he had to run back twice to get his notepad and lock the doors.

Chapter Twenty-two

The sensational courtroom drama of the caped crusaders sitting on the front row, while the joker of the judge dissed them, bristled over the airwaves. It was bounced from radio tower to radio tower throughout the Carolinas. Don Imus picked it up, embellishing as only he could, and Paul Harvey told the rest of the story. While Hammer was back and forth to SICU and aware of little else, West drove Charlotte's streets, looking for Brazil, who had not been seen since Thursday. It was Saturday morning now.

Packer was out with the dog again when West called. He got on the phone, irritable and perplexed. He had heard nothing from Brazil, either. In Davidson, Mrs Brazil snored on the living-room couch, sleeping through Northside Baptist's televised service, as usual. The phone rang and rang, an overflowing ashtray and bottle of vodka on the coffee table. West was driving past the Knight-Ridder building, hanging up her portable phone in frustration.

'Goddamn it!' she blurted. 'Andy! Don't do this!'

* * *

Mrs Brazil barely opened her eyes. She managed to sit up an inch, thinking she heard something. A choir in blue with gold stoles praised God. Maybe that was the noise. She reached for her glass, and it shook violently as she finished what she had started the night before. Mrs Brazil fell back into old sour couch cushions, the magic potion heating blood, carrying her away to that place nowhere special. She drank again, realizing she was low on fuel with nothing open but the Quick Mart. After noon, she could get beer or wine, she supposed. Where was Andy? Had he been in and out while she was resting?

Night came, and West stayed home and did not want to be with anyone. Her chest was tight and she could not sit long in any one spot or concentrate. Raines called several times, and when she heard his voice on the machine, she did not pick up. Brazil had vanished, it seemed, and West could focus on little else. This was crazy. She knew he wouldn't do anything stupid. But she was revisited by the horrors she had worked in her career.

She had seen the drug overdoses, the gunshot suicides not discovered until hunters returned to the woods. She conjured up images of cars covered by the clandestine waters of lakes and rivers until spring thaws or hard rains dislodged those who had chosen not to live.

Even Hammer, with all her problems and preoccupations, had contacted West several times, voicing concern about their young, at-large volunteer. Hammer's weekend, so far, had been spent at SICU, and she had sent for her sons as their father settled deeper into the valley of shadows. Seth's eyes stared dully at his wife when she entered his room. He did not speak.

He did not think complete thoughts, but rather in

shards of memories and feelings unexpressed that might have formed a meaningful composite had he been able to articulate them. But he was weak and sedated and intubated. During rare lucid flickers during days he could not measure, when he might have given Hammer enough to interpret his intentions, the pain pinned him to the bed. It always won. He would stare through tears at the only woman he had ever loved. Seth was so tired. He was so sorry. He'd had time to think about it.

I'm sorry, Judy. I couldn't help any of it ever since you've known me. Read my mind, Judy. I can't tell you. I'm so worn out. They keep cutting on me and I don't know what's left. I punished you because I couldn't reward you. I have figured that out too late. I wanted you to take care of me. Now look. Whose fault is it, after all? Not yours. I wish you would hold my hand.

Hammer sat in the same chair and watched her husband of twenty-six years. His hands were tethered to his sides so he would not pull out the tube in his trachea. He was on his side, his color deceivingly good and not due to anything he was doing for himself, but to oxygen, and she found this ironically typical. Seth had been drawn to her because of her strength and independence, then had hated her for the way she was. She wanted to take his hand, but he was so fragile and inflexible and trussed up by tubes and straps and dressings.

Hammer leaned close and rested her hand on his forearm as his dull eyes blinked and stared and looked sleepy and watery. She was certain that at a subconscious level he knew she was here. Beyond that, it was improbable much registered. Scalpels and bacteria had ravaged his buttocks and now were fileting and rotting his abdomen and thighs. The stench was awful, but Hammer did not really notice it anymore.

'Seth,' she said in her quiet, commanding voice. 'I know you may not hear me, but on the off chance you can, I want to tell you things. Your sons are on their way here. They should arrive sometime late this afternoon and will come straight to the hospital. They are fine. I am hanging in there. All of us are sad and sick with worry about you.'

He blinked, staring. Seth did not move as he breathed oxygen and monitors registered his blood pressure and pulse.

'I have always cared about you,' she went on. 'I have always loved you in my own way. But I realized long ago that you were attracted to me so you could change me. And I was drawn to you because I thought you'd stay the same. Rather silly, now that I look at it.' She paused, a flutter around her heart as his eyes stared back at her. 'There are things I could have done better and differently. You must forgive me, and I must forgive myself. You must forgive me and you must forgive yourself.'

He didn't disagree with this, and wished he could somehow indicate what he thought and felt. His body was like something unplugged, broken, out of batteries. He flipped switches in his brain and nothing happened. All this because he drank too much in bed, while playing with a gun to punish her.

'We go on from here,' Chief Judy Hammer said, blinking back tears. 'Okay, Seth? We put this behind us and learn from it. We move ahead.' It was hard to talk. 'Why we got married isn't so important anymore. We are friends, companions. We don't exist to procreate or perpetuate endless sexual fantasies for each other. We're here to help each other grow old and not feel alone. Friends.' Her hand gripped his arm.

Tears spilled from Seth's eyes. It was the only sign he

gave, and his wife dissolved. Hammer cried for half an hour as his vital signs weakened. Group A strep oozed toxins around his soul, and did not give a damn about all those antibiotics and immunoglobulin and vitamins being pumped into its plump host. To his disease, he was a rump roast. He was carrion on life's highway.

Randy and Jude entered their father's SICU room at quarter of six, and did not see him conscious. It was not likely Seth knew they were by his bed, but knowing they were coming had been enough.

West cruised past the Cadillac Grill, Jazzbone's, and finally headed to Davidson, deciding that Brazil might be hiding out in his own house and not answering the phone. She pulled into the eroded driveway, and was crushed that only the ugly Cadillac was home. West got out of her police car. Weeds grew between cracks in the brick walk she followed to the front door. She rang the bell several times, and knocked. Finally, she rapped hard and in frustration with her baton.

'Police!' she said loudly. 'Open up!'

This went on for a while until the door opened and Mrs Brazil blearily peered out. She steadied herself by holding on to the door frame.

'Where's Andy?' West asked.

'Haven't seen him.' Mrs Brazil pressed her forehead with a hand, squinting, as if the world was bad for her health. 'At work, I guess,' she muttered.

'No, he's not and hasn't been since Thursday,' West said. 'You're sure he hasn't called or anything?'

'I've been sleeping.'

'What about the answering machine? Have you checked?' West asked.

'He keeps his room locked.' Mrs Brazil wanted to return to her couch. 'Can't get in there.'

West, who did not have her tool belt with her, could still get into most things. She took the knob off his door and was inside Brazil's room within minutes. Mrs Brazil returned to the living room and settled her swollen, poisoned self on the couch. She did not want to go inside her son's room. He didn't want her there anyway, which was why she had been locked out for years, ever since he had accused her of taking money from the wallet he tucked under his socks. He had accused her of rummaging through his school papers. He had blamed her for knocking over his eighteen-and-under singles state championship tennis trophy, badly denting it and breaking off the little man.

The red light was flashing on the answering machine beside Brazil's neatly made twin bed with its simple green spread. West hit the play button, looking around at shelves of brass and silver trophies, at scholastic and creative awards that Brazil had never bothered to frame, but had thumbtacked to walls. A pair of leather Nike tennis shoes, worn out from toe-dragging, was abandoned under a chair, one upright, one on its side, and the sight of them pained West. For a moment, she felt distressed and upset. She imagined the way he looked at her with blue eyes that went on forever. She remembered his voice on the radio, and the quirky way he tested coffee with his tongue, which she had repeatedly told him wasn't a smart way to determine whether something was too hot. The first three calls on his machine were hang-ups.

'Yo,' began the fourth one. 'It's Axel. Got tickets for Bruce Hornsby . . .'

West hit a button.

'Andy? It's Packer. Call me.'

She hit the button again and heard her own voice looking for him. She skipped ahead, landing on two more hang-ups. West opened the closet door, and her fear intensified when she found nothing inside. She, the cop, went into drawers and found them empty, as well. He had left his books and computer behind, and this only deepened her confusion and concern. These were what he loved the most. He would not abandon them unless he had embarked upon a self-destructive exodus, a fatalistic flight. West looked under the bed and lifted the mattress, exploring every inch of Brazil's private space. She did not find the pistol he had borrowed from her.

West drove around the city much of the night, mopping her face, popping Motrin, and turning the air conditioner on and off as she vacillated between hot and cold. On South College, she slowly passed street people, staring hard at each, as if she expected Brazil to have suddenly turned into one of them. She recognized Poison, the young hooker from Mungo's videotape, undulating along the sidewalk, smoking a cigarette and enjoying being watched. Poison followed the dark blue cop car with haunted, glassy eyes, and West looked back. West thought of Brazil, of his sad curiosity about bad people and what had happened to make them that way.

They make choices, West said that all the time, and it was true.

But she envied Brazil's freshness, his innocent clarity of vision. In truth, he saw life with a wisdom equal to her own, but his was born of vulnerability, and not of the experience that sometimes crowded West's compassion and cloaked her feelings in many hard layers. Her condition had been coming on for a long time, and most likely was irreversible. West accepted that when one is exposed to the worst elements of life, there comes a point of no return. She had been beaten and shot, and she had killed. She had crossed a line. She was a missionary, and the tender, warm contours of life were for others.

On Tryon Street, she was stopped at a traffic light near Jake's, another favorite spot for breakfast. Thelma could do anything with fried steak and biscuits, and the coffee was good. West stared ahead, several blocks away, just past First Union Bank with its giant painted hornet bursting out of one side of the building. She recognized the dark car's boxy shape and conical tail lights glowing red. She wasn't close enough to see the tag yet, and was going to do something about that.

The light turned green and West gunned the Ford's powerful engine until she was on the old BMW's bumper. Her heart thrilled as she recognized the plate number. She honked her horn and motioned, and Brazil kept going. West followed, honking again and longer, but clearly he had no intention of acknowledging her as she followed his shiny chrome bumper through downtown. Brazil knew she was there and didn't give a damn as he threw back another gulp from the tall-boy Budweiser he was holding between his legs. He broke the law right in front of Deputy Chief West, and knew she saw it, and he didn't give a shit.

'Goddamn son of a bitch,' West exclaimed as she flipped on flashing lights.

Brazil sped up. West couldn't believe what was happening. How could he do anything this stupid?

'Oh for fuck's sake!' She hit the siren.

Brazil had been in pursuits, but he had never been the lead car. Usually, he was back there sitting in the front seat with West. He drank another swallow of the beer he had bought at the 76 truck stop just off the Sunset East exit. He needed another one, and decided he might as well hit I-77 off Trade Street, and cruise on back for a refill. He tossed his empty in the back seat, where several others clinked and rolled on the floor. His broken speedometer faithfully maintained its belief that the BMW was going thirty-two miles per hour.

In fact, he was going sixty-three when he turned onto the Interstate. West doggedly pursued as her alarm and anger grew. Should she call for other cars, Brazil was ruined, his volunteer days ended, his real troubles only begun. Nor was there a guarantee that more cops would effect a stop. Brazil might decompensate further. He might feel desperate, and West knew how that might end. She had seen those final chapters before, all over the road, crumpled metal sharp like razors, glass, oil, blood, and black body bags on their way to the morgue.

His speed climbed to ninety miles per hour, and he maintained it, with her steadily behind him, lights and siren going full tilt. It penetrated his fog that she had not gotten on the radio for help. He would have heard it on his scanner, and backup cars surely would have shown up by now. He didn't know if this made him feel better or worse. Maybe she didn't take him seriously. Nobody took him seriously, and nobody ever would again, because of Webb, because of the unfairness, the heartlessness of life and all in it.

Brazil shot onto the exit of Sunset Road East and began to slow. It was finished. In truth, he needed gas. This chase had its limits anyway. He might as well stop. Depression settled heavier, crushing him into his seat as he parked at the outer limits of the tarmac, far away from eighteen-wheelers and their bright-painted shiny cabs with all their chrome. He cut the engine and leaned back, shutting his eyes, as punishment approached. West wouldn't cut him any slack. She, in her uniform and gun, was above all else a cop, and a hard, unkind one at that. It mattered not that they were partners and went shooting together and talked about things.

'Andy.' She loudly rapped a knuckle on his window. 'Get out,' she commanded this common lawbreaker.

He felt tired as he climbed out of a car that his father, Drew, had loved. Brazil took off his father's jacket and tossed it in the back seat. It was almost eighty degrees out, gnats and moths swarming in sodium vapor lights. Brazil was soaked with sweat. He tucked the keys in a pocket of the tight jeans that Mungo believed pointed to Brazil's criminal leanings. West shone her flashlight through the back window, illuminating aluminum tallboy beer cans on the mat in back. She counted eleven.

'Did you drink all these tonight?' she demanded to know as he shut his door.

'No.'

'How many have you had tonight?'

'I didn't count.' His eyes were hard and defiant on hers.

'Do you always elude police lights and sirens?' she said, furious. 'Or is tonight special for some reason?'

He opened the back door of his BMW, and angrily grabbed out a T-shirt. He had no comment as he peeled off his wet polo shirt, and yanked on the dry one. West had never seen him half naked.

'I ought to lock you up,' she said with not quite as much authority.

'Go ahead,' he said.

Randy and Jude Hammer had flown into the Charlotte-Douglas International Airport within forty-five minutes of each other, and their mother had met them downstairs in baggage. The three were somber and distracted as Hammer returned to Carolinas Medical Center without delay. She was so happy to see her boys, and old memories were reopened and exposed to air and light. Randy and Jude had been born with their mother's handsome bones and straight white teeth. They had been blessed with her piercing eyes and frightening intelligence.

From Seth, they had received their four-cylinder engines that moved them slowly along, and with little direction or passing power or drive. Randy and Jude were happy enough simply to exist and go nowhere in a hurry. They drew gratification and joy from their dreams, and from regular customers in whatever restaurant employed them from one year to the next. They were happy with the understanding women who loved them anyway. Randy was proud of his bit parts in movies no one saw. Jude was thrilled to be in any jazz bar he and the guys got gigs in, and he played the drums with passion, whether the audience was ten people or eighty.

Oddly, it had never been their rocket-charged mother who could not live with the sons' something less than stellar accomplishments in life. It was Seth who was disgusted and ashamed. Their father had proved so totally lacking in understanding and patience, that the sons had moved far away. Of course, Hammer understood the psychological dynamics. Seth's hatred for his sons was his hatred for himself. It didn't take great acumen to deduce that much. But knowing the reason had changed nothing. It had required tragedy, a grave illness, to reunite this family.

'Mom, you holding up?' Jude was in back of Hammer's personal car. He was rubbing her shoulders as she drove.

'I'm trying.'

She swallowed hard as Randy looked at her with concern from the front passenger's seat.

'Well, I don't want to see him,' said Randy, cradling flowers he had bought for his father in the airport.

'That's understandable,' Hammer said, switching lanes, eyes in the mirrors. It had begun to rain. 'How are my babies?'

'Great,' Jude said. 'Benji's learning to play sax.'

'I can't wait to hear it. What about Owen?'

'Not quite old enough for instruments, but she's my boogie baby. Every time she hears music, she dances with Spring,' Jude went on, referring to the child's mother. 'God, Mom, you'll die when you see it. It's hilarious!'

Spring was the artist Jude had lived with in Greenwich Village for eight years. Neither of Hammer's sons was married. Each had two children, and Hammer adored every fine golden hair on their small lovely heads. It was her bleeding, buried fear that they were growing up in distant cities with only infrequent contact with their rather legendary grandmother. Hammer did not want to be someone they might someday talk about but had never known.

'Smith and Fen wanted to come,' said Randy, taking his mother's hand. 'It's gonna be all right, Mom.' He felt another stab of hate for his father.

West didn't know what to do with her prisoner of the evening. Brazil was slumped down in the seat, arms crossed, his posture defiant and decidedly without remorse. He refused to look at her now, but stared out the windshield at bugs and bats swirling beneath lights. He watched truckers in pointed cowboy boots and jeans strolling out to their mighty steeds, and leaning against cabs, propping a foot on the running board, hands cupped around a cigarette, as they lit up like the Marlboro Man.

'You got your cigarettes?' Brazil asked West.

She looked at him as if he had lost his mind. 'Forget it.'

'I want one.'

'Yeah, right. You've never smoked in your life, and I'm not going to be the reason you start,' she said, and she wanted one, too.

'You couldn't possibly know whether I've ever smoked a cigarette or pot or anything else,' he said in the strange tone of intoxication. 'Ha! You think you know so much. You don't know shit. Cops. And their dark, narrow alleyways for minds.'

'Really? I thought you were a cop. Or have you quit that, too?'

He stared miserably out his side window.

West felt sorry for him, mad as she was. She wished she knew what was wrong, exactly.

'What the hell's gotten into you?' She tried another tactic, poking Brazil, this time not playfully.

He did not respond.

'Trying to ruin your life? What if some other cop spotted you first?' She was no-nonsense. 'Got any idea how much trouble you'd be in?'

'I don't care,' he said, and his voice caught.

'Yes, you do, goddamn it! Look at me!'

Brazil stared out, his eyes swimming as he dully watched bleary images of people in and out of the truck stop, men and women whose lives were different from his, and who would not understand what it was like to be him. They would look at all that he was and despise him for being privileged and spoiled, because they could not comprehend his reality.

* * *

Bubba felt precisely this, and just so happened to be parking his King Cab at the pumps. He spotted the BMW first, then the cop car with the enemy in it. Bubba could not believe his good fortune. He went in for Pabst Blue Ribbon and Red Man, and picked up the latest *Playboy*.

Brazil was struggling to control himself, and West could be hard but so long. She cared about him in a way that fit no easy definition, and this was partly why he unsettled and confused her so much. She enjoyed him as a talented, precocious recruit, someone she could mentor and get a kick out of watching as he learned. She did not have a brother and would have liked one exactly like him, someone young, smart, sensitive and kind. He was a friend, although she did not give him much of a chance. He was a pretty incredible-looking guy and didn't seem to notice.

'Andy,' she quietly said, 'please tell me what happened.'

'Somehow he got in my computer basket, my files. Everything over the news channels before the paper came out. Scooped.' His voice trembled, and he did not want West to see him like this.

West was stunned. 'He?' she asked. 'Who's he?'

'Webb.' He could barely bring himself to say that name. 'Same piece of shit screwing your deputy chief!'

'What?' Now West was truly lost.

'Goode,' he said. 'Everybody knows.'

'I didn't.' West wondered how she could have missed intelligence like that.

Brazil's heart was broken forever. West wasn't quite sure what to do as she mopped her face again.

* * *

Bubba stealthily made his way back to his truck, his thick face with its misshapen nose averted and shadowed by an Exxon baseball cap. Climbing up into his cab with his purchases, he sat watching the cop car out his windshield. For a while, he flipped through his magazine, pausing at the really big stories. There were many of them, and he tried not to think about his wife or make comparisons as he calculated the best method of attack.

He had packed light tonight, just a Colt .380 caliber seven-shot pistol in an ankle holster, which would not have been his first choice had he known he might have a standoff with the cops. It was a good thing he had a backup between the seats, a Quality Parts Shorty E-2 Carbine, .223 caliber, with thirty-shot magazine, adjust able sights, chrome-lined barrel finished in manganese phosphate that didn't shine at night. For all practical purposes, this was an M-16, and with it, Bubba could riddle West's car Bonnie and Clyde style. He turned a page, and massaged more big ideas as he enjoyed the dark.

West had never really been called upon to comfort a member of the male gender. Rarely was such a thing needed or requested, and having no precedent to follow, she used common sense. Brazil was hiding his face in his hands. She felt terribly sorry for him. What an unfortunate state of affairs.

'It's not that bad, really,' she kept saying. 'Okay?' She patted his shoulder. 'We'll find a way out of this. Okay?'

She patted him again, and when this did not make a dent, she finally broke down. 'Come here,' she said.

West put an arm around him, and pulled him close. Suddenly, he was in her lap, his arms clamped around her, as he held her like a child, which he was not. West's hot flashes seemed worse as she thought fast and hormones spiked. He nuzzled her, holding tight, and her insides woke up, startling her. Brazil was suffering from a similar response, and moved up her body, to her neck, until he found her mouth. For moments, at least, they were completely out of control and out of orbit. Their traumatized brains went into shock, allowing other instincts to have their way, for Mother Nature worked in this fashion to trick couples into procreating.

West and Brazil had not gotten to the point of worrying about what sort of birth control was best suited to their anatomies, needs, tastes, belief systems, personal choices, fantasies, secret pleasures, or faith in consumer reports. This way of communicating with each other was new, so they took the time to linger in places they had always wondered about. Then reality asserted itself with alacrity, and West suddenly sat up and looked out the windows of her police car, remembering she was on duty with a man in her lap.

'Andy,' she said.

He was busy.

'Andy,' she tried again. 'Andy, get up. You're on my . . . gun.'

She tried to move him, with no energy or enthusiasm, not wanting him to go anywhere ever again. Hell was here and she was finished.

'Sit up,' she said, wiping her face again. Her life was ruined. 'This is incest, pedophilia,' she muttered, taking a deep breath as he went on with what he was doing.

'You're right, you're right,' he mumbled with absolutely no conviction, as he explored the wonders of her existence in a way that was unknown and overwhelming to her.

It was difficult to predict exactly where this might have gone had Bubba not intervened. There was a Holiday Inn Express not too far away on I-77, and it had an indoor pool, 42-channel cable TV, and free local calls and newspaper, and complimentary continental breakfasts. Possibly, West and Brazil would have made their way to one of those rooms before morning, and gotten into even more trouble at a bargain price. They possibly would have slept together, and that was where West always drew the line. Sex was one thing, but she did not sleep with someone she was not in love with, meaning she slept with no living soul except Niles.

Again, such contemplations are moot when there is a sharp rap on the window and one peers into the barrel of a carbine rifle reminiscent of Bosnia, or perhaps Miami. West did not have her glasses on, but the redneck with his assault rifle outside her police car looked familiar in a fuzzy sort of way.

'Sit up very slowly,' she said to Brazil.

'What for?' He wasn't ready yet.

'Trust me,' she told him.

It was just as well that condensation had formed on the glass. Bubba could not see exactly what was going on inside the dark blue Ford Crown Victoria, but he had a pretty good idea. This heightened his excitement, making him more certain that he was going to waste these two after doing something really, really bad to them first. If there were two things Bubba could not endure in life, they were queers making out, and straights making out. When he saw queers flirting, touching, Bubba wanted to beat the shit out them and then leave them dying in a ditch. When he saw what he thought he was looking at right now inside this police car, he felt pretty much the same impulse. People with money, importance, or a good sex life, and especially all three, made Bubba insane with righteous outrage. It was his calling, he was sure, to smite them in the name of America.

West was not as frightened by the rifle with thirty rounds as most people would have been, and her brain was powering up. It seemed this was the creep from the Firing Line who had gotten arrested for exposing himself in Latta Park. She had a pretty good idea why she had found Super Glue in her shrubs, and she wished like hell that Brazil hadn't busted the guy's nose. All the same, West was ready for violence. When anyone pointed a gun at her, there was a true cause and effect that rapidly clicked into gear. Unhooking the mike, she placed it next to her hip. She keyed it with her right hand, locking out all radio traffic in her response area. Dispatchers, cops, reporters, and criminals with scanners, could hear nothing but her. She rolled down her window a few inches.

'Please don't shoot,' she said loudly.

Bubba was surprised and pleased by her rapid submission. 'Unlock the doors,' he ordered.

'Okay, okay,' West continued in the same loud, tense voice. 'I'm going to unlock the doors real slowly. Please don't shoot. Please. We can work this out, all right? And if you start shooting here, everyone at the Seventy-six truck stop will hear, so what good will it do?'

Bubba had already thought about this, and she was

right. 'The two of you are getting in my truck,' he said. 'We're taking a ride.'

'Why?' West kept on. 'What do you want from us? We have no problem with you.'

'Oh yeah?' He gripped the carbine tighter, loving the way the bitch in uniform was groveling before him, the great Bubba. 'How about at the range the other night, when Queerbait there hit me?'

'You started it,' Brazil said to him and all listening to channel two.

'We can work this out,' West said again. 'Look. Let's just get right back on Sunset, maybe meet somewhere where we can talk about this? All these trucks coming in here, they're looking. You don't want witnesses, and this isn't a good place to be settling a dispute.'

Bubba thought they had already gone over this point. What he planned to do was shoot them out near the lake, weigh their bodies down with cinder blocks, and dump them where no one would find them until mud turtles had eaten important features. He heard that happened. Crabs were bad on dead bodies, too, as were household pets, especially cats, if locked up with dead owners and not fed, and eventually having no choice.

As Bubba deliberated, eight Charlotte patrol cars with flashing lights were speeding along I-77, now within minutes of the truck stop. Shotguns were out and ready. The police helicopter was lifting from the helipad on top of the LEC, sniper shooters poised. The SWAT team had been deployed. The FBI had been called and agents were on standby, in the event hostage or terrorist negotiators, or the Child Abduction Serial Killer Unit, or the Hostage Rescue Team, might be what it took to save the day.

'Get out of the car,' said Bubba.

In his mind, he was not in plaid shorts, white tube

socks, Hush Puppies, and a Fruit of the Loom white T-shirt that had never been washed with bleach. In his mind, he was in military fatigues, with black grease under his eyes, hair a buzz cut, sweaty muscles bunching as he gripped his weapon and prepared to score two more points for his country and the guys at the hunt club. He was Bubba. He knew the perfect sliver of undeveloped lake property where he could do his duty, having his way with the woman first. *Take that*, he would think as he drove home his point. *Now who's got the power, bitch?*

Police cars turned onto Sunset East. They traveled single file, lights going, in a neat flashing line. Inside the truck stop, several truckers, who believed they had been stagecoach drivers in an earlier life, had lost interest in microwave nachos, cheeseburgers, and beer. They were looking out plate glass, watching what was going on at the edge of the parking lot as pulsing blue and red lights showed through trees.

'No way that's a rifle,' Betsy was saying as she chewed on a Slim Jim.

'Oh yeah it is too,' said Al.

'Then we should go on out and help.'

'Help which one?' asked Tex.

All contemplated this long enough for police cars to get closer and the sound of chopper blades to be barely discernible.

'Looks to me like Bubba started it,' decided Pete.

'Then we should go get him.'

'You hear about the guns he's got?'

'Bubba ain't gonna shoot us.'

* * *

The argument was moot. Bubba could feel dark armies closing around him, and he got desperate.

'*Git out now or I'm going to let loose!*' he screamed, racking a cartridge into a chamber that already had one.

'Don't shoot.' West held up her hands, noting the double feed that had just jammed his gun. 'I'm opening the door, okay?'

'NOW!' Bubba pointed and yelled.

West positioned herself before the door as best she could, and planted a foot on it. She raised the handle, and kicked with all her strength, as eight police cars roared in, sirens ripping the violent night. Bubba was slammed in his midsection, and flew back, landing on his back, the rifle skittering across tarmac. West was out and on him before her feet hit the ground. She did not wait for her backups. She didn't care a shit about the big, burly drivers boiling out of the truck stop to help. Brazil leapt out, too, and together they threw Bubba on his fat belly and cuffed him, desperate to beat him half to death, but resisting.

'*You goddamn son-of-a-bitch piece of chicken-eating shit!*' Brazil bellowed.

'*Move and your head's all over with!*' exclaimed West, her pistol pressed hard against the small of Bubba's thick neck.

The force hauled Bubba away, with no assistance from the truckers, who returned their attention to snacks for the road, and cigarettes. West and Brazil sat in silence for a moment inside her car.

'You always get me into trouble,' she said, backing up.

'Hey!' he protested. 'Where are you going?'

'I'm taking you home.'

'I don't live at home anymore.'

'Since when?' She tried not to show her surprised pleasure.

'Day before yesterday. I got an apartment at Charlotte Woods, on Woodlawn.'

'Then I'll take you there,' she told him.

'My car's here,' he reminded her.

'And you've been drinking all night,' she said, buckling her shoulder harness. 'We'll come back and get your car when you're sober.'

'I am sober,' he said.

'Compared to what?' She drove. 'You won't remember any of this tomorrow.'

He would remember every second of it for the rest of his tormented life. He yawned, and rubbed his temples. 'Yeah, you're probably right,' he agreed, deciding it had meant nothing to her. It also meant nothing to him.

'Of course, I'm right.' She smiled easily.

She could tell he was indifferent. He was one more typical asshole-user guy. What was she, anyway, but a middle-aged, out-of-shape woman who'd never been to a city bigger or more exciting than the one she had worked in since she had graduated from college? He was just trying her on for size, taking his first test drive in an old, out-of-style car that he could afford to make mistakes in. She felt like slamming on the brakes and making him walk. When she pulled into the tidy apartment complex parking lot and waited for him to get out, she offered not a word of friendship or meaning.

Brazil stood outside her car, holding the door open, staring in at her. 'So, what time tomorrow?'

'Ten,' she said, shortly.

He slammed the door, walking away fast, hurt and upset. Women were all the same. They were warm and wonderful one minute, and turned-on and all over him the next, which was followed by moody and distant and didn't mean what happened. Brazil didn't understand how he and West could have had such a special moment at the truck stop, and now it was as if they weren't even on a first-name basis. She had used him, that's what. It was empty and cheap to her, and he was certain this was her modus operandi. She was older, powerful, and experienced, not to mention good-looking, with a body that caused him serious pain. West could toy with anyone she wanted.

So could Blair Mauney III, his wife feared. Polly Mauney could not help but worry about what her husband might engage in when he traveled to Charlotte tomorrow, on USAir flight number 392, nonstop from Asheville, where the Mauneys lived in a lovely Tudor-style home in Biltmore Forest. Blair Mauney III was from old money, and had just come in from the club after a hard tennis match, a shower, a massage, and drinks with his pals. Mauney had come from many generations of banking, beginning with his grandfather, Blair Mauney, who had been a founding father of the American Trust Company.

Blair Mauney III's father, Blair Mauney, Jr., had been a vice president when American Commercial merged with First National of Raleigh. A statewide banking system was off and running, soon followed by more mergers, and the eventual formation of North Carolina National Bank. This went on, and with the S&L crisis of the late 1980s, banks that had not been bought up were offered at fire sale prices. NCNB became the fourth-largest bank in the country, and was renamed USBank. Blair Mauney

III knew the minutiae about his well-respected bank's remarkable history. He knew what the chairman, the president, the vice chairman and chief financial officer, and CEO got paid.

He was a senior vice president for USBank in the Carolinas, and routinely was required to travel to Charlotte. This he rather much enjoyed, for it was good to get away from wife and teenaged children whenever one could, and only his colleagues in their lofty offices understood his pressures. Only comrades understood the fear lurking in every banker's heart that one day Cahoon, who tolerated nothing, would inform hard workers like Mauney that they were out of favor with the crown. Mauney dropped his tennis bag in his recently remodeled kitchen, and opened the door of the refrigerator, ready for another Amstel Light.

'Honey?' he called out, popping off the cap.

'Yes, dear.' She briskly walked in. 'How was tennis?'

'We won.'

'Good for you!' She beamed.

'Withers must have double-faulted twenty times.' He swallowed. 'Foot-faulted like hell, too, but we didn't call those. What'd you guys eat?' He barely looked at Polly Mauney, his wife of twenty-two years.

'Spaghetti Bolognese, salad, seven grain bread.' She went through his tennis bag, fishing out cold sweat-soaked, smelly shorts, shirt, socks, and jock strap, as she always had and would.

'Got any pasta left?'

'Plenty. I'd be delighted to fix you a plate, dear.'

'Maybe later.' He fell into stretches. 'I'm really getting tight. You don't think it's arthritis, do you?'

'Of course not. Would you like me to rub you down, sweetheart?' she said.

While he was drifting during his massage, she would bring up what her plastic surgeon had said when she had inquired about a laser treatment to get rid of fine lines on her face, and a copper laser treatment to eliminate the brown spot on her chin. Polly Mauney had been filled with terror when her plastic surgeon had made it clear that no light source could substitute for a scalpel. That was how bad she had gotten.

'Mrs Mauney,' her plastic surgeon had told her. 'I don't think you're going to be happy with the results. The lines most troublesome are too deep.'

He traced them on her face so gently. She relaxed, held hostage by tenderness. Mrs Mauney was addicted to going to the doctor. She liked being touched, looked at, analyzed, scrutinized, and checked on after surgery or changes in her medication.

'Well,' Mrs Mauney had told her plastic surgeon. 'If that's what you recommend. And I suppose I am to assume you are referring to a face lift.'

'Yes. And the eyes.' He held up a mirror to show her.

The tissue above and below her eyes was beginning to droop and puff. This was irreversible. No amount of cold water splashes, cucumbers or cutting down on alcohol or salt would make a significant difference, she was informed.

'What about my breasts?' she then had inquired.

Her plastic surgeon stepped back to look. 'What does your husband think?' he asked her.

'I think he'd like them bigger.'

Her doctor laughed. Why didn't she state the obvious? Unless a man was a pedophile or gay, he liked them bigger. His gay female patients felt the same way. They were just better sports about it, or pretended to be, if the one they loved didn't have much to offer.

'We can't do all of this at once,' the plastic surgeon warned Mrs Mauney. 'Implants and a face lift are two very different surgeries, and we'd need to space them apart, giving you plenty of time to heal.'

'How far apart?' she worried.

Chapter Twenty-three

It did not occur to West until she was home and locking herself in for the night that she would have to set her alarm clock. Perhaps one of her few luxuries in life was not getting up on Sunday morning until her body felt like it, or Niles did. Then she took her time making coffee and reading the paper, as she thought about her parents heading off to Dover Baptist Church, not far from the Chevon, or from Pauline's Beauty Shop, where her mother got her hair fixed every Saturday at ten in the morning. West always called her parents on Sunday, usually when they were sitting down to dinner and wishing her place wasn't empty.

'Great,' she muttered to herself, grabbing a beer as Niles sat on the window sill over the sink. 'So now I've got to get up at eight-thirty. Can you believe that?'

She tried to figure out what Niles was staring at. From this section of Dilworth, West would have no reminders of the city she protected were it not for the top thirty stories of USBank rising brightly above West's unfinished fence. Niles had gotten really peculiar lately, it struck West. He sat in the same spot every night, staring out, as if he were ET missing home.

'What are you looking at?' West ran her fingernails down Niles's silky, ruddy spine, something that always made him purr.

He did not respond. He stared, as if in a trance.

'Niles?' West was getting a bit worried. 'What is it, baby? You not feeling well? Got a hairball? Mad at me again? That's probably it, isn't it?' She sighed, taking a swallow of beer. 'I sure wish you'd try to be more understanding, Niles. I work hard, do everything I can to provide you a secure, nice home. You know I love you, don't you? But you gotta try and cut me a little slack. I'm out there all the live-long day.' West pointed out the window. 'And what? You're here. This is your world, meaning your perspective isn't as big as mine, okay? So you get pissed because I'm not here, too. This isn't fair. I want you to give some serious thought to this. Got it?'

The words of the owner were chatter, the buzzing of insects, the drone of sounds drifting out of the radio on the table by the bed. Niles wasn't listening as he stared out at the forlorn King Usbeecee staring back at him. Niles had been called. There was disaster looming in the land of the Usbeeceeans, and only Niles could help, because only Niles would listen. All others looked up to the mighty King and mocked him in their minds and among themselves, thinking the benevolent monarch could not hear. They, the people, had wanted His Majesty to come. They had wanted his child-care centers and frescos, his career opportunities, and his wealth. Then they had turned jealous of his omniscience, of his all-powerful and praiseworthy presence. Those here and from distant ports were lustful and plotting a takeover that only Niles could stop.

'Anyway,' West was saying, popping open another beer as her weird-ass cat continued staring out at the night. 'I'm chasing him south on Seventy-seven at about ninety miles an hour? Can you believe it? He should be in jail right now, you ask me.'

She took another swallow of Miller Genuine Draft, wondering if she should eat something. For the first time since she'd had the flu several years ago, West was not hungry. She felt light and foreign inside, and awake. She thought back on how much caffeine she'd had this day, wondering if that might be the problem. It wasn't. Hormones, she decided, even though she knew that the beast was no longer raging, and in fact had been quiet most of the day, on its way back to its cave until the moon was in position again.

King Usbeccee was a potentate of few words, and Niles had to watch carefully to hear what the King was saying. Sunrise and sunset were the King's most chatty times, when windows flashed white and gold in a firestorm of pontifications. At night, Niles mainly studied the red light winking on top of the crown, a beacon saying to him, repeatedly, *wink-wink-wink*. After a barely perceptible pause, three more winks, and so on. This had gone on for weeks, and Niles knew that the code was directing him to a three-syllable enemy, whose armies this very minute were marching closer to the Queen City that the King ruled.

'Well, since you're so friendly,' West said in a snippy tone to her cat, 'I'm going to do laundry.'

Startled, Niles stretched and stared at her, his eyes

crossed as a similar firestorm flared inside his head. What was it the King had said? What, what, what? Earlier this evening, when Niles had been watching the King send him signals with the sun, hadn't the King flashed an agitated pattern, light going round and round the building, back and forth, back and forth, very similar to how the owner's big white box worked when she did *laundry*? A coincidence? Niles thought not. He jumped off the sill, then the counter, and followed his owner into the utility room. The fur stood up on his back when she dipped into pants pockets, pulling out *money* before wadding clothes and dunking them into the machine's basket. Other flashes of insight exploded in Niles' brain. He frantically rubbed against his owner's legs, and nipped her, sharpening his claws on her leg, trying to tell her.

'Goddamn it!' West shook the cat off. 'What the hell has gotten into you?'

Brazil lay back in the sleeping bag on the floor of his new, one-bedroom, unfurnished apartment. He had a headache and couldn't seem to get enough water. He'd been drinking beer for two days, and this frightened him. His mother had probably started exactly the same way, and here he was following her path. He knew enough from all the interest in genetics these days to deduce that he might have inherited his mother's proclivity for self-destruction. Brazil was deeply depressed by this realization, and he was ashamed of his behavior and knew for a fact that West had only humored a drunk kid, and the performance would never be repeated.

He lay still, hands beneath the back of his head, staring up at the ceiling, lights out, music on. Beyond his window he could see the top of the USBank Corporate Center almost touching the slivered moon, a red light blinking at the top of the crown. Brazil stared, zoning out again, an unsettling realization coming over him. Tomorrow would be two weeks since the last Black Widow slaying.

'Christ.' He sat up, sweating, and breathing hard.

He kicked off sheets and stood. He began pacing, with nothing on but gym shorts. He drank more water and stood in his bare kitchen, staring out at USBank, thinking, worrying. Out there somewhere was another businessman about to become a victim! If only there were some way to prevent it. Where was the killer now? What was the bastard thinking as he loaded his gun, and thought his evil thoughts, waiting on the web of Five Points for the next rental car to innocently creep into the city?

Niles was following West all over the house. She was certain the cat had gone haywire, and knew this was a danger with Siamese, Abyssinians, and all overbred, cross-eyed creatures that had been around for thousands of years. Niles wound through her moving legs, almost tripping her twice, and she had no choice but to boot him across the room.

Niles cried out, but persisted, then he got angry. One more boot, he thought, and you've had it. West gave him the side of her foot, sending him under the bed, scoring another point.

Niles watched from his dark space between the box spring and hardwood floor, his tail twitching. Niles waited until his owner had taken off shoes and socks, then he shot out and bit the soft spot at the back of her heel, right behind the ankle bone. He knew this hurt, because he'd tested it before. His owner chased him around the house for ten minutes, and he ran with sincerity, because he recognized true homicidal rage when he saw it. Niles returned to the bed and stayed under it until his owner got tired and wanted to sleep. Sneaking out, Niles returned to the kitchen. He curled up on the sill, where his kind and loving King kept watch over him during dark, lonely nights.

Morning came and brought rain. The unfriendly alarm clock buzzed loudly and stung West awake. She groaned, lying in bed, refusing to get up as heavy drops of water drummed the roof. This was perfect sleeping weather. Why should she get up? Memories of Brazil and his stranded BMW, of Niles and his outrageous behavior last night, depressed and excited her at the same time. This made no sense. She pulled the covers up around her chin, and images came, disturbing ones somehow relating to whatever she had dreamt. When she was absolutely still, she could almost feel Brazil's hands and mouth all over her. She was horrified and stayed in bed for quite some time.

Niles, having free rein of the house for a bit, had crept into the laundry room. He was interested in the big white box with wet clothes in it. On top were several folded bills and some change. He jumped up, having yet another idea of how to pass along King Usbeecee's message to Niles's owner. Of course, Niles knew with joy that his owner could do something about the King's endangerment. She could act on it, roar in wearing her important suit with all its leather and metal and dangerous toys. That's what this was all about, Niles was convinced. The King had spoken to him, and wanted him to pass along the information to his owner. She in turn would alert other fierce leaders. The troops would be called, the King and all Usbeeceeans saved.

Niles spent a difficult five minutes flipping open the

cover on top of the washing machine. He dipped in a paw and pulled out a small, wet article of clothing. He grabbed a folded five-dollar bill in his mouth, and jumped back down, excited, knowing his owner would be so pleased. She wasn't. His owner did not seem the least bit thrilled to see Niles, and sat up in a rage when her face was draped with a pair of wet panties that had been dragged across the house. She stared at the panties, and the five-dollar bill on her chest, and a chill settled over her.

'Wait a minute,' she said to Niles, who was fleeing. 'Come back. Really.'

Niles stopped, and looked at her, thinking, his tail twitching. He didn't trust her.

'Okay. Truce,' West promised. 'Something's up. This isn't just your acting kooky, is it? Come here and tell me.'

Niles knew her tone was honest, and maybe even a little contrite. He walked across the bedroom, and hopped three feet up to the bed, like it was nothing. He sat staring at her as she began to pet him.

'You brought me a pair of panties and money,' she said. 'Mean something?'

His tail twitched, but not enthusiastically.

'Has to do with panties?'

His tail went still.

'Underwear?'

No response.

'Sex?'

He didn't budge.

'Shit,' she muttered. 'What else? Well, let me retrace this thing, work it like a crime scene. You went to the washing machine, opened the lid, fished this out, it's wet, and not been in the dryer yet. So what, exactly, did you intend to fetch and then bring to me? Clothes?'

Niles was getting bored.

'Of course not,' West reprimanded herself. Niles could get clothes from anywhere, the chair, the floor. He had gone to a lot of trouble for one pair of panties. 'You went into the laundry,' she said.

Niles twitched.

'Ah, getting warm. Laundry? It that it?'

Niles went crazy, twitching and nuzzling her hand. West next started on the five-dollar bill. It took only two tries to affirm that *money* was the operative word.

'Laundry money,' West muttered, mystified.

Niles could help her no further, and believed he had carried out his assignment. He jumped off the bed and returned to the kitchen, where water washed out the King's morning greeting to his faithful subject. Niles was disappointed, and West was late. She dashed out the door, then dashed back in, having forgotten the most important item, the little box she disconnected from her own telephone. She sped along East Boulevard to South Boulevard, and turned off on Woodlawn. Brazil was wearing a windbreaker with a hood, and waiting in the parking lot, because he did not want her to see his small place with nothing in it.

'Hi,' he said, getting in.

'Sorry I'm late.' She could not look at him. 'My cat's lost his mind.'

Well, this was certainly starting off well, Brazil dismally realized. He was thinking about her, and she was thinking about her cat.

'What's wrong with him?' Brazil asked.

West pulled out of the parking lot as rain sprinkled. Her tires swished over wet streets. Brazil was acting as if nothing had happened. It just went to corroborate her belief that all males were the same. She supposed that his foray through her private possessions was no different than flipping through a magazine full of naked women. A thrill. A passing turn-on like a vibrating motorcycle seat or the right person sitting in your lap when the car was packed with too many passengers.

'He's just crazy, that's all,' West said. 'Stares out the window all the time. Drags things out of my washing machine. Bites me. Makes weird yowling noises.'

'This is new and different behavior?' asked Brazil, the psychologist.

'Oh yeah.'

'What kind of yowling sounds?' Brazil went on.

'He goes *yowl-yowl-yowl*. Then he's quiet, and does the same thing again. Always three syllables.'

'Sounds to me like Niles is trying to tell you something, and you're not listening. Quite possibly he's pointing out something right under your nose, but either you're caught up in other preoccupations, or you don't want to hear it.' Brazil enjoyed making this point.

'Since when are you a cat shrink?' West glanced at him, experiencing that same giddy sensation again, that wiggling in her bowels, as if tadpoles had hatched somewhere down there.

Brazil shrugged. 'It's all about human nature, animal nature, whatever you want to call it. If we take the time to try and look at reality from someone else's perspective, try a little compassion, it can make a difference.'

'Gag,' West said, and she flew right by the Sunset East exit.

'You just passed the truck stop. And what you do you mean, *gag*?'

'You sure got your lines down pat, don't you, boy?' She laughed in a not-so-nice way.

'I'm not a boy, in case you haven't noticed,' he said, and

he realized for the first time, to his shock, that Virginia West was scared. 'I'm a legal adult, and I don't deliver lines. You must have met a lot of bad people in life.'

This honestly amused her. She started laughing as rain fell harder. She turned on wipers and her radio, while Brazil watched her, a smile playing on his lips, although he was clueless as to what he had said to amuse her so.

'*Met a lot of bad people*.' She sputtered, almost helpless. 'What do I do for a living, for Christ's sake? Work in a bakery, serve ice cream cones, arrange flowers?' More peals of laughter.

'I didn't mean just what you do for a living,' Brazil said. 'The bad people you meet in policing aren't the ones who really hurt you. It's people off the job. You know, friends and family.'

'Yeah. You're right.' She sobered up fast. 'I do know. And guess what?' She shot him a glance. 'You don't. You don't know the first thing about me and all the shits I've come across when least expecting it.'

'Which is why you're not married or close to anyone,' he said.

'Which is why we're changing the subject. And you're one to talk, by the way.' She turned the radio up loud as rain beat the top of her personal car.

Hammer was watching the rain out the window of her husband's room in SICU, while Randy and Jude sat stiffly in chairs by the bed, staring at monitors, watching every fluctuation in pulse and oxygen intake. The stench got worse every hour, and Seth's moments of consciousness were like weightless airborne seeds that seemed neither to go anywhere nor land. He drifted, not here or there, and his family could not tell whether he had any awareness of their presence and devotion. For his sons, this was especially bitter. For them, this was more of the same. Their father did not acknowledge them.

Rain streaked glass and turned the world gray and watery as Hammer stood in the same position she had maintained for most of the morning. Arms crossed, she leaned her forehead against the window, sometimes thinking, sometimes not, and praying. Her divine communications were not entirely for her husband. Hammer was more worried about herself, in truth. She knew she had reached a crossroads, and something new was meant for her, something more demanding, that she might never do with Seth weighing her down, as he had all these years. Her children were gone. She would be alone soon. She needed no specialist to tell her this as she watched the continuing ravenous ingestion of her husband's body.

Whatever you want, I'll do, she told the Almighty. *I don't care what. Why does it matter, really, anyway? Certainly, I'm not much of a wife. I would be the first to confess that I haven't been much in that department. Probably not been much of a mother, either. So I'd like to make it up to everyone out there, okay? Just tell me what.*

The Almighty, who actually spent more time with Hammer and was more related to her than she knew, was pleased to hear her say this, for the Almighty had a rather big plan in store for this special recruit. Not now, but later, when it was time. Hammer would see. It was going to prove rather astonishing, if the Almighty didn't say so for Its-Almighty-self. As this exchange went on, Randy and Jude fixed their eyes on their mother for the first time that day, it seemed. They saw her head against the glass, and how still she had gotten for one who generally never stopped pacing. Overwhelmed with the profound love and respect they felt for her, they both got up at once. They came up behind her, and arms went around her.

'It's okay, Mom,' Randy sweetly said.

'We're here,' promised Jude. 'I wish I could've grown up into some big-shot lawyer or doctor or banker or something, so you'd know you were going to be taken care of.'

'Me, too,' Randy sadly agreed. 'But if you're not too ashamed of us, we'll at least be your best friends, okay?'

Hammer dissolved into tears. The three of them hugged as Seth's heart slowed because it could not go on, or perhaps because some part of Seth Bridges knew it was okay for him to leave just now. He coded at eleven minutes past eleven, and the cart and team could bring him back no more.

Chapter Twenty-four

West had missed the Sunset East exit deliberately. Retrieving Brazil's BMW was not what she intended to take care of first. It was quarter past eleven, and most of the world sat in church and wished the minister would hurry up and end the sermon. West was deep inside her preoccupations. She felt a terrible heaviness that she could not explain, and she wanted to cry, which she blamed on the time of month, which, of course, had passed.

'You all right?' Brazil felt her mood.

'I don't know,' she said, depressed.

'You seem really down,' he said.

'It's weird.' She checked her speed, glancing around for sneaky state troopers. 'It just hit me all of a sudden, this really bad feeling, as if something is horribly wrong.'

'That happens to me sometimes, too,' Brazil confessed. 'It's like you pick up on something from somewhere, you know what I mean?'

She knew exactly what he meant, but not why she should know it. West had never considered herself the most intuitive person in the world.

'I used to get that way about my mom a lot,' he went on. 'I would know before I walked in the house that she was not in good shape.'

'What about now?'

West was curious about all this, and not certain she knew what was happening to her. She used to be very pragmatic and in control. Now she was picking up extraterrestrial signals and discussing them with a twenty-two-year-old reporter she had just made out with in a police car.

'My mother's never in good shape now.' Brazil's voice got hard. 'I don't want to sense much about her anymore.'

'Well, let me tell you a word or two, Andy Brazil,' said West, who did know about some things in life. 'I don't care if you've moved out of her house, you can't erase her from the blackboard of your existence, you know?' West got out a cigarette. 'You've got to deal with her, and if you don't, you're going to be messed up the rest of your life.'

'Oh good. She messed up all my life so far, and now she's going to mess up the rest of it.' He stared out his window.

'The only person who has the power to mess up your life is you. And guess what?' West blew out smoke. 'You've done a damn good job with your life so far, if you ask me.'

He was silent, thinking about Webb, the memory of what had happened washing over him like icy water.

'Why, exactly, are we going to my house?' Brazil finally got around to asking that.

'You get too many hang-ups,' West replied. 'You want to tell me how come?'

'Some pervert,' Brazil muttered.

'Who?' West didn't like to hear this.

'How the hell do I know?' The subject bored and annoyed him.

'Some gay guy?'

'A woman, I think,' said Brazil. 'I don't know if she's gay.'

'When did they begin?' West was getting angry.

'Don't know.' His heart constricted as they pulled into the driveway of his mother's home, and parked behind the old Cadillac. 'About the time I started at the paper,' he quietly said.

West looked at him, touched by the sadness in his eyes as he looked out at a dump he had called home, and tried not to think of the terrible truths it held.

'Andy,' West said, 'what does your mother think right now? Does she know you've moved out?'

'I left a note,' he answered. 'She wasn't awake when I was packing.'

By now West had ascertained that *awake* was a code word for reasonably sober. 'Have you talked to her since?'

He opened his door. West gathered the Caller ID system from the backseat and followed him inside the house. They found Mrs Brazil in the kitchen, shakily spreading peanut butter on Ritz crackers. She had heard them drive up, and this had given her time to mobilize her defenses. Mrs Brazil did not speak to either one of them.

'Hello,' West said.

'How ya doing, Mom?' Brazil tried to hug her, but his mother wanted none of it, and waved him off with the knife.

Brazil noticed that the knob had been removed from his bedroom door, and he looked at West and smiled a little. 'I forgot about you and your tools,' he said.

'I'm sorry. I should have put it back on.' She looked around as if there might be a screwdriver somewhere.

'Don't worry about it.'

They walked inside his bedroom. She took off her raincoat, hesitating, looking around as if she had never been here before. She was disturbed by his presence in this intimate corner of his life, where he had been a boy and turned into a man, and where he had dreamed. Another hot flash was coming on, her face turning red as she plugged the Caller ID system into his phone.

'Obviously, this won't help when you get your new phone number at your apartment,' she explained. 'But what's more important is who has been calling this number.' She straightened up, her work complete. 'Does anybody besides your mother and me know you've moved?'

'No,' he replied, his eyes on her.

There had never been a woman in his room before, excluding his mother. Brazil glanced about, hoping there was nothing here that might embarrass him or reveal something to her that he did not want her to know. She was looking around, too, neither of them in a hurry to leave.

'You've got a lot of trophies,' she remarked.

Brazil shrugged, moving closer to look at crowded shelves he paid no mind to anymore. He pointed out especially significant awards and explained what they were. He gave her a few highlights of dramatic matches, and for a while they sat on his bed as he reminisced about days from his youth that he had lived with no audience, really, but strangers. He told her about his father, and she gave him her own vague recollection of Drew Brazil.

'I only knew who he was, that was about it,' she said. 'Back then I was pretty green, too, just a beat cop hoping to make sergeant. I remember all the women thought he was good-looking.' She smiled. 'There was a lot of talk about that, and that he seemed nice.'

'He was nice,' Brazil told her. 'I guess in some ways he was old-fashioned, but that was the time he lived in.' He picked at his fingernails, his head bent. 'He was crazy about my mother. But she's always been spoiled. She grew up that way. I've always thought the biggest reason she couldn't deal with his death is she lost the person who doted on her the most and took care of her.'

'You don't think she loved him?' West was curious, and she was very aware of how close they were sitting on his bed. She was glad the door was partially open, the knob off.

'My mother doesn't know how to love anybody, including herself.'

Brazil was watching her. She could feel his eyes like heat. Thunder and lightning played war outside the window as rain came down hard. She looked at him, too, and wondered if life would ruin his sweetness as he got older. She felt sure it would, and got up from the bed.

'What you've got to do is call the phone company first thing in the morning,' she advised him. 'Tell them you want Caller ID. This little box won't do you a bit of good until they give you that service, okay?'

He watched her, saying nothing at first. Then it occurred to him, 'Is it expensive?'

'You can manage it. Who's been hitting on you at work?' she wanted to know as she moved closer to the door.

'Axel, a couple women back in composing.' He shrugged. 'I don't know, don't notice.' He shrugged again.

'Anybody able to get into your computer basket?' she said as more thunder cracked.

'I don't see how.'

West looked at his computer.

'I'm going to move that to my apartment. I didn't have room in my car the other day,' he volunteered.

'Maybe you could write your next story on it,' she said.

Brazil continued to watch her. He lay back on the bed, hands behind his head. 'Wouldn't do any good,' he said. 'Still has to go into the newspaper computer one way or another.'

'What if you changed your password?' West asked, slipping her hands in her pockets and leaning against the wall.

'We already did.'

Lightning flashed, rain and wind ripping through trees.

'We?' West said.

Brenda Bond was sitting at her keyboard in her room of mainframes, working on Sunday because what else did she have to do? There was little life held for her. She wore prescription glasses in expensive black Modo frames, because Tommy Axel looked good in his. She imitated him in other ways, as well, since the music critic looked like Matt Dillon, and was clearly cool. System Analyst Bond was going through miles of printouts, and was not pleased by whatever she was finding.

The general architecture of the newspaper's computerized mail system simply had to be reconfigured. What she wanted was plain and not so much to ask, and she was tired of trying to convince Panesa through presentations that the publisher obviously never even bothered to look at. Bond's basic argument was this: When a user sent a mail message for the UA to relay to the local MTA, the

MTA then routed the message to the next MTA, which then routed it to the next MTA, and the next, until the message reached the final MTA on the destination system. With a Magic Marker, Brenda Bond had vividly depicted this in Figure 5.1, with colorful dashed lines and arrows showing possible communication paths between MTAs and UAs.

Bond's ruminations crystallized and she stopped what she was doing. She was startled and confused as Deputy Chief Virginia West, in uniform, suddenly walked in at quarter past three. West could see that Bond was a cowardly little worm, middle-aged, and exactly fitting the profile of people who set fires, sent bombs by mail, tampered with products like painkillers and eyedrops, and harassed others with hate notes and anonymous ugly calls over the telephone. West pulled up a chair, and turned it backwards, straddling it, arms resting on the back of it, like a guy.

'You know it's interesting,' West thoughtfully began. 'Most people assume if they use a cellular phone, the calls can't be traced. What they don't realize is calls come back to a tower. These towers cover sectors that are only a mile square.'

Bond was beginning to tremble, the bluff working.

'A certain young male reporter has been getting obscene phone calls,' West went on, 'and guess what?' She paused pointedly. 'They come back to the same sector you live in, Ms Bond.'

'I, I, I . . .' Bond stammered, visions of jail dancing through her head.

'But it's breaking into his computer basket that bothers me.' West's voice got harder, police leather creaking as she shifted in the chair. 'Now that's a crime. Leaking his stories to Channel Three. Imagine! It would be like someone stealing your programs and selling them to the competition.'

'No!' Bond blurted. 'No! I never sold anything!'

'So you *gave* stories to Webb.'

'No!' Bond panicked. 'I never talked to him. I was just helping the police.'

For an instant, West was quiet. She wasn't expecting this.

'What police?' she asked.

'Deputy Chief Goode told me to.' Bond confessed all, out of fright. 'She said it was part of an undercover departmental operation.'

The chair scraped as West got up. It was when she called Hammer's home that she learned the terrible news about Seth and felt sick.

'Oh my God,' West said to Jude, who had answered the phone. 'I had no idea. I don't want to bother her. Is there anything at all I can do . . . ?'

Hammer took the phone away from her caretaking son. 'Jude, it's all right,' she said to him, patting his shoulder. 'Virginia?' she said.

Goode was watching a videotape of *True Lies*, and relaxing on the couch with her gas fire lit and the air conditioning on high, waiting for Webb to call. He had promised to sneak by before the six o'clock news, and she was getting anxious. If he didn't show up within minutes, there wouldn't be time to do or say a thing. When the phone rang, she snatched it up as if all in life depended on whoever it was. Goode was not expecting Chief Hammer. Goode was not expecting Hammer to somberly tell her that Seth had died, and she, the boss, would see Goode in Goode's office at four-thirty sharp. Goode jumped off the couch, energized and euphoric. This could mean but one thing. Hammer was taking a long leave to get her pathetic affairs in order, and she was naming Goode acting chief.

Hammer had quite another scenario in mind for Deputy Chief Jeannie Goode. Although those around Hammer did not entirely understand how she could think of work at a time like this, in fact, nothing could have been more therapeutic for Hammer. Her mind cleared. She woke up, anger a blue flame burning through her veins. She felt she could vaporize someone just by looking at him, as she dressed in gray polished cotton slacks and blazer, a gray silk blouse, and pearls. She worked on her hair, and sprayed a light mist of Hermès on her wrists.

Chief Judy Hammer went out to her midnight-blue police car, and flicked on wipers to slough out leaves knocked down by rain. She backed out of her drive, and turned onto Pine Street as sun broke through moiling clouds. A lump formed in her throat, and she swallowed hard. Tears burned her eyes, and she blinked and took a deep breath, as she saw her street and the world around it, for the first time, without him. Nothing looked different, but it was. Oh, it was. She took deep breaths as she drove, and her heart felt bruised while her blood roared for righteous revenge. Goode could not have picked a worse time to pull such a stunt and get caught, of this Hammer was certain.

Goode was filled with confidence and self-importance, and she didn't see any point in putting on her uniform or a suit that might have suggested respect and consideration for her troubled leader. Instead, Goode drove back downtown, dressed in the short khaki skirt and T-shirt she had been in all day, waiting for Webb, who was busy working in the yard, his wife keeping a close eye on him these days. Goode parked her Miata in her assigned spot, and was more arrogant than usual to all she met as she took the elevator to the third floor, where her fine office was just around the corner from the suite that soon would be hers.

She shut her door and began her usual routine of dialing Webb's number and hanging up if someone other than the handsome news reporter answered. Goode enjoyed a feature on her police line that scrambled signals and rendered Caller ID useless. She was hanging up on Webb's wife when Goode's door suddenly flew open. Chief Hammer walked in, about to live up to her name. Goode's first reaction was how sharp her boss looked in gray. Goode's second and final reaction was that Hammer did not seem to be in mourning as she strode to the desk and snatched up Goode's brass nameplate.

'You're fired,' Hammer said in a voice not to be questioned. 'I want your badge and gun. Your desk gets cleared out now. Let me help you start.'

Hammer threw the nameplate into the trash. She turned without another glance and walked out. Hammer was fury traveling down the corridors of her department, yet she was forthcoming in her nods and salutations to troops she passed. Word was already out on the radio about her husband, and members of the Charlotte Police Department were overwhelmed with sorrow and newfound respect for their leader. Throughout it all, she was here, damn it, and she wasn't going to let them down. When a sergeant saw Goode sneaking out to her car with her office crammed in bags and boxes, there was rejoicing throughout Adam, Baker, Charlie, and David response areas, and investigations and support. Cops high-fived and low-tenned in the parking deck and the roll call room. The duty captain lit a rum crook cigar in his nonsmoking office.

Brazil got the good word by pager as he was out in the parking lot changing the oil in his car. He went inside and dialed West's home number.

'Bond won't be bothering you anymore.' West tried to be cool, but she was intensely proud of herself. 'Goode won't be getting your stories from the little shit and leaking them to Webb.'

Brazil was shocked and ecstatic. 'No way!'

'Oh yeah. It's done. Hammer's fired Goode and Bond is in a state of paralysis.'

'Bond was making those calls?' To Brazil, this seemed incongruous.

'Yup.'

He was oddly disappointed that it wasn't someone more dynamic and attractive thinking such thoughts about him.

West sensed this and told him, 'You aren't looking at this the right way.'

'Looking at what?' He played dumb.

'Andy, I see this kind of thing all the time, doesn't matter whether it's a man or woman doing it, except that women aren't likely to expose themselves to you, so at least you can be grateful for that,' she explained. 'This sort of thing is not about sex or being attracted to someone in the normal sense of things. It's all about control and power, about degrading. A form of violence, really.'

'I know that,' he said.

He still wished his verbal assailant had been someone

halfway pretty, and he couldn't help but wonder what it was about him that prompted people like the creep at the car wash, and now Brenda Bond, to select him. Why? Did he send out signals that made them think they could take advantage of him? He bet that no one dared do such a thing to West or Hammer.

'Gotta go,' West said, leaving Brazil disappointed and irritable.

He got back to changing his oil, in a hurry to finish now. He had an idea.

West had one, too. She called Raines, and this definitely was unexpected and abnormal. West never called him or anyone, except Brazil, as all around her knew and accepted as fact. Raines had the night off and was looking forward to watching a just-released sports bloopers video he had acquired over the weekend. West was thinking about pizza. They decided they probably could collaborate on this quite nicely, and he headed over to her house in his rebuilt, fully loaded, black on black '73 Corvette Stingray, with headers, tinted glass top, and window sticker. West usually could hear him coming.

Brazil thought he should come up with a way of showing his appreciation to West for resolving his life's crisis. He also imagined the two of them celebrating, and why not? This was a big day for both of them. She had rid him of Bond and Webb, and she and the entire police department were free of Goode. Brazil sped to the nearest Hop-In and picked up the nicest bottle of wine he could find in the glass cooler, a Dry Creek Vineyard 1992 Fume Blanc, for nine dollars and forty-nine cents.

She would be surprised and pleased, and maybe he could pet Niles for a while. Maybe Brazil could spend a little more time inside West's house and learn something more about her. Maybe she would invite him to watch TV with her, or listen to music, the two of them sipping wine in her living room, talking, and telling stories about their early years and their dreams.

Brazil drove toward Dilworth, overflowing with happiness that his problems had cleared up, and he had a friend like her. He thought about his mother, wondering how she was doing, and was pleased that she didn't seem to get him down so much anymore. He didn't seem to feel that her choices were because of what he did or did not do for her.

The lights were out, the TV on in West's living room. She and Raines were on the couch, eating a Pizza Hut triple decker. Raines was perched on the edge of his cushion, drinking a Coors Light, and crazed over his new videotape. Without a doubt it was the best yet, and he wished West would let him watch it undistracted. She was all over him, kissing, nibbling, running her fingers through his thick, curly black hair. She was getting on his nerves, really, and acting out of character, in general.

'What the hell's gotten into you?' he absently said.

He tried to look around her as he twirled her hair with the creative enthusiasm of Niles kneading the rug.

'Yes! Yes! What a dunk! Rip that backboard down! Oh shit! Ahhhh! Look at that! Christ! *Right into the pole*. Oh, man.' Raines sat back down.

The next five minutes was ice hockey. The goalie got a stick between his legs. A puck ricocheted off two face masks and hit a referee in the mouth. Raines was going wild. There was nothing he liked better than sports and injuries, especially if the two went together. With each tragedy, he imagined rushing in with his medical kit and stretcher, Raines to the rescue. West was unbuttoning her blouse. She threw herself on top of him, devouring his mouth, and desperate. Raines put down his pizza.

'Hormones again?' He had never seen her this frustrated.

'I don't know.' She worked on more buttons and hooks.

They seriously made out on the couch while Niles remained in his sanctuary above the sink. He was not a fan of Tire Man, as Niles called Raines, after noticing some radial ad in the newspaper lining his litter box. Tire Man was offensively loud and never warm and appreciative of Niles. Several times, Tire Man had launched Niles off the couch, and this would have been one of those times, should Niles have tested his luck, which he did not.

He looked adoringly at his distant, sad King. *I'll help you. Fear not. My owner knows about laundry money. She is very powerful and will protect you and all Usbeeceeans.* Niles twitched an ear, detecting another engine sound, this one a pleasant, deep purring that he recognized. It was Piano Man, the nice one who played his fingers over Niles's spine and ribs, and right behind his ears, until Niles fell over from sheer pleasure, rattling window panes. Niles got up and stretched, excited that Piano Man seemed to be slowing behind the house, where he had parked in the past, on the few times he had stopped by for one reason or another.

West and Raines were not in a good space when the doorbell rang. By now, Raines was completely focused on what he was doing, and was within minutes, at most, of victory. It was most inconvenient and inconsiderate for someone to dare and drop by, unannounced. Raines experienced an intense wave of homicidal rage as he withdrew to his end of the couch, sweating and out of breath.

'Goddamn son of a bitch,' he furiously blurted.

'I'll get it,' West said.

She got up, pulling, zipping, and buttoning, as she walked and combed her fingers through her hair. She was a mess, and as the bell rang again, she hoped it wasn't Mrs Grabman from two doors down. Mrs Grabman was a nice enough old woman, but she tended to drop by every weekend West was home, usually offering vegetables from her garden as an excuse to meddle and complain about someone suspicious in the neighborhood. West already had a long row of ripening tomatoes on the counter, and two drawers full of okra, green beans, squash, and zucchini in the refrigerator.

Safety-conscious West, who had never gotten around to installing a burglar alarm, yelled through the door, 'Who is it?'

'It's me,' Brazil said.

From the bottom of the steps, where he waited with wine, he was excited, and clueless. He assumed the old black Corvette on the street belonged to a neighborhood kid. It had never occurred to him that Denny Raines might drive anything besides an ambulance. West opened the door, and Brazil lit up at the sight of her. He offered her the bottle of wine in its brown paper bag.

'I thought we should at least drink a toast . . .' he started to say.

West awkwardly took the wine from him, acutely conscious of his reaction to her tousled hair, to the red marks on her neck, and her blouse buttoned crooked. Brazil's smile faded as his eyes wandered around her crime scene. Raines appeared behind his woman, and looked down the steps at Brazil.

'Hey, what'cha know, sport?' Raines grinned at him. 'Like your stories . . .'

Brazil ran back to his car as if someone were chasing him.

'Andy!' West yelled after him. 'Andy!'

She hurried down the steps as his BMW roared off into the setting sun. Raines followed her back into her living room as she buttoned her blouse properly, and nervously smoothed her hair. She set the wine on a table, where she did not have to look at it, and be reminded of who had brought it.

'What the hell's his problem?' Raines wanted to know.

'Temperamental writer,' she muttered.

Raines wasn't interested. He and West had several downs yet to go, and he tackled her from behind, grabbing, fondling, and working his tongue into her ear. The play was incomplete as she broke free, leaving him yards behind, and taking the ball with her.

'I'm tired,' she snapped.

Raines rolled his eyes. He'd had enough of her poor sportsmanship and penalty flags.

'Fine,' he told her as he ejected his bloopers tape from the VCR. 'Let me just ask you one thing, Virginia.' He furiously strutted to the door, pausing long enough to fix smoldering eyes on hers. 'When you're eating and the phone rings, what happens after you hang up? Do you go back to your meal, or do you forget that, too? Do you just *quit* because you had a tiny interruption?'

'Depends on what I'm eating,' West told him.

* * *

Brazil's dinner was late and spent at Shark Finn's, on Old Pineville Road, at Bourbon Street. After roaring away from West's house, he had driven around, getting angrier by the moment. It had not been one of his wiser moves, perhaps, to stop by Tommy Axel's Fourth Ward condominium with its blush rose front door. Brazil noticed a number of men noticing him during his approach from the parking lot. Brazil wasn't especially friendly to them, or even to Axel.

What Axel considered a first date and Brazil considered revenge began in Shark Finn's Jaws Raw Bar, where a mounted sailfish caught in a net protested with an open mouth and startled glass eyes. Wooden tables were uncovered, the plank floor unvarnished. There were faces carved on coconuts, and curled starfish and stained glass. Brazil nursed a Red Stripe beer and wondered if he might be going insane as he considered the senseless and impulsive behavior that had landed him here in this place at this moment.

Axel was burning holes in him, living a fantasy, and fearful the vision would vanish if he looked away for even a second. Brazil was certain that other people slipping down raw oysters and getting drunk had figured out Axel's intentions and were miscalculating Brazil's. This was unfortunate since most of the men drove pickup trucks and believed it was their higher calling to get women pregnant, own guns, and kill queers.

'You come here a lot?' Brazil swirled beer in its dark brown bottle.

'Whenever. You hungry?' Axel grinned, displaying his very nice white teeth.

'Sort of,' Brazil said.

They got up and moved into the crab shack, which was no different than the raw bar, except there were captain's chairs at the tables, and the ceiling fans were working so hard they looked like they might take off. Jimmy Buffet was playing over intercoms. A candle and Tabasco sauce were on their table, which rocked, requiring Brazil to fix it with several packets of Sweet & Low. Axel started by ordering a Shark Attack with lots of Myers's rum, and he convinced Brazil to try a Rum Runner, which had enough liquor in it to turn the lights out in half of Brazil's brain.

As if Brazil were not in enough trouble already, Axel ordered a tin bucket filled with iced-down bottles of Rolling Rock beer. This was going to work just fine, the music critic was sure of it. Brazil was a puppy and could be trained. Axel was stunned to suspect that the guy might never have been drunk in his life. Incredible. What did he grow up in, a monastery, the Mormon church? Brazil was wearing another pair of slightly too-small jeans left over from high school days, and a tennis team T-shirt. Axel tried not to think about what it might be like to get those clothes off.

'Everything here's good,' Axel said without looking at the menu, as he leaned into candlelight. 'Conch fritters, crab cakes, Po-Boy sandwiches. I like the baskets, and usually get fried scallops.'

'Okay,' Brazil said to both Axels sitting across from him. 'I think you're trying to get me drunk.'

'No way,' Axel said, signaling for the waitress. 'You've hardly had a thing.'

'I don't usually. And I ran eight miles this morning,' Brazil pointed out.

'Man,' Axel said. 'You're sheltered. Looks like I'm gonna have to educate you a little, pull you along.'

'I don't think so.' Brazil wanted to go home and hide in bed. Alone. 'I don't feel too good, Tommy.'

Axel was insistent that food would prove the cure, and what he said was true to a point. Brazil felt better after he threw up in the men's room. He switched to iced tea, waiting for his internal weather to clear.

'I need to go,' he said to an increasingly sullen Axel.

'Not yet,' Axel said, as if the decision was his to make.

'Oh yes. I'm out of here.' Brazil was politely insistent.

'We haven't had a chance to talk,' Axel told him.

'About what?'

'You know.'

'Do I have to guess?' Brazil was getting annoyed, his mind still in Dilworth, really.

'You know,' Axel said again, his eyes intense.

'I just want to be friends,' Brazil let him know.

'That's all I want.' Axel couldn't have agreed more. 'I want us to get to know each other real well so we can be great friends.'

Brazil knew a line when he heard one. 'You want to be better friends than I want to be. And you want to start right now. No matter what you say, I know how it works, Tommy. What you're saying is insincere. If I told you this minute that I'd go home with you, you'd go for it *like that.*' He snapped his fingers.

'What's so wrong about it?' Axel liked the idea quite a lot, and wondered if it were remotely possible.

'See. A contradiction. That's not called being friends. That's called being laid,' Brazil enlightened him. 'I'm not a piece of meat, nor do I care to be a one-night stand.'

'Who said anything about one night? I'm a long-term kind of guy,' Axel assured him.

Brazil could not help but notice the two guys with bulging muscles and tattoos, in greasy coveralls, drinking long-neck Budweisers, glaring at them as they eavesdropped. This didn't bode well, and Axel was so obsessed, he wasn't picking up on the stubby fingers drumming the table and toothpicks agitating in mean mouths, and eyes cutting, as plans were being made for the dark parking lot when the fags returned to their vehicle.

'My feelings for you are very deep, Andy,' Axel went on. 'Frankly, I'm in love with you.' He slumped back in his chair, and dramatically threw his hands up in despair. 'There. I've said it. Hate me if you want. Shun me.'

'Puke,' said Rizzo, whose visible tattoo was of a big-breasted naked woman named Tiny.

'I gotta get some air,' agreed his buddy, Buzz Shifflet.

'Tommy, I think we should be smart and get out of here as fast as we can,' Brazil suggested quietly, and with authority. 'I made a mistake and I apologize, okay. I shouldn't have come over and we shouldn't be here. I was in a mood and took it out on you. Now we're going to make tracks or die.'

'So you do hate me.' Axel was into his crushed, you-have-deeply-wounded-me routine.

'Then you stay here.' Brazil stood. 'I'm pulling your car up to the front porch, and you're going to jump in. Got it?' He thought of West again, and anger returned.

Brazil was looking around, as if expecting a gunfight any moment, and ready for one, but aware of his limitations. There were rednecks everywhere, all drinking beer, eating fried fish with tartar and cocktail sauces, and ketchup. They were staring at Axel and Brazil. Axel saw the wisdom in Brazil getting the car by himself.

'I'll pay the bill while you do that,' Axel said. 'Dinner's my treat.'

Brazil was completely cognizant of the fact that the two big boys in coveralls were this very second out in the dark parking lot, waiting for the two queers. Brazil wasn't especially concerned by their erroneous impression of him and the choices he made in life, but he was not interested in having the shit beat out of him. He thought fast, and tracked down the hostess in the raw bar, where she was parked at a table, smoking and writing tomorrow's specials on a chalk board.

'Ma'am,' he said to her. 'I wonder if you could help me with a serious problem.'

She looked skeptically at him, her demeanor changing somewhat. Guys said similar words to her every night after they'd been through buckets of beer. The problem was always the same thing, and so easy to remedy if she didn't mind slipping off behind the restaurant for maybe ten minutes and dropping her jeans.

'What.' She continued writing, ignoring the jerk.

'I need a pin,' he said.

'A what?' She looked up at him. 'You mean, something to write with?'

'No, ma'am. I mean a pin, a needle, and something to sterilize it with,' he told her.

'What for?' She frowned, opening her fat vinyl pocketbook.

'A splinter.'

'Oh!' Now that she understood. 'Don'cha hate it when that happens? This place is full of 'em, too. Here you go, sugar.'

She fished out a small sewing kit in a clear plastic box that she'd gotten from the last hotel some rich guy took her to, and she slid out a needle. She handed him a bottle of nail polish remover. He dipped the needle in acetone, and bravely retreated to the porch. Sure enough, the two thugs were prowling near cars, waiting. They lurched in his direction when they spotted him, and he quickly stabbed his left index finger with the needle. He stabbed his right index finger and thumb. Brazil squeezed out as much blood as he could, and smeared in on his face, which he then held in his hands, as if he were reeling.

'Oh God,' he moaned, staggering down steps. 'Jesus.' He fell against the porch railing, groaning, holding his disgusting, gory face.

'Shit.' Rizzo had gotten to him, and was completely taken aback. 'What the fuck happened to you?'

'My cousin in there,' Brazil weakly said.

'You talking about that fag you was sitting with?' asked Shifflet.

Brazil nodded. 'Yeah, man. He's fucking got AIDS, and he threw up blood on me! You believe that! Oh God.'

He staggered down another step. Shifflet and Rizzo moved out of the way.

'It went in my eyes and mouth! You know what that means! Where's a hospital around here, man? I got to get to the hospital! Could you drive me, please?'

Brazil staggered and almost stumbled into them. Shifflet and Rizzo ran. They leapt into their Nissan Hard Body XE with its four-foot-lift oversized tires that spun rocks.

Chapter Twenty-five

The next night, Monday, Blair Mauney III was also enjoying an agreeable meal in the Queen City. The banker was dining at Morton's of Chicago, where he typically went when business called him to headquarters. He was a regular at the high-end steak house with stained-glass windows, next to the Carillon, and across from First Presbyterian Church, which also had stained glass, only older and more spectacular, especially after dark, when Mauney felt lonely and in the mood to prowl.

Mauney needed no explanation from the pretty young waitress with her cart of raw meat and live lobster waving bound claws. He always ordered the New York strip, medium rare, a baked potato, butter only, and the chopped red onion and tomato salad with Morton's famous blue cheese dressing. This he downed with plenty of Jack Black on the rocks. Tomorrow he would have breakfast with Cahoon, and the chairman of corporate risk policy, and the chairman of the credit corp, in addition to the chairman of USBank South, plus a couple of presidents. It was routine. They'd sit around a fancy table in Cahoon's fancy Mount Olympus office. There was no crisis or even good news that Mauney knew of, only more of the same, and his resentment peaked.

The bank had been started by his forebears in 1874. It was Mauney who should be ensconced within the crown and have his black and white portrait regularly printed in the *Wall Street Journal*. Mauney loathed Cahoon, and whenever possible, Mauney dropped poison pellets about his boss, spreading malicious gossip hinting at eccentricities, poor judgement, idiocy, and malignant motives for the good in the world Cahoon had done. Mauney requested a doggie bag, as he always did, because he never knew when he might get hungry later in his room at the luxurious Park Hotel, near Southpark Mall.

He paid the seventy-three-dollar-and-seventy-cent bill, leaving two percent less than his usual fifteen-percent tip, which he figured to the penny on a wafer-thin calculator he kept in his wallet. The waitress had been slow bringing his fourth drink, and being busy was no excuse. He returned to the sidewalk out front, on West Trade Street, and the valets scurried, as they always did. Mauney climbed into his rental black Lincoln Continental, and decided he really was not in the mood to return to his hotel just yet.

He briefly thought of his wife and her endless surgeries and other medical hobbies, as he cataloged them. What he spent on her in a year was a shock, and not one stitch of it had improved her, really. She was a manikin who cooked and made the rounds at cocktail parties. Buried somewhere deep in Mauney's corporate mind were memories of Polly at Sweetbriar, when a carload of Mauney's pals showed up for a dance one Saturday night in May. She was precious in a blue dress, and wanted nothing to do with him.

The spell was cast. He had to have her that moment. Still, Polly was busy, hard to find, and cared not. He started calling twice a day. He showed up on campus, hopelessly smitten. Of course, she knew exactly what she was doing. Polly had been mentored thoroughly at home, at boarding school, and now at this fine women's college. She knew how men were if a girl acknowledged their attentions. Polly knew how to play hard to get. Polly knew that Mauney had a pedigree and portfolio that she had been promised since childhood, because it was her destiny and her entitlement. They were married fourteen months after their first meeting, or exactly two weeks after Polly graduated cum laude, with a degree in English which, according to her proud new husband, would make her unusually skilled in penning invitations and thank-you notes.

Mauney could not pinpoint precisely when his wife's many physical complications began. It seemed she was playing tennis, still peppy and enjoying the good fortune he made possible for her, until after their second child was born. Women. Mauney would never figure them out. He found Fifth Street and began cruising, as he often did when he was deep in thought. He began getting excited as he looked out at the night life and thought about his trip tomorrow afternoon. His wife thought he would be in Charlotte for three days. Cahoon and company believed Mauney was returning to Asheville after breakfast. All were wrong.

While family traveled from the distant airports of Los Angeles and New York, the bereft chief and her sons went through closets and dresser drawers, carrying out the painful task of dividing and disposing of Seth's clothing and other personal effects. Hammer could not look at her late husband's bed, where the nightmare had begun as he got drunk and fantasized about what he could do to really hurt her this time. *Well, you did it, Seth. You figured it out*, Hammer thought. She folded extra-extra-large shirts, shorts, underwear, socks, and placed them in paper bags for the Salvation Army.

They made no decision about Seth's valuables, such as his four different Rolex watches, the wedding band that had not fit him in more than ten years, the collection of gold railroad watches that had belonged to his grandfather, his Jaguar, not to mention his stocks, and his cash. Hammer cared nothing about any of it, and frankly expected him to zing her one last time in his will. She had never been materialistic and wasn't about to begin now.

'I don't know the details about any of his affairs,' she said to her sons, who cared nothing about them, either.

'That figures,' said Jude as he removed another suit from a hanger and began folding it. 'You would think he might have discussed his will with you, Mom.'

'Part of it is my fault.' She closed a drawer, wondering how she could have endured this activity alone. 'I never asked.'

'You shouldn't have to ask,' Jude angrily said. 'Part of the whole point of living with someone is you share important things with each other, you know? Like in your case, so you could maybe plan for your future in the event something happened to him? Which was a good possibility with his rotten health.'

'I've planned for my own future.' Hammer looked around the room, knowing that every molecule within it would have to go. 'I don't do so badly on my own.'

Randy was younger and angrier. As far as he was concerned, his father had been selfish and neurotic because he was spoiled and made no effort to think about others beyond what function they might have served in his wasteful, rapacious existence. Randy, especially, seethed over the way his mother had been treated. She deserved someone who admired and loved her for all her goodness and courage. He went over and wrapped his arms around her as she folded a Key West shirt she remembered Seth buying on one of their few vacations.

'Don't.' She gently pushed her son away, tears filling her eyes.

'Why don't you come stay with us in LA for a while?' he gently said, holding on to her, anyway.

She shook her head, getting back to the business at hand, determined to get every reminder of Seth out of this house as fast as she could, that she might get on with life.

'The best thing for me is to work,' she said. 'And there are problems I need to resolve.'

'There are always problems, Mom,' Jude said. 'We'd love it if you came to New York.'

'You know anything about this Phi Beta Kappa key on a chain?' Randy held it up. 'It was inside the Bible in the back of this drawer.'

Hammer looked at the necklace as if she had been struck. The key was hers, from Boston University, where she had enjoyed four very stimulating years and graduated near the top of her class, with a double major in criminal justice and history, for she believed that the two were inexorably linked. Hammer had grown up with no special privileges or promise that she would amount to much, since she was a girl amid four brothers in a household with little money and a mother who did not approve of a daughter thinking the dangerous thoughts hers did. Judy Hammer's Phi Beta Kappa key had been a triumph, and she had given it to Seth when they had gotten engaged. He wore it for a long time, until he began to get fat and hateful.

'He told me he lost it,' Hammer quietly said as the telephone rang.

West felt terrible about bothering her chief again. West apologized on the cellular phone inside her police car, as she sped downtown. Other units and an ambulance roared to the heart of Five Points, where another man from out of town had been brutally slain.

'Oh Lord,' Hammer breathed, shutting her eyes. 'Where?'

'I can pick you up,' West said over the line.

'No, no,' Hammer said. 'Just tell me where.'

'Cedar Street past the stadium,' West said as she shot through a yellow light. 'The abandoned buildings around there. Near the welding supply company. You'll see us.'

Hammer grabbed her keys from the table by the door. She headed out, not bothering to change out of her gray suit and pearls. Brazil had been driving around, in a funk, when he'd heard the call on the scanner. He got there fast, and now was standing beyond crime-scene tape, restless in jeans and T-shirt, frustrated because no one would let him in. Cops were treating him as if he were a reporter no different than others out foraging, and he didn't understand it. Didn't they remember him in uniform, out with them night after night, and in foot pursuits and fights?

West rolled up seconds before Hammer did, and the two women made their way to the overgrown area where a black Lincoln Continental was haphazardly parked far off Cedar and First Streets, near a Dumpster. The welding company was a looming Gothic silhouette with dark windows. Police lights strobed, and in the far distance a siren wailed as misfortune struck in another part of the city. A Norfolk Southern train loudly lumbered past on nearby tracks, the engineer staring out at disaster.

Typically, the car was rented, and the driver's door was open, the interior bell dinging, and headlights burning. Police were searching the area, flashguns going off and video cameras rolling. Brazil spotted West and Hammer coming through, reporters moiling around them and getting nothing but invisible walls. Brazil stared at West until she saw him, but she gave him no acknowledgment. She did not seem inclined to include him. It was as if they had never met, and her indifference ran through him like a bayonet. Hammer did not seem aware of him, either. Brazil stared after them, convinced of a betrayal. The two women were busy and overwrought.

'We're sure,' Hammer was saying to West.

'Yes. It's like the others,' West grimly said as their strides carried them beyond tape, and deeper inside the scene. 'No question in my mind. MO identical.'

Hammer took a deep breath, her face pained and outraged as she look at the car, then at the activity in a thicket, where Dr Odom was on his knees, working. From where Hammer stood, she could see the medical examiner's bloody gloves glistening in lights set up around the perimeter. She looked up as the Channel 3 news helicopter thudded overhead, hovering, its camera securing footage for the eleven o'clock news. Broken glass clinked under feet as the two women moved closer, and Dr Odom palpated the victim's destroyed head. The man had on a dark blue Ralph Lauren suit, a white shirt missing its cufflinks, and a Countess Mara tie. He had graying curly hair and a tan face that might have been attractive, but now it was hard to tell. Hammer saw no jewelry but guessed that whatever this man had owned wasn't cheap. She knew money when she saw it.

'Do we have an ID?' Hammer asked Dr Odom.

'Blair Mauney the third, forty-five years old, from Asheville,' he replied, photographing the hateful blaze-orange hourglass spray-painted over the victim's genitals. Dr Odom looked up at Hammer for a moment. 'How many more?' he asked in a hard tone, as if blaming her.

'What about cartridge cases?' West asked.

Detective Brewster was squatting, interested in trash scattered through briars. 'Three so far,' he answered his boss. 'Looks like the same thing.'

'Christ,' said Dr Odom.

By now, Dr Odom was seriously projecting. He continually imagined himself in strange cities, at meetings, driving around, maybe lost. He thought of suddenly being yanked out of his car and led to a place like this by a monster who would blow his head off for a watch, a wallet, a ring. Dr Odom could read the fear the victims had felt as they begged not to die, that huge .45 pointed and ready to fire. Dr Odom was certain that the soiled undershorts consistent in each case were not postmortem. No goddamn way. The slain businessmen didn't lose control of bowels and bladder as life fled and bled from them. The guys were terrified, trembling violently, pupils dilated, digestion shutting down as blood rushed to extremities for a fight or flight that would never happen. Dr Odom's pulse pounded in his neck as he unfolded another body bag.

West carefully scanned the interior of the Lincoln as the interior alert dinged that the driver's door was ajar and the lights were on. She noted the Morton's doggie bag, and the contents of the briefcase and an overnight bag that had been dumped out and rummaged through in back. USBank business cards were scattered over the carpet and she leaned close and read the name Blair Mauney III, the same name on the driver's license Detective Brewster had shown her. West pulled plastic gloves out of her back pocket.

She worked them on, so consumed by what she was doing, that she was unaware of anyone around her or the tow truck that was slowly rolling up to haul the Lincoln to the police department for processing. West had not worked crime scenes in years, but she had been good at it once. She was meticulous, tireless, and intuitive, and right now she was getting a weird feeling as she looked at the clutter left by the killer. She lifted a USAir ticket by a corner, opening it on the car seat, touching as little of it as possible as her misgivings grew.

Mauney had flown to Charlotte from Asheville today, arriving at Charlotte-Douglas International Airport at five-thirty P.M. The return, for tomorrow afternoon, was not back to Asheville, but to Miami, and from there Mauney was flying to Grand Cayman, in the West Indies. West carefully flipped through more tickets, her heart picking up, adrenalin coursing. He was scheduled to fly out of Grand Cayman on Wednesday, and stop over in Miami for six hours. Then he would return to Charlotte, and, finally, to Asheville. There were more disturbing signs that were likely unrelated to Maundy's murder, but pointed to other crime possibly surrounding his life.

This was always the bitter irony in such cases, she couldn't help but think. Death ratted on people who were closet drug abusers, drunks, or having affairs with one and/or the other sex, or those who liked to whip or be whipped, or to string themselves up by pulleys and nooses and masturbate. Human creativity was endless, and West had seen it all. She had gotten out a ballpoint pen and was using it to turn pages of other paperwork. Though her forte was not cash and equivalents, treasury and agency securities, derivatives, investment banking, commercial and corporate banking, West knew enough to get a sense of what Mauney might have been intending on his travels.

In the first place, he had an alias, Jack Morgan, whose picture IDs on passport and driver's license showed Mauney's face. There were a total of eight credit cards and two checkbooks in the names of Mauney and Morgan. Both men seemed to have a keen interest in real estate, specifically a number of hotels along Miami Beach. It appeared to West that Mauney was prepared to invest some one hundred million dollars in these old pastel dumps. Why? Who the hell went to Miami Beach these days? West flipped through more paperwork, perspiring in the humid heat. Why was Mauney planning to drop by Grand Cayman, the money-laundering capital of the world?

'My God,' West muttered, realizing that Grand Cayman was three syllables.

She stood up, staring at the bright skyline, at the mighty USBank Corporate Center rising above all, its red light slowly blinking a warning to helicopters and low flying planes. She stared at this symbol of economic achievement, of greatness and hard work on the part of many, and she got angry. West, like a lot of citizens, had checking and savings accounts at USBank. She had financed her Ford through it. Tellers were always pleasant and hard-working. They went home at the end of the day and did their best to make ends meet like most folks. Then some carpetbagger comes along and decides to cheat, steal, hoodwink, make out like a bandit, and give an innocent business and its people a bad name. West turned her attention to Hammer and motioned to her.

'Take a look,' West said quietly to her chief.

Hammer squatted by the open car door and examined documents without touching them. She had been making investments and saving money most of her life. She knew creative banking when she saw it, and was shocked at first, then disgusted as truth began to whisper. As best she could tell, and of course none of it could be proven at this precise moment, it appeared Blair Mauney III was behind hundreds of millions of dollars loaned to Dominion Tobacco that seemed to be linked to a real-estate development group called Southman Corporation, in Grand Cayman. Associated with this were multiple bank account numbers not linked by identification numbers. Several of the same Miami telephone numbers showed up repeatedly, with no description other than initials that made no sense. There were references to something called *USChoice*.

'What do you think?' West whispered to Hammer.

'Fraud, for starters. We'll get all this to the FBI, to Squad Four, see what they make of it.'

The news helicopter circled low. The cocooned body was loaded into the ambulance.

'What about Cahoon?' West asked.

Hammer took a deep breath, feeling sorry for him. How much bad news did anybody need in one night? 'I'll call him, tell him what we suspect,' she grimly said.

'Do we release Mauney's ID tonight?'

'I'd rather hold out until morning.' Hammer was staring beyond bright lights and crime-scene tape. 'I believe you have a visitor,' she said to West.

Brazil was at the perimeter taking notes. He was not in uniform this night, and his face was hard as his eyes met West's and held. She walked toward him, and they moved some distance away from others, and stood on different sides of crime-scene tape.

'We're not releasing any information tonight,' she said to him.

'I'll just do my usual,' he said, lifting the tape to duck under.

'No.' She blocked him. 'We can't let anybody in. Not on this one.'

'Why not?' he said, stung.

'There are a lot of complications.'

'There always are.' His eyes flashed.

'I'm sorry,' she told him.

'I've been inside before,' he protested. 'How come now I can't?'

'You've been inside when you've been with me.' West began to back away.

'When I've . . . ?' Brazil's pain was almost uncontainable. 'I am with you!'

West looked around and wished he would lower his voice. She could not tell him what she had found inside the victim's car, and what it quite likely implied about the not-so-innocent victim Blair Mauney III. She glanced back at Hammer. The chief was still leaning inside the Lincoln, looking through more paperwork, perhaps grateful for the distraction from her own private tragedies. West thought of Brazil's behavior at her house while Raines was watching the videotape. This was a mess, and it could not go on. She made the right decision and could feel the change inside her, the curtain dropping. The end.

'You can't do this to me!' Brazil furiously went on. 'I haven't done anything wrong!'

'Please don't make a scene or I'm going to have to ask you to leave,' West, the deputy chief, stated.

Enraged and hurt, Brazil realized the truth. 'You're not going to let me ride with you anymore.'

West hesitated, trying to ease him into this. 'Andy,' she

said, 'it couldn't go on forever. You've always known that. Jesus Christ.' She blew out in frustration. 'I'm old enough to . . . I'm . . .'

Brazil backed up, staring at her, the traitor, the fiend, the hard-hearted tyrant, the worst villain ever to touch his life. She didn't care about him. She never had.

'I don't need you,' he cruelly said.

Brazil wheeled around and ran. He ran as fast as he could, back to his BMW.

'Oh for God's sake,' West exclaimed as Hammer suddenly was at her side.

'Problem?' Hammer stared after Brazil, her hands in her pockets.

'More of the same.' West wanted to kill him. 'He's going to do something.'

'Good deduction.' Hammer's eyes were sad and tired, but she was full of courage and support for the living.

'I'd better go after him.' West started walking.

Hammer stood where she was, strobing lights washing over her face as she watched West duck reporters and trot off to her car. Hammer thought about new love, about people crazy about each other and not knowing it as they fought and ran off and chased. The ambulance beeped as it backed up, carrying away what was left of a person who Hammer, in truth, did not feel especially sorry for at this point. She would never have wished such horrendous violence upon him, but what a piece of shit he was, stealing, hurting, and more than likely perpetuating the drug trade. Hammer was going to take this investigation into her own hands, and, if need be, make an example of Blair Mauney III, who had planned to screw the bank and a hooker during the same trip.

'People die the way they lived,' she commented to Detective Brewster, patting his back.

'Chief Hammer.' He was loading new film in his camera. 'I'm sorry about your husband.'

'So am I. In more ways than you'll ever know.' She ducked under the tape.

Brazil must have been speeding again, or perhaps he was hiding in another alleyway. West cruised West Trade street, looking for his old BMW. She checked her mirrors, seeing no sign of him, the scanner a staccato of more problems in the city. She picked up the portable phone and dialed the number for Brazil's desk at the *Observer*. After three rings, it rolled over to another desk, and West hung up. She fumbled for a cigarette, and turned onto Fifth Street, checking cars driven by men checking the late night market. West whelped her siren and flashed her lights, messing with those up to no good. She watched hookers and sh'ims scatter as potential clients sped away.

'Stupid bastards,' West muttered, flicking an ash out the window. 'Is it worth dying for?' she yelled at them.

Cahoon lived in Myers Park on Cherokee Place, and his splendid brick mansion was only partly lit up because its owner and his wife and youngest daughter had gone to bed. This did not deter Hammer in the least. She was about to do a decent thing for the CEO and great benefactor of the city. Hammer rang the doorbell, her fabric worn in places she had not known she had. She felt an emptiness, a loneliness, that was frightening in its intensity. She could not bear to go home and walk past places Seth had sat, lain, walked, or rummaged through. She did not want to see remnants of a life no more. His favorite coffee mug. The Ben & Jerry's Chocolate Chip

Cookie Dough ice cream he'd never had a chance to eat. The antique sterling-silver letter opener he had given her the Christmas of 1972, still on the desk in her study.

Cahoon heard the bell from his master suite upstairs, where his view above sculpted boxwoods and old magnolia trees included his building encrusted with jewels and topped by a crown. He threw back fine monogrammed sheets, wondering who on earth would dare to drop by his home at this obscene hour. Cahoon went to the Aiphone on the wall, and picked up the receiver. He was startled to see Chief Hammer on the video monitor.

'Judy?' he said.

'I know it's late, Sol.' She looked into the camera and spoke over the intercom. 'But I need to talk to you.'

'Is everything all right?' Alarmed, he thought of his children. He knew Rachael was in bed. But his two older sons could be anywhere.

'I'm afraid not,' Hammer told him.

Cahoon grabbed his robe from the bedpost, and flung it around himself. His slippers patted along the endless antique Persian runner covering stairs. His index finger danced over the burglar alarm keypad, turning off glass breakers, motion sensors, contacts in all windows and doors, and bypassing his vault and priceless art collection, which were in separate wings and on separate systems. He let Hammer in. Cahoon squinted in the glare of bright lights that blazed on whenever anything more than a foot tall moved within a six-foot radius of his house. Hammer did not look good. Cahoon could not imagine why the chief was out so early in the morning, so soon after her husband's sudden death.

'Please come in,' he said, wide awake now and more gentle than usual. 'Can I get you a drink?'

She followed him into the great room, where he repaired

to the bar. Hammer had been inside Cahoon's mansion but once, at a splendid party complete with a string quartet and huge silver bowls filled with jumbo shrimp on ice. The CEO liked English antiques and collected old books with beautiful leather covers and marbled pages.

'Bourbon,' Hammer decided.

That sounded good to Cahoon, who was on a regimen of no fat, no alcohol, and no fun. He might have a double, straight up, no ice. He pulled the cork out of a bottle of Blanton's Kentucky single barrel, and didn't bother with the monogrammed cocktail napkins his wife liked so much. He knew he needed to be medicated because Hammer wasn't here to hand him good news. *Dear Lord, don't let anything bad have happened to either of the boys.* Did a day go by when their father didn't worry about their partying, and flying through life in their sports cars or Kawasaki one-hundred horsepower Jet Skis?

Please let them be okay and I promise I'll be a better person, Cahoon silently prayed.

'I heard on the news about your . . .' he started to say.

'Thank you. He had so much amputated, Sol.' Hammer cleared her throat. She sipped bourbon and was soothed by its heat. 'He wouldn't have had a quality of life, had they been able to clear up the disease. I'm just grateful he didn't suffer any more than he did.' She typically looked on the bright side as her heart trembled like something wounded and afraid.

Hammer had not and could not yet accept that when the sun rose this morning and each one after the next, there would be silence in her house. There would be no night sounds of someone rattling in cupboards and turning on the TV. She would have no one to answer to, report to, or call when she was late or not going to make it home for dinner, as usual. She had not been a good wife. She had not even been a particularly good friend. Cahoon was struck speechless by the sight of this mighty woman in tears. She was trying hard to muster up that steely control of hers, but her spirit simply could not take it. He got up from his leather wing chair and dimmed the sconces on dark mahogany that he had salvaged from a sixteenth-century Tudor manor in England. He went to her and sat on the ottoman, taking one of her hands.

'It's all right, Judy,' he kindly said, and he felt like crying, too. 'You have every right to feel this way, and you go right on. It's just us, you and me, two human beings in this room right now. Who we are doesn't matter.'

'Thanks, Sol,' she whispered, and her voice shook as she wiped her eyes and took another swallow of bourbon.

'Get drunk if you want,' he suggested. 'We have plenty of guest rooms, and you can just stay right here so you don't have to drive.'

She patted Cahoon's hand, and crossed her arms and drew a deep breath. 'Let's talk about you,' she said.

Dejected, he got up and returned to his chair. Cahoon looked at her and braced himself.

'Please don't tell me it's Michael or Jeremy,' he said in a barely audible voice. 'I know Rachael is all right. She's in her room asleep. I know my wife is fine, sound asleep, too.' He paused to compose himself. 'My sons are still a bit on the wild side, both working for me and rebellious about it. I know they play hard, too hard, frankly.'

Hammer thought of her own sons and was suddenly dismayed that she might have caused this father a moment's concern. 'Sol, no, no, no,' she quickly reassured him. 'This is not about your sons, or about anyone in your family.'

'Thank God.' He took another swallow of his drink. 'Thank you, thank you, God.'

He would tithe more than usual to the synagogue

next Friday. Maybe he would build another child-care center somewhere, start another scholarship, give to the retirement center and the community school for troubled kids, or an orphanage. Damn it all. Cahoon was sick and tired of unhappiness and people suffering, and he hated crime as if all of it were directed at him.

'What do you want me to do?' he said, leaning forward and ready to mobilize.

'Do?' Hammer was puzzled. 'About what?'

'I've had it,' he said.

Now she was very confused. Was it possible he already knew what she had come here to tell him? He got up and began to pace in his Gucci leather slippers.

'Enough is enough,' he went on with feeling. 'I agree with you, see it your way. People being killed, robbed, and raped out there. Houses burglarized, cars stolen, children molested. In this city. Same is true all over the world, except in this country, everybody's got a gun. A gun in every pot. People hurting others and themselves, sometimes not even meaning to. Impulse.' He turned around, pacing the other way. 'Impaired by drugs and alcohol. Suicides that might not have happened were there not a gun right there. Acci . . .' he caught himself, remembering what had happened to Hammer's husband. 'What do you want me – want us at the bank – to do?' He stopped and fixed impassioned eyes on her.

This wasn't what she'd had in mind when she'd rung his doorbell, but Hammer knew when to seize the day. 'You certainly could be a crusader, Sol,' she thoughtfully replied.

Crusader. Cahoon liked that, and thought it time she saw he had some substance, too. He sat back down and remembered his bourbon.

'You want to help?' she went on. 'Then no more

shellacking what really goes on around here. No more bullshit, like this one hundred and five percent clearance rate. People need to know the truth. They need someone like you to inspire them to come out swinging.'

He nodded, deeply moved. 'Well, you know, that clearance rate crap wasn't my idea. It was the mayor's.'

'Of course.' She didn't care.

'By the way,' he said, curious now. 'What is it really?'

'Not bad.' The drink was working. 'Around seventy-five percent, which is nowhere near what it ought to be, but substantially higher than in a lot of cities. Now, if you want to count ten-year-old cases that are finally cleared, or jot down names from the cemetery, or decide that a drug dealer shot dead was the guy responsible for three uncleared cases . . .'

He held up his hand to stop her. 'I get it, Judy,' he said. 'This won't happen again. Honestly, I didn't know the details. Mayor Search is an idiot. Maybe we should get someone else.' He started drumming his fingers on the armrest, plotting.

'Sol.' She waited until his eyes focused on her again. 'I'm afraid I do have unpleasant news, and I wanted you to know in person from me before the media gets on it.'

He tensed again. He got up and refreshed their drinks as Hammer told him about Blair Mauney III and what had happened this night. She told him about the paperwork in Mauney's rental car. Cahoon listened, shocked, the blood draining from his face. He could not believe that Mauney was dead, murdered, his body spray-painted and dumped amid trash and brambles. It wasn't that Cahoon had ever particularly liked the man. Mauney, in Cahoon's experienced opinion, was a weak weasel with an entitlement attitude, and the suggestion of dishonesty did not surprise Cahoon in the least, the more it sank in. He was chagrined about *USChoice* cigarettes with their alchemy and little crowns. How could he have trusted any of it?

'Now it's my turn to ask,' Hammer finally said. 'What do you want me to do?'

'Jesus,' he said, his tireless brain racing through possibilities, liabilities, capabilities, impossibilities, and sensibilities. 'I'm not entirely sure. But I know I need time.'

'How much?' She swirled her drink.

'Three or four days,' he said. 'My guess is most of the money is still in Grand Cayman, in numerous accounts with numbers that aren't linked. If this hits the news, I can guarantee that we'll never recover the cash, and no matter what anybody says, a loss like that hurts everybody, every kid with a savings account, every couple needing a loan, every retired citizen with a nest egg.'

'Of course it does,' said Hammer, who also was a faithful client of Cahoon's bank. 'My eternal point, Sol. Everybody gets hurt. A crime victimizes all of us. Not to mention what it will do to your bank's image.'

Cahoon looked pained. 'That's always the biggest loss. Reputation and whatever charges and fines the federal regulators will decide.'

'This isn't your fault.'

'Dominion Tobacco and its secret, Nobel-potential research always bothered me. I guess I just wanted to believe it was true,' he reflected. 'But banks have a responsibility not to let something like this happen.'

'Then how did it?' she asked.

'You have a senior vice president with access to all commercial loan activities, and trust him. So you don't always follow your own policies and procedures. You make exceptions, circumvent. And then you have trouble.' He was getting more depressed. 'I should have watched the son of a bitch more closely, damn it.'

'Could he have gotten away with it, had he lived?' Hammer asked.

'Sure,' Cahoon said. 'All he had to do was make sure the loan was repaid. Of course, that would have been from drug money, unbeknownst to us. Meanwhile, he would have been getting maybe ten percent of all money laundered through the hotels, through the bank, and my guess is we would have become more and more of a major cash interstate for whoever these bad people are. Eventually, the truth would have come out. USBank would have been ruined.'

Hammer watched him thoughtfully, a new respect forming for this man, who prior to this early morning, she had not understood, and in truth had unfairly judged.

'Just tell me what I can do to help,' she said again.

'If you could withhold his identification and everything about this situation so we salvage what we can and get up to speed on exactly what happened,' he repeated. 'After that, we'll file a Suspicious Activity Report, and the public will know.'

Hammer glanced at her watch. It was almost three A.M. 'We'll get the FBI on it immediately. It will be in their best interest to buy a little time, too. As for Mauney, as far as I'm concerned, we can't effect a positive identification just yet, and I'm sure Dr Odom will want to withhold information until he can get hold of dental records, fingerprints, whatever, and you know how overworked he is.' She paused, and promised, 'It will take a while.'

Cahoon thought of Mrs Mauney III, whom he had met only superficially at parties. 'Someone's got to call Polly,' he said. 'Mauney's wife. I'd like to do that, if you have no objections.'

Hammer got up and smiled at him. 'You know something, Sol? You're nowhere near as rotten as I thought.'

'That works both way, Judy.' He got up.

'It certainly does.'

'You hungry?'

'Starved.'

'What's open at this hour,' he wondered.

'You ever been to the Presto Grill?'

'Is that a club?' He grabbed his car keys.

'Yes,' she said. 'And guess what, Sol? It's about time you became a member.'

Chapter Twenty-six

For the most part, only people up to no good were out this hour, and as West drove seedy streets looking for Brazil's car, her mood became more grim. In part she was worried. She was also so irritated that she wanted to slug him. What was he, crazy? Where did these irrational, angry fits come from? Were he a woman, she'd wonder about PMS and suggest he go back to the gynecologist. She grabbed the portable phone and dialed again.

'Newsroom,' an unfamiliar voice answered.

'Andy Brazil,' West said.

'He's not in.'

'Has he been in at all the last few hours?' West asked, frustration in her tone. 'Have you heard from him?'

'Not that I know of.'

West hit the end button, and tossed the phone on the seat. She pounded the steering wheel. 'Damn you, damn you, Andy!' she exclaimed.

As she cruised, her phone rang, startling her. It was Brazil. She was sure of it as she answered. She was wrong.

'It's Hammer,' her chief said. 'What in the world are you doing still out?'

'I can't find him.'

'You certain he's not home or at the paper?'

'Positive. He's out here courting trouble,' West said rather frantically.

'Oh dear,' Hammer said. 'Cahoon and I are about to have breakfast, Virginia. Here's what I want you to do. No information about this case, and no identification until I tell you otherwise. For now, the case is pending. We need to buy some time here because of this other situation.'

'I think that's wise,' West said, checking her mirrors, looking everywhere.

She had missed Brazil by no more than two minutes, and in fact, unwittingly had done so a number of times during the past few hours. She would turn onto one street just before he drove past where she had been. Now, he was cruising by the Cadillac Grill on West Trade Street, and staring out at boarded-up slums haunted by the rulers of the night. He saw the young hooker ahead, leaning inside a Thunderbird, talking to a man looking for a good investment. Brazil wasn't in a shy mood, and he pulled up closer, watching. The car sped off, and the hooker turned hostile, glazed eyes on Brazil, not at all happy with the intrusion. Brazil rolled down his window.

'Hey!' he called out.

Poison, the prostitute, stared at the one known on the street as Blondie, mockery in her eyes. She started strolling again. This pretty-boy snitch followed her everywhere, had a thing about her, and was still working up his nerve, maybe thought he was going to get something more to leak to the police and the newspaper. She thought it was funny. Brazil unfastened his seatbelt. He reached to roll down the passenger's window. She wasn't going to get away from him this time. No sir, and he tucked the .380 out of sight beneath his seat, as he crept forward, calling out to her.

'Excuse me! Excuse me, ma'am!' he said again and again. 'I need to talk to you!'

Hammer was rolling past at this very moment, Cahoon following in his Mercedes 600S V-12 sedan, black with parchment leather interior. He wasn't entirely within his comfort zone in this part of the city, and he checked his locks again as Hammer got on her police radio and told the dispatcher to ten-five Unit 700. Immediately, she and West were on the air.

'The subject you're looking for is at West Trade and Cedar,' Hammer said on the air to West. 'You might want to head this way in a hurry.'

'Ten-four!'

Officers in the area were perplexed, even a little lost, as they overheard this transmission between their highest leaders. They were still mindful of their chief's feelings about being followed and harassed. Maybe it was wise to sit this one out for a minute or two, until they had a better idea about what exactly was going down. West gunned the engine, racing back toward West Trade.

Poison stopped and slowly turned around, seduction smoldering in her eyes as she entertained notions this snitch in the BMW couldn't even begin to imagine.

* * *

Hammer wasn't so sure this was the right time to introduce Cahoon to the Presto Grill. Trouble seemed to rise from the street like heat, and she had not gotten where she was in life by ignoring her instincts. Only in her personal life had she looked the other way, turned the volume down low, and denied. She swung off into the All Right parking lot across from the grill, and motioned out her window for Cahoon to follow. He stopped by her unmarked car and his window hummed down.

'What's going on?' he asked.

'Park and get in,' she said.

'What?'

She furtively scanned their surroundings. Something bad was out there. She could feel its foulness, detect the scent of the beast. There was no time to waste.

'I can't leave my car here,' Cahoon reasonably pointed out, because the Mercedes would be the only car in the lot, and possibly the only vehicle within fifty miles, that cost roughly one hundred and twenty thousand dollars.

Hammer got the dispatcher on the air. 'Send a unit to the All Right parking lot, five hundred block West Trade, to watch a late-model black Mercedes until I give further notice.'

Radar, the dispatcher, was none too fond of Hammer, for she, too, was female. But she was the chief, and he, at least, had the good sense to be afraid of the bitch. Radar had no idea what she was doing out on the street, especially at this hour. He sent two units while Poison smiled knowingly and took her time reaching the passenger's window of Brazil's car. She leaned inside like she did all the time, and took an inventory of the groomed leather interior. She noted the briefcase, pens, *Charlotte*

Observer notepads, old black leather bomber jacket, and, most of all, the police scanner and two-way radio.

'You po-lice?' she drawled, a little confused about just who the hell Blondie was.

'A reporter. With the *Observer*,' Brazil said, because he was not police anymore. West had made that clear.

Poison appraised him with dangerous flirtation. A reporter's money was as good as any, and now she knew the truth. Blondie wasn't a snitch. He was the one writing those stories that had Punkin Head so cranky and out of control.

'What you trading, little boy?' she asked.

'Information.' Brazil's heart was thudding hard. 'I'll pay for it.'

Poison's eyes gleamed, her lips parting in an amused, gap-toothed smile. She slinked around to his side of the car, and leaned in his window. Her fragrance was cloying, like incense.

'What kind you want, little boy?' she asked.

Brazil was wary but intrigued. He'd never dealt with anything like this, and he imagined experienced, worldly men and their secret pleasures. He wondered if they were scared when they let someone like this in their car. Did they ever ask her name or want to know anything about her?

'What's been going on around here,' he nervously went on. 'The murders. I've seen you around, in the area, I mean. For a while. Maybe you know something.'

'Maybe I do. Maybe I don't,' she said, trailing a finger down his shoulder.

West was driving fast, passing the same bad places Brazil had moments earlier. Hammer wasn't too far behind her, Cahoon riding shotgun, wide-eyed as he surveyed a reality far removed from his own.

'Will cost you fifty, little boy,' Poison said to Brazil.

He didn't have that much in the bank, and wasn't about to let her know. 'Twenty-five,' he negotiated, as if he did it all the time.

Poison backed up, appraising him and thinking about Punkin Head in its van, watching. It had yelled at her and slapped her around this morning. It had hurt her in places no one could see, because of what Blondie had put in the paper. Poison started feeling hateful about it, and made a decision that perhaps wasn't very wise, considering she and Punkin Head had already whacked one rich dude tonight, meeting their quota for the week, and cops were all around.

She seemed amused by something Brazil didn't know, and she pointed. 'See that corner there, little boy?' she said. 'That old apartment building? Nobody in it no more. Meet you back there, 'cause we can't be talking here.'

Poison stared into a dark alleyway across the street, where Punkin Head watched from inside its windowless van in dark shadows. It knew what she was up to, and was aroused by it, and in a mood to murder, since it was taking less and less time for it to cool down and get the tension again. Punkin Head felt an insatiable rage toward Blondie that was more exciting than sex. It couldn't wait to watch that fucking snitch soil his fancy jeans and beg on his knees before the almighty Punkin Head. It had never wanted to ruin anything more in its despicable, low, nasty, hate-filled life, and its excitement mounted unbearably.

* * *

West spotted Brazil's car up ahead. She saw the hooker walking off as Brazil drove to the corner and took a right. She saw the old, windowless van slide out of the dark alleyway, like an eel.

'Christ!' West panicked. 'Andy, no!'

She grabbed the radio and slammed down the accelerator, flipping on strobing lights. 'Seven hundred requesting backups!' she screamed on the air. 'Two hundred block West Trade. Now!'

Hammer heard the broadcast, too, and sped up. 'Shit,' she said.

'What the hell's going on?' Cahoon was on red alert, in military mode, ready to take out the enemy.

'Don't know, but it's not good.' She threw on her lights, whelping her siren as she passed people.

'You got an extra gun handy?' Cahoon asked.

He was in the Marines again, launching grenades at North Koreans, crawling through the blood of his buddies. Nobody went through that and came out the same. Nobody messed with Cahoon, because he knew something they didn't. There were worst things than dying, the fear of it being one of them. He unfastened his seatbelt.

'Put that back on,' Hammer told him as they flew.

West was trying to find a place to do a U-turn, and finally gave up. She bumped and slammed over the concrete median, rubber squealing as she headed the other way. She had lost sight of Brazil, the hooker and the van. West was as frantic and frightened as she had ever been.

'Please God, help!' she fervently said. 'Oh please God!'

* * *

Brazil turned behind haunted ruins of graying old wood, and broken windows gaping ragged and black, where there was no sign of life. He stopped and sat in silence. He looked around, increasingly jumpy. Maybe this wasn't such a good idea. He dug in a pocket of his jeans, and was taking an inventory of crumpled bills, when suddenly the young hooker filled his window, smoking a cigarette, holding a washcloth, and smiling in a way that increased Brazil's misgivings. It was the first time he'd noticed how crazed her eyes were, or maybe something was different now.

'Get out,' she said, motioning to him. 'I see the money first.'

Brazil opened his door and stepped out as an engine roared in from the rear. A dark, old van with no windows bumped toward them at a high rate of speed. Brazil was shocked. He scrambled back inside his BMW, throwing it into reverse. But it was too late. The van blocked him, and there was nothing ahead but a thicket and a deep gully. Trapped, Brazil watched the driver's door open. He took in the big, ugly sh'im with pumpkin-colored hair woven in cornrows close to its skull. It jumped out, its smile serpentine as it walked towards Brazil, a large-caliber pistol in one hand, the other rattling a can of spray paint.

'We got us a sweet one,' Punkin Head said to Poison. 'Might have some fun. Teach him what we do with snitches.'

'I'm not a snitch,' Brazil let Punkin Head know.

'He's a reporter,' Poison said.

'*A reporter*,' it mocked, its anger raging out of control as memories of Black Widow stories unfurled and flashed and infuriated all over again.

Brazil's stories were the furthest thing from his mind

as he thought fast. Poison laughed. She zipped open a switchblade.

'Get out of the car and give me the keys,' Punkin Head moved closer to its prey, a .45 caliber pistol pointed between Blondie's eyes.

'All right. All right. Please don't shoot.' Brazil knew when to cooperate.

'We got us a beggar.' Punkin Head made a harsh, horrid sound that was supposed to be a laugh. '*Please don't shoot*,' it mimicked.

'Let's cut him first.' Poison waited outside the BMW's door, knife ready to carve this reporter boy where it hurt.

Brazil turned off the engine. He fumbled with the keys, dropping them to the floor. He groped for them as West squealed around the corner, turning behind the abandoned apartments. Gunshots exploded. BAM-BAM, and BAM-BAM. Her siren screamed and screamed as a gun fired four more times. Hammer turned in four seconds after West, hearing the gunshots, too, flipping on her siren, while backups closed in from all directions of the Queen City, the night a red-and-blue flashing war zone.

West had her gun drawn as she bolted out of her car. Hammer, her partner, was right behind West, pistol racked back and ready. The two women scanned the parked van with running engine. They took in the two bloody bodies not breathing near an open switchblade and a can of spray paint. They locked on Brazil clenching the borrowed .380, as if his victims might hurt him, the gun jumping in his locked hands. Cahoon walked closer to the crime scene, staring at the dead, and then all around at the lit-up skyline, where his building towered.

West went to Brazil. She carefully took the gun from

him and enclosed it in a plastic evidence bag, along with spent cartridge cases.

'It's okay,' she said to him.

He blinked, shivering, as his shocked eyes met hers.

'Andy,' she said. 'This is very traumatic. I've been through it, know all about it, and I'm going to help you every step of the way, okay? I'm here for you now. Got it?'

She took him in her arms. Andy Brazil dug his fingers in her hair. He shut his eyes and held her hard.

Southern Cross

To Marcia H. Morey
World champion in juvenile justice reform
and all you've ever done

For what you've taught me

chapter one

The last Monday morning of March began with promise in the historic city of Richmond, Virginia, where prominent family names had not changed since the war that was not forgotten. Traffic was scant on downtown streets and the Internet. Drug dealers were asleep, prostitutes tired, drunk drivers sober, pedophiles returning to work, burglar alarms silent, domestic fights on hold. Not much was going on at the morgue.

Richmond, built on seven or eight hills, depending on who counts, is a metropolitan center of unflagging pride that traces its roots back to 1607, when a small band of fortune-hunting English explorers got lost and laid claim to the region by planting a cross in the name of King James. The inevitable settlement at the fall line of the James River, predictably called 'The Falls', suffered the expected tribulations of trading posts and forts, and anti-British sentiments, revolution, hardships, floggings, scalpings, treaties that didn't work and people dying young.

Local Indians discovered firewater and hangovers, and traded herbs, minerals and furs for hatchets, ammunition, cloth, kettles and more firewater. Slaves were shipped in from Africa. Thomas Jefferson designed Monticello, the Capitol and the state penitentiary. He founded the University of Virginia, drafted the Declaration of Independence and was accused of fathering mulatto children. Railroads were constructed. The tobacco industry flourished and nobody sued.

All in all, life in the genteel city ambled along reasonably well until 1861, when Virginia decided to secede from the Union and the Union wouldn't go along with it. Richmond did not fare well in the Civil War. Afterward, the former capital of the Confederacy went on as best it could with no slaves and bad money. It remained fiercely loyal to its defeated cause, still flaunting its battle flag, the Southern Cross, as Richmonders marched into the next century and survived other terrible wars that were not their problem because they were fought elsewhere.

By the late twentieth century, things were going rather poorly in the capital city. Its homicide rate had climbed as high as second in the nation. Tourism was suffering. Children were carrying guns and knives to school and fighting on the bus. Residents and department stores had abandoned downtown and fled to nearby counties. The tax base was shrinking. City officials and city council members didn't get along. The governor's antebellum mansion needed new plumbing and wiring.

General Assembly delegates continued slamming desktops and insulting one another when they came to town, and the chairman of the House Transportation Committee carried a concealed handgun onto the floor.

Dishonest gypsies began dropping by on their migrations north and south, and Richmond became a home away from home for drug dealers traveling along I-95.

The timing was right for a woman to come along and clean house. Or perhaps it was simply that nobody was looking when the city hired its first female police chief, who this moment was out walking her dog. Daffodils and crocuses were blooming, the morning's first light spreading across the horizon, the temperature an unseasonable seventy degrees. Birds were chatty from the branches of budding trees, and Chief Judy Hammer was feeling uplifted and momentarily soothed.

'Good girl, Popeye,' she encouraged her Boston terrier.

It wasn't an especially kind name for a dog whose huge eyes bulged and pointed at the walls. But when the SPCA had shown the puppy on TV and Hammer had rushed to the phone to adopt her, Popeye was already Popeye and answered only to that name.

Hammer and Popeye kept a good pace through their restored neighborhood of Church Hill, the city's original site, quite close to where the English planted their cross. Owner and dog moved briskly past antebellum homes with iron fences and porches, and slate and false mansard roofs, and turrets, stone lintels, chased wood, stained glass, scroll-sawn porches, gables, raised so-called English and picturesque basements, and thick chimneys.

They followed East Grace Street to where it ended at an overlook that was the most popular observation point in the city. On one side of the precipice was the radio station WRVA, and on the other was Hammer's nineteenth-century Greek Revival house, built by a man in the tobacco business about the time the Civil War ended. Hammer loved the old brick, the bracketed cornices and flat roof, and the granite porch. She craved places with a past and always chose to live in the heart of the jurisdiction she served.

She unlocked the front door, turned off the alarm system, freed Popeye from the leash and put her through a quick circuit of sitting, sitting pretty and getting down, in exchange for treats. Hammer walked into the kitchen for coffee, her ritual every morning the same. After her walk and Popeye's continuing behavioral modification, Hammer would sit in her living room, scan the paper and look out long windows at the vista of tall office buildings, the Capitol, the Medical College of Virginia and acres of Virginia Commonwealth University's Biotechnology Research Park. It was said that Richmond was becoming the 'City of Science', a place of enlightenment and thriving health.

But as its top law enforcer surveyed edifices and downtown streets, she was all too aware of crumbling brick smokestacks, rusting railroad tracks and viaducts, and abandoned factories and tobacco warehouses with windows painted over and boarded up. She knew that bordering downtown and not so far from where she lived were five federal housing projects, with two more on Southside. If one told the politically incorrect truth, all were breeding grounds for social chaos and violence and were clear evidence that the Civil War continued to be lost by the South.

Hammer gazed out at a city that had invited her to solve its seemingly hopeless problems. The morning was lighting up and she worried there would be one cruel cold snap left over from winter. Wouldn't that be just like everything else these days, the final petty act, the eradication of what little beauty was left in her horrendously stressful life? Doubts crowded her thoughts.

When she had forged the destiny that had brought her to Richmond, she had refused to entertain the possibility that she had become a fugitive from her own life. Her two sons were grown and had distanced themselves from her long before their father, Seth, had gotten ill and died last spring. Judy Hammer had bravely gone on, gathering her life's mission around her like a crusader's cape.

She resigned from the Charlotte P.D., where she had been resisted and celebrated for the miracles she wrought as its chief. She decided it was her calling to move on to other southern cities and occupy and raze and reconstruct. She made a proposal to the National Institute of Justice that would allow her to pick beleaguered police departments across the South, spend a year in each, and bring all of them into a union of one-for-all and all-for-one.

Hammer's philosophy was simple. She did not believe in cops' rights. She knew for a fact that when officers, the brass, precincts and even chiefs seceded from the department to do their own thing, the result was catastrophic. Crime rates went up. Clearance rates went down. Nobody got along. The citizens that law enforcement was there to protect and serve locked their doors, loaded their guns, cared not for their neighbors, gave cops the finger and blamed everything on them. Hammer's blueprint for enlightenment and change was the New York Crime Control Model of policing known as COMSTAT, or computer-driven statistics.

The acronym was an easy way to define a concept far more complicated than the notion of using technology to map crime patterns and hot spots in the city. COMSTAT held every cop accountable for everything. No longer could the rank and file and their leaders pass the buck, look the other way, not care, not know the answer, say they couldn't help it, were about to get around to it, hadn't been told, forgot, meant to, didn't feel well or were on the phone or off duty at the time, because on Mondays and Fridays Chief Hammer assembled representatives from all precincts and divisions and gave them hell.

Clearly, Hammer's battle plan was a northern one, but as fate would have it, when she presented her proposal to Richmond's city council, it was preoccupied with infighting, mutiny and usurpations. At the time, it didn't seem like such a bad thing to let someone else solve the city's problems. So it was that Hammer was hired as interim chief for a year and allowed to bring along two talents she had worked with in Charlotte.

Hammer began her occupation of Richmond. Soon enough stubbornness set in. Hatred followed. The city patriarchs wanted Hammer and her NIJ team to go home. There was not a thing the city needed to learn from New York, and Richmonders would be damned before they followed any example set by the turncoat, carpetbagging city of Charlotte, which had a habit of stealing Richmond's banks and Fortune 500 companies.

Deputy Chief Virginia West complained bitterly through painful expressions and exasperated huffs as she jogged around the University of Richmond track. The slate roofs of handsome collegiate Gothic buildings were just beginning to materialize as the sun thought about getting up, and students had yet to venture out except for two young women who were running sprints.

'I can't go much farther,' West blurted out to Officer Andy Brazil.

Brazil glanced at his watch. 'Seven more minutes,' he said. 'Then you can walk.'

It was the only time she took orders from him. Virginia West had been a deputy chief in Charlotte when Brazil was still going through the police academy and writing articles for the *Charlotte Observer.* Then Hammer had brought them with her to Richmond so West could head investigations and Brazil could do research, handle public information and start a website.

Although one might argue that, in actuality, West and Brazil were peers on Hammer's NIJ team, in West's mind she outranked Brazil and always would. She was more powerful. He would never have her experience. She was better on the firing range and in fights. She had killed a suspect once, although she wasn't proud of it. Her love affair with Brazil back in their Charlotte days had been due to the very normal intensity of mentoring. So he'd had a crush and she had gone along with it before he got over it. So what.

'You notice anybody else killing himself out here? Except those two girls, who are either on the track team or have an eating disorder,' West continued to complain in gasps. 'No! And guess why! Because this is stupid as shit! I should be drinking coffee, reading the paper right now.'

'If you'd quit talking, you could get into a rhythm,' said Brazil, who ran without effort in navy Charlotte P.D. sweats and Saucony shoes that whispered when they touched the red rubberized track.

'You really ought to quit wearing Charlotte shit,' she went on talking anyway. 'It's bad enough as is. Why make the cops here hate us more?'

'I don't think they hate us.' Brazil tried to be positive about how unfriendly and unappreciative Richmond cops had been.

'Yes they do.'

'Nobody likes change,' Brazil reminded her.

'You seem to,' she said.

It was a veiled reference to the rumor West had heard barely a week after they had moved here. Brazil had something going on with his landlady, a wealthy single woman who lived in Church Hill. West had asked for no further information. She had checked out nothing. She did not want to know. She had refused to drive past Brazil's house, much less drop by for a visit.

'I guess I like change when it's good,' Brazil was saying.

'Exactly.'

'Do you wish you'd stayed in Charlotte?'

'Absolutely.'

Brazil picked up his pace just enough to give her his back. She would never forgive him for saying how much he wanted her to come with him to Richmond, for talking her into something yet one more time because he could, because he used words with clarity and conviction. He had carried her away on the rhythm of feelings he clearly no longer had. He had crafted his love into poetry and then fucking read it to someone else.

'There's nothing for me here,' said West, who put words together the way she hung doors and shutters and built fences. 'I mean let's be honest about it.' She wasn't about to paint over anything without stripping it first. 'It sucks.' She sawed away. 'Thank God it's only for a year.' She pounded her point.

He replied by picking up his pace.

'Like we're some kind of MASH unit for police departments,' she added. 'Who were we kidding? What a waste of time. I don't remember when I've wasted so much time.'

Brazil glanced at his watch. He didn't seem to be listening to her, and she wished she could get past his broad shoulders and handsome profile. The early sun rubbed gold into his hair. The two college women sprinted past, sweaty and fat-free, their muscular legs pumping as they showed off to Brazil. West felt depressed. She felt old. She halted and bent over, hands on her knees.

'That's it!' she exclaimed, heaving.

'Forty-six more seconds.' Brazil ran in place like he was treading water, looking back at her.

'Go on.'

'You sure?'

'Fly like the wind.' She rudely waved him on. 'Damn it,' she bitched as her flip phone vibrated on the waistband of her running shorts.

She moved off the track, over to the bleachers, out of the way of hard-bodied people who made her insecure.

'West,' she answered.

'Virginia? It's . . .' Hammer's voice pushed through static.

'Chief Hammer?' West said loudly. 'Hello?'

'Virginia . . . You there?' Hammer's voice scattered more.

West pressed a hand over her other ear, trying to hear.

'. . . That's bullshit . . .' a male voice suddenly broke in.

West started walking, trying to get into a better cell.

'Virginia . . . ?' Hammer's voice barely crackled through.

'. . . can do it anytime . . . usual rules apply . . .' The male voice was back.

He had a southern drawl and was obviously a redneck. West felt instant hostility.

'. . . time to . . . kill . . . Got to . . . or score . . .' The redneck spoke in distorted blurts.

'. . . an ugly dog not worth . . . lead to shoot it . . .' A second redneck suddenly answered the first redneck. 'How much . . . ?'

'Depends on . . . Maybe a couple hundred . . .'

'. . . Just between us . . .'

'. . . If . . . body . . . finds . . .'

'. . . not invited . . .'

'What?' Hammer's voice surfaced and was gone.

'. . . Use a . . . cold nose . . . Not your piece . . . shit . . . ! Blue . . .'

'Chief Hammer . . .' West started to say more, then caught herself, realizing the rednecks might be able to hear them, too.

'. . . coons . . .' The first redneck came back. '. . . not one born too smart for . . . Dismal Swamp . . .'

'. . . Got that right, Bubba . . . We covered . . . a blanket . . .'

'Okay, Smudge . . . buddy . . . early morning?'

West was silently shocked as she listened to two men plan a homicide that clearly was racially motivated, a hate crime, a score to settle that involved robbery. It sounded as if the murder would go down early in the morning. She wondered if a *cold nose* was slang for a snub-nosed revolver and if *blue* referred to a gun that was blue steel versus stainless steel or nickel-plated. Clearly, the psychos planned to wrap the body in a blanket and dump it in the Dismal Swamp.

Static.

'. . . Loraine . . .' Bubba's fractured voice was back. '. . . At old pumps . . . cut engine . . . headlights off so don't wake . . .'

Static, and the cell cleared.

'Chief Hammer?' West said. 'Chief Hammer? Are you still there?'

'Bubba . . .' the second stranger crackled again. 'Somebody's on . . .'

Static, scratch, blare, blip.

'Goddamn it,' West muttered when her phone went dead.

Bubba's real name was Butner Fluck IV. Unlike so many fearless men devoted to pickup trucks, guns, topless bars and the Southern Cross, he had not been born into the tribe of Bubbas, but rather had grown up the son of a theologian in the Northside neighborhood of Ginter Park, where old mansions were in disrepair and Civil War cannonballs on porches were popular. Butner came from a long line of Butners who always went by the nickname 'But', and it was lost on his erudite father, Dr. But Fluck III, that calling his son But in this day and age set the child up for problems.

By the time little But had entered the first grade, the slurs, the slander and the derision were on every tongue. They were whispered in class, shouted on buses and playing fields, and drawn on sheets of notebook paper slipped from desk to desk or left inside little But's locker. When he wrote his name it was But Fluck. In the teacher's grade books he was Fluck, But.

Any way he looked at it, he was screwed, really, and of course his peers came up with any number of other renditions. *Mother-But-Flucker, Butter-Flucker, But-Flucking-Boy, Buttock-Fluck,* and so on. When he retreated into his studies and went to the head of the class, new pet names were added to the list. *But-Head, Fluck-Head, Mother-Flucking-But-Head, Head-But-Head,* et al.

For But's ninth birthday he requested camouflage and several toy guns. He became a compulsive eater. He spent a lot of time in the woods hunting imaginary prey. He immersed himself in a growing stash of magazines featuring mercenary soldiers, anarchists, trucks, assault weapons, Civil War battlefields and women in swimsuits. He collected manuals on simple car care and repair, automotive tools and wiring, wilderness survival, fishing, and hiking in bear country. He sneaked cigarettes and was rude. His tenth year he changed his name to Bubba and was feared by all.

This early Monday morning Bubba was driving home from third shift at Philip Morris, his CB and two-way radios turned on, his portable phone plugged into the cigarette lighter, Eric Clapton on the CD player. His stainless steel Colt Anaconda .44 with its eight-inch barrel and Bushnell Holo sight on a B-Square base was tucked under his seat within quick reach.

Multiple antennas bobbed on his red 1990 Jeep Cherokee, which Bubba did not realize had been listed in the *Used Car Buying Guide* as a used car to avoid, or that it had been wrecked and had a hundred thousand more miles on it than the odometer showed. Bubba had no reason to doubt his good buddy, Joe 'Smudge' Bruffy, who last year had sold the Jeep to Bubba for only three thousand dollars more than the Blue Book value.

In fact, it was Smudge who Bubba had been talking to on the portable phone moments earlier when two other voices broke in. Bubba hadn't been able to make out what the two women were saying, but the name 'Chief

Hammer' had been unmistakable. He knew it meant something.

Bubba had been raised in a Presbyterian atmosphere of predestination, God's will, inclusive language, exegesis and colorful stoles. He had rebelled. In college he had studied Far Eastern religions to spite his father, but none of Bubba's acting out had eradicated the essence of his early indoctrination. Bubba believed there was purpose. Despite all setbacks and personal flaws, he had faith that if he accumulated enough good karma, or perhaps if yin and yang ever got along, he would discover the reason for his existence.

So when he heard Chief Hammer's name over the cell phone, he experienced a sudden release of gloominess and menacing persecution, a buoyant happiness and surge of power. He was transformed into the warrior on a mission he had always been destined to become as he followed Midlothian Turnpike to Muskrat's Auto Rescue, this time for another windshield leak. Bubba snapped up the mike of his two-way Kenwood radio and switched over to the security channel.

'Unit 1 to Unit 2.' He tried to raise Honey, his wife, as he followed the four-lane artery of Southside out of Chesterfield County and into the city limits.

No answer. Bubba's eyes scanned his mirrors. A Richmond police cruiser pulled in behind him. Bubba slowed down.

'Unit 1 to Unit 2,' Bubba tried again.

No answer. Some shithead kid in a white Ford Explorer was trying to cut in front of Bubba. Bubba sped up.

'Unit 1 to Unit 2!' Bubba hated it when his wife didn't respond to him immediately.

The cop remained on Bubba's tail, dark Oakleys staring straight into Bubba's rearview mirror. Bubba slowed again. The punk in the Explorer tried to ease in front of Bubba, right turn signal flashing. Bubba sped up. He deliberated over what form of communication to use next, and picked up his portable phone. He changed his mind. He thought about trying his wife again on the two-way and decided not to bother. She should have gotten back to him the first and second times. The hell with her. He snapped up the mike to his CB, eyeing the cop in his mirrors and keeping a check on the Explorer.

'Yo, Smudge,' Bubba hailed his buddy over the CB. 'You on track come back to yack.'

'Unit 2,' his wife's out-of-breath voice came over the two-way.

Bubba's portable phone rang.

'Sorry . . . oh my . . .' Honey said sweetly as she gasped. 'I was . . . oh dear . . . let me catch my breath . . . whew . . . was chasing Half Shell . . . she wouldn't come . . . That dog.'

Bubba ignored her. He answered the phone.

'Bubba?' said Gig Dan, Bubba's supervisor at Philip Morris.

'Trackin' and yackin', buddy,' Smudge came back over the CB.

'Unit 2 to Unit 1?' Honey persisted anxiously over the two-way.

'Yo, Gig,' Bubba said into the portable phone. 'What's goin' on?'

'Need ya to come in and work the second half of second shift,' Gig told him. 'Tiller called in sick.'

Shit, Bubba thought. Today of all days when there was so much to do and so little time. It depressed the hell out of him to think about showing up at eight o'clock tonight and working twelve straight hours.

'Ten-4,' Bubba replied to Gig.

'When you wanna shine on yellow eyes?' Smudge hadn't given up.

Bubba didn't really like coon hunting all that much. His coon dog Half Shell had her problems, and Bubba worried about snakes. Besides, Smudge always got a higher score. It seemed all Bubba did was lose money to him.

'Before slithers wake up, I guess.' Bubba tried to sound sure of himself. 'So go ahead and shake out a plan.'

'Ten-fo, good buddy,' Smudge came back. 'Gotcha covered like a blanket.'

chapter two

Smoke was a special needs child. This had become apparent in the second grade when he had stolen his teacher's wallet, punched a female classmate, carried a revolver to school, set several cats on fire and smashed up the principal's station wagon with a pipe.

Since those early misguided days in his hometown of Durham, North Carolina, Smoke had been written up fifty-two times for assault, cheating, plagiarism, extortion, harassment, gambling, truancy, dishonesty, larceny, disruptive dress, indecent literature and bus misconduct.

He had been arrested six times for crimes ranging from sexual assault to murder, and had been on probation, on supervised probation with special conditions, in an Alternative to Detention Program, in detention, in a wilderness camp therapeutic program, in a community guidance clinic where he received psychological evaluation and in an anger-coping group.

Unlike most juveniles who are delinquent, Smoke had parents who showed up for all of his court appearances. They visited him in detention. They paid for attorneys and dismissed one right after the other when Smoke complained and found fault. Smoke's parents enrolled him in four different private schools and blamed each one when it didn't work out.

It was clear to Smoke's father, a hardworking banker, that his son was unusually bright and misunderstood. Smoke's mother was devoted to Smoke and always took his side. She never believed he was guilty. Both parents believed their son had been set up because the police were corrupt, didn't like Smoke and needed to clear cases. Both parents wrote scathing letters to the district attorney, the mayor, the attorney general, the governor and a U.S. senator when Smoke was finally locked up in C. A. Dillon Training School in Butner.

Of course, Smoke didn't stay there long because when he turned sixteen, he was no longer a minor according to North Carolina law and was released. His juvenile record was expunged. His fingerprints and mug shots were destroyed. He had no past. His parents thought it wise to relocate to a city where the police, whose memories were not expunged, would not know Smoke or harass him any more. So it was that Smoke moved to Richmond, Virginia, where this morning he was feeling especially mean-spirited and in a mood to cause trouble.

'We got twenty minutes,' he said to Divinity.

She was leaning against him as he drove the Ford Escort his father had bought him when Smoke had gotten his Virginia driver's license. Divinity started kissing Smoke's jaw and rubbing her hand between his legs to see if anybody was home.

'We got all the time you want, baby,' she breathed in

his ear. 'Fuck school. Fuck that little kid you pick up.'

'We got a plan, remember?' Smoke said.

He was in running shoes, loose-fitting sweats, a bandanna around his head, tinted glasses on. He wound his way through streets within a block of the Crestar Bank on Patterson Avenue, in the city's West End, and spotted a small brick house on Kensington where there was no car or newspaper – no one home, it seemed. He pulled into the driveway.

'Anybody answers, we're trying to find Community High School,' Smoke reminded her.

'Lost in space, baby,' Divinity said, getting out.

She rang the doorbell twice and was met with silence. Smoke got into the passenger's seat and Divinity drove him back to Crestar Bank. The sky was pale and clear, and traffic was picking up as people began a new work week and realized they needed cash for parking and lunch. The bank's ATM wasn't doing any business at the moment, and that was good. Smoke climbed out of the car.

'You know what to do,' he said to Divinity.

He walked toward the bank as she drove off. He went around to the drive-thru where he could not be seen. It wasn't long before a young man in a Honda Civic hatchback parked in front of the ATM. Smoke came out from behind the bank, taking his time. The young man was busy making his transaction and didn't notice Smoke's angled approach out of range of the camera.

Smoke was so swift his victims were always too shocked to move. He slapped duct tape over the camera lens and the man's eyes. Smoke jabbed the barrel of his Glock pistol into the small of the man's back.

'Don't move,' Smoke said quietly.

The man didn't.

'Hand the money behind you real slow.'

The man did. Smoke looked around. Another car was pulling off Patterson, heading to the ATM. Smoke snatched the duct tape off the camera lens and ran behind the bank. He started jogging, turning on Libbie Avenue, then Kensington. He slowed to a walk in the driveway of the small brick house where Divinity was waiting in the Escort.

'How much you get, baby?' she asked as Smoke casually climbed in.

'Twenty, forty, sixty, eighty, a hundred,' he counted. 'Let's get the fuck outta here.'

•

Judy Hammer couldn't believe it. This had to be one of the most bizarre things that had ever happened to her. Two white supremacists named Bubba and Smudge were going to murder a black woman named Loraine. She lived near some sort of old pumps where the killers would park and wait with engines and headlights off. Money was involved, perhaps several hundred dollars. Hammer paced, Popeye anxiously at her heels. The phone rang.

'Chief Hammer?' It was West.

'Virginia. What the hell was that?' Hammer asked. 'Any way we can trace it?'

'No,' West's voice returned. 'I don't see how.'

'I'm assuming we both heard the same thing.'

'I'm still on a cell phone,' West warned. 'Don't think I should go into it. But it sounds like something we'd better take very seriously.'

'I completely agree. We'll talk about it after the presentation. Thanks, Virginia.' Hammer was about to hang up.

'Chief? What were you calling me about when I was on the track?' West quickly reminded her.

'Oh. That's right.'

Hammer searched her thoughts, trying to bring up what she was calling West about when the rednecks broke into their conversation. She paced, Popeye with her every step.

'Oh, I remember. We're already getting responses to our new website,' Hammer said, pleased. 'Since Andy's op-ed piece.'

'That worries me,' West replied. 'I think we should have done a little troubleshooting, Chief.'

'It will all be fine.'

'What are they saying?'

'Complaining,' Hammer replied.

'I'm shocked.'

'Don't be cynical, Virginia.'

'Any reaction to what he said about escalating juvenile crime? And *Richmond's gang mentality* about not having gangs, or however he put it? About the country's *desperate need for radical juvenile justice reform?*'

It was not lost on Hammer that whenever West talked about Brazil, West's attitude was sharp to bump up against. Hammer knew when West was hurt. Hammer recognized a sadness in Brazil as well, a light not quite so bright in his eyes, a sluggishness in the creative energy that so profoundly singled him out. Hammer wished the two of them would get along again.

'The phones started ringing off the hook about that the minute the newspapers hit the driveways,' Hammer replied. 'We're shaking people up. And that's exactly what we're here to do.'

Hammer got off the phone. She retrieved Brazil's op-ed piece from the coffee table and glanced through it again.

> . . . This past week our city's *children* committed at least seventeen cold-blooded felonies, including rape, armed robbery and malicious wounding. In eleven of these violent, seemingly random acts, the *child* hadn't even turned fifteen yet. Where do children learn to hate and harm? Not just from the movies and video games, but from each other. We do have a gang problem, and let's face it, kids who commit adult crimes aren't kids anymore . . .

'I expect my popularity just took another dip,' Hammer said to Popeye. 'You need a bath. A little of that good cream rinse?'

Popeye's black-and-white coat was handsomely reminiscent of a tuxedo, but her fur was very short, her freckled, pink skin very sensitive and prone to get dry and irritated.

Popeye loved it when every few weeks her owner would put her in a sink of warm water and lather her up with

Nusalt antiseborrheic therapeutic shampoo, followed by the Relief antipruritic oatmeal and pramoxine cream rinse that her owner kneaded into Popeye's fur for exactly seven minutes, as the directions prescribed. Popeye loved her owner. Popeye stood on her hind legs and nuzzled her owner's knee.

'But a bath will have to wait, I guess, or I'll be late.' Her owner sighed and got down to Popeye's level. 'I shouldn't even have brought it up, should I?'

Popeye licked her owner's face and felt pity. Popeye knew her owner was denying the grief and the guilt she felt about her late husband's sudden death. Not that Popeye had known Seth, but she had overheard conversations about him and had seen photographs. Popeye could not imagine her owner being married to a lazy, independently wealthy, fat, whiny slob who did nothing but eat, work in his garden and watch television.

Popeye was glad Seth wasn't around. Popeye adored her owner. Popeye wished there was more she could do to comfort this heroic, kind lady who had saved Popeye from being an orphan or being adopted by some unhappy family with cruel children.

'All right.' Her owner got up. 'I've got to get going.'

Hammer showered quickly. She threw a robe around her and stood inside her cedar-lined closet, deliberating over what to wear. Hammer understood the subliminal power of clothing, cars, office decor, jewelry and what she ate at business lunches and dinners. Some days required pearls and skirts, other days called for unfriendly suits. Colors, styles, fabrics, collars or no collars, patterns or plain, pockets or pleats, watches, earrings and perfumes and fish or chicken all mattered.

She shoved hangers here and there, deliberating, envisioning, intuiting and finally settling on a navy blue suit with trousers that had pockets and cuffs. She selected low-heel lace-up black leather shoes and matching belt, and a blue and white striped cotton shirt with French cuffs. She dug through her jewelry box for simple gold post earrings and her stainless steel Breitling watch.

She picked out a pair of gold and lapis cufflinks that had belonged to Seth. She fumbled with them as she put them on and remembered those times when Seth followed her around the house like Popeye, unable to manage buttons, lapels, matching socks or combinations, on those rare occasions when Seth dressed up.

It would have made sense to divide her late husband's jewelry, leather briefcases, wallets and other things male between their sons, but Hammer held on. When she wore something of Seth's, she had the eerie feeling that he wanted her to be the man he never was. He wanted her to be strong. Maybe he wanted to help her because now he could. Seth had always had a good heart. But he had spent his life at war with his compulsions and privileged past, spreading misery like the flu. He had left Hammer wealthy, relieved, pained, pissed off and as burdened with anxieties as he had been with his weight.

'Popeye, come here,' Hammer called out.

Popeye was lazy in a bar of sunlight on the kitchen floor. She had no intention of changing venues.

'Let's get in our crate, Popeye.'

Popeye regarded her owner through slitted eyes. She yawned and thought it silly that her owner always used the *we* word, as if Popeye wasn't smart enough to see through it. Popeye knew her owner had no intention of climbing inside that little plastic crate with Popeye any more than her owner was going to eat a heartworm pill or get a shot at the vet when the *we* word was used about those, either.

'Popeye.' Her owner's tone firmed up. 'I'm in a hurry. Come on. In the crate. Here's your squirrel.'

She tossed Popeye's favorite stuffed squirrel inside the crate. Popeye couldn't care less.

'All right. Here's your fuzzle.'

She tossed in the filthy lambs' wool chick that Popeye had chewed the eyes off and routinely flung into the toilet. Popeye was indifferent. Her owner walked with purpose across the kitchen and picked up Popeye. Popeye went into her Salvador Dalí limply-drape-over-everything-and-play-possum manifestation. Her owner tucked Popeye into the crate and fastened shut the wire grate door.

'We need to behave better than this,' her owner said, feeding Popeye several little pieces of lung treats. 'I'll be back real soon.'

Hammer set the burglar alarm and went out to her unmarked midnight-blue Crown Victoria. She drove down East Grace, passing the back of St. John's Church and turning on 25th where Tobacco Row was now upscale apartments and Pohlig Bros still manufactured 'paper boxes of every design.' A graffiti artist had spray-painted 'Meat is Murder' and 'Eat corn' and 'Anita Hill started it' on an abandoned tobacco warehouse, and rusting fire escapes and dead vines held on to old brick shells. One could get a bargain on used tires at Cowboy Tire, and Strickland Foundry and Machine Company had refused to quit.

On the other side of Broad Street, past the coliseum, was the police department where Hammer now spent her days in an ugly precast building with a blue mosaic trim missing many of its tiles. The Richmond Police Department was dim and too small, with windowless corridors, asbestos and the stale smell of dirty people and dirty deeds.

She said good morning to cops she passed, and out of fear they returned her greeting. Hammer understood the trauma of change. She understood a distrust of any influence that came from the outside, especially if its sanction was federal. Resentment and hostility were nothing new, but never had she experienced it quite like this.

At precisely seven o'clock, she walked into the conference room. It was crowded with some thirty unenthusiastic commanders, captains, detectives and officers who followed her with stares. Computer mapping of the city projected onto a large screen showed statistics for murder, rape, robbery, aggravated assault, burglary, larceny and auto theft, or the big seven, during the most recent twenty-eight-day COMSTAT period and also year-to-date. Charts showed time frames and probability and days of the week when crimes occurred, and in what precincts and during what shifts.

Hammer took her seat at the head of the table between West and Brazil.

'Another ATM,' West said in a low voice in Hammer's ear.

Hammer looked sharply at her.

'We just got the call, are still at the scene.'

'Damn,' Hammer said as anger stirred. 'I want the details ASAP.'

West got up and left the room. Hammer looked around the table.

'Nice to see all of you here,' she began. 'We've got a lot to discuss this morning.' She didn't waste time as she looked around and smiled. 'We'll start with first precinct. Major Hanger? I know it's early.'

'Always is,' Hanger grumbled. 'But I know that's how they do things in New York.'

He nodded at Officer Wally Fling, Hammer's administrative assistant, who was new at working the computer-mapping software that everyone hated. Fling hit several keys and a pie chart filled the screen.

'I don't want the pie chart yet, Fling,' Hanger said.

Fling hit several more keys and another pie chart popped up, this one for fourth precinct.

'Sorry,' Fling said as he nervously tried again. 'I guess you want first precinct.'

'That would be nice. And I don't want pies.'

Hanger got one anyway, this time for second precinct. Flustered, Fling hit more keys and the department's shield flashed on screen, with its motto, *Courtesy, Professionalism and Respect,* or CPR, which Hammer also had borrowed from NYPD.

Several people groaned and booed. Brazil gave Hammer an *I've tried to warn you* look.

'Why can't we have our own logo?' asked Captain Cloud, who was a commander for the day and felt he had a right to speak.

'Yeah,' other disgruntled voices joined in.

'It makes us look like second string.'

'Maybe we can get their hand-me-down uniforms, too.'

'That's one of the things that's griping us, Chief.'

Two more pie charts flashed by on the screen.

'Officer Fling,' Hammer said. 'Put it back on the logo, please. Let's talk about this.'

A pin map of handgun seizures filled the screen, little yellow revolvers pointed at the problem areas of the city.

'Go, Fling!'

'Check out *COMSTAT for Dummies.*'

'Shit,' Fling said when he somehow ended up back at the main menu.

'Go back to your day job, Fling.'

He banged the enter key four times and an error message told him to stop it.

'All right, all right,' Hammer quieted the room. 'Captain Cloud? I want to hear what you have to say.'

'Well,' Cloud picked up where he'd left off, 'it's like the city seal, George Washington on his horse. I gotta ask you, what's George Washington got to do with Richmond? I guess we what? Borrowed that from D.C., from another big city, in other words?'

'Amen.'

'I agree totally.'

'I bet he never even slept here.'

'It's an embarrassment.'

'D.C., and now we're swiping ideas from New York. How bad does that make us look?' Cloud said.

'Okay,' Hammer raised her voice. 'I'm afraid there's not a thing we can do about the city seal at this time. So let's get back to our motto. Captain Cloud, remember that part of accountability is to suggest a solution when you point out a problem. Do you have a new motto in mind?'

'Well, I played around with one a little bit last night.'

Cloud had high blood pressure. His white uniform shirt was too tight around the neck, and his face was almost purple. He was center stage and sweating.

'I was thinking about what would be simple but direct, and, now don't get your hopes up that this is real creative or poetic or anything, but if you ask the question, what are we all about? I think the answer can be summed up in three words. *Tough On Crime.*' Cloud looked around the table. 'TOC, in other words, which is real easy to remember and doesn't take up any more room than CPR if we're gonna paint it on things or add it to our patches.'

'Doesn't do anything for me.'

'Me either.'

'Naw.'

'Okay, okay,' Cloud rushed forward. 'I had a backup just in case. How about *Tough In Court and Tough On Crime*? TIC TOC.'

'I don't like it.'

'Ditto.'

'Wait a minute,' Cloud went on with conviction.

'Everybody's always complaining how slow we are getting to scenes, to their house after their alarm's gone off, right? And how many times do we hear the public bitch about how long it takes to solve a case? I think TIC TOC sends a positive message about a new attitude, about us trying harder.'

'It also makes it sound like we're watching the clock. Like we can't wait for shift change.'

'Or something bad's about to happen.'

'Besides, it would be TOC TIC because being *tough on crime* is gonna come before you get to court.'

'It doesn't work, Cloud.'

'Forget it.'

Cloud was crushed. 'Never mind,' he said.

Hammer had been silent through all this because she wanted to give her troops a chance to be heard. But she could take no more.

'It's something for all of us to think about,' she said abruptly. 'I'm always open for something new. Thank you, Captain Cloud.'

'Actually, I had a thought on the subject,' Andy Brazil said.

No one spoke. Cops started shuffling through notes and shifting in chairs. They got up for more coffee. Cloud opened a little bag of Fisherman's Friend throat lozenges, paper tearing loudly. Fling rebooted the computer and it beeped and honked as it tried to come back.

Hammer felt sorry for Brazil. She was indignant that he was discriminated against for reasons beyond his control. It wasn't his fault that women and gay men of all ages could not take their eyes off him. He couldn't help that he was only twenty-five and talented and sensitive. Nor was there a thing he had done or intimated that gave credence to the vicious rumor that she had brought him with her to Richmond for sexual pleasure and then he had run off with his landlady.

'Go ahead, Officer Brazil.' Hammer tended to be brusque with him. 'But we need to move along.'

'I really think we'd be better off without a motto,' Brazil said.

Silence.

'CPR makes it sound like we need to be resuscitated,' he added.

No one would look at him. Papers shuffled. Duty belts creaked.

'That we're in extremis,' he said.

Silence.

Then Cloud spoke up, 'I've always thought that. It's about time somebody said it before it got painted on all the cars.'

'It's just one more thing for people to make fun of,' Brazil pointed out. 'Especially since the core of COMSTAT is *accountability.* And what happens if somewhere down the road someone decides to add *accountability* to our motto?'

More silence as everyone puzzled. Some wrote words and letters on paper, rearranging acronyms, like Jumble. Hammer knew instantly where Brazil was going with this.

'CARP,' Fling read from his notepad.

'PARC?' Captain Cloud volunteered.

'You get CRAP,' Brazil told them.

'Interesting,' Hammer said loudly, restoring order. 'All of you have made me see this in a different light. Maybe we shouldn't have a motto. Those in favor, raise your hand.'

All did except Cloud. He sipped his coffee, eyes cast down at his half-eaten glazed doughnut, a sour expression on his face.

'So I guess I can delete the motto from the computer,' Fling said, tapping keys again.

'I don't want you deleting anything,' Hammer told him.

chapter three

Puff Daddy & the Family were rapping on the CD player and air was blowing through a stuck back window of Smoke's Escort. He had changed clothes in the car and Divinity was gone, the scent of her cloying perfume lingering as Smoke and fourteen-year-old Weed Gardener headed west to Mills E. Godwin High School.

Smoke had money in his pocket. Tucked under the seat was the Glock nine-millimeter pistol he had traded twenty rocks of crack cocaine for on the street. He was high as he replayed the robbery again and again, a favorite scene in the movie that was his life. He was getting better. He was getting bolder.

He thought how cool it would be to walk into the band room and take out twelve, thirteen, maybe fifteen students and their fucking band director, Mr. Curry, who thought he knew so much and wouldn't let Smoke play in the marching band because Smoke was tone deaf and couldn't keep rhythm on the snare drum. But Weed got to play the cymbals when he didn't know them from garbage can lids, and why? Because Weed was good in art and never got into trouble. Well, all that was about to change.

'*. . . Who you know do it better . . .*' Smoke rapped along, out of sync and off key, his blood heating up. '*Don't make an ass out of yourself . . . I'm gonna make you love me baby . . .*'

Weed joined in on percussion, playing his hands on his thighs and the dashboard and jumping in his seat as if he had a synthesizer for a central nervous system and a drumbeat for a pulse. Smoke hated it. He hated that Weed saw rainbow colors and pictures to draw everywhere he went. He was tired of Weed's art being put on display in the library. At least Weed was stupid. He was so stupid he had no clue that the only reason Smoke had befriended him and started giving him rides to school was that Smoke intended to use Weed up.

'*Ri-dicu-u-lous . . . you're in the danger zone you shouldn't be alone . . .*' Smoke's monotone got louder.

Smoke turned up the volume on the CD player and pumped up the bass as far as it would go. He kept working the switch for the left back window and swearing when the glass remained stuck open halfway. Air slapped and the music throbbed as Weed played on.

'Hey, retard, cut it out,' Smoke said, grabbing one of Weed's hands to make him stop his solo.

Weed went still. Smoke imagined he could smell Weed's fear.

'Listen to me, retard,' Smoke went on. 'Maybe I'm coming around to giving you what you been dreaming about, the biggest offer in your puny nothing life.'

'Oh.' Weed dreaded what Smoke was about to say.

'You want to be cool, right? You want to be just like me, right?'

'I guess so.'

'You *guess* so?' Smoke blurted.

He flicked Weed's nose so hard it started bleeding. Tears jumped into Weed's eyes.

'Now, what was that you said, retard?' Smoke's voice was flat with hate.

Blood trickled down Weed's face and dripped onto his Route 66 sand-blasted, relaxed-leg jeans.

'You get blood in my car, and I'm gonna throw your ass out. How'd you like to be a skid mark on the road?' Smoke told him.

'I wouldn't,' Weed said quietly.

'I know how much you want to be a Pike and been waiting for my answer,' Smoke said. 'And after a lot of consideration, I've decided to let you have a shot at it, even though you don't measure up to the standards.'

Weed didn't want to be a Pike. He didn't want to be part of Smoke's gang. They beat people up, stole things, broke into cars, cut holes in restaurant roofs and carried off cases of liquor. They did all kinds of things that Weed didn't even want to know about.

'So, what do you say?' Smoke had his hand up, fingers poised to flick Weed again.

'Yeah, man.'

'First you say *thank you,* retard. You say, *I'm so honored I'm about to shit in my pants.*'

'It would be fucking cool, man.' Weed dressed his fear in cocky words that started strutting off his tongue. 'Think of the shit we could do, man. And I get to wear the colors?'

'Chicago Bulls, like you're fucking Michael Jordan. Maybe it will make you taller. Maybe it will pump up that flat inner tube between your legs and you can start juicing girls.'

'Who says I don't juice 'em now?' Weed talked big.

'You ain't juiced anything in your puny little motherfucking life. Not even fruit.'

'You don't know that.'

Smoke laughed in his cruel, mocking way.

'You ain't got no idea,' Weed went on, acting like a hardass, knowing what would happen if he didn't because weakness made Smoke meaner.

'You wouldn't know what to do with pussy if it rubbed up against your leg and purred.' Smoke guffawed. 'I've seen your tool. I've seen you whiz.'

'Whizzing and juicing ain't the same thing,' Weed let him know.

Smoke turned into the parking lot of Mills E. Godwin High School, named after a former governor of Virginia and home of the Eagles. Smoke stopped and waited for Weed to get out.

'Ain't you coming?' Weed asked.

'I'm busy right now,' Smoke said.

'But you'll be tardy.'

'Oh, I'm scaaaarrrred.' Smoke laughed. 'Get out, *retardy.*'

Weed did. He opened the back door and gathered his cheap knapsack of books, papers and the bologna-and-mustard sandwich he had fixed before Smoke picked him up.

'After school, you get your ass right back here,' Smoke said. 'Right in this exact spot. I'm gonna take you over to the clubhouse so you can get initiated and make your dream come true.'

Weed knew about the clubhouse. Smoke had told him all about it.

'I got band practice,' Weed said as his spirit trembled inside him.

'No you don't.'

'Yeah I do. Every Monday, Wednesday and Friday, we got marching practice, Smoke.' Weed's blood lost its heat and his stomach made itself smaller.

'Today you're busy, re-tardy. Your ass better be right here at three.'

Tears welled in Weed's eyes again as Smoke sped off. Weed loved band. He loved going outside on the practice baseball field and marching with his Sabian eighteen-inch bronze cymbals and dreaming of the red-and-white toy-soldier uniform with its black hat and plume that he'd get to wear in the Azalea Parade on Saturday. Mr. Curry said Sabians were the best made, and Weed was responsible for keeping them bright and shiny, the leather straps tied nice and tight in their special flat, braided knots.

Flags were waving in front of the tidy blond-brick school, where nineteen hundred boisterous upper-middle-class students were jostling and shuffling into classrooms. Weed's mood lifted. At least his father lived in the right school district. Weed kept clothes and other belongings in his father's house, pretending he lived there, too. If Weed couldn't go to Godwin, there would be no art or music in his life.

The 8:35 tardy bell was ringing as Weed slammed shut the door to his bright orange locker and ran through empty corridors of different colored walls, the classrooms he passed filled with chatter and laughter and the thud and flutter of books opening on desktops. Weed had a phobia of being late that preceded this moment by many years.

His mother worked all the time and was rarely home or awake to get Weed up for school. Sometimes he overslept, sending him flying down to the corner bus stop in a panic, without books or lunch, barely dressed. In his mind, *missing the bus* meant missing life and being left alone in an empty house that echoed with past fights between parents who had split and the loud, full-of-himself sounds of Weed's big brother, Twister, who was dead.

Weed galloped around a corner to the science department just as Mr. Pretty began hall duty from the table outside Mrs. Fan's biology class, where this second Weed was supposed to be getting ready to take a quiz.

'Whoa,' Mr. Pretty called out as Weed ran past and the tardy bell stopped and doors up and down the halls shut.

'I'm going to Mrs. Fan's class,' Weed gasped.

'Do you know where it is?'

'Yes, sir, Mr. Pretty. Right there.' Weed pointed at the red door less than twenty steps away, and wondered what kind of stupid question was that.

'You're late,' Mr. Pretty told him.

'The bell just quit,' Weed said. 'You can almost still hear it.'

'Late is late, Weed.'

'I didn't mean to be.'

'And I don't guess you have a pass,' said Mr. Pretty, who taught ninth-grade Western Civilization.

'I don't got a pass,' Weed said as indignation gathered, ''cause I wasn't planning on being late. But my ride just got here and there wasn't nothing I could do about it and I ran all the way so I wouldn't be late. And now you're making me later, Mr. Pretty.'

Mr. Pretty's compulsion was to pull kids but not ticket them. He was young and nice-looking and had an insatiable need for captive audiences. He was notorious for holding kids in the hall as long as possible while they fidgeted and stared at the rooms where they were supposed to be as classes and quizzes went on without them.

'Don't blame me or your ride for being tardy,' said Mr. Pretty from behind his small table in the empty intersection of shiny, empty hallways.

'I'm not blaming. I'm just saying the way it is.'

'If I were you, I'd watch my mouth, Weed.'

'What you want me to do, walk around with a mirror?' Weed sassed him.

Mr. Pretty might have let Weed go on to class, but Mr. Pretty was pissed and decided to draw things out.

'Let's see, I believe you're in my third period,' he said. 'You remember what we talked about on Friday?'

Weed didn't remember anything about Friday except

that he wasn't looking forward to spending the weekend with his father.

'Ah. Maybe this will jog your memory,' Mr. Pretty said curtly. 'What happened in 1556?'

Weed's nerves were tangling and popping. He could hear Mrs. Fan's voice through her shut door. She was passing out the quiz and going over instructions.

'Come on, I know you know it.' Mr. Pretty picked on Weed some more. 'What happened?'

'A war.' Weed threw out the first thing that came to mind.

'A fairly safe guess since there were so many of them. But you're wrong. Fifteen fifty-six was when Akbar became emperor of India.'

'Is it okay if I go in Mrs. Fan's class now?'

'And then what?' Mr. Pretty demanded. 'What happened next?'

'What?'

'I asked you first.'

'About what?' Weed was getting furious.

'About what happened next?' Mr. Pretty asked.

'Depends on what you mean by *next,*' Weed smarted off.

'*Next* as in what's *next* in the chronology of events that I handed out to every person in my class,' Mr. Pretty answered with an edge. 'Of course, you probably never looked at it.'

'I did too. And it says right on it we don't have to memorize nothing unless it's in bold, and the India thing and what happened next ain't in bold.'

'Oh really?' Mr. Pretty got haughty. 'And how can you

remember whether something was in bold or not if you don't remember anything in the first place?'

'I remember when something's in bold!' Weed raised his voice, as if he were suddenly talking in bold.

'No you don't!'

'Yes I do!'

Mr. Pretty angrily grabbed a ballpoint pen out of his shirt pocket. He began scribbling words on the Hall Duty *passes* and *no passes* sheet.

'All right, smarty pants,' said Mr. Pretty as self-control slipped further out of reach. 'I've written down ten words, some in bold, some not. You get one minute to look them over.'

He handed the list to Weed: *forfend, **effigy**, pogrom, Versailles, **mead**, Fabergé, Fabian, Waterloo, edict, **pact**.* Not one word was familiar. Mr. Pretty snatched back the list.

'Which words were in bold?' Mr. Pretty demanded.

'I can't pronunciate them.'

'Versailles,' Mr. Pretty prodded him.

Weed looked at the list in his head and located the only word that began with a V.

'Fourth one, not in bold,' he said.

'Pogrom!'

'Third, not in bold.'

'Fabian!' Mr. Pretty fired back.

'He's four before last. Not in bold, either.'

'Effigy!' Mr. Pretty blurted out, his attractive face distorted by anger.

'It's in bold,' Weed said. 'Just like five and ten are.'

'Oh really?' Mr. Pretty was beside himself. 'And just

what are five and ten since you think you know so much?'

Weed saw *mead* and *pact* in his head and pronounced them his own special way. 'Med and paced.'

'What do they mean!'

Mr. Pretty was talking loudly and Mrs. Fan cracked open her door, out of concern, to check on things.

'Shhhhhhhhh!' she said.

'What do they mean, Weed?' Mr. Pretty lowered his scornful voice.

Weed did the best he could.

'*Med* is what you feel when someone disses you. And *paced* is what we use in art class,' he guessed.

Officer Fling was guessing, too. He had gone to the *next layer control,* then hit function 3 for *thematic display,* and selected *remove* to get rid of the latest pie, and brought up *priority one, two and three calls* for fourth precinct, which was not what anyone was interested in at the moment.

Hammer flipped on the overhead lights. The presentation was never supposed to run over an hour and it was well past the limit. She was discouraged and frustrated and determined not to let it show.

'I realize we're all new at this,' she said reasonably. 'I understand that things don't happen overnight. We're going to leave computer mapping until Friday morning at seven hundred hours, by which time I'm sure we will be well versed in it?'

No one responded.

'Officer Fling?' she said.

His hands were lifeless on the keyboard. He looked dejected and defeated.

'Do you think you will be able to make this work by Friday's COMSTAT presentation?' Hammer persisted.

'No, ma'am.' Fling was honest about it.

The door opened and West returned to the room and took her seat.

'Okay, Officer Fling, that's fair enough,' Hammer said in a positive tone. 'Is there anybody else who might want to learn how to work this program? It's really very user-friendly. The point was not to design it for programmers and engineers, but for police.'

No one spoke.

'Officer Brazil, help me out here,' Hammer said.

'Sure,' he said dubiously.

'Maybe for now you'd better pitch in,' Hammer said. 'Deputy Chief West? You're also very familiar with the software. See if the two of you can't work to get this thing up and running. I expect smooth sailing by our next COMSTAT presentation.'

'Who's willing to learn?' West asked, looking around the table. 'Come on guys, show some guts.'

Lieutenant Audrey Ponzi raised her hand. Captain Cloud's hand went up next, and Officer Fling decided to give it another try.

'Excellent,' Hammer said. 'Major Hanger? If you'll resume with your presentation. We'll proceed without the computer. And we really need to wind this up.'

Hanger hastily looked through his notes and took a nervous sip of coffee.

'Nothing much has changed since our last meeting,' he began. 'We got the same rash of petit larcenies from autos, mostly Jeeps, broken into for their airbags.'

'CABBAGES,' Fling interjected.

All eyes turned toward Captain Cloud, who had come up with Car Air Bag Breaking And Enterings and its acronym CABBAE, which the media had immediately mistaken for CABBAGE, or CABBAGES, and continued to do so, despite the police department's numerous corrections.

'Anyway,' Hanger resumed, 'we suspect most of the stolen airbags are ending up at two body shops recently opened by Russians. Possibly the same clan of Russians who opened the kiosk at the farmer's market last summer, on Seventeenth Street directly across from Havana '59. Selling cabbages, the kind you make slaw with, which has done nothing but add to the confusion.' He glared at Cloud.

'But the CABBAGES might be related because the Russians possibly are,' Fling figured.

'We're thinking that,' Hanger said.

'Let's get back to the airbags,' Hammer said.

'Well, the MO remains the same in these most recent petit larcenies.' Hanger avoided using the term CABBAGE. 'Owner returns to his vehicle, finds a window smashed, the airbags gone. These same cars go in to one of the Russian body shops to get the airbags replaced and ironically the stolen airbags installed to replace the ones stolen could be the very ones stolen out of the vehicle in question. So you're really paying for the same airbags twice, thinking you're getting new ones for three hundred bucks apiece, when in fact you're getting stolen ones. It's gotten to be a pretty big racket all over the world.'

'But if you're getting your same airbags back, they're really not secondhand because they were never owned by a second person,' said Fling. 'Does that . . . ?'

'What are we doing about this situation?' Hammer raised her voice.

'We're coordinating with investigations to get an undercover guy in at least one of the body shops,' Hanger replied.

'Are the airbags traceable?' Hammer asked.

'Not unless they start putting VINs on them,' Hanger said, referring to the Vehicle Identification Numbers that were etched on the edge of all driver's doors. 'I was thinking maybe we could get some kind of grant to help out. Maybe NIJ would be interested.'

'To help out in what way?' Hammer frowned.

'To do a study on the usefulness of ABINs.'

'ABINs?'

'That's what we could call them,' Hanger explained. 'Air Bag Identification Numbers. Thing is, if your same stolen airbags are put back in your vehicle, then for sure the ABINs are going to match.'

'True.'

'That would make it pretty easy.'

Hanger nodded. 'Not only could we start making cases here, but I'm pretty sure a lot of these stolen airbags are going overseas. So if we developed a system of ABINs, we could get Interpol involved, too. It might bring us some recognition.'

'I see.' Hammer fought a growing sense of hopelessness. 'Anything else?'

'Two more stolen Saturns. We got a pattern going on.'

'How many so far?'

'Twelve General Motors cars stolen in the past month.'

'Any breaks?' Hammer asked.

'It appears several kids are involved. We think they bought master keys for Saturns from some kid named Beeper, supposedly in the area of Swansboro Elementary School on Midlothian Turnpike.'

'Gang-related?' Hammer asked.

'Can't say for sure,' Hanger answered.

'What does that mean?'

'Well, all we got to go on is this one snitch who's lied to us before.'

Hammer jumped ahead. 'We just had another ATM robbery, I'm sorry to say. I'm going to let Deputy Chief West give the details.'

'Victim is an Asian male, age twenty-two.' West looked at her notes. 'Pulled up to the Crestar ATM at 5802 Patterson. Nobody else was there. Nothing seemed out of the ordinary, says duct tape was suddenly slapped over his eyes, a gun jammed into his back. A male, he couldn't tell race, demanded money. By the time the victim removed the tape, the perp was long gone.'

'The duct tape is different,' Hammer said.

'Absolutely,' West said.

'That makes six ATM robberies,' Hammer said. 'Four on Southside, two in the West End. An average of one per week since early February.'

'Let me just say that I'm extremely concerned about this latest one, assuming it's related,' West spoke up. 'Let's just go through it. We have the first four ATMs late night or early morning when it's dark. There's a male-female team. She diverts by asking the victim where the nearest post office, pay phone, whatever, is. The male appears, opens his jacket just enough to show the handle of a gun and says, *I want the money you took out of the machine.* Maybe the gun's real, maybe it's not. The perp takes the money and runs.

'Then we have a fifth ATM in Church Hill. Again, when it's dark out, but this time the male perp actually displays the gun. He gets into the victim's car, turns out the interior light so the victim can't see his face. Threatens if the victim ever tries to help cops ID him, he knows the guy's plate number and will find him and kill him. Then he forces the victim to drive several blocks. The perp jumps out with the money. Now we've got an ATM in the West End, and this time it's daylight. I'm seeing a possible pattern of escalation here. An escalation that could end in violence.'

'We got anything more on these cases?' Cloud asked.

'Not anything helpful. Some of the victims think the female perp's black, some think he is, and vice versa. Age unknown, assumed to be juveniles. No sign of a vehicle, if they use one,' West replied. 'Bottom line is we don't know.'

'And bank tapes?'

'Of no use.'

'Why not?' Hammer asked.

'In the first one, all you see is the back of her and it was dark,' West said. 'On the next four you don't see anything at all.'

'And the cameras were functioning?'

'Nothing wrong with them.'

'And the one this morning?'

'Seems fine.'

'Anybody have anything even remotely similar going on in other parts of the city?' Hammer then asked.

No one did.

'What about third precinct? We haven't heard from you, Captain Webber,' Hammer pushed ahead.

'Some Russians opened up an antique store on Chamberlayne, near Azalea Mall,' Webber said. 'They haven't done anything illegal yet.'

'Any reason to think they will?' Hammer inquired.

'Well, it's just this Russian thing going on.'

'How do we know they aren't gypsies?' burglary detective Linton Bean asked.

'Can gypsies be Russian?'

'Seems to me they can be anything as long as they drift around and con people.'

'Yeah, but the ones we've had coming through here are mostly Romanian, Irish, English and Scotch. The Travelers. Well, that's what they call themselves. They get real pissed if we call them gypsies.'

'How 'bout if we just call them tramps and thieves?'

'I've never heard of Russian gypsies.'

'My sister went over to Italy last year and said they have gypsies over there.'

'I know for a fact they got Hispanic ones in Florida.'

'See, that's the whole thing,' said Detective Bean. 'There's no such country as 'Gypsy'. You can be from anywhere and be a gypsy, including Russia . . .'

'What are we doing about this problem?' Hammer interrupted.

'Stepping up patrols in neighborhoods like Windsor Farms, where you have mostly older people with money,' said Bean. 'Maybe forming a task force.'

'Do it,' Hammer said, glancing at her watch and conscious of the time. 'Lieutenant Noble is commander for a day in second precinct. What do you have to report?'

'This week we arrested a domestic violence recidivist,' said Noble, who spoke the proper police language and was resented by all.

'Very good,' Hammer said.

'We're also doing warrant sweeps but so far haven't surfaced the suspect in the stairwell rapes,' Noble added. 'And if it's all right, Chief Hammer, I have a comment to make.'

'Please,' Hammer said.

'I'm not so sure it was a good idea to piss off all the citizens with this gang crap Brazil wrote about for the Sunday paper.'

'It wasn't crap,' Brazil said.

'Name one gang,' Noble challenged him.

'It's all a matter of semantics,' Brazil answered. 'It depends on how you label *gangs.*'

Hammer agreed. 'Juveniles are committing the worst

crimes. They mentor each other, influence each other, form packs, gangs. We have them here and need to identify them.'

'Most of the kids that go in schools and blow everybody away aren't in gangs. They're loners,' Noble argued.

'Let's look at Jonesboro,' West countered. 'A fourteen-year-old recruits an eleven-year-old to pull the fire alarm, right? So what would happen if you had four, five, six kids involved? Maybe twenty kids and teachers would have died.'

'She's got a point.'

'Got to admit, it makes you think.'

'You'd have to call in the damn National Guard.'

'Kids are scary. They don't have any boundaries. They think killing's a game,' West added.

'It's true. There's no concept of consequences.'

'What happens if you get some charismatic gang leader and he really organizes? Imagine,' Brazil said.

Insights and arguments were volleyed back and forth as Hammer deliberated over how to broach the next subject.

'Recent intelligence,' she began, 'indicates that two white males may be planning a hate crime, the robbery and murder of a black woman possibly named Loraine. The males may go by the names or aliases of Bubba and Smudge.'

No one spoke for a moment, faces perplexed.

Then, 'You don't mind my asking, Chief, where'd this come from?'

Hammer looked to West for help.

'We're really not at liberty to reveal the source at this

time,' West said. 'You just need to be aware, keep your eyes and ears open.'

'If there's nothing further?' Hammer said.

There wasn't.

'Then I do have two commendations to present and I believe both people are here.' Hammer smiled. 'Communications Officer Patty Passman and Officer Rhoad?'

They came forward. Hammer handed each a certificate and shook hands. Applause was weak.

'Communications Officer Passman, as you know, handled a nine-one-one last month that saved a man from choking on a hot dog,' Hammer said. 'And Officer Otis Rhoad issued three hundred and eighty-eight parking tickets last month. A department record.'

'Booooo!'

'Yeah, a lot of 'em on our cars!'

Passman glared at Rhoad.

'He wins the prize for talking on the radio!'

'Rhoad Hog!'

Passman bit her lip, her face an angry red.

'*Rod*eo!' Fling had to toss in, although the aspersion made no sense.

'That's enough,' Hammer said. 'I'll see all of you back here on Friday.'

The Ford Explorer's turn signal was beating like a panicking heart as its driver, who had already missed his exit, tried once again to ease in front of Bubba. Bubba accelerated and the Explorer swerved back into its lane, where it belonged. The cop was still on Bubba's bumper and Bubba slowed to send the message that he wouldn't tolerate tailgaters no matter who they were. Bubba was a cowboy herding cattle on the open prairie of motoring life.

'Unit 2 to Unit 1.' Honey was sounding increasingly concerned over the two-way.

Bubba was too busy to talk to his wife.

'Smudge,' he got back to his good buddy, 'Queen Bee's buzzing, got a city kitty tailwind, and a sixteener with a low seater's trying to wipe my nose.' Bubba spoke in code, letting Smudge know that Bubba's wife was trying to get hold of Bubba, he had a city cop riding his ass and a 4x4 driven by a punk was trying to swipe in front of him.

'I'll leave ya lonely.' Smudge signed off.

'Throwin' ya back. Catch ya later, good buddy.' Bubba signed off, too.

By now, the kid in the Explorer seemed challenged and might have become violent but for the cop one lane over. The kid decided to default. He got in the last word by laying on his horn and giving Bubba the finger and mouthing *Fuckhead.* The Explorer disappeared in the current of other traffic. Bubba slowed to communicate to the cop one more time to get off his rear bumper. The cop communicated back by flashing his red-and-blue emergency lights and yelping his siren. Bubba pulled over into a Kmart parking lot.

chapter four

Officer Jack Budget took his time collecting his silver anodized aluminum Posse citation holder and dual clipboard. He climbed out of his gleaming blue-and-red-striped white cruiser, adjusted his duty gear and approached the red Jeep with the Confederate flag rear bumper sticker and BUB-AH vanity plate that he had been staring at for miles. Its redneck driver rolled down the window.

'Am I to assume you go by the name Bub-ah?' Budget asked.

'No, it's *Bubba,*' Bubba said rudely.

'Let me see your license and registration.' Officer Budget was rude, too, although he might not have been had Bubba not started it.

Bubba pulled his nylon wallet out of his back pocket. Velcro ripped as he opened it and got out his driver's license. He fished around in the glove box for his registration, then handed both proofs of identification and ownership to the cop, who studied them for several long minutes.

'You have any idea why I stopped you, Mr. Fluck?'

'Probably because of my bumper sticker,' Bubba stated.

Budget stepped back to look at the Jeep's rear bumper, as if just now noticing the Confederate flag on it.

'Well, well,' he said as images of white pointed hoods and burning crosses violated his mind. 'Still trying to win that war and round up Negroes to pick your cotton.'

'The Southern Cross has nothing to do with that,' Bubba indignantly said.

'The *what?*'

'The Southern Cross.'

Budget's jaw muscles knotted. It had not been so long ago that he had been bused to one of the city's public high schools and had watched seats empty one by one as other black kids got locked up or killed on the street. He had been *Buckwheat*, *Sambo*, *drone*, *porch monkey*, *Uncle Tom*. He had grown up in the *niggerhood*. Even now on some calls, white complainants asked him to go around to the back door.

'I guess you know it as the Confederate flag,' the white redneck asshole was explaining to him. 'Although it was really the battle flag, versus the Stars and Bars or Stainless Banner or Naval Jack or Pennant.'

Budget knew nothing of the various official Confederate flags that had gone in and out of vogue for various reasons during the war. He only knew that he hated the bumper stickers and tattoos, tee shirts and beach towels he saw everywhere in the South. He was enraged by Confederate flags waving from porches and graves.

'It's all about racism, Mr. Fluck,' Budget said coldly.

'It's all about states' rights.'

'Bullshit.'

'You can count the stars. One for each state in the Confederacy plus Kentucky and Missouri. Eleven stars,' Bubba informed him. 'There's not a single slave on the Southern Cross. You look for yourself.'

'The South wanted out because it wanted to keep its slaves.'

'That's only part of it.'

'So you admit that it's at least part of it.'

'I'm not admitting anything,' Bubba let him know.

'You were driving erratically,' said Officer Budget, who wanted to grab Bubba out of the Jeep and smack him around.

'Was not.' Bubba refused to admit it.

'Yes, you were.'

'Not me.'

'I was right behind you. I ought to know.'

'That kid in the Explorer was trying to cut in front of me,' Bubba said.

'He had his turn signal on.'

'So what.'

'Have you been drinking?' demanded Budget.

'Not yet.'

'Are you on any kind of medications?'

'Not this minute.'

'But you are sometimes?' Budget asked, for he knew that some drugs and poisons, such as marijuana and arsenic, stayed in the blood for a while.

'Not anything you need to know about,' said Bubba.

'I'll be the judge of that, Mr. Fluck.'

Officer Budget leaned closer to the open window, hoping he might smell alcohol. He didn't.

Bubba got out a cigarette. He smoked Merit Ultima instead of other brands because Merits, along with Marlboros and Virginia Slims, to name a few, were manufactured by Philip Morris. Bubba was very loyal to his employer and to all products made in America.

Bubba had no intention of telling Officer Budget that he took Librax for cranky bowel syndrome and that now and then he needed Sudafed to control his allergic responses to dust mites, mold and cats. None of this was Officer Budget's business.

'Advil,' Bubba answered the cop.

'That's all?' Officer Budget asked with severity.

'Maybe Tylenol.'

'Mr. Fluck, you . . .'

'What did you say?' Bubba interrupted.

'. . . certain you aren't on anything else?' Budget finished his sentence.

'I heard what you said and I'm going to report you to the chief!' Bubba exclaimed in rage.

'You do that, Mr. Fluck. In . . .'

'See!'

'In fact, I'll make the appointment. You can see her, Mr. Fluck, face . . .'

'That's it!'

An entire population of cruel schoolchildren stampeded through Bubba's brain. They chanted those awful names, shrieking with laughter. Bubba saw himself fat and in camouflage. Enough was enough, he could take no more.

'What's it?' Budget raised his voice, too.

'I don't have to listen to this!'

'You can tell the chief that face to face!' Budget exclaimed. 'I don't give a flying . . .'

'Stop!'

'Man, you got a problem,' Budget said.

Weed did, too. He made it to biology class in time to watch all completed quizzes passed up to the front and to hear Mrs. Fan go over homework he had not done.

His miserable eyes wandered around the room to worms, deer embryos, rhinoceros beetles, termite eggs and dog intestines suspended in formaldehyde, and butterflies and snakeskins pinned to boards. He felt trapped by Smoke.

Later, in Western Civilization, Mr. Pretty picked on Weed three times, and Weed knew the answer to nothing. Weed's fears gathered force.

His escape was Mrs. Grannis's class. She taught Art IV and V during fifth period, and was very young and pretty, with soft blond curls, and eyes as green as summer grass. She had told Weed more than once that he was the first freshman ever, in the history of the school, to attend her class. Ordinarily, only juniors could take Art IV, and only seniors and Advanced Placement students could take V. But Weed was special. He had a gift that was rare.

There had been much debate about pushing Weed so far ahead so fast, especially since he clearly lagged miles behind the troops on most other fronts. Questions about his maturity and social adjustment had been discussed at length among faculty and counselors. Even Mrs. Lilly, the principal, had been brought in at the end, and had proposed that Weed take a class at Virginia Commonwealth University or perhaps specialized classes at the Center for Arts. But the county did not provide transportation beyond the morning and afternoon buses Weed was afraid of missing. He had no way to get around in the middle of the day. Godwin decided to take a chance.

Weed had free period and lunch between 11:40 and 12:31 and he needed to hide. He did not want to run into Smoke somewhere. Weed was desperate and had come up with a secret, brazen, bizarre plan. At 11:39 he walked into Mrs. Grannis's classroom. His self-esteem was low. He was frightened about what lay ahead and could tell by the way Mrs. Grannis looked at him that she sensed he wasn't himself.

'How are you today, Weed?' she asked with an uncertain smile.

'I was wondering if it would be all right if I worked in here through free period,' he said.

'Certainly. What would you like to work on?'

Weed stared at the computers on a back counter.

'Graphic art,' he said. 'I'm working on a project.'

'I'm delighted to hear it. There are many, many job opportunities in that field. You know where the CDs are,' she said. 'And I'll see you back here fifth period.'

'Yes, ma'am,' Weed said as he pulled out a chair and sat in front of a computer.

He opened a drawer where graphic software was neatly arranged in stacks, and picked out what he wanted. He inserted CorelDRAW into the CD drive and waited until Mrs. Grannis left the room before logging onto America Online.

Lunch followed free period and Weed had no intention of eating. He hurried down the hallway to the band room, which was empty except for Jimbo 'Sticks' Sleeth, who was doing his thing on the red Pearl drums.

'Hey, Sticks,' Weed said.

Sticks was rolling on the snare, his feet keeping rhythm on the high hat and kick. He had his eyes squeezed shut, sweat running down his temples. Weed went over to a cabinet and retrieved the hard plastic Sabian case. He opened it and lovingly lifted out the heavy bronze crash cymbals. He checked the leather straps to make sure the knots were holding tight. He gripped the straps, index fingers and thumbs touching. He held the cymbals at an angle, the edge of the right one lower than the left.

Sticks opened his eyes and gave Weed the nod. Weed struck the left cymbal, glancing it off the right, punctuating toms and snare with his euphoric bright sound.

'Do it, baby!' Sticks yelled, and he started in.

It sounded like a musical war going on as Sticks beat and throbbed and boomed in a rhythm that made the blood wild, and Weed was march-dancing around the room, crashing and flipping up, flashing and spinning.

'Go! Go! Oh yeah!' Sticks was frenzied.

Weed was moonwalking, his bright sound rolling out from the edges, then crashing staccato, then crashing long. He didn't hear the bell ring but he finally noticed the clock on the wall. He packed up the cymbals and made it back to Mrs. Grannis's art room with two minutes to spare. He was the first one there. She was writing on a white board and turned around to see who had come in.

'Did you get a lot done during your free time?' she asked Weed.

'Yes, ma'am.' Weed wouldn't meet her eyes.

'I wish everybody liked the computer as much as you do.' She started writing again. 'You have a favorite software so far?'

'QuarkXPress and Adobe Illustrator and Photoshop.'

'Well, you have a real knack for it,' she said as he chose his place at one of the tables and tucked his knapsack under his chair.

'It's no big deal,' Weed mumbled.

'Have you written your story of the power behind your fish?' Mrs. Grannis asked as she continued writing this week's project on the white board in long, looping letters.

'Yea, ma'am,' Weed sullenly answered, opening his notebook.

'I can't wait to hear it,' she continued to encourage him. 'You're the only person in the class to pick a fish.'

'I know,' he said.

The assignment for the past two weeks had been to make a papier-mâché figure that was symbolic to the student. Most picked a symbol from mythology or folklore, such as a dragon or tiger or raven or snake. But Weed had constructed a cruel blue fish. Its gaping mouth bared rows of bloody teeth, and Weed had fashioned glittery eyes from small compact mirrors that flashed at anyone walking past.

'I'm sure all of the students can't wait to hear about your fish,' Mrs. Grannis went on as she wrote.

'We doing watercolor next?' Weed asked with interest as he made out what she was writing.

'Yes. A still-life composition that includes reflective objects, texture.' She wrote with flourish. 'And a 2-D object that gives the illusion of a 3-D object.'

'My fish is three-dimensional,' Weed said, 'because it takes up real space.'

'That's right. And what are the words we use?'

'Over, under, through, behind and around,' he recited.

Weed could remember words in art, and they didn't have to be in bold.

'Freestanding, or surrounded by negative areas,' he added.

Mrs. Grannis put down her Magic Marker. 'And how do you think you'd make your fish three-dimensional if it was actually two-dimensional?'

'Light and shadow,' he said easily.

'Chiaroscuro.'

'Except I can never pronunciate it,' Weed told her. 'It's what you do to make a drawing of a wineglass look three-dimensional instead of flat. Same for a lightbulb or an ice chicle or even clouds in the air.'

Weed looked around at boxes of pastels and the 140-weight Grumbacher paper he only got to use on final sketches. There were shelves of Elmer's glue and colored pencils and carts of the Crayola tempera paints he had used on his fish. On a counter in the back of the room the computer terminals for graphics reminded him of the secret thing he had done.

By now, students were wandering into the room and scooting out chairs. They greeted Weed in their typically affectionate, smack-him-around fashion.

'Hey, *Weed Garden,* what's going on?'

'How come you're always in here before we are? Doing your homework early?'

'You finished the Mono Lisa yet?'

'You got paint on your jeans.'

'Whoa, doesn't look like paint to me. You been bleeding, man?'

'Uh uh,' Weed lied.

Mrs. Grannis's eyes got darker as she looked at him and his jeans. He could see a question mark in a little balloon over her head. Weed had nothing to say.

'Everybody ready to read what you wrote about your symbols?' She returned her attention to the class.

'Groan.'

'I can't figure out what mine means.'

'No one said we had to *write.*'

'Let's take a minute to talk about symbols.' Mrs. Grannis hushed them. 'What is a symbol? Matthew?'

'Something that means something else.'

'And where do we find them? Joan?'

'In pyramids. And jewelry.'

'Annie?'

'In the catacombs, so the Christians could express themselves in secret.'

'Weed? Where else might we find symbols?' Mrs. Grannis's face got soft with concern as she looked at him.

'Doodles and what I play in the band,' Weed said.

Brazil was at his desk, drawing designs on a legal pad, trying to come up with a newsletter logotype as the chairman of the Governor's Blue Ribbon Crime Commission drove him crazy over the speakerphone.

'I think it is a dread-filled miscalculation,' Lelia Ehrhart's emphatic, haughty voice sounded.

Brazil turned down the volume.

'To even suggest much less implicate we might have a gang here is to cause one,' she proclaimed.

The logo was for the website and needed to attract attention, and since it was agreed that CPR was out the window, Brazil had to start over. He hated newsletters, but Hammer had been insistent.

'And not every children are little mobsters. Many of them are misguided and misled astray, mistreated and abusive and need our help, Officer Brazil. To dwell on those few bad, especially those to band together in little groups you call gangs, is to give the public a very wrong, untrue and false view. My committee is completely all about prevention and doing that first before the other. That's what the governor has mandated to tell us to do it.'

'The last governor,' Brazil politely reminded her.

'What is relevant about that and how does it matter?' retorted Ehrhart, who had been raised in Vienna and Yugoslavia and did not speak English well.

'It matters because Governor Feuer hasn't gotten around to appointing a new commission yet. I don't think it's a good idea for us to be making assumptions about his policies and mandates, Mrs. Ehrhart.'

There was a high-pitched, outraged pause.

'Are you implicating that he might dissolute my commission and undo it? That he and I may be a problem in my relationship?' said Ehrhart.

Brazil knew that a good nameplate should attract attention without overdoing it. Perhaps because they were on the subject of gangs, Brazil suddenly scrawled *Richmond P.D.* graffiti-style.

'Wow,' he muttered in excitement.

'Wow which?' Ehrhart's angry voice filled the office.

'I'm sorry.' Brazil came to. 'What were you saying?'

'I demand you tell me when you were saying *wow* about just there,' she demanded.

Chief Hammer filled the doorway. Brazil rolled his eyes and put his finger to his lips.

'I think you were became impertinent!' Ehrhart went on.

'No, ma'am. I wasn't saying *wow* about anything that has to do with you,' Brazil answered honestly.

'Oh really? And did *that* supposedly mean what?'

'I'm working on something here, and was saying *wow* about it.'

'Oh, I see. Here I am taken my costly time to call your phone, and you're working on something else in addition to our conversing while I'm talking to you?'

'Yes, ma'am. But I'm listening.' Brazil tried not to laugh as he looked at Hammer, who was never amused by Ehrhart.

West walked in.

'What . . . ?' she started to say.

Hammer motioned for her to be silent. Brazil clamped his pencil between his teeth and crossed his eyes.

'The upshoot, Officer Brazil, is I simple will not allow to permit you a commission quote for whatever your next column might be about in terms of so-called gangs. *You're hanging out by a thread on a limb all alone on this one!*'

Brazil snatched the pencil out of his mouth and wrote down the quote. West scowled. Hammer shook her head in disgust.

'We members on the Blue Ribbon Crime Commission are children pro-advocates, not bounty hunting,' she preached on. 'Even if children do formulate little groups, what by the when is perfect and normal, certainly all of us had our little clichés where we were in school and to start labels them as *gangs* is like all this millions of misspoken facts about well-meaning mens who play Santa Claus at Christmas all being children molesters, or that clowns are, or that the Internet becomes that. And this is how there things all get their inception. Because of the power of suggesting that the media has. Don't you view how you've opened a flooded gate? So I'm asking you reasonable to square a peg in that round hole right now.'

Brazil was biting his hand. He cleared his throat several times.

'I understand what you're . . .' His voice went up an octave and cracked.

He cleared his throat again, tears in his eyes, face bright red as he held back laughter that was fast becoming hysterical. Hammer looked like she wanted to break Lelia Ehrhart's neck, as usual. West's expression pretty much mirrored her boss's.

'Then am I to happily assumption that we won't hear no more about this gang paraphernalia?' said Ehrhart, who was famous for her creativity with self-expression.

Brazil simply could not speak.

'Are you where?'

Brazil mashed several buttons on the phone at the same time to give the impression there was trouble on the line. He quietly depressed the hang-up button and returned the receiver to its cradle.

'*Gang paraphernalia!*' He was weak with laughter.

'Oh great,' West said. 'Now she'll call us. Way to go, Andy. Every time you get with her on the fucking phone, this happens. Then she calls the chief or me. Thanks a hell of a lot.'

'We have things to discuss,' Hammer announced, coming inside the office. 'We'll leave Lelia for later. She takes up far too much of our time as is.'

'Why can't you say something to Governor Feuer?' Brazil said as he took a deep breath and wiped his eyes.

'I will if he asks me,' Hammer replied. 'We need a very simple user's manual for COMSTAT. We've got to get this computer business straight. We're what? Three months into this? A fourth of our year is up. And they still can't use the computer? Both of you see how bad that is?'

'Yes.' Brazil got serious. 'I do. If we don't leave that much with them, I guess we've failed.'

'I'm sorry to heap more on you.' Hammer began pacing. 'But we need the manual ASAP.'

'How soon is *as soon as possible?'* West asked suspiciously.

'Two weeks from today, at the outside.'

'Jeez.' West sat down on the small couch. 'I'm already working days and riding with patrol, detectives, inspectors, you name it.'

'Me, too,' Brazil said. 'Plus I've got this website stuff.'

'I know, I know.' Hammer stopped to look out the window at the downtown skyline. 'I have my computer at home. I'll add my thoughts, too. We're all in this together. I think the thing to do is give each of us our own responsibility. Andy, you're more into programming, commands and all that. You can handle the how-to technical part of it, and Virginia, you can help put it in very basic, black-and-white terms, nuts and bolts, that the cops will be able to follow.'

West wasn't sure if she'd been insulted or not.

'I'll try to add the concepts, philosophies, put it all in context,' Hammer said. 'Then – Andy, you're the writer – you can compile the whole thing.'

'I agree this has to be done,' West said, 'but if you ask me, the only thing that's going to really turn the guys on to COMSTAT is if they see it works.'

'They aren't going to see if it works if they can't work it,' Hammer replied logically.

Hammer walked out of the office. Brazil and West looked at each other.

'Shit,' West said. 'Look what you've gotten us into.'

'Me!' Brazil exclaimed.

'Yes, you.'

'She suggested the user's manual, not me.'

'She wouldn't have suggested one if you weren't a writer.' West saw the holes in her logic but would not back down.

'Oh, I see. So now everything's my fault just because I know how to do something in general that I've been told to do specifically and that you've been asked to help with, sort of.'

West had to unravel this for a moment.

'What do you mean, *sort of?'* she asked. 'It sounds to me like my involvement is more than a sort of.'

Brazil's phone rang.

'Brazil. Oh, hi.' His voice softened and he paused as the other person talked. 'You're so thoughtful,' Brazil said, listening again. 'The usual place is fine,' he said as the voice chattered on. 'I'll look forward to it,' Brazil said. 'I've got to go.

'Sorry,' he said to West.

'Do you have any idea how much I'm going to hate writing computer instructions?' she asked in an uneven, strained voice as she imagined Brazil's wealthy, beautiful landlady. 'And you're not supposed to make personal calls at work!'

'I didn't make it. She called me. And you're not the one who has to do the writing. I am,' Brazil replied.

'Well, writing, after all is said and done, is the easy part.'

Brazil's anger mounted.

'You don't have any right to say it's easy,' he said.

'I can say anything I want,' she replied.

'No you can't.'

'Yes I can,' she asserted.

'Then you write it.'

'Fuck no,' she answered. 'I've got enough to do.'

'Excuse me,' a voice behind them spoke up.

Fling was holding his schedule book, standing outside the door, afraid to walk in. West and Brazil stopped their bickering and stared at him.

'I'm out of here.' West left.

'Officer Brazil,' Fling said, 'I just wanted to remind you of your 1:56 appointment at Godwin High School. I believe you're speaking in the auditorium to all the students?'

'Dammit,' Brazil muttered as he checked the time. 'Do you know how to get there from here?'

'No,' Fling said. 'I didn't go there.'

'Huh?' Brazil's mind was racing.

'I went to Hermitage,' Fling said.

'Wait.' Brazil popped up from his desk. 'Virginia, come back here!'

'On Hungary Springs Road.' Fling was warmed by the memories. 'You know, Godwin isn't the only good school around.'

West walked back into the office, defiant in a khaki suit that complemented the darkness of her eyes and deep red of her hair. Her body was far finer than she deserved for as little as she did to help it along.

'What?' she asked impatiently.

'You ought to go out to Hermitage, too. Talk with the students there, you know,' Fling was going on and on. 'That's the thing about doing one school. What about the others?'

'In case you've forgotten,' Brazil said to West as he tightened the laces of his Rocky boots, 'you're supposed to go with me to Godwin.'

'Shit,' she said.

chapter five

Muskrat's Auto Rescue was Bubba's home away from home, and today especially, he was grateful. It didn't matter that Officer Budget had let Bubba go with only a warning. Bubba was traumatized. The cop had called Bubba names. The cop had brought back old injuries and humiliations and then had been so unfair and ugly as to accuse Bubba of being the one with prejudices.

Muskrat's shop was behind his brick rancher on several junk-scattered acres off Clopton Street, between Midlothian and Hull. The fence bordering Muskrat's garage and its outbuildings was built of old railroad ties piled like Lincoln Logs. Transmissions littered the hard-packed dirt tail housings covered with plastic quart oil bottles to keep out the rain. Cars, vans, pickups, a tractor trailer and an old fire truck used each year in the Azalea Parade were parked wherever Muskrat had left them last. Bubba pulled up to the shop's open bay door, cut the engine and climbed out.

He was momentarily cheered by Muskrat's automotive kingdom, which could very well have passed for a chop shop were most of the parts not rusty and from an earlier stage of vehicle evolution. Bubba stepped around an ancient air jack and a bearing press. He made his way through miscellaneous flowerpots, coils of garden hoses, fenders, headlights, hoods, bumpers, car seats, stacks of split firewood and fifty-five-gallon drums overflowing with junk parts.

Bubba was convinced, although he spoke of it rarely, that there was a Bermuda Triangle for vehicles. He believed cars and trucks swept up in floods and tornadoes, or perhaps gone and believed stolen, ended up in places like Muskrat's shop, where they would be cared for and used to help humans continue their journeys through this life. Bubba intended to write this insight to Click and Clack's Car Talk on the Internet or perhaps to his favorite, Miss Lonely Parts, a syndicated columnist who was really a man.

'Hey Scrat!' Bubba called out.

He walked inside the garage, where an old furnace burned a mixture of dirty motor oil and firewood.

'Scrat? Where the hell are ya?' Bubba tried again.

Muskrat wasn't always easy to locate within the jumbles of heater cores, batteries, oil pans, grease guns, chains, tow ropes, bungee straps, gas lines, vacuum hoses, homemade jumper cables, stands made of old Ford wheels, clutches. Pressure plates were stacked like doughnuts on sections of exhaust pipes. There were grinders, a chain horse to lift out engines, and hundreds of American and metric wrenches, ratchets, pliers, chisels, awls, vises, presses, springs, drill bits, spark plugs, dead blow mallets and brass hammers.

'How come you got the heat on, Scrat?'

'To keep my joints from aching. What'dya try to fix this time?' Muskrat's voice was muffled under a jacked-up 1996 Mercury Cougar.

'*Who* tried to fix?' Bubba accused.

Muskrat was flat on his back on a creeper. He rolled out from underneath the car, suddenly there, a wizard in a mechanic's blue work pants and shirt and a NAPA Auto Parts cap.

'What do you mean, I tried?' asked Muskrat, who was at least seventy, with hands rough and hard like horn.

'Windshield's leaking again,' Bubba let him know. 'You fixed it last, Scrat.'

'Uh huh,' Muskrat said blandly as he snatched toilet paper from an industrial roll overhead and began cleaning his glasses. 'Well, drive her on in here, Bubba. I'll take a look but I keep telling you to get the boys at Harding Glass to put in a new windshield. Or dump the damn thing altogether and get something that don't break down every other minute.'

Bubba walked out of the garage, not listening. He got into his Jeep and cranked the engine as anger pecked at him. He could not and would not believe that his buddy Smudge had cheated him. It couldn't be that Smudge had sold him a piece of shit. The possibility of it resurrected other injustices as Bubba parked inside the garage, in the bay next to the Cougar, and climbed out.

'I got to tell you right now, Scrat, there's police brutality in this city,' Bubba announced.

'Oh yeah?' Muskrat mumbled as he started looking at the windshield.

'I think something's telling me to do something about it.'

'Bubba, something's always telling you something.'

'There're reasons too complicated to go into that the new chief, that new woman who just moved here, needs my help, Scrat.'

'And you always got complicated reasons, Bubba. I'd stay out of it if I were you.'

Bubba could not stop thinking about Chief Hammer. He had heard her name on his cell phone this morning. There was a reason for this; it was not random.

'It's time we mobilize, Scrat.'

'Who's *we?'*

'Citizens like us,' Bubba said. 'We gotta get involved.'

'I can't find your leak,' Muskrat said.

'Right here.' Bubba pointed to the top of the windshield, near the rearview mirror. 'The water drips in from this spot here. Want a cigarette?'

Bubba pulled out a pack.

'You need to cut back, boy,' Muskrat said. 'Chew gum. That's what I do to kill the craving when I'm around gasoline and what all.'

'You forget I got TMJ. My jaws are killing me.' Bubba clicked them side to side.

'I told you not to get all those damn crowns,' Muskrat said as he retrieved a Windex spray bottle full of water and uncoiled an air hose. 'You'd probably be better off if he just yanked all of 'em out and fixed you up with a pair of clackers like I got.'

Muskrat grinned, showing off his dentures.

'I'll get on the inside with the hose, and when I tell you to, you start spraying,' said Muskrat.

'Same thing we did last time,' Bubba said. 'And a lot of good it did.'

'It's like fixing those crowns of yours,' Muskrat wouldn't let up as he sat in the driver's seat. 'All you do is go to the dentist. I'd get new ones that don't look like piano keys if I were you. And you sure as hell ought to replace this windshield. The car's been wrecked.' Muskrat had told him this before. "That's why everything keeps going wrong with it, that and the fact that you're always trying to fix it yourself, Bubba.'

'It ain't been wrecked, good buddy,' Bubba said.

'It sure as hell has. Where you think all that Bondo came from, the factory?'

'I won't have you talking about Smudge that way,' Bubba told him.

'I didn't say a word about Smudge.'

'Smudge has been my good buddy since we were in Sunday school together, way back.'

'Way back when you used to go to church and listen to your daddy,' Muskrat reminded him. 'Don't forget, you was the preacher's kid.'

Bubba was shocked by another memory of name-calling. *The flucking preacher's kid.* He had forgotten all about it. For a moment, he couldn't speak. His bowels came alive.

'I'm just pointing out, for your own good, Bubba, that it didn't hurt Smudge one bit to be on the preacher's good side. Not everybody has as high opinion of Smudge as you do.'

Muskrat had heard every tale there was about everybody in the city who had ever owned a car that needed fixing, including the Dodge Dart belonging to Miss Prum, who happened to be the director of Christian education at the historic downtown Second Presbyterian Church, where Dr. But Fluck had been the senior minister.

'Look, it's already six-thirty and I gotta start my shift early tonight, as if my day hasn't been bad enough. So I guess we'd better get this leak taken care of,' Bubba said as an Escort drove up and parked outside the shop.

'I'm going as fast as I can,' Muskrat said.

He peeled the Jeep's headliner and its cardboard away from the ceiling and examined the rubbery black polyurethane in the pitch well.

'Least you didn't try to fix this one yourself,' Muskrat observed.

'Didn't have time,' Bubba said.

'Good thing, since you're always screwing up things worse,' Muskrat said candidly.

They did not see the clean-cut kid walk in until he was so close he startled them.

'Hi,' the kid said. 'Didn't mean to scare you.'

'Don't go sneaking up on people like that, son,' Muskrat said.

'I got a stuck window,' the kid told him.

'Well, you just stand on back and hold your horses,' Muskrat said. 'I'll get with you as soon as I wind up here.'

Bubba hadn't finished arguing yet.

'I did my own pigtail wiring on my trailer hitch,' he said.

'And you got the turn signal lights backwards,' Muskrat countered.

'So what, big deal.'

'Well, I'll remind you of a *big deal.* Remember the serpentine belt?' Muskrat talked on.

'The directions weren't clear,' Bubba answered.

'Well, you fought it out with that one for five hours and still put it on wrong-ribbed against smooth instead of ribbed against ribbed and smooth against smooth, and next thing you've lost the alternator, power steering, water pump. You're just lucky you didn't lock up the engine and have to get a new one. Bubba, you can start spraying.'

'Excuse me?' the kid said politely. 'You know how long you'll be?'

'You'll have to hold off for just a minute,' Muskrat told him.

Bubba worked the Windex bottle along the top of the windshield, spraying water near the rearview mirror while Muskrat blasted compressed air at the seal from the inside.

'Before that,' Muskrat picked up where he'd left off, 'you replaced the mercury switch in the trunk and did that wrong, too. So the trunk light stayed on all the time and your battery kept going dead. Before that it was replacing your brakes and putting the pad in backwards, and the time before that, you left out the antirattle spring, the horseshoe clip in the emergency brake, and the lever fell into the drum.'

Bubba winked at the kid as if to imply that Muskrat was exaggerating. Muskrat walked over to a workbench, where the heater box was warming up several tubes of SikaTack Ultrafast polyurethane. He picked up a caulking gun and dropped a tube inside it.

'Remember the time you forgot the cotter pin and the tire rod fell off and both wheels went out spread-eagle?' Muskrat kept on.

'He can tell a story,' Bubba said to the kid.

Water trickled down the inside of the glass. Muskrat ran a thick bead of black polyurethane, licking his finger and pressing it flat. He stepped out of the car and ran a thin bead on the outside of the glass.

'We need to wait about fifteen minutes to test it again,' he said. 'Truth is, none of the seals in this thing are tight. Bet you get a lot of wind noise.'

Bubba wasn't going to admit it. Muskrat walked over to the solvent bin and dipped his hands in the murky fluid.

'What'cha need?' Muskrat finally said to the kid.

'My left rear power window won't work.' The young man was courteous, but his eyes were hard.

'The motor's probably gone bad,' volunteered Bubba the ace mechanic. 'But you're gonna have to wait. I was here first.'

'We got a few minutes,' Muskrat told Bubba. 'Let me go on and take care of him.'

Muskrat dried his hands and walked outside to the Escort. He opened the back door and popped the panel off as the young man scanned his surroundings.

'Bubba, how 'bout bringing me the wire strippers,' Muskrat said. 'You're lucky,' he told his young customer. 'It ain't the switch or the motor. You got a broke wire between the door and the jamb. All I gotta do is splice it. What's your name, by the way?'

'Smoke.'

'Now that's a new one,' Muskrat commented.

'What everybody calls me.' Smoke shrugged. 'Hope you get your problem taken care of,' he then said to Bubba. 'I'm new around here. People seem really nice.'

'It's the South,' Bubba bragged.

'I guess you're from here.'

'Couldn't be from anyplace else. In fact, I'm even more southern than I used to be.'

'How so?' Smoke asked with a smile that might have been interpreted as a faint sneer had Bubba paid attention.

'Born on Northside and moved to Southside.'

'Oh yeah? Where 'bouts?'

'Forest Hills. Over on Clarence,' said Bubba, who was flattered by the boy's interest and his respectful way of addressing him. 'Can't miss my house. The one with the coon dog in the pen. Half Shell. She barks nonstop and wouldn't hurt a flea.'

'Not much of a watchdog if she barks all the time,' Smoke said.

'You got that right.'

'You hunt with her?'

'Big into that,' Bubba said.

'Seems all us southern guys are big on guns.'

'You bet.'

Muskrat twisted the wires he'd stripped and was done.

'When I was your age,' Bubba said to Smoke, 'I started fixing things like this myself.'

'I'm not very mechanically inclined,' Smoke said.

'You can work on it, son.' Bubba beamed. 'Go out and get the proper tools, some books, and it's trial and error. Same with things around the house. You build your own deck and fix your own roof – hell, just the other day I bought a new garage door at Sears. Installed it myself.'

'No kidding,' Smoke said. 'Remote control and all?'

'You bet. Gives satisfaction money can't buy,' Bubba said.

'You must have quite a shop,' Smoke said.

'Had to add an addition to the garage. Everything from grove joint pliers to a DeVilbiss air compressor rated at 7.6 CFM at 40 PSI and 5.6 CFM at 90 to diagnostic tools like a Sunpro Sensor Probe so you can test manifold absolute pressure, mass air flow and vane air flow sensors.'

'Don't need shit like that, and neither do you, Bubba,' Muskrat let him know. 'At least I know how to use what I got.'

Muskrat replaced the door panel and got up. He climbed into the driver's seat, started the engine and tested the window. It hummed up.

'Smooth as silk,' he announced proudly, wiping his hands on his pants.

'Gee, thanks,' Smoke said. 'How much do I owe you?'

'The first time's on the house,' Muskrat said.

'Gee. Thanks a lot,' Smoke said.

'Hey, the Gun and Knife Show's coming in two weeks,'

Bubba suddenly remembered. 'Looking for a couple after-market clips, twenty rounds, for my new 92FS M9 Special Edition, finest military handgun in the world. Now that I gotta show you, Muskrat. Comes with pistol belt and holster, magazine pouch. Same thing used in Just Cause, Desert Storm, Desert Shield, Restore Hope, Joint Guard.'

'Do tell,' said Muskrat.

'I'm debating if I should've got the presentation case. Walnut, etched glass cover. And the walnut grips,' Bubba agonized.

'Wouldn't be as practical if you ever plan to shoot it.'

'I sure as hell do. Winchester 115-grain Silvertip high-power.'

'How come you ain't in school?' Muskrat asked Smoke.

'Free period. In fact, I gotta get back.'

Muskrat waited until Smoke was in his car, driving off.

'You notice that boy's eyes?' Muskrat said. 'Looked like he'd been drinking.'

'As if you and I didn't at that age,' Bubba said. 'So what d'ya think? This urethane hard enough yet?'

'Should be. But don't get your hopes up.'

They used the air hose and spray bottle again. The leak was still there. Muskrat took his time studying the problem until he'd figured it out.

'You got a hairline crack in the roof line,' he said.

chapter six

Weed refused to read his story, causing Mrs. Grannis to doubt that he had written one. This disappointed her greatly, and the other students in the class did not know what to think. Weed had always been so eager, the little boy-wonder in art class. Now, suddenly, he was uncommunicative and uncooperative, and the more Mrs. Grannis pressed him, the more obstinate he got. Finally, he was rude.

'Why I did the fish is my business,' he said, reaching under his desk for his knapsack.

'You had an assignment, just like everyone else,' Mrs. Grannis said firmly.

'No one else did a fish.' Weed looked up at the clock.

'That's all the more reason we want to hear about yours,' Mrs. Grannis answered.

'Come on, Weed.'

'Read it to us.'

'Hey, it's not fair. You heard ours.'

It was 1:48. Fifth period ended in three minutes. Mrs. Grannis felt terrible. Weed was impossible, sitting rigidly in his chair, head bent, as if he were about to be beaten.

His classmates shifted uncomfortably, waiting for the bell.

'Well,' Mrs. Grannis broke the silence. 'Tomorrow we start watercolors, and don't forget, we have a special program next period.'

Henry Hamilton was the star pitcher of the baseball team, and he hated any activity that kept him sitting past two in the afternoon. He made a face, slumped in his seat and sighed loudly. Eva Grecci did the same because she had an aching crush on Hamilton. Randy Weispfenning wasn't happy, either.

'We have two very important police officers who have been sent to Richmond by the National Institute of Justice,' Mrs. Grannis said. 'They have generously agreed to come today and talk with us.'

'About what?'

'Crime, I suppose,' Mrs. Grannis said.

'I'm sick of hearing about it.'

'Me, too. My mom won't even read the paper anymore.'

'My dad thinks I should start wearing a bulletproof vest to class.' Hamilton laughed, ducking when Weispfenning tried to cuff him.

'That's not funny,' Mrs. Grannis said.

The bell rang. Everyone jumped up as if there was a fire.

'Off to see the wizzz-aarrrddd . . .' Hamilton sang and started skipping down an imagined Yellow Brick Road.

Eva Grecci laughed too hard.

'Weed,' Mrs. Grannis said. 'I need to see you for a minute.'

He sullenly shuffled up to her desk. The room emptied, leaving the two of them alone.

'This is the first time you've not turned in an assignment,' she said softly.

He shrugged.

'Do you want to tell me why?'

'Because.' He shrugged again as tears smarted.

'That's not an answer, Weed.'

He blinked, looking away from her. Feelings boiled up in him. In an hour he was supposed to meet Smoke in the parking lot.

'I just didn't get around to it,' he said as he thought of the five-page story hiding inside his knapsack.

'I'm very surprised you didn't get around to it,' she measured her words.

Weed said nothing. He had spent half of Saturday writing four drafts of it before painstakingly making the final copy in black felt-tip ink, letters perfectly formed in the calligraphy that he had learned from a kit and then modified to his bold, funky, completely unique style. The second bell rang.

'We need to go on to the auditorium,' Mrs. Grannis said.

He felt her searching his face, looking for a clue. Weed knew she was hoping the faculty had not made a mistake advancing him to the outer limits of Godwin's art instruction.

'I don't want to listen to no cops,' Weed told her.

'Weed?' It wasn't negotiable. 'You're going to sit with me.'

Brazil parked his marked patrol car on the circle outside the high school's front entrance, and despite his constant complaining during the drive, felt happy to be here as he climbed out of the car and students milling about stared. It did not occur to Brazil that his tall, chiseled, uniformed presence was striking, that this might have something to do with the attention he so often got.

He had never really accepted his physical self. In part this was because he was an only child left to the mercy of a mother who had always been too miserable and eventually too drunk to see him as someone separate from herself. When she looked at him, she saw a bleary projection of her husband, who had been killed when Brazil was ten. In her rages, it was Brazil's dead father she ranted to and struck and begged not to leave her.

'You got any idea where the hell we're going?' West asked as she pushed shut the car door.

Brazil scanned the notes Fling had given him.

'"Go in, take a left,"' he read.

'Go in where?'

'Uh,' Brazil scanned some more. 'Doesn't say. We "go through doors ahead to green hallway through more doors to a blue one until see a bulletin board with photographs."'

'Fuck,' West said as they walked.

'After that,' Brazil said, 'we "can't miss it."'

'It's a conspiracy. I'm telling you, Andy. They deliberately had Hammer inherit Fling to fuck her.'

'I don't know,' Brazil said as he opened one of the front

doors for her and they entered the commons. 'The former chief had him for three years.'

'The former chief also got fired for incompetence.'

'Ah.' Brazil spied a pretty young teacher walking with one of her students. 'Excuse me,' Brazil said to her with a smile. 'We're trying to find the auditorium. I'm Officer Brazil and this is Deputy Chief West.'

'Of course,' Mrs. Grannis answered with enthusiasm. 'You're exactly who we're on our way to see. I'm Mrs. Grannis and this is Weed. You can just follow us. It's just straight ahead. I'm sure everybody else is already seated and waiting with great anticipation.'

'What'cha say?' Brazil said to Weed.

'Nothing,' Weed said.

'Ah come on,' West said. 'I hear they teach a lot more than nothing here.'

'Weed's our star artist,' Mrs. Grannis said proudly, patting Weed's shoulder.

He moved away from her, his lower lip protruding in a combination of hostility and near-tears.

'That's cool,' Brazil said, shortening his long strides. 'What kind of art, man?'

'Whatever kind I want,' Weed said.

'Oh yeah?' Brazil said. 'You do sculpture?'

'Yeah.'

'How about pen and ink?'

'Yeah.'

'Watercolors?'

'Going to.'

'Papier-mâché?'

'Easy.'

'Impressionism. You like Cézanne? "Le Château Noir"?'

'Huh?' Weed looked up at Brazil. 'Say what?'

'Cézanne. He's one of my favorites. Go look him up.'

'Where's he live?'

'He doesn't anymore.'

Weed frowned, following the two cops and Mrs. Grannis into the auditorium. It was full, students turning around in their seats, wondering what Mrs. Grannis and Weed were doing with the two important guests. Weed held his head up, walking cool in his baggy look of the day. He and Mrs. Grannis slipped into the second row, near other teachers. Brazil and West made their way onto the stage and sat in chairs on the dais, spotlights on them. West tapped her microphone and it thudded loudly.

'Can everybody hear?' she asked.

'Yes,' voices returned.

'All the way in the back?'

'Yes.'

'Where's your gun?'

Laughter started rolling through the rows.

'We'll start with that,' West said, her voice booming. 'What's all this crap about guns? Yeah, sure, I've got one on.'

'What kind?'

'The kind I don't like,' she answered. 'Because I don't like any gun. I don't even like being a cop, and you know why? Because I wish we didn't need guns or cops.'

She and Brazil talked for about twenty minutes.

Afterward the principal, Mrs. Lilly, made her way up to the front of the auditorium as the applause continued. Brazil bent down and handed Mrs. Lilly the microphone. She squinted in the glaring lights and announced there was time to take a few questions.

Smoke had returned to school after a quick stop at Sears, where he had shoplifted ten garage remote controls. He stood up from an aisle seat on the tenth row.

'I was wondering,' he spoke loudly and sincerely, 'if you think some kids are born bad.'

'I think some are,' the lady cop answered bluntly.

'I'd like to believe that's not true,' Mrs. Lilly piped up.

'We'd all like to believe it's not true,' the blond uniformed cop said. 'But I think what's important is that at the end of the day, people make choices. Nobody makes you cheat on that test or steal that car or beat somebody up.'

Smoke continued to stand in the darkness, listening attentively, his expression innocent and thoughtful. He wasn't finished yet.

'But what do you do if someone's really bad and nothing's going to change him?' he asked in a loud, sure voice.

'Lock him up.' The lady cop meant it.

Laughter.

'About all you can do is protect society from people like that,' the blond cop added.

'Isn't it true though that genetically bad people are usually smarter and harder to catch?' Smoke asked.

'Depends on who's trying to catch them.' The blond cop was a little cocky.

Laughter swelled as the bell rang. Smoke slipped out of the auditorium first, through a side door, heading straight for the parking lot. A cold smile played on his lips as he envisioned the blond cop and his sidekick with the big tits and imagined himself in direct combat with them. The thought aroused him.

Power lifted him and pumped through his blood as he trotted to his Escort and unlocked it. He sat behind the wheel, working himself into intense excitement as he stared at the circle of yellow school buses and the hundreds of kids suddenly streaming out of doorways, cheerful, playful and in a hurry.

Smoke started the car and drove to the appointed spot in the parking lot, forcing other students to go around him or turn and head out the other way. He wasn't going to move for anyone. Traffic and voices were loud as he sat watching for Weed, who was about to hurt like hell and make Smoke famous.

Smoke wanted to touch himself again, but resisted. When he deprived himself, he couldn't be stopped. He could do anything. He would get a faint metallic taste in his mouth as energy rushed up from between his legs and lifted the top of his head. He could work himself into anything.

All he had to do was play the same fantasy over and over again in his mind. He was sweaty and dirty on a downtown rooftop with an AR-15, taking out half the fucking cops in the city, slapping magazine after magazine into his assault rifle, shooting down helicopters and slaughtering the National Guard.

Smoke never carried the fantasy much beyond that point. A rational part of his brain realized that the last scenario most likely would be his death or imprisonment, but neither was enough to get his attention when he was consumed by lust so intense and seething that these days he did little beyond playing with plans.

It was five past three when Weed walked up to the car, knapsack limp in his hand. Smoke was silent as Weed climbed in, shut the door and fastened his shoulder harness. Smoke drove off, slowly making his way out of the parking lot. He turned onto Pump Road and followed it south to Patterson Avenue while Weed got increasingly nervous, licking his lips, staring out his side window.

'So how come you asked the cops all those questions?' Weed finally mustered up the courage to ask.

Smoke said nothing.

'I thought they was good questions.'

Smoke was silent as he turned east on Patterson Avenue. He started driving faster. He felt Weed's fear, and the heat of rage pressed against Smoke like a wall of fire.

'I thought the cops were fuckin' stupid.' Weed tried to sound big. 'Hey. You hungry, Smoke? I didn't eat my sandwich at lunch. You want it?'

A long silence followed. Smoke turned south on Parham Road.

'Hey, Smoke, how come you ain't talking to me?' Weed's voice jumped. 'I do something?'

Smoke's right hand flew out as if it were alive on its

own. It chopped Weed hard between the legs.

'What time I tell you to meet me in the parking lot?' Smoke yelled as Weed shrieked, doubled over, arms locked under his crossed legs, head practically in his lap. 'What time, you fuckin' little shit!'

'Three!' Weed cried, tears running down his face in little rivers. 'Why'd you do that? I didn't do nothing.' He hiccuped. 'Smoke, I didn't!'

'And what time was it when you walked up to my car, you little fuck!' Smoke grabbed the back of Weed's woolly cornrows. 'It was *five after three!'*

He yanked. Weed screamed again.

'*When I say three, what does that mean, retard?'*

'I couldn't get away from Mrs. Grannis!' Weed choked, gasping and making awful faces as Smoke gripped Weed's hair, tearing some of it out by the roots. 'I'm sorry, Smoke! I'm sorry! Oh please don't hurt me no more.'

Smoke shoved him away and started laughing. He turned up 2 Pac on the CD player, every other word *fuck* and *nigger.* Smoke reached under his seat and snatched out the Glock. He shoved it between Weed's ribs, getting off on how bad the little shit was shaking. Weed put his hands over his face. He farted and burped.

'You pee or shit in here, and I'll blow your dick off,' Smoke told him.

'Please, Smoke,' Weed begged in a tiny, pitiful voice. 'Please don't, Smoke.'

'You gonna do what I say from now on?'

'Yes. I'll do anything you want me to, Smoke. I promise.'

Smoke tucked the pistol back under his seat. He turned up 2 Pac and started rapping along. There was no further conversation as Smoke headed across the river toward Huguenot Road, winding here and there, cutting over to Forest Hill, avoiding tolls whenever he could. Weed had gotten very quiet. He dried his eyes and kept his legs tightly crossed. The kid was so puny his Nikes barely touched the floor. Smoke knew all about timing. He knew exactly how to make people do what he wanted.

'Feeling better?' Smoke asked, turning down 2 Pac.

'Yes,' Weed answered politely.

They were on Midlothian Turnpike now, passing German School Road.

'You know what an oath is?' Smoke asked.

He was nice now, relaxed and taking his time, as if they were going out for a hamburger or just cruising.

'No,' Weed answered softly.

'You need to speak up,' Smoke said. 'I can hardly hear you.'

'I don't know what it is,' Weed said more loudly.

'You ever been a Boy Scout?'

'No.'

'Well, to be one you got to take an oath. On my honor I promise to do my best and on and on, whatever. That's an oath. Something you swear to, and if you break it, something really bad happens.'

Businesses along this stretch of Midlothian Turnpike were all about cars and trucks and everything that went with them. A Cheers restaurant had gone out of business, and an adult bookstore had only one car in the lot. Smoke cut up an unpaved side street and drove through the middle of a trailer park, where balding, muddy yards were littered with metal chairs, flowerpots and ceramic lawn ornaments. Scrawny cats darted out of the way. Wind chimes tinkled, and parked trucks reflected the sun.

They turned into the cracked, weed-infested parking lot of the Southside Motel, which had been out of business and boarded up for years. A chain was strung across either end of the drive leading into it, air conditioning units outside the rooms rusted, a breeze sucking dingy white curtains in and out of broken windows. Junipers had grown out of control in clumps, shielding entire blocks of rooms, and grass was dead and treacherous with broken glass. Smoke drove around to the back of the motel and parked next to a Dumpster.

'Remember when I drove you through here last week?' Smoke said. 'Remember, the first rule is, nobody parks back here. You see all the No Trespassing signs?'

'Yeah,' Weed answered, looking around and scared.

'Well, the cops don't come here, but I can't take the chance. They see your car, and you're fucked.'

He put the Escort in gear and drove back around to the front. Weed was quiet as Smoke backtracked and parked on the side of a rutted, muddy road on the outskirts of the trailer park.

'This is how I go in,' Smoke said, cutting the engine and reaching down for his Glock. 'You gonna have to come in another way because they don't have nothing in here but white trash and you'll attract attention. They might even call the cops.'

'Then what do I do?' Weed asked, climbing out and casting furtively about.

'Cut in through Fast Track, Jiffy Tune, Turnpike Auto Parts, one of those other places on the strip, and just come through the woods behind the motel,' Smoke said, sticking the pistol down the front of his jeans and pulling his Chicago Bulls sweatshirt over it.

He kept a good pace along the unpaved road, Weed limping along as fast as he could, obviously hurting. Smoke knew his latest recruit was wondering if he was going to get his brains blown out behind an abandoned motel in the middle of nothing, and Smoke let him worry. Smoke understood fear. The gratification was instant when he made something suffer. He had learned this as a little boy when he could see panic in the eyes, when he could feel terror in the rapidly beating heart of the weaker creature he tortured to death.

Smoke came from a better home than most, one of comfortable, open-minded parents who had never gotten in his way or tried to hold him back or believed their son could be bad. They preferred to give permission rather than force the child into clandestine behavior. They believed if they were trusting and fair-minded, their three children would make the right choices. Smoke's older brother and sister had seemed to prove the philosophy right. They were making good grades in college and associated with nice people and had normal ambitions.

Smoke had always been different. During the interminable evaluations and counseling sessions in Durham and training school at Butner, he had not complained about his family or a single event that had or hadn't happened to him. He had blamed no one for who he was, and in fact, took full credit. He had diagnosed himself as a psychopath. He worked hard to be a good one. Smoke had no doubt that one day the world would know his name.

Smoke wasn't giving Weed a hard time right now, and Weed was grateful and appropriately cooperative. Their feet clinked bits of broken bottles and dislodged rocks, and acres of dense woods shielded the back of the motel from busy highways and streets just blocks away. Smoke headed straight for a large sheet of plywood propped against a wall behind a clump of junipers. His eyes narrowed as he looked around and listened. He slid the plywood to one side and stepped through the empty bent aluminum frame of what was left of sliding glass doors.

'Who's bartending?' Smoke announced to the girl and three boys inside the boggy, musty-smelling suite. 'We got something to celebrate. Weed, meet your new family. That's Divinity, and the three assholes there are Dog, Sick and Beeper.'

'That's their real names?' Weed couldn't help but ask.

'Their slave names,' Smoke replied.

chapter seven

The Pikes were sipping vodka out of Dixie cups and smoking cigarettes. They looked at Weed and seemed amused, their eyes laughing at him as they lounged on stained, sour-smelling mattresses.

Divinity was dark-skinned, but Weed didn't think she was black, maybe Hispanic or a little bit of everything. She wasn't wearing a bra, and her tight sheer black undershirt showed more than Weed had ever seen in person. Her slender legs in their worn-out jeans were spread wide. She was really pretty.

Dog was big and looked mean and stupid, and Sick had acne and a dark buzz cut and five loops in his right ear. Beeper seemed a little nicer, or maybe it was just that he was small like Weed. Each of them had a number tattooed on the right index finger and seemed oblivious to the nasty mattresses and the rotting wall-to-wall brown carpet beneath them.

Strewn about were plain oak chairs that Weed associated with school, and TV trays, and boxes of paper napkins and Dixie cups. Candles of all description sat in puddles of hardened wax on windowsills, and the motel furniture was so warped the Formica lamination was curling up. Piled in corners were boxes of chalk, erasers, a slide projector, library books, a corkboard, throw pillows, and at least a dozen empty wallets and ladies' purses and just as many pairs of leather tennis shoes of different sizes. Cases of liquor were stacked up to the water-stained ceiling. Smoke lit one of the candles while Divinity poured Smirnoff into a Dixie cup and handed it to him.

'Are you gonna change my name?' Weed asked.

'Give him some,' Smoke ordered Divinity.

She poured a cup of vodka for Weed and laughed when he hesitantly took it from her.

'Go on.' Smoke jerked his head at Weed.

Weed's daddy drank straight liquor all the time, but Weed never had. He knew it made his daddy mean and sent him out running around and not coming back, sometimes the entire weekend Weed was visiting. The vodka burned and almost gagged Weed. Instantly his face heated up and his brain got lighter.

'Naw,' Smoke said as he held out his cup for more and gestured for Divinity to refill Weed's as well. 'You got such a fucking stupid name, I'm just gonna leave it. We couldn't do much better than *Weed* if we tried, could we?' he said to his gang.

'No, baby.' Divinity sighed as she laid back on her mattress, hands beneath her head, breasts pointed up at the ceiling.

Smoke caught Weed staring.

'You never seen tits before, retard?' he asked.

Weed downed his second cup of vodka and thought he might be sick.

'Sure I seen 'em,' he stuttered.

'Bet you haven't either, retard.' Smoke laughed. 'Except maybe in pictures when you try to jerk off that little golden rod of yours.'

Everybody laughed with him, including Weed. Weed tried to get cocky and show no fear.

'Fuck,' Weed strutted. 'I seen tits bigger 'an hers.'

'Show him.' Smoke snapped his fingers at Divinity.

She pulled up her shirt and smiled at Weed. He stared, his mouth falling open, his face so hot he thought he had a bad fever. She had tattoos of targets and flower petals in places he could not believe.

'You can look, but you touch and I shoot your balls off,' Smoke said in a menacing tone. 'Everybody knows the rule, right?'

Beeper, Sick and Dog nodded blearily. They didn't seem the least bit interested in Divinity or her equipment. Smoke dropped down next to her on the mattress. He started feeling her and kissing her, his tongue about to get dislocated from his mouth. Weed had never seen anybody act like that in front of other people. It didn't make any sense to him, and he wanted to run as fast as he could and wake up in another city.

'All right, baby, you ready to cook?' Smoke asked, his tongue in her ear.

'Yeah, sugar.'

She languidly reached behind her and got hold of a box of syringes and a Bic ballpoint pen. Weed watched with growing terror as Smoke started heating a needle in the candle flame while Divinity smashed the pen with the butt of the vodka bottle. She pulled out the slender ink tube and dabbed a dot of black ink on her wrist, as if she were testing the warmth of baby's milk.

'We got it, sugar,' she said.

'Get your ass over here,' Smoke ordered Weed.

Weed was paralyzed.

'What'cha gonna do, Smoke?' His voice got small again.

'You gotta get your slave number, retard.'

'I don't need one. Really I don't.'

'Yeah you do. And you don't get your puny ass right here right now' – he patted the mattress where he and Divinity sat – 'then I'm gonna have to get the boys here to convince you.'

Weed walked over and sat on the mattress, a musty, yeasty smell assaulting his nostrils. He held his legs close together and wrapped his arms around his knees, his fists clenched to hide his fingers as best he could. Smoke slowly turned the needle in the flame.

'Hold out your right hand,' he commanded.

'I don't need no number.' Weed tried not to sound like he was begging, but knew he did.

'You don't hold it out now, I'm gonna chop it off.'

Divinity poured another cup of vodka and handed it to Weed.

'Here, honey, this will help. I know it don't feel good, but we all had it done, you know?' she said, holding out her delicate finger with its homemade 2 tattoo.

Weed drank the vodka and caught on fire. His mind went somewhere and when he put out his hand, he was surprised that he could tolerate the sticks and deep scratches of the red-hot needle. He didn't cry. He threw a switch that turned off pain. He didn't look as Divinity dripped ink into the wounds and rubbed it in good. Weed swayed and Smoke had to tell him twice to sit still.

'Your slave number's five, little shit,' Smoke was saying. 'Pretty good, huh. That makes you in the top ten – hell, it makes you in the top five, right? That makes you a first-string Pike. And a fucking lot is expected of a first-string Pike, right, everybody?'

'Sure as fuck is.'

'Fucking got it fucking straight.'

'Honey, don't you fret. You're gonna be just great,' Divinity reassured Weed.

'We're going to initiate you, retard,' Smoke said as again he stuck the needle in Weed's right index finger, above the first knuckle. 'You're gonna do a little paint job for us.'

Weed almost fell over and Divinity had to hold him up. She was laughing and rubbing his back.

'We're gonna show this city who we are once and for all,' Smoke went on, full of liquor and himself. 'You got paints, don't you, little art fag?'

Smoke's words whirled inside Weed's head like the Milky Way.

'He's gone, man,' Beeper said. 'Whatta we do with him?'

'Nothing right now,' Smoke said. 'I got an errand to run.'

It was almost eight P.M., and Virginia West was glad. Working long hours meant she didn't have the energy to get emotional about the dishes in the sink, the dirty clothes on the floor, the clean ones draped over chairs and falling off hangers.

She didn't have to wait for Brazil to ring her up and suggest a pizza or just a walk like he used to back in Charlotte. She knew from her InLog of calls that he never tried, but why should he? She made sure he knew she was never home. If it even crossed his mind to call, he wouldn't because it was pointless. She was busy, out, not thinking of him, not interested.

In fact, eight P.M. was earlier than usual. West preferred to roll in around ten or eleven, when it was too late to even call her family on the farm, where she rarely visited anymore because she now lived so far away. Time had become West's enemy. A pause in it echoed with an unbearable emptiness and loneliness that sent her fleeing from the nineteenth-century town house she rented on Park Avenue, once known as Scuffletown Road, in Richmond's Fan District.

Although the name 'Fan' meant nothing to outsiders or even the majority of Richmond residents who were not interested in the history of their city, a quick look at a map brought much clarity to the matter. The neighborhood *fanned out* several miles west of downtown, spreading fingers of quaint streets with names like Strawberry, Plum and Grove. Homes and town houses of distinctive designs were brick and stone with slate and shingle roofs, stained glass transoms, elaborate porches and parapets, finials and even medallions and domes. Styles ranged from Queen Anne to Neo-Georgian and Italian Villa.

West's town house was three stories with a gray and brown granite front on the first floor and red brick on the two above. There were stained glass bands around the sashes on the second-floor windows and a white frame sitting porch in front. Although Park Avenue had once been one of the most prominent addresses in the city, much of the area had become more affordable as Virginia Commonwealth University continued to expand. Quite frankly, West was growing to hate the Fan, finding its unrelenting noises were causing her mood swings, which in turn seemed to be causing the same in Niles, her Abyssinian cat.

The problem was that West had unwittingly picked a location several houses down from Governor Jim Gilmore's birthplace, which had become increasingly overrun by tourists. She was across the street from the crowded Robin Inn, a popular hangout for students and cops who liked big servings of lasagne and spaghetti and baskets full of garlic bread. As for finding parking on the street, it was a chronic lottery with chances always slim to none, and West had grown to despise students and cars. She even hated their bicycles.

She dropped her briefcase in the foyer, and Niles slinked out of the office and regarded his owner with crossed blue eyes. West threw her suit jacket on the living-room couch and stepped out of her shoes.

'What were you doing in my office?' West asked Niles. 'You know not to go in there. How did you anyway? I know I locked the door, you little fleabag.'

Niles was not insulted. He knew as well as his owner did that he didn't have fleas.

'My office is the worst room in the house,' his owner said as she walked into the kitchen and Niles followed. 'What is it about going in there, huh?'

She opened the refrigerator, grabbed a Miller Genuine Draft and screwed off the cap. Niles jumped on the windowsill and stared at her. His owner was always in such a hurry that she just thought she closed doors, cabinets, windows and drawers, and put away things Niles might enjoy in her absence, such as loose nails and screws, balls of string, half-and-half or part of an egg and sausage sandwich left in the sink.

His owner took a big swallow of beer and stared at her Personal Information Center, an expensive gray phone with a video screen, two lines, caller ID and as many stored telephone numbers as Niles's owner decided to program into memory. She checked for messages, but there were none. She scrolled through the Caller ID InLog to see if anyone had called and not left a message. No one had. She took a big swallow of beer and sighed.

Niles stayed on the windowsill and stared down at his empty food bowl.

'I get the hint,' his owner said, taking another swig of beer.

She walked into the pantry and carried out the bag of Iams Less Active.

'I'm gonna tell you this right now,' his owner said as she filled Niles's handmade ceramic food bowl, 'if you walked on my keyboard again or screwed around under my desk and unplugged anything, you've had it.'

Niles jumped down silently and crunched on his boring, fat-free, meatless food.

West left the kitchen for her office, dreading what she might find. Abyssinians were unusually intelligent cats, and Niles certainly went beyond the norm, which was a problem since he was curious by nature and didn't have enough to do.

'Goddammit,' West exclaimed. 'How the fuck did you do that?'

Glowing on her computer screen was a crime map of the city. That simply could not be possible. She was certain the computer had been turned off when she left the house that morning.

'Holy shit,' she muttered as she seated herself in front of the terminal. 'Niles! Get your butt in here right now!'

Nor did she remember the map's colors being orange, blue, green and purple. What happened to the pale yellow and white spaces? What were all these small, bright blue fish icons clustered in second precinct's beat 219? West looked at the icons one could click on at the bottom of the screen. Homicides were plus signs, robberies were dots, aggravated assaults were stars, burglaries were triangles, vehicle thefts were little cars. But there were no fish, blue or otherwise.

In fact, there was no such thing as a fish icon in COMSTAT's computer network, absolutely not, and she could think of no explanation whatsoever for why beat 219 was filled with fish, or why the beat was outlined in flashing blood red. West reached for the phone.

chapter eight

Andy Brazil also lived in the Fan, but on Plum Street in a fifteen-foot-wide row house with a flat roof and cornices of plain brick, and old plumbing and appliances, and creaking hardwood floors scattered with worn-out braided rugs.

The house was furnished and owned by the old spinster Ruby Sink, a shrewd businesswoman and busybody, one of the first who heard the NIJ team was coming to town and might need a place to stay. As it so happened, she had one vacant rental property she had been trying to fill for months. Brazil had taken it sight unseen.

Like West, he regretted his choice in living accommodations. The trap he had fallen into was plain to see. Miss Sink was rich, lonely, cranky and a compulsive talker. She popped over whenever she wished, ostensibly to check on the small patch of landscaping in front, or to make sure no repair work or touch-ups were needed, or to bring Brazil homemade banana bread or cookies and to inquire about his job and personal life.

Brazil climbed the steps to the front porch, where a package was propped against the front screen door. He recognized Miss Sink's fussy cursive penmanship on the brown wrapping paper and got depressed. It was late. He was exhausted. He hadn't eaten. He hadn't gone to the store in days. The last thing he wanted was another one of Miss Sink's cakes or tins of cookies, which was sure to be followed by yet another visit or a phone call.

'I'm home,' he irritably and sarcastically announced to nobody as he tossed his keys on a chair. 'What's for dinner?'

He was answered by a dripping faucet in the guest bath down the dark paneled hall. Brazil began unbuttoning his uniform shirt as he walked in the direction of the master bedroom, on the first floor and barely big enough for the double bed and two chests of drawers.

He unsnapped his holster and slipped out the Sig Sauer nine-millimeter pistol, setting it on a bedside table. He unbuckled his duty belt, took off his boots, pants and lightweight body armor. He rubbed his lower back as he headed to the kitchen in his socks, briefs and sweaty undershirt. His office was set up in the dining room, and as he passed by it, he was shocked by what was on his computer screen.

'My God,' he exclaimed as he pulled out a chair and placed his hands on the keyboard.

Glowing on his computer screen was the city crime map. Beat 219 was filled with little blue fish and outlined in flashing red. That particular area of second precinct was bordered by Chippenham Parkway to the west, Jahnke Road to the north, railroad tracks to the east and Midlothian Turnpike to the south. Brazil's first thought was that some terrible disaster had happened within those boundaries since he had marked End Of Tour twenty minutes ago. Perhaps there had been a riot, a bomb threat, an overturned chemical truck, a hurricane watch.

He got on the phone and called the radio room. Communications Officer Patty Passman answered.

'This is unit 11,' Brazil announced abruptly. 'Is something big going down on Southside, specifically in beat 219?'

'You marked EOT at 1924 hours,' Passman came back.

'I know,' Brazil ten-foured.

'Then why are you asking about 219? Are you monitoring the scanner?'

'Ten-10,' Brazil let her know he wasn't. 'Is something on it about 219?'

'Ten-10,' Passman said as radio chatter sounded in the background.

'Oh. I thought when you asked if I was monitoring 219 maybe you meant that something was going on,' Brazil said, realizing that ten-codes were not necessary over the phone.

'Ten-10, unit 11,' said Passman, who no longer knew how to talk in anything but. 'Ten-12, unit 11,' she told him to stand by. 'Ten-10,' she came back. 'Nothing 10-18,' she let him know nothing urgent was afoot.

'What about anything at all?' Brazil couldn't let it go.

'How many times do I have to 10-9 myself?' She was getting increasingly impatient as she let him know she wasn't going to repeat herself again.

'What about a fish truck overturning, for example?'

'What?'

'Anything that might have to do with fish? Blue ones, maybe?'

'Ten-12,' she told him to stand by again. 'Hey, Mabie!'

Passman inadvertently keyed the mike. Brazil and all on the radio, including felons and hobbyists with scanners, could hear every word.

'Anything come in about fish?' Passman was saying in a loud voice to dispatcher Johnnie Mabie.

'Fish? Who wants to know?'

'Eleven.'

'What kind of fish?'

'Blue fish. Maybe a truck overturning or a problem with one of the fish markets or something.'

'I'll have to get hold of an inspector. Unit 709.'

Horrified, Brazil snapped on his scanner.

'Seven-oh-nine,' the inspector's voice blurted into Brazil's dining room.

'Anything going on with fish in second, specifically in 219?' dispatcher Mabie came back.

'Who's fish?' 709 responded.

'Anybody's.'

'I meant is Fish a subject?' 709 qualified. 'Or are you referencing fish?'

'Fish,' Passman bullied Mabie out of the way. 'A fish spill, for example.'

'Ten-10,' 709 replied after a long pause. 'Possible fish could be an a.k.a.?'

Passman got back on the phone without ever having gotten off it, really. She posed the question to Brazil. He could think of no wanted subject with the alias *Fish* or *Blue Fish.* Brazil thanked her and hung up as other units began calling in with insincere questions and mocking tips about *fish* and *fishy* people, incidents, situations, false alarms, mental subjects, prostitutes and pimps named one or the other, and vanity plates. Brazil snapped off the scanner, furious that the Richmond cops now had one more thing to ridicule him about.

Reporters and camera crews were out in force this night, stalking La Petite France, waiting for Governor Mike Feuer and his wife, Ginny, to emerge from a power dinner of fine French food and warm chats with the chef.

The media wasn't necessarily interested in the Virginia Economic Development Section of the *Forbes* magazine CEO kickoff banquet going on inside. But Governor Feuer had appeared on *Meet the Press* over the weekend. He had made controversial statements about crime and tobacco, and *Richmond Times-Dispatch* police reporter Artis Roop felt dissed because the governor had not given the quotes to him first.

For weeks Roop had been working on a significant series about the impact of black-market cigarettes on crime and life in general. Roop believed if the price of Marlboros, for example, climbed as high as thirteen dollars and twenty-six cents a pack, as predicted by financial analysts as recently as the end of trading today, citizens would start growing tobacco in hidden places, such as cornfields, wooded backyards, backyards enclosed by high walls, greenhouses, logging roads, private gardens, private clubs and anywhere that ATF might not look. Citizens would begin illegally manufacturing their own cigarettes, and who could blame them.

The country would revert to the days of stills, or *smokes,* as Roop called the imagined contraption necessary to make bootleg tobacco products. He further theorized that in Virginia, especially, people would get away with operating smokes, since not a day went by when there wasn't controlled burning, a forest fire, a fire in a landfill or on a hearth somewhere. Smoke drifting from acres of trees or refuse or out of the chimneys of historic homes would not necessarily raise suspicions.

Roop was smart enough to know that if he was one of the twenty or thirty aggressive members of the media perched outside the restaurant door, he would not get special treatment. He had wisely chosen to sit in his car, monitoring the scanner as usual. He had been perplexed and excited when he picked up something about a fish spill in second precinct's beat 219. Roop was a streetwise investigator. He was certain *fish spill* was a code for big trouble, and he would get the scoop as soon as he finished with the governor.

Even as he was thinking *Shit,* and staring at the computer screen, it suddenly came to Brazil that what he was seeing was not COMSTAT computer mapping at all, but a clever, creative screen saver that someone had downloaded into the police department's new website.

'I'll be damned.' He was incredulous.

He noticed the light flashing on his answering machine. He played his messages. There were three. The first was from his mother, who was almost too drunk to talk and demanding to know why he never called. The second was Miss Sink making sure he had gotten the sweet potato pie she'd delivered, and the third was from West, wanting him to call right away.

Brazil knew her number, even though he never dialed it. He switched to speakerphone, his pulse running harder, hands busy on the keyboard to no avail. He could not get rid of the screen saver or alter it in any way.

'Virginia?' He ran his fingers through his hair and strangled his nervousness before it could speak. 'I'm returning your call,' he said easily.

'There's something bizarre going on with the computer.' She was all business.

'Yours too?' He couldn't believe it. 'Fish?'

'Yes! And get this. I leave home this morning and my computer's off, right. Then I come home and not only is it on now, but there's this map of 219 with all these little blue fish swimming around in it.'

'Has anyone been inside your house today?'

'No.'

'Your alarm was set?'

'Always.'

'You sure you didn't just *think* you turned your computer off?'

'Well, I don't know. It doesn't matter. What are all these fucking fish? Maybe you should come over.'

'I guess you're right,' Brazil hesitated to say as his heart beat harder to make itself heard.

'We've got to get to the bottom of this,' West said.

Chief Hammer had been fighting with her computer for the past hour, trying to figure out how the city crime map had gotten on her screen and why there were fish in it. She tapped keys and rebooted twice while Popeye restlessly paced about, in and out of her toybox, scratching, standing on her hind legs, and jumping on furniture and finally into Hammer's lap.

'How am I supposed to concentrate?' Hammer asked for the tenth time.

Popeye stared up at Hammer as she pointed the mouse at an X and tried again to exit the map on her screen. This was crazy. The computer was locked. Maybe Fling had screwed up the software. That was the risk when all PCs had to log into the microprocessor downtown. If Fling put a bug in the system, everybody on the Richmond network was infected. Popeye stared at the screen and touched it with her paw.

'Stop it!' Hammer said.

Popeye stepped on several keys that somehow jumped Hammer off the map and landed her on an unfamiliar screen with the heading RPD PIKE PUNT. Under it were strings of programming that made no sense: *IM to $im__on* and *available* and *AOL% findwindow('AOL Frame2.5' , 0&),* and so on.

'Popeye! Now look what you've done. I'm in the

operating system where I absolutely don't belong. Let me tell you something, I'm not a neurosurgeon. I don't belong here. I touch one thing and I could braindamage the entire network. What the hell did you hit and how am I supposed to get out?'

Popeye stepped on several keys again, and the map and fish returned. She jumped to the floor, stretched and trotted out of the room. She came back with her stuffed squirrel and started slinging it. Hammer swiveled her chair around and looked at her dog.

'Listen to me, Popeye,' Hammer said. 'You've been home all day. When I left the house this morning, my computer was on the main menu. So how could it be that when I walked in just a little while ago I find this map with all those little fish? Did you see anything? Maybe the computer made noises and things started happening on it? We don't have fish in any of our COMSTAT applications that I am aware of.'

She reached for the phone and called Brazil, catching him just before he was out the door.

'Andy? We've got trouble,' she said instantly.

'Fish?' he asked.

'Oh God. You too,' she said.

'And Virginia. Same thing.'

'This is awful.'

'I'm on my way to her house right now.'

'I'm coming,' Hammer said.

chapter nine

The adult bookstore was enjoying a steady business at twenty minutes past eight, when Smoke parked between a Chevrolet Blazer with eight-inch superlift and 39x18.5 custom tires, and a granny-low Silverado 2500. He turned the engine off, waiting for a break in spent, dazed, afraid-the-wife-or-mother-would-find-out male traffic exiting the small sex shop.

A gimpy old man in overalls emerged from the door, looking this way and that, Viagra worn off, face wan, exhausted and paranoid in the sick glow of neon lights. He stuffed a bandanna into his back pocket and checked his fly and touched the side of his neck to see what his pulse was doing. He was unsteady as he made a dash for his El Camino. Smoke waited until it was spitting gravel and lurching onto Midlothian Turnpike. He knew his way through the woods so well he didn't turn on the flashlight until he reached the plywood entrance of his clubhouse.

Candles had long since been snuffed out, the gang gone except for its newest member. Weed was sitting in his own vomit on a mattress, hands and ankles bound with belts. He was shaking and whimpering.

'Shut up,' Smoke said, shining the light in Weed's terrorized face.

'I didn't do nothing,' Weed muttered repeatedly.

Smoke quickly undid the belts, keeping his distance and not breathing.

'Maybe I ought to dump your ass,' he said in disgust. 'You're nothing but a puny little pussy. Throwing up all over the place and crying like a queer. Well, I'll tell you one thing, Mr. Picasso. You're cleaning up this place before you go anywhere.'

West was running around her house, picking up, straightening up, throwing out pizza and fried chicken boxes, stuffing dishes into the dishwasher while Niles stuck with her feet like a soccer ball.

'Get out of my way,' West told Niles. 'Where's your mouse? Go get your mouse.'

Niles wouldn't. West trotted into the bedroom. She sat on the left side, where she didn't sleep, and bounced up and down. She punched the pillow and rumpled the spread. She ran back into the kitchen and got two wineglasses out of a cupboard. She dusted them, swirled a small amount of Mountain Dew in each, raced back to the bedroom and placed them on the bedside tables. She dropped a pair of athletic socks that could have passed for a man's.

She was out of breath when she hurried inside her office and began digging in drawers for a greeting card, maybe a letter that looked suspiciously personal from someone besides Brazil, who had written her often back in days that meant nothing to her anymore. She came across a florist's card still in its envelope, her name typed on it. She walked quickly into the foyer and dropped the card on a table, in plain view of anyone who came through the front door.

Bubba was late, the night without a moon or stars or possibility of redemption. He had no choice but to exceed the speed limit on Commerce Road. He had no time to indulge in nostalgia as he sped by the Spaghetti Warehouse, where he had taken Honey last Mother's Day, despite their not having children. Bubba did not want them, because Bubba believed the Flucks, especially those named Butner, were overbred and had reached the end of the line.

Bubba smoked and rode hard past Sieberts Towing, and Fire Station # 13, Cardinal Rubber & Seal, Estes Express, Crenshaw Truck Equipment Specialists, Gene's Supermarket, John's Seafood & Chicken, and all the other businesses paralleling I-95. It had begun to rain, limber drops diving through the crack in the Jeep's roof and kicking below the rearview mirror and over polyurethane before touching the dashboard in record time. The Lucky Strike water tower and tip of the Marlboro sign loomed on the horizon no matter which way Bubba turned, reminding him that cigarette making, like life, went on.

Bubba felt hateful toward Muskrat because he had refused to do anything further to Bubba's leaky Jeep. Bubba was angry with Honey, who had not lived up to her name when he had finally gotten home. She had not apologized for gummy Kraft macaroni and cheese and charred Tombstone pizza, both dashed with too much Parm Plus! Seasonal Blend. Honey cared not that Bubba's ritual glass of Capri Sun was tepid, the Jell-O cheesecake warm, or that the Maxwell House left over from breakfast could have blacktopped the driveway.

Honey had gone from ridiculing the Cheez Whiz and Miracle Whip that Philip Morris had spread over the earth, to launching into a weepy litany that Bubba could not escape because she had hidden his car keys. He did not know what had gotten into her. Before this night, she had never caused him to be late for work, even though she had no way of knowing that he wasn't really late because he was going in early to cover the second half of Tiller's shift.

Philip Morris sparkled like a jewel and was as perfectly pitched as a tuning fork amid the depressing tarnish and unbearable discord of the awful traffic and endless road repairs of I-95. The grounds of the 1.6-square-mile administrative offices and manufacturing plant were immaculate, the expansive green often used as a helipad by those of a higher order that Bubba revered and rarely saw. Shrubs were perfectly sculpted. Japanese maple, crabapple, Bradford pear and oak trees were lush and precisely placed.

Over the years, Bubba had become increasingly convinced that Philip Morris had been sent to earth on a mission that, like God's will, wasn't entirely revealed but merely hinted at, even to its well-paid chosen employees. Bubba had never been inside a building with so much varnished parquet and sparkling glass surrounded by gardens so splendid they had been dedicated by Lady Bird Johnson.

Big video screens communicated to workers from all corners, the industry's technology so secret that not even Bubba understood half of what he did every day. Bubba knew it was all too enlightened to be of this world. He had come up with a theory that he discussed only with those who had, over time, been drawn into the secret society of Alien Ship Helpers, or ASH.

ASHlings believed the fourteen thousand cigarettes produced per minute, twenty-four hours a day, seven days a week, were really fuel rods needed by the massive throbbing engine room that propelled the spacecraft through dimensions one could accept only on faith. These fuel rods were inert unless burned, and this required millions of humans to help out by lighting up and causing the collective combustion needed to keep the spacecraft moving at warp speed through its secret dimension.

It made perfect sense to Bubba that the good and loving Consciousness had figured out long ago the planet wasn't going to make it unless IT intervened. It followed logically, according to Newton's Third Law, that if all actions cause an equal and opposite reaction, there would have to be an Evil Force who liked things exactly the way they were and wanted them to get worse.

Thus it was, as more combustible fuel rods were produced and ignited around the planet, the Evil Force got increasingly desperate and irritable. It studied history to figure out what had worked in the past. It came up with a destructive and divisive campaign of nonsmokers' rights that instantly resulted in discrimination, hate groups, censorship and fame for the surgeon general. Sweeping anti-smoking campaigns, lawsuits, horrendous taxes and bloody skirmishes on the Senate floor unfurled like the Southern Cross and sent litigious and greedy troops into a senseless war that could be watched by all on CSPAN and CNN.

The ASHlings alone knew that if the campaign of evil aggression caused people to quit lighting up, soon there would be no more combustion, except by cars, which didn't count. The production of fuel rods would cease. The engine room would be silenced. The alien spacecraft would have no choice but to change course lest it be powerless and adrift.

Bubba was thinking about all this and was in quite a state by the time he stopped at the guard booth and Fred, the guard, opened his window.

'How ya doing, Bubba?' Fred asked.

'I'm late,' Bubba said.

'Seems to me you're early. You don't look like you're in a good mood.'

'I didn't read the paper today, Fred. Didn't have time. How're we doing?'

Fred's face darkened. He was a closet ASHling and often conspired with Bubba when Bubba rolled up in his piece-of-shit Jeep and displayed his parking permit.

'You saw the video board downtown, that Dow Jones display in front of Scott and Stringfellow?'

'Didn't get there.'

'Bubba, it's getting worse,' Fred told the truth in a hushed voice. 'It's up to eleven ninety-three a pack. Help us, Lord.'

'No, it can't be right,' Bubba said.

'Oh yeah it is. Let me tell ya, they're talking about taxes and settlements pushing up the price even higher, as much as twelve dollars a pack, Bubba.'

'And then what?' Bubba angrily blurted out. 'Black market. Bootlegging. Layoffs. And what about the cause?'

'Won't help the cause, no sir,' Fred agreed, shaking his head as Bubba held up traffic.

'You got that straight. Most of the rods, especially Marlboros, will end up overseas. Meaning the ship will head that way, following the smoke to the Far East. And where does that leave America?'

'Farther down the drain, Bubba. I'm glad I'm past sixty-five, can retire tomorrow if I want, have a drawer in the new mausoleum at Hollywood Cemetery and know if I pass on tonight, I spent my life in the right camp.'

Fred lit a Parliament and shook his head again as the line of cars behind Bubba got longer.

'People these days don't see beyond their damn hood ornaments, which are a helluvalot nicer than yours and mine, Bubba, because of all these people suing and getting rich for faking coughs and blaming ailments on deep pockets. And I ask you, Bubba. Did we stick the goddamn things in their mouths and tell 'em to inhale? Did we blindfold 'em and line 'em up against the wall and say we're gonna shoot 'em if they didn't light up? Did we force 'em off the highway into Seven-Elevens at all hours of the night? Did we make Bogart smoke in the movies?'

The unfairness and downright criminality of it all sent Fred into a fury. The line of cars was almost out to Commerce Road, dozens of other Philip Morris employees about to be late as Bubba was no longer early.

'Tell it, brother.' Bubba couldn't agree more. 'Why don't we just sue waste treatment plants because it's their fault we shit.'

'Amen.'

'Why don't we just drag KFC to court because we're gonna drop dead of a stroke.' Bubba was inspired.

'How's your cholesterol doing, by the way, Bubba?'

'Honey keeps bugging me to get a checkup. Who the hell has time?'

'Well, I have a new attitude about it,' Fred said. 'I've decided if your body says "Eat eggs" or "Sprinkle a little salt," it's talking to you, telling you what it needs.' Fred crushed out the cigarette. 'Course, if I get high blood pressure, I'll just sue the umbrella right out of that little Morton Salt girl's hands!'

Bubba guffawed. Fred laughed so hard his eyes watered. He began waving cars around them. Drivers were panicked as they sped past the guard booth, competing for parking.

brazil was panicking, too. It occurred to him that neither he nor anyone else would be able to fix the new website he had begged Hammer to delay until the department had someone other than Fling banging away on the keys every day.

Brazil was computer literate and actually quite good at understanding instructions and help files, unlike West, who had no patience for any sort of tool or material she couldn't grip in her hand or saw in two. But Brazil could not cure computer viruses, and he was convinced the blue fish were a fulminating eruption caused by a fatal new strain that had slipped in unnoticed, perhaps because it was widely assumed if one abstained from practicing unsafe disks, there was nothing to worry about. How could he have been so naive? How could he have been so careless when he knew damn well that viruses could be transmitted over the Internet, and therefore his website had put all of COMSTAT in jeopardy?

Brazil's heart battered his ribs as he drove his cosmos V6 BMW Z3. The leather still smelled new, the paint was without a flaw, yet he didn't love the car the way he did the vintage BMW 2002 that had belonged to his father. When Brazil had covered it and left it at his childhood home in Davidson, he had thought it was the thing to do. It was time to start over. It was time to leave his past. Maybe it was time to finally get away from his alcoholic mother.

He passed through the endless intersections and one-way streets of the Fan, avoiding bicycles and pedestrians and the crowds trying to get in and out of Helen's, Joe's Inn, Soble's, Konsta's, Commercial Tap House, Southern Culture and various markets and Laundromats. Brazil was terrified of telling Hammer the truth about COMSTAT, and worse, parking wasn't possible in West's part of town. Brazil had no luck, and groaned when he saw Hammer turning up and down narrow streets, impatient and picking up speed, for whenever she could not get somewhere, she did it in a hurry.

Brazil parked in front of a fire hydrant as a Mercedes V12 roared away from a curb and a Jeep Cherokee tried to bulldoze its way into the space. Brazil jumped out of his car, trotted over to the Jeep and held up his hand to halt. Shari Moody was at the wheel. She scowled as she rolled down her window.

'Look, I was here first,' she said.

'That's not the issue,' Brazil told her.

'It sure as hell is.'

'I'm Richmond Police.'

'The whole department?' she scoffed.

'An officer.'

'*An officer?* Just one?' she said sarcastically.

'There's no point in being rude, ma'am.'

'Police officers don't drive BMWs and you're in jeans,' she retorted. 'I'm so sick and tired of people trying to cheat me out of parking just because I'm a woman.'

Brazil got out his creds and displayed them as he noted Hammer racing by again.

'We drive all kinds of cars and aren't always in uniform,' Brazil explained to Shari Moody, whose parking place he was going to appropriate. 'Depends on what we're doing, ma'am, and gender has nothing to do with it.'

'Bullshit,' she said, popping gum as she argued. 'If I was a guy, you wouldn't be standing here.'

'Yes, I would.'

'What are you going to do, anyway? Give me a ticket for something I didn't do, as usual. You know how many tickets I get just because I'm a woman in a four-by-four?'

Brazil had no idea.

'Lots,' she said. 'If I had a Suburban or, God forbid, a Ford F-350 Crew Cab with a four-hundred-and-sixty-cubic-inch engine, a brush guard and tow package, I'd probably be on fucking death row.'

'I'm not giving you a ticket,' Brazil told her. 'But I'm afraid you're in a U.Z. and I'm going to have to ask you to leave for your own protection.'

'An Uzi?' She was suddenly frightened and locked her doors. 'You mean drug dealers with machine guns are in this neighborhood, too?'

'This is an Unsafe Zone,' Brazil explained in his best police tone. 'We've been having an epidemic of Jeeps broken into around here.'

'Ohhhhh,' she said as it dimly came to her. 'I've read about that. The cabbage thing.'

'You definitely don't want to park your Jeep here, ma'am,' Brazil told her as Hammer flew by again, going faster the other way.

'Well, gee,' Ms. Moody said, finally easing up and appreciating how good-looking and helpful the cop was. 'I sure am glad you told me. You new around here? Some way I can get hold of you if I need further information about U.Z.s and the cabbage problem?'

Brazil gave Ms. Moody his card and moved her along. He managed to flag down Hammer as she was racing through the intersection again. He motioned her into the space at the curb, got back into his car and had to park five blocks away, close to a rundown section of West Cary where citizens stared at him from porches and calculated how much a chop shop would pay for his car.

chapter ten

Bubba hurried along in his blue uniform and safety shoes and earplugs, already getting sweaty as he race-walked through two filter rooms. He trotted under the observation deck that had not been used since Philip Morris had started giving scheduled tours on small trains.

He ran and walked and ran and walked over shiny floors filled with spotless beige Hauni Protos II and G.D. Balogna making machines, computers and OSCAR units in bays where the roar and rat-a-tatting of production never ceased and there was no such thing as dirt or killing time.

Driverless, bright yellow robotic cars loaded with cases of cigarettes hummed back and forth, pausing to recharge at computerized magnets, never tiring or loitering or forming unions. Gray-uniformed maintenance workers zipped back and forth in supply carts and were careful turning corners and passing through busy intersections.

Huge spools spun cellulose too fast to see while thousands of pristine white cigarettes flowed down tracks and were fed into veins that configured them in rows of

7-6-7 for soft packs and 6-7-7 for flip-top boxes before a plunger kicked them into a pocket where they were wrapped in double-wide foil which was married to blanks that were labeled and glued on the sides and fed into big wheel drying drums and finished in cellophane and tear tape and marched single file into stacker towers where ten-packs were pushed into cartons that were carried by elevators up to exit stations with conveyor belts that eventually carried cases out of the building to awaiting trucks.

Bubba was breathless when he reached Bay 8, where he was a maker operator, or more formally, a tech 3, the highest pay grade. His responsibility was huge. He was the sole captain of a module that had been predicted to produce exactly 12,842,508 cigarettes by the end of this day's twenty-four-hour period, or 4,280,836 cigarettes during Bubba's eight-hour shift.

No module was ever unattended at Philip Morris, and Bubba's supervisor, Gig Dan, had been forced to fill in for the last half of second shift and the first sixteen minutes of third. Dan was relieved but unhappy when Bubba appeared, dripping sweat and panting.

'What in the hell has gotten into you, Bubba?' Dan said loud enough for both of them to hear through their earplugs.

'I got pulled by the cops,' Bubba bent the truth.

'And getting a ticket took four and a half hours?' Dan didn't buy it.

'He spent a long time warning me and then the radio was down or something. I'm telling you, I was pissed.

There's a lot of police bullying going on out there, Gig. It's time some of us got involved and . . .'

'Right now, I just want you to get involved in your module, Bubba!' Gig Dan yelled above machines. 'Our goal today was fifteen million and we were some 719,164 below that even before you decided to take your time smelling the roses!'

'I wasn't . . .' Bubba tried to protest.

'So guess what? The latest readout has us at 3,822,563.11 this shift, which is exactly 458,272.0 below what we were gonna make when we were already below what we were damn supposed to make. And why? The tipping paper's already broke twice, rejects is three times the usual because the circumference dropped below 24.5 and the weight didn't hit even close to nine hundred and the dilution was minus eight percent, and then the glue got a bubble because there was air in the line, and why?

'Because you weren't here to hand-feed five lousy cigarettes into the Sodimat. You didn't inspect the quality. You didn't check out the machines because you were too goddamn busy getting stopped by the police or whatever the hell it was you were supposedly doing!'

'Don't worry,' Bubba told him loudly. 'I'll make up the slack.'

Brazil was late, too, through no fault of his own. He had jogged in the dark from his endangered car, back to Park Avenue, and when he reached West's apartment he took a moment to settle down. He rang the bell and she wasn't the least bit warm as she let him in.

'Where have you been?' she asked, standing in front of the foyer table.

'Trying to find a deli,' Brazil said dryly.

'What for?'

'A deli, a restaurant, a bank. Anyplace I could maybe park.'

'Obviously you succeeded,' she said.

'Depends on if my car's still there after we're done.'

She oddly continued to stand in front of the table, and he sensed there was something on it she didn't want him to see.

'We're in my office. On the left, just past the bedroom.' She waited for him to go first as she continued to stand in front of the table.

Brazil was already getting a sick feeling. He didn't want to see what was on the table. He walked past the bedroom and refused to look inside. He entered West's office and didn't look around. Hammer was sitting close to the desk, reading glasses on, eyes fixed on the strange map on the computer screen.

'What were you saying to that woman in the Jeep?' Hammer asked him right off. 'The one whose parking place I took.'

'I told her she was in a garbage zone.'

'A what?' West said as she walked in.

'Where trucks pull in and out all night as they make their rounds to restaurant Dumpsters. I showed her my badge and she complied.'

'You probably shouldn't have done that,' Hammer told him. 'You got anything to drink in this house, Virginia?'

'Good stuff?'

'I'm driving my police car.'

Brazil found a chair and set it down near Hammer.

'Water and Sprite,' West said.

'What about Perrier?' Hammer asked.

'Not since the benzene scare.'

'That's ridiculous, Virginia. When chickens get avian flu, do you never eat them again?'

'Has that happened recently? I got Diet Coke.'

'Tap water is fine,' Hammer said. 'Andy, we've been sitting here talking and not getting anywhere at all. Do you have a clue as to what this is about? Please explain how fish got into COMSTAT.'

'Well, they didn't, not directly, Chief Hammer,' Brazil said. 'And I'd love some water, too,' he said to West. 'But I can get it. I can get Chief Hammer's, too, if you want. I'd be happy to.'

'I'll do it. And don't be so polite, it makes me sick.'

'I'm sorry.' Brazil was polite again.

It was awful being inside West's home and reminded that she had never invited him over, not even once since they had moved to Richmond. It was the first time he had seen her in anything but business suits or running clothes, and she was wearing the worn-out jeans that had always driven him crazy. Her gray tee shirt was made out of really soft cotton that clung to every contour of full breasts he was no longer allowed to see, much less touch. He ached all over.

'If you look at the top of the screen here.' He ran his finger across the monitor, addressing Hammer as if West had been caught up in the rapture, never to be seen again. 'This tells you what we're looking at is our website, because that's its address.'

'No,' Hammer said in disbelief.

''Fraid so,' Brazil said.

Hammer and West bent close to the screen and stared in shock at:

http://www/sen__orrin__hatch__r__utah.govsen__bill__10/sen__judic__commit/dept__justice/nij/nypd__1__pol__plaza/comstat/comp__map__center__dc/interpol/scot__yrd/fbi/atf/ss/dea/cia/va__nat__guard/va__state__pol/va__corr__dept/va__crim__just__serv/juv__just__serv/va__att__gen/va__gov__off/va__dept__health/va__dept__safety/city__mang/gsa/city__hall/city__counc//rich__pol__dept/off__pub__info/qa/rich__times__disp/ap/upi/link_ntwk/all_rights_resrv/classfyd/asneed/othrwyz/pub__domain.html

'Andy, I've never seen such shit as this,' Hammer exclaimed. 'Please don't tell me this is how the public accesses our website.'

'I'm afraid that's it,' Brazil told her anyway.

'How the hell do you expect anyone to remember something like that?' West asked, scowling at the screen.

Brazil ignored her. 'At least it works,' he said. 'We know that much since we've gotten some responses.'

'But why the hell is ours so goddamn complicated?'

Hammer wanted to know. 'How many responses are we going to get with an address like that?' She paused for a minute, a shadow falling over her face. 'Don't tell me Fling had something to do with this.'

Silence.

'Oh God,' Hammer muttered.

'Well,' Brazil answered her, 'you wanted this ASAP, Chief Hammer. It was a matter of finding gateways to pass through en route to our website, sort of the way mail is routed here and there before it finally gets to you, or the way you may have to change planes at four different airports before you get where you need to go . . .'

'Oh great,' West said. 'So Fling has people going to fifty different airports just to get from one end of the city to the other. He has the post office routing a letter through twenty different states just to travel two blocks.'

'To give Fling a little credit, the more gateways, the more secure your system is,' Brazil said objectively.

'Ha!' West really snorted this time. 'We're safe, all right! The damn website's been up and running for a few days and we have fucking fish all over the place and are locked out of COMSTAT!'

'It would also seem to me,' Hammer followed the bread crumbs of what little logic there seemed to be in this dark forest, 'that the security situation is rather much the opposite of what you said, Andy. It would seem to me that the more gateways, the more possibility of outsiders getting in. Like doors in your house. The fewer the better.'

'There's that side of it, too,' Brazil agreed. 'Look, to be

honest, I had no idea Fling put together an address like that until it was too late.'

Hammer peered at the screen some more. Her disgust grew.

'Let me make sure I've got this straight,' she said. 'The first gateway to our small Richmond website is Senator Orrin Hatch, the chairman of the judiciary committee, the patron of Senate Bill 10?'

'Yes,' Brazil replied calmly as he imagined pepper-spraying Fling and throwing him off an overpass.

'What does the Violent and Repeat Juvenile Offender Act of 1997 have to do with our website, Andy?' Hammer demanded.

Brazil didn't have a clue.

'And from that we go through Interpol and Scotland Yard? And FBI, ATF, DEA, Secret Service and CIA gateways?'

Hammer got up abruptly and began pacing.

'And NYPD at One Police Plaza? And the Virginia governor's office? And goddamn city hall, yada, yada, yada?'

She threw up her hands in despair.

'Is there any fucking place on the earth where inquiries from the Richmond public won't land before they get to our website?' Hammer's voice rose dangerously.

Niles fled out from under the table, where he had been asleep on top of West's foot.

'Look!' Brazil could take no more. 'I had nothing to do with the Internet address, okay? All the important programming was done by NIJ's Computer Mapping

Center. Fling was just supposed to come up with a very simple address.'

'And now we have fish!' Hammer exclaimed.

'We don't know that the address has anything to do with the fish getting in.' Brazil didn't believe what he was saying. 'They might have gotten in anyway, no matter how short the address.'

West got up for another Miller.

'Let's forget the address shit for a minute,' she called out from the kitchen. 'This web thing is new.'

'As new as slick-soled shoes,' Brazil said to Hammer instead of answering West.

West glared at him as she returned to the table. She hated it when he made analogies. She hated it more when he pretended she was a lamp, a chair, some mundane object he didn't notice.

'Yes, it's exactly like that,' said Hammer, who had slipped across marble and hardwood quite enough in life whenever new shoes had all-leather soles that needed to be roughed up by bricks, pavement or perhaps a serrated knife.

'So how does somebody know enough about our brand-new website to download fish?' West asked. 'I mean, come on. We all know damn well the fucking Fling address is how the fish got in.'

'That's a very good point,' said Hammer.

'The op-ed that ran Sunday a week ago. Remember? I said we were starting a web page so citizens could write in their questions, concerns, complaints, whatever. They were told the new address would be ready in a couple days and they could call HQ for it. Obviously Fling gave it out.'

'That's how the fish swam in then,' West said again, gulping Miller. 'Got to be unless someone inside the department did this.'

'Sabotage. A virus,' Brazil thought out loud.

'I'm afraid that's also possible,' Hammer said. 'But saying it's not a virus or a deliberate attempt to crash the system, then there is the other thought that the fish might be a symbol, perhaps a code of some sort.'

'Probably making a joke of us, as usual,' West said. 'First we're the *Ninjas*, then the *Ni-Jays*, then the *Nee-gees.* Now we're fish. Maybe *fish out of water*, implying that everyone wants us to go home.'

'I don't think this is about us being fish out of water or fish, period,' Hammer stated.

'Maybe we're *fishing* for something, then.' West wouldn't let it go.

'Like what?' Brazil asked. 'And you know, if you don't mind, Chief, I think I'd like a beer.'

'I don't care.'

Brazil got up and went into the kitchen.

'Fishing for clues? For crime patterns? For hot spots?' West kept on.

'This is nonsense.' Hammer was pacing.

Niles slinked back into the dining room. Brazil was right behind him, sipping a Heineken.

'Took the good stuff,' he said politely to West. 'Hope you don't mind.'

'That's Jim's good stuff, not mine.'

Brazil sat down and drained half the bottle in one swallow.

'Andy,' Hammer was thinking. 'Is there any way to trace this fish-thing?'

He cleared his throat, his cheeks burning, his heart pounding irregularly and dully.

'I doubt it,' he said.

'Let's break it down for just a minute.' Hammer stopped pacing and leaned closer to the brilliantly colored map on the screen. 'Sector 219 is outlined in flashing bold red and there are one, two, three, four . . . , eleven bright blue fish inside it. Everywhere else we find just the usual icons.'

She looked at both of them.

'Possible this could be a warning of some sort?' she suggested.

'Fish?' Brazil thought about it. 'There are only a few fish markets in 219. No lakes or reservoirs or even many seafood restaurants except Red Lobster and Captain D's.'

'What possible illegal use could there be for fish?' Hammer explored. 'I can't imagine a black market in them, not unless there's a proposed fish bill we don't know about yet, a huge fish tax in the works and the lawsuits that would inevitably follow.'

'Hmmmm.' Brazil was willing to consider anything at this point. 'Let's just go down that path for a minute. Let's say this is going on in the Senate and no one knows about it yet. Well, since one of the primary gateways is the Senate Judiciary Committee, and saying fish is a big issue, then could it be we somehow picked up some of their coding as our data passed through?'

'I'm getting a headache,' Hammer said. 'And Virginia, would you please get your cat off my foot. He won't move. Is he dead?'

'Niles, come here.'

chapter eleven

Weed tried to get to his feet and fell back on his butt. He crawled across the floor, his new tattoo throbbing. Smoke lit half a dozen fat candles and carried over several gallon jugs of water and a roll of paper towels. Weed started cleaning up his mess and would have thrown up again had anything been left.

'Now, go outside and take your shirt and pants off,' Smoke said.

'What for?' Weed barely asked as his stomach heaved like a small boat on an upset ocean.

'You're not getting in my car stinking like that, retard. So go dump water over yourself until you're clean, unless you want to walk from here.'

Weed made his way carefully in wavering candlelight, stepping through the sliding glass door frames. He peeled off his shirt and jeans. It wasn't as warm out as it had been, and he shivered uncontrollably as he dumped three gallons of water over himself, his slight body clad in nothing but soaked boxer shorts and Nikes that sloshed when he walked.

'You got something for me to wear?' Weed asked Smoke, who was throwing down vodka again.

'What's wrong with what you got on?'

'I can't go anywhere like this!' Weed begged. 'Oh, man, my head hurts so bad. I feel real sick and I'm freezing, Smoke.'

Smoke handed him a Dixie cup of vodka. Weed just stared at it.

'Drink it. You'll feel better,' Smoke said.

He went behind cases of liquor and returned with a pair of folded Gottcha jeans, a black tee shirt, and Chicago Bulls jersey, windbreaker and cap.

'Your colors,' Smoke said proudly.

For an instant, Weed was happy and forgot his head throbbed. He felt important as he worked the relaxed-leg jeans over his soaked hightops and pulled the tee shirt and jersey over his head. He didn't want any more vodka but Smoke forced it on him.

Weed had very little awareness as he struggled and tripped after Smoke through dark woods and ended up at the adult bookstore, hiding behind cars until the coast was clear, then jumping inside the Escort and speeding away. Weed was beginning to think that things weren't too bad when Smoke stopped on a dark street corner in Westover Hills. He reached in back and pulled out two dark blue pillowcases. One was empty, the other filled with things that clanked and clacked together.

'Get out and keep your fucking mouth shut,' Smoke said. 'Don't make a fucking sound.'

Weed barely breathed as he followed Smoke along

Clarence Street to a simple white frame house surrounded by a picket fence that leaned this way and that and had uneven spaces between the boards. The redwood deck listed as if sailing into a stiff wind, and the big add-on garage was out of proportion to the rest of the house. An old Chevy Cavalier wagon was in the drive, lights were on in several rooms of the house and a dog was baying in its pen.

'Do exactly what I do,' Smoke whispered.

'What about the dog?' Weed said.

'Shut up.'

Smoke scanned the empty street, bent close to the ground and darted across the yard, ducking behind trees and finally crouching around the corner from the shut garage door. Weed was right behind him, his heart hammering as Smoke reached inside the pillowcase and pulled out a handful of remote controls. He tried one after another.

'Fuck,' he whispered as nothing happened.

On the eighth try, he got his reward. The Sears home-installed garage door cranked up slowly and sounded ill. No other lights went on inside, the dog barking and barking. Weed thought of running and Smoke seemed to know it because he grabbed him by the collar.

'Don't fuck with me,' he snarled in Weed's ear.

Smoke slid a small Mag-Lite out of a pocket. He looked around. The same windows in the house were lit up. There was no sign of motion.

'Follow me,' Smoke whispered.

Weed's brain was sliding around inside his skull like an

egg yolk. His vision was blurred. He grabbed Smoke's shirttail and crept along behind him, catching his toe on concrete, lurching inside the garage. Smoke stopped. He scanned, breathing hard, listening. He turned on the flashlight and the bright finger probed hundreds of shiny saws, drills, hammers and other tools Weed didn't recognize.

'Fucking unbelievable,' Smoke whispered. 'The asshole can't even hammer a nail straight and look at all this shit.'

He shone the light on a tall cabinet with a padlock that promised treasure inside. He didn't bother with the bolt cutters in the pillowcase because there was a better pair hanging on the peg rack. Smoke lifted it off the hooks and opened and closed the cruel steel beaks. He seemed pleased. He snapped through the lock as if it were soft lead and it pinged into the darkness, clanking against the floor.

Smoke quietly opened the doors. He ran the light over shelves of camouflage, targets, boxes of ammunition, revolvers, pistols, rifles and shotguns. His hands flew as he stuffed everything he could into the pillowcases Weed held open for him. Smoke filled the pockets of his relaxed-leg jeans, tucked handguns into his waistband. He snapped open a black plastic thirty-gallon bag and stuffed it and handed it to Weed. Smoke slung the bulging pillowcases over his shoulder like Santa Claus making the rounds for the NRA.

'Run!' Smoke whispered to Weed.

They clanked and banged across the yard and along the street, not going anywhere fast. They were sweating and miserable. They were slowing down when Smoke spotted a thick boxwood hedge and stashed the bags out of sight. Light of foot, they ran back to the Escort.

They jumped in and drove back to Clarence Street and parked by the hedge. The loot was where they'd left it. Smoke emptied his pockets and shut everything he had stolen inside the trunk. Not a single car passed. Nothing stirred. Bubba's dog barked the way it always did.

Smoke started laughing hysterically as he drove off. Weed had no idea where they were going. He had never broken the law in his life except for the time he drew a disrespectful picture of a teacher he didn't like and was sent to in-school suspension for two days.

'I just held the bag, so I didn't really steal anything, did I, Smoke?' Weed asked. 'I mean, I'm not keeping any of it, either. It's all yours, right?'

Smoke laughed harder.

'Where we going?' Weed dared to ask.

Smoke started digging through CDs.

'Can I go home now?' Weed asked.

'Sure,' Smoke said.

He started rapping to Master P.

'It don't look like we're going the right way.' Weed raised his voice.

Smoke told him to shut up. Somehow they ended up on West Cary Street, which was nowhere near Weed's neighborhood. Smoke stopped the car in the middle of the road.

'Get out,' he said.

'What for?' Weed protested. 'I can't get out here!'

'You're walking for a while. To make sure you're wide

awake when we pick you up later.'

Weed didn't know a thing about later. He didn't dare ask. Smoke's meanness was coiling and about to strike.

'Get out, retard,' Smoke warned.

'I don't know where I am.'

'Keep walking that way and you'll get to your street in a couple miles.'

Weed didn't move as he stared wide-eyed into the night, his head pounding. Smoke was checking his mirrors.

'Meet you two blocks from your house at three A.M. At Schaaf and Broadmoor,' Smoke said.

Weed didn't understand. His stomach was pushing everything the wrong way again.

'Bring your paints, retard. Whatever will work on a life-size metal statue in a graveyard.'

Weed opened his door and spat up bile on the pavement. He got out and almost fell again.

'Remember what happened last time when you were late,' Smoke reminded him. 'And anybody finds out what you're doing, I'm going to hurt you real bad.'

Weed stumbled to the side of the road and grabbed a speed-limit sign to steady himself. He watched Smoke's taillights vanish down the dark road. Weed sat down hard and begged God to help him. He got up and couldn't remember which way to go or where he was. He ducked behind walls and trees whenever headlights appeared, sometimes lying flat on his face and playing dead.

Niles was playing dead, too. He had given up trying to hint that he had been sitting right on top of his owner's desk the instant the fish appeared on the computer screen, which had been at exactly 12:47 this afternoon.

Niles had done nothing to cause this unusual event, and frankly had assumed his owner had loaded a new screen saver for Niles's benefit, since he was very fond of fish and his owner was always looking for ways to please him and occupy his attention so he'd stay out of trouble.

Hammer moved her feet again under the table. Niles held on, paws snugly around her ankles, claws tucked in so he didn't run her hose.

'What about using fish to body-pack cocaine,' West said.

'Virginia, that's brilliant,' Hammer said, shaking her feet again.

'Drugs could get in undetected from Maine, Miami, from almost anywhere,' West went on.

'I want narcotics on it right away,' Hammer said. 'And Andy, call NIJ's Crime Mapping Center first thing in the morning and see what they can tell us. We'll hope the fish problem's not pervasive, not an indication of a virus.'

'With an address like that,' Brazil was frank, 'I'm worried about how many sites on the network might have been affected.'

'Tell NIJ our situation is urgent, that we're locked out of COMSTAT until we can resolve this,' Hammer said. 'I've really got to head on and let Popeye out. Virginia, please get your cat so I can move.'

'Niles, enough!'

Niles draped over Brazil's shoe. Brazil leaned over and played Niles's ribs like piano keys. Niles purred. Niles was very fond of Brazil and had nicknamed him Piano Man when all of them lived in Charlotte and Piano Man and Niles's owner used to get along and play tennis and go shooting and watch movies and talk about Piano Man's eventually leaving the *Charlotte Observer* and becoming a cop so he could write stories about crime that would change the way people thought.

Niles wanted his owner and Piano Man to get along again, even if it meant being thrown off the bed every night. Niles was irritated with his owner. She wasn't being the least bit friendly to Piano Man and was annoyed that Niles was purring for him. Niles jumped in Piano Man's lap.

'Sorry. Gotta go,' Piano Man said to Niles.

'Thanks for the beer,' Brazil said politely to West as he scooted back from the table. 'Chief Hammer, I'll get you safely to your car.'

West showed them out. She stood in front of the foyer table again, but not in time. Brazil saw the florist's card with West's name typed on it.

'Good night,' West said to them.

chapter twelve

Brazil was jittery and angry as he trotted under streetlights along Mulberry, worrying that he would find his BMW gone or vandalized. He was tempted to turn around and show up at West's house, demanding an explanation.

It was true that their relationship in Charlotte had been somewhat complicated by their differences. She was older and accomplished. She had power. Her personality was the opposite of his. But she had been his mentor when he worked the police beat for the paper and rode the streets at night as a volunteer cop. Those had been the best stories Brazil had ever written. They had won prizes and changed the way people thought. They had changed the way he thought, too.

He had decided to become a real cop, as his father had been, and West had given Brazil the courage. She had helped him and loved him even through fights that were violent storms. When they made up it was always unbelievable. Brazil could not think of her without reliving every taste and touch. He did not know why she had changed so abruptly, and when he had asked, she would not say. It was as if they had never been lovers or even close friends. He did not push because maybe his primal fear was true. He just wasn't worth it. No one in his life had ever made him feel he was. His father had died when Brazil was a boy and Brazil's mother did not love herself and wasn't capable of loving anyone. For a while, West had filled a terrible space in Brazil's life. He hated Jim. How dare Jim send her flowers.

Smoke ordered Sick, Beeper, Dog and Divinity to keep an eye on Weed and make sure he didn't try taking a detour that might screw up their plans for the night.

So the Pikes set out in Dog's '69 Pontiac Lemans, cruising dark stretches of West Cary looking unsuccessfully for any sign of the drunk little motherfucker.

'I'm thirsty,' Divinity said.

'Fucking yeah,' said Beeper.

'Come on, Dog. Let's see you do your trick,' Divinity said.

Dog didn't like being thought of as a dog that did tricks. He never said anything, though. He pretty much just went along and did what he was told.

'What flavor you want this time?' Dog asked.

'Lemme see,' Divinity considered. 'How about something *ice,* baby? Maybe Michelob Ice? I'm fucking sick of Bud and all that other shit you're always getting that tastes like piss. 'Sides, baby, ice got more spin in it. You know, makes your head go round and around.'

She thought she was very funny and just loved laughing with herself. Dog pulled into a 7-Eleven and used his fake ID to buy a second six-pack of Michelob Ice while Beeper and Sick caused a diversion by Beeper's pretending to slip on the floor and Sick's having to help him up as Divinity browsed shelves and tucked whatever she wanted inside her denim bag.

'I think we find him we have some fun,' Dog said as he peeled out of the parking lot and started thinking about Weed again. 'I don't like him.'

'That's 'cause he paints, baby, and you can't do a fucking thing,' Divinity said.

Dog felt himself get meaner. 'He needs to learn about life,' Dog said. ''Bout showing respect.'

'You go about making him show respect and Smoke's gonna tear your ass off and feed it to a pit bull,' Divinity said as she sipped her beer.

'Fuck Smoke.' Dog turned back onto West Cary Street. 'I'm not fucking afraid of him.'

It wasn't true. Dog hadn't been Dog until last Christmas when he'd just turned fifteen and was shopping around for a little crack and ran into Divinity and Smoke at the mall on Chimborazo Boulevard. Smoke sold Dog a couple rocks and then pulled a pistol and stole the rocks back and kept Dog's money.

'Hey, gimme my money if you ain't giving me the rocks,' Dog told him.

'Not unless you earn it,' Smoke said.

Smoke talked Dog into robbing some woman at gunpoint downtown near the Monroe Building. Dog turned over forty-seven dollars to Smoke. Dog would never forget what Smoke said to him next.

'Now you're mine. I own you.' He pointed his Glock between Dog's eyes. 'You're my slave. Know why?'

Dog said he didn't.

'Because you ain't got shit in life. You go home to shit. You've got shit for brains. You're so fucking shitting stupid you came out here buying crack and robbed some poor old lady, probably gave her a heart attack. That could be murder if she dies. I might just have to tell the po-lice.'

'You can't.' Dog was so confused. 'But you can't do that.'

Smoke started laughing at Dog and Divinity joined in. Dog was named Dog and became a Pike. He started cutting school so much he got suspended all the time, which gave him permission to keep cutting school, which was kind of confusing, to him. So much was confusing, and whenever Dog questioned and maybe said he didn't want to rob nobody else or break into another car or restaurant, Smoke got in his bad way.

He knew how to hurt Dog and make Dog scared for his life. Smoke didn't mind killing. Dog had seen Smoke run over animals on purpose, like a cat the other day, and a puppy that was all the way off the road on someone's driveway. Smoke had a game he called 'Squash the Squirrel', which was just what it sounded like. Smoke would swerve all the hell over the place to run over a squirrel and he kept count. Smoke bragged he had killed somebody before in the city in North Carolina where he used to live.

He said he walked right into a crippled lady's house and stabbed her fifty times just so he could take her handicap van for a drive. He said he came back after ditching the van and stole whatever he wanted and fixed a sandwich and ate it, staring at her dead, bloody body and then opening up her clothes. He said she was so ugly he cut on her a little more in places he wasn't even supposed to look at. He said his grandmother used to live with his family until he punched her in the face and she decided to move. He said she had nagged him one last time and that was that.

Smoke said he got locked up for killing the crippled lady and was let loose free as a bird the minute he turned sixteen, and no one except his family knew what he had done and never would, because that was the way the law worked. Dog knew it wouldn't be long before Smoke killed somebody again. He had that need. Dog didn't want to be the one who filled it.

'Baby, oh baby,' Divinity suddenly said as she twisted the top off another beer. 'Look at that ride. Ummmm ummmm.'

'We gotta keep looking for Weed,' Beeper reminded her.

'Oh no,' Divinity told him. 'Uh uh, baby. Stop right here 'cause I'm getting out.'

At West Cary Street, the alarm sounding inside Brazil's head seemed as audible as a fire truck moving traffic out of the way. Three teenage boys and a girl who looked like a hooker were fondling Brazil's car as if they wanted to gang-rape it.

The boys were laughing, making their cool moves in wide-legged jeans half falling off, one leg rolled up, one down, big hightops, Chicago Bulls jerseys and stocking caps. The girl was dressed in a short tight black skirt and low-cut black tee shirt. They stared defiantly at Brazil and he stared back.

Brazil walked directly to his car, keys in hand, a Colt Mustang strapped around his right ankle under the leg of his worn-out jeans. His mood had been bad before he got here. Now it was dangerous.

'This your car, baby?' the girl asked.

'Yup,' Brazil replied.

'Where you get it?'

'Crown BMW on West Broad,' Brazil said with a smart-ass smile. 'They got a good selection.'

'Oh yeah?' the girl said. 'Well, Pretty Boy, that don't matter 'cause I just picked this one.'

Divinity decided she was the spokesperson for the gang. For one thing, she wasn't as drunk as the others. For another, the car man was as fine-looking as hell and she might just enjoy herself a little.

'Listen, baby.' Divinity stepped closer to him. 'Why don't you take little Divinity here on a little ride in that bad car of yours?'

She stepped closer. Pretty Boy moved back. The other three closed in. Pretty Boy was standing by the driver's door, street punks all around him.

'What's the matter, sugar?' Divinity brushed her fingers over Pretty Boy's chest. 'Euuuuu. What a man! Ummm-ummm.'

She pressed both of her hands against his muscular chest and liked what she was feeling.

'Don't touch me,' Pretty Boy said.

Beeper got in Pretty Boy's face.

'What'd you say to her, motherfucker?'

'I told her not to touch me. And get out of my face, asshole,' Pretty Boy said without raising his voice.

'Get outta my way,' Divinity told Beeper. 'He's mine.'

Beeper stepped aside. Divinity wanted to touch Pretty Boy again. She was getting interested in him touching her back. She leaned her breast against Brazil's arm.

'How's that feel, baby?' she cooed. 'It sure do feel good to me.'

'What the fuck you doing?' Dog exclaimed, grabbing her elbow and pulling her away.

'Man!' Sick started walking in cocky circles. 'Smoke see you, he kill all our asses!' he almost screamed.

Only Beeper kept his thoughts to himself. He seemed tired of Divinity showing off her parts as if she was some kind of V10 Viper that everybody wanted to drive.

'Let go of the white-meat boy,' Beeper suggested to her.

'Let's just take his car and get the fuck outta here,' Dog said nervously, looking around and wetting his lips.

'I'm not giving you the car,' Pretty Boy told them. 'It's not paid for.'

Divinity laughed and got close to him again.

'It's not paid for!' she hollered. 'It's not paid for! Oh baby, well it's good to know that 'cause we sure wouldn't want to steal no car that wasn't paid for!'

Sick, Dog and Beeper got into it. They started laughing and sneering, strutting around like badass chickens in a barnyard, pants hanging lower, boxer shorts riding higher.

Divinity put her hands on Brazil again, and she smelled like incense and her breath was bad. Her fingers trailed over his chest, and when she pressed up against him, grinding her pelvis into his, he shoved her away.

'You don't touch me unless I give permission,' Brazil told her in a tone that was four-star general.

'Motherfucker,' she hissed. 'Nobody pushes away Divinity.'

She reached under her short skirt and slipped out a thin switchblade. It zipped open, the long steel blade glinting in the uneven light of the street.

'Man, it's time to go,' the little mean kid with the buzz cut said.

'Put the fucking knife away,' the dumb one told Divinity.

'Get outta my face!' Divinity spat. 'You fuckheads leave, now. I got business to do and a nice new car to ride.'

'We leave you, Smoke will kill us,' the dumb one matter-of-factly stated.

'You don't and I'll kill you,' Divinity promised.

The three guys ran off. They disappeared around the

corner toward Robinson Street. Divinity pointed the knife at Brazil's throat, moving in.

'I thought you wanted to be alone with me,' Brazil said as if nothing had ever scared him or ever could. 'What kind of way is that to start?'

'Don't fuck with me,' Divinity said in a soft, menacing voice.

'I thought that's what you wanted me to do. Fuck with you.'

'When I'm finished with you, baby, you won't be fucking nothing no more.'

Brazil pointed the remote key at the BMW's door and the lock clicked free.

'You ever been in one of these?' he asked her as the knife caught light.

He knew he could grab her faster than she could stab, but he would get cut, probably badly. He had something else in mind. He opened the car door.

'What do you think?' he said.

Divinity couldn't keep her eyes from wandering inside, taking in the dark, soft leather upholstery and thick carpet.

'Climb in,' Brazil said.

She looked uncertain.

'What's the matter? You afraid to be seen with me?' Brazil asked. 'You afraid your boyfriend will do something?'

'I'm not afraid of nothing,' she snapped.

'Maybe I just need to look the part, huh?' Brazil said. 'Maybe I'm not dressed right, huh?'

He sat sidesaddle in the driver's seat. He pulled his Polo shirt over his head and tossed it in back. Divinity stared at his bare chest. Sweat was rolling down it. He picked a Braves baseball cap off the dashboard and put it on backward.

Divinity grinned. She lowered the knife.

'I got Nikes on already.' Brazil held up his right foot. 'So all I gotta do is roll up the pants leg and then you climb in with me, baby. And we'll drive the night away.'

Divinity started giggling. She started laughing harder when Brazil reached down and started rolling up his right pants leg. She gasped when Brazil was suddenly pointing the Colt Mustang between her eyes. The switchblade clattered to the pavement. Divinity started running. An old shark-gray Lemans roared around the corner and slammed on the brakes. The back door flew open and Divinity dove in. Brazil stood in the middle of West Cary Street, the gun by his side, his heart pounding.

He thought about chasing them, but his better judgment told him to leave well enough alone. The Lemans was gone so fast, Brazil got only a glimpse of a Virginia plate. He got back in his BMW and drove along West Cary toward home.

The first time the Lemans rolled by slowly, its muffler was dragging the pavement and making a terrible noise, sparks flying as if the car were a match trying to light the street.

The bass was up so high the night throbbed worse than

Weed's head, and he had scraped both palms when he dove into a ditch just in time. He had peeked through weeds and made out four people jumping around to the rap inside the car. One of them turned to look back as she drank out of a bottle. Weed had realized with horror that Divinity, Beeper, Sick and Dog were in that car and probably looking for him.

It was past ten the second time Weed heard the awful rumble of the souped-up engine and the clanging of the muffler and the boom-boom of the bass coming from a distance. He vaulted over a wall and crouched behind a spruce on the property of some rich person who lived in a brick mansion with big white pillars.

The Pikes disappeared down the road. Weed waited a good five minutes before he came out of hiding. He climbed back over the wall at the precise moment a small sports car purred around the bend, its high beams on and pinning Weed against the night like a moth against a window.

chapter thirteen

Bubba was too busy to take so much as one sip of Tang, which had been room temperature when Honey had spitefully filled his thermos, and therefore would still be room temperature if he ever had time to drink it. There wasn't the slightest chance Bubba would make it to the break room to microwave his Taco Bell Lunchable, which Honey had not ruined because she couldn't.

Bubba had not a moment to think about the Icehouse or Molson Golden or Foster's Lager filling the refrigerator in the mud room, waiting for him when he finally rolled in, exhausted, around half-past seven every morning except Tuesday and Wednesday, his days off. Bubba did not eat, drink or smoke anything that wasn't Philip Morris. He would have bought nothing but Philip Morris stock if he didn't spend so much on its products and his Jeep and tools.

Bubba Fluck's feelings were lacerated to the point of rage. He was being treated like shit as he tried like hell to speed things along in Bay 8. Sure, there had been a lot of rejects flying into the bins on the floor, destined for the ripper room, where they would be fed into a machine, the precious tobacco separated from the paper and reclaimed. Bubba refused to accept defeat. He figured if three shifts could crank out thirty million packs of cigarettes every twenty-four hours, then he, by God, could whip out an extra half a million cigarettes or twenty-five thousand packs before shift change.

Bubba worked like one possessed, dashing back and forth between the computer and the maker. When the resistance to draw got a little too close to the red line, Bubba was right there making the adjustment. He intuitively knew when he was going to run out of glue and made sure the attendant pulled up the cart early. When the tipping paper broke again, Bubba spooled it back through the air channel, up into the feed rollers, threaded it into the garnisher and hit reset in a record thirty-one seconds.

When the paper broke another time, he realized he had dull knives in the cutting head and summoned a fixer to take care of the problem. Bubba sweated through more lost minutes and worked even faster to make up the time. He ran three hours without another mishap, without stopping, and by four A.M., the production report on the computer screen showed Bubba was only 21,350 dual-rods, or less than two minutes, behind Bay 5.

Production supervisor Betty Council monitored quality and oversaw fixers and electricians, and coordinated shifts. She had been keeping her eye on Bubba for weeks because he seemed to have more technical problems than any of the other operators. Gig Dan had told her he was getting fed up with him.

'How are we doing?' she called out to Bubba as the vacuum in the maker sucked blended tobacco down, and rods formed almost faster than the eye could follow.

Bubba was too busy to answer.

'You don't have to kill yourself,' said Council, who was on her way to being promoted again because she was smart, hardworking, and several months ago had increased production three percent by encouraging competition among the bays.

'I'm fine,' Bubba said as rods were glued, cut, plucked into the transfer drum, carried to another knife and flipper, then to another drum. Plugs from the plug hopper were cut and married to the rods.

'I'm absolutely amazed,' she yelled above the roar and strike of machines. 'You and Smudge are almost neck and neck.'

Brazil stepped on the gas in pursuit of the kid half-falling and zigzagging on the side of the road. It was commonly accepted in policing that if a subject was running, usually there was a reason. Brazil rolled down his window.

'What's going on?' he called out as he drove and the kid continued to dash about.

'Nothing,' the kid gasped, the whites of his eyes showing all the way around as fear propelled his Nikes.

'Something is, or you wouldn't be running,' Brazil called back. 'Stop so I can talk to you!'

'Can't.'

'Yes, you can.'

'Uh-uh.'

Brazil pulled off the road ahead of him and jumped out. The kid was exhausted and intoxicated. He was wearing a Bulls jersey and looked vaguely familiar, even in the dark.

'Leave me alone!' he screamed as Brazil grabbed him by the back of his jersey. 'I didn't do nothing!'

'Whoa,' Brazil said. 'Calm down. Wait a minute. I've met you before. You're that kid at Godwin, the artist. A different sort of name. What was it . . . ? *Week? Wheeze?*'

'I'm not telling you nothing!' The kid was heaving, sweat shining on his face and dripping off his chin.

Brazil looked around, wondering, listening. He didn't see anyone else. There was no burglar alarm hammering anywhere, the road dark, the night silent.

'Weed,' he suddenly remembered. 'Yeah, that's it.'

'No it ain't,' Weed said.

'Yeah, it is. I'm sure of it. I'm Andy Brazil.'

'You're that cop who came to school,' Weed accused him.

'Something wrong with that?' Brazil asked.

'So how come you're out here in a BMW?' Weed demanded to know.

'A better question is how come you're drunk and running like a maniac?'

Weed looked up to where the moon would be, were it not covered in clouds.

'I'm taking you home,' Brazil said.

'You can't make me,' Weed defied him, his words slurring and knocking one another down.

'Sure I can.' Brazil laughed. 'You're drunk in public. You're a juvenile. You can either come downtown or I'm taking you to your house, and if I were you, I'd choose the latter and take some aspirin and go to bed.'

Weed was thinking. A U-Haul truck rumbled past, then a station wagon. Weed was still thinking, wiping his face on his sleeve. A VW Rabbit buzzed by, then a Jeep that reminded Brazil of CABBAGES. Brazil shrugged and walked over to his car. He opened his door.

'I'll call a unit to come take you downtown,' he said. 'I'm not hauling prisoners in my personal car.'

'You said you'd drive me home in it,' Weed countered. 'Now you saying you ain't.'

'I said I'm not hauling your butt downtown.'

Brazil shut his door.

Weed yanked open the passenger's door and slid onto the leather seat. He fastened his shoulder harness and didn't say a word. Brazil pulled back onto West Cary.

'What's your real name?' Brazil asked him.

'Weed.'

'How'd you end up with a name like that, huh?'

'I dunno.' Weed stared down at his untied hightops.

'Sure you do.'

'My daddy works for the city.'

'And?' Brazil encouraged him.

'Cuttin' grass and stuff. Pullin' weeds. Called me Weed 'cause he said I'd grow like one.'

Instantly he was humiliated and alarmed. It was obvious he had never grown like a weed, and he had told the cop way too much. He watched the cop write down

Weed on a little notepad. Shit! If the cop figured out Weed was a Pike, Weed would die. Smoke would see to that.

'What's your last name?' Brazil then asked.

'Jones,' Weed lied.

Brazil wrote this down, too.

'What's the five for?'

'Huh?'

'The five tattooed on your finger.'

Fear turned to panic. Weed's mind went blank.

'I don't got no tattoo,' he said stupidly.

'Yeah? Then what am I looking at?'

Weed examined one hand, then the other as if he had never taken a good look at himself before this moment. He stared at the 5 and rubbed it with his thumb.

'It don't mean nothing,' he said. 'I just did it, you know?'

'But why the number five?' Brazil persisted. 'You picked it for a reason.'

Weed was beginning to shake. If the cop figured out that 5 was Weed's slave number, one thing might lead to another.

'It's my lucky number,' Weed said as sweat trickled from his armpits, down his sides, beneath his Bulls colors.

Brazil fiddled with the CD player, jumping around from Mike & The Mechanics to Elton John before deciding on Enya.

'Man, how you listen to that?' Weed said finally.

'What about it?'

'It ain't got nothing to it. No good drums or cymbals or words that mean something.'

'Maybe the words mean something to me,' Brazil answered him. 'Maybe I don't care about drums or cymbals.'

'Oh yeah?' Weed got mad. 'You're just saying that because I play cymbals and pretty soon gonna learn drums.'

'You mind telling me where we're going?' Brazil said. 'Or is it a secret?'

'I bet you don't know nothing about cymbals.' Weed's logic was fading in and out, the dark smooth ride sedating him further. 'We're in the Azalea Parade, too.'

'I know you have to live somewhere near Godwin or you couldn't go to school there.' Brazil was getting increasingly frustrated.

Weed was falling asleep. He smelled bad and Brazil still didn't know why the kid had been out on the street drunk and running as if Jack the Ripper were after him. Brazil reached over and gently shook him. Weed practically jumped through the roof.

'*No!*' he screamed.

Brazil turned on the light above the visor and took a long hard look at Weed. Brazil noticed that the number 5 on his right index finger was crude and puffy.

'Tell me where you live,' Brazil said firmly. 'Wake up, Weed, and tell me.'

'Henrico Doctor.'

'The hospital?'

'Uh huh.'

'You live near Henrico Doctors' Hospital?'

'Uh huh. My head hurts so bad.'

'That's not in Godwin's district.'

'My daddy live in the district. My mama don't.'

'Well, who are you going home to, Weed? Your mother or your dad?'

'I don't hardly ever go near him. Just now and then, maybe a weekend every two months so he can go out and leave me alone, which is all right by me.'

'What street does your mother live on?'

'Forest and Skipwith. I can show you.' Weed's tongue was sticking to the roof of his mouth.

Brazil plucked Weed's right hand out of his lap.

'What'd you go and get a tattoo for?' he said again. 'Somebody talk you into that?'

'A lotta people get 'em.' Weed pulled his hand away.

'Looks to me like you just got it,' Brazil said. 'Maybe even today.'

chapter fourteen

Apparently Governor Feuer and his party had gone on to other courses and conversations. They had yet to emerge from La Petite France, and Roop was tired of waiting. He decided he might as well gather a little intelligence on the fish problem and dialed Hammer's home number, thanks to Fling, who had stupidly given it to Roop.

'Hammer,' she answered.

'Artis Roop here.'

'How are you doing, Artis?'

'I guess you're wondering how I got your home number . . .'

'It's in the phone book,' Hammer said.

'Right. Listen, Chief Hammer, I'm looking into this fish spill business . . .'

'Fish spill?' She sounded alarmed. 'Who told you about a fish spill?'

'I can't reveal my sources. But if there's a fish spill, I do think the public needs to know for its own protection, or if for no other reason, so they can choose alternate routes for work in the morning.'

'There is no fish spill that I know of,' Hammer answered firmly.

'Then what are people talking about?'

'This is simply a housekeeping matter you're referring to, Artis.'

'I don't understand.'

Roop was getting anxious as the door to the restaurant remained closed with no sign of activity. It suddenly occurred to him that the governor might try escaping through the service entrance. Maybe he had already gone. Roop unplugged the phone from the cigarette lighter and scrambled out of the car, still talking.

'How can fish or a fish spill be an internal matter?' he persisted.

'A computer glitch,' she replied.

'Oh,' he said, baffled. 'I still don't get it. Is fish some sort of virus?'

'We hope not,' said Hammer, who was always straightforward unless she refused to comment.

'So the COMSTAT telecommunications system is down?' Roop got to the raw nerve of the matter.

Hammer hesitated, then said, 'At the moment.'

'Everywhere?'

'I have nothing more to say,' Hammer replied flatly.

Roop was certain the fish problem was big. But he also had other fish to fry. Executive Protection Unit state police officers were coming out of La Petite France, the governor not far behind. Camera lights and flash guns fired from all sides, the governor gracious and unflappable, as was his wife, because they were used to this shit. Roop listened to *governor this* and *governor that* and was pleased that Feuer had no comment. Roop casually strolled over to Jed, the governor's EPU driver.

'I don't want to bother him,' Roop said. 'I feel sort of sorry for him being bothered like this all the time. Can't even eat dinner without everyone stalking him.'

'I wish everybody else felt like that,' Jed said.

'How the hell do you park that thing?' said Roop as he looked over every curve and inch of the gleaming black stretch Lincoln limousine.

Jed laughed as if it were nothing.

'I mean, really,' Roop went on as the governor and his wife were briskly escorted to the car. 'I couldn't be a driver to begin with. I get lost everywhere. You know how hard it is to roll up on a crime scene when you don't know where the hell you are?'

Roop had gathered intelligence on Jed, who was known by all, except the governor, to be directionally compromised and deceitful about it.

'You're kidding?' said Jed as he opened the back door for the first family and they climbed inside.

'Good evening, Governor and Mrs. Feuer,' Roop bent over to say politely.

'And to you,' replied the governor, who was a very gracious man if you could get to him.

'I saw you on *Meet the Press,'* Roop said.

'Oh, did you?'

'Yes, governor. You were great. Thank God someone's sticking up for the tobacco industry,' Roop gushed.

'It's common sense,' said Feuer. 'Personally, I don't smoke. But I believe it's a choice. Nobody forces it on anybody, and unemployment and black market cigarettes are not a happy prospect.'

'Next it will be alcohol,' Roop said with righteous indignation.

'Not if I have a say about it.'

'*There'll be smokes instead of stills,* governor,' Roop pitched the line that he believed would win him a Pulitzer Prize.

'I like that,' Feuer said.

'So do I,' said the first lady.

'*Smokes.*' Governor Feuer smiled wryly. 'As if ATF doesn't have enough to do. By the way,' he said to Roop, 'I don't believe we've met.'

The small house around the corner from Henrico Doctors' Hospital was brick with freshly painted blue shutters, and a well-cared-for yard. The driveway was gravel. There was no car. Brazil pulled in, small white rocks pinging under the BMW. He deliberated over what to do.

'When does your mom come home?' he asked Weed.

'She's home.' Weed was a little more alert.

'She doesn't own a car?'

'Yes she does.'

'It's not here,' Brazil said. 'It doesn't look to me like she's home.'

'Oh.' Weed sat up straighter and stared out the

windshield, his fingers on the door handle. 'I want to go to bed. I'm tired. Just let me out now, okay?'

'Weed, where does your mother work?' Brazil persisted.

He was eager to go home and call it a day, too, but he felt very uneasy about leaving this evasive little kid alone.

'She works at the hospital,' Weed said, opening the door. 'She does stuff in the operating room.'

'She a nurse?'

'I don't think so. But she could be here about midnight.'

'Could?'

'Sometimes she's gone longer. She works real hard 'cause what she makes is all we got, and my daddy gambles a lot and got us bad in debt. I wanna go to bed. Thanks for the ride. I never been in a car this nice.'

Officer Brazil drove off the minute Weed locked the front door. He looked around the empty living room, wishing his mother was home and glad she wasn't. There was leftover meat loaf and cold cuts, and Weed wasn't sure if eating would make things better or worse. He gave it a try, grilling a ham and cheese sandwich, which helped calm down his stomach.

He went down the hall, pausing to open the door to Twister's bedroom. Weed stared at all the basketball trophies and posters, the bed unmade, throw rug rumpled, University of Richmond tee shirt on the floor, the computer on the desk with its Bad Dog screen saver. Everything was exactly the way Twister had left it the last time he had been in his room, August 23, a Sunday, the last time Weed had ever seen him alive.

Weed wandered inside and imagined he could smell Twister's Obsession cologne and hear his laughter and teasing talk. He envisioned Twister sitting in the middle of the floor, long muscular legs folded up as he put on his shoes and called Weed his 'little minute.'

'See, it takes sixty of those to make an hour,' he would say. 'Now I know you can't add worth shit, but trust me on this one. Soon you'll be an hour, then a day, then a week, then a month. And you'll be big like me.'

'No I won't,' said Weed. 'You was twice as big as me when you was my age.'

Then Twister would unfold himself and start dribbling an invisible basketball. He would take on Weed, faking left and right, keeping the ball tight against him, elbows going this way and that.

'Time's running out on the clock and I got just one *little minute!'* Twister would laugh as he snatched up Weed and dunked him on the bed, bouncing him up and down until Weed was dizzy with delight.

Weed walked over to the desk and sat down. He turned on the computer, the only thing he ever touched inside his brother's room, because Twister had taught Weed how to use the computer and Weed knew Twister would want him to keep using it. Weed logged onto AOL. He sent e-mail to Twister's mailbox and checked to see if anybody else had.

Other than the notes Twister got daily from Weed, there was nothing else.

Hi Twister
You reading my letters? They ain't been opened, but I bet you don't have to open them the way other people do. I ain't changed nothing in your room. Mama don't come in it. She always keeps the door shut.

Weed waited for an instant message. He somehow believed that one of these days Twister was going to contact Weed through the computer. He was going to say, *What's ticking, little minute? I sure am glad you're writing me. I see everything you're doing so you better be keeping your ass straight.*

Weed waited and waited. He logged off and turned out the light. He stood in the doorway for a while, too depressed to move. He wandered into his bedroom and set the alarm clock for 2:45 A.M.

'Why you not here?' he said to Twister.

The dark had no answer.

'Why you not here, Twister! I don't know what to do no more, Twister. Mama quit coming home, works so much it's like she got hit on the head or something. Just sleeps and gets up and goes. She hardly talks no more ever since you went on. Daddy gives her a real hard time and now I got Smoke. He might kill me, Twister. He wouldn't if you was here.'

Weed went to sleep talking to Twister. Weed slept hard, his head full of cruel dreams. He was being chased by a garbage truck that made horrible scraping sounds as it rumbled down a dark road looking for him. It was on his tail no matter which way he went. He was sweating, his heart hammering when the alarm clock buzzed. He snatched it from the bedside table and turned it off. He listened, hardly breathing, hoping his mother was still asleep.

He turned on the light and dressed quickly. He went over to the small card table beneath the window and sat down to think about what he would need to paint the metal statue, and wishing he could have come right out and told Officer Brazil what was going on and why he had the tattoo. But Weed knew Smoke would get him. Somehow he would.

The big question was whether Weed should use oils or acrylics. He rummaged through shelves of his precious art supplies, lovingly looking through the Bob Ross master paint set his mother had worked overtime to buy for him last Christmas. It had cost almost eighty dollars, and included eight tubes of oil paint, four brushes and a Getting Started videotape which Mrs. Grannis had let Weed watch at school since he didn't have a VCR.

Weed opened the caps of sap green, cadmium yellow and alizarin crimson. He looked through his Demco Collegiate set and thought about how long it took oil paints to dry and how much cleaning up he'd have to do. He didn't want to smell like turpentine.

He studied his tubes of Apple Barrel acrylic gloss enamel paints. He had forty-six colors to choose from, but to really get a good effect he needed to sand the statue first and apply two coats. That would take forever, and in truth, the last thing Weed wanted was to do something to a statue. If nothing else, God would do something to Weed. Messing with the statue of someone famous would be as bad as painting graffiti on a church or putting a mustache on Jesus.

Weed came up with a daring plan. Maybe he could use poster paints. He had bags full of them. They were inexpensive and didn't make a mess. In fact, they could be washed off with soap and water, but there was no way Smoke could know that when Weed was painting away.

Weed had never used water-based tempera on metal, and tried a little green on the metal trash basket in his room. He was thrilled and a little surprised when the paint went on smooth and stuck. He gathered every jar he had and stuffed them inside his knapsack and a grocery bag. He dug through his box of perfectly clean paintbrushes and decided on two aquarelle for thin lines and two wash/mops for broad washes. He threw in one Academy size 14 round style just in case.

chapter fifteen

The New York City Police Department was beyond Artis Roop's usual scope of things. He had started with directory assistance and been bounced from Midtown North Precinct to the Rape Hotline to the Crack Hotline to the College Point Auto Pound and finally to a property clerk in Queens who gave him a number for the radio room. From there, Roop was able, by lying, to get Sergeant Mazzonelli to talk to him.

'Yeah, I know what COMSTAT is. Who you think started it?' Mazzonelli was saying.

'Of course, I know you guys did,' said Roop from his cluttered desk inside the *Richmond Times-Dispatch* newsroom.

'You're damn right we did.'

'We're having a problem in the mapping center,' Roop said.

'What mapping center? I ain't heard nothing about no mapping center.'

'At NIJ.'

'In New Jersey?'

'NIJ. Not NJ,' Roop corrected Mazzonelli.

'So where the hell are you calling from?' Mazzonelli asked. He put his hand over the phone. 'Yo! Landsberger! You going out to Hop Shing's?'

'Who wants to know?'

'Your mother.'

'Yeah? What's she want? *Fish?*'

Roop got excited.

'Hey! That ain't even funny,' another cop said.

'Stromboli. Provolone, extra onions. The usual,' Mazzonelli said.

He took his hand off the mouthpiece and was back. 'So you was saying?' he said to Roop.

'We're showing a problem with the COMSTAT computer network.'

'Who's *we?*'

'Look, this is Washington, we've got a problem.' Roop said it the way he'd heard it in the movies. 'A possible virus has infected the network and we want to know how extensive it is.'

Silence.

'It may show up as fish,' Roop added.

'Shit,' Mazzonelli barely said. 'So youze guys got it in D.C., too, the same thing? All these goddamn little blue fish swimming around in 219, wherever the hell that is?'

'Richmond, Virginia,' Roop informed him. 'We believe that's the wormhole the virus entered through. The carrier, in other words.'

'Richmond is?'

'We think so, sergeant. This is worse than I feared. If

your COMSTAT telecommunications system is locked out as well,' Roop went on, writing furiously, 'then everybody's down.'

'Shit. It's the weirdest friggin' thing I ever seen. We got three experts up here right now trying to get the damn thing off the screen, but we're totally down. Now, I don't do the computer shit myself, you know? But I got eyes and ears and know when something's real bad. From what they're saying, we can't find hot spots or patterns at all.'

'Exactly.' Roop flipped a page. 'Apparently no one can.'

Roop's editor Clara Outlaw stopped by his desk to see what was going on and if he planned on making the last edition deadline. He gave her a big thumbs-up. She started to say something. He scowled and put his finger to his lips. She tapped her watch. He nodded and gave her an okay sign. She didn't believe him. She tapped her watch again. He shook his head and motioned her to hold on a minute.

'It was early afternoon, so I hear, and all a sudden this fish map flashed on the screen and we can't get it off. It just came outta friggin' nowhere,' Mazzonelli went on and on.

Roop scrawled *Fishsteria* on a piece of notepaper. He ripped it off and handed it to Outlaw. She frowned and wrote *Pfiesteria?* Roop shook his head. This was not to be confused with the microbe responsible for massive fish kills on the East Coast, or was it? What did anybody know right now? Roop grabbed the piece of paper back from her and underlined *Fishsteria* four times.

At ten minutes to three in the morning, Weed crept out of his bedroom, pausing before his mother's shut door, hoping she was snoring. She was, as loud as ever. Weed left the house and waited on the street corner where Smoke had told him to be.

Minutes later, the Lemans sounded in the distance and Weed was reminded of his nightmare about the garbage truck. His hands started shaking so badly he worried he wouldn't be able to paint. He started feeling sick again, and he was tempted to run back inside the house and call the police or at least grab his acrylics, just in case Smoke figured he'd been tricked.

The back door of the Lemans was pushed open. Weed climbed in and protectively set the knapsack and bag of paints in his lap as he stared at the back of Smoke's head. Divinity was in the front seat, against Smoke's shoulder.

'I guess the others aren't coming,' Weed said, doing his best to keep his voice steady.

'Don't need 'em,' Smoke said.

'How come you're not driving your own car?' Weed asked as his terror swelled like a wave about to crash.

'Because I don't want my own car parked out where someone might find it,' Smoke said.

'Dog don't care if someone sees his car?' Weed asked.

'Don't matter if he cares,' Smoke said coldly. 'And you can shut the fuck up, retard. When it comes to questions, I do the asking. You got that straight?'

Divinity laughed and stuck her tongue in Smoke's ear.

'Yes,' Weed barely said as tears flooded his eyes and he

wiped them away so fast they didn't have time to go anywhere.

He said not another word as Smoke headed downtown and through the row houses of Oregon Hills where they left the car in a small park on the river. The cemetery fence was thick with ivy and about ten feet high. Weed saw no easy way to climb it, but Smoke did. Weed had never heard of a business advertising on a cemetery fence, but apparently Victory Rug Cleaning thought the idea was a good one. Its large metal sign was fastened to the fence at the intersection of South Cherry and Spring Street.

Smoke showed Weed and Divinity how simple it was to grip the edges of the sign and boost themselves up far enough to grab the thick overhanging branch of an ancient oak tree on the other side of the fence. In no time, the three of them had dropped to the ground and were inside the dark, silent cemetery. To Weed it was a ghost city with narrow lanes winding everywhere and headstones and spooky monuments as far as he could see. It suddenly occurred to him that Smoke and Divinity might think it was funny to leave him here.

Maybe that was their real plan. It caused shivers right up his bones and through his teeth. Weed had heard stories of pimps punishing hookers by tying them to trees inside graveyards and leaving them overnight. Some of the ladies lost their minds. Some died when their hearts attacked and beat themselves to death, trying to get out. One hooker chewed her hand off to escape while another committed suicide by holding her breath. Weed willed his teeth not to chatter. He knew he could not show fear.

'Cool,' he said, looking around. 'Man, I could paint in here for weeks.'

He and Divinity were following Smoke, who seemed to know where he was going.

'You know, all these gravestones, like clean canvases and sketching paper. Ummm um. I could paint my ass off in here,' Weed went on. 'After the statue, can I do a few more?'

'Shut up,' Smoke told him.

Weed got quiet. It felt like little bugs were crawling on him, and he was sweating and cold at the same time. He wondered how many dead people were in here. More than he could count, that was for sure, especially since Weed usually got an F in math. It amazed him how many of them were PAXes. No one in his school was a PAX, although there were quite a few Paxtons, and one Paxinos who had moved down from New York and thought he was the only one who knew how to talk.

But it was the dead rich people who bothered Weed most, all of them inside little marble houses with all kinds of carvings and names chiseled above huge heavy metal doors. There were windows, too, and the thought of looking through them raised every hair on Weed's body. Images jumped in his mind and started messing with him bad. A moldy face with sunken eyes and green rotting hands held a white Bible and any minute was going to turn to a page with a curse on it saying Weed was going to hell. A grinning skeleton in a long satin dress, bony hands folded around a dried-up rose, was about to sit up and fly after him, rattling and rustling.

Weed's legs almost collapsed. He dropped his knapsack and the straps grabbed his feet. He stumbled and got more entangled and crashed through a sculpted boxwood and almost regained his balance before tripping over an urn and landing flat on his face, his head just missing an Indiana limestone marker shaped like a tree. Weed didn't know who Lt. Col. Peachy Boswell was, but Weed had just stepped all over his grave.

Smoke and Divinity were laughing their asses off, hands over their mouths, trying not to make any noise, choking, bent over and hopping around like the ground was hot. Weed took his time getting up, taking an inventory of his parts to make sure nothing was missing or damaged, but his elbow stung a little and he realized blood was running down his arm. He knelt in the grass and replaced clods he had kicked up. He collected his knapsack and bag of paints. He shrugged as if it didn't bother him in the least that he had just desecrated a grave, for which there was usually a curse like the one he'd imagined in the white Bible.

Divinity dug inside her denim bag and pulled out a pint of Wild Turkey. She and Smoke started swigging. Smoke handed Weed the bottle. Weed refused. Smoke shoved it at him. Weed wouldn't budge.

'It'll mess me up,' Weed whispered. 'You want me to paint, don't you?'

'Sure fucking do.' Smoke started to laugh. 'The statue's right over there, retard. And guess what? You're on your own. We ain't hanging around.'

Weed tried to keep cool.

'Okay,' he said. 'But how do I get home?'

'Any way you can!' Smoke grabbed Divinity's hand and they ran away, laughing and drinking and not caring where they stepped.

Weed looked around, trying to figure out where he was. It was a part of the cemetery that was very close to the river and populated with a lot of rich people, many of them so important they had their own squares of grass big enough for the entire family. Weed saw the silhouette of the statue two streets and one circle away, and his heart swelled with awe. It was tall and erect against the night, a man standing proud, his profile handsome and sharp.

As Weed got closer, he could see there were six walkways leading to the statue, meaning the man must have been some kind of hero, maybe the most famous person alive when he was. He wore a long coat and knee-high boots, hat in one hand, the other on his hip. He stood on a marble base surrounded by azaleas and ivy. Two redneck flags were planted at his feet.

Weed did not recognize the name Jefferson Davis. Weed knew nothing about the man whose statue he was about to paint, except that Davis was 'an American soldier and defender of the constitution' who had been born in 1808 and died in 1889. The math took Weed a few minutes to figure out. He opened his knapsack and began pulling out paints and brushes and bottles of water.

Eighty-nine minus oh-eight, he moved his lips as he calculated. He drew a blank and tried again. *Nine minus eight was one. And eight minus zero was still eight.* So Jefferson

Davis was only eighteen when he died. Weed was overwhelmed by sadness.

He looked around at the marble sculpture of a mournful woman holding an open Bible. An angel with big wings was sitting nearby. They seemed to be watching him and waiting. Weed suddenly knew why he had been brought here. It had nothing to do with Smoke, not in the big scheme of things. There was no curse but an unexpected gift. Joy filled his heart. Weed knew what he was supposed to do. He didn't feel lonely and he wasn't afraid.

chapter sixteen

Sleep was a stranger that would have no part of Brazil's life at the moment. He kicked the sheets off again, got up for water, walked around in the dark for a few minutes, sat down in front of the computer screen and stared at the map and its blue fish. He drank more water and imagined that West was tormented, too.

He hoped she was fitful and full of bad dreams, her heart aching as she thought of him. Then his fantasy was shattered by a face he did not know, someone named Jim. Brazil thought hard of every cop he knew West was acquainted with, and he could think of no one named Jim she would be remotely interested in. West liked tall, well-built men who were intelligent, funny and sensitive, men she could watch movies and go drinking and shooting with. She was tired of being hit on. She required patience and a gentle touch. Indifference sometimes worked, too.

Brazil stalked back into his bedroom. It was almost five. West had made it clear she didn't intend to run with him this morning because she hated running and needed a day off. Brazil put on sweats and went out by himself.

He ran fast through the Fan, picking up speed as he obsessed about Jim. All Brazil knew about him was that he drank Heineken, or at least had brought a six-pack to West's house, so it was also possible that he simply thought she liked Heineken. Jim might not drink beer at all. He might be into Scotch or fine wine, although Brazil had noticed neither in West's kitchen. Of course, he hadn't looked in her cabinets.

He hadn't looked in her bedroom as he had walked past because he knew he couldn't bear seeing men's clothing in a pile on the floor, the bed a mess. Brazil clipped off five miles. He worked with free weights and did ab crunches until his upper body was on fire. He took a long, hot shower, miserable and furious.

Brazil shaved and brushed his teeth in the shower and decided he couldn't let West get away with this any longer. Damn her. He played and rewound and played again and again the last time they had touched, on Christmas Eve, when he'd gone to her house to deliver her Christmas present. He'd saved money for months to buy her a gold and platinum bracelet that she had stopped wearing days after they moved to Richmond.

Brazil felt used. He felt lied to and trivialized. If she really loved him as much as she used to say she did, then how could she suddenly get involved with someone named Jim and how long had it been going on? Maybe she'd been cheating on Brazil from the start, was seeing some other Jim back in Charlotte, had Jims all over the world. Brazil was going to call her and demand an explanation. He toweled his hair dry as he rehearsed what he would say. He put on his uniform, taking his time as he debated.

Hollywood Cemetery usually came alive around dawn. Clay Kitchen worked maintenance and took his job very seriously. He also liked overtime and found that if he showed up around seven each morning, he could add a good ten hours, or two hundred eighty-five dollars and eighty cents, to his twice-monthly paycheck.

Kitchen drove his blue Ford Ranger slowly through the Confederate soldiers section where eighteen thousand brave men and General Pickett's wife were buried, their simple marble markers closely spaced in perfect rows that were hard to mow around. Kitchen parked by the ninety-foot-high Confederate Monument pyramid, built of granite quarried from the James River in 1868 when the only machinery was strong bodies and fearlessness and a derrick.

Kitchen had heard the stories. There had been accidents. The workers had gotten very nervous. The project's timetable had stretched into a year and everyone was getting tired. When all that was left was to climb to the top and guide the capstone into place, the crew balked. Forget it. You got to be kidding. No one would do it, so an inmate at the nearby state penitentiary allegedly volunteered and performed the perilous task without incident, on November 6, 1869, while a happy crowd cheered.

The grass was getting a little high about the pyramid's

base and in need of string trimming. But that would have to wait until Kitchen finished his inspection of the one hundred and thirty-five acres that kept him so busy. He moved on, cruising along Confederate Avenue, then Eastvale and onto Riverside, which took him to Hillside and on the Presidents Circle, to Jeter and Ginter, eventually approaching Davis Circle where he saw the problem immediately and from a distance.

Jefferson Davis was wearing a red-and-white basketball uniform. The hat he held in his left hand had been turned into a basketball, although an oddly shaped one. His skin had been painted black. The marble base he stood on had been turned into a gym floor.

Kitchen sped ahead, shocked, crazed, almost out of control. He slammed on the brakes to get a closer look. The number on the jersey was 12. Kitchen was a sports fan and knew without a doubt the University of Richmond Spiders uniform. The number 12 on the jersey was that of Bobby Feeley, who was one of the most pathetic recruits Kitchen had ever seen. Kitchen yanked the portable radio off his belt and raised his supervisor on the air.

'Someone's turned Jeff Davis into a colored basketball player!' Kitchen declared.

chapter seventeen

Niles would not leave West alone. The cat had never been easy, but there was one sin he wasn't allowed to commit. No cat or anyone else kept West awake unless she chose to be awake, and she had chosen no such thing.

'What the hell's wrong with you?' West complained, turning over and punching the pillow under her head.

Niles wasn't asleep, but he wasn't moving, either. He'd been in the same position since midnight when his owner had finally decided to toss aside that silly *Chicken Soup for the Soul* book that promised a hundred and one happy heartwarming stories that meant nothing to Niles.

'Shut up!' his owner said, kicking the sheets.

Niles's ribs silently rose and fell as he breathed. He wondered when his owner would figure out that she always got cranky whenever Piano Man had been sighted in the area.

'I can't take this anymore,' his owner announced.

She sat up. She picked up Niles and dropped him on the floor. He had put up with quite a lot in the past few hours, but enough was enough. He jumped back up on the bed and batted her chin with his paw, keeping his claws tucked in.

'You little shit!' She popped Niles's head.

Niles jumped on her abdomen as hard as he could, knowing how much she hated that in the morning when she had to pee. His owner threw him off the bed again, and he jumped back and hissed and nipped her little finger and leaped back off the bed and ran like hell. She jumped out of bed in pursuit.

'Come back here, you little fuckhead!' she yelled.

Niles ran faster, taking the corner into his owner's office and springing on the top shelf of her bookcase, where he waited with swishing tail, crossed eyes staring. His owner made the turn not quite as gracefully, hitting her hip on the door frame and swearing some more. She pointed her finger at Niles. Niles wasn't intimidated. He wasn't even tired. She came closer and reached up, trying to grab him.

Niles sprang over her head, landing on her desk. He hit InLog on her Personal Information Center phone until he found the number he wanted. Then he hit Speaker and Dial. He waited until his owner almost had her hand on the back of his neck. He bopped her nose and was gone again as a phone loudly rang and rang over the speaker.

'Hello?' Piano Man answered.

West froze.

'Hello?' Brazil asked again.

She snatched up the phone.

'How'd I call you when I didn't?' she demanded to know as she read Brazil's number on the video screen.

'Who is this?' Brazil asked.

'Niles did it, not me,' West said.

'Virginia?'

'I didn't do it,' she said, glaring at Niles, who was stretching one leg after another from a safe distance.

'It's not like it's a crime if you called me,' Brazil said.

'That's not the point.'

'You want to have breakfast or are you tied up?' Brazil said haltingly, as if he was just being nice and had no interest whatsoever in seeing her.

'God, I don't know,' she replied as she ran through a list of other fabricated options. 'What time is it? Niles kept me up all night.'

'It's almost seven.'

'I'm not running with you if that's what you're really asking,' West shot back as her heart forgot its rhythm.

'I've already done that,' Brazil said. 'River City Diner? You been there?'

'I can't remember the names of everything around here.'

'It's really good. You mind picking me up since you get to take home a car and I don't?'

'So I guess you know all the places around here,' West said.

Popeye would not give Hammer a moment's peace this morning, either. She jumped all over Hammer.

She brazenly ran into Hammer's office and jumped into the desk chair and stared at the computer screen and the fish on it. She would not let Hammer sit and drink a first cup of coffee or glance at the paper. Popeye was stubborn on her walk. Treats were of no interest. She wouldn't sit, lie down, come or stay.

'What good does it do for me to read all those books and consult with an animal behaviorist?' Hammer asked in exasperation. 'I don't need this, Popeye. I have tried reasoning with you. I've talked with you at great length about how important it is to cooperate and be a pleasure to have around. I've asked you many times if something traumatic might have happened to you before I got you from the SPCA, something that has caused you to start nipping at people and jumping in their faces.

'But whatever it is, you won't let me know, and it's not fair, Popeye. You know how much I care. You know my life is hard and I need no more stress. You know I will be sued if you bite someone and they fake emotional distress, disfigurement and sexual dysfunction because they know I have money and don't need bad publicity. Now sit, and I mean it.'

Hammer squatted, holding a treat in her fist.

Popeye assumed her defiant stance and just stared at her.

'Sit.'

Popeye wouldn't.

'Lie down.'

Popeye didn't.

'What's gotten into you?' Hammer asked.

The shockwaves traveled quickly and with alarming repercussions. Hollywood Cemetery's maintenance supervisor immediately alerted the cemetery association president, Lelia Ehrhart, who instantly called every member of the board, including Ruby Sink, the association secretary and the most likely person to spread the news.

Miss Sink decided to go out and get her newspaper at the precise moment Chief Hammer was walking by with Popeye. Hammer quickly moved past the two-story brick town house with its Doric front porch and original cornices and windows. Miss Sink picked up speed, shuffling down steps and over cobblestones.

'Come back here,' Miss Sink called out.

Hammer did not appreciate being ordered about.

'Good morning, Miss Sink,' she said politely without slowing down.

'I need to speak to you.'

Hammer stopped while Popeye did her best to continue on course.

'It's just a darn good thing you showed up,' Miss Sink answered.

'Be good, Popeye.' Hammer pulled the leash.

Popeye pulled back.

'Popeye,' Hammer warned.

'What an awful name for a dog,' said Miss Sink. 'What's wrong with her eyes?'

'It's normal for the breed.'

'Did you have her tail chopped off?'

'No,' Hammer replied.

Miss Sink leaned over to get a better look at the stumpy, cock-eyed tail that covered nothing important. Popeye began to lick herself in a naughty place and suddenly sprang straight up into the air, her tongue darting into Miss Sink's mouth. Miss Sink jumped back and screamed. She rubbed her lips and looked sick as she thought about where that tongue had just been. Popeye grabbed the hem of Miss Sink's pink robe and almost pulled the frail old woman off her feet.

'Now Popeye, you behave. Sit,' Hammer said emphatically.

Popeye sat. Hammer fed her a Lung Chop. Miss Sink was mortified and momentarily speechless. She rubbed her mouth and checked the hem of her robe, looking for damage.

'What was it you wanted to talk to me about?' Hammer asked.

'You mean you don't know?' Miss Sink raised her voice. She glared hatefully at Popeye as she bent over to pick up the paper.

'Know what?' Hammer asked, irked that there might be something Miss Sink might know before Hammer did.

'Someone vandalized Hollywood Cemetery!' Miss Sink's fury gathered. 'Graffiti all over the statue of Jefferson Davis!'

'When did you find this out?' asked Hammer as Confederate troops rose up and began marching through her mind.

'I want to know what the police are doing,' Miss Sink demanded.

'Have we been called?' Hammer asked.

Miss Sink thought for a moment.

'This is the first I've heard of it,' Hammer went on as Popeye got interested in Miss Sink's ankles.

'I don't know if anyone called,' Miss Sink said. 'That's not my responsibility. I just assumed whoever happened upon the crime would have called the police. Of course, I just got the call myself a few minutes ago. They think some U of R basketball player did it.'

'Who's *they?*'

'You can ask Lelia Ehrhart that. She's the one who called me.'

Hammer's resentment blossomed and flourished.

'And how did Lelia find out?' Hammer asked.

'She's the president of Hollywood,' Miss Sink replied as if there was only one Hollywood. 'The city's being ruined. And if we had more police out doing their jobs, this sort of thing wouldn't happen. Not to mention the continuing deterioration of this neighborhood. *Here* of all places.'

Hammer feared that one of these days she was going to tell the nagging, horse-faced woman to go to hell.

'The people coming in here,' Miss Sink railed on. 'As if this is some sort of subdivision with McDonald's and aluminum siding!'

Miss Sink used to feel perfectly safe and sequestered on her famous tree-lined street, where in 1775 Patrick Henry had stood inside St. John's Episcopal

Church, in the third pew from the left, and declared '. . . Give me liberty or give me death!' It was here, just several houses down, that Elmira Royster Shelton and Edgar Allan Poe had been reunited and began a second courtship not long before he died.

Although Miss Sink was not Episcopalian and had never been engaged and did not read frightening stories, she revered history and the famous people in it. More to the point, Miss Sink had an inspired indignation when any outsider violated the sanctity of her restored neighborhood, and that included Judy Hammer, who was not from Richmond, but from Arkansas, which as far as Miss Sink was concerned was not the true South.

Popeye emptied her bladder on a blooming yellow forsythia bush. She began sniffing tulips and the lamppost, ready to claim other territory.

'Actually, crime is down six percent in our neighborhood, Miss Sink,' Hammer reminded her without adding that it was soaring everywhere else. 'Thanks in part to the community effort here, thanks to our crimewatch people like you, the eyes and ears of the street.'

'Six percent my foot.' Miss Sink stamped her pink slipper and yanked the plastic wrapper off the newspaper. 'Tell me why someone stole the fountain from Libby Hill Park?'

'It was recovered and is back right where it always was, Miss Sink.'

'Doesn't matter. It was stolen. Right out from under us like a rug. An entire iron fountain, and nobody saw a thing. So much for eyes and ears.' She dug in a pocket and pulled out a tissue. 'Not to mention rocks thrown at gas lamps and cars. Most of my friends and family are in Hollywood Cemetery.'

Miss Sink dabbed her nose and gave Hammer's ugly little dog the fish eye. She opened the newspaper to see what else was going on in the city. The headline above the fold stood up in huge black type:

FISHSTERIA HYSTERIA!

MYSTERIOUS VIRUS CRASHES POLICE COMPUTER NETWORK

Hammer snatched the paper out of Miss Sink's hands.

'Excuse me,' Miss Sink said indignantly. 'That was rude.'

Hammer didn't give a shit. She read the story, incredulous. It even included an artist's rendition of the little blue fish that were suspected, according to the article, to be the carrier of the virus.

'Oh God. So it's hit New York, too,' Hammer said as she read. 'It's everywhere. That goddamn Roop. The media doesn't care. This is only going to make matters worse, rewarding some hacker with front-page news. Oh great, great, great. Whatever happened to people trying to work together? When I was getting started, you could plant a story with the local media and they would run things that would actually help the police.

'But can you imagine such a thing happening now?' Hammer went on. 'Does it ever occur to self-serving people like Roop that when we can't do our jobs, he suffers too? What happens when his airbag is stolen?'

'I've read about that. Why do you call it CABBAGES?'

'What happens when he's robbed at gunpoint at an ATM?' Hammer went on.

'Those are awful,' Miss Sink said with a shudder. 'I see they had another one yesterday. Of course, look how early it was. People have no business getting money out of machines at night when nobody's around.'

Popeye lunged again. She got up on her hind legs, dancing about, front paws held out as if she wanted to hug Miss Sink. It made no sense.

'What's wrong with that dog?' Miss Sink said. 'It's like she's trying to tell me something.'

'Popeye is very intelligent. She's intuitive. Frankly, she knows so much it scares me,' Hammer confessed.

'And for the record,' Miss Sink went on, 'I think ATMs and the Internet are the 666 in Revelation. The beast leading up to Armageddon.'

Popeye jumped at Miss Sink again. Popeye growled. She hopped over to Miss Sink and tried to hug the old woman. Miss Sink smacked the newspaper against her hand as a warning. Popeye darted behind her owner's legs, wrapping her leash around them. She was shaking.

'It's all right, little baby.' Hammer was distressed and furious.

She squatted and put her arms around her dog and held her close. She gave Popeye another treat.

'Please don't do that again,' she said sternly to Miss Sink.

'Next time I'm going to smack her little bottom,' Miss Sink promised.

'Actually, you won't,' Hammer said in her dry *don't fuck with me* tone of voice.

'That dog's going to bite someone,' Miss Sink chastised Hammer. 'You wait. And then won't you be in Dutch? These days people sue just like that.' She tried to snap her fingers and missed.

Popeye growled.

'Well, I've got to go in and call all the other board members. I guess telling you is the same thing as calling the police,' Miss Sink said.

She headed back down her walk, her feet loud on her Doric porch, her cat darting out from behind a hedge.

chapter eighteen

despite Bubba's incredible efforts, no matter his eight straight hours of relentless work in Bay 8, his productivity had fallen short by 3,901 cigarettes. He was devastated. It was the last night of the competition of the month, and the second month in a row that Bay 5 had claimed victory.

'Don't take it so hard,' Smudge said.

'I can't help it,' Bubba replied despondently.

They stopped outside the cafeteria and Bubba inserted his ID card into the cigarette machine, selecting the free pack all workers got daily. Bubba chose his usual Merit Ultima. Smudge did, too, and sold his pack to Bubba at the slightly discounted price of eight dollars and twenty-five cents. Smudge smoked Winstons, which were not made by Philip Morris. For the first time it bothered Bubba that Smudge didn't offer his daily allotted pack to Bubba for nothing, since it cost Smudge nothing. It bothered Bubba that it just so happened that Smudge and Gig Dan played golf together.

'I guess Gig had a long day,' Bubba commented as he and Smudge headed out of the building.

'He looked pretty tired when he left,' Smudge agreed. 'Too bad you were so late.'

'Wouldn't've been if that asshole Tiller wasn't supposedly sick again.'

Smudge made no comment.

'Funny how he always gets sick on the night the competition ends,' Bubba made another casual remark.

'Maybe losing is something he can't face,' Smudge suggested.

'Also funny how nothing in my module works worth a shit the last night of the competition. Know how many times the tipping paper broke? Or how many glue bubbles I got? Had a dull knife, too. So I clean up right before shift change, and find dust in the machine and glue balled up on the glue roller,' Bubba said.

Smudge stopped at his gleaming red Suburban. He got out his keys.

'See, I think someone gets to Kennedy on first shift and sucks him into the conspiracy. So Kennedy works the first half of second shift because Tiller's called in sick, because he's been told to. Then Kennedy fucks up everything he can so when I'm supposed to come in and work one and a half shifts, I've got all this dust, glue balls and shit waiting for me.'

'Sounds rather elaborate, like a spy thriller. Don't be paranoid, Bubba.' Smudge patted Bubba's shoulder.

But it wasn't just paranoia. Bubba wasn't stupid. He knew Gig Dan was involved in the plot as well or he would have said something to somebody about how dirty the machine was. He had to have known, since he inadvertently had to fill in for Bubba because Bubba was late being early and then ended up late for being on time because Fred held him to a conversation. Bubba kept his conviction to himself as he began to see just what Smudge was really made of. Whatever it was, it was beginning to stink.

'You owe me and everyone else in Bay 5 two cases of beer, good buddy,' Smudge said as he cranked the Suburban.

'Yeah, I know,' Bubba said. 'What will it be?'

'Hmmmm. Let me think,' Smudge jerked Bubba around. 'I guess Corona.' He added insult to injury.

Corona was not a Philip Morris product, and Smudge knew Bubba would rather eat poison than spend a nickel on anything not Philip Morris.

'Okay, but you gotta give me a chance to get you back,' Bubba said.

Smudge laughed. 'Lay it on me.'

'Tomorrow night. Highest score. Let's raise the stakes higher, more than two hundred dollars,' Bubba said.

Smudge's face lit up as he lit up a Winston.

'You're on. Rain or shine,' Smudge said.

Bubba thought of the leak in his Jeep and everything else Muskrat had to say about it. Bubba tested Smudge one more time this morning.

'You want me to drive?' Bubba said.

'We'll be better off in my hunting truck.' Smudge said exactly what Bubba anticipated. 'I'll drive, you can pay for gas. Meet me at my house.'

Brazil was watching out the window for West's unmarked Caprice, and every other minute, he ran back to the bathroom and wet his fingers and ran them through his slightly gelled hair, giving it that wet look, making sure one strand fell down the middle of his forehead. He had brushed his teeth four times and couldn't stand still.

When West parked in front of his house, he took his time. He waited for her to come to the door. He waited until she had knocked five times.

'Andy? Are you in there?' she said loudly.

He ran to the door and opened it, tucking in his uniform shirt, adjusting his duty belt as if he was busy with many things and running behind.

'Gosh, I'm sorry,' he said politely. 'I was on the phone.'

It wasn't quite a lie because Brazil had been on the phone. He just didn't say *when* he'd been on it.

'I don't have much time,' West smacked the volley back. 'We'd better go. This was probably a bad idea,' she continued as she went down the steps. 'I've got the day from hell. I'm not even hungry.'

Brazil locked the door and followed her to the car, his feelings stung again.

'It doesn't matter to me,' he said. 'If you need to get to HQ, you can go on. You don't even have to give me a ride. It's not a problem.'

'I'm already here,' she retorted.

'I'm not that hungry either,' Brazil announced.

West put the car in gear and pulled away from the curb.

'You should fasten your seatbelt,' Brazil told her.

'Forget it.'

'Look, I want to be able to get out of the car fast, too, if something goes down. But I don't want to be thrown out, like through the windshield. Besides, how long does it take you to unbuckle a seatbelt, if you're really honest?'

'You work the streets as long as I have, you don't have to be really honest.' She reminded him of his inexperience and her high rank.

'Have you ever been to The Forest?' Brazil asked.

'What forest?'

'The neighborhood hangout on Forest Hill.'

'That's the other side of the river.'

'There's more parking there than downtown where the River City Diner is.'

'Since when are we eating breakfast again? I thought we'd decided that issue,' West said.

She turned on the radio, tuning in to WRVA. Adrenaline was shorting out Brazil's central nervous system as he groped for just the right words. He had a right to know why she treated him the way she did. He had a right to know about Jim.

'I guess I'm realizing if I don't eat something now, I don't know when I will,' Brazil said, making sure she understood how busy he was, too.

'River City is closer to HQ.'

'Try parking on Main Street during rush hour.'

West decided to head Southside.

'How did you find out about The Forest?' she asked as the radio broke the news of Fishsteria.

'I've been there a couple times.' Brazil's thoughts were tangled like fishing line.

'. . . believed to be a new strain of computer virus that cannot be detected by the standard antivirus software most of us have,' Johnny, of the popular *Johnny in the Morning Show,* went on.

'I pretty much stick to the Fan,' West said. 'There are so many good restaurants, bars, like Strawberry Street Vineyard. Why go anywhere else?'

'Strawberry Street Vineyard is a wine shop,' Brazil corrected her.

'I didn't say it wasn't,' she fired back.

'Best wine in the city. They can get anything. I picked up a Ken Wright Cellars Pinot Noir the other week. Outstanding.' Brazil had to rub it in.

'. . . hibernates in bottom sediments,' explained *Johnny in the Morning*'s special guest, Dr. Edith Sandal-Viverette, a biologist with the Virginia Institute of Marine Science. 'And releases toxins that are stunning and killing all these fish. Crabs are falling victim, as well. What's curious, Johnny, is the microbes like the temperature of the water to be eightyish. It's a little early for that.'

'But Fishsteria isn't related to Pfiesteria, right?' Johnny worried.

'I'm not sure we can say that at this moment.'

Brazil felt stubborn again. He didn't care enough to ask West anything. She didn't matter.

'I've really gotten into French burgundies, too,' Brazil rubbed it in some more.

'I get tired of red wine,' West said.

'Then you ought to try a white burgundy.'

'What makes you think I haven't?' West fired back.

'Well, it's really scary,' Johnny said as Brazil and West continued not to listen.

Bubba knew what had happened when he was half a block away from his house. The garage door was wide open. His heart was seized by fear. He pulled into the driveway and jumped out of his car, screaming his wife's name.

'Honey!' he yelled as he ran up the front steps. 'Honey! Oh my God! Honey! Are you all right!'

Bubba dropped his keys three times before he managed to unlock the front door. He burst into the living room as Honey's slippers swished along the hallway. He ran to her and hugged her hard.

'Why, what on earth is the matter?' Honey said, rubbing his back.

Bubba started sobbing.

'I was so scared something happened to you,' he cried into her permed, honey-blond hair.

'Of course nothing's happened to me, sweetie,' she said. 'I just this minute got up.'

Bubba stepped back from her, his mood suddenly skipping discs. He was enraged.

'How the hell could you sleep through someone breaking into the workshop?' he yelled.

'What?' Honey was dazed. 'The workshop?'

'The garage door's wide open! You leave it open for

some reason, like the awful Jell-O and room temperature Tang? Is this the final blow to hurt me? Is that how they got in?'

'I don't go near that door,' said Honey, who knew better than to ever set foot inside his workshop. 'Would rather take the Lord's name in vain and be a Mormon or a queer or a feminist than dare to get near your shop!' exclaimed Honey, who was Southern Baptist and knew the party line by heart. 'I don't want to go near your tools, much less touch them. I never ask anything about them even if I can see them plain as day when you're working on some project that never turns out quite right.'

Bubba ran back out the door. Honey held her robe together and followed. Bubba walked into the garage. He held his breath, hands clenched as he took in what had to be the biggest disaster of his life. Tools were scattered everywhere, and all of his handguns were gone. Someone had pissed all over Bubba's electronic caliper and it would convert inches into metric dimensions no more. The dual sander and air hammer had been cruelly dropped into the ten-gallon drum of dirty oil that Bubba saved for Muskrat's heater.

Bubba staggered back out into the sunlight. Honey grabbed his arm to steady him.

'Maybe I should call the police,' she said.

West and Brazil were close to The Forest when several things happened at once.

Brazil's flip phone trilled. The police radio broadcast a

possible B&E on Clarence Street, and WRVA played an ad for Hollywood Cemetery's new Chapel Mausoleum, located in one of the oldest sections of the cemetery, adjacent to a convenient roadway and with no additional expenses for a vault or monument, one price covering everything including the inscription.

'Hello?' Brazil said into his phone.

'. . . Any unit in the area,' the police radio was repeating, '. . . possible B and E at 10946 Clarence Street.'

'. . . the Hollywood Cemetery Chapel Mausoleum reflects a combination of both beauty and dignity . . .' the ad continued, jazz playing in the background.

'Andy? It's Hammer,' Chief Hammer said over the phone.

'Three,' West answered the radio.

'Our computer problem's hit the national news. I guess you saw this morning's paper,' Hammer said to Brazil.

'Go ahead, 3,' said Communications Officer Patty Passman, who was surprised that the head of investigations was answering the call.

'Actually, I didn't know,' Brazil replied honestly to Hammer.

'Front page,' Hammer said. 'They're making fun of us, fun of COMSTAT, saying we've crashed around the world because of a virus called *Fishsteria.*'

'*Fish* versus *Pfiesh?*' Brazil asked.

'Figure it out, Andy.'

'. . . designed to reflect the classic elements found with Hollywood's hills . . .' said the ad.

'We're just a couple blocks from there,' West told

Communications Officer Passman. 'We'll take the call.'

'And a vandal or vandals hit Hollywood Cemetery last night,' Hammer went on.

'Ten-4, 3. Complainant's a Mr. Butner Fluck.'

'Appears a Spiders basketball uniform was painted on the statue of Jefferson Davis,' Hammer explained.

Brazil was stunned. He started laughing and could not stop.

'And I'm afraid his race was altered,' she went on.

'You mean, he got Michael Jordanized?' Brazil choked.

'This isn't funny, Andy.'

'I think I'm gonna be sick.' Brazil was doubled over, hardly able to talk.

West made a U turn on Forest Hill and accelerated.

'Lelia Ehrhart's called an emergency meeting of city leaders tomorrow morning at eight,' Hammer told Brazil.

'I hope she's not going to speak!' Brazil's voice went up an octave. He couldn't help himself.

'What's wrong with you?' West glanced over at him as she drove fast out of habit, taking every shortcut she could to get to the scene.

'Look into it,' Hammer said to Brazil.

'*Fishsteria* or *Magic Jeff?*' Brazil's stomach hurt, his eyes watering.

'All of it,' she said to him.

The house on Clarence Street was very peculiar, but not for obvious reasons at a glance. Rather it was the sort of phenomenon that caused an unsettled, odd feeling of disharmony and something just not quite right that was discarded, like a lost file, the instant the person drove or walked past or delivered the newspaper and moved on.

But to someone with a trained eye who took a hard look, the problem was clear.

'Good God,' West said, stopping the car in the middle of the road as she stared in wonder.

'Wow,' Brazil chimed in. 'I think he home-improved when he was drunk.'

Dark green shutters were askew, the paint not quite as white to the left of the red front door as it was to the right. The white picket fence was the worst West had ever seen. Clearly the soil was unstable and the builder had not driven the 4x4 posts far enough into the ground or set them in cement, nor had he bothered with a plumb line, it didn't appear, or chamfered the tops of the posts, meaning rainwater did not run off and the wood was beginning to rot. The rails sloped uphill on one side of the ill-fitting gate and downhill on the other. The pickets were unevenly spaced like bad teeth.

Apparently this same well-intentioned but misguided builder had expanded his garage by adding on a homemade shed that leaned north, suggesting the pressure-treated posts had not been sunk below the frost line and the new addition had shifted during the winter. Nothing was right. Shingles were not aligned, window boxes were different sizes, the stone garden fountain in front was dry, the herringbone pattern of the outdoor bench near the slumping brick barbecue was chaos. A long dog pen of torqued and drooping chain link was near the woods, and a blanket-back coon hound was perched on top of a barrel, bawling.

West turned into the driveway and a gas-station bell announced Mr. Fluck had company. A curtain in a window moved, and immediately a man emerged from the house. He was fat and didn't have much hair, his round head and small eyes bringing to mind a smiley face that wasn't. Mr. Fluck looked depressed and bereft, as if his wife had just walked out or come back, depending on how he felt about her.

'Uh oh,' Brazil said, unfastening his seat belt.

'No kidding,' said West.

Bubba followed his uneven brick walk to the driveway, where the unmarked white Chevrolet Caprice had pulled in. His mind was dark with ruined dreams, cruel predestination and bad karma.

His father, Reverend Fluck, had always disapproved of Bubba's fondness for guns, and Bubba was suspicious that his father had prayed for such a thing to happen. It was just too coincidental that, for the most part, only guns had been stolen. His expensive tools had been left. The burglar had not tried to break into Bubba's house or Honey's station wagon.

A tall, well-built blond man in uniform climbed out of the Caprice. The driver was a woman in plain clothes, a detective, Bubba assumed. They walked up to him, radios chattering.

'Are you Mr. Fluck?' the woman asked.

'Yes,' he said. 'Thank God you came. This is the worst thing that's ever happened to me.'

'I'm Deputy Chief Virginia West, and this is Officer Andy Brazil,' West said.

Bubba felt better. He sighed. The police had sent a deputy chief. This had to be Chief Hammer's doing. She was looking after Bubba. Somehow she had been touched as had he, their destinies entwined. Chief Hammer knew that a terrible injustice had been perpetrated against Bubba.

'I sure appreciate Chief Hammer contacting you,' Bubba said.

Both cops looked mystified.

'She did, didn't she?' Bubba's faith wavered. 'Just now, when I called nine-one-one?'

'Actually,' Brazil faltered. 'Well, yes. How did you know she just called me?'

Bubba looked heavenward and smiled, despite his pain.

West started walking toward the workshop. Brazil followed. Both of them stood on the driveway, looking at the mess. Brazil recorded the month, day, year and victim's name and address on the offense report attached to his clipboard.

'What a disaster,' Brazil said.

'It's unspeakable,' Bubba said.

'Do you have any idea when the B and E occurred?' West asked.

'Sometime between eight o'clock last night and seven-thirty this morning.'

'I need your home and business phone numbers.' Brazil was writing.

Bubba gave them to him.

'I got home from work and found this,' Bubba said, almost in tears. 'Exactly like this. I didn't touch anything. I didn't move anything, so I'm not a hundred percent sure what's missing.'

West's expert eye skimmed over stand-alone tools such as a drill press, a drum sander, bench grinder, jointer, thickness planer, shaper, and all the expected chisels, Forstner bits, wire-brush wheels, brad-point bits, plug cutter, countersink set. There was protective gear of every description, and more hand tools than Bob Vila probably had in his workshop.

'It's interesting that you have so many expensive tools, yet the burglar or burglars didn't take them,' West observed.

'He was after guns,' Bubba said. 'I know they're missing.'

He pointed to the cabinet and its severed padlock on the floor.

'You got bolt cutters?' West asked.

'Toolsmith, eighteen-inchers.'

'Still have them?' Brazil said.

'I can see them from here,' answered Bubba.

'What kind of lock was on the gun cabinet?' West asked.

'Just a plain Master lock.'

'*Case hard?*'

Bubba looked ashamed.

'I was meaning to get around to it,' he said.

'So it *wasn't* case hard,' Brazil wanted to make sure as he took the report.

Bubba shook his head.

'That's too bad,' West said with feeling. 'I've never seen a pair of bolt cutters that can go through a case hard Master lock. And considering what you had in your cabinet, you should have had the best.'

'I know, I know,' Bubba said as his shame deepened. 'I know how foolish I was.'

West walked in to inspect more closely, noting that Bubba had painted his initials in white on all tools and equipment. She stepped over dozens of step-by-step books on plumbing, deck and patio upgrades, painting and wallpapering, pruning, and home repair problem solving.

She picked her way around a Stanley thirty-foot heavy-duty tape measure and its Nicholas leather holder, a Makita tool holster, a McGuire-Nicholas wide saddle-leather belt, a top-grade cowhide Longhorn hammer holder, red Nicholas heavy-duty suspenders, and a foam rubber knee pad with double straps that had become separated from its mate.

West recognized top quality. She knew all the brands and how much they cost. She was curious. She was envious.

'And you have no alarm system,' Brazil said.

'The "No Trespassing" sign and the bell in the driveway. I can hear anybody drive in.'

'I didn't know they used those anymore,' Brazil said.

'Muskrat's Auto Rescue has a bunch of them,' Bubba said.

'What about your dog?' West asked.

'Half Shell bawls all day and night. Nobody listens to her anymore.'

'So Half Shell and the gas-station bell were your only alarm system?' West gave him a skeptical look.

Bubba could tell she wasn't impressed with him. He was suddenly conscious of how pretty she was. Bubba felt fat, dirty, unattractive and inferior. He felt the way he had most of his life. Deputy Chief West saw through his guns and tools and home repairs. She saw Bubba as a persecuted little boy with an awful name and a world that ridiculed him. Bubba could see it in her eyes. It suddenly occurred to him that she might have gone to school with him.

'Are you from around here?' he asked her.

'No,' she said.

'You sure?'

'What do you mean, *am I sure?*'

He was paranoid and obsessed. He had to be convinced.

'So you're not from Richmond,' he said.

'No.' She was getting curt with him.

'It's just that you look like someone I went to school with whose name was Virginia,' Bubba lied.

'We didn't go to school together,' West told him.

'Did the burglar or burglars urinate in here?' Brazil asked.

'Yes.' Bubba pointed. 'Does that mean something?'

'Oftentimes burglars urinate or defecate in the place they've broken into,' West explained. 'It's part of an MO, and may or may not matter.'

Brazil made a note of it.

'The sort of thing your police computer might have picked up on if it didn't have the fish virus,' Bubba said. 'I heard about it on the news when I was driving home. So you won't be able to check for a pattern.'

'Don't you even worry about it.' Brazil avoided the subject. 'You got a list of the guns and their serial numbers?'

'I got them all at Green Top,' Bubba said. 'Never buy guns anywhere else.'

'That helps,' Brazil said. 'But I want to list on the report what's missing so the detective can follow up.'

'I guess you won't be able to use the computer to see if someone else got broken into like this,' Bubba said, disappointed. 'Because of the fish problem.'

'Don't worry about how we do our jobs,' Brazil told him. 'Now, about the list.'

'One Browning Buck Mark Bullseye .22,' Bubba recalled, 'a Taurus eight-shot M608 .357, Smith and Wesson Model 457 alloy frame .45 ACP and its Bianchi Avenger holster, a Pachmayr pocket cleaning kit, a mini-Glock G26 nine-millimeter with night sights, Sig P226 nine by nineteen millimeter, same thing used by Navy SEALs. Let's see. What else?'

'Jesus,' West said.

Brazil was writing at top speed.

'A Daisy Model 91 Match pistol, air gun, in other words. Ruger Blackhawk .357 revolver, and a couple Ruger competition handguns.'

'Are you a competition shooter?' West asked.

'Haven't had time,' Bubba said.

'Is that it?' Brazil asked.

'I just got a M9 Special Edition nine mil, fifteen-round clips, still in the box. It makes me sick. I never even got to try it out. And I had a bunch of speed loaders and about twenty boxes of cartridges. Most of them Winchester Silvertips.'

'What about anything else?' West asked.

'It's hard to tell,' Bubba said. 'But the only other thing I'm not seeing anywhere is my Stanley tool belt. It's really nice. Black nylon with a padded yellow belt, lightweight and not as hot as leather. Can fit everything but the kitchen sink.'

'I've always wanted one of those,' West confessed. 'They cost about sixty bucks.'

'That's if you get a discount,' Bubba said.

'What about suspects?' Brazil had gotten to that part of the report. 'Anybody you think might have done this?'

'It had to be somebody who knew what I had inside my shop,' Bubba said. 'And the door wasn't forced, so the person had a remote, too.'

'That's interesting,' Brazil commented.

'You can buy them at Sears,' West said, looking up at the retracted Sears garage door. 'Mr. Fluck, I'm going to see to it that a detective comes by before the day's out to look for any possible evidence, prints, tool marks, whatever.'

'My prints will be in here,' Bubba worried.

'We'll have to print you, now that you mention it, to know what's yours and what's not,' West said.

They walked out of the workshop, careful where they

stepped. Half Shell was bawling and jumping in circles.

'Thank Chief Hammer again for me,' Bubba said, following West and Brazil to their car.

'*Again?*' Brazil looked baffled. 'Have you spoken to her?'

'Not directly,' Bubba said.

chapter nineteen

Hammer was extremely sensitive to racial issues and had studied the Richmond metropolitan area's thoroughly. She knew it wasn't so long ago that blacks couldn't join various clubs or live in certain neighborhoods. They couldn't use golf courses or tennis courts or public pools. Change had been slow and in many ways was deceptive.

Memberships and neighborhood associations began to accept blacks, and in some cases women, but making it off the waiting list or feeling comfortable was another matter. When the future first black governor of Virginia tried to move into an exclusive neighborhood, he was turned down. When a statue of Arthur Ashe was erected on Monument Avenue, it almost caused another war.

Chief Hammer was worried as she and administrative assistant Fling drove through Hollywood Cemetery to inspect the damage and find out if the descriptions of it were exaggerated. They weren't. Hammer parked on Davis Circle, where the painted bronze statue was clearly visible in the distance, rising amid a background of magnolias and evergreens, small Confederate flags fluttering at the marble base, the perimeter secured with yellow crime-scene tape.

'Looks like he's hogging the basketball and won't pass it to anyone,' Fling observed. 'He looks kind of stuck-up, too.'

'He was,' Hammer commented.

She stifled laughter, her blood fluttering with peals of it that were almost impossible to suppress. The statue of Davis had always been described as having a proud and haughty air. He had worn the southern gentleman's dress typical of his day, before the graffiti artist, remarkably, had transformed the long coat into a baggy jersey and voluminous shorts to the knees. Trousers had become muscular legs and athletic socks. Boots had been turned into hightop Nikes.

Hammer and Fling got out of the Crown Victoria as the throaty roar of a black Mercedes 420E came up from behind. The sedan, with its sunroof and saddle interior, swerved around Hammer's car and parked in front of it.

'Shit,' Hammer said as Lelia Ehrhart gathered something off the Mercedes's front seat and opened her door. 'Where's the interpreter?'

Although Ehrhart had been born in Richmond, she had spent most of her growing-up years in Vienna, Austria, where her father, Dr. Howell, a wealthy, prominent music historian, had labored for years on an unauthorized psychological biography of the very gentle, sensitive Mozart and his fear of the trumpet. Later the family had moved to Yugoslavia where Dr. Howell explored the subliminal influence of music on the Nemanjic dynasty. German was

Lelia Ehrhart's first language, Serbo-Croatian followed, then English. She spoke nothing well and had combined the three, stirring and folding, as if making a cake.

For a moment, Ehrhart stood, transfixed by the statue, her lips slightly parted in shock. She wore yellow Escada jeans, a full yellow-striped blouse with an E on the breast pocket, a black belt studded with brass butterflies and shoes to match. Although Hammer mostly wore Ralph Lauren and Donna Karan, she knew other designers and recognized that the butterflies were several seasons old. This gave Hammer a little satisfaction, but not enough.

'This will excite a riot,' Ehrhart exclaimed, moving in closer to the crime scene, a Canon Sure Shot in hand. 'Nothing like this has even happened before this.'

'I'm not sure I'd go so far as to say that,' Hammer replied. 'Not so long ago someone painted graffiti on the statue of Robert E. Lee.'

'That was different.'

'He wasn't changed into a black basketball player,' Fling agreed. 'Not saying he wouldn't have been, but he's on a horse with a sword, and right there on Monument Avenue where if you spent a lot of time, someone's bound to notice. So I really don't see how you could easily do him. Or doing anybody on Monument Avenue. Arthur Ashe's holding a tennis racket and the other guys are on horses. Unless you did polo, I guess.'

'I want to know how you're doing about this?' Ehrhart said to Hammer as a sudden gust of wind stirred trees and whipped the Southern Cross at Davis's feet. 'And where were your officers when some vandal came in here like

Michelangelo in the Sistine Chapel?'

'The cemetery is private property,' Fling reminded her.

'If a serial killing shows up on my private property, is that a *so-what* also?' Ehrhart replied indignantly.

'Not if we know he's a serial killer,' Fling retorted.

'The truth is,' said Hammer, 'we do patrol the cemetery.'

'That's even worst,' Ehrhart said. 'You certainly must have somewhere been elsewhere last night.'

'The beat car is very busy in that area, Lelia. We've got VCU, Oregon Hills. We get many, many calls,' Hammer said. 'When calls involve living people, they take priority.'

'As if I would know this!' Ehrhart indignantly answered.

'It's confusing what's city and what isn't.' Fling tried to gloss over his misinformation. 'And Mrs. Ehrhart, my earlier point that I wanted to emphasize was you shouldn't take this so hard when it may simply be a random choice because of how remote being in a place like this is if you're up to no good.'

'That's easier to say,' said Ehrhart.

Hammer felt as if she were listening to aliens.

'When about Bobby Feeley?' Ehrhart was becoming more accusatory.

'We're working hard on this, Lelia,' Hammer replied.

'He's twelve,' she persisted. 'That ought to add up for something.'

'We are investigating this with great seriousness,' said Hammer, who frankly thought the statue was much improved by the new outfit.

'He probably alibied his way from there to here and you take it at fact value.' Ehrhart wouldn't let it rest.

'I think he wasn't feeling good last night and didn't go out,' Fling offered. 'There are witnesses.'

Hammer glared at Fling, who had just divulged sensitive information about the case.

'Well, we'll put this up at my meeting. And by the way, I've had to move it earlier to seven A.M. in the morning, Judy.' Ehrhart started taking photographs of the crime scene. 'The Commonwealth Club private boarding room. If you don't know where it is, they'll ask you at the door when you cash your coat.'

'It's a little warm for a coat,' Fling said.

For the past century, Lelia Howell Ehrhart's alleged ancestors had been laid to rest in stately family plots and tombs, and remembered by obelisks and urns, and blessed by crosses, and guarded by Carrara marble angels of grief and a cast-iron dog, and embellished with ornamental metalwork.

It was well known that her family tree included Jefferson Davis's wife, Varina Howell, although genealogists had thus far been unsuccessful in tracing Ehrhart's bloodline back to any geographic region even close to Mississippi, where Mrs. Davis was from.

Ehrhart was traumatized and personally outraged. She took the vandalism personally and couldn't help but think it was directed at her, and therefore gave her the right to find the monster who had done it and lock him up for the rest of his life. Ehrhart didn't need the police. What good were they anyway?

What mattered most and got things done was connections, and Ehrhart had more than the Internet. She was married to Dr. Carter 'Bull' Ehrhart, a millionaire dentist and alleged descendant of Confederate General Franklin 'Bull' Paxton. Bull Ehrhart was a University of Richmond alumnus. He was on the Board of Visitors. He had donated hundreds of thousands of dollars to U of R and rarely missed a basketball game.

It had been no great matter for Lelia Ehrhart to call Spiders head coach Bo Raval and find out exactly where she might get her hands on Bobby Feeley. Probably the gym, she had been told. She turned off Three Chopt Road onto Boatwright and followed it to the U of R campus. She turned into the private lot, where members of the Spiders Club parked during the games. She tucked her Mercedes at an angle, taking two spaces, far away from those less expensive cars that might hit her doors. She walked with purpose up the Robins Center's front steps.

The lobby was empty and echoed with the memory of many games won and lost that Ehrhart had not enjoyed. Eventually, she had refused to attend them with her husband, nor would she subject herself to football. She simply would not watch sports on TV anymore. Bull could get his own beer and make his own microwave popcorn. He could point the remote as often as he wanted, playing God, controlling, master designing, making things happen, and she didn't care.

A basketball bouncing beyond shut doors sounded lonely and determined. Ehrhart entered Milhouser Gym, where Bobby Feeley was shooting foul shots. He was tall, as expected, with long sculpted muscles and a shaved head and a gold loop earring, like all basketball players. His skin glistened with sweat, gray tee shirt soaked in back and front, shorts baggy down to his knees and swirling as he moved. Feeley paid no attention to Ehrhart as he tried again and hit the rim.

'Shit,' he said.

She said nothing as he dribbled and faked, rushed, elbows flying, turning, faking again, fast breaking, leaping and slam-dunking, hitting the rim again.

'Fuck,' he said.

'Excuse me,' Ehrhart announced herself.

Feeley slowly dribbled the ball, looking at her.

'Are you Bobby Feeley?'

She stepped onto the gym floor in high-heeled shoes with brass butterflies.

'That's not a good idea,' he said.

'Excuse me?'

'Your shoes.'

'Who's not right with them?'

'They aren't tennis shoes.'

'Yours aren't wearing tennis shoes,' she said.

He dribbled some more, frowning.

'What do you call these?' he asked.

'Basketballs shoes,' she said.

'Ah. A purist. Okay,' said Feeley, an honors English student. 'But you still can't walk on the floor in those shoes. So you can take them off or go somewhere else, I guess.'

Ehrhart slipped out of her shoes and drew closer to him in knee-high hose.

'So, what can I do for you?' Feeley asked as he pulled the ball away, elbows out and dangerous, eluding an imaginary adversary.

'You're number twelve,' Ehrhart said.

'Not that again,' Feeley exclaimed as he dribbled. 'What is this anyway? You people think I have nothing better to do? That I would do something as sophomoric as painting graffiti in a cemetery?'

He dribbled between his legs and missed a jump shot.

'This is not just graffiti as you watch on subway trains. It's not 'The Screech' and schmucks you watch on buildings.'

Feeley stopped dribbling and wiped sweat off his brow, trying to interpret.

'I think you mean *scream,*' he tried to help her out. 'As in Edvard Munch's 'The Scream'. And maybe you mean *schmoe?* Schmuck's not a nice word, although those unfamiliar with Yiddish usually don't get it.'

'Spray painting Mountain Rushmore, how about then?' she said indignantly.

'Who did?' Feeley asked.

'So you can go paint your basketball uniform, number twelve included, on my ancestor!'

'You're related to Jeff Davis?'

Feeley ran and dunked. The ball bounced off the backboard.

'I'm related to Vinny,' Ehrhart stated.

'As in Pooh?'

'Varina.'

'I thought that was a place or maybe something else we shouldn't allude to.'

'You are vulgarly rude, Mr. Feeler.'

'Feeley.'

'It disdains me that people from your generation respect not a thing that's gone before in the past. And the point is, it isn't gone even if it started before you in. I'm standing here, as evident.'

Feeley frowned. 'How 'bout ringing me up again. I think we have a bad connection.'

'I wouldn't,' she said flatly.

He cradled the ball under his arm. 'What did I do?'

'We know both what you did.'

He dribbled into a hook shot that swished below the net.

'Sorry,' Feeley said, 'but I didn't do a job on Mr. Davis's statue, although I must say that it was about time somebody put him in his place.'

'How dare can you!'

Feeley flashed his big smile. He dribbled back and forth from one hand to the other and hit his foot.

'Indicted for treason but never tried. First and last president of the Confederacy. Ha!' He missed another foul shot. 'Got to feel sorry for him, when you think about it. Inferior railroad, no navy, no powder mills or shipyard and forget arms and equipment.' A jump shot sailed over the backboard. 'Congress fighting like cats and dogs.' Feeley walked and hit his toe again. 'Lee surrenders without asking Davis if it's all right.' He trotted after the ball. 'Jeff Davis finds himself in leg irons and ends up an insurance salesman in Memphis.'

'Not truth.' Ehrhart was incensed.

'Sure as hell is, ma'am.'

'Where were you last night?' she demanded to know.

'Right here, practicing.' A last-second shot from half court hit the stands. 'I didn't go to the cemetery and have never been inside that cemetery.'

He trotted after the ball again and started spinning it on his middle finger.

Ehrhart misinterpreted. 'Are you giving to me an obscenity gesture?'

The ball wobbled off. Feeley tried again. He tossed it around his back and missed.

'Rats,' he said.

'I fine you most lacking in respect,' Ehrhart said loudly and with emotion. 'And you can alibi from then on and in the end, what comes and goes around!'

'Look, ma'am.' Feeley tucked the ball under his arm. 'I had nothing to do with the statue. But I sure do intend to go take a peek.'

Many people in the Richmond area had decided the same thing. Clay Kitchen had never seen such a solid line of cars without headlights on. He had never in his twenty-seven years of faithful service observed such unbecoming behavior.

People were cheerful. They had rolled windows down and were enjoying the premature spring weather. They were playing rock & roll, jazz and rap.

Kitchen and West zipped along in the truck, avoiding the flow of traffic by entering the crime scene from Lee Avenue. West looked out the window, rather amazed by the interest. When the statue came in view she almost lost her proper police decorum. She almost said *fucking unbelievable.*

'Stop right here,' she said to Kitchen. 'I don't want people seeing me getting out of your truck.'

Kitchen completely understood. West was here in plain clothes and would not tell him why, but he was quite a reader. He knew what was going on. Criminals often returned to the scene of the crime, especially if they were pyromaniacs or wanted to apologize or had forgotten to take a souvenir. Kitchen had talked to police when they patrolled the cemetery on slow days. Kitchen had heard the stories.

He remembered the man who stabbed his wife almost a thousand times and slept with her body for days, bringing her breakfast in bed, watching TV with her, talking about the good times. Of course, that really wasn't the same thing as returning to the scene since he'd never left it, Kitchen supposed. He did know for a fact that up north a few years back, a woman ground up her husband in a wood chipper and came back several days later to burn up his pieces in the backyard. A neighbor apparently got suspicious.

The crowd was pressing too close to the statue and threatened any moment to duck under or even break the crime-scene tape. West got on her radio and requested backups. There was a near riot situation at the cemetery, hundreds of people. Many of them had been drinking and probably still were.

'Three,' Communications Officer Patty Passman came back. 'Is this 10-18?'

West checked her annoyance. People pushed against her. Passman was always questioning West's calls, and now she had the nerve to ask if the situation was urgent. *No, why don't you get around to it when you can,* West felt like saying. *After I've been stampeded.*

'Three, 10-10. At the moment.'

'Three, what's your exact 10-20?'

'I'm exactly at the statue,' West answered tersely.

'Hey! Who's the chick with the radio?' some man yelled.

'We got undercover cops here!'

'FBI.'

'CIA.'

'Yay!'

'You want my fingerprints, baby?'

The smell of alcohol was strong as bodies pressed closer and jeering people got in West's face. Her body space wasn't there. People were jostling her, touching her, laughing. She got back on the radio and suddenly noticed the small blue fish painted on the statue's base, just below Jefferson Davis's left Nike. A kid came up behind her and pretended to go for her gun. She lifted him off the ground by his belt and tossed him like a small bag of garbage. He laughed, running off.

'Three, 10-18!' West exclaimed over the air as she stared at the fish, her thoughts crashing into each other.

'Any unit in the area of Hollywood Cemetery, an officer needs assistance,' Passman broadcast calmly.

'Step back!' West shouted to the crowd. 'Step back now!'

She was against the crime-scene tape, the crowd getting frenzied and moving in.

West whipped out her red pepper spray and pointed it. People paused to reflect.

'What the hell's gotten into you?' West yelled. 'Step back now!'

The crowd inched back a little, faces twitching with indecision, fists balled, sweat rolling, the air throbbing with the heat of violence about to erupt.

'Someone want to tell me what this is all about!' West yelled again.

A youth wearing a Tommy Hilfiger shirt and stocking cap, one relaxed-pants leg rolled up, one down, spoke for the group.

'Nobody wants us in here,' he explained. 'Maybe it gets to you, you know? And then one day something happens and you snap.'

'Well, there'll be no snapping here,' West told all sternly. 'What's your name?'

'Jerome.'

'Seems like these people listen to you, Jerome.'

'I don't know any of them, but I guess so.'

'I want you to help me keep them calm,' West said.

'Okay.'

Jerome turned around and faced the mob.

'CHILL!' he shouted. 'EVERYBODY FUCKING BACK OFF AND GIVE THIS LADY SOME FUCKING SPACE!'

Everybody did.

'Now listen up.' Jerome stepped into his new role and had no problem with it. 'The deal is you people don't know what it's like,' he told West.

'Tell it!' a woman yelled.

'You think anybody wants us in here?' he whipped up the crowd.

'Fuck no!' they screamed.

'You think anybody wants us dropping by?'

'Fuck no!' the crowd chanted.

'You-think-you-go-Hollywood-who's-gonna-let-you-they're-gonna-get-you-throw-your-ass-in-the-grass-cemetery-in-the-hood?' Jerome started rapping.

'Never!'

'The-mon-u-ment-like-the-mom-u-meant-is-cold-I'm-told-how-many-times-I-gotta-tell-it.' Jerome was strutting before the crowd. 'What's-it-take-to-taste-and-smell-it-when-you-got-no-chance-to-sell-it-'cause-everything's-for-sale-except-for-me-and-you-no-matter-what-we-do-we're-the-boys-in-the-hood-ain't-no-fuck-in-Hollywood.'

'AND-THE-*GIRLS*-IN-THE-HOOD!'

'Boys-and-*girls*-in-the-hood-ain't-no-fuck-in-Hollywood,' Jerome politically corrected himself.

'AIN'T-NO-FUCK-IN-HOLLY-WOOD!' the crowd rapped back.

'Thanks, Jerome,' West said.

'AIN'T-NO-FUCK-IN-HOLLY-WOOD!' The crowd was out of control.

'Jerome, that's enough!'

'Say it again, brothers!' Jerome was spinning and kick-boxing. 'AIN'T-NO-FUCK-IN-HOLLY-WOOD!'

'AIN'T-NO-FUCK-IN-HOLLY-WOOD!'

Sirens sounded in the distance.

chapter twenty

The Robins Center, where the Spiders played basketball before great crowds, was between the private lot where Ehrhart had tucked her Mercedes, and the X lot where commoners parked, no more than two rows of parking spaces or approximately fifty yards from the track, where this moment Brazil was running hard for the second time this day.

It was late afternoon. He had spent hours working on the COMSTAT computer crisis while the media continued to kick around mean-spirited stories about Fishsteria and the vandalism of Jefferson Davis's statue. Comments of low intelligence and terribly poor taste streaked through e-mail and were passed word-of-mouth through offices, restaurants, bars and health clubs before at last finding their way to the ears of the police.

Cops finally *catch* something, no longer let crooks *off the hook*.

Knock knock. Who's there? Police. Police who? Plice get rid of the fish.

Jeff Davis *coloredized*.

What's black and white and red all over? (Jeff Davis.)

Brazil had been desperate for a break. He needed to clear his head and work off stress. What he did not need was to see Lelia Ehrhart walking out of the Robins Center, heading toward her black Mercedes parked in the Spiders Club lot. He knew instantly what she was up to and was furious.

Brazil sprinted off the track and through the gate. He got to her as she was backing up. He tapped on her window as the car continued to move. She braked, made sure her doors were locked and the window down an inch.

'I'm Officer Brazil,' he said, wiping his face with the hem of his tank top.

'I didn't recognize you,' Ehrhart said, appraising him as if thinking about a purchase.

'I don't mean to be rude,' Brazil said, 'but what were you doing in the gym?'

'Fact finishing.'

'Did you talk to Bobby Feeley?'

'Yes.'

'I wish you hadn't done that, Mrs. Ehrhart,' Brazil said.

'Someone had to, and I have a personal interested in this that has to do with me. Aren't you visiting outsiders from Charlotte always telling us to community police? Well, here I am. How old are you?'

'Community policing does not include interfering with an investigation,' Brazil told her.

She stared at his legs.

'You are quite the athletic,' she flitted. 'I have a trainer. If ever you want to work in together, the both of us, wouldn't that be nice?'

'It's generous of you to offer.' Brazil was courteous, professional and respectful.

'Which gym do you work in out of?' She rolled the window down the rest of the way, caressing every part of him with eyes that had huge purchasing power.

'I've gotta go,' Brazil said as she stared at his crotch.

'How often do you hang yourself out here?' she inquired, continuing her physical examination of him. 'You are very sweating. It's running all down you in little rivets and you look very hots. You should take your shirts off and drinks some Gatorades.' She patted the passenger's seat. 'Come sits, Andy. Out of the heats. I have a swimmer pool at my house. We could go and jump on it. Think how good that would feeling when you are so hots.'

'Thank you, Mrs. Ehrhart.' Brazil couldn't get away fast enough. 'But I've got to head out.'

He ran off. Her window hummed up. Her tires sounded angry when she sped away.

Brazil took two steps at a time and ran inside the Robins Center, dashing into the gym, where Bobby Feeley was working on defense and fouling imaginary Cavaliers.

'Mr. Feeley?' Brazil said from the sidelines.

Feeley dribbled the ball over to him. He started laughing.

'What is this? The inquisition? Or are you just looking for the track, man?'

'I'm with the Richmond Police Department, investigating the vandalism that occurred in Hollywood Cemetery last night,' Brazil explained.

'You always go to work dressed like that?' Feeley tried another jump shot and the ball didn't even come close.

'I just happened to be out running when I saw Lelia Ehrhart drive off,' Brazil said.

'Now that's a piece of work.' Feeley retrieved the ball. 'How long's she been on this planet?'

'Look, Mr. Feeley . . .'

'It's Bobby.'

'Bobby, do you have any idea why someone would paint a statue to look like you?' Brazil said. 'Assuming you didn't do it.'

'I didn't do it.' Feeley faked passes. 'And although it's very flattering to think there's a statue of me in a historic white cemetery, I don't think so.' He missed a layup. 'I'm a pretty sorry basketball player and not likely to be anybody's hero.'

'How'd you get on the team?' Brazil had to ask as he watched Feeley miss another layup.

'I used to be better than this,' Feeley said. 'I pretty much ripped up the court in high school, got recruited a million places and decided on Richmond. So I get here and something goes haywire. I'm telling you, man, I started worrying that maybe I had lupus, muscular dystrophy, Parkinson's.'

Feeley sat on the basketball, resting his chin in his hand, depressed.

'Doesn't help that I'm wearing Twister Gardener's jersey,' Feeley said despondently. 'I've wondered if that's part of it. Getting psyched out, you know, because everybody looks at my number twelve and remembers him.'

'I'm not from here.' Brazil sat beside him. 'More into tennis than basketball.'

'Well, let me tell you,' Feeley said, 'Twister was the best player this school's ever seen. I got no doubt he'd be playing for the Bulls right now if he hadn't got killed.'

'What happened?' Brazil asked as something started stirring deep in his mind.

'Car wreck. Some fucking drunk driver on the fucking wrong side of the road. Last August, right before his sophomore year.'

The story pained Brazil. It enraged him that an extraordinary talent could be completely annihilated in a second by someone who had decided to throw back a few more beers at the bar.

'I'm just glad I got to see him play. I guess you could say he was my hero.' Feeley got up and stretched his limber seven-foot frame.

'Pretty tough to wear your hero's jersey,' Brazil commented as he got up, too.

Feeley shrugged. 'It's part of running with the big dogs.'

'Maybe you should get your number changed,' Brazil suggested.

Feeley was startled. His face got hard, eyes flashing.

'What did you say?' he asked.

'Maybe you should retire the number, let someone else have it,' Brazil explained.

Feeley's eyes snapped. His jaw muscles bunched.

'Fuck no.'

'Just a suggestion,' Brazil said. 'But I don't understand

why you'd want to keep it if you get psyched. Give it up, Bobby.'

'No fucking way!'

'Just do it.'

'Fuck you!'

'It really makes sense,' Brazil went on reasonably.

'Motherfucking never!'

'Why not?'

'Because nobody would fucking care about it as much as I do!'

'How do you know?'

Feeley threw the basketball as hard as he could and it swished in without touching the rim.

'Because nobody would respect Twister, treat him right, spread the word about him like I would!'

Feeley ran full speed for the ball, dribbled with his right hand and left and slam-dunked.

'And I'll tell you what, too, you'll never see that jersey dirty or tossed in a corner somewhere!' He dunked the ball over the back of his head, the rim vibrating. 'Some little spoiled piece of shit coming in here and wearing Twister's number!'

He hooked it in, rebounded, slam-dunked, snapped it up, thundered to the top of the key and banked it in, wrestled it away from grabbing hands and jumped a good two feet off the floor, sinking it.

'Does Twister have family around here?' Brazil asked.

'I remember going to the home games and seeing him with some little kid. Twister would sit the little guy right behind the bench,' Feeley said, hitting free throws and talking at the same time. 'I got the impression it might be his little brother.'

At James River Monuments, Ruby Sink was doing a little investigating on her own. The noise of air hammers and pneumatic tools was awful, and someone was bouncing a four-point bumper on Southern Georgia granite. The sandblaster was going and an overhead crane was lifting a thirteen-hundred-pound monument that was chipped and stained green along the top from moss.

White Vermont marble was very difficult and not used anymore and Floyd Rumble had a chore on his hands. He was a bit overwhelmed, anyway. It had been one of those days. His back hurt and his son was stuck at the desk inside the office because the secretary was on vacation.

Then Colonel Bailey, who had Alzheimer's, had come in for the fourth time in a week to say that he was to be buried in uniform and wanted something very patriotic engraved on his Saint Cloud Gray marble monument. Each time, Rumble made out a new order because the last thing he'd ever do was humiliate anyone.

Rumble picked up a knife and resumed cutting a leaf on Nero Black marble, thinking how bad he'd felt when stockbroker Ben Neaton had suddenly dropped dead of a heart attack and the wife had to come in here, too distraught to think, much less pick out something.

So Rumble had suggested the elegant black stone because Mr. Neaton had always driven shiny black Lincolns and worn dark suits. The inscription, *Not Gone,*

Just Reinvested, had been stenciled into a sheet of rubber which was placed over the face of the stone. The sandblaster had etched the letters in a matter of minutes, but Rumble always cut the detail work, such as ivy or flowers, by hand.

It was common for bereft, shocked people to ask Rumble to make all decisions and unfold the story of their lost loved one's life, and what the person had last said or eaten or worn, or had intended to do the next day. Always there was that *one little thing* that gave the person a bad feeling.

Rumble would hear endless renditions of how the husband didn't go out and get the paper like he always did while his wife was fixing breakfast and school lunches and getting the kids up and ready for school and making sure they didn't miss the bus before she fixed his eggs the way he liked them and asked what he might like for supper and what time he'd be home.

Ruby Sink had worn out Rumble's patience. She had been planning her monument ever since her sister died eleven years ago, and it wasn't uncommon for Miss Sink to wander in once a month just to see what sorts of things Rumble was working on. First she wanted an angel, then a tree, then a plain African granite headstone with raised lilies, then she got into marbles and went through them like a woman rifling through her closet trying to figure out what color dress to wear. She had to have Lake Superior Green, then Rainbow, then Wausau, then Carnelian, then Mountain Red, and so on.

Rumble's business had been in the family for three

generations. He had dealt with all sorts and was smart enough to quit placing orders for Miss Sink after the third time she had changed her mind.

'Good afternoon, Floyd,' Miss Sink walked right in talking loudly above the chop chop chop and rat-a-tats of machines and blasting of carbon sand and whirring of the exhaust fan and roaring of compressors.

'I guess so,' he said.

'I don't know how you stand all the dust in here.' She always said that.

'It's good for you,' he always replied. 'Same thing they use in toothpaste. All day long your teeth get cleaned. You ever see a Rumble with bad teeth?'

In part, he went down this path to distract Miss Sink. Sometimes it worked. Today it didn't.

'I guess you heard.' She moved close to confide in him.

The thirteen-hundred-pound monument hung perilously midair and Rumble thought about what a chore restoring it was going to be. All duplications of old work like that had to be chiseled by hand, and there was no way he was going to start on it while Miss Sink was within a mile of his shop. She'd decide she had finally found what she wanted. She'd know without a spark of doubt that she had to have soft white Vermont marble chiseled by hand.

He started looking through trays of stencil types, preparing to etch a Hebrew inscription on Sierra White marble while his crew lowered the damaged monument into a cart.

'You heard what they did to Jefferson Davis,' Miss Sink told him.

'I heard something about it.'

Rumble started laying out stencil types. They had to be plastic so one could see through them, but they broke all the time.

'As you know, Floyd, I'm on the board.'

'Yes, ma'am.'

'The overwhelming matter that must be taken care of is how badly is the statue damaged, how do we go about restoring it and how much will it cost.'

Rumble hadn't gone into the cemetery to look yet. Nor would he bother at all unless he was offered the job.

'He paint any of the marble base or just the bronze?' Rumble inquired.

'Mostly the bronze.' Just the thought of it made her sick. 'But he did paint the top of the base to look like a basketball floor. So yes, some of the marble was involved.'

'I see. So he's standing on a basketball floor. What else?'

'Well, the worst part. He painted a basketball uniform on him, tennis shoes and the whole bit, and changed his race.'

'Sounds like we got two problems here,' Rumble said as he tossed out another broken letter and the diamond saw in a corner started cutting through stone. 'To fix the marble, I'm going to have to chisel it down and put on a new surface. As for the bronze, if we're talking about oil-based paints . . .'

'Oh we are,' she said. 'I could tell. Nothing spray-painted here. This was all done in thick coats with a brush.'

'We'll have to strip that down, maybe with turpentine,

then refinish with a polyurethane coating so we don't get oxidation.'

'We'll study this, then,' Miss Sink announced.

'We should,' Rumble said. 'Eventually we'll have to get Jeff Davis in my shop. I can't be doing all this work on him in the middle of a public cemetery with people all over the place. Means we'll have to hoist him up with a crane and a sling, lower him in a truck.'

'I 'spect we should close the cemetery while you're doing all this,' Miss Sink said.

'During the removal, for sure. But I'd do it now anyway in case other people get ideas about other monuments. And I suggest you get security patrolling around there.'

'I'll get Lelia to take care of it.'

'In the meantime, I don't want anyone touching that statue. Now that's saying you're asking me to fix it.'

'Of course you're the one, Floyd.'

'It will take me a day or so to get it out of the cemetery, and then I don't know how long after that.'

'I guess all this is going to cost a pretty penny,' the parsimonious Miss Sink said.

'I'll be as fair as I can be,' Rumble said.

Bubba had no intention of being fair. There had been too much trauma and disruption for him to even think about sleep, and as soon as the detective had left with lifted prints and other evidence, Bubba had returned to his shop. He had cleaned up fast and hard, anger giving him boundless energy while Half Shell bawled and bawled and ran around in circles and jumped up and down from the overturned barrel.

Bubba's karma had not been favorably inclined so far this day. He had bought a bag of large white marbles and a bottle of iridescent yellow paint. His attempts at drilling holes through the marbles were disastrous. They kept slipping out of the vise, and when he tightened the vise more, the marbles cracked. The drill bit kept sliding off, then broke. This went on and got no better until he came up with a clever idea.

At several minutes past three P.M., Honey poked her head inside the shop, a concerned expression on her face.

'Sweetie, you haven't eaten a thing all day,' she worried.

'Don't have time.'

'Sweetie, you always have time.'

'Not now.'

She spotted what was left of her favorite large pearl necklace on the workbench.

'Sweetie, what are you doing?'

She dared to venture several inches inside his shop. The pearls were loose and Bubba was widening the holes through them with a 5/64th-inch drill bit.

'Bubba? What are you doing to my pearls? My father gave me those pearls.'

'They're fake, Honey.'

Bubba threaded black string through one of the pearls and tied a tight knot. He did the same thing with another pearl and took the two lengths of string and tied them together maybe four inches below the pearls. He slowly whirled this above his head like a lasso. He liked the way it felt, and proceeded to make several more.

'Honey, you go on back inside the house,' Bubba said. 'This is something you don't need to see or tell anybody about.'

She wavered in the doorway, her eyes uneasy.

'You're not doing something sneaky, are you?' she dared to ask.

Bubba didn't reply.

'Precious, I've never known you to do anything sneaky. You've always been the most honest man I've ever met, so honest everybody's always taking advantage of you.'

'I'm meeting Smudge at his house around six and we're heading out to Suffolk.'

She knew what that meant. 'Dismal Swamp? Please don't tell me you're going there, Bubba.'

'May or may not.'

'Think of all the snakes.' She shivered.

'There's snakes everywhere, Honey,' said Bubba, who was acutely phobic of snakes and believed no one knew it. 'A man can't spend his life worrying about snakes.'

Smudge had his own workshop, which was much better organized than Bubba's and equipped with only the essentials. He had the expected table, power miter, radial-arm and band saws, a thickness planer, wood lathe, workbench and shop vacuum. Smudge wasn't fond of snakes, either, but he used common sense.

The weather had been unseasonably warm. Water moccasins might be stirring in the Dismal Swamp, meaning Smudge had no intention of hunting coons down there. Southampton County would be better, although probably not for Bubba. Smudge was at his workbench Super-Gluing a real rattlesnake rattle to the tail of a long rubber snake. He snagged the snake with a simple eagle-claw hook threaded with twenty feet of monofilament.

chapter twenty-one

Smudge loaded the portable dog pen on the back of his coon-hunting fully loaded V10 Dodge Ram.

'Get in, Tree Buster,' Smudge commanded.

The open-spotted male coon hound jumped eagerly into the truck and got inside his pen. Tree Buster was born to tree coons and that's all he lived to do, that and eat. Tree Buster was a Grand Show Champ. He had a horn bawl with a lot of volume, which was the best voice a coon dog could have, unless one was hunting in the mountains, and then a higher pitch would carry better.

Smudge was proud of Tree Buster and fed him Sexton dry food ordered out of Kentucky. Tree Buster had tight cat feet, strong legs and good muscles, his ears reached the end of his nose, his bite was good and he could carry his tail up like a saber. This was not quite the quality of hound Smudge had encouraged Bubba to order from an ad in *American Cooner*.

Bubba was certain he'd gotten a great deal. The dog was already broken in and was sired by Thunder Clap, who had placed high in a number of world hunts. Bubba had bought the dog for three thousand dollars sight unseen, not knowing she'd been raised tracking coyotes, deer, bear, bobcats. She was especially good at sniffing out armadillo, or *possum on the half shell* as the good ole boys called them, thus explaining the dog's name.

Bubba parked his Cherokee in Smudge's driveway. Bubba slid his portable dog pen out the back and loaded it into Smudge's truck. Half Shell stopped bawling. Her tail was wagging furiously.

'Kennel up,' Bubba told his dog.

Bubba tossed in his knee-high waders, headlamp, flashlight, gloves and oilcloth Barbour coat, a portable phone, a compass, a Bucktool and a lock-blade Spyderco knife. He set his knapsack on the floor in front of his seat. It was packed with many things, including Cheez Whiz sandwiches, Kool-Aid, his Colt Anaconda and tricks.

'Looks like you packed for a snowstorm,' Smudge commented as he backed out of the driveway.

'Never know what the weather might do this time of year,' Bubba replied.

'It's pretty warm, Bubba. I don't know about the Dismal Swamp. Snakes might be squirming.'

Bubba acted as if he didn't care while the hair stood up all over his body.

'We can talk about it at Loraine's,' Bubba said.

They drove through peanut country, mulch plants and bleak stretches of newly plowed farmland. Nothing much had changed in Wakefield over the years, except for the new National Weather Service WSR-88-D Doppler radar installation. It looked like a huge high-tech water tower and had stirred up superstitions among neighbors who didn't particularly want the thing even close to their yards.

Bubba, for one, always got an eerie feeling when the radar dome appeared over the tops of trees. Sure, he had no doubt that it was used to track towering storm clouds, wind direction and provide county-level coverage of tornado threats. But he also believed there was more to it than that. Aliens were involved. Perhaps they used the radar installations to communicate to the mother ship, in whatever wrinkle of time or plane of reality that might be. After all, the aliens had been sent here by someone. They needed a way to call home.

There had been a time when Bubba might have confided such a theory with Smudge, but no more. He glanced at his good buddy and felt resentment. When they passed the Shrine of the Infant Jesus in Prague church, Bubba did not feel like turning the other cheek. When they cruised by Purviance Funeral Home, Bubba experienced dark feelings about Smudge's longevity. When they entered Southampton County, where buzzards on the road were looking for snacks, Bubba thought about how Smudge had picked Bubba's bones clean ever since they'd been friends in church.

Just beyond wetlands, Loraine's Restaurant offered Fast, Friendly Service, a neon sign out front advertising FR ED SHR P OYST & CRA LE S $13.25 with a blinking arrow pointing to the small cream building with red trim. The parking lot was an old truck stop with piles of gravel, and islands where there used to be gas and diesel pumps. A Norfolk-Southern train rumbled behind the building as Bubba and Smudge parked and walked past front windows hung with Smithfield hams.

Loraine's was a favorite hangout for coon hunters, although not as busy in chasing season as it was in killing season, which was fine with Myrtle, the cashier. She supposed she could understand killing coons years back when pelts were going for twenty dollars apiece. But no one bothered once the price dropped to eight dollars. Whatever the boys shot usually stayed in the woods.

Myrtle was always happy to see Smudge and Bubba. They hunted for the joy of putting their dogs through their paces, it seemed. They only killed coons when it was important to rev up the dogs again, make them believe if they treed a coon, maybe they'd get to kill it. Myrtle couldn't count all the times coon hunters came into the restaurant dressed in Delta Wings camouflage covered with blood. The guys smoked and chewed. They ordered lots of hot coffee and All-U-Can-Eat fried oysters and shrimp, Captain's Platters and meat loaf.

Tables were plastic-covered and designated with bingo numbers. Bubba and Smudge chose B4, with its cheery message, 'Come Back Real Soon.' Bubba started digging in the little wicker basket of A-1, Worcestershire, sugar, Tabasco, and packets of jellies to see if there were any captain's wafers hiding in there. A ceiling fan turned slowly. Smudge and Bubba looked at the specials on the board, next to a sign that read 'We reserve the right to refuse service to anyone.'

'Let's put it all out on the table, Bubba,' Smudge said, taking off his Ducks Unlimited cap. 'How much?'

'How much you want?' Bubba tried to sound macho and confident, but inside he was Jell-O.

'Five hundred,' Smudge said, studying Bubba carefully to see his reaction.

'I'll raise it to a thousand,' Bubba said as his gut turned to ice.

'You on the map, good buddy? Or just mud flapping.'

'I got it in my pocket,' Bubba said.

Smudge shook his head. 'That old hound of yours has treed a chicken on top of a chicken pen and a goat on top of a stump. Closest it got to a coon was treeing one on top of a telephone pole. She won't go across water, just barks at it when she's not hanging around your feet. Half Shell ain't worth the lead to shoot her, Bubba.'

'We'll see,' Bubba said as Myrtle came up to the table, notepad in hand.

'You boys decided yet?'

'Iced tea, fried shrimp and oysters,' Bubba said.

'One-time plate or all-u-can-eat?'

'Lay it on me,' Bubba said.

Myrtle laughed, chewing gum. 'And Smudge?'

'The same.'

'You boys sure are easy,' she said, brushing crumbs off their table and walking back to the kitchen.

'Where we headed?' Bubba asked.

'Gonna start out at the intersection of 620 and 460 right over there.' Smudge pointed. 'And head left way up in the middle of nowhere. Just muddy roads, forest and creeks. I did some checking into the Dismal Swamp and you definitely don't want that right now. Apparently when it's warm during the day, snakes are balled up like earthworms, there's so many of 'em. When it cools off at night, you run over 'em like sticks on the road.'

Bubba was having a hard time breathing.

'You all right, good buddy?' Smudge said.

'Allergies. I forgot to bring my Sudafed.'

'Chances are where we're going the snakes aren't going to be near that bad,' Smudge went on. 'And if we see a snake, just let it be. They're more scared of us than we are of them.'

'Who says?' Bubba blurted out. 'Did a snake actually tell someone that? It's like saying dogs have no sense of time. Did someone ask Half Shell if it's true? I've heard tales of a snake going up somebody's pants leg. So how scared is that?'

'Good point,' Smudge replied thoughtfully. 'I've heard the same thing. I must admit I've also heard of snakes chasing people and cobras spitting you in the eye, although I can't say whether it's true.'

divinity tried to calm Smoke and get him out of his dangerous mood. But when he got like this, there was no point ranting and raving about something unless she wanted to get the treatment.

'Baby, it's just I don't want nothing bad to happen to you,' she tried one more time as he sped along Midlothian Turnpike, away from the slum he called a clubhouse where he now had enough of an arsenal to take out an entire police precinct.

'I find him, he's dead,' Smoke said.

Wu-Tang was playing 'Severe Punishment.' Smoke turned it up louder.

'What'd I tell him to do?' Smoke glared at Divinity.

'You told him to paint up the statue,' she said quietly, watching his hands to make sure he didn't head them her way.

'I told him to *paint up*, as in *fuck up*, as in *ruin*.' Smoke gripped the wheel hard. 'I knew I shoulda stayed there and watched. Goddamn it. Shit! Then he paints that little fucking blue fish and the whole fucking world thinks that fish virus has got something to do with it! Where's our credit, huh? Where does it say the *Pikes?*'

'Don't look like we got credit, baby.' She was freezing up inside, waiting for that beast in him to jump out.

'Well, I'm gonna fucking fix that, and you know how?'

'No, baby,' Divinity said, rubbing his neck.

'Don't touch me!' Smoke shoved her away. 'My mind's working.'

The newsroom at this hour was left to a certain breed, the cave fish of journalism, those who slept through the sun and monitored life at its darkest hours. Artis Roop did not keep to a schedule.

He was energized and almost crazed as he hammered on about 'Smokes,' Fishsteria and the same blue fish painted ever so subtly on the base of Basketball Jeff. There had been no real breaks. Roop was rearranging old information, and he knew it. There was nothing else going on except the same old drug shootouts and fights in city council.

'Shit.'

He leaned back in his chair and stretched, cracking his neck to the right and left.

'Got anything for last edition?' night editor Outlaw called out.

'Working on it,' Roop called back.

'How big?'

'How much space I got?' Roop asked.

'Depends on what comes in over the wire,' Outlaw said.

Roop was about to confess that he had nothing worth shit when his phone rang.

'Roop,' he answered.

'How do I know for sure?'

'Huh?' Roop asked.

'How do I know I'm talking to Roop?' the tough male voice came back.

'What is this, some kind of crank call?' Roop was about to hang up.

'I'm the blue fish guy.'

Roop was silent. He flipped open his notepad.

'You ever heard of the Pikes, man?'

'No,' Roop confessed.

'Who the fuck you think painted that fucking statue? What the hell do you think the fucking fish is?'

'A pike?' Roop was fascinated. 'The fish is a pike?'

'You fucking got it.'

'There've been suggestions the fish is actually the

state fish, a trout,' Roop let him know.

'It ain't no trout and you better pay attention 'cause there's a lot going down in this city that the Pikes are taking charge of.'

'So is it fair to say that the Pikes are a gang?' Roop asked.

'No, fuckhead, we're a Girl Scout troop.'

'Then it's all right if I refer to the Pikes as a gang in my article. Who are you?' Roop asked cautiously.

'Your worst nightmare.'

'I mean, really.'

'The leader. I'm whatever I decide to be and I do whatever I want. Your fucking city ain't seen nothing yet. And you can print that in red. Remember the Pikes. You're going to hear from us again.'

'But why a basketball player, and does the fish tag have anything to do with the computer crash . . . ?'

Roop was answered by a dial tone. He called the police.

At this point, tables B3, B6, B2 and B1 had gotten caught up in Bubba and Smudge's conversation.

'Let me tell you what happened to me one time,' said an old man in overalls. 'Found one in my toilet. Lifted the lid and there it was, all curled up, its tongue sliding in and out.'

'Oh my!' exclaimed a woman at the other table. 'How could that have happened?'

'Can only figure it was a hot summer and he wanted to cool off.'

'Snakes are cold-blooded. They don't have to cool off.'

'Might've come up from the sewer.'

'I was out in my johnboat one early morning before it was light, looking for duck when a damn water moccasin dropped into my boat, right on top of my foot, I kid you not. He must've been that big around.' He made a huge circle with his fingers.

'Every time you tell that story, Ansel, the darn thing gets bigger.'

'What'dya do?' Smudge asked as Bubba sat in silence, his face ashen.

'Kicked the damn thing as hard as I could. It sailed right over my head, all wriggly, and I could feel it brush my hair as it went past before splashing in the water.'

'We had one right here in the cooler.' Myrtle came over to join in. She pulled out a chair as if dinner no longer mattered.

'It was the worse scare of my life, fellas. Apparently he was out back sunning hisself on the loading dock when Beane went into the walk-in cooler to get a barrel of pickles. Must've walked right by that God-awful rattlesnake and neither noticed the other. All we could figure after the fact is while Beane had the cooler door open, the snake went on in and got locked up. So little ole me goes in there the next morning for bacon and the minute I opened that door and step inside, I hear something rattling.'

She paused, shivering, shutting her eyes. Everyone was silent and horror-struck as they hung on to every word.

'Well,' Myrtle went on, 'I didn't move. I looked around

and couldn't see nothing at first and then I heard the rattle again. By then I pretty much knew what it was. I mean a rattlesnake's rattle has a rattle all its own and that's what I was hearing sort of in the direction of the ten-gallon buckets of potato salad and coleslaw.' She paused again.

'Where was it?' The man in overalls could wait no longer.

'I'll bet it was eating a rat back there.'

'We don't got rats in the cooler,' Myrtle was quick to defend.

'Then where the hell was it, Myrtle?' Smudge said.

'That far from me.' She held her index fingers six inches apart.

Everybody gasped.

'It was coiled up right next to the mop, its tail sticking up and rattling to beat the band.'

'What'cha do!' Voices chimed in.

'Why, I got bit,' Myrtle said. 'Right there on my left calf. Happened so fast I hardly felt a thing and then that snake was gone like a streak of grease. I was in the hospital a week, and let me tell you, my leg swole up so big they thought they might have to cut it off.'

No one spoke. Myrtle got up.

'Your food ought to be ready,' she said, heading back to the kitchen.

Ruby Sink tried for hours to get Lelia Ehrhart on the phone, but when call waiting kicked in, whoever was on the line simply ignored it.

Agitation and loneliness usually sent Miss Sink into the kitchen, where she had no one to cook for these days except that sweet young police officer renting one of her many properties. She had often thought about inviting him in for dinner, but she didn't have time to cook a big meal.

Making shortbread cookies was one thing. But pot roast and fried chicken were another. Her various boards and associations consumed her, really. It was a wonder she could ever get around to fixing that boy anything. She dialed his pager and left her number, assuming he was probably busy at a crime scene.

The page landed in Brazil's beeper as he was knocking on Weed's front door. It hadn't taken much investigation to check the city directory and see that the Gardeners, not the Joneses, lived in the small house behind Henrico Doctors' Hospital where Brazil had dropped off Weed last night.

When Roop tipped off the police that a gang called the Pikes had claimed responsibility for the cemetery vandalism, Brazil knew Weed quite possibly was into something deep and dangerous.

Brazil knocked again and no one answered. It was dark out with no moon. There were no sounds coming from inside the house and no car in the driveway.

'Anybody home?' Brazil loudly tapped the door with his Mag-Lite.

West covered the back door, and after several minutes

of silence she came around to the front.

'He knows we're looking for him,' West said, slipping her nine-millimeter Sig back into the shoulder holster.

'Maybe,' Brazil said. 'But we can't assume he's figured out we know who his brother was.'

They were walking back to the unmarked car. Brazil shone the flashlight on his pager and read the number. He got out his phone and dialed. Miss Sink answered immediately.

'Andy?'

'Hi,' Brazil said sweetly as he thought of the florist's card on the table in West's hallway.

'We're closing the cemetery to the public,' she told him right off.

West took her time unlocking her door. Brazil was certain she wanted to know who he was talking to.

'I think that's a great idea,' Brazil said.

'The statue's going to have to go into the shop, which is no easy thing when you think how much it weighs. So until we can get it out of the cemetery, the association has decided to keep everybody out except funeral parties, of course.'

'What time?' Brazil said in a hushed voice.

'What?' Miss Sink said. 'I can't hear you.'

'Right now?'

'Oh.' Miss Sink sounded confused. 'You mean is it closed right this minute?'

'Yes.'

'It is. Do you like pot roast?'

'Don't tease me,' Brazil whispered as West jerked open her door.

'I'm not wheezing,' Miss Sink said. 'But this time of year, the pollens are awful, especially if you're in the garden very much. Well, I guess pot roast isn't what young people eat these days. Not fried chicken either.'

'Oh yes I do,' Brazil said as he went around to his door and got in.

'You know what the secret is?' Miss Sink's mood was considerably uplifted.

'Let me guess. Honey.'

West abruptly pulled out onto the street and gunned the engine.

'Exactly right,' Miss Sink exclaimed. 'How did you know that?'

'Had it before. About time I had it again.'

'Now that's talking,' Miss Sink said. 'I'll get back with you and we'll do something about it.'

'I sure hope so,' Brazil said. 'Gotta go.'

West was driving as if she hated the car and was determined to punish it.

'At least I don't make personal calls on the job,' she exclaimed.

Brazil was silent. He stared out his window. He took a deep breath and sighed. He glanced over at her, his feelings a volatile mixture of euphoria and heartache. She was jealous. She must still care. But he couldn't stand to hurt her. He almost told her the truth about Miss Sink. But when he remembered the florist's card, he thought, *forget it.*

Bubba was not in good spirits as Smudge drove through the tar-black night, rocking over ruts and splashing. Stars were out and stingy with their light. Bubba wished he'd never come. He felt awful. He thought he might throw up.

'We really haven't gone over the rules,' Smudge said cheerfully.

'I thought we said they'd be the same as always,' Bubba replied despondently.

'No, I think we ought to add a default clause,' Smudge proposed. 'Since so much is at stake and this is a one-on-one competition.'

'I don't understand,' Bubba commented as suspicions gathered.

'Let's say Half Shell's being her typical loudmouth cold nose and starts treeing about two or three trees away from the tree where the coon is. And Half Shell's doing it every time. You might just want to bag it instead of staying out in the woods all night. Same thing goes for me.'

'So if I default, you get the thousand dollars. If you default I get it. If both of us default, neither of us get a thing,' Bubba deduced.

'You got it, good buddy. We'll go one hundred and twenty minutes, five minutes' rest between each segment, regular competition rules.'

Bubba had no idea where he was when Smudge finally parked the truck on a muddy road and climbed out, leaving the headlights on so they could see. They sat on the tailgate and put on their boots and coats.

'Left my Bucktool inside,' Bubba mumbled.

He crawled into the front seat, far out of Smudge's view, and dug inside his knapsack for the pearls on black string. He stuffed them into a pocket. He slipped out his Colt Anaconda .44. It was not his gun of choice for the night. But Bubba had nothing left. The rest had been stolen. He slid the monster revolver into a Bianchi on-belt HuSH nylon holster beneath his long, full coat.

'We all set?' Smudge asked.

'Let's get on with it,' Bubba replied bravely.

They let their dogs out of the pens and both began howling and baying, tails wagging as Bubba and Smudge restrained them with heavy nylon leashes.

'Good girl,' Bubba said as he kneaded Half Shell behind her long silky ears.

Bubba loved his dog, no matter her deficits. She looked like a long-legged, sleek Beagle with surprisingly soft fur. She loved to lick Bubba's hand and face. Bubba was reluctant to let her go crashing through those woods. If she got snake-bit or a coon tore her up, Bubba couldn't live with it.

Smudge had out the stopwatch. Bubba was petting Half Shell and encouraging her to find a coon this time.

'Go!' he said before Bubba was ready.

Weed ran through the dark along Cumberland Street until he neared I-195's Cherry Street overpass. Banking either side of it were thick growths of trees and shrubs closed in by a high chain-link fence.

He walked over a grassy bank, furtively looking left

and right as he reached the fence, which he could not see through because the foliage was too dense. He almost didn't care what was on the other side. So what if he fell fifteen feet into rushing traffic? What was left in life but for Smoke to find him?

Weed climbed the fence and pushed branches away from his face as he worked his way down the other side. He held his breath as his feet touched ground and blindly pushed his way through tall grass and shrubs, holding his arm in front of his face to protect his eyes. He found himself in a clearing where he could just make out a small camp and a figure sitting in the middle of it, the tip of a cigarette glowing. Weed's heart flipped.

'Who's there?' an unfriendly voice sounded. 'Don't try anything. I can see in the dark and I know you're puny and don't got a gun.'

Weed didn't know what to say. He had no place to run unless he tried to get back over the fence or decided to jump the wall and land on the expressway.

'What's the matter, kitty got your tongue?' the man asked.

'No, sir,' Weed said politely. 'I didn't know nobody was here. I'll be glad to leave.'

'No place to go. That's why you're here, now ain't it?'

'Yes, sir.'

'You can stop all that yes sir shit. My name's Pigeon.'

'That ain't your real name.' Weed ventured a little closer.

'I don't remember my real one anymore.'

'How come they call you that?'

'Because I eat 'em. When I can, that is.'

Weed's stomach flopped.

'What's your name, and why don't you come a little closer so I can get a good look at you.'

'Weed.'

'That ain't your real name,' Pigeon mimicked him.

'Yes, it is, too.'

Weed was hungry and thirsty, and the constant thunder of traffic frightened him. A chill had settled over the night and he was cold in his baggy jeans and Bulls jersey. Pigeon lit another cigarette and Weed caught a glimpse of Pigeon's face in the spurt of flame.

'You're pretty old,' Weed said.

'Older than you, that's for damn sure.' He inhaled deeply and held it.

Weed stepped closer. Pigeon smelled as if he were rotting alive.

'Once you been in here awhile, your eyes start seeing again. Notice? I think all those lights from the cars below us have something to do with it,' Pigeon said. 'You don't look like you're much older than ten.'

'Fourteen,' Weed replied indignantly.

Pigeon dug in a trash bag and pulled out part of a submarine sandwich. Weed's mouth watered but he felt kind of sick, too. Pigeon dug in the bag again and set down a two-liter bottle of Pepsi that was half empty. He flicked the cigarette butt into the night.

'Want some?' Pigeon asked.

'I ain't eating or drinking nothing that came out of the garbage,' Weed said.

'How you know it came out of the garbage?'

''Cause I seen people like you digging things outta the garbage. You go around with shopping carts and don't live anywhere.'

'I live here,' Pigeon said. 'That's somewhere, isn't it? Get your butt closer. I'll show you something.'

Weed tried to block out the smell as he walked all the way to the blanket Pigeon sat on. Pigeon reached into a pocket of his ragged Army jacket and showed Weed a Baggie filled with something.

'Peanut butter crackers,' Pigeon confided in his rough, raspy voice. 'Didn't come outta the trash. The soup kitchen downtown is where.'

'You swear?' Weed said as his stomach begged him to help out a little.

Pigeon nodded.

'I gotta bottle of water that's never been opened. Soup kitchen again. I guess I can share with a little lost boy.'

'I'm not lost,' Weed said.

Bubba was. The minute the dogs had been cut loose, Half Shell had taken off through the woods in one direction while Smudge and Tree Buster had gone in another. The dogs crashed through underbrush for a good ten minutes before Half Shell barked three times.

'STRIKE, HALF SHELL!' Bubba hollered.

The crashing in Smudge's direction stopped. Bubba started running as best he could, breaking branches so he could find his way back, stepping over logs and wading through creeks, his headlamp clearing the way. He stamped and crackled, hoping if there was a snake in the area, it would think twice about getting near all that noise. Bubba's heart was pounding and he was gasping for breath as he followed the sound of his dog.

Half Shell's front paws were up an old pine tree and she was barking and bawling, her tail wagging, when Bubba appeared. Bubba had no doubt that Half Shell had either backtracked and followed the scent of where the coon had been instead of where the coon was going, or Half Shell had found yet one more slick tree that no more had a coon in it than an iceberg had sugarcane. Bubba shone his submersible Super SabreLite up into the branches, sweeping the beam from high to low, disappointed but not surprised.

He dug out two iridescently painted pearls on a string and whirled them over his head. He flung them as high as they would go and was relieved when they snagged halfway up the pine tree. He shone his light on them and they glowed yellow, two perfect coon eyes. Bubba's heart swelled with euphoria as Half Shell continued barking at nothing and Tree Buster crashed in on them, Smudge right behind him.

'TREE, HALF SHELL!' Bubba yelled.

'No way,' Smudge said, trying to catch his breath and sweating.

'Look for yourself.'

Bubba shone the light on the bright yellow eyes high up in the black branches of the tree.

'If there's a coon up there, then how come Tree Buster's

just sitting here and isn't trying to tree it, too,' Smudge declared as Tree Buster panted and stared.

'That's your problem, good buddy,' Bubba said. 'And you can't tell me you don't see it.'

'I see it,' Smudge had to admit. 'Damn thing sure is crouched up there at a funny angle. Looks like he's sideways.'

Bubba got out his score card.

'A hundred points for the strike and another hundred and twenty-five for the tree,' he said, jotting the numbers in the Tree column.

Smudge was sullen. They put the dogs back on the leashes and walked through the woods for five minutes. Smudge started the timer and again they let the dogs loose. Tree Buster bolted off as if he knew something. Half Shell disappeared no more than a hundred feet into the woods before she hit a creek and barked three times.

'STRIKE, HALF SHELL!' Bubba let loose his battle cry.

Tree Buster barked three times much farther away.

'STRIKE, TREE BUSTER!' Smudge yelled.

The two men went after their dogs. Bubba almost tripped over a root and stepped into a hole as he tried not to think about snakes. It was on his mind that if Smudge caught on to what Bubba was doing, Smudge might just leave Bubba out here. Hunters would find Bubba's skeleton years later.

Half Shell continued barking at the shallow creek and Bubba picked her up and carried her across it, setting her under another thick, winter-bare oak tree.

'Bark at that,' Bubba told her.

Half Shell wasn't interested.

'Come on, girl,' Bubba begged.

Half Shell sat, tongue hanging out. Bubba sighed. He reached inside a pocket and pulled out another pair of marbles and a Cheez Whiz sandwich on white bread. Half Shell started barking and drooling as Bubba waved the sandwich in front of her nose. The dog went crazy. Bubba reached up and stuffed the sandwich in a knothole. Half Shell started jumping up at it, barking and baying as Bubba flung another set of eyes high up in the branches of another slick tree.

This went on until there were only twenty minutes left of the two-hour competition. Bubba had amassed nine hundred points. Smudge had nothing. He had stopped talking forty-five minutes ago. He no longer petted his dog.

'We may as well call it a day,' Bubba proposed. 'There's no way you can catch up, Smudge.'

'It ain't over 'til it's over,' Smudge let him know.

The last chance was for Bubba to default, to quit before the competition was over. Smudge knew he had no choice as they walked deeper into the woods during their five-minute break between segments.

Smudge quietly reached inside his knapsack and grabbed hold of the rubber snake, closing his hand around the rattle to silence it as he withdrew the rattler and uncoiled the monofilament attached to it. Smudge cast the snake over Bubba's head. It landed about six yards in front of Bubba's feet.

'What the hell was that?' Bubba asked with fear in his voice.

'What was what?' Smudge asked as he started jerking the line and the rattle sounded.

'Oh God!' Bubba exclaimed, standing perfectly still and shining his light on a huge rattlesnake wriggling toward him at great speed.

'AHHHHHHHHH!!' Bubba screamed, crashing this way and that, tearing open his coat as the snake jumped and tumbled and rattled after him.

'Run! Run!' Smudge yelled, darting wherever necessary to keep the snake where he wanted it.

Bubba suddenly wheeled around, his .44 Anaconda revolver with its eight-inch barrel and scope gripped in both shaking hands. He fired again and again and again as pieces of the snake flew straight up into the air and Smudge dove over a dead tree and rolled through bushes and over a bank and into the creek.

chapter twenty-two

Weed was chilled and achy as he stared out at the city from the dark, stinking camp he shared with Pigeon, who had fallen asleep after drinking a quart of Colt 45.

Weed wondered what Officer Brazil was doing and if everybody was out looking for him. Weed wondered if the cops had found anything that might cause him a problem. Maybe they could make him doodle on some kind of lie detector and figure out he was the one who painted the statue.

Pigeon had shared two peanut butter crackers with Weed. He had given Weed four sips of water, saying it had to last. Weed decided his hideaway stunk worse than the Pikes' clubhouse, and he thought of his nice home and good food and clean bed.

Weed would never go back to his mama again. He'd probably never see her again. He'd never spend another weekend with his father, not that he really wanted to, anyway. Weed would have to live like Pigeon because the Pikes would always be looking for him. He could never be free again. He had a slave number to remind him in case he forgot.

Pigeon rolled over and came to about the time his beer wore off. He fluffed the mound of dirty clothes that served as his pillow. His yawn was an open garbage can Weed could smell two yards away.

'You awake?' Weed said.

'Not by choice.'

'How come you live the way you do, Pigeon?' Weed asked. 'You always lived this way?'

'I was a little kid like you once,' Pigeon said. 'Grew up and fought in Vietnam, came home and didn't want to be part of nothing.'

'How come?'

'Way I felt. Still do.'

'Me, too,' Weed said. 'Maybe I'll just hang out with you from now on.'

'The hell you will!' Pigeon said in a voice that startled Weed. 'You ever been shipped off to war, had your foot shot off, part of your hand, too? Ever been in mental hospitals 'til they can't keep you no more so they dump your ass out on the street? Ever slept on the sidewalk in the dead of winter, nothing but a newspaper for a blanket? You ever eaten rats?'

Weed was horrified. 'Did you really get your foot shot off?'

Pigeon raised his right leg and showed his stump. Weed couldn't see it in detail because it was covered with a sock and the morning was still pretty dark.

'How come you were in mental hospitals?' Weed got

around to the most important question as he had second thoughts about staying with Pigeon.

'Crazzzzzzy.' Pigeon shook his body and rolled his eyes.

'No you ain't.'

Weed thought of the fence again and if he could get back over it fast.

'Well, I am. Sometimes I see things that aren't there. Especially at night. People coming at me with knives, guns. Cut off arms, legs, blood flying everywhere. They got all kinds of names for it, but it don't matter in the long run, Weed. No matter what you call something, it's still the same thing.'

Pigeon fished another cigarette butt out of his pocket, and when he lit it, Weed saw his mangled hand. All that was left was part of the index finger and thumb.

'What you running from?' Pigeon asked.

'Who says I am?'

'I do.'

'So what.'

'Cops after you for something?' Pigeon asked. 'Don't be shy, boy. They been after me a time or two.'

'So what if they is?' Weed said.

'Huh.' Pigeon blew out smoke, wheezing in the dark. 'Someone's after you for sure. I bet it's some other kid out there. Maybe you stole his drugs or something.'

'No, I didn't! I never even seen drugs! He's just mad 'cause I didn't do what he told me to!'

'How mad? Like maybe he's gonna really get you?'

Tears filled Weed's eyes. He wiped them away, hoping Pigeon couldn't see.

'Huh, one of those *bad* kids. Shoot people for the hell of it,' Pigeon went on. 'Whole new breed. And they get away with it too, for the most part.'

Weed's fury burned hot like the cigarette filter burning Pigeon's lips. Pigeon tossed it and seemed disappointed.

'Kids worse than what I saw in 'Nam. All strapped up with bombs. *Hi, nice to meet ya. KABOOM!*' Pigeon went on. 'Least over there we had a reason. Sure as hell wasn't no goddamn sport, tell you what.'

'He already hurt me more 'an once,' Weed blurted out. 'Made me join his gang and tattooed my finger when I didn't want to and now I'm not in school and ain't been to art class or the last two band practices! And he knows where I live and if I go anywhere he'll find me and blow my head off. He's worse than the devil!'

'Sounds like only one thing to do.' Pigeon pondered the situation. 'You said the cops might be looking for you?'

'Maybe.'

'What'd you do?'

'Painted a statue in the cement-tary.'

'Let them catch you.'

Weed was shocked.

'Why would I want to do that?' he asked.

''Cause you get locked up, the devil can't get you.'

'I don't want to go to no jail!'

'They put you in a home for kids, right across the street from the jail. You get clothes, three meals a day, your own little room, play basketball, watch TV, go to class. You want a doctor, a shrink, they give it to you. How bad's that? Oughta hear the kids on the street. *Vacation. Where you been, man? Man, I been on vacation.* Rotten little bastards.

'Now kids, I'm afraid of. Been beat up, robbed, rolled, cut on, kicked in the nuts. One time they set me on fire for the helluvit. And what happens to 'em? They go away on fucking *vacation* for two, three weeks. Come right back out, laughing, strutting under streetlights, big wads of cash in their pockets.'

'I don't want to go on vacation,' Weed said.

'You want to die?'

'No. Uh uh, Pigeon. I don't.'

'Then get locked up somewhere 'fore the devil gets you,' Pigeon said. 'Maybe by the time you get out, someone will've got him first. People like him don't live too old.'

Three blocks south on Spring Street, Brazil and West were inspecting a section of fence encircling the final resting place of presidents, governors, Civil War heroes, Richmond's first and finest families, and more recently, citizens of all sorts who wished to be interred there, realizing, of course, that all lots with river views were taken.

Early morning sunlight was touched by cool fingers of shade in a remote section of Hollywood Cemetery where low-lying ground gave way to brambles and the river. West and Brazil had discovered a hole in the fence that was big enough to allow unlawful passage to an average-size adult. But there was too much rust to suggest the chain links had been cut in recent months or possibly years.

'He didn't come in this way,' Brazil decided as he looked around.

West was irritated by the deduction, mainly because she had not made it first.

'Didn't realize you were a detective. Thought you were flack,' she said.

'I'm not flack.'

'All right, P.R., a reporter, a novelist.'

Brazil was reminded of the op-ed piece due pretty soon and he hadn't even started it. He couldn't do anything about the newsletter for the website, either, because the computer system was still frozen on the same fish map. Nor had Brazil given even a moment's thought to the computer manual he was supposed to help write, as if it mattered right now, anyway.

'My obvious point is he certainly could have gotten in easily,' West said.

Brazil stepped through the hole, careful not to snag his uniform or cut himself.

'You're right,' he said. 'You coming in?'

'No. This is your hunch, not mine. I, for one, don't think he's going to return to the scene of the crime, as you put it. What makes you so sure of that?'

'Because what he did was very personal and emotional,' Brazil said. 'I think he won't be able to resist taking another look. To him the statue's not Jeff Davis. It's a monument to Twister. There's got to be a lot of stuff going on inside Weed's head, and I intend to get to him before the Pikes find him first.'

'Maybe they've already found him,' West said.

Brazil thought about that as he scanned leaning headstones so old the inscriptions were ghosts of words no longer readable. Trees that had been around before the Civil War cast thick shadows, and leaves rustled with breaths of wind.

'Look, Virginia, I'm going to hang out here for a while,' Brazil said. 'I'll radio someone to come get me when I'm done.'

She hesitated. Brazil sensed she was bothered that he would stay, that he didn't seem to care if she went on without him.

'Well, anyway.' West hesitated again, then was disagreeable. 'All I can say is it's amazing the problems in this fucking city and what? They'll spend a fucking fortune on a fucking cemetery.'

'Actually,' said Brazil, who had done much research on Richmond and its surroundings, 'Hollywood's a non-profit, nonstock corporation owned by its lot owners, not the city.'

'Huh,' retorted West as she stalked off. 'Who cares.'

Lelia Ehrhart did. She was serving her eighth term as chairman of Hollywood Cemetery's board of directors, which required very little of her time, really. The majority of lot owners were dead, the annual meeting with the board always poorly attended, suggestions and complaints few.

Ehrhart had never needed anyone at meetings. She

had never needed the opinions or suggestions of others. It had been her idea, and her idea alone, to ban picnics, snacks, alcoholic beverages, bicycles, jogging, motorcycles, skateboards, Rollerblades, recreational vehicles, vehicles pulling trailers and boom boxes from the grounds. Ehrhart was passionately devoted to the cemetery and its importance as a tourist attraction and celebration of lives faded but not forgotten, especially those Ehrhart claimed as her relations.

'This is far more than vandals,' Ehrhart declared in the private boardroom of the Commonwealth Club, where she had called the meeting and then changed the time of it. 'This is a front to our unalien rights, to their liberty and happiness, to our very civilization. These vandals, these unrepentent, cold-bloody juvenile delinquents that call themselfs Pikes have descegraded everyone sitting in their room.'

This did not include Chief Judy Hammer, since she was originally from Arkansas. She ran through the ivy-framed entrance and up the old brick front steps of the historic and aristocratic club where women could not be members, but as guests of husbands or male friends were welcome to enjoy all amenities except the Victorian bar, Men's Grill, swimming pool, gym, steam and sauna rooms, squash and racquetball courts and reading rooms.

Such restrictions were of little concern to public-service minded women busy with forming various committees for the Bal du Bois and its debutantes, or supporting the arts with auctions of wine, vacations, fine jewelry and other luxury items, or planning wedding receptions or exhibits for the Maymont Flower & Garden Show, or lunching with the Virginia Federation of Garden Clubs, Daughters of the American Revolution or Daughters of the Confederacy, and with the Junior League, and of course, first families of Virginia and wives of legislators.

Hammer was twenty minutes late. She rushed into the marble foyer, impervious to the splendid Oriental rug, the antique crystal chandelier, the velvet love seat and gilt mirrors and wall-size portrait of George Washington. She did not pause to check her coat or to admire the stunning paintings of Robert E. Lee and Lighthorse Harry. Judy Hammer had little interest in a hundred-and-eight-year-old club founded by former Confederate officers who, according to the original charter, wished to promote social intercourse and maintain a library.

The door to the board room on the first floor was shut. She opened it slowly and quietly as Lelia Ehrhart held forth. Hammer scanned the faces of City Councilman Reverend Solomon Jackson, Mayor Stuart Lamb, Lieutenant Governor June Miller, NationsBank president Dick Albright, *Richmond-Times Dispatch* publisher James Eaton, and Metropolitan Richmond Convention & Visitors Bureau president Fred Ross.

The men glanced at Hammer. Several of them nodded. All of them looked restless and ready to tell Ehrhart to commit suicide. Hammer found a seat.

'. . . It's so much and more than the city of the deads,' Ehrhart was saying with authority. 'It is the Valhalla of we brave mens who carried the Southern Cross into their bosom of deadly, waving it for the because of states' right, to at last be buried, many we don't know who, in Hollywood.'

Ehrhart would have been a stunning blond were it not for several physical flaws that caused her to be more unpleasant and driven than she otherwise might have been. Her hair wasn't really as blond as she let on, and as she got older it was getting darker, requiring frequent trips to the Simon & Gregory hair salon. Nor did arduous hours with her personal trainer remedy her genetically coded long neck, narrow shoulders, tiny breasts and broad hips.

Ehrhart covered up as best she could, exclusively in Escada. This morning she was dazzling in a blaze orange skirt and blouse with matching earrings, pumps and purse. Hammer, out of breath and perspiring beneath her gray pinstripe suit, thought Ehrhart looked like a traffic cone.

'Two presidents and five governors are restful there,' she preached. 'Not to forget, also, Brigadier Generals Armistead, Gracie, Gregg, Morgan, Paxton, Stafford and Hill.'

'Hill was a *major* general,' Lieutenant Governor Miller remarked blandly. 'And all the generals you just mentioned were interred in Hollywood only for a time. Aren't still there, in other words.'

Ehrhart had found the seven names in the back of a booklet listing Confederate States of America generals, and had not noticed nor comprehended the parenthetical phrase *interred for a time*. Indeed, it wasn't until this moment she realized her husband's alleged ancestor, General Bull Paxton, was among the seven war heroes whose remains she was now being told had been moved out of the cemetery. Ehrhart refused to stand corrected.

'I believe I'm in the right.' She smiled coolly at the lieutenant governor.

'You're not,' he matter-of-factly replied in a voice that rarely rose or showed strain. 'There are twenty-five generals in Hollywood, but not those seven. You might want to go back and check your booklet.'

'What booklet?'

'The one you didn't read very carefully,' he said.

chapter twenty-three

Bubba, Smudge, Half Shell and Tree Buster had spent the night in the woods. This was not by choice. When Bubba had blasted the rubber rattlesnake and Smudge had taken a flying leap, Smudge had ended up with a bump on his head.

Smudge was confused and disoriented and bleeding a little. This left navigation entirely in Bubba's hands. It meant he alone had to restrain two dogs on leashes to make sure that one or both of them didn't go after a coon.

'Watch the root there,' Bubba said to Smudge as they trudged through brush and trees so thick they could have been in a rain forest for all Bubba knew.

'How far?' Smudge slurred.

'Can't be much farther.' Bubba said what he had been saying for the past eight hours.

Smudge wasn't going to be able to walk much longer. It was a good thing Bubba had brought food, although it was a shame he had stuffed half of his Cheez Whiz sandwich in a knothole. Boy, what he wouldn't give for that now. At least water wasn't a problem. The fucking stuff was everywhere, and each time they happened upon it, Half Shell would dig in her feet and bark, and Bubba would have to carry her over another creek, some of which were very swift and deep. The only thing that kept Bubba going was anger.

'I still can't get over what a rotten thing that was to do,' he said to Smudge yet once again.

Smudge was too exhausted and disoriented to answer.

'I could've had a heart attack. You're just lucky I'm a nice guy.'

They reached another creek, this one a trickle, but Half Shell didn't care.

'I've had it,' Bubba said to the dogs. 'I can't drag your asses another step.' He unhooked their leashes. 'You're on your own.'

Tree Buster shot off like a rubber band, crashing through brush and barking three times for a strike that no one gave a goddamn about. Half Shell went off to the left. She kept looking back at Bubba every couple of steps, her eyes intense and caring.

'What is it?' Bubba asked her.

Half Shell ran ahead ten feet and looked back again.

'We supposed to follow you?' Bubba asked his dog.

Half Shell barked. Bubba and Smudge followed her for another forty-five minutes while Tree Buster treed coons and wondered why nobody showed up. Mist was rising, the world silent, sunlight breaking through the canopy of trees. It seemed a miracle when suddenly they were in a clearing, Smudge's truck straight ahead on the muddy road.

It was important that Pigeon venture out at dawn to avoid the thunder of rush hour, and more important, to forage before Dumpsters were emptied behind restaurants that would not open for hours.

Often he discovered unexpected treasures such as money, jewelry and doggie bags that drunk people dropped on their way back to their cars. Once he found a Rolex watch and got enough money from the pawn shop to keep him happy for months. He had found a number of portable phones, calculators and pagers, and an occasional gun.

'You can stay here if you want,' Pigeon said to Weed.

Weed was sitting on the blanket and didn't know what to do. In daylight, his predicament seemed even worse, maybe because it was harder to hide when the sun was looking him in the eye.

'There's got to be places the devil won't go,' Pigeon said.

Weed gave it some thought.

'I guess he wouldn't go back to the cement-tary,' Weed decided.

Pigeon got an idea.

'People ever leave good stuff on the graves? Like the dead person's favorite food, whiskey, wine, cigars, sort of like they used to do in the Pyramids?'

'It was dark when I was in there,' Weed told him. 'I

didn't see nothing 'cept those little flags you see everywhere. But it's a big place.'

The world was no longer big enough to accommodate traffic, and this was fortunate for Officer Otis Rhoad. It was almost seven-thirty and rush hour was out of the gate.

Soon there would be thousands of personal cars driven by solitary commuters indifferent to the wear and tear of the ozone and jealous of their right to come and go when and how they pleased in whatever they could afford to drive, using their own flight plans.

He steered his cruiser with a bony knee as he lit a Carlton Menthol, one eye in the rearview mirror, the other on a traffic light that was about to turn red and the guy in the Camaro next to him who thought he was going to make it. He did. Rhoad was disappointed.

Rhoad was tall, skinny, slightly cross-eyed and close to sixty. When he had been growing up south of the river, he had dreamed of being a radio disc jockey or perhaps a singer.

This had gone nowhere, and after high school he signed on with the Richmond Police Department. His first week in the academy he learned the assigned radio frequencies and areas, the proper operation of the radio, the correct procedures for relaying confidential information, the disposition of codes, the phonetic alphabet and, most important, ten signals.

When he was finally let loose on city streets, he was

relentless, fluent, precise and omnipresent on the mike. He rode radio waves like the DJ he had never become, and cops, dispatchers and 911 operators dreaded his unit number and resonating voice.

They resented and loathed his habit of running his colleagues off the airways and into one another, and hogging the communication system in general. He was 'Rhoad Hog.' He was 'Talk in a Box,' and all wished the brass would transfer him out of traffic, into the silence of the property room, information desk, maintenance division or tow lot.

But the chiefs preceding Hammer were zealous about quotas, and Rhoad was a relentless one-person posse pursuing citizens who exceeded the speed limit, went the wrong way, ran red lights and stop signs, made U turns where not allowed, drag raced, drove drunk and ignored Rhoad's lights and siren.

As time passed and maturity waved Otis Rhoad through new intersections of his life, he realized that more important than his war against moving violations was an insidious disease that clearly was becoming the epidemic of modern times. The world was running out of parking spaces.

He began punishing those who left their cars at expired meters, in handicap spaces or in more selfish and ruder appropriations such as lawns, shoulders, driveways that did not belong to them, businesses or churches they did not visit, and bicycle paths. He started carrying his ticket book off duty, especially after the city changed to twenty-four-hour meters.

Rhoad tapped an ash and gripped the mike. In exactly six minutes and forty seconds it would be eight-forty A.M., and Communications Officer Patty Passman's meter would expire.

It was possible that Smudge had a slight concussion, but he refused to be taken to the hospital, and Bubba refused to let Smudge drive. Bubba had to admit that he'd never driven a truck quite as nice as Smudge's and he felt the bitterness once again, a resentment that had pickled a part of Bubba since the beginning of time. In his own way, Smudge was no different from all who had mocked and wounded Bubba throughout his life.

'Some good buddy you are,' Bubba muttered because Smudge seemed asleep. 'Sell me that piece-of-shit Jeep. Sabotage Bay 8 so you can win the competition every month. Get your free packs of cigarettes and sell 'em to me.'

'You say something?' Smudge mumbled as Bubba turned into Smudge's driveway, where Bubba had left his crappy Jeep last night.

'I guess you owe me a thousand dollars,' Bubba told him.

Smudge suddenly became alert. He sat up straight in his seat and blinked several times, taking in his surroundings.

'Where are we?' he asked.

'In your driveway,' said Bubba. 'Don't be changing the subject on me, Smudge. I won.'

He started to say *fair and square* but saw his manufactured coon eyes glowing in trees.

'Won?' Smudge acted drugged. 'Won what?'

'Our bet, Smudge.'

'What bet?'

'You know what bet!'

'Huh?' Smudge slurred. 'Think I have amnesia. Don't even know where we are. Don't recognize a thing. Where are we?'

'Your expensive house in Brandermill!' Bubba wanted to give Smudge a more serious concussion. 'The one with the swimming pool and the brand-new Range Rover in front. Because you don't give a shit about buying American or being loyal to Philip Morris who doesn't pay you enough to live like this! So you're cheating, lying, stealing all over the world!'

Smudge grappled with the door handle and almost fell getting out of the truck. Bubba got Half Shell out and she jumped into the back of his Jeep. Smudge's wife boiled out the front door to assist Smudge. She threw Bubba a menacing look as he backed out of the driveway. He didn't care. He didn't stop to explain. He sped through Smudge's rich neighborhood with its big homes and wooded lots. He darted out on Midlothian Turnpike and passed everyone.

Bubba was having a hard time staying awake, but this didn't stop him from driving aggressively. He wouldn't let anyone into his lane. If someone got too close to his rear bumper, he slowed down more abruptly than he usually did.

He turned off his CB because there was no good buddy to talk to anymore. He didn't raise Honey on the two-way because he would be seeing her soon enough. He unplugged his phone so it wouldn't ring.

At Cloverleaf Mall, misfortune, or perhaps bad karma, began to swarm in. It started with a tattooed woman on a Harley-Davidson. She thundered around Bubba, flying between two lanes, dyed blond hair streaming out from her bright red helmet.

'Hey!' Bubba yelled as if anyone could hear. 'What the fuck you think you're doing?'

The woman rode on. Bubba sped up. He wove through traffic and floor-boarded it after her, squealing off on Oak Glen after she did and backtracking to Carnation and Hioaks, past the Virginia Department of Corrections Headquarters, and down Wyck Street and over to Everglades Drive.

Bubba was too exhausted, his mood too foul, to realize the woman was having a good time with him. When she shot back onto Midlothian Turnpike, Bubba took the turn too wide and didn't bother checking for cars. Horns blared. People cursed. An old woman in a Toyota Corolla pointed her finger at him like a gun and fired.

A city police cruiser darted in behind Bubba, blue-and-red lights flashing in Bubba's rearview mirror. This time Officer Budget yelped his siren as he pulled Bubba into the same Kmart where they had met before.

chapter twenty-four

Communications Officer Patty Passman was overweight, with prematurely gray hair and bad skin. She was single, antisocial, and suffered from hypoglycemia, but she was no fool. She, too, knew that her parking meter on 10th Street was about to expire.

If she didn't get to her car before Otis Rhoad, he would anchor yet one more ticket beneath her wiper blade. What was it now? An average of two a week at sixteen dollars each? Of course she would be better off parking in the nice new safe parking deck one street over, but there were no spaces left today. Whenever this happened she was forced out on the street, where Rhoad was always chalking tires and stalking expired meters.

Officer Budget recognized the red Jeep Cherokee immediately and couldn't believe he was pulling it again in the same damn parking lot. What was wrong with this guy? Was he doing it on purpose? Did he have some kind of dysfunction like those people who were always getting sick so they could go to the doctor?

The Jeep pulled into the Kmart parking lot, in front of First Union Bank, same as last time. Budget got out and approached the driver's door. Bubba was wearing camouflage. He was glassy-eyed and filthy. A dog was in a pen in the back. Budget rapped on the glass with his portable radio. Bubba rolled down his window.

'Step out of the car,' Budget said.

'If you don't mind, I'll just give you my license and registration like last time, Officer Budget. I've been up all night lost in the woods coon hunting.'

The racial slur was astonishing.

'Not a good time to say something like that, Mr. Fluck,' Budget said in an icy voice. 'How many you catch, huh? You hang 'em from trees or shoot 'em?'

'We get 'em in trees if we can,' Bubba said. 'It's not legal to shoot 'em right now.'

Budget jerked open the door and looked down at Bubba. He wanted to beat him up. It occurred to him that he might be able to get away with it since this was Rodney King in reverse. But they weren't in California.

'Once we get 'em up in the trees,' Bubba was talking too much because his nerves were frayed, 'we shine a light in their eyes. Course, it's the dogs that get them first, really. The dogs track 'em down.'

Budget looked back at Half Shell. The dog seemed docile enough.

'And just what kind of dog? Pit bulls? Dobermans?' Budget said hatefully.

'No, no. Coon dogs.'

'That's a *coon dog* in the back?'

'One of the best.'

Budget continued to stare at Half Shell. She stared back. She started barking and tried to break out of her pen.

'You sit right here and don't you move.' Budget backed away from the Jeep. 'And that dog gets out, you're in a lot of trouble.'

Passman was about to dash out to her car when 218 sounded in her headphones.

'Unit 218. Traffic stop,' Budget let her know.

'Go ahead, Unit 218.' Passman was stressed as she looked up at the clock.

'Sixty-eight hundred block Midlothian Turnpike with Boy-Union-Boy-hyphen-Adam-Henry.'

'Ten-4, 218 at 0748 hours,' Passman said, getting desperate.

Bubba punched in the cigarette lighter and noticed the tip of his .44 Magnum Colt Anaconda protruding from underneath his seat. Fear seized him. He broke into a cold sweat. He had a concealed weapon and no permit for such.

He kicked at the revolver, trying to shove it out of sight. It resisted his efforts, stainless steel glinting in plain view. Bubba slowly sneaked his right hand down to the floor, but his arm wasn't long enough to reach the gun unless he bent over or got on the floor. He knew it would not be a good idea to give the impression he was hiding something or had hidden something under his seat.

Bubba shoved some more and realized that his monster revolver was hung up on something. He envisioned the release lever or a bolt or maybe an exposed spring pushing against the trigger. He imagined rotted fabric caught in the hammer. With the slightest motion the gun would go off.

Brazil had gotten off to a miserable start. He was hot. Gnats had begun to pay attention to him. His urge to use the bathroom overrode decorum and he'd finally relieved himself behind azalea bushes near a plot of realistic tree-shaped markers that had something to do with the Woodmen of the World.

Brazil was tired of waiting for Weed to show up. Brazil couldn't bear to admit that West had been right. Worse, he had to tell the radio room he needed a ride. The thought was awful.

All cops on the air and people with scanners would know Brazil was alone on foot in Hollywood Cemetery. He could hear the jokes. He could imagine the sniggers. *The pretty boy's been reassigned to the dead beat.*

'Unit 11,' Brazil got on the air.

'Go ahead, 11,' Patty Passman quickly came back.

'At Hollywood Cemetery. Need a unit to 10-25 me here.'

'Ten-4, 11, 0749 hours. 562.'

'Unit 562,' Rhoad came back.

Brazil recognized Talk in a Box's unit number and cringed. *Oh please don't ask him to pick me up.*

'Five-six-two. Need you to 10-25 a party at Hollywood Cemetery ASAP.' Passman's voice was strained as it came back.

Passman had fabricated calls in the past to divert Rhoad from her illegally parked car, and he wasn't about to fall for it this time.

'What's your 10-20?' Passman asked Rhoad over the air.

'Unit 562. Broad and Fourteenth,' he answered.

'Ten-4, 562, 0750 hours.'

'Unit 562,' he got back to her

'Five-six-two.'

'Unit 562,' he said. 'Got to make one stop first. Can 10-30 11 with an estimated 10-26 of 0830 hours.'

'Eleven,' Brazil shoved his way on the air. 'Radio, can you send another unit? Need to get out of here long before then.'

Passman was in a panic as she glanced up at the clock. She frantically stuffed the other half of a chocolate eclair into her mouth.

'Eleven, that's 10-10,' she informed Brazil. 'All other units are 10-6.'

'Can you 10-9 that?'

'All other units are 10-6,' she repeated.

It was a lie. Everyone on the air knew radio traffic had been light so far, with no indication whatsoever that all other units, or even half of them, were tied up.

'Ten-12.' She told Brazil to stand by.

'Eleven.' Brazil's voice was getting irritated. 'Ten-5 562 and ask his 10-20.'

'Five-six-two.' Rhoad didn't wait for the message to be relayed, since he clearly heard what unit 11 asked and was capable of being direct. 'Ten-20's Broad and 9th.'

'Well, can you 10-25 me now or not?'

'Ten-10. Got to make a stop first.'

'Radio, can you please get me another ride?' Brazil asked again.

'Ten-10, 11. Five-six-two's en route.'

'Five-six-two. No I'm not. I got to make a stop first.'

Passman finished the eclair.

'I need someone to 10-25 me ASAP,' Brazil answered back.

'Five-six-two. Can't do it, 11.'

Mikes began clicking as other cops on the air voiced their amusement and encouraged Rhoad and Brazil to keep it up.

'Units 562 and 11,' Passman snapped into her microphone. 'Ten-3.'

Passman's order to *stop transmitting* brought about complete silence, but only temporarily.

'Five-six-two.' Rhoad could not stop. He was addicted. 'Could you 10-9 that?' he said.

'Ten-3.' Passman ordered him for the last time, in the secret language of cops, to shut up.

'Eleven?' Rhoad could not.

There was no response.

'Eleven?' Rhoad repeated, talking faster, doing his best to outrun Communications Officer Passman, whose habit it was to cut him off and speak unkindly whenever she could. 'Everything 10-4?'

'No!' Passman blurted into her mike. 'Everything's not 10-4, unit 562! It's *10-10!*' she exclaimed.

Her hands were shaking. She felt faint. Patty Passman was furious at a damn city that had no parking for loyal employees like her who worked eight-hour shifts in the windowless, dimly lit radio room, talking to lump-heads like Otis Rhoad. Her blood sugar spiked. Insulin dumped.

Her blood sugar went crashing lower than before. Her vision blacked out and she almost fainted when she jumped to her feet, turning over her coffee. Other dispatchers answered other calls as she ran out of the radio room.

Officer Budget had been waiting ten minutes for Communications Officer Passman to get back to him. Budget finally got another dispatcher to run a 10-27 and 10-28 on Bubba's red Jeep.

Budget was disappointed but not surprised to learn that Butner U. Fluck IV's driver's license was still valid through 2003 with no restrictions, and that the Jeep continued to be registered to the same party with an address on Clarence Street in the city.

'Shit,' Budget said.

He climbed out of his cruiser and approached the Jeep again, pleased to find Bubba seemed appropriately scared for once.

'I'm charging you with reckless driving,' Officer Budget said severely, doing his best to make the asshole feel even worse. 'But you're lucky it's not a lot worse. So Mr. Fluck, head . . .'

'Please,' Bubba interrupted, holding up an arm as if he were about to be struck.

'About time you showed some manners,' Budget said, returning Bubba's identification and registration.

Passman's stubby feet rang loudly on worn metal steps as she raced up to the street, her heart startled like a deer or a duck fired upon. Her chest heaved as she shoved through double glass doors.

Rhoad was parking his patrol car next to her 1989 white Fleetwood Cadillac. The toe of her left New Balance jogging shoe caught on a crack in the sidewalk. She stumbled but caught herself, flailing and out of alignment.

'Stop!' she yelled at Rhoad as he approached her car, ticket book in hand, pen out. '*No!*' she screamed.

The digital reading clearly showed the time on the meter had expired.

'Sorry,' Rhoad told her.

'You're not sorry, you son of a bitch!' Passman jabbed her finger at him as she fought to catch her breath.

Rhoad was unflappable as he filled in the meter number, the vehicle make and license plate number, and the mode, which in this case was an *A* for automobile. Rhoad slipped the ticket inside its envelope. He tucked it under the wiper blade. Passman moved closer to him, glaring, panting, sweating, her blood roaring. She drilled small dark homicidal eyes into him.

'I would have gotten here sooner and moved my car if you could shut the fuck up on the air!' she bellowed. 'It's your goddamn fault! It's always your goddamn fault, you stupid, cow-brained loser, cross-eyed, dickless, son-of-a-mother-fucking-bitch-dumb-fuck!'

She marched to her Cadillac and snatched the summons off the windshield. She violently wadded it in his face and stuffed it down the front of his neatly pressed uniform shirt, knocking loose his clip-on tie.

'Now you've done it,' Rhoad told her indignantly.

She flipped him a double bird.

'You're under arrest!' he exclaimed.

Traffic slowed, people ready for a good fight on an otherwise meaningless Wednesday morning.

'Stuff it up your ass!' Passman screamed.

'Go, girlfriend!' a woman called out from her Acura.

Rhoad fumbled with the handcuffs on the back of his Sam Browne belt as Passman yelled more obscenities, her blood sugar dipping lower into its dark crevice of irrationality and violence as an audience gathered and encouraged her.

Rhoad grabbed Passman's wrists. She kicked him in both shins and spat. He sputtered, wrenching her left arm behind her back as her right fist knuckle-punched him in the neck. Rhoad had not handcuffed anyone in many years, and steel cracked against Passman's wrist bone as he snapped and missed. Passman howled in pain as he jerked and smacked and steel jaws finally locked around her wrist and bit hard.

'Do it! Do it!' someone yelled from a black Corvette.

Passman's free hand grabbed Rhoad between his legs and twisted.

chapter twenty-five

Ruby Sink's one-year-old grandniece, Loraine, was running a fever and had kept her mother awake all night.

'Poor baby,' Miss Sink said over the phone. 'Are you rocking her? Did you give her a baby aspirin?'

'Yes, yes,' Miss Sink's niece, Frances, said. 'I don't know what else to do. If I miss another day of work, well, there're plenty of people out there wanting my job.'

Miss Sink could hear Loraine squalling and imagined the child's bright red face. Day care was out of the question. Miss Sink simply would not allow the sick child to stay with strangers, nor did she want Loraine to pass on whatever she had to others.

'I'll be pleased as punch to keep her while you're at work,' Miss Sink said. 'And I bet you're frantically trying to get ready even as we speak.'

'Yes,' Frances said in despair. 'I haven't even showered yet.'

'I'm on my way right now,' Miss Sink said. 'I'll pick up Loraine and we'll have a grand day.'

'And if her fever doesn't break you'll call Dr. Samson? Just to make sure she's all right?'

'Of course, dear.'

'Oh, thank you, Aunt Ruby.'

'I was going to get out anyway at some point,' Miss Sink said. 'I've got only two dollars in my billfold and I owe the yard man and probably half of everybody else in this town.'

'You always say that, Aunt Ruby. The most broken record I ever heard. Mother said you were the richest poor person she ever knew.'

Miss Sink was saddened by the thought of her dead sister. Miss Sink had no one left except Frances and Loraine. Her spirit settled in that low place she could not tolerate.

'Why don't you have supper with me after work,' Miss Sink said. 'When you pick up our little angel child.'

'Depends on what you're cooking,' Frances said.

'I might just invite this lovely police officer I know,' Miss Sink said. 'The handsomest young man you ever saw, and so sweet. The one who writes editorial pieces for the paper. He rents my little place on Plum Street.'

'Him? Lord have mercy, I've seen his picture. He's too young for me, Aunt Ruby.'

'Why, that's nonsense,' Miss Sink said. 'Things aren't like they used to be.'

'He wouldn't be interested in me. He's so good-looking and all.'

'And you're pretty as a rosebud.'

'I'm older than him and have a child, Aunt Ruby.

Reality, you know?'

'I'm going to make my sesame-honey fried chicken. Cheese grits and fresh tomatoes with balsamic vinegar,' Miss Sink said.

'And just where are you going to get fresh tomatoes this time of year?'

'You forget I can them,' Miss Sink said. 'Now quit talking so I can be on my way.'

Smoke's girlfriend, Divinity, was the first to notice the red Jeep Cherokee abandoned in the Kmart parking lot, no more than a hundred feet from the First Union Bank.

'Well, look at that,' Divinity said to Smoke. 'That Jeep just sitting there, nobody in it and engine running, waiting for us, baby.'

'No it's not 'cause we don't want it,' Smoke told her.

Smoke's mind was going through its routine, his concentration focused. He had turned off Puff Daddy when he'd picked up Divinity at the McDonald's on West Broad Street, where she'd let him know by pager that she was waiting for him. She had her hand on his thigh, but at the moment, he was aroused by other things as he watched an ancient Chevy Celebrity driven by an old woman park in front of the twenty-four-hour money stop.

'Oh, now don't be telling me you're into that one,' Divinity complained. 'Some old bitch driving that piece of shit?'

'It's the people with new cars that don't have money,'

Smoke said as he watched the old woman rummage in her purse.

He drove past her and tucked his Escort out of sight behind the bank.

'Get in line behind her,' Smoke ordered Divinity.

'For what? She probably only gonna get twenty, thirty dollars. I'd rather do the Jeep.'

She looked longingly back at it, wondering why someone would be so stupid to leave it like that in times like these days. Smoke rubbed his hand between her legs. Divinity laughed and grabbed him back.

'All right, all right,' she said. 'Whatever you say, baby.'

Miss Sink felt perfectly safe as she continued digging in her purse. She had no reason to worry about withdrawing cash from this particular location because it was just across from the Kmart parking lot, and Kmart opened at eight. Already there were quite a number of cars pulling in for bargains.

Loraine was awfully quiet in the back. She was strapped in and warmly dressed, and at the moment, not crying. Miss Sink got out of the car, still digging for her wallet. Her heart got tight as she tried to remember where she had shopped last, and if she might have left her billfold there. Her memory wasn't as good as it used to be and she was always making up all kinds of excuses to deny it.

At first, she didn't pay much attention to the young woman who stepped up behind her and started grabbing things out of a faded denim bag.

'I can't find nothing inside this thing, either,' the young woman said, rummaging loudly. 'Drives me crazy!'

Miss Sink turned around and was rather taken aback. The young woman was hard-looking in a very short skirt, tight black tank top and red Chicago Bulls windbreaker. She had rings in her ears, nose and one eyebrow, the style of the day, which in Miss Sink's opinion was no different from the mutilation she used to see in *National Geographic.*

'I don't know where I put it,' Miss Sink muttered in irritation.

She glanced back at her car, hoping the baby aspirin had helped and Loraine was asleep. The young woman stepped a little closer and something inside Miss Sink suddenly woke up. She got uneasy. She was relieved when a nice-looking young man came around from the back of the bank.

'Save any for me?' he said in a friendly voice.

He was well groomed and neatly dressed in the baggy, sand-blasted, Chicago Bulls fashion of the day. Miss Sink gave him an uncertain smile.

'Morning, ma'am,' he said to her.

Miss Sink didn't like his eyes. They were so intense, more like a stare, and there was something in them that spoke to her but she didn't want to listen. The young woman was standing oddly to one side of the machine, as if avoiding the camera. Miss Sink was beginning to feel frightened. She wanted to believe the young man would protect her.

'Worst thing ever invented. Spits out money like it's

Monopoly,' the young man said as he also stayed out of range of the camera.

'Tell me about it,' the young woman said. 'I go through it like candy these days. Or would if some people'd hurry on up.'

He seemed like the sort of boy who might live in Miss Sink's part of town. He was probably getting money on his way to school, and she bet he went to one of the private schools like Saint Christopher's or Collegiate.

'You know, some of us gotta be somewhere,' the young woman said loudly. She was making faces, sighing, looking around and rolling her eyes. 'I can't be standing here all day!' She glared at Miss Sink.

'I'm sorry,' Miss Sink stammered, her nervous hands fluttering through her purse. 'I just hope I haven't lost it. Oh dear, oh dear.'

'You can't find it, old woman, then just get outta the way!'

'Hey, cool it,' the young man suddenly said.

He stepped closer to Miss Sink, but still off to the side.

'She was here first,' the young man told the little tramp.

'Well, I got my Visa card out, ready to go. Nobody tells Divinity what to do. Why you think they call me that? Because I am as divine as Jesus, that's why.'

'A terrible way to talk!' Miss Sink exclaimed. 'You better pray for forgiveness.'

'You better pray I don't take that tongue of yours and tie it around your old-ass neck.'

'That's enough!' the young man said to her.

'Fuck you, pretty boy.'

Miss Sink was trembling when she finally found her credit card. She promptly dropped it on the sidewalk. She almost lost her balance as she snatched it up, her heart drilling. She fumbled and dropped it again while the nasty young woman named Divinity made exaggerated sighs and swore.

Miss Sink managed to insert her MasterCard into the machine, and typed in her PIN and answered all questions. She could smell Divinity's cloying perfume and feel her evil spirit as ten twenty-dollar bills were ejected from the machine.

'That's a lot of bus money,' Divinity said to her sarcastically.

'Please leave me alone,' Miss Sink said in a shaky voice.

'Don't you tell me what to do, old bitch,' Divinity said in a tone mean enough to break the skin.

'Come on,' the young man said to Miss Sink. 'I'll walk you to your car, ma'am.'

'Oh thank you.' Miss Sink almost grabbed his hand. 'Oh you're so nice. I can't thank you enough.'

Miss Sink caught a glimpse of Divinity tearing off a strip of duct tape and slapping it over the money machine's camera.

'We should call the police!' Miss Sink whispered to her escort as he opened the driver's door for her.

She didn't understand why he went around and opened the passenger's door, too.

'I want to ride with you maybe half a block just to make sure you're okay,' he explained as Divinity hung around the money machine, waiting to cause trouble for the next poor person who showed up, Miss Sink assumed.

She turned around to check on Loraine. Thank goodness she was sleeping. Miss Sink started the engine and locked the doors.

'I don't like the looks of that girl,' the young man said. 'Sometimes people like that work in pairs, like snakes. I'm worried there might be someone else around. You know, there's just something about all this that doesn't feel right. And I guess you've heard about these ATM robberies.'

'Oh, yes!' Miss Sink exclaimed. 'Thank God you came along when you did! You must be my guardian angel. I don't believe I know your name.'

'People call me Smoke.'

'Well, I hope you don't. Once upon a time I did. Can't tell you how hard it was to quit.'

'That's not why they call me that.'

Miss Sink backed up as the camera's blind eye observed nothing.

'They call me Smoke because I used to burn up things when I was a kid,' he said between clenched teeth as he snatched a gun out of the back of his pants and rammed it hard into her ribs.

'Oh dear God!' Miss Sink exclaimed. 'Oh no!'

'Keep driving,' Smoke snapped. 'That way. Around the back of Kmart.'

'Oh please, for God's sake,' Miss Sink begged. 'There's a child in the car. Just take what you want and leave us be.'

'Shut up, bitch!' he said.

Smoke watched Divinity drive the Escort from behind the bank, where it had been hidden. She inserted herself into the solid line of traffic creeping toward downtown, early morning light winking off windshields. He smelled shit and pee and at first thought it was the kid in the back seat.

'Fuck,' he said when he realized his victim had lost control of her bowels and bladder. 'I wish you hadn't done that.'

'I'm sorry. Please don't . . .'

'Shut the fuck up, bitch. You're going to drive real normal and you try anything I'm gonna blow your sweet little baby's brains all over the back of the car while you watch.'

'Take anything,' she cried. 'Just don't hurt her. Anything you want. Oh please! Anything . . . !'

'Shut up!' Smoke hissed.

Miss Sink was crying so hard her teeth were chattering. They drove behind Kmart and parked where asphalt gave way to acres of woods. Smoke grabbed her wallet out of her purse. He took the ten crisp twenties she had gotten from the money stop.

He robbed her of an additional two dollars and sixty-two cents, and quarters and tokens for tolls. Her watch and necklace weren't worth the trouble, and pawn shops were risky. She stunk so bad he was about to gag, and the fucking kid was waking up and beginning to cry.

'Loraine, it's all right, sweetie. Please be quiet, honey. My name's Miss Sink and this is my grandniece, Loraine,' Miss Sink prattled on. 'You don't want to hurt us. For

God's sake, you must have a mother, a grandmother . . .'

'SHUT UP! QUIT NAGGING ME, YOU UGLY OLD BITCH!'

Smoke turned the radio up loud. The kid began to howl.

'SHUT THE FUCK UP!' Smoke yelled at the baby.

'Oh God in heaven! Please don't hurt us! Dear God! Think about what you're doing! You look like a smart young man. You don't want trouble like this!'

'I hate ugly old women like you. So you better shut the fuck up and consider yourself lucky I don't do other things to you. But you stink too bad,' he said in a low, cold voice. 'So now you're gonna bend over. So you don't see me when I get out. Okay?'

'Okay,' Miss Sink whimpered.

She pressed her face against the steering wheel. She squeezed her eyes shut and tightly covered them with her hands. She didn't move. She barely breathed. Annie Lennox was stepping on broken glass on the radio as Smoke dug through the glove box and the kid screamed. Smoke emptied the purse on the floor mat and helped himself to a pack of spearmint Freedent gum, fingernail clippers and a prescription bottle of Atavan.

'Thanks, *Miss Sink,'* he said. 'Grow up to be a good girl, *Loraine.* Y'all don't forget me, promise?' He laughed.

He popped a stick of Freedent into his mouth and scanned the area. No one was around.

'You know what I look like, bitch?' he said. 'I mean, you gonna recognize me on the street?'

'No. No. I didn't see you! Please,' Miss Sink begged.

'What 'bout that ugly little motherfucker of yours in her little seat back there. She know what I look like?'

'No! She's just a baby! You don't want to hurt us!'

Miss Sink was shaking as if she was having a seizure.

'Let me think about this. What's a guy to do?'

Smoke smacked his gum. He pulled back the slide of his Glock and it snapped forward with a loud clack.

He felt the power. Smoke was high and hard with it as he pumped three Winchester hollowpoints into the back of Miss Sink's head.

chapter twenty-six

Brazil stood with his hands in his pockets, impatiently staring out at sloped, loamy land sutured by railroad tracks and tangled with brambles and trees. Steam billowed from the Fort James Paper Company, and the river was soft music played with fingers of wind and bright notes of sun.

The portable radio on Brazil's belt was a staccato of dispatchers and cops cutting in and out in spurts and codes. Nothing was going on. A handicap van was abandoned on a roadside, traffic was tied up because a light wouldn't flash, a driver had been stopped at a Kmart.

Unit numbers and military time peppered the air, but Passman and Rhoad were strangely silent. Passman dispatched no calls. Rhoad answered no one. Brazil was furious. He was certain the cops were messing with him.

'Eleven,' Brazil tried again.

'Go ahead, 11,' answered a communications officer whose name Brazil did not know.

'Radio, I'm still at the cemetery,' Brazil said, trying to keep the anger out of his voice. 'Need someone to 10-25 me right away.'

'That's Hollywood.'

'Ten-4.'

'Any unit in the area of Hollywood Cemetery, need someone to 10-25 unit 11 there.'

'Unit 199.'

'Go ahead, 199.'

'Just two blocks away, I'll swing by the cemetery, 10-25 11.'

'Ten-5, 199, 0812 hours.'

Brazil turned away from the river as he heard a rustle. He caught a flash of red on the other side of the cemetery fence where Spring and South Cherry streets intersected. The chain link was dense with ivy. Through it Brazil could just make out the back of the large metal sign advertising Victory Rug Cleaning, an arrow pointing to the business a block away. He turned off his radio and didn't move.

The fence began to shake as someone gripped the edge of the sign and hoisted himself up. Brazil was hidden by the thick shadows of holly trees as he watched Weed reach for a tree branch and pull himself up with ease, swing over the fence and drop branch by branch to the ground. Brazil took cover behind a monument.

'Come on, it's easy,' Weed said to someone on the other side.

The fence shook harder. Brazil was baffled when a scraggly, bearded face was followed by a filthy, raggedly dressed body missing part of a hand and an entire foot. The street person grabbed a branch, got snagged a couple times, but somehow made it over.

'Can't believe I did that,' the street person said. 'Haven't done anything that agile in years.'

He looked around at the mute stony tongues of the dead speaking from the grass, as if searching for something.

'Shit,' he said. 'It ain't all too promising so far unless I plan on a steady diet of flowers.'

Weed nervously wiped sweat off his face with the tail of his extra-extra-large Bulls jersey and rubbed his hands on his relaxed-leg jeans.

'Go on,' the street person said to Weed. 'I'll scrounge around and catch you later.'

Weed trotted off in untied Nikes as if he knew exactly where he was going. Brazil ducked behind more monuments, boxwoods and trees as he tailed Weed and kept an eye on the street person Weed had brought with him.

Weed jogged past the Presidents Circle and the graves of Jeb Stuart and John Tyler, on to Jeter Avenue and Bellvue, directly to Davis Circle where the vandalized statue of the first and last president of the Confederacy was still dressed for the game, lumpy basketball in hand. Weed stood in front of it and stared in reverence. Every now and then he cast about, his furtive gaze sweeping over the marble sarcophagus where Brazil this moment was hiding.

A swarm of histamines rushed forth to combat the dust mites storming into Bubba's sinuses and lungs as he probed with a flashlight on the floor of his Jeep. He began to sneeze. His throat and eyes itched and his nose started to run.

'Goddamn!' he said.

The Anaconda's Holo sight was hung on the position spring wire running from one seat to the other. The exposed CB antenna wires Bubba had installed himself and covered with a mat and his work rag were snagged on the trigger.

Smudge's voice came over the CB because Bubba had not been able to stand the silence and had turned radios and the phone back on. Smudge must be feeling better, Bubba thought snidely. Bubba had nothing to say.

'Shit!' Bubba cried when he bumped his funny bone on the door handle and numbness shot up his arm.

He sneezed three more times as he carefully groped under the seat, the engine running.

'Smudge to Bubba. You stealthing on me, good buddy? Called Queen Bee, says you're no show.'

Bubba's eyes were on fire and streaming. He couldn't breathe out of his nose. The stick shift kept grabbing his shirt. Smudge wouldn't shut up and Bubba's portable phone rang. He answered no one. He laid his head against old carpet, straining to see what was required to free his Colt revolver with its eight-inch barrel. He sneezed so hard his nose began to bleed.

Something hard tapped loudly and with authority on his driver's window, startling Bubba. He jumped and yelled and his shoulder banged the gear shift and knocked the Jeep into reverse. Bubba jammed down the brake with his right hand. He shoved the Jeep back into park and crawled up into his seat, in pain and gasping for breath. He was dazed when Officer Budget jerked open the door.

'You almost ran me over, you son of a bitch!' Budget's eyes were wild, his pistol pulled. 'Get out with your hands up. Now!'

'What did I do?' Bubba cried, mopping his face with his sleeve and sneezing.

'Get out!'

Bubba did. He was dazzled by sunlight. He was bloody and congested and filthy.

'Legs spread, hands against the car!' Budget meant it.

He frisked Bubba, finding nothing useful.

'What were you doing hiding on the floor?' Budget demanded as he holstered his pistol.

'Nothing,' Bubba lied.

'Bullshit!'

'Queen Bee's gonna sting your butt,' Smudge was back. 'Buzz is you ain't touched down since we faced last. Where you truckin', buddy?'

'You mind if I tell him I can't talk right now?' Bubba asked Budget.

'Don't you move!'

Budget peered through the window at a mat bunched on the floor. Bubba could tell by his reaction that he saw the revolver protruding from under the seat. Bubba froze, despair and terror rocking him like an earthquake while he watched, as if in slow motion, Budget snatch handcuffs off the back of his belt and snap them hard on Bubba's wrists and tensely radio for a backup unit and a detective.

brazil didn't hear the call because his radio was still turned off, and Weed was staring at the statue, as if in a trance. Brazil's legs were cramping. His expandable tactical baton and Mag-Lite were digging into his ribs. He was sweltering in his Progressive Technologies body armor, and his knees had seen too many years of hard tennis to take squatting or kneeling for very long.

He was about to make his move when Weed touched the statue. He traced the number on the uniform. He hung his head, his narrow shoulders shaking as he sobbed quietly.

Weed wiped his eyes on the sleeve on the back of his hand and was glad no one was around to see him cry. He never got weak like that, not even when his daddy smacked him or when Smoke was mean.

Weed didn't feel anything when people forgot his birthday or other kids ignored him and didn't invite him to parties or when basketball started up and he didn't get to go anymore. The last time Weed Gardener remembered crying hard out of sadness was in August when Twister was jogging and got hit by a car that kept on going.

So why Weed was crying that way now made no sense to him, unless it was being alone in a graveyard and reminded of Twister, who was buried in Forest Lawn Cemetery on the north side of the city. It was Twister who had always encouraged Weed's art, laughing and making a big fuss over Weed's wild designs and cartoons, because

Twister was famous and made good grades, but he couldn't draw. He couldn't match colors when he fixed up his dorm room or got dressed.

He used to tell Weed all the time that Weed was a *fucking genius.* Those were his exact words. Weed wanted Twister to admire what Weed had done to the statue. He wanted Twister to be flattered. He wanted Twister to beat up Smoke or maybe even kill him so Weed wouldn't have to hide anymore, so he could go back to art class and practice with the band.

Tears streamed down Weed's face and he swallowed hard as he remembered TV people and the newspapers calling Twister *a tornado on the basketball court.* Twister was tall like a tree, good-looking, and girls taped posters of him up in their bedrooms. He could have been a model or a movie star if he wanted.

He and Twister had no one but each other, and Twister used to take Weed swimming in the quarry, and to Regency Mall, and to Bullets for burgers and of course to the games, where he sat right behind Twister, who now and then turned around to wink at him in front of all those thousands of people. Weed missed Twister so much, he refused to believe Twister was gone for good.

'You lookin'?' Weed sobbed as he talked to his dead big brother. 'See what I done? I worked real hard all alone in the dark. How come you ain't here, Twister?'

A loud voice suddenly sounded behind him, and Weed almost came out of his shoes and screamed, his eyes huge.

'Don't move!' Officer Brazil exclaimed.

Brazil was standing so close he could tackle Weed.

'What, what, what?' Weed stammered.

'What are you doing here?' Brazil demanded in that tone cops use to remind people that the law rules.

'Looking,' Weed said. 'Nothing wrong with looking,' he added, hoping it was true.

'Looking at what?'

'The paint job. I heard about it,' Weed said. 'So I came to look.'

'Who were you talking to?'

'I wasn't talking.'

'I heard you,' Brazil said.

Weed had to revise. It took him a minute.

'I was praying to Jesus,' he said.

'About what?'

Brazil was trying to be mean, but Weed didn't think he really was.

'About all these dead people,' Weed said.

'How did you get here. You walk?'

Weed nodded.

'Nobody gave you a ride? You're by yourself?'

Weed shook his head.

'*No* to which?'

'Being here by myself,' Weed answered.

'Meaning you are here by yourself or you're not?'

'Yeah.'

'Yeah?' Brazil had to get it straight. 'You're here by yourself?'

Weed nodded.

'And you got in by climbing over the fence.'

'Huh?'

'I saw you. You grabbed the Victory Rug Cleaning sign and climbed over.'

'Why you think they advertise on a cement-tary fence? Who they think gonna get their rugs done? Dead people?' Weed tried to divert the conversation.

'Why did you climb over the fence?' Brazil asked him.

'It was quicker.' Weed was trying to act cool but his heart was attacking him.

'Why aren't you in school?'

'It's a holiday.'

'Oh really?' Brazil asked. 'Which one?'

'Can't remember.'

'I'm pretty sure today isn't a holiday,' Brazil said.

'Then how come there's no school?' Weed said.

Brazil didn't find Weed threatening in the least, but Brazil looked him over to make sure he wasn't carrying anything Brazil ought to know about.

'Then what are you doing way over here?' Brazil asked.

Brazil stepped closer to the statue to get a better look at Magic Jeff. He couldn't help but smile.

'I think it was one of those teacher work days,' Weed offered lamely. 'All I know is it was something, you know, something they was doing and we didn't have to go. And my mama had to go to work. So I'm just hanging, you know?'

'It would only take me a minute to find out whether you're telling me the truth,' said Brazil, who was distracted and upset that West had left him and 199 hadn't shown up yet. 'What I ought to do is haul your tiny butt back to Godwin and let them deal with you. But guess what? All they'd do is suspend you and that would only keep you out of school longer, right? So that'd just give you what you want, right?'

'I don't want to be out of school!' Weed fired back. 'I'd be there now if . . .'

'I thought you said it was a holiday,' Brazil said.

Weed was horrified that he'd just tripped over his lie and landed flat on his ass. There was no going back. His eyes danced around, looking for some place to run.

'All right, Weed,' Brazil said. 'Let's get down to business.'

'What kind of business?'

'It's time for the truth,' Brazil said as Pigeon suddenly appeared, heading toward them, his gait listing and awkward.

'For one thing, your last name isn't Jones, now is it?' said Brazil, who could not see Pigeon at his back.

'No,' Weed said.

'It's Gardener, and your brother was Twister.'

Weed was speechless.

'Weed, tell me what the five's for?'

'Huh?'

'The five tattooed on your finger. Let's try that story again and see if it comes out better this time.'

Fear turned to panic. Weed's mind went blank.

'I told you before it don't mean nothing,' Weed said.

'I know it does,' Brazil persisted. 'The Pikes. The gang taking credit for painting the statue, right?'

Weed was beginning to shake, Pigeon right behind them. Brazil probably smelled him and suddenly spun around, hand on his gun.

'Don't go shooting me, I ain't worth it,' Pigeon said calmly as he eyed the statue. 'Now that's special.'

'Who are you?' Brazil asked Pigeon, relaxing his shooting hand a little.

'Pigeon. I've seen you before,' Pigeon said. 'Usually with some hot-looking lady cop. Can't be on the street as much as I am and not see everybody eventually.'

Pigeon studied the statue again. Weed wasn't sure, but he thought he saw admiration shining in Pigeon's eyes. For an instant, Weed felt joy.

'So,' Brazil said, 'either one of you got any idea who painted this statue to look like Weed's brother?'

Weed tensed.

Pigeon waited.

'Well,' Weed said in a tight voice, 'they was both eighteen. Maybe that's why somebody did it.'

Pigeon squinted at the inscription on the statue's base.

'What?' Brazil frowned.

'It says right there.' Weed pointed. 'The man in the statue was eighteen just like Twister was.'

'You need to recheck your math,' Pigeon said to Weed. 'Jeff Davis was eighty-one when he died.'

'What'd he do anyway?' Weed asked.

'Went to jail for a while,' Pigeon said. 'About two years, leg irons and the whole bit, as I recollect.'

Weed stared at the statue and got a frightened expression on his face. He wondered if leg irons were like big handcuffs and if he'd have to wear them, too. He didn't want to go to jail for two years. He tried to console himself by hoping Mr. Davis had done something worse than paint a statue.

'What you do to him if you catch him?' Weed said.

'Catch who?' Brazil asked.

'The one who did the paint job.'

'Can't say for sure. I'd have to talk to him first and find out why he did it,' Brazil replied thoughtfully. 'Whoever it is, your brother must be very special to him.'

'Lock him up right this minute,' Pigeon was quick to volunteer. 'That's what I'd do with him.'

'Naw,' Brazil replied. 'If all he did was paint this statue, what good would it do to lock him up? Better to get him to do something helpful to the community.'

'Like what?' Weed asked.

'Like cleaning up what he's done.'

'You mean getting rid of it? Even if it's good?' Weed said.

It didn't matter that his artwork wouldn't survive the first rain or spray of a hose. Weed couldn't stand the thought of cleaning it up himself. It would just kill him to wash Twister away.

'Doesn't matter if it's good,' Brazil was saying.

But it did to Weed, and he couldn't resist asking, 'You think it is?'

'I sure as hell think so,' Pigeon said. 'I think the artist ought to open a gallery in goddamn New York.'

'That's not the issue,' Brazil said to Pigeon. 'There's someone running around out there who's unusually gifted, I'll admit that. But this isn't the way to show it.'

'What does gifted mean?' Weed said.

'Special. Really good at something. You *sure* you don't know who might be doing this?' Brazil asked.

Brazil knew. Weed could tell.

'Come on, Weed, fess up,' Pigeon ratted on him. 'Remember what we talked about, huh? Remember the devil out there?'

Weed ran like hell, his knapsack flapping on his back. Two paintbrushes flew out and landed on Varina Davis's grave.

chapter twenty-seven

At the Commonwealth Club, Hammer was losing her polish and becoming argumentative. She had not eaten breakfast and unwisely had washed down a Multi-Max 1 sustained release multivitamin, two Advils, two BuSpars and three tropical-fruit-flavored Tums calcium supplements with black coffee. Her stomach burned.

'I think we need to put things in perspective,' Hammer announced.

'I think there's exactly why we're doing it,' Ehrhart answered her.

'The point is not our reverence of monuments and a historic cemetery,' Hammer said, knowing she was venturing into an Indian burial ground.

'It's not a matter of reverence but of a far-stretching perception,' Ehrhart butted in. 'Hollywood Cemetery is a symbolism of the prospering advancement of culture that midway in the middle of the nineteenth century catapulted our marveling city into the twenty-fifth bigger of the others in America.'

'Anybody know how many big cities there were back then?' challenged Reverend Jackson.

'Anybody know what she just said?' Mayor Lamb whispered in Hammer's ear.

'At least thirty-five,' offered publisher Eaton.

'Closer to forty. South Dakota entered the union in 1859,' Lieutenant Governor Miller quietly corrected the mayor.

'I'd like to finish what I was saying,' Hammer pushed forward. 'The important point is that a painted statue is not the worst crime that's ever happened here.' She looked pointedly at Ehrhart. 'It might be a better idea to focus on gangs and escalating juvenile crime, and on the community's refusal to participate in protecting and taking care of itself. Which is what brought me here to begin with.'

'Why did you thinking were in here there morning if not to *participate?*' Ehrhart said with emotion. 'And for the records, it's never been my believe we needed Charlotte to telling us how to ruin our police department and our city.'

'Well, they're sure as hell running things a whole lot better than we are,' commented NationsBank president Albright, who had worked out of the headquarters in Charlotte before transferring to Richmond.

'We're not here today to talk about Charlotte,' the mayor said irritably.

'Nothing wrong with learning from somebody else,' said the lieutenant governor.

'I suggest the Blue Ribbon Crime Commission pave the way, Lelia,' Hammer said to Ehrhart, who was looking at her gold and diamond Rolex watch and getting anxious. 'You're in a strong position to mobilize citizens and state and city officials. You have a voice.'

'It's the responsible *police,* not the *citizens* what do away with crime. You already know the commission's subscription. We need to hire another additional more one hundred officers. We need more patrols on feet. Police officers should be forced even if they don't want to, to live with the city and carry there police cars home so there's more in our neighborhoods to be visible.'

'Who's going to pay for all that?' the mayor wanted to know. 'You never have explained that part, Lelia.'

Hammer's flip phone vibrated. She absented herself from the gathering umbrage at the conference table and went out the door.

'Chief?' West's voice came over the cell.

'Now's not a good time,' Hammer said.

'I'm at 6807 Midlothian Turnpike,' West said. 'I think you'd better come.'

The handcuffs around Bubba's wrists had been snapped on with contempt and no nonsense. Steel teeth bit into his soft flesh. The air conditioning inside the patrol car was up too high and Bubba's cranky bowel syndrome had rumbled out of remission.

Bubba had always known it was risky to tuck his Anaconda .44 under the seat, but he had never imagined he might get into this much trouble. Police were everywhere, some of them detectives. Moments ago, two fire trucks and an ambulance had screamed past, heading around to the back of Kmart. The media was rolling in and a helicopter was circling the area.

Officer Budget was standing outside the car talking to

the woman deputy chief who had come to Bubba's house after the break-in. He recalled her name was West. She kept glancing in at Bubba, her face hard, eyes sharp with anger that Bubba was certain was directed at him, although he didn't know why. He didn't understand why the cops had wanted his filthy tee shirt.

No one would tell him anything except that he had committed a class one misdemeanor by concealing a weapon from common view, a weapon that Budget had freed from beneath the seat and checked to see how many cartridges were inside the cylinder. With growing panic Bubba watched a tow truck turn off Midlothian Turnpike and park beside his Jeep.

Bubba tapped his manacled hands against his window. Budget glared in at him. West stopped talking. Bubba tapped again. Budget opened the front passenger's door and leaned inside the car.

'What?' Budget asked in a most unfriendly way.

'I need to use the bathroom.' Bubba lowered his voice because he didn't want West to hear.

'Yeah, yeah,' Budget said with no compassion.

'I can't wait,' Bubba told him quietly.

'You're gonna have to.'

'Can't.' Bubba gritted his teeth, pressing his buttocks together tightly.

'Too bad.' Budget shut the door.

Hammer rolled up in her midnight-blue Crown Victoria as a detective and two crime-scene technicians searched for evidence. The twenty-four-hour money stop had been cordoned off with yellow tape, and two more officers were standing sentry around a red Jeep Cherokee. West and another officer were talking by a patrol car, a suspect in back.

Hammer parked and got out as a blue medical examiner's van turned off Midlothian Turnpike and drove slowly through the Kmart parking lot, heading to the crime scene.

'Chief.' Budget greeted Hammer.

'What's going on?' Hammer asked West.

'We've got a white female shot in the head behind the Kmart, found at 0832 hours inside her vehicle, a baby in the back seat, strapped in a car seat.'

'God,' Hammer said. 'The baby all right?'

'Screaming, seems feverish,' West replied.

'How young?' Hammer asked.

She stared through the patrol car window at the suspect, a white man with thinning brown hair and a pudgy, flushed face. She thought he looked rather ill.

'I'd say less than a year old,' Budget replied. 'Child Protective Services just removed her from the scene, taking her to Chippenham Hospital to make sure she's okay while we try to find next of kin.'

'We might have a lead on that,' West said. 'There was a note in the victim's purse. Possibly written by the mother. Something about the baby's doctor whose office might be on Pump Road. The note refers to a sick baby named 'Loraine'. We're also making arrangements for temporary foster care, which we hope we won't need.'

Hammer stared at the red Jeep, noting the Confederate flag bumper sticker. She noted the BUB-AH vanity plate. She took a closer look at the suspect. He was shirtless and wearing camouflage pants.

'What's the victim's name?' Hammer asked.

Budget flipped back pages of his notepad.

'Ruby Sink,' he said. 'Seventy-two years old with a Church Hill address.'

'*Miss Sink?*' Hammer interrupted in horror. 'Oh my God! She's one of my neighbors. I can't believe it.'

'You knew her?' Budget was startled.

'Not well. Dear God! She's on the Hollywood Cemetery board of directors. I just talked to her.'

'Christ!' West said, throwing Bubba a killing look.

'Another ATM?' Hammer asked as a terrible darkness settled over her.

'We know she withdrew two hundred dollars at 0802 hours,' Budget answered. 'We found the receipt. The cash is gone.'

Pieces were fitting together, although not without a little forcing. Hammer recalled the fragmented cell phone conversation between two men named Bubba and Smudge. They were planning to rob and murder a woman. The name Loraine and something about pumps were in the mix. Hammer had supposed their intended victim was black. But perhaps she had misunderstood. Hammer stared at the suspect again.

'Tell me about him,' she said.

'Butner Fluck the fourth, but goes by Bubba,' West replied. 'Oddly enough, Brazil and I responded to a B and

E at his house just yesterday. A lot of guns allegedly stolen from his workshop.'

'Interesting,' Hammer said.

'Appears he was parked here at the time the homicide occurred,' Budget added.

'Did he see anything?' Hammer asked.

'Says he didn't. I recovered a forty-four Magnum that was concealed under the seat. One of these eight-inch-barrel jobs with a scope. Recently fired, four rounds missing. Plus, I'd stopped him maybe a half hour earlier, pulled him over to the exact spot where his Jeep is now . . .'

'Wait a minute.' Hammer held up her hand. 'Start over.'

'I know it's rather bizarre,' West tried to clarify. 'But the suspect was driving erratically shortly after seven this morning and Officer Budget pulled him over here, exactly where the Jeep is now. No outstanding warrants, nothing on him. He was charged with reckless driving and released. Less than an hour later, the victim's discovered behind Kmart.'

'I heard the call over the radio and responded,' Budget explained. 'And there's the same Jeep right where I'd seen it last, the suspect hiding on the floor, the gun in plain view.'

'So he never moved after you pulled him,' Hammer said. 'The Jeep was right here when the victim was robbed at the money stop and then murdered behind Kmart.'

'That's how it appears,' West said.

'What about his demeanor?' Hammer stared at Bubba.

'Extremely agitated, sweating profusely,' Budget replied. 'He has blood on his tee shirt. We said we'd like to take the shirt to the lab, but he was under no obligation to let us. He was compliant.'

'Anything else that might link him to the homicide?' Hammer asked.

'Not so far. Not until we can see if the bullets in the victim were fired from his gun. But it's kind of doubtful, to be honest. The shells we found in the car are nine-millimeter, ejected from a pistol.'

'This is all very strange,' Hammer said. 'And it sounds like all we've really got on him is a class one misdemeanor.'

'Yes, ma'am.'

Hammer stared again at the fat man in the back seat of the cruiser. He stared back at her with exhausted, miserable eyes.

'Well, it doesn't appear to me that we have probable cause to hold him,' Hammer said with extreme disappointment.

'We don't,' West agreed. 'But we couldn't be sure of that at first.'

'It's hard for me to imagine he was sitting here while a woman was robbed and never saw a thing,' Hammer remarked angrily as she thought again of Bubba and Smudge and their broken conversation.

'Nobody ever sees a thing,' West said.

chapter twenty-eight

Governor Mike Feuer was a tall, lanky man in his early sixties, with piercing eyes that burned with compassion and fierce truth. Republicans often compared him to Abraham Lincoln without a beard. Democrats called him *The Fuhrer.*

'I understand completely. And of course I'm upset, too,' he was saying into a secure phone in the back of his bulletproof black limousine as he rode through downtown.

'Governor, have you seen it already yet?' Lelia Ehrhart's voice came over a line that could not be tapped or picked up by cell phones, scanners or CB radios.

'No.'

'You must be able to.'

He sighed, glancing at his watch. Governor Feuer had ten meetings scheduled today. He was supposed to call at least six legislators who were fighting hard for and against House and Senate bills flowing through a typically turgid General Assembly.

He was supposed to be prepped for an interview with *USA Today,* sign a proclamation, meet with his cabinet, be briefed by the House Finance Subcommittee and hold two press conferences. It was his mother's eighty-sixth birthday and he had yet to get around to sending flowers. His back was acting up again.

'If you could just have time to take to drive through and see it for yourself in person, Governor,' said Ehrhart. 'I think you'll be shocking, and if you aren't taking a look today, it's a risk because it has eventually to be removed at some point to be restored. It won't do any good at the most if you are looking later, because by then it will be original again.'

'Then the damage must not be too extensive,' he replied reasonably as plainclothes Executive Protection Unit state police officers rode in unmarked Chevrolet Caprices in front of his limousine and behind it.

'It's the action of it that matters, Governor,' she went on in her unique accent.

Governor Feuer imagined her on the floor as a child, laboring over building blocks that she could not quite get in the right order.

'The vile deliberation of it,' she was saying.

'Frankly, I'm more concerned with . . .'

'Please take a minutes. And I wasn't intentioned to interrupt.'

She did mean to, but the governor let it pass because he was a secure, fair man. He believed in second chances. Lelia Ehrhart was entitled to one more this day before he hung up on her.

'Of course, the cemetery's closed and won't be opening to the public this minutes,' Ehrhart said. 'But I'll make sure it's unlocked isn't hooked for you to get in.'

The governor pressed the intercom button.

'Jed?'

'Yes, sir,' Jed replied from the other side of the glass partition, his attentive eyes in the rearview mirror.

'We need to swing over to Hollywood Cemetery.' Governor Feuer glanced at his watch again. 'We'll have to make it quick.'

'Whatever you say, sir.'

'Lelia,' the governor said into the phone. 'Consider it done.'

'Oh, you're so wonderful!'

'I'm not, really,' he replied wearily as he thought of his mother's birthday again.

Lelia Ehrhart returned the portable phone to its charger inside her completely equipped gym on the third floor of her brick mansion behind wrought-iron gates on West Cary Street. Her brow was damp, her arms quivering from working latissimus dorsi, rhomboids, trapezius, triceps, deltoids and pectoralis on the incline, chest and shoulder presses, and the lat pulldown, and the low row, just before the governor had returned her phone call.

'When now?' she cheerfully asked her trainer, Lonnie Fort.

'Seated row,' he said.

'No most rowing. I simply can never.' She sipped Evian and dabbed her face with a towel. 'I think we've got to all those muscles, Lonnie. I really don't like working it out this early, anyway. My entire system's in the state of shock. It's like getting out of bed and jumping on the Arctic Ocean. And I'm not a little bit penguin,' she said in a cute voice. 'Nothing cold-natured with me.'

'I'm sorry we had to meet so early, Mrs. Ehrhart.'

'Not your fault, not in the smallest. I forgot you had a damn dental appointed.'

Lonnie studied the circuit Ehrhart was supposed to complete this morning, recording the number of reps and their weights.

'Thanks for fitting me on,' she said. 'But it wasn't very nice that Bull to scheduled you at the same time of nine A.M. in the morning when we always do this. Of course, he has so much people working for him. He probably knew nothing to remember about it since others always do for him so he doesn't.'

'I'm sure you're right, Mrs. Ehrhart.'

The son of a bitch. She thought of her wealthy dentist husband with all his radio ads and strip mall offices and sycophantic employees. He'd had affairs with three dental hygienists that she knew of, and although the number most likely far exceeded that, what difference did it make? Lelia Ehrhart would never forgive him for the first one.

'So tell to me, Lonnie, will Bull go to crown all your teeths like he does all everybody else's?' Ehrhart asked her trainer, who was so beautifully constructed she wanted to trace her fingers and tongue over every inch of him.

'He says he can give me a Hollywood smile,' Lonnie answered.

'Ha! He says this always to everyone.'

'I don't know. His hygienists sure have pretty smiles. They told me he crowned all their teeth.'

Just the word *hygienist* pierced Ehrhart like a foil.

'But I don't know,' Lonnie said again.

'Don't do it! No!' Ehrhart told him. 'One time it's done there's no to undone it and it's permanently. Bull's grinded up all the teeths in the city, Lonnie.'

'Well, he's sure made a good living,' said Lonnie.

He attached the short extension cable to the lower pulley of the Trotter MG2100 total fitness machine. He attached the revolving straight bar, his sculpted muscles sliding and bunching beneath smooth, tan skin.

'You'll end up with at the end with all this little nibs, looking like a man-eating cannibals. You'll get TMJ and lisps when you talk and end up with several roots canals,' the dentist's wife warned him. 'Your teeths are so beauty!'

'I have this space between my two front ones.' He showed her.

'They're perfect! Some peoples think space is really sexual.'

'You're kidding?' He looked at his teeth in one of the many wall-size mirrors.

'Oh no, I'm never.'

She looked intensely at his mouth and was enraged that she'd ever let her husband talk her into crowning all her teeth. She felt ruined. The crowns weren't as natural as the teeth he'd ground away, and she got frequent headaches and had pressure and temperature sensitivity in three molars. Lelia Ehrhart envied natural teeth, even if they weren't perfect. She envied beautiful bodies. She was obsessed with both and would never have either.

'Arm curls.' Lonnie got back to business, holding the bar in both hands to demonstrate.

'My arms are shaken,' she complained with a flirty porcelain smile. 'You need to show me another again one more time. I never can get these one right. I always feel them behind my back and I know that's not supposedly to be.'

He moved the pin to one hundred and fifty pounds and demonstrated, his biceps bunching like huge swells in an ocean, a gathered energy capable of great force, a slope for her to climb and conquer.

'Lift just with your arms,' he said. 'Don't lean back. You use your back, you're cheating.'

He lowered the weight to twenty pounds. Ehrhart took the bar and held it shoulder-width apart with an underhand grip, palms facing up, elbows close to her sides, just as she had been taught. She eyed her form in mirrors, not sure her blue Nike tights had been a good choice. The red stripes emphasized her wide hips. When all was said and done, black was always best for lower body, bright colors for upper, such as the chartreuse sports bra she had on today.

'Twenty reps,' Lonnie told her.

She was energized by her conversation with Governor Führer. How many people could ask to speak to the governor of Virginia and have him on the phone twenty-two minutes later? Not many, she told herself as she strained. Not many at all, and this time it had nothing to do with her husband's power and contributions.

'All of us have our complexions,' she said to Lonnie as she struggled for breath. 'Our insecure hidden secret places that others can't see. Even I do. I've lost counting.' She huffed.

'Sixteen.'

'Seventeen, eighteen. Goodness, you're wearing me in!'

'What complexes could you possibly have? How many women your age work out like you do and have their own gym? Not to mention a house like this.'

The comment seared Ehrhart's ego and self-worth. She wanted him to say that no other woman on earth looked like her, that age and a wealthy husband had nothing to do with it. She wanted to hear him say she was divine, her face so beautiful it turned all mortals to stone, her body fatal to those who dared look at it. She wanted Lonnie to taste blood when his eyes wandered over her. She wanted him possessive, obsessive, jealous. She wanted him to feel a raging lust that kept him up all night.

'I supposedly my most big complexion is worrying I don't have enough times for my husband,' she lied. 'Filling his endlessly needs, which are unsatisfying. I suppose I worry anxiously my rule in state government carries with it such huge responsibles I often neglected family and many, many friends and don't have times for them. I worry anxiously about getting over muscled. I didn't want to be over developing.'

Lonnie looked her up and down.

'Oh, you shouldn't worry about that,' he reassured her. 'You don't have the kind of body that will get overbuilt, Mrs. Ehrhart.'

'I suppose I'm much the soft, female typed,' she decided.

'Next time we'll measure your body fat again.'

'And then the children,' she went on with her complexes, which were multiplying the more Lonnie talked. 'Last night I was too busy and spend much too little times with thems individually, either one, because of my commission meeting I had to call to order and make it earlier. And I barely had times for that. And why?' She gave him a coquettish smile. 'To be here with you an hour earlier than before the usual.'

'I admire your dedication,' Lonnie said, glancing at his watch and setting the clipboard on a weight bench. 'That's what it takes. No pain, no gain.'

'Don't crowns your teeths!' she told him with feeling. 'And don't you dare tell Bull I lost away his business.' She winked at Lonnie. 'When next?'

'Abs,' Lonnie said. 'And then we're almost done.'

'I can't tell if I see any progression.' She placed her hands on her abdomen and looked in the mirror. 'All that misery for a thing more. I hate abs so much more intensively than others.'

He studied her rectus abdominus and lliopsoas, sweat staining his gray MetRex tank top and buffing his skin.

'Why bother it?' she went on.

'You forget where you were when you started,' he said. 'You don't see how much you've improved because you look at yourself every day. Your abs are definitely better, Mrs. Ehrhart.'

'I am very doubting. You look.'

She took his reluctant hands and placed them on her abdomen.

'Well?'

He had no response.

'Maybe when you get to be my older age at this stage of life, it's hopeless and can't be changed. Nature is just won't collaborating and do what you want it to do.'

Lonnie didn't move. She slid his hands up a little.

'You're in great shape,' he exaggerated.

'Bull's out crowning every tooths in North of America,' Ehrhart answered, sliding his hands up more. 'You know why he nicked his name Bull? It's not because of the general he thinks he's relations with, Lonnie.'

'I thought maybe it had to do with the stock market.'

'The reason is because of . . .'

'I've really got to go, Mrs. Ehrhart.'

She pressed his large, strong hands against her, finally cupping them over her very small breasts.

'What's the oldest older woman you once ever had before?' she whispered.

'I guess my eighth-grade teacher,' he said.

'What was that have been?'

'When I was in the eighth grade.'

'My, you must have been bigger for your age then.'

'Mrs. Ehrhart, I've gotta go so I'm not late for my appointment. Your husband's really hard to schedule. Well, I guess I wouldn't get in at all if it wasn't for you.'

Lelia Ehrhart removed his hands. She angrily grabbed a towel and wrapped it around her neck.

'So what's the next place where we go from here?' she demanded as all her phobias and insecurities roared at her.

'You haven't done squats,' he said.

chapter twenty-nine

Governor Feuer neatly folded the *New York Times*, *Wall Street Journal*, *Washington Post*, *USA Today* and the Richmond paper. He stacked them on the black carpet and stared out the tinted window at pedestrians staring at him.

Everyone knew that a black stretch limousine with 1 on the license plate was not Jimmy Dean or Ralph Sampson. It was not kids going to the prom.

'Sir?' Jed said over the intercom. 'I'll just shoot over on Tenth, cut across Broad to avoid all that traffic, then wind around the courthouse onto Leigh and get on Belvidere. From there it's pretty much a straight shot into the cemetery.'

'Ummmm.'

'If that suits, sir,' added Jed, who was obsessive-compulsive and needy.

'That's fine,' said the governor, who had worked his way up from attorney general to lieutenant governor to governor, and therefore had not navigated Richmond's streets alone for more than eight years, but rather had watched his travels throughout his beloved Commonwealth from a back seat through tinted glass, police escorts leading the way and protecting his rear.

'I've got the package,' Jed said loudly in his two-way, secure radio. 'Going to be turning on Tenth.'

'Gotcha covered,' the lead car came back.

The altercation between Patty Passman and Officer Rhoad had gone beyond a squabble or fit of pique that might have been reasonably resolved, forgiven or perhaps forgotten.

Cars were double-parked and parked on an angle and within fifteen feet of a fire hydrant and on the wrong side of the street and on the sidewalk along 10th. Drivers and pedestrians had gathered around a fight in progress as police cruisers with sirens screaming and lights flashing raced in from all directions.

Passman had Rhoad on hold. He was running around in circles, screaming 'MAYDAY' into his portable radio while she twisted and squeezed.

'God! God!' Rhoad shrieked as she doggedly followed his every move, on his heels, killing him. 'Let go! Please! Please! Ahhhhhhhhh! AHHHHHHHH!'

The crowd was frenzied.

'Go, girlfriend!'

'Yank it hard!'

'Get him!'

'In the nuts! Hooo-a hooo-a hooo-a!'

'Hey! Punch her! Man, fucking poke her eyes out!'

'Yeah! Knock her nose to the back of her head so she

can smell her ass!'

'Pull that banana off the tree, girlfriend!'

'Shift him into neutral, baby!'

'Let go, fatso!'

'Untie his balloon!'

'Go, girl!'

The crowd cheered on as a gleaming black stretch limousine and two unmarked black Caprices with multiple antennas floated across Broad Street. The convoy pulled off to the side of 10th Street, making way for two cruisers with flashing lights and screaming sirens. Other police cars were screeching in from Marshall and Leigh. A fire truck wailed and rumbled along Clay.

•

Jed was desperate to jump out of the limousine and get involved. The cops must be after a fugitive, someone on the FBI's ten most wanted list, maybe a serial killer. Clearly, the fat lady was a psycho of some sort, and it was obvious that the uniformed officers could not restrain her.

'What's going on?' Governor Feuer inquired over the intercom.

'Some wacko woman, probably high on PCP or crack. Wow, look at her go, like a damn pit bull! She's got half a dozen cops playing Ring Around the Rosie and falling on their butts!'

The governor made his way to the other side of the black leather horseshoe-shaped seat that could comfortably accommodate six. He strained to see over the back of Jed's big head.

Governor Feuer was startled by the obese woman flying after a tall, rather elderly skinny cop. A pair of handcuffs dangled off one of her wrists and her free hand was shoved up the poor fellow's crotch. She was twisting and crushing, cursing, kicking. She was whirling and swinging the loose handcuff like a numchaku, scattering arriving troops.

'Wow!' Jed exclaimed.

'How awful,' said the governor. 'How perfectly awful.'

'We need to do something, sir!'

Governor Feuer agreed, his anger rising. There was nothing funny about this. There was nothing entertaining about violence. He jerked open his car door. Before Jed or EPU police could stop him, the governor popped the trunk and snatched out a fire extinguisher.

He ran into the melee and to the astonishment of all blasted Patty Passman with Halon 1301. Shocked, she released Rhoad. Cops tackled her to the ground. Four EPU police officers quickly escorted Governor Feuer back to his limousine.

'Way to go, sir!' Jed was very proud of his commander-in-chief.

The governor checked his black cashmere pinstripe suit for a Halon residue, but the miracle extinguisher left not a trace. He watched the cuffed, crazed woman as she was stuffed into the back of a patrol car. The poor officer was on his knees in the middle of the street, clutching himself and crying. The media was rolling in, advancing with television cameras and microphones like drawn swords.

'On to Hollywood,' Governor Feuer ordered.

'There's really not time, sir,' Jed suggested.

'There's never time,' the governor said, waving him on.

Weed decided he had stayed long enough in the big hole with broken clay pipes in the bottom of it. Water was leaking from somewhere. A Bob Cat was parked nearby and lots of shovels and hoes were scattered on the ground.

He had begun to worry that the hole was really a grave, even though it wasn't at all shaped like one. Maybe everybody was on an early lunch break or something. Maybe all of a sudden dirt would start falling in and Weed would be buried alive.

He peeked out and didn't see a sign of Brazil or anyone else. He listened hard. Only birds were talking. He climbed out of the hole and made a dash for the cemetery fence. He climbed to the top of it as the Lemans slowly cruised into view. Dog, Beeper and Sick were looking for him so Smoke could shoot Weed and dump him in the river. Weed dropped back inside the cemetery and ran with no particular destination in mind, zigzagging around graves and leaping over monuments.

brazil too was running fast and could have continued his seven-minute-mile pace for hours, although boots would not have been his footwear of choice and his shins were beginning to hurt. The more frustrated he got, the faster he ran.

He cut over to Riverview, flying past memorials, monuments, plaques, sculptures, vases and tablets. Tiny Confederate flags waved him on. A groundskeeper with extra spools of nylon twine tied on his belt trimmed around stones, the weed-eater popping and buzzing as he maneuvered it with the skill of a surgeon.

'You seen a kid in Chicago Bulls stuff?' Brazil called out as he got close.

'Like the statue?'

'Only smaller,' Brazil said, running past.

'Nope,' the groundskeeper said as he trimmed.

Brazil wove between a marble lamb and a mausoleum, jumped over an English boxwood and to his amazement landed almost on top of Weed. Brazil grabbed him by the back of his jersey, kicked his feet out from under him and sat on him. He pinned Weed's arms to the ground.

'I changed my mind,' Weed yelled. 'You can lock me up.'

bubba had lost control and it was obvious to all. He was humiliated and sick to his stomach when Officer Budget opened the back of the patrol car and exclaimed, '*Shit, man*.' Bubba felt sure one more hideous nickname had just been added to the list.

'I'm sorry,' Bubba said. 'But I told you . . .'

'Man, oh man!' Budget cried.

He was beside himself, almost gagging as he unlocked Bubba's handcuffs while Chief Hammer and West looked on.

'And just who's going to clean this up! Man, oh man! I can't believe it!'

Bubba's shame could not have been deeper. He had been so certain it was his destiny for his path to cross with Hammer's. But not like this. Not half naked, dirty, fat and soiled. He could not look at her.

'Officer Budget,' Hammer said flatly, 'if you'll just leave me alone with him for a few minutes, please. Major West? I'll meet you behind the Kmart?'

'We'll let you know what the medical examiner says,' Budget told Hammer, 'in case you don't get there before he leaves.'

'*She,*' West corrected him.

Hammer turned her attention to Bubba. He was stunned that she did not seem to notice his unspeakable predicament.

'Chief Hammer?' he stammered. 'I, uh . . .' He swallowed hard. 'I didn't mean . . .'

She held up a hand to silence him.

'Don't worry about it,' she told him.

'How can I not!' he cried. 'And all I wanted to do was help!'

'Help who?'

She seemed interested and sincere. Bubba hadn't realized she was so attractive, not in a pretty way, but strong and striking in her pinstripe pants suit. He wondered if she had a gun. Maybe she carried one in her black handbag. His thoughts moiled crazily as the wind shifted to Hammer's disadvantage. She moved several feet to her right.

'Who is it you're trying to help?' she asked. 'The woman who just got murdered? Did you see something, Mr. Fluck?'

'Oh my God!' Bubba was shocked. 'A lady was just murdered, right here! When?'

'While you were parked here, Mr. Fluck.'

Bubba's bowels were irritably gathering again, like dark clouds about to release another lashing, violent storm. He thought of his sweaty tee shirt, covered with blood and on its way to the police labs.

'You sure you didn't see anything?' The chief continued to press.

'My Anaconda was hung,' he answered.

She just stared at him.

'I couldn't get it off,' he said.

Still, she said nothing.

'So I got down and started tugging on it, you know, manipulating it as best I could. See, I was afraid it might go off. Then I got a nosebleed.'

'This was when?' Hammer asked.

'I guess when the lady got killed. I swear. I was on the floor ever since Officer Budget left me. That's all I was doing until he was knocking on my window. I couldn't have seen anything, because I was on the floor, is what I'm saying, ma'am.'

He couldn't tell if she believed him. There was nothing cruel or disrespectful about her demeanor, but she was shrewd and very smart. Bubba was in awe of her. For a moment he forgot his plight until Channel 8's cameraman trotted toward them, heading straight for the chief, then getting a disgusted look on his face. He stared at Bubba's camouflage pants and changed course.

'It appears the victim was robbed right here at the money stop,' Hammer spoke to Bubba. 'I'm not telling you anything confidential. I'm sure you'll be hearing all about it on the news. You were parked less than fifty feet from the money stop, Mr. Fluck. Are you absolutely certain you didn't hear anything? Maybe voices, arguing, a car or cars?'

Bubba thought hard. Channel 6 headed toward them and quickly went the other way. Bubba would have done anything to help this brave woman, and it broke his heart that the one time he had a chance, he could do nothing but stink.

'Shit,' muttered a WRVA reporter as he stopped and backed up. 'Wouldn't go over there if I was you,' he said to a crew from Channel 12.

'What's going on?' *Style Magazine* called out to *Richmond Magazine.* 'A sewer line break?'

'Hell if I know. Shit, man.'

Bubba went on red alert.

'"Shit man" is right.' A *Times-Dispatch* reporter waved his hand in front of his face.

Bubba's blood heated up. He didn't hear a word Chief Hammer was saying to him. Bubba was completely focused on the knot of reporters, cameramen, photographers and technicians gathered by his Jeep. They were restless and angry, talking and bitching loudly amongst themselves and calling him *Shit Man.*

'Anybody seen what's going on back there behind the building?'

'They won't let anybody close.'

'You can forget it. The minute you get to the garden center, the cops push you back.'

'Yeah, one asshole put his hand over my lens.'

'Shit, man.'

Bubba's mind whited out the way it always did when he heard the voices and the laughter shrieking from dangerous, painful convolutions in his brain. He saw a legion of little faces distorted by taunts and cruel grins.

'My editor's gonna kill me. Shit, man!'

'*Stop It!*' Bubba screamed at the press.

His eyes suddenly focused. Hammer was staring at him, rather startled. The media wasn't interested.

'Maybe the body's decomposing,' one of them was saying.

'It's back behind the store.'

'Could've been here first. Maybe they moved it for some reason.'

'That wouldn't make sense.'

'Well, they wouldn't want to leave it here right in front of the bank.'

'No way it could have been here long enough to decompose without someone spotting it before this morning.'

'Oh, so now you're a medical examiner.'

'Maybe it was dumped. You know, the victim's been dead for a while, is getting ripe and the killer dumps her.'

'It's a her?'

'Maybe.'

'Dumps her *here?'*

'I'm just throwing things out.'

'Yeah, asshole, 'cause you want the rest of us to write them down and make fools out of ourselves.'

'Then what stinks so bad?'

'Chief Hammer?' A reporter raised his voice without getting any closer. 'Can I get a statement?'

'Don't talk to them!' Bubba said to her in a panic. 'Don't let them do this to me! Please!'

'Truth is, I think our source is him,' a reporter broke the news. 'Look at his pants. Not all of that's camouflage.'

'Shit, man.'

'See!' Bubba hissed.

'How can she stand there like that? It's bad enough way back here.'

'I've heard she's tough.'

'I'm interested in your vanity plate,' Hammer said to Bubba.

Officer Horace Cutchins wasn't interested in anything except his pocket Game Boy Tetris Plus as he drove the detention wagon at a good clip along Leigh Street.

He'd been on duty only three hours and had already transported two subjects to lockup, both of them gypsies caught burglarizing a Tudor-style home in Windsor Farms. Cutchins didn't understand why people didn't learn.

Gypsies passed through the city twice a year on their migrations north and south. Everyone knew it. The press ran frequent stories and columns. Sergeant Rink of *Crime Stoppers* offered impassioned warnings and prevention and self-defense tips on all local television networks and radio stations. 'Gypsies Are Back' signs were prominently posted as usual.

Yet wealthy Windsor Farmers, as Cutchins jealously called them, still went out to get the newspaper or worked in their gardens and yards or sat by their pools or chatted with neighbors or frapped around the house with alarm systems off and doors unlocked. So what did they expect?

Cutchins was just turning into Engine Company #5's back parking lot, where he was looking forward to resuming his puzzle game, when the radio raised him.

'Ten-25 unit 112 on Tenth Street to 10-31 a prisoner,' the communications officer told him.

'Ten-4,' he answered. 'Fuck,' he said to himself.

He'd heard the mayday earlier and knew that Rhoad Hog was involved in an altercation with a disorderly female. But when it appeared that an arrest had been made, Cutchins just assumed the subject would be transported in a screen unit.

After all, it wasn't likely that a female could kick out the Plexiglas, and even if the partition didn't fit right because the numb nuts with General Services had taken one from a Caprice, for example, and retrofitted it for a Crown Vic, it didn't matter in this case. A female prisoner was not equipped to pee on the officer through gaps and spaces caused by improper installment.

Cutchins made a U turn. He shot back out on Leigh Street, stepping on it, wanting to get the call over with so he could take a break. He swung over to 10th and rolled up on the problem as Detective Gloria De Souza climbed out of her unmarked car.

Rhoad Hog and three other uniformed guys were waiting for Cutchins, their prisoner an ugly fat woman who looked vaguely familiar. She was sitting on the curb, wrists cuffed behind her back, hair wild. She was breathing hard and looked like she might do something unexpected any minute.

'Okay, Miss Passman, I'm going to have to search you,' said Detective De Souza. 'I need you to stand up.'

Miss Passman didn't budge.

'Cooperate, Patty,' one of the officers urged her.

She wouldn't.

'Ma'am, you're going to need to stand up. Now don't make this harder than it has to be.'

Passman wasn't trying to make things harder. She simply could not rise to the occasion on her own, not with her hands shackled behind her.

'Get up,' De Souza said sternly.

'I can't,' Passman replied.

'Then we'll have to help you, ma'am.'

'Go ahead,' Passman said.

De Souza and another officer got Passman under each arm and hoisted her up while Rhoad hung back at a safe distance. Cutchins hopped out of his white Dodge van and went around to the back to open the tailgate. De Souza bent over and briskly slid her hands up Passman's stout legs, over sagging pantyhose with runs, feeling her way up into areas where no woman, other than Passman's gynecologist, had ever gone before. Passman tried to kick De Souza and almost fell.

'Get the flex cuffs!' De Souza demanded as she held Passman's legs still. 'You do that again, ma'am, and I'm gonna hogtie you!'

De Souza held on as an officer looped the plastic flex cuff around Passman's ankles, jerking it tight as if she were a tall kitchen bag.

'Ouch!'

'Hold still!'

'That hurts!' Passman screamed.

'Good!' Rhoad cheered.

Detective De Souza resumed her search, running experienced hands over Passman's topography, into its crevices, through its canyons, between its foothills and under and over them while Passman cursed and yelled and called her a diesel dyke and cops helped Passman to her feet.

'Get your fucking hands off me, you queer!' Passman shouted. *'That's right! You sleep with the coach of your fucking queer softball team the Clit Hits and everybody in the entire police department and radio room knows it!'*

Cutchins momentarily forgot his puzzle game. He'd always thought it a waste that a good-looking woman like De Souza was *into same,* not that he minded lesbians, and in fact watched them whenever he had access to pay TV.

He simply objected to discrimination. De Souza did not share herself with men, and Cutchins didn't think that was fair.

'Nothing on her but an attitude,' De Souza said.

Unfortunately, Cutchins had parked on the other side of 10th and it was shift change at the Medical College of Virginia hospital. Instantly, traffic was heavy, sidewalks and streets congested with nurses, dietitians, orderlies, custodians, security guards, administrators, resident doctors and chaplains, all of them worn out, underpaid and cranky. Cars stopped to let the tied-up lady and the cops cross to the awaiting wagon. Pedestrians slowed their impatient get-out-of-my-way steps as Passman hopped ahead awkwardly.

'Fuckheads! What are you staring at!' she yelled to all.

'Go jump!' a secretary yelled back.

'Jumpin' Jack Flash! Jumpin' Jack Flash! Jumpin' Jack Flash!' chanted a group of sleep-deprived residents.

'Hop-a-long!'

'Motherfuckers!' screamed Passman, whose blood sugar was as low as it had ever been while she was conscious.

'Jumpin' bean!' cried a records clerk.

Passman struggled, writhing like a python, hissing and baring her teeth at her detractors. Officers did their best to move her along while bystanders and drivers got more worked up and Rhoad tagged along out of range.

Pigeon had gotten bored with the cemetery and was rooting through a trash can, where so far he had salvaged part of a 7-Eleven breakfast burrito and a twenty-two-ounce cup of coffee that was half full.

He watched the heartless parade pass by, some woman hopping along as if she were in a sack race. He suddenly felt self-conscious of his stump and was angered by the crowd.

'Don't pay any attention to them,' he counseled the fat lady as she hopped past and he took a bite of the burrito. 'People are so rude these days.'

'Shut up, you crippled garbage-picker!' the woman yelled at him.

Pigeon was sorrowed by yet another rotten example of human nature. He continued his treasure hunting, always drawn by crowds that might throw things away.

de Souza gripped Passman's arm like a vise.

'He started it!' Passman twisted around to glare at Rhoad. 'Why don't you lock his ass up!'

Cops shoved her inside the wagon and slammed the tailgate shut.

it was Chief Hammer's NIJ mission to implement the New York City Crime Control Model in the Richmond Police Department, as she had in Charlotte and would do in other cities should health, energy and grant money allow. Understandably, this created a bit of a dilemma for her.

She was losing stamina and professionalism as she stood

close to Bubba and listened to him talk. She wanted out but simply could not and would never pass the buck, look the other way, walk off and make this a problem for someone else. Hammer was here, and that was that. When a cop asks a suspect a question, the cop must listen to the answer, no matter how long and drawn-out it is.

Bubba was telling her about his vanity plate, recalling his trip to the DMV on Johnston Willis Drive, between Whitten Brothers Jeep and Dick Straus Ford, where he had waited in line at customer service for fifty-seven minutes only to learn that *BUBBA* was taken, as were *BUBA, BUBBBA, BUUBBBA, BUBEH, BUBBEH, BUBBBEH, BG-BUBA, BHUBBA* and *BHUBA*. Bubba had been crushed and exhausted. He could think of nothing else that didn't exceed seven letters. Despondent and emotionally drained, he had accepted that the vanity plate was not meant to be.

'Then,' he seemed momentarily energized by the tireless account, 'the lady at the counter said *Bubah* would work, and I asked if I could hyphenate it and she didn't care because a hyphen doesn't count as a letter and that was good because I thought it would be easier to pronounce *Bubah* with a hyphen.'

Hammer believed that Bubba had an accomplice named Smudge, and a graphic and believable scenario was materializing in her mind even as Bubba droned on and reporters continued to keep their distance. Bubba and Smudge somehow knew that Ruby Sink and Loraine were headed to the First Union money stop near the Kmart.

Possibly the men had been lying in wait for the wealthy

Miss Sink, headlights and engines off, and when she left her residence, Smudge and Bubba tailed her, weaving in and out of traffic, keeping tabs on each other over cell phones and CBs.

It was at this point that Hammer's re-creation of the crime became less well defined. Frankly, she couldn't figure out what might have happened next and was not the sort to make things up. Yet she simply could not, would not walk away with no accountability and tell her troops the murder was their problem.

Somehow, Hammer had to get Bubba to answer the question of Smudge without Bubba thinking she had asked.

chapter thirty

Governor Mike Feuer had been on the car phone for the past fifteen minutes, and this was fortunate for Jed, who had made five wrong turns and sped through an alley-way, losing both unmarked Caprices, before finding Cherry Street and driving past Hollywood Cemetery and ending up at Oregon Hill Park, where he had turned around and gone the wrong way on Spring Street, ending up on Pine Street at Mamma'Zu, reputed to be the best Italian restaurant this side of Washington, D.C.

'Jed?' The governor's voice sounded over the intercom. 'Isn't that Mamma'Zu?'

'I believe so, sir.'

'I thought you said it closed down.'

'No, sir. I think I said it *was closed* when you wanted to take your wife there for her birthday,' Jed fibbed, for it was his modus operandi to say a business had closed or moved or gone under if the governor wanted to go there and Jed did not know how to find it.

'Well, make a note of it,' the governor's voice came back. 'Ginny will be thrilled.'

'Will do, sir.'

Ginny was the first lady, and Jed was scared of her. She knew Richmond streets far better than Jed was comfortable with, and he feared her reaction if she learned that Mamma'Zu had not closed or moved or changed its name. Ginny Feuer was a Yale graduate. She was fluent in eight languages, although Jed wasn't certain if that included English or was in addition to English.

The first lady had quizzed Jed repeatedly about his creative, time-killing routes. She was on to him and could get him reassigned, demoted, kicked off the EPU or even fired from the state police with a gesture, a word, a question in pretty much any language.

'Jed, shouldn't we be there by now?' the governor's voice sounded again.

Jed eyed his boss in the rearview mirror. Governor Feuer was looking out the windows. He was looking at his watch.

'In about two minutes, sir,' Jed replied as his chest got tight.

He picked up speed, following Pine the wrong way. He took a hard right on Oregon Hill Parkway which ran him into Cherry Street where the ivy-draped cemetery fence on the left embraced and welcomed him like the Statue of Liberty.

Jed followed the fence, passing the hole in it and the Victory Rug Cleaning sign. He drove through the cemetery's massive wrought-iron front gates that Lelia Ehrhart had made sure would be unlocked for them. He passed the caretaker's house and business office, following Hollywood Avenue. Jed would have rolled up on the statue in a matter of moments had he not turned onto Confederate Avenue instead of Eastvale.

It was clear to Brazil why the media, the unimaginative, the insensitive, the resentful, and those citizens not indigenous to Richmond often trivialized Hollywood Cemetery by referring to it as the City of the Dead.

As Brazil and Weed walked deeper into having-no-idea-where-they-were, Brazil's respect for history and its dead was greatly diluted by fatigue and frustration. The famous cemetery became nothing more than a heartless, unhelpful metropolis of ancient carriage paths, now paved and named, that had been laid out by first families who already knew where they were going.

It wasn't possible to find sections or lot owners or the way out unless one had a map or an *a priori* knowledge or was lucky as hell. Brazil, sad to say, was heading west instead of east.

'Is it hurting?' Brazil asked his prisoner.

Weed had cut his chin when Brazil tackled him. Weed was bleeding and Brazil's day had just gotten worse, if that was possible. The sheriff's department would not accept a juvenile who was visibly injured. Weed would have to get a medical release, meaning Brazil would have no choice but to take Weed to an emergency room where the two of them would probably sit all day.

'I don't feel nothing.' Weed shrugged, holding one of Brazil's socks against his chin for lack of any other bandage.

'Well, I'm really sorry,' Brazil apologized again.

They were walking along Waterview to New Avenue where Weed stopped to gawk at tobacco mogul Lewis Ginter's granite and marble tomb. He couldn't believe the heavy bronze doors, Corinthian columns and Tiffany windows.

'It's like a church,' Weed marveled. 'I wish Twister could have something like that.'

They walked in silence for a moment. Brazil remembered to turn his radio back on.

'You ever had anybody die on you?' Weed asked.

'My father.'

'Wish mine was dead.'

'You don't really mean that,' Brazil said.

'What happened to yours?' Weed looked up at him.

'He was a cop. Got killed on duty.'

Brazil thought of his father's small, plain grave in the college town of Davidson. The memories of that spring Sunday morning when he was ten and the phone rang in his simple frame house on Main Street were still vivid. He could still hear his mother screaming and kicking cabinets, wailing and throwing things while he hid in his room, knowing without being told.

Again and again the television showed his father's bloody sheet-covered body being loaded into an ambulance. An endless motorcade of police cars and motorcycles with headlights on rumbled through Brazil's head, and he envisioned dress uniforms and badges striped with black tape.

'You ain't listening to me,' Weed insisted.

Brazil came to, shaken and unnerved. The cemetery began closing in, suffocating him with its pungent smells and restless sounds. The radio reminded him that he should call again for a 10-25, but he wasn't going to do it. Brazil was not going to let the entire police department, including West, know he was lost inside Hollywood Cemetery with a fourteen-year-old graffiti artist.

They headed out again on New Avenue. It eventually curved around the western edge of the cemetery and turned into Midvale, where in the distance they could see what appeared to be a long black hearse traveling toward them at a high rate of speed.

Cemetery monuments and markers and holly trees streamed past Governor Feuer's tinted windows as he ended another phone call, having by now lost all patience and willingness to give second chances.

Jed was driving too fast. It was taking longer to find Jefferson Davis's statue than it had probably taken to paint it. The unmarked Caprices and their EPU drivers were nowhere to be seen.

'Jed.' This time Governor Feuer hummed down the glass partition first. 'What happened to our backups?'

'They went on, sir.'

'Went on where?'

'Back to the mansion, I believe, sir. I'm not sure, but I think Mrs. Feuer needed to run an errand or something.'

'Mrs. Feuer is on her way to the Homestead.'

'I hear that's quite a resort, up there in the mountains

with spas, unbelievable food and skiing and everything. I'm glad she's going to relax a little,' Jed prattled on nervously.

'Where the hell are we, Jed?' Governor Feuer restrained himself from raising his voice.

'There's a lot of detours, sir,' Jed replied. 'From funerals, I guess.'

'I don't see any funerals or any sign of them.'

'Not on this street, no sir.'

'In fact, I haven't seen another car,' the governor said testily.

'This is for through traffic, sir.'

'*Through* traffic? *Through* to where? There is no *through.* There's only one way in and out of the cemetery. If you went *through,* you'd end up in the James River.'

'What I meant, sir, was that this isn't a funeral route,' Jed explained, slowing down a bit.

'For God's sake, Jed.' The governor lost his cool. 'There's no such thing as a funeral route in a cemetery. The cars go where the person's being buried. You don't bury people along routes. We're lost.'

'Not at all, sir.'

'Turn around. Let's go back,' Governor Feuer said as a cop and a little kid suddenly flowed past his right window.

Governor Feuer turned around in his seat, staring out the back window at a uniformed officer and a boy dressed like the Bulls. They were walking slowly and unsteadily, as if their legs would go out from under them any minute.

'Stop the car!' Governor Feuer ordered.

Jed slammed on the brakes, sending newspapers sliding across the carpeted floor.

The scene behind Kmart was slowing down and thinning out. The medical examiner's van was en route to the morgue where Ruby Sink would be autopsied later this day, and uniformed officers had begun to scatter, returning to the streets.

Detectives sought out witnesses and Miss Sink's next of kin while the media tried to get there first. The fire department was long gone, leaving West and two crime-scene technicians to finish up.

So far, dozens of latent prints in addition to the three nine-millimeter cartridge cases had been recovered from inside the car, which soon would be carried off in a flatbed truck for further processing by forensic scientists in the shelter of a bay. Eventually, firing pin impressions would be scanned into ATF's computer system to determine if they matched those recovered from other crimes.

Prints would be run through the Automated Fingerprint Identification System known as AFIS. Hairs, blood and fibers would go to DNA and the trace evidence labs.

'We need to get this out of the sun, or the blood and any other biological evidence are going to start decomposing really fast,' West said to crime-scene technician Alice Bates, who was taking photographs of the inside of the Chevy Celebrity.

'We've got it covered,' Bates said.

A second technician named Bonita Wills was focusing on the scattered contents of the victim's pocketbook that were strewn on the floor of the passenger's side. West leaned inside the open driver's door to look, her suit jacket brushing against the frame.

'Oh great,' she muttered as she tried to brush black fingerprint powder off her jacket.

West studied blood spatter on the rearview mirror, on the roof near it, the drips on the steering wheel and the pool of coagulating blood on the passenger's seat. When she had first arrived at the scene, Miss Sink had been slumped over on her right side, her head on the passenger's seat. There were blood spatters on her forearms and elbows and the roof above the driver's seat, and all this gave West a depressing picture.

It appeared that Ruby Sink had been sitting behind the wheel, elbows raised, hands under something, perhaps her face, when she had been shot execution style. Then the killer had climbed out of the car, and Miss Sink's body had slumped over on the passenger's seat where she had bled very briefly before dying.

'The bastard,' West said. 'Doing that in front of a baby. For two hundred fucking bucks. Goddamn son of a bitch.'

'Don't touch anything,' Wills warned her, as if West had sat behind a desk all her life.

West checked her temper. She was tired of being treated like an interloper, like an idiot, when it hadn't been so long ago that she was regarded with respect and even friendliness by a department a lot bigger and better than this one.

She stepped back from the car, looking around, hot and impatient in her smudged suit. The perimeter behind Kmart was secured by yellow crime-scene tape and West had no intention of letting anyone in anytime soon, and this included drivers making deliveries to the department store.

'Where's the truck?' West was all business. 'I don't like this. Everybody's flown the coop and other than the body, the car is the most important piece of evidence.'

'I wouldn't sweat it too much,' Wills said. 'This thing's a pigpen of prints. They could be anybody's, depending on how many people have been inside it, outside it, whatever. Most will probably be hers.'

'Some will be his,' West said. 'This guy doesn't wear gloves. He doesn't care if he leaves spit, hairs, blood, seminal fluid because he's probably some fucking piece of shit who's just got out of some juvenile training school and all his records have been destroyed to protect his precious confidentiality.'

'Hey, Bates,' Wills called to her partner, 'make sure you get the trunk good around the lock. In case he went in there.'

'I'm way ahead of ya.'

West got on her radio and requested an officer to guard the crime scene. She got back in her car and drove around to the front of Kmart. The parking lot was full of shoppers looking for a deal. A few of them were standing in front of the store, staring at First Union Bank and speculating in hushed, excited voices. Most were inside, probably pushing carts up and down aisles, oblivious.

West pulled up to the bank and was surprised to see that Hammer was still talking to Bubba, both of them standing in the bright sun. West got out and walked toward them. She slowed her pace when the stench reached her. She stared at Bubba's camouflage.

'Certainly I think it's a good idea for citizens to get involved,' Hammer was saying to Bubba. 'But within limits. I don't want our volunteer police carrying guns, Mr. Fluck.'

'Then a lot of us won't do it,' he let her know.

'There are other ways to help.'

'What about pepper spray or tactical batons? Could they carry those?'

'No,' Hammer replied.

West knew exactly what her boss was doing. Chief Hammer was an expert at playing people, dribbling the conversation in many directions, faking and passing until she saw an opening to score. West went along with it.

'Well, Chesterfield's auxiliary police carry guns,' Bubba pointed out, swatting at flies. 'I know a bunch of the guys. They work hard and really like it.'

Hammer noticed West's suit. She stared at the black fingerprint powder on the jacket.

'How'd you get smudge on . . .' Hammer said without finishing, laying the trap.

'I didn't,' Bubba replied. 'Actually he's been trying to get me on, but I'd have to move to Chesterfield.'

Hammer gave him a feigned puzzled look. 'Excuse me?'

'My buddy Smudge.' Then Bubba looked puzzled, too.

'How'd you know about him?'

'Sorry for your inconvenience, Mr. Fluck,' Hammer said. 'Why don't you go on home and freshen up. Deputy Chief West? A word with you.'

The two women walked away from Bubba.

'That was pretty clever,' West marveled. 'I guess you were referring to my jacket but made it sound like you knew about Smudge.'

'I was lucky,' Hammer said as a car pulled into the parking lot and sped toward them. 'And I want him under surveillance. *Now.*'

Roop jumped out in such a hurry he didn't bother turning off the engine or shutting the door.

'Chief Hammer!' he said excitedly. 'I got another phone call. Same guy.'

'You sure?' Hammer asked.

'Yes!' Roop exclaimed. 'The Pikes are claiming responsibility for the ATM homicide!'

chapter thirty-one

Brazil had never met Governor Feuer and it did not register that this indeed was the man walking briskly toward him and Weed on Midvale Avenue.

The man was tall and distinguished in a dark pinstripe suit. He was in a hurry and seemed very anxious about something. Brazil wiped sweat out of his eyes, his mouth so parched he could barely speak.

'Is everything all right?' Brazil asked.

'I was about to ask you that, son,' the man said.

Brazil paused as he processed the familiar voice and fit it with the face.

'Oh,' was all Brazil said.

'I seen your picture all over the place!' exclaimed Weed.

'Looks like you two have been through it,' the governor said. 'What did you do to your chin?' he asked Weed.

'Cut myself shaving.'

The governor seemed to accept this.

'How on earth did you end up out here? Are you hurt? No backup? Doesn't your radio work?' Governor Feuer asked Brazil.

'It works, sir.'

Brazil's words were sticky, as if he had communion wafers in his mouth. His tongue got caught on every syllable. He sounded a little drunk and wondered if he was delirious. Maybe none of this was happening.

'Let's get both of you some water and out of the sun,' the governor was saying.

Brazil was too exhausted and dehydrated to have much of an emotional reaction.

'You should know I've got a prisoner,' Brazil mumbled to the governor.

'I'm not worried unless you are,' Governor Feuer said. 'My driver's state police.'

Jed smiled as he stood attentively by the limousine. He opened a back door and the governor got in. Jed nodded at Brazil and Weed to do the same.

'Jed, you've got water, don't you?' Governor Feuer said.

'Oh yes sir. Chilled or unchilled?'

'Doesn't matter,' Brazil said.

'Chilled would be good,' Weed answered.

Brazil was overwhelmed by air conditioning and an expanse of clean, soft gray leather. He sat on the carpeted floor and nodded for Weed to do the same. The governor gave them an odd look.

'What are you doing?' he asked Brazil.

'We're pretty sweaty,' Brazil apologized. 'Wouldn't want to mess up your upholstery.'

'Nonsense. Have a seat.'

Air conditioning blasted their drenched clothes. Jed slid open the glass partition and handed back a six-pack of chilled Evian. Brazil drained two bottles, barely breathing between swallows. A stabbing sensation ran up his sinuses to the top of his head. He bent over in agony and rubbed his forehead.

'What is it?' the governor asked, alarmed.

'Ice cream headache. I'll be fine.'

'Those are miserable. Nothing worse.'

'Uhhh.'

'I get 'em when I drink Pepsi too fast,' Weed commiserated.

Jed's voice came over the intercom. 'Where to, sir?'

'Where can we take you?' the governor asked Brazil. 'Home? Back to headquarters? The jail?'

Brazil rubbed his forehead. He poured water on a napkin and gently cleaned Weed's cut and wiped dried blood off his neck.

'What will it be?' the governor asked.

'Honestly, Governor, you don't have to do that. I can't let you go to the trouble,' Brazil said.

Governor Feuer smiled. 'What's your name, son?'

'Andy Brazil.'

'As in the NIJ fellow who wrote the op-ed on juvenile crime?'

'Yes, that's me.'

The governor was favorably impressed.

'And you?' he asked Weed.

'Weed.'

'That's your real name, son?'

'How come everybody always asks me that?' Weed was tired of it.

'I guess headquarters would be good, sir,' Brazil said.

'Swing by headquarters,' the governor told Jed. 'I guess you'd better call my scheduler and tell him I won't make it to whatever.'

Time had stopped for Patty Passman as she sat in the urine-sticky dark on the cold metal floor of the wagon, arms wrenched behind her, ankles immobilized. Her hands and feet were numb. She was chilled to the core. She envisioned gangrene and amputations and lawsuits.

The scales of her unfortunate chemistry were back in balance. Although weak and somewhat banged up, she was thinking with clarity and premeditation. She knew exactly what Rhoad was doing. The wagon could not carry her to lockup for processing until he filled out at least one arrest sheet. The son of a bitch was trumping up every charge imaginable, filling out the paperwork on every single one because the longer he took, the longer she sat, trussed up like a turkey inside an icebox.

Passman wriggled backward across unforgiving metal, finally finding a side of the van to lean against. She shifted positions every few seconds to relieve the bite of the handcuffs and the ache in her shoulders.

'Oh please hurry,' she begged in the dark as the tears came. 'I'm so cold. Oh God, I hurt! Please! You're so mean to me!' She burst into sobs that no one heard or would have been moved by were she standing in the middle of a packed coliseum.

No one cared. No one ever had.

Patty Passman's first mistake in life was being born a

girl to parents who already had six girls and were devastated when they had yet one more on their last try. Passman spent her childhood trying to make it up to them.

She pounded on her sisters and told them they were ugly, stupid and flat-chested. She broke toys, dismembered dolls, drew obscene pictures, passed gas, belched, spat, didn't flush the toilet, was insensitive, hoarded candy, kept quarters meant for the Sunday school offering, lost her temper, teased the dog, played Army, played doctor with other girls in the neighborhood and refused to play the piano. She did all she could to act like a boy.

She toned it down as years passed, only to find she had been gender contraire for so long she had fallen too far behind in the female race to ever catch up or even come in last. She was disqualified and defaulted by all except Moses Pharaoh, who nominated her for the wrestling homecoming court because, he told her as he escorted her across the spotlit basketball court that illustrious night, he was turned on by fat women with small teeth.

Afterward the two of them ate lasagne, garlic bread, salad and cheesecake at Joe's Inn. On the way home in his '69 high-performance Chevelle, with its 425 horsepower and 475 pounds of torque, Moses drove her up to the observation point at the end of East Grace Street.

What Passman knew about kissing she had learned from movies. She was not prepared for the huge garlic-tasting thick tongue thrust down her throat. She was shocked when Moses shoved his hands down her chiffon neckline, groping for the Promised Land. He parted her, crossed her, broke all ten commandments, or seemed to, on that awful night when her long pink satin dress was pushed up and crushed, all because she had not been born a boy.

She was shivering and feeling crazed again when the wagon rumbled awake. It pulled ahead. With each turn it took she rolled on her side like a log in the tide. Minutes seemed forever. The van finally halted.

'Sally Port One, put the gate up,' a male voice announced.

Passman heard what sounded like a grate lurch and begin slowly rolling up. The van drove ahead and stopped again. The grate screeched back down. The van's tailgate swung open, a cop standing there, chewing gum.

He was disheveled, his waist drooping over his duty belt like excess pizza dough hanging off the pan. One eye was hazel, the other brown, his graying hair slicked back, ears and nostrils bristly like stiff paintbrushes. Wagon drivers were the flatworms of law enforcement, a throwback to a spineless, lazy, lower order of life Passman had grown to despise.

'O-kie do-kie,' he said to her. 'Let's head 'em up and move 'em out.'

Passman squinted at him from her supine position on the floor.

'I can't,' she said.

He clicked her a *giddy-up* out of the side of his mouth.

'I'm not going anywhere until you at least undo my ankles.' She meant it.

Her dress was pushed up to her padded hips and she could do nothing about it. He was staring. She knew if she lost her temper again, it would only ensure further bondage.

'Please undo my ankles so I can get out,' she said again. 'Pretty please with sugar on top?'

She thought she recognized his voice, then was certain. 'You're unit 452,' she said.

'Guess I'm famous. Now I'm gonna cut off these flex cuffs, but you so much as twitch and I'm gonna keep you busy.'

She did not know his name, but one thing Passman did know was voices. She had total recall when it came to words uttered on the air by hundreds of units she never saw. Unit 452 cut off the flex cuffs with a pocketknife and the feeling rushed back to her feet in swarms of tiny pins. She worked her way to the open rear of the van, her skirt hiking higher, far above the brown tops of her panty hose, up to the waistband. He stared, chomping gum. She inchwormed her way to the ground.

Unit 452 pushed a button on the wall to open the door to lockup, and on his way in used a key from his snap holder to secure his pistol inside the gun safe. He got out another key, this one tiny, and unlocked her handcuffs.

'Unit 452,' Passman mimicked him. *'Go ahead, 452. I'm 10-7 2600 block of Park. Ten-4, 452. That'd be the Robin Inn, for a meal. Uh, 10-4 . . .'*

'You!' Unit 452 was shocked and deeply offended. 'You're the one! That bitch in the radio room!'

'You're that dumb shit who's always hiding out at Engine Company Number Nine playing your fucking nutless puzzle games. Tetris Plus, Q*Bert, Pac Man, Boggle!' Passman accused.

'What, what?' Unit 452 stammered.

Passman had him.

'Everyone knows,' she went on as Deputy Sheriff Reflogle took the arrest sheets from unit 452 and began to search Passman.

'Looks like you're getting the book thrown at you, girl,' Reflogle said. 'Must've been a bad time at home to act out like this.'

Passman wasn't listening.

'You're a joke in the radio room!' she railed on to Unit 452. '*B* is *boy,* not *bravo,* and *H* is *Henry,* not *hotel,* you shit dick! What do you think you are, an airplane pilot?'

'Now you quiet down,' Deputy Reflogle said to her as he fished eight quarters out of her skirt pockets.

He rolled Passman's fingers on an ink pad and transferred her loops and whirls to a ten-print card. He took mug shots. He asked her about aliases. He asked about a.k.a's in case she didn't know what aliases were. He locked her inside a holding cell. It was not much bigger than a locker, a hard bench to sit on, a small square screen to see through. She ate cherry Jell-O, cottage cheese and fish sticks for lunch.

The magistrate's office for the city of Richmond was on the first floor of the police department, past the information desk and in close proximity to lockup and Sally Port 1.

It was not quite four o'clock in the afternoon. Vince Tittle wasn't feeling good about his job or life. It wasn't hard to look back and see where he had cracked the glass, chipped the china, scorched the sweet milk in the pot. He had succumbed to a favor. He had sold his soul for an office that looked very much like a tollbooth.

Tittle had not always thought the worst about himself. Until four years ago he had enjoyed a fulfilling career as a photographer at the morgue. He had been proud of taking pictures perfectly to scale. He had been a magician with lighting and shutter speeds. His art went to court. It was viewed by prosecutors, defense attorneys, judges and juries.

The chief medical examiner adored him. Her deputy chiefs and the forensic scientists did, too. Defendants hated him. Tittle's lust for justice was what got him into trouble. His road to hell began when Tittle joined the Gentleman's Bartering Club, which included hundreds of people with training, skills and talents that Tittle couldn't always afford. He took family portraits, and photos for Christmas cards, calendars, graduations and debutante balls, swapping his skills for virtual cash minus a ten percent commission that went to the club.

Tittle rarely shopped in reality after that. He could take wedding pictures, for example, and earn a thousand virtual dollars, which in turn he might virtually spend on roof repair. Tittle was addicted to his camera. Soon he became virtually wealthy, which is how he met Circuit

Court Judge Nicholas Endo, who was at war with his wife and losing.

Judge Endo believed Mrs. Endo was having an affair with her dentist, Bull Ehrhart, and wanted to catch her in the act. Tittle would never forget what Judge Endo said to him one night when they were drinking bourbon in the clubhouse.

'Vince, you've got virtually everything a man could want,' said the judge as he paid five virtual dollars for a drink that was real. 'But there's got to be one thing in this club you can't buy, and I bet I damn well know what it is.'

'What?' Tittle said.

'You love court. You love the law,' said the judge. 'Taking photographs of stiffs is getting boring. Has to be. Should always have been, Vince.'

Tittle slowly swirled ice in his Maker's Mark. The truth pained him deeply.

'Come on. Come on.' The judge leaned across the table and said in the tone that reminded Tittle of *come here, kitty, kitty, kitty*, 'I mean, Vince, how goddamn challenging can it be to shoot a liver on a scale, a brain on a cutting board, stomach contents, little cups of urine and bile, bite marks, axes in the back of people's heads?'

'You're right,' Tittle muttered, motioning for Seunghoon the cocktail waitress. 'This round's on me.'

'What will it be, sugar?' Seunghoon asked.

'Another round. You got Booker's?'

'Shoot. I don't think so, cutie. But you know what? I believe Mr. Mack carries it in his restaurant. He has quite a bar.'

'We ought to get that in.' Judge Endo rendered his verdict. 'Best damn bourbon known to man. Hundred twenty proof, knock you back to China. Maybe next time a movie comes to town, Vince, you could take a couple shots of Mack with a celebrity or two? He can hang them in his restaurant. Charge him two hundred virtual dollars, turn around and buy the Booker's with it.'

'Okay,' Tittle agreed.

Their conversation went on for quite a while before the judge got into the substance of his case.

'I think you'd make a damn good magistrate, Vince,' he said, puffing on an illegal Cuban cigar. 'I've always thought so.' He blew a smoke ring.

'It would be an honor,' Tittle said. 'I would like a chance to punish bad people. I've always wanted that.'

'How 'bout we make a trade?'

'I'm always doing it,' Tittle said.

Judge Endo went on to say that he wanted explicit photographs of Mrs. Endo's adultery. He didn't care if they were doctored. He didn't care how Tittle did it. Judge Endo just wanted to keep his house, his car and his dog, and have his grown children take his side.

'It won't be easy,' the judge said, jaw muscles clenching. 'I know, I've tried everything I can think of. But you pull it off, I'll take care of you.'

The next day, Tittle went to work. He discovered soon enough that Mrs. Endo's MO was so simple it was complicated. Bull Ehrhart had forty-three strip mall offices throughout the greater Richmond area, and twenty-two additional ones as far away as Norfolk, Petersburg,

Charlottesville, Fredericksburg and Bristol, Tennessee.

Twice a week, Mrs. Endo used a different alias to make a late-day appointment at a different office. When she'd done the circuit, she'd start again. She'd change her accent, hair color and style, experimenting with makeup, glasses and designer clothes.

For weeks, Tittle failed. The adulterous couple was too careful and clever. Just when Tittle was about to give up, he found a crow that had flown into his kitchen window because it didn't see the glass and died of a head injury, Tittle could only suppose. Tittle got an idea. He put the dead crow in the freezer. He painted a camera and tripod yellow.

Late that afternoon he followed Mrs. Endo to dental office number 17 on Staples Mill Road, near Ukrops, and set up his faux surveyor's equipment in the parking lot. It was five-thirty P.M. The only office lit up was a corner one, the windows covered by shut Venetian blinds. Tittle gave Mrs. Endo and Dr. Ehrhart fifteen minutes to get into it as Tittle pointed the twelve-hundred-millimeter telephoto lens and attached the cable release.

He pulled the frozen crow out of a pocket of his coat and hurled it at the window, where it hit with a sickening thud, shaking the glass. The blinds suddenly flashed open. The naked dentist looked out and around and down at the ground, discovering the poor bird that had flown into the glass. The naked Mrs. Endo put a hand over her mouth, shaking her head in pity.

They paid no attention to the surveyor walking off the job with his bright yellow equipment. The divorce turned out favorably for Judge Endo. In return, he gave Tittle the appointment, as promised in their bartering agreement.

Magistrate Tittle's guilt grew with the years. He became increasingly depressed and intimidated when Judge Endo called from time to time to remind him of the favor and the necessity of going to the grave, in this case Hollywood Cemetery, with the secret swap that had brought about Tittle's dream-come-true. Magistrate Tittle never told a soul.

He confessed his sin to God and swore to make restitution. Tittle took photographs no more. He resigned from the barter club. He reported its members to the IRS. He turned in the neighbor who illegally hooked up cable. Tittle exposed the lady in the grocery store who was trying to pass expired manufacturers' coupons. He admitted when something was his fault. He was humble and hard-working.

Magistrate Tittle became known for his zero tolerance of felons, fools, rotten kids and stupid cops. He was admired for his fairness and truth if one was unjustly accused. This was both good and bad for Officer Rhoad, who had not made an arrest in over twenty years. When Rhoad had flipped through the Virginia code, looking for charges to bring against Patty Passman, he had been certain Magistrate Tittle would empathize and go with life imprisonment with no TV or chances for appeals and lawsuits.

Tittle was reaching back to the coffeemaker to pour another cup, his grim gray suit jacket draped over a chair, when Officer Rhoad appeared at his window.

'I need to get some warrants,' Rhoad said.

'What makes you think I can see you right this minute?' said Tittle.

'Because you don't look busy, I guess.'

'Well, I am,' he said through the small opening in the bulletproof glass. 'I should make you sit over there for an hour or two, but I'm about to go home. So let's get this over with.'

Tittle shoved out a metal drawer. Rhoad placed his thick stack of arrest sheets in it. Tittle pulled them in and started looking through them. Tittle was silent for a long time while Rhoad watched through the glass.

'Officer?' Tittle finally spoke. 'You ever heard of piling on charges?'

'Certainly,' said Rhoad, who was used to quotas and assumed the magistrate was paying him a compliment.

'Use of police radio during commission of a crime,' Tittle started going through the charges.

'Obstructing justice. Subject did knowingly attempt to impede this officer from engaging in his duties.'

Tittle went to the next one. 'Using abusive language.'

'You should have heard her,' Rhoad said indignantly.

'Disorderly conduct in public places. Resisting or obstructing execution of legal process.' Tittle peered up over his reading glasses. 'Crimes against nature?'

'She grabbed me.' Rhoad's face got hot.

'She carnally knew you by anus?'

'No, sir.'

'What about by mouth?'

'Just the things she said.'

'This isn't about *things said,* officer. What about bestiality?'

'Yes! She was a beast! She was awful!'

'Officer Rhoad,' Tittle said in a hard tone. 'Bestiality means screwing animals. No probable cause.' He tossed the arrest sheet in a to-be-shredded basket. 'Let's see.' He continued. 'Keeping, residing in or frequenting a *body* place.'

'She wouldn't let go,' Rhoad said, the memory clearly smarting.

'B-A-W-D-Y, not B-O-D-Y,' Tittle said slowly and deliberately as he tossed the report in the basket. 'Entering property of another for purpose of damaging it.'

'Same thing. She touched my property, sir.'

'What property, Officer Rhoad?'

'Well, my privates. She tried to damage my privates.'

That report went into the basket with the others.

'Trespass after having been forbidden to do so,' Tittle read.

'I told her to stop.'

'Aggravated sexual assault. How did you arrive upon that one?'

'Because it was my privates she went after,' Rhoad reminded him.

'I suppose *attempted rape* is for the same reason.'

'What if it were you?'

'Sexual battery, rape. No probable cause,' Tittle said, strained. 'And oh. Here we have *threatening the governor or his immediate family?'*

'She said, "I'm going to find the governor or his wife or

children or relatives. And then you'll be sorry!"'

Rhoad averted his eyes. He wasn't really sure of this one. So much was a blur now. Tittle balled up the arrest sheet and tossed it on the floor.

'Oral threats. Bodily injuries caused by prisoners. Assault and battery. Malicious bodily injury. Aggravated malicious wounding.'

Tittle balled up each sheet, pummeling them at the trash basket.

'Shooting, stabbing with intent to maim, kill. Failure to obey order of conservator of the peace. Treason. *Treason?*'

'Subject did resist the execution of the laws under color of its authority,' Rhoad cited. 'She levied war against the Commonwealth when she attacked me.'

'You need a therapist.'

'I'm a citizen of the Commonwealth, aren't I?' Rhoad argued.

'Why did this woman grab your genitals, Officer Rhoad?' Tittle had never met such an idiot in his life. 'Did she swoop in out of nowhere? Was she provoked? A spurned lover?'

'She tried to stop me from putting a parking ticket on her car,' Rhoad explained.

'I don't buy it.'

'Well,' Rhoad said, 'I'd done it a few times before.'

Brazil was wise enough to ask Governor Feuer to drop off his guest passengers a block from the police department, thus avoiding a scene that would be difficult, if not impossible, to explain.

'I'm going to take you to MCV,' Brazil said to Weed as they walked along the sidewalk. 'Then let's get your mother to come for you. You don't want to be locked up all night.'

'Yes I do,' Weed told him.

Brazil noticed Weed was very agitated, looking all around as if afraid someone was following them.

'You're not making any sense to me,' Brazil went on. 'And you know why?' He opened double glass doors on the lower lot of headquarters. 'Because you're not telling me everything, Weed. You're holding back.'

Weed had nothing to say. Brazil checked out a car and let the radio room know where he was going. He and Weed sat in MCV's emergency room, where Weed could not be treated without one of his parents being present. Weed's mother didn't answer the phone and she wasn't at work. Weed's father was out cutting grass somewhere and didn't return Brazil's call. Brazil's radio would not transmit from inside the hospital. He felt cut off from the world, angry, helpless and miserable.

Brazil finally had to get a judge to grant permission for treatment, which would have resolved the matter had there not been a school-bus accident midafternoon. The E.R. could not get to Weed until almost eleven P.M., when a nurse cleaned Weed's cut and put a butterfly bandage over it.

'I don't get it,' Brazil was saying to Weed as they drove back to headquarters. 'Are you sure you have a mother?'

The remark hurt Weed. Brazil could tell.

'She don't answer the phone very much, especially when she's sleeping, and she sleeps a lot in the day.'

'Why wouldn't she answer the phone otherwise?'

''Cause Daddy's always calling. He says real mean things to her. I don't know why, and he has to have the number 'cause I stay with him sometimes.'

They parked in the back lot and Brazil escorted Weed inside the police department. They walked past the information desk and Weed didn't seem to care where he was being taken. His mood continued to sink.

'You know something,' Brazil told him. 'You know something big. Something so big you're scared, real scared.'

'I ain't scared of nothing,' Weed told him.

'We're all scared of something,' Brazil replied.

Handcuffed prisoners drifted in and out, heading to lockup, muttering, staggering and swaggering, some wearing sunglasses and cool clothes, many of them high or drunk. The air smelled of body odor, alcohol and marijuana. Brazil turned right, passing through another set of double doors. He opened one leading into a small drab room with desks built into the walls, and plastic chairs, and ugly green upholstered benches stained with unpleasant, recalcitrant life.

Brazil went to a phone and dialed the pager number of the intake officer on call. There was an old radio on a table and Brazil tuned it in to 98.1. He sat on top of a desk and looked at Weed.

'Talk to me,' Brazil said.

'Got nothing to say.' Weed sat on a bench.

'Why did you decide to paint the statue?'

'Felt like it.'

'Did someone tell you to do it? One of the Pikes?'

'I don't know nothing about Pikes.'

'Bullshit,' Brazil said. 'Where'd you get that number tattooed on your finger?'

A radio announcer was going on and on about the ATM homicide, and at first the news and the name of the victim did not penetrate Brazil's fatigue and frustration. Then he caught it.

'. . . confirmed her identity as a seventy-one-year-old Church Hill woman named Ruby Sink . . .'

'Wait a minute!' Brazil turned up the volume.

'. . . made a withdrawal at the ATM, was abducted and shot to death in her own car. A gang known as the Pikes has claimed responsibility. This is the same gang that claimed responsibility for the vandalism of Jefferson Davis's statue in Hollywood Cemetery . . .'

Brazil was beside himself. He paced furiously, his fists clenched. He was confused and disbelieving as he envisioned Ruby Sink and remembered when she had called him last.

'No!' he exclaimed. *'No!'*

Brazil pounded the wall and kicked the trash can. It clanged across the floor, paper, fried chicken boxes and fast food wrappers spilling.

'How could someone do that to a helpless old woman!'

His last conversation with her sounded in his mind. He could hear her voice. He had used her to make West jealous. Brazil clenched his fists so hard his nails dug into his palms. He grabbed Weed by the shoulders.

'*You know them, I know you do!*' he said in fury. '*They just murdered someone, Weed!* Someone I knew! Someone who never did anything to anybody! A human being with a name and a family and now people who loved her have to deal with what happened just like you do with Twister!'

Weed stared at him in shock.

'You're going to protect monsters like that?'

Brazil let go of Weed and walked across the room. Brazil tried to control himself. He was trembling, his heart pounding so hard he could feel it in his neck.

'I tried to tell you on the computer,' Weed said sadly.

'Tell me? Tell me what?'

'The fish map.'

Brazil's mind had an electrical outage.

'On AOL. A map with pikes on it,' Weed explained.

'Pikes as in fish?' Brazil came back.

'Uh huh. I did a papier-mâché pike in Mrs. Grannis's class. Trying to tell somebody where they are.'

'Wait a minute.' Brazil pulled up a chair and sat down. 'The fish on the map. That's where the Pikes have their clubhouse?'

Weed nodded. 'In the back of Southside Motel. Behind a big piece of wood.'

'You've been there?'

'I didn't wanna be. I swear. But Smoke made me go and he hit me, too.' Weed wouldn't look up.

'Who is Smoke?' Brazil said.

'He broke in the garage and took all them guns. He made me go along and I held pillowcases for him. So I guess I get locked up for that and everything and I don't care 'cause if I go out, Officer Brazil, Smoke gonna kill me. I know it. He's looking for me now. That's why I told you to lock me up.'

'Do you know Smoke's real name?'

'He's just Smoke. Never heard no other name.'

'He go to school with you?'

'Uh huh.'

'And you don't know his real name?'

'He's a senior and I don't know no seniors except the ones in art class, and Smoke never been in one of my art classes. Not the band, either.'

'He get in a lot of trouble in school?' Brazil asked.

'I never even noticed him until he come looking for me and found me after school in the band room. He asked if I wanted a ride to school in the morning and something told me not to tell him no. And next thing he's talking about guns and the Pikes and how nobody in the school deserved to be a Pike except the ones he picked. He said he had special things to do.'

'Did he tell you what these special things were?'

'All he kept saying was everybody was going to know him. He'd be more famous than Twister ever was, 'cause there's still pictures of Twister and trophies in the glass cases so I guess that's how Smoke heard about him.'

'Think hard, Weed.' Brazil put his hands on Weed's shoulders. 'Was Smoke planning something that might make him famous? Maybe something bad?'

'I think he wants to shoot people,' Weed said.

chapter thirty-two

Brazil tried to figure out what to do. If Smoke was planning to show up at school with semiautomatics and take out as many people as he could, Brazil had to do something fast. He grabbed the phone and called West, waking her up.

'Get down here right away,' Brazil said. 'Don't ask why, just come.'

'Where's *here?*' she asked groggily.

'HQ. We need to get as many cops as we can at Godwin tomorrow to make sure Smoke doesn't show up, and we need to get that going now.'

West tried to wake up. Brazil could hear her moving around.

'I'll meet you in the detective division in maybe two hours,' Brazil said.

'Yeah,' she said.

Weed was getting increasingly frightened. He picked at his jersey and kept sighing as if he was having a hard time breathing.

'He made me do things. He put a gun to my head and said he'd shoot me if I didn't. Then a couple weeks ago he stopped showing up at school.'

'So he didn't give you rides anymore.' Brazil was taking copious notes.

'He'd drop me off and leave. Then he started making me late, started dragging me around, making me miss band practice. And I was supposed to play in the Azalea Parade on Saturday.' The light went out of his eyes. 'I been practicing all year. And now I guess I can't.'

The phone rang, startling both of them. Brazil answered it. He was wired and somewhat impatient as he explained Weed's transgressions to Intake Officer Charlie Yates.

Brazil charged Weed with violating Code 18.2-125, *Trespass at night upon any cemetery,* a class 4 misdemeanor, and 18.2-127, *Injuries to churches, church property, cemeteries, burial grounds, etc.,* class 1 misdemeanor, and 182.2-138.1, *Willful and malicious damage to or defacement of public or private facilities,* a class 1 misdemeanor or a felony, depending on how much damage was done.

'So which is it?' Yates wanted to know.

'Misdemeanor, class one,' Brazil said. 'We don't know how much cleaning up the statue's going to cost. If it's more than a thousand dollars, we'll deal with it at the trial.'

Weed was staring wide-eyed at Brazil. It was obvious Weed did not understand. He was terrified.

'Hearing's set for Friday,' Yates went on. 'He got someone . . . ?'

'I want the hearing in the morning,' Brazil interrupted. 'It's really important, Charlie.'

'Hey, no big deal.' It made no difference to Yates.

It did to Brazil. He knew from this month's court calendar that Judge Maggie Davis was on the bench. She had a policy that her courtroom was not open to the public unless the juvenile had committed a felony, and the last thing Brazil wanted was Weed's hearing open to the public. He didn't want some reporter making the rounds and walking in. He didn't want anyone except the attorneys and judge to hear what he and Weed might have to say.

'He got someone to pick him up tonight and take him home?' Yates was asking.

'We haven't been able to locate his mother.'

She was in the operating room and could not be disturbed, not that Brazil had tried very hard. Weed didn't want to go home and Brazil didn't want him to, either.

'There's no beds in detention. I just checked,' Yates said.

'Never are,' Brazil replied.

'So if he can't go home, he's going to end up in a holding cell until the morning.'

'That's fine,' Brazil said, not taking his eyes off Weed. 'As soon as you can get here, I'll sign the petition and take him on over. And try to make it fast, Charlie. There's a lot going on.'

Weed had an intake room without much of a view, a cell no bigger than a closet, everything stainless steel, including the bed. He could not sleep. He stared out a small grate and watched other kids brought in who reminded him of Sick, Beeper, Divinity and Dog. No one reminded him of Smoke. Smoke didn't look like what he was.

It was dark when Officer Brazil had transported Weed to this place. They called it the Juvenile Detention Home, but it wasn't like any home Weed had ever been in. He couldn't see what the outside of it was like but he knew it was in a bad part of town, because right before he'd gotten here they'd driven past the jail. It was all lit up, rolls of razor wire shining like knife blades waiting to cut someone. Weed's stomach got hollow and he had a cold feeling in his heart.

Weed was still mad they had made him take off all his clothes and go into the shower. When he came out they had a uniform for him to wear. It was nothing to make Weed proud. He was reminded of what his daddy wore cleaning out gutters and clipping hedges when he wasn't gambling away what he earned.

'Hey!' Weed banged on the door.

Someone was cussing and a deputy was telling a cocky badass boy everything he had done wrong and why he was going to pay for it.

'Hey!' Weed pounded the metal door with his fist, standing on his tiptoes to see through the grate.

Suddenly a deputy was in his face, nothing but a crisscross of metal between them. Weed could smell cigarettes and onions on his breath.

'You got a problem?' the deputy asked.

'I wanna see my police officer,' Weed told him.

'Yo!' the deputy called out. 'He wants to see *his po-lice officer!'*

Laughter and bad-mouthing followed.

'What, you got your own personal po-lice officer?' the deputy smarted off to Weed. 'Now ain't that something.'

'He's the one who brought me in,' Weed said. 'Tell him I got to talk to him.'

'You can tell him in court.'

'When's that?'

'Nine in the morning.'

'I need to find out if he called my mama!' Weed exclaimed.

'Maybe you should've thought about your mama before you broke the law,' the deputy said.

chapter thirty-three

At shortly after three A.M. a SWAT team raided the Pikes' clubhouse at the Southside Motel and found the room abandoned. Police recovered no guns or ammunition. They found nothing but liquor and trash and filthy mattresses.

Brazil was on one phone, West on another, each of them in a cubicle inside the detective division. Brazil had called Godwin's principal, Mrs. Lilly, at home, and when she realized what it was about, she met the registrar at the high school and they started going through records.

Eventually they figured out that Smoke's real name was Alex Bailey, but the address listed in his school records didn't exist, the phone number didn't work, and there was no photograph of him on file. Although the yearbook wasn't out yet, a check of those who had gotten their pictures taken for it did not include him. All anyone really knew was the classes he had been in and that last summer he had moved here from Durham, North Carolina, where the obscure private high school he supposedly had transferred from didn't exist.

Brazil called every Bailey in the city directory, waking

people up. No one seemed to have a family member named Alex who went to Godwin High School.

'How the hell did he get away with it?' Brazil said to West. 'He uses a bogus address, phone number, name of his former high school and who knows what else.'

West was smoking a Carlton. She'd sort of quit months ago, but at times like this she needed a friend.

'Who's going to check?' she said. 'You ever had your high school call you at home or come see you?'

'I don't remember.'

'Well, I sure as hell didn't. Most people don't unless they get in trouble. And it sounds like he was just your average kind of keep-to-yourself nobody until a couple weeks ago. Then he cuts classes or doesn't show up at all. Maybe the school starts calling. But guess what? By then it's too late.'

'I wonder what his parents know.' Brazil reached for his Styrofoam cup of what once was drinkable coffee.

'Denial. Maybe protecting him. Don't want to face it and never have. No question in my mind this kid's not new to the system. No pictures of him anywhere, including the yearbook, just like all these other little felons, so we don't know what they look like. I bet you anything he's got a record in North Carolina, probably transferred from *Dillon* High School.' She sarcastically referred to the juvenile training school in Butner, North Carolina. 'His fucking family probably moved him here when he turned sixteen and all his records were expunged. So the asshole gets to start all over again, clean as a Boy Scout.'

Brazil swirled the coffee in his cup. He took a deep

breath and let it out slowly.

'So. You going to bother going to bed tonight?' West said.

'There's no night left,' Brazil said.

'You want to come over, maybe scramble up a few eggs or something?'

Sadness walked through Brazil's eyes.

'As long as we stop at my house first,' he said. 'There's something I've got to get.'

The Azalea Motel on Northside's Chamberlayne Avenue was not where the police would have expected to find Smoke. He also liked the irony of the name, since the Azalea Parade was the day after tomorrow. Smoke had big plans.

He sat on his single bed in his single room and thought where he was staying wasn't much better than the clubhouse. The Azalea Motel was the sort of place where people did drugs and got murdered and nobody cared. Smoke got room 7 for twenty-eight dollars a night. He stared blankly at the TV and drank vodka from a plastic cup. Smoke had been monitoring the news. At five after six A.M., his phone rang.

'What,' he answered.

It was Divinity.

'Baby, they raided our place just like you said they would,' she told him in an excited voice.

Smoke smiled as he stared at the trash bags full of guns and ammunition in the corner.

'Sick and me parked the car at the dirty bookstore and we was in the woods watching, you know, baby. It was all we could do not to laugh. Them busting in there with all their stuff on and big guns and all. You sure was right about getting out when we did, sugar. But I wanna know when I'm gonna see you, huh?'

'Not now,' Smoke told her without much interest as he spun around the cylinder of a Colt .357.

'I sure could do with a little more *I miss you* enthusiasm.' Divinity's voice was hurt on the way to being mad.

Smoke wasn't listening. His mind wandered back to the old woman and her fear. Smoke had never scared anybody that much. He was awed by his power and as drunk from it as he was from vodka. He loved the way it felt to squeeze the trigger. He had been so high he barely heard the explosions when he blew apart her head. He threw back another swallow of vodka.

'What'cha gonna tell the others?' Divinity was asking.

Smoke came to.

'About what?' he said.

'You ain't even listening.' Her voice was getting sharp.

One thing Smoke avoided was fighting with Divinity. She could make a scene, and that was what he didn't need right now.

'I'm just so tired,' he said, sighing. 'And I miss you and it makes me crazy I can't see you until Saturday night. That's when we'll be free and clear.'

'How?'

'You'll see.'

'What about Dog and the rest of them?'

'I don't want them anywhere near me,' Smoke said. 'None of you come anywhere near the Azalea Parade.'

'I don't understand this big shit about some little parade named after a bush.' Divinity hadn't softened much.

'Baby, I'm gonna be the king of it,' Smoke said.

'What'cha gonna do, ride on a float?'

He couldn't stand it when she got sarcastic. He slammed down the vodka bottle and snapped the revolver's empty cylinder in place. He dry-fired at the TV.

'Shut up!' he said in his voice from hell, that tone he got when the change came over him. 'You just do what I say, bitch.'

'I always do.' Divinity backed down.

'Don't you call anymore. Don't you come around, and the others don't know where I am, right?'

'I ain't told 'em nothing. So you dumping me?'

'For two days.'

'Then we're good?'

'As good as it gets,' he said.

Brazil ran into his house for only a moment and when he returned to West's car, he was carrying a grocery bag with something in it. He had a strange look on his face.

'What's that?' West asked.

'You'll see,' he said. 'I don't want to talk about it right now.'

'You got a body part in there or something?'

'In a way,' Brazil said morbidly.

West knew about Ruby Sink. The word had traveled like electricity. Everyone in the police department found out Miss Sink was Brazil's landlady, and when West heard the truth, she felt sick with guilt. She felt stupid and ignorant. Brazil's so-called girlfriend had been a seventy-one-year-old woman who rented a row house to him. West felt absolutely terrible and for hours had been trying to think of what to say.

She drove through the Fan. Nothing was open, not even the Robin Inn. She parked in front of her town house and turned off the engine but didn't get out. She looked at Brazil in the dark. Her heart stirred as she stared at his face, sharply defined by shadows from the streetlight.

'I know,' she said.

He was quiet.

'I know about Ruby Sink. That she was your landlady. The landlady I heard you were seeing.'

Brazil turned to her, baffled.

'Seeing?' he said. 'Where the hell did you hear something like that?'

'The talk was all around the department from day one,' West replied. 'People told me you had a thing going with your landlady. Then I heard you on the phone with her and . . . well, it sounded like it was true, in a way.'

'Why? Because I was nice to her when she paged me?' Brazil said with emotion. 'Because she was lonely and always bringing me cookies, cakes and things?' His voice wavered. 'Leaving them on my doorstep because I was never fucking home and never gave her the fucking time of day!'

'I'm sorry, Andy,' West said gently.

'It's like my mother.' He dissolved. 'I don't call her. She's so fucking drunk all the time and I can't stand it and won't listen to the awful things she says. I don't know. I don't know.'

West moved over and put her arms around him. She held him close to calm him. Her blood got hot and her chemistry woke up.

'It's all right, Andy,' she said. 'It's going to be all right.'

She wanted to hold him forever, but suddenly the awkwardness of it overtook the magic. She thought of her age. She thought of his talent, of everything that made him so unusual and special. He was probably hugging her back because he was terribly upset, no other reason. His heart probably wasn't pounding like hers. He probably wasn't as aware of their bodies touching as she was. She abruptly pulled away.

'I guess we should go in,' she said.

Niles heard them long before they gave a thought to him. He was waiting by the front door when his owner and Piano Man walked in.

Piano Man took a moment to pet Niles, while Niles's owner couldn't be bothered. Niles stayed where he was, tail switching. He watched with crossed eyes and plotted as they went into the kitchen.

When they were out of view, Niles jumped up on the

table in the foyer. He hooked a claw into the florist's card. He jumped down, landing silently on three legs.

West did not think she could eat the sweet potato pie. She stared at the slice Brazil set before her. The idea that Ruby Sink had made it before her cold-blooded murder was too much for West to process.

'I can't throw it away.' Brazil sat across from West at the kitchen table. 'It would be heartless to throw it away. I just can't. You couldn't either, Virginia. She would want us to eat it.'

'This is kind of sick,' West said, blinking, focusing, looking at him. 'I don't think I can.'

Brazil picked up his fork. He flinched as he cut off the point of his slice. He raised it. He took a deep breath and put it in his mouth. West watched him chew once or twice and swallow. It surprised her that he looked enormously relieved. Tension left his face. His eyes brightened and got that fierce blue flame in them that she had learned to recognize and take very seriously.

'It's okay,' he told her in a strong voice. 'Trust me.' He nodded for her to eat.

West had never backed down from a challenge, especially in front of him. It was one of the hardest things she'd ever done when she took a bite of that pie. It surprised her that it didn't taste weird or dead or who knows what. She had no idea what she had expected.

'Brown sugar, coconut milk, cinnamon,' said Brazil,

who spent more time in the kitchen than West did.

He took another bite, this time without hesitation. West matched him.

'Raisins, vanilla extract.' Brazil concentrated on his tongue as if he were tasting fine wine. 'Ah. Ginger. A hint of it. And a breath of nutmeg.'

'*Breath* of nutmeg?' West said. 'Where the hell does that shit come from?'

Brazil took another bite. So did she. She might just eat another slice to spite him.

Neither of them heard Niles, not that they ever did. He walked in holding up a paw, a white square of paper caught on one of his claws.

'Baby?' West said in alarm, certain he was injured. 'Oh sweetie, what did you do to yourself?'

She didn't realize what was on his claw until Niles was in Brazil's lap and the florist's card from the hallway table was in plain view. Brazil got a confused expression on his face.

'Schwan's Flowers and Gifts? Charlotte?' he read aloud what was on the envelope as he pulled out the card. '"Thinking of you, Andy,"' his voice trailed off.

West tried to act nonchalant and failed. She hated Niles and would pay him back for this.

'How did this end up on your hallway table?' Brazil wanted to know.

'How do you know it was on the table?' she said coolly as she imagined leaving Niles out in a hailstorm.

'I saw it there when we were here working on the computer!'

'Why were you looking at anything on any table?' Old anger and hurt jumped off the shelf where she had been storing them for months.

'Because you put it there so I would see it,' he exclaimed.

'How arrogant of you!'

'Then why?' he said. 'And don't tell me Niles did it.'

West pushed away her plate and stared past him. She tried to think how to say it. Confessing feelings was as dangerous as counting money when you walked down a dark street in a bad part of town.

'Because you didn't care about me anymore.' She was out with it.

'That's because you didn't care about me first,' he argued.

'And that's because I thought you dumped me the minute we got to town and started seeing someone else without even having the courtesy to tell me.'

'Virginia, I haven't seen anybody,' Brazil said in a softer tone.

He reached out and took her hand. She had a hard time swallowing.

'And I didn't dump you,' he said.

He moved his chair next to hers and kissed her. In the bedroom he discovered the wineglasses of Mountain Dew.

Hammer wanted to dump the entire NIJ project. Her mind was a riotous crowd of dissenting, unhappy people who would not let her sleep. She thought about Bubba and how badly she had maligned him. She obsessed over how badly she had handled Lelia Ehrhart and those like her.

Part of Hammer's mission was to enlighten people. She saw no evidence that she had. Part of her plan was to modernize the police department. And what happened? The entire COMSTAT telecommunications network crashed. The ATM robberies escalated to murder. There were gangs. There was Smoke.

Hammer didn't think she could ever again endure seeing Ruby Sink's house or even the block Miss Sink had lived on. Miss Sink, in her pink robe and slippers, had shuffled through Hammer's mind all night. Hammer could not get away from their last conversation on Miss Sink's sidewalk. Hammer could see the old woman in such detail it hurt her heart and pierced her with guilt.

'I'm a failure,' Hammer said to Popeye.

Popeye was under the covers, between Hammer's feet.

'I've caused harm. I should never have come here. I bet you wish you still lived in Charlotte where you had a yard, don't you?'

Her eyes filled with tears. Popeye burrowed up to her and licked her face. Hammer couldn't remember the last time she had cried. She had been so stoical when Seth had died because she believed she had to be. She had been rational about the reasons her sons did not seem to want to see her. Hammer had been courageous, innovative, community-minded. All of it so she would be too busy to be lonely, and it hadn't worked. She got up and dressed.

There was no answer at Brazil's house when Hammer called from her car phone. She tried West next and was relieved that he and West were there.

'I've got something important to say to both of you,' Hammer said over the line.

Parking in the Fan wasn't as much of a problem at this early hour, and she managed to squeeze into a space on the curb right across the street from West's town house. Hammer was numb. She did not feel present, nor did she want to be when Brazil opened the front door.

'Thank you for seeing me,' Hammer said to Brazil as they walked into the living room.

'Thank *you,*' he replied. 'It's kind of messy.'

Hammer didn't care. She didn't even notice her surroundings, messy or not. She sat in a straight-back chair while West and Brazil sat across from her on the couch.

'Virginia, Andy,' she began, 'I'm going to resign.'

'Oh God,' West said, shocked.

'You can't,' Brazil said, sick.

'Basically,' Hammer went on, 'I've pretty much screwed up everything here. I used to be a good police officer, a good chief. Everybody hates us.'

'Not *everybody,*' Brazil said.

'Most of them,' said West. 'I mean, let's be honest about it.'

'Well, I guess the Charlotte connection doesn't help,' Brazil supposed.

'Or our locking up the COMSTAT network pretty much around the globe,' Hammer said.

'Or our failure to crack the ATM cases before they progressed to a horrible murder. Or a communications officer getting in a fight with a traffic cop, both of whom had just received commendations several days before.' West helped her out with the list.

Hammer folded her hands in her lap and kept them still. She did not interrupt. She did not get up and pace.

'Judy,' West said. 'Where are you going to go? Back to Charlotte?'

Hammer shook her head.

'Nowhere,' she answered. 'If I can't handle Richmond, I'm not going to be able to handle someplace else. When the horse dies, get off. I'm retiring from police work. I don't know where I'll live. It doesn't matter.'

'That reminds me,' West said. 'We need to talk about the Azalea Parade.'

'How did what she just said remind you of that?' Brazil asked.

'The horse comment. We've got mounted cops in the parade,' West said. 'And' – she looked at Hammer – 'Andy and I are supposed to ride in your convertible.'

'What kind of convertible is it?' Hammer looked distracted.

'Dark blue Sebring,' Brazil said. 'Modest, not showy, although one of the big guys at Philip Morris wanted to drive you in his red Mercedes V12 convertible.'

'Not a good idea,' Hammer muttered.

'I don't think you should be in the parade at all,' West said with conviction. 'The parade could be a possible target for Smoke. And I hate for you to be riding slow in a convertible anyway. There're a lot of kooks out there.'

Hammer got up. She really didn't care what happened to her.

'It's important,' she said dully. 'Every little thing we do to reach the community is helpful. I won't back out of a promise.'

'Well, we're going to have fifty off-duty cops there in addition to the regular shifts,' West told her. 'To the public, it will appear we're there mainly for traffic control. And we're mobilizing about twenty plainclothes guys to mingle, just in case Smoke shows up or someone else decides to cause a problem.'

bubba was thinking the same thing. He believed Chief Hammer should not be riding in an open car in the Azalea Parade, and worse, it had been in the newspaper so everybody knew it. It was possible this was where all roads met. Bubba had been called to save her from a terrible danger. Bubba also figured the Pikes somehow factored in.

At eight o'clock this morning, he was already parking in front of Green Top Sporting Goods on U.S. Route 1, some twenty minutes outside of Richmond. There was no place Bubba would rather be. The minute he walked through the door and was greeted by thousands of fishing rods and all that went with them, his pulse quickened. When he turned to the right and saw hundreds of rifles, shotguns, pistols and revolvers, he got flushed. He felt lust in a way he had never experienced with Honey.

'Hey, what'cha know.' He was enthusiastically greeted by Fig Winnick, the assistant manager.

By Virginia law, a citizen could buy one handgun every thirty days and no more. This had given rise to the tongue-in-cheek Gun-of-the-Month Club. It was a small but clever group of one hundred and eighty-nine men and sixty-two women who sent each other reminders when their thirty days, loosely interpreted as a month, were up. It was April 2.

'If only I'd come in two days ago, I could have bought a gun then and another one today,' Bubba misinterpreted, as usual.

'Wishful thinking,' Winnick told him again. 'Doesn't work that way, Bubba. And it sure as hell is too damn bad.'

'So you're saying it's not once a month,' Bubba challenged what he refused to believe.

'Not literally. But sort of. If you start with the first day of each month.'

'You know, someone stole all my guns.' Bubba browsed.

'The guys were talking about it,' Winnick sympathized.

'So all I got left's the Anaconda and I need something I can pack easier,' Bubba spoke the language.

'I got just the thing.'

Winnick lovingly opened a showcase and gently pulled out a Browning 40 S&W Hi-Power Mark III pistol. He handed the beauty to Bubba.

'Oh God,' Bubba muttered as he fondled the silver chrome pistol. 'Oh, oh, oh.'

'Molded polyamide grips with thumb rest,' Winnick said. 'Weighs thirty-five ounces, four and three-quarters barrel. Feels great to the hand, huh?'

'Boy. No kidding.'

Bubba pulled back the slide and snapped it forward. There was just no better sound than that.

'Low profile front sight blade, drift-adjustable rear sight,' Winnick went on. 'Ambidextrous safety, ten-round magazine.'

'Imported from Belgium.' Bubba wasn't going to be fooled. 'The genuine thing.'

'Nothing but.'

'What about a matte blue finish?' Bubba inquired. 'It doesn't show up as much.'

'Sorry,' Winnick apologized. 'Damn. If only you had come in yesterday. We had about eleven left.'

'Well, I guess this one will have to do,' Bubba said.

Patty Passman also was thinking ahead. She hadn't missed an Azalea Parade in twelve years and she didn't intend to miss this one. Although Rhoad had unfairly charged her with many things, it was only *assault on a police officer* that had stuck. She wished bail bondsman

Willy 'Lucky' Loving would show up to get her the hell out of here.

Lockup was just a holding area and inmates wore their own clothes, giving up only their belts to make it trickier to commit suicide. Passman was sticky, her panty hose so torn up she'd had no choice but to take them off right in front of her cellmate, Tinky Meaney, a truck driver for Dixie Motorfreight, who had gotten picked up for getting into a scuffle in the parking lot of the Power Clean Grill on Hull Street. Passman didn't know the details, but of one thing she was certain, Tinky Meaney wasn't on the list of those Passman might have invited to a slumber party.

'I sure wish he'd hurry up,' Passman said from her narrow steel pull-down bed.

She said this often to make certain Meaney didn't think that Passman enjoyed Meaney's company and was in no hurry to leave it. Meaney was a big woman. She was the sort who always said they weren't fat, just big-boned and solid. This was nonsense.

Meaney's thighs were thicker than the biggest Smithfield hams Passman had ever seen, and every time Meaney stalked about the tiny cell, her jeans swished as her upper legs rubbed together. Her hands were thick with stubby fingers and big knuckles that were scraped and bruised from the fistfight that had landed her here. She had no neck. As she sat on the edge of her bed staring at Passman, Meaney's breasts sagged over her empty belt loops. Unshaved pale legs showed between the hem of her jeans and the top of her hand-tooled black and red cowboy boots.

'What the hell are you staring at?' Meaney caught Passman looking.

'Nothing,' Passman lied.

Meaney stretched out on her side and propped up on an elbow, chin in hand. She stared without blinking, a look in her tiny dark eyes that Passman recognized instantly. At the same time Passman realized in amazement that Meaney's breasts were even bigger than Passman had thought. One was hanging over the side of the bed, almost touching the floor, and brought to mind a sandbag. Passman realized Meaney wasn't wearing a bra under her Motor Mile Towing & Flatbed Service sweatshirt.

Passman was painfully reminded of yet one more lousy card she'd been dealt in life. No matter how much weight she had put on over the years, her breasts were elusive. Their fat cells dodged any opportunity for growth and development and always had. She suspected that when, as a young girl, she had tried to be a boy, that part of the programming never got deleted when she later returned to her proper gender.

It was unbearably humiliating in eighth-grade health class to watch the films on menstruation, the female outline on the screen developing right before Passman's eyes, the breasts rounding, the pear-shaped muscular uterus discharging its menses in little hatch-marks flowing through the mature female outline, then out of it, on the screen.

All the other girls could relate. Passman could not. She could have gotten by in life without a bra, had she been honest about it. Her periods were more like commas, brief pauses each month that exacerbated her hypoglycemia and made her very cranky.

Passman was still staring, lost in tortured memories of puberty. Meaney smiled like a jack-o'-lantern and stretched provocatively. Passman came to. She quickly averted her gaze.

'I sure wish he'd hurry up,' Passman said again, this time with more emphasis.

'It ain't so bad in here,' Meaney said in her twangy drawl. 'I recognize your voice. Hear you all the time when I'm in the vincinity, riding through. Channels one, two and three, know 'em by heart. Four-sixty point one hundred megs, 460.200, 460.325. I always thought you had a nice voice.'

'Thank you,' Passman said.

'So, what'd you do?'

Passman thought it wise to send out a warning.

'Beat the shit out of some guy,' she answered. 'I lost control and should've held back a little more than I did. Huge son of a bitch. Had it coming.'

Meaney nodded. 'Mine had it coming, too, fucking son of a bitch. I'm sitting in the bar minding my own business, you know, after a long day on the road, I mean long. He comes over to my table, this big ole trashy fucker in a cowboy hat. I recognized him.' She nodded. 'And he recognized me.' She nodded again. 'He was in his personal car this night. Nineteen ninety-two Chevy Dually, lowered, loaded, four-fifty-four, aluminum wheels, tinted windows, air ride, all the hitches.

'It was in the lot and he asked if I liked it. I said I did.

He asked what I drove. I told him a Mack. He asked if I'd ever drove a Peterbilt. I said I'd driven all there was. He asked if I'd ever had a blowout in a Peterbilt. I said I hadn't. He asked if I wanted to. I said, *Why would I?* And he yanked down his zipper, so I threw him up against his Chevy Dually.

'Then I musta really gone at him because he looked like hamburger, a bunch of broke bones, teeth everywhere but in his mouth, most of his hair yanked out, ear tore off. What I hate about someone pissing me off like that is later on I can't remember a thing. I guess I must have a spell of some sort, like an epilepick.'

'I'm the same way,' Passman said.

'So, you live around here?'

'We're over near Regency Mall.'

'Who's *we?*' Meaney's eyes got smaller and darker.

'Me and my boyfriend.' Passman lied out of self-defense.

'I had one once,' Meaney reminisced. 'Then I was in lockup one day. I forget what for. And there was another girl in there with me.' Meaney nodded and laid on her back, hands behind her head, body spilling everywhere.

Passman was beginning to panic. She was going to kill the bondsman Lucky Loving if he didn't hurry up. She didn't want to encourage Meaney, not in the least, but she had to know the rest of the story. She needed to get as much information as she could. Forewarned is forearmed, her mother always used to say.

'What happened?' Passman asked after a long, intense silence.

'The things we did. Ha!' Meaney grinned, enjoying the memory. 'Let me tell you something, honey. There ain't a thing a man's got that you can't find under your own hood, if you know what I mean.'

chapter thirty-four

The Oliver Hill Courts Building was modern and full of light and Ayokunle Odeleye mahogany carvings. Brazil had never seen a court building that looked less like one, and it made him feel a little more optimistic when he walked in, Weed's case file under his arm. It was five minutes before nine, and unlike other juvenile systems, this one had an exact time schedule docket.

If the arraignment was at nine, it would begin at nine, and that's exactly what time it was when the intercom announced, 'Weed Gardener, report to courtroom number two, please.'

Judge Maggie Davis was already on the bench, formidable and distinguished in her black robe. She was young to be a judge, and when the General Assembly had appointed her, she had charged in and made changes. Although she protected the confidentiality of juveniles who committed lesser crimes, she did not coddle or shield violent offenders.

'Good morning, Officer Brazil,' Judge Davis said as Brazil seated himself on the first row and the clerk handed the judge Weed's file.

'Good morning, Your Honor,' said Brazil.

A deputy escorted Weed in from the back and positioned him in front of the judge, where he seemed even smaller in his ill-fitting blue jumpsuit and detention-issue black Spalding hightops. But Weed held his head up. He didn't seem dejected or ashamed and in fact seemed to be looking forward to the arraignment, unlike Commonwealth's Attorney Jay Michael or Sue Cheddar, the public defender on his heels, or Mrs. Gardener, who was at the door explaining to a deputy who she was.

'. . . yes, yes, my son,' Brazil heard Mrs. Gardener say.

'Mrs. Gardener?' Judge Davis inquired.

'Yes,' Mrs. Gardener whispered.

Weed's mother had put on a crisp blue dress and matching shoes, but her face belied her neat facade. Her eyes were puffy and exhausted, as if she had been crying all night. Her hands shook. She had burst into tears and called herself a failure as a mother when Brazil had finally gotten her on the phone to tell her about Weed. She had told Brazil that she'd quit feeling or facing anything after Twister died.

'You can come up here,' the judge said kindly to Mrs. Gardener.

Mrs. Gardener came to the front of the courtroom and sat quietly in a corner of the first row, as far from Brazil as she could get. Weed did not turn around.

'Are you expecting any other family?' the judge asked Mrs. Gardener.

'No ma'am,' she barely said.

'All right,' Judge Davis said to Weed, 'I'm going to tell you your rights.'

'Okay,' he said.

'You have the right to counsel, to a public hearing, to the privilege against self-incrimination, to confront and cross-examine witnesses, to present evidence, and the right to appeal a final decision of the court.'

'Thank you,' Weed said.

'Do you understand them?'

'No.'

'What this means, Weed, is you have a right to an attorney and you don't have to say anything this morning that might incriminate you. Those other rights don't apply unless you go to trial. Does that make sense, do you understand?'

'What does incriminalate mean?'

'For example, saying something that will be used against you.'

'How do I know what that is?' Weed asked.

'I'll stop you if you start doing it, how's that?'

'What if you don't stop me quick enough?'

'I will, don't worry.'

'You promise?'

'Yes,' Judge Davis answered. 'Now.' She looked at Weed. 'The purpose of this arraignment is to determine whether I should keep you locked up in detention before your trial date or let you go.'

'I wanna stay locked up,' Weed said.

'We'll talk about that as we proceed,' said the judge.

She looked at the petition Brazil had signed.

'Weed, you've been charged with 18.2-125 of the Virginia code, *Trespass at night upon any cemetery*, and 18.2-127, *Injuries to churches, church property, cemeteries, burial grounds, etc.*, and 182.2-138.1, *Willful and malicious damage to or defacement of public or private facilities.'* She leaned forward. 'Do you understand the seriousness of these charges?'

'I only know what I did or didn't do,' Weed said.

'Do you believe you're guilty or not guilty?'

'Depends on what happens if I say one or another,' Weed said.

'Weed, it doesn't work that way.'

'I just wanna have my say.'

'Then plead not guilty and you can have your say at the trial,' she told him.

'When's that?'

'We'd have to set a date.'

'Could we do it tomorrow?'

'Twenty-one days from now.'

Weed looked crushed.

'But the Azalea Parade's Saturday,' he explained. 'Can't I have my say now so I can march in it and play the cymbals?'

Judge Davis seemed to find this juvenile a little more interesting than most. Commonwealth's Attorney Michael was befuddled. Public Defender Cheddar had a blank expression on her face.

'If you want to have your say, Weed, then plead not guilty.' The judge tried to make him get the drift.

'Not unless I get to be in the parade,' he told her stubbornly.

'If you don't plead not guilty, the alternative is guilty. Do you understand what a guilty plea means?' Judge Davis asked with surprising patience.

'Means I done it.'

'It means I have to sentence you, Weed. Maybe I'll put you on probation, maybe I won't. You may lose your freedom, go back to detention, in other words, and if that's the case, there's absolutely no chance of your being in any parade anytime soon.'

'You sure?' Weed asked.

'Sure as I'm sitting here.'

'Not guilty,' he said, 'even if I am.'

Judge Davis looked at Mrs. Gardener. 'Do you have an attorney?'

'No, ma'am,' Mrs. Gardener replied.

'Can you afford to hire one?'

'How much would it cost?'

'It could be expensive,' said the judge.

'I don't want an attorney,' Weed piped up.

'I'm not talking to you,' the judge warned.

'Don't hire one, Mama!' he said.

'Weed!' the judge said sternly.

'I'm gonna defend myself.' Weed wouldn't stop.

'No, you're not,' Judge Davis replied.

She appointed Sue Cheddar to defend Weed, and Cheddar moved to Weed's side and smiled at him. She wore a lot of makeup, her mascara so thick it reminded Weed of asphalt right after they put it down. Little gold stars had been painted on red nails so long her fingers never touched anything first. Weed wasn't impressed.

'I don't want her,' he said. 'I don't need nobody to talk for me.'

'I've decided you do,' said the judge. 'Mr. Michael, please present evidence to the state for continued custody,' she said to the commonwealth's attorney, who looked over at Brazil and passed the baton.

'Your Honor, I think the arresting officer is better able to do that at this time,' Michael said. 'I haven't really looked at anything yet.'

Weed didn't like the way Sue Cheddar was handling things. Every time he tried to say what was what, Cheddar told him to hush. He didn't understand how the truth ever got out if people weren't allowed to tell it because they might get in trouble when they ought to be in trouble anyway.

After a while, when Brazil was leading up to the crime, Weed got tired of Cheddar basically telling him to shut up. He was insulted and indignant. She didn't seem to object to anything except Weed, and she was supposed to be on his side. So he took over. He decided that if Officer Brazil was going to tell Weed's story, Weed would object for himself all he wanted, even if he agreed with Brazil.

'About two o'clock Tuesday morning, Weed climbed over the Hollywood Cemetery fence, trespassing on private property.' Brazil was standing before the judge and summarizing.

'We didn't even get there until after three,' Weed corrected him again.

'That's immaterial,' Judge Davis said as she had numerous times before.

'Shhhhh . . .' Cheddar hissed.

'Apparently he was with a gang and was coerced . . .' Brazil went on.

'No, I wasn't,' Weed objected. 'I was just with Smoke and Divinity. Dog, Sick and Beeper wasn't there.'

'Immaterial,' said the judge.

'Point is,' Brazil went on, 'Weed carried paints into the cemetery with the intention of defacing Jefferson Davis's statue.'

'I didn't know who it was,' Weed cut in. 'And I didn't de-face him. He still has a face. You go look.'

'Your Honor.' Public Defender Cheddar's voice was tight and high. 'I don't think my client understands the bit about self-incrimination.'

'He said he did,' Judge Davis replied.

'Yeah,' Weed told Cheddar.

'Please continue, Officer Brazil,' said the judge.

'Weed painted a Spiders basketball uniform on the statue and at or around five A.M. left the cemetery by climbing over the fence again.'

'It wasn't that early,' Weed protested. 'I know, 'cause the sun was starting to show up and that always happens after six 'cause that's when I get up, too, because I gotta make my own toast and jelly before I go to school 'cause my mama works too late to get outta bed that early.'

Mrs. Gardener bent her head. She hid her face, wiping tears.

'Immaterial,' said Judge Davis.

'And besides,' Weed declared, 'it's just poster paint. You go look. A hose will get it off, but they been so busy studying what to do about it they never even wet their finger and touched it to see if it would stick. First rain's gonna ruin it,' he concluded with a trace of disappointment.

No one spoke for a moment.

Papers shuffled.

The C.A. was staring off, not present.

Brazil was amazed.

It took several synapses before Cheddar got it.

'Then it's not really defaced,' Cheddar announced as if her voice was a gavel.

'How do you know?' Weed objected to his attorney. 'Anybody looked at it today?'

Nobody had.

'Then don't be telling . . .' he started to say before Cheddar clamped her hand over his mouth.

'How many times I gotta tell you to keep your mouth shut so I can do my job!' Cheddar exclaimed.

Weed bit her.

'Lord in heaven!' Cheddar exclaimed. 'He bit me!'

'Not hard,' Weed said. 'But she started it. What if she cut me with those nails? You seen them things up close?' He rubbed his mouth with his sleeve.

'Order!' Judge Davis declared.

'What if I clean up the statue?' Weed said. 'If you want

me to, I will.' It was a big sacrifice for Weed to make, but he knew Twister's monument couldn't last forever. 'All I want is to be locked up except for Saturday when the Azalea Parade is.'

'We're not there yet, Weed,' Judge Davis told him firmly. 'I can't decide anything until I've heard the evidence. And please refrain from biting your counsel again.'

'What if I promise to fix the police computer? Would you let me play my cymbals in the parade?' Weed went on.

'He's referring to what the press has been calling "Fishsteria,"' Brazil told her.

Cheddar was visibly alarmed. 'He has that?' she asked, her face stricken.

'He caused it,' Brazil said.

'Your Honor, may I approach the bench?' Cheddar panicked.

She lunged forward and grabbed the edge of the bench, standing on her tiptoes, leaning as close to the judge as she could.

'Your Honor,' she whispered excitedly, but everyone could hear. 'If what's being said here is my client's the one spreading that fish sickness, then I need to know if others are in danger of catching it!'

Cheddar shot Weed a menacing look.

'Others meaning me,' Cheddar went on. 'He bit my hand, Your Honor.'

'I don't think we're talking about that sort of disease,' Judge Davis told her with a glint of irritation.

'Your Honor,' Cheddar said in a more demanding tone, her nails flashing as she gestured. 'How do I know for an absolute true fact that he doesn't have some sort of bug of some type that all of us should be concerned about! Especially me because his teeth made contact with my skin!'

She held up her hand like the Statue of Liberty.

'Doesn't look like he broke the skin,' the judge observed.

'Then you're saying you're not going to send him to mental health or someplace where they can do tests?' Cheddar's voice rose to a shriek.

'That's what I'm saying,' Judge Davis said.

'Then I quit!' Cheddar threw her hands up, red and gold flashing.

'No you don't 'cause I fired you first!' Weed called out as Cheddar grabbed her falling-apart briefcase, papers spilling, and rushed out of the courtroom.

'Your Honor,' Brazil spoke up. 'The truth is, we really need our COMSTAT telecommunications system up and running again.' He was out of line, but didn't care. 'The network's down all over the world because of the fish thing.'

'Officer Brazil, that is irrelevant to this case.'

'Of course,' Brazil mumbled a deliberate challenge to Weed, 'he probably couldn't fix it anyway.'

'Can too,' Weed said.

'Oh yeah?' Brazil taunted. 'Then how?'

'Just take out the program I did when I punted and messed up the HTML interpreter in AOL.'

Judge Davis couldn't help herself because like all else in the world, she used AOL and lived in fear of color bombs, IM bombs, HTML Freeze/Lag, HTMO errors, a combination of the above, or possibly the less innocuous but more annoying Blank IM bombs.

'What's *punting?'* she asked Weed.

'The bug's in autowrap in the text handler,' he informed her as if his explanation was as obvious as colors. 'See, if you use VBMSG subclassing, you know? To hold the window open and do some other things I told it to do, you know? 'Cause, see, like I said, there's this bug. So I told it to put my map on there and hold it. And the Anti-Punt program won't work, either, because I made my program hit Reply on the IM.'

Amazement stilled the room. Brazil was writing everything down. The C.A.'s mouth was open in disbelief.

'But I never meant for my fish screen to go everywhere,' Weed added. 'Someone must've stuck all these addresses together, and it ain't me who did.'

'Does anybody understand what he just said?' the judge asked.

'I sort of do,' Brazil said. 'And he's right about the addresses.'

'It won't take me but a minute to show him how to fix it, then you can lock me up,' Weed said. 'And I can do the parade and get locked up again.'

He looked up at her, fear shining in his eyes. He could tell Judge Davis understood something bad would happen if she let him go home. He turned around and looked at his mother.

'It's okay, Mama,' he said. 'It ain't got nothing to do with you.'

Tears filled her eyes, and his got a little swimmy, too.

The C.A., whose job it was to punish to the fullest extent of the law, finally argued the case.

'The release of him is an unreasonable danger to the property of others.' He quoted the code. 'I think there is clear and convincing evidence *not* to release him.'

The judge leaned forward and looked at Weed. She had made up her mind. Weed's heart jumped.

'I find there is probable cause for the state,' the judge let everybody know, 'and an adjudicatory hearing will be held twenty-one days from today. The state may summon witnesses, and the juvenile will remain in detention. But I order that the juvenile be released into the custody of Officer Brazil this Saturday.' She looked at Weed. 'What time is the parade?'

'Ten-thirty,' Weed said. 'But I gotta be there earlier than that.'

'When does it end?'

'Eleven-thirty,' Weed said. 'But I gotta stay longer than that.'

'Nine A.M. to one P.M.,' the judge said to Brazil. 'Then back in detention pending the court date.'

chapter thirty-five

The morning of the Azalea Parade Weed's soul was as light as light itself. He wished he could paint the way he felt and the way the morning looked as Officer Brazil drove him to George Wythe High School, where the Godwin marching band was waiting and warming up.

Weed was proud and sweating in his polyester and wool blend red-and-white uniform with its many silver buttons and its stripes down the legs. His rolled-heel black shoes looked like new, the Sabian cymbals polished and safely in their black case in the back seat.

'Too bad you haven't had more time to practice,' Brazil said.

Weed knew that out of the 152 members of the band, he was probably the only one who had missed a week of practice. He hadn't had a chance to look at his drill charts or work on forward march, pull mark time, pull halt, high mark, backward march, his favorite freeze-spin and especially the crab step, which was unique to the percussion section of Godwin's finely tuned precision marching band.

'I'll be all right,' Weed said, staring out the window, his heart thrilled.

Already crowds were gathering. It was predicted this might be the biggest turnout in the history of the parade. The weather was perfect, in the seventies, a light breeze, not a cloud. People were spreading out blankets, setting up lawn chairs, parking strollers and wheelchairs, and those who lived along the parade route had decided it was a good day for a yard sale. Cops were everywhere in reflective vests and Weed had never seen so many traffic cones.

Brazil was worried. Thousands of people were gathering and those participating in the parade filled the George Wythe High School parking lot. If Smoke had a plan, Brazil didn't see how it was possible to pluck one teenager out of such congestion, especially if no one, except Weed, seemed to know what Smoke really looked like.

'Weed, I want you to make a promise, okay?' Brazil said as Weed collected his cymbal case from the car. 'You'd recognize Smoke or any of his gang.'

'So.'

Weed was in a hurry, anxiously staring off at his marching band, which from this vantage was a patch of bright red and white somewhat lost in a swarm of colorful uniforms and flashing instruments and swords and twinkling batons and twirling flags. Floats hovered restlessly in an endless line. Masons were dressed like clowns. Mounted police were letting kids pet the horses. Antique cars rattled.

'We're better than that,' Weed said, watching the Navy

League Cadet Corps practice marching. 'Look at that bus! That band came all the way from Chicago! And there's one from New York!'

'Weed, did you hear what I said?' Brazil asked out his open window.

Sergeant Santa worked the crowd. One of the Florettes lost track of her baton and it bounced several times on the road. People dressed for the Old West were showing off miniature horses that had azalea blossoms in their manes. The Independence Wheelchair Athletic Association was ready to go. Weed was dazzled.

'Weed!' Brazil was about to get out of the car.

'Don't you worry, Officer Brazil,' Weed said. 'I'll let you know.'

'How?' Brazil wasn't going to take any bullshit.

'I'll do a real long crash and flash my cymbals good when I'm not supposed to,' Weed said.

'No way, Weed. How am I going to notice that with everything else going on?' Brazil countered.

Weed thought. His face got tense, his shoulders slumped and he looked heart-broken when he said, 'Then I'll cut one loose. You can't miss that. Course you'll have to explain later why I did or I won't be playing cymbals in the band no more.'

'Cut one loose?' Brazil was lost.

'Let go of the strap. You ever seen an eighteen-inch cymbal roll down the road?'

'No,' Brazil confessed.

'Well, you see one,' Weed told him, 'then you know I'm telling you trouble's about to start.'

Lelia Ehrhart was already having trouble. She was closely inspecting the Blue Ribbon Crime Commission's red Cadillac convertible, with its streamers of blue ribbons that would float and flutter beautifully once the car was rolling along the parade route. She realized with horror that there wasn't a single azalea blossom, not even one.

'We must carry on to the theme and message of the parade,' she told Commissioner Ed Blackstone.

'I thought the blue ribbons did that,' replied Blackstone, who was eighty-two but maintained that age didn't matter. 'I thought it was called the Azalea Parade because of azaleas, which are everywhere, and it wasn't expected that we fill the car with them, especially since we don't have many seats anyway.'

Ehrhart could not be persuaded, and she directed that the white leather front passenger's side and most of the back were to be lush and dense with pink and white azalea bushes. This reduced the number of waving and smiling commissioners from three to one.

'I guess I'll have to ride alone by myself,' Ehrhart said.

'Well, I'm going to tell you something, Lelia,' said Blackstone as he leaned against his walker, straining to see through the huge glasses he'd been wearing since his last cataract surgery. 'You're going to have bees. That many blossoms, and bees will show up, mark my words. And don't say I didn't warn you about making those streamers so long. Twenty feet.' Blackstone was severe on this point. 'Anybody gets close to your rear with all those streamers of blue ribbons endlessly flying, something's going to get tangled up.'

'Where's Jed?' Ehrhart frowned.

'Over there.' Blackstone pointed at a tree.

Ehrhart searched the masses and spotted Jed hanging around an antique fire truck, talking to Muskrat, who had fixed her car a time or two. She didn't like to be reminded that Governor Feuer had declined to participate in the parade, even after Ehrhart had offered to ride with him. At least he had volunteered Jed to drive the commission's car, which was on loan from one of Bull Ehrhart's patients.

'Tell to him it's times to come now,' Lelia Ehrhart ordered Blackstone.

Blackstone motioned at the tree to hurry along.

Neither Brazil nor West liked crowds, but Chief Hammer refused to bask in the limelight alone, especially since she hated parades and other public celebrations more than West and Brazil did.

'I can't believe you're doing this,' West complained from the back seat of the dark blue Sebring. 'You got this psycho kid out there waiting to make himself a legend by doing something really, really bad, and what do you decide?' She slid into the driver's seat and began adjusting mirrors. 'You decide to ride in an open convertible.'

'I don't like it, either,' said Brazil as he climbed in back, next to Hammer. 'You sure you don't want me to drive?' he asked West.

'Forget it,' she replied.

Brazil got out paperwork.

'We need to find the Mustang Club,' he said, 'because

we're in front of them. And' – he traced his finger down a list – 'right behind Miss Richmond.'

'Yuck,' West said.

Pigeon and a fat man were within two feet of each other at Westover Hills and Bassett, across from Brentwood South.

The fat man seemed ready for action as he clandestinely searched the crowd through a pair of Leica binoculars. Pigeon was rooting for half a hot dog with mustard and relish that a little kid had just tossed into a trash can, as if hot dogs grew on trees.

Pigeon never missed the Azalea Parade. People were so wasteful. Not one kid this day and age knew the value of a dollar, not even those folks on food stamps. He fished out an almost entire bag of potato chips that some little brat couldn't toss without violently squeezing, crushing and pulverizing first.

'What we need is another good war,' he said to the fat man, although they were not acquainted.

'I've been saying that for years.' The fat man couldn't have agreed more. 'No one understands what it's like.'

'How could they?' Pigeon said, peering inside the bag, unable to find a chip bigger than a dime.

'My name's Bubba,' Bubba said as he continued his sweep with the binoculars.

'I'm Pigeon.'

'Nice to meet you.'

Pigeon homed in on another kid who dropped his

bubble gum on the sidewalk after three chews, when there was still plenty of flavor left. A woman in jogging clothes stepped on it.

'Thanks a lot!' she called out to the kid as he popped open a can of Orange Crush and walked off.

She lifted her foot and stared at strings of pink gum leading to a blob fixed to the tread of her right Saucony running shoe.

'I hate you!' she screamed at the kid as people walked around her, looking for a spot with a decent view. 'I hate all children! I hate people!'

'That would piss me off, too,' Pigeon said. 'Nobody cares anymore.'

Bubba focused on Smudge and his wife opening lawn chairs in a yard no more than fifty feet to Bubba's right.

'He probably doesn't even know those people,' Bubba mumbled with fresh fury. 'Just helps himself like he does with everything in life.'

'All the world's like that now,' Pigeon said.

'He knows I'm here, too,' Bubba said. 'The son of a bitch knows he owes me a thousand dollars. Says he has amnesia, doesn't remember the bet, so it doesn't count.'

'I don't know what happened to honesty,' Pigeon said.

Bubba watched Smudge open a checkered tablecloth and spread it out in the grass. He set down a blue ice chest, opened the lid and rummaged.

Pigeon searched in vain for a cigarette butt. He could tell the price had shot way up. People were smoking closer to the filter, leaving nothing for him.

He was shocked yesterday morning when he was picking his way along Main Street, downtown, and observed on the Dow Jones electronic message board outside Scott and Stringfellow brokers that the price per pack had increased another two dollars and eleven cents. If only Pigeon had bought more when he had the money from the pawn shop. He could have done some quick trading. He'd probably be rich.

Even as Pigeon was thinking that, Bubba reached into his shirt pocket for a pack. He shook out a cigarette without lowering the binoculars.

'Those Merit Ultimas any good?' Pigeon asked as Bubba lit up. 'That's one I haven't tried yet.'

'Oh yeah,' Bubba said. 'Anything Philip Morris makes is the best.'

'I've always thought so. How are those different from regular Merits?' Pigeon asked slyly.

'Want to try one?'

'That would be nice,' Pigeon said as Bubba passed him the pack. 'Why, thank you very much.'

Wailing police sirens and the thunder of cops on motorcycles sounded in the distance, signaling that the parade was starting. Weed was so excited his knees were shaking.

He was positioned to the right of Lou Jameson on the

snare drum, who was wearing sunglasses like all the drummers did. He had never been very friendly to Weed and more than once had commented that anybody could play cymbals and he'd seen girls doing it in other bands.

Western Guilford High School in white and black was directly in front of Godwin. Lakeview Junior High in gold and green was to the rear. Bright, brave uniforms of all colors and designs must have stretched for a mile, Weed calculated. The parade was starting to move. The lead band out of New Jersey exploded into 'God Bless America,' which wasn't very original and the trumpets were a little off.

Weed stood tall and proud. He did a few toe lifts to loosen up.

'Left foot out and point flex and point flex and really stretch it,' he recited.

Jameson looked at him with disdain.

'Left heel two inches off ground while ball and toe remain touching the ground.' Weed practiced a *low mark time* with a quick, snappy motion. 'Ankle touches knee on end of each beat, toe pointed straight down the leg, feet flat.' He executed a perfect *high mark.* 'Push down on beat on left foot, then *mark time.'*

'Hey, cut it out,' Jameson said.

'No,' Weed retorted.

He used to be intimidated by Jameson. But after being arrested, getting locked up in detention, mouthing off to a defense attorney and striking a deal with a judge, Weed wasn't scared of anyone.

'Three, four, halt. To left, right, foot crosses over, mark

time hut, and one, two, three, four, weight on toes.' His crab step was flawless.

'I told you to fucking cut it out,' Jameson whispered.

'Make me.'

'I'll beat your ass.'

'Hope you beat it better than you do that drum,' Weed said.

'TO THE READY!' the drum major shouted from the front.

Weed came to attention. One thing about his cymbals, they sure got heavy.

'BAND, TEN-HUT!'

He strained to see what the color guard was doing way ahead. When the woodwinds started forward marching, he knew he was next.

There was nothing random about Smoke's decision to steal the black nylon Stanley tool belt when he broke into Bubba's workshop. Its extra deep pockets were perfect and he had known it at the time, because Smoke had been planning for a while.

He was dressed in worn-out, soiled jeans, a filthy tee shirt and dirty scuffed Red Wing boots. A paint-spattered baseball cap was low over his eyes. He wore Oakleys and hadn't shaved in days. No one paid any attention to him as he walked across yards, trying to see the parade like everybody else.

Smoke had conducted a thorough surveillance in the George Wythe parking lot while the parade was lining up.

He knew where everyone was. He had spotted Weed. Smoke had walked right past the police chief and the two cops who had spoken in Godwin's auditorium. It was hilarious. Smoke's nerves were humming. He was pumping adrenaline and almost manic.

Concealed inside the pouches around his waist were the stolen Beretta and four ten-round clips and two fifteen-round clips and his Glock with three seventeen-round clips. That made a grand total of one hundred and twenty-one Winchester 115 grain Silvertip high-power cartridges.

He watched antique Jaguars and Chryslers cruise by, then the Corvette Club. People were waving and clapping, the weather great, everybody in a good mood. He spotted a sloping lawn that was a little higher above the street than those around it. Some jerk and a mousy woman were having a picnic on a red-checked tablecloth. Smoke had found the perfect spot. He walked right up to them, crossed his arms and looked out as the Veterans of Foreign Wars and the Red Cross rolled by.

bubba recognized the Stanley tool belt immediately. Some construction guy was wearing it. The big black belt with its deep pouches was exactly like the one missing from Bubba's garage. Bubba focused the binoculars a little more, zooming in on the guy's face.

He looked about fifteen or sixteen, kind of puny and pale. The pouches were bulging and looked heavy. He had the padded yellow belt pulled as tight as it would go, the entire rig huge on him because it was an extra-large and the kid couldn't weigh more than a hundred and twenty pounds. Bubba didn't see a single tool, no tape measure, no nails, nothing in the hammer holder, not so much as a handle protruding.

'That's my belt,' Bubba said as his heart picked up speed. 'I know it is!'

Pigeon looked where Bubba was looking, squinting as he smoked another Merit Ultima that Bubba had been pleased to give him.

'How do you know?' Pigeon inquired.

'I see a little white mark on the quick-release belt buckle. It might be my initials. I paint my initials in white on all my tools, on everything, to make sure when Smudge borrows something he can't turn around and say it's his!'

'Who's Smudge?' Pigeon asked, tapping an ash.

The last of some band in black and white was marching by, playing 'Take the "A" Train.' The drum major of the Godwin band was right behind it. Bubba stared through the binoculars, blood rushing to his head, his heart beating faster than a snare drum as he focused on the dark blue convertible carrying Hammer, West and Brazil. They were one band behind Godwin.

The guy wearing Bubba's tool belt seemed tense. His right hand was twitching. He seemed to be waiting for something or someone. He was searching the ranks of the Godwin band, then looking straight at Chief Hammer. Bubba was sure of it.

Godwin started in on the theme from *Titanic.* The

construction guy looked left and right and slipped his right hand into a pouch and kept it there. Bubba's stolen guns flashed in his head. He ran out into the street as the woodwinds were going by. He wanted to pull out his new Browning but thought better of it.

'*Stop him!*' he yelled at the top of his lungs.

The fat man Smoke had met at Muskrat's Auto Rescue and soon after burglarized was pointing right at Smoke and yelling. Smoke was cool. He looked around and shrugged.

'What a wacko,' he said to the man and woman picnicking next to him.

Cops were running out. One galloped up on a horse. They were trying to calm the fat man and get him out of the street. Smoke smiled. This was going to be better than he thought. He zoomed in on Weed. The little retard was crashing and flashing his cymbals, the dude to the left trying to outdo him on the snare drum. Smoke took his time. He didn't want to slip his hand into the pouch again until the fat man quit pointing at him.

'*Somebody do something!*' the fat man was screaming as two cops grabbed his arms. '*Get him, not me! The kid up there in the Stanley tool belt!*'

Pigeon was concerned. He walked out on the street as Bubba struggled with the cops and continued to yell.

'Look, he's with me,' Pigeon told the cop on the horse.

'Stand back!' the cop yelled at Pigeon.

'It's his tool belt. You can see the white initials on the buckle. I mean with binoculars you can.' Pigeon wasn't to be deterred. 'The kid stole it.'

Bubba's binoculars flew off. A pistol fell out of somewhere and clattered to the street. This seemed to upset the cops quite a lot. All of them snatched handcuffs and red pepper spray off their belts. The Godwin band quit playing and froze as some little kid suddenly broke out of formation and rolled his cymbal down the street. Pigeon realized it was Weed.

Chief Hammer had no idea what was going on. The parade halted as what sounded like a huge bronze hubcap rolled toward her car.

'What's happening?' Hammer asked, standing up in the back seat, trying to see.

West stopped the car.

'GET DOWN!' Brazil yelled as he pushed Hammer to the floor and band members jumped out of the way and the cymbal hit a little dip in the road and picked up speed, flying past loudly, scattering the Mason clowns, sending Sergeant Santa scurrying, almost running the mayor's car into the crowd. The Florettes dropped their batons.

Jed saw the cymbal coming before Lelia Ehrhart did, and he suddenly threw the red Cadillac into reverse.

Azalea bushes jumped off the back seat, clay pots breaking, bees darting out of harm's way, dirt flying everywhere as streamers of blue ribbons changed direction and flew in Ehrhart's face.

The blond cop Jed had picked up in the cemetery the other day had just leaped out of Chief Hammer's car and was running like hell. Jed slammed on the brakes. A pink azalea bush sailed over the back of the front seat and Ehrhart shrieked. The cymbal went screaming past, flashing in the sun like a runaway gold chariot wheel.

Jed jumped out of the Cadillac without opening the door, neglecting to put the car in park. It began moving forward on its own as Ehrhart fought with streamers of blue ribbons, getting more entangled, and Patty Passman, nearby in the rioting crowd, threw down her Death by Chocolate ice cream cone and pushed people out of the way.

'MOVE, FUCKHEADS!' She shoved and punched, sugar-charged and unstoppable.

She chased the red Cadillac and hurled her fat body over the driver's door, landing with her feet in the air, grabbing the gear shift and jamming it into park.

Smoke was momentarily confused by the commotion. The plan in his head turned to page three and stopped. He looked around and backed up a little, almost slipping on the grass. At first it didn't register that the blond cop he had heard at school, and Weed and a street person were running toward him at top speed.

'EVERYBODY GET DOWN!' the blond cop was yelling.

The crowd started panicking. The cops lost interest in the fat man. They charged toward Smoke, too, the blond cop running the fastest.

'YOU SON OF A BITCH!' the fat man screamed at Smoke.

The picnicking couple dove out of the way as the fat man ran across their red-and-white-checkered tablecloth. Smoke panicked and pulled out the Beretta. In his confusion he forgot how to take the safety off.

People were thundering toward Smoke from all directions, with Weed in the lead, the plume on his black hat straight back as he ran at incredible speed. Smoke dropped the Beretta and groped for his Glock as Weed leaped five feet in the air and punched Smoke in the nose and grabbed his hair, knocking Smoke to the ground. They struggled over the Glock. Smoke let go of it when Weed bit his wrist hard.

'I'M GOING TO KILL YOU, YOU PIECE OF SHIT!' Weed kept yelling as he pummeled Smoke with his fists.

Brazil struggled to handcuff Smoke, who was rolling in the grass and yelling, clips of ammunition falling out of the stolen tool belt around his waist. At this point, community involvement was making matters worse.

Bubba was poised, taking jabs at Smoke whenever Weed left an opening. Pigeon was on the ground, trying to hold Smoke's ankles. Other cops were grabbing at Smoke and getting in Brazil's way. Unfortunately, one of them started squirting pepper spray. Then everyone was rolling on the ground, hands over their eyes, yelling in pain.

Smoke kicked straight up and caught one of the cops in the groin and grabbed the Sig Sauer pistol out of the other cop's holster. Smoke was bloody and breathing hard as he gripped the pistol in both shaking hands, his eyes watering and crazed with rage. He didn't see the two women cutting through the space between the two houses behind him.

Hammer and West had their pistols out and were moving in fast. It seemed Smoke was trying to figure out who to shoot. He wildly pointed the gun at a fat man Hammer recognized as Bubba. Then the gun was pointed at Brazil and the other cops on the ground, then out at the fleeing crowd and participants in the parade.

Hammer didn't have a clear shot because a street person and a little kid in a band uniform were in the way. Drifting pepper spray irritated Hammer's eyes and lungs. She and West split up as Smoke wheeled around, apparently hearing the sound of approaching feet. The barrel of his pistol seemed huge and unreal as he pointed it straight at Hammer's face. She couldn't shoot first. There were too many people in the way.

Hammer hadn't been in a good fight in a while but she hadn't forgotten her training. She hurled her pistol at Smoke as hard as she could, and it sailed and spun like a boomerang, and Smoke involuntarily raised his arms to ward it off, giving Hammer an opportunity to dive at his feet, knocking him down. They struggled over his gun.

'*GIVE IT UP!*' Hammer demanded.

He tried to point the gun into her ribs and she managed to get a good purchase on one of his thumbs. She bent it straight back, an old and reliable police trick. He howled in pain. She wrested the gun away from him and shoved it hard under his chin.

'*MOVE I'LL BLOW YOUR MOTHERFUCKING HEAD OFF!*' she yelled at him.

Her finger was on the trigger. She wanted him to give her an excuse.

'*You goddamn little bastard,*' she said in his face. '*That helpless old woman you murdered was my neighbor.*'

Brazil had recovered enough to help West handcuff Smoke and haul him away. Bubba sat up, tears streaming down his cheeks. Pigeon was facedown, still covering his eyes. The sock had come off his stump. Weed was unsteady as he got to his feet. He looked at Chief Hammer with red, watering eyes. She was standing very still, a gun at her side, pointed at the grass.

'Thanks,' Weed said to her. 'I sure am glad you're here.'

chapter thirty-six

That night it rained. Water spilled from the sky in waves that reminded Weed of pictures he had seen of oceans. Next, hail was bouncing off streets, the wind pushing so strong, Weed bet it could ring doorbells.

'Who is it?' he whispered in the dark, messing with the powers that be. 'Come in,' he talked to himself. 'Oh 'cuse me, I guess I forgot how to unlock the door.'

Tears filled his eyes, his attempts at being funny not amusing anyone else since no one else was there. Lightning flashed in his barred window and snapped and cracked like popping bubble wrap. Weed imagined a tornado and thought of Twister. Weed had heard he wasn't supposed to walk around with a golf club, play the cymbals or talk on the phone when lightning was flying everywhere, and here he was sitting on a stainless steel bed.

Oh well. Who cared if he was dead.

Somewhere in a different part of the detention home, in what was called a pod, Smoke was locked up, too. The thought of that made Weed feel little bugs all over his skin. He scratched and brushed himself off, his heart bouncing everywhere. He was having difficulty breathing and couldn't seem to get warm. He pulled the covers more tightly around him and thought of his steel bed again when lightning flamed like a big gun.

Chief Hammer hated lightning and usually stayed away from windows and objects that conducted electricity. But she couldn't sit still. She was pacing in her living room before windows and near lamps and iron fireplace tools and beneath the brass chandelier while Brazil and West sat restlessly on her couch, relentlessly replaying the day's events.

'I don't care what anyone says,' Brazil repeated his biggest concern as the power went out. 'Weed shouldn't be in the same facility Smoke's in. Different pods or not. Smoke's already proven how clever, how diabolical he is.'

'Didn't prove it enough to stay out of lockup,' West reminded them. 'But I don't like the situation either.'

'I'm going to tell you right now,' Brazil went on. 'If Smoke wants to do something, he will.'

'Yes, yes, yes,' Hammer said as she moved this way and that while Popeye snored from a wing chair and thunder boomed.

Brazil was worried to the point of taking drastic action, although he wasn't sure what that was. Apparently, Smoke hadn't wanted Divinity, Beeper, Dog and Sick running loose while he was locked up. He had told the police how to find every one of them, and now all of the Pikes were supposedly in different pods in detention, maybe one or two corridors away from where Weed was being held in his single room with its steel toilet and fold-down bed.

'We're going to need Weed to testify against all of them,' Brazil went on.

'Don't care who's sleeping where,' West added, 'Weed could end up in recreation with Smoke or any of the guys. And Miss Divinity's a snake, too.'

'Andy, Virginia, both of you are absolutely right.' Hammer stopped pacing long enough to light several candles. 'We need to get him out tonight.'

This required an unusual, unorthodox plan, and Hammer had one. At quarter past eight, she called Judge Maggie Davis at home.

'I'm glad you're there,' Hammer said quickly.

'Wouldn't want to be anywhere else on a night like this,' said the judge. 'I'm sorry I missed the parade. Good God. Way to go, Judy. Wish I'd been there to see you take out the little shit.'

'I didn't do much.' Hammer dismissed the compliment. 'We've got to get Weed Gardener out of detention as soon as possible.'

'I thought he wanted to be in detention.'

'That was then,' Hammer said. 'Now you've got Smoke and his gang in there. That's not good, Maggie. Not good at all.'

The judge deliberated for a moment.

'What do you propose?' she finally asked the chief.

Hammer was well aware that what she was about to

suggest could not happen. But most of what she had accomplished in life could not happen, according to those who stood around and watched.

'Can you get hold of the commonwealth's attorney and the public defender?' Hammer asked.

'Of course,' Judge Davis replied.

'I'll make sure the gates are unlocked.'

'What gates?' Judge Davis asked.

At nine o'clock, the six of them pulled up in four cars at the front iron gates of Hollywood Cemetery. Rain lashed ancient boxwoods and trees, and headstones and monuments were wet and eerie as headlights swept over them.

The chief, Brazil and West were in the lead car. Behind them was Judge Davis in her Volvo and Commonwealth's Attorney Michael in his Honda Accord. Trailing from a bit of a distance was an old Mercury Cougar carrying Sue Cheddar, who had quit and then been fired by Weed and was now ordered by Judge Davis to stay on the case.

'I sure as hell hope he was telling the truth,' West said to Hammer and Brazil.

Wipers beat and the rain beat back. Hammer was driving very slowly, leaning over the steering wheel and squinting to read street signs.

'He was,' Hammer said as if she knew Weed very well.

They splashed along Waterview Avenue, tree branches whipping and violently grabbing at them. Silhouettes of angels watched them pass. Dark tombs drew Hammer's imagination through windows of stained and leaded glass, and she remembered childhood fears. She was ten when her next-door neighbor, Mrs. Wheat, was buried in the Baptist church cemetery a block away, her gray granite headstone in plain view from the street. Every morning on Hammer's way to school, she would run past the cemetery as fast as she could because she had never liked Mrs. Wheat and was certain Mrs. Wheat knew it now that she was in heaven.

Hammer still hated cemeteries. She did not like anything about them. She was afraid of their pungent smells and insect sounds and subtle mounds. She was afraid of death. She was afraid of what she felt about Seth's. She was afraid of being alone. She was afraid of failure. She was afraid of fear. All of her many fears took energy, and frankly, at this moment, she was fucking fed up.

'This is ridiculous,' she said to West and Brazil. 'I'm not going to quit, retire, do nothing, whatever.'

'Well, if you do, I'm not hanging around here,' West retorted.

'I'm history, too,' Brazil let his boss know as they neared Davis Circle.

'Are they still behind us?' Hammer peered in the rearview mirror.

'You absolutely shouldn't quit, Chief Hammer,' Brazil advised her. 'Especially now. I think the more people pick on you, the more you should offend them with your presence.'

'That's very astute.' Hammer considered Brazil's words. 'I rather like that thought.'

Not everyone had praised Hammer for tackling Smoke and putting a gun to his head while yelling obscenities. The mayor told all TV networks in time for the six o'clock news that the incident should never have happened to begin with and he had gone on to label Hammer's heroics a self-serving publicity stunt. Lelia Ehrhart told Q94 that Hammer was a 'Jack Footed Thung' who didn't give a 'hoo' about prevention. The city manager had called for a thorough investigation by internal affairs.

'Don't be discouraged by today.' Brazil seemed to know what she was thinking. 'Don't forget, Governor Feuer was impressed. He called to congratulate you. He ought to count more than the other ones do.'

'Aren't we supposed to turn somewhere?' Hammer couldn't see a damn thing.

Brazil saw Jefferson Davis first.

'I'm melting! I'm melting!' Brazil mimicked the Wicked Witch in *The Wizard of Oz*.

'Well, I'll be damned,' West said as the statue was fully exposed by Hammer's high beams.

She stopped her Crown Victoria and turned the police spotlight on the statue.

'Hot dog!' Brazil exclaimed. 'Shit, I wish Weed could be here to see this.'

'I don't know,' Hammer said thoughtfully. 'He'd probably be disappointed.'

'Yeah.' Brazil reconsidered sadly. 'I guess you're right. Twister's moved on.'

Jeff Davis was fast losing his newly acquired race and position on the University of Richmond Spiders basketball team. His face was streaked black, his red-and-white uniform in pools around his no-longer-Nike footwear and the orange-smeared marble base that supported him. The basketball he held in his left hand had turned back into a hat.

Car doors were opening and shutting, lights scattered with rain. Feet sloshed and sounded wetly over stone. Judge Davis was a native of New York. She walked up to the statue and looked it over carefully. She bent down and plucked a tiny Southern Cross out of the sod. She waved it from its slender stick as if trying to see how it worked or what the big fuss was all about.

'I think it's clear this isn't vandalism anymore,' Hammer announced. 'Nor was it ever. We just thought it was.'

Sue Cheddar was under a bright pink parasol and only her long, animated nails were visible as she spoke.

'See,' she said as red claws flashed at Commonwealth's Attorney Michael.

He was getting soaked and looked like a defeated Confederate soldier in his ill-fitting gray suit and skinny dark tie. His hair was plastered to his head, rain running down his tired face as he watched the president of the Confederacy lose his glory once more.

'Point is, Weed meant to do damage,' Michael said with no conviction. 'Goddamn, will this rain ever stop? You ought to see my yard. The road in front, too, since the city doesn't do a damn thing to maintain it. Water must be six inches deep.'

'Do we have any further arguments?' Judge Davis faced all of them as rain turned back into hail and began to click and clatter.

'Not me,' West said.

'Of course not,' said Hammer.

'Nope,' Brazil agreed with everyone.

'Then I rule that the charge against Weed Gardener be dismissed,' Judge Davis decided as a marble woman with an open Bible and an angel looked on. 'Officer Brazil.' She nodded at him. 'Let's get the paperwork. I want him released immediately.'

'Right this minute,' Hammer agreed. 'Virginia, Andy? Straight to detention. We're taking Weed home.'

Brazil cheered and put his arm around West. Chief Hammer began to clap. West did, too. Cheddar joined in, although it wasn't possible for her hands to touch. Commonwealth's Attorney Michael shrugged. Paperwork was completed and the six of them returned to their cars. Jefferson Davis receded into the night as the small motorcade followed Waterview through rain that no longer seemed so harsh, past monuments that did not seem quite so sad.